The New
Olympia Reader

The New Olympia Reader

Edited by Maurice Girodias

SELECTIONS FROM THE TRAVELLER'S COMPANION SERIES,
OPHELIA PRESS, INC., AND THE OLYMPIA PRESS, INC.

ILLUSTRATED BY KASOUNDRA

QUALITY PAPERBACK BOOK CLUB
NEW YORK

CONTENTS

REPENTANCE, DESIRE AND NATALIE WOOD

Check it out, here is the afterword to a chapter from *Oracle of the Thousand Hands* which appears in this volume:

> Barry Malzberg lives with his wife and daughter in Manhattan and is worried about having recently reached the ominous age of thirty . . . . Mr. Malzberg's first hardcover novels, *Oracle of the Thousand Hands* and *Screen* are seriously-intentioned works which, according to the author, were neither fun to write nor fun in retrospect. Major influences on his work in no particular order are Norman Mailer, J. D. Salinger, Saul Bellow, James Agee, Vladimir Nabokov, Fyodor Dostoyevsky and Nikolai Gogol.

Not quite. The *major* major influences upon the author's "seriously-intentioned" hardcover novels, as well as eight paperbacks done for the Olympia Press America between 1968 and 1973 were really: Jayne Mansfield, Natalie Wood, Hope Lange, repentance, desire, lust, resentment, ambition and the collected opi of the Four Coins, Four Preps, Four Seasons and the Belmonts. (Dion, too.) Heady stuff for the kid, though, writing for Nabokov's publisher, citing Gogol and Dostoyevsky as influences; I recommend this experience to everyone having real or even slight pretensions to artistry.

Girodias *fils* left Paris in a flurry of debt, lawsuit and governmental revulsion in 1967, decamped to New York, found financial backing (but not too much) from obscure sources, set up active shop here as the reincarnation of that insouciant and eclectic Left Bank spirit which in the 1950s had given bewildered culture lovers the works of Akhbar del Palumbo, Henry Miller, Terry Southern and even Vladimir Nabokov whose *Lolita* had come to Paris in 1955 at the behest of an author whose agent had been unable to place the novel anywhere.

Maurice Girodias, 49 when he came to New York, 36 then, had been unable to sell many copies of *Lolita*; he hadn't done too well with Miller either (Akhbar on the other hand had been a staple) but he had ideas, he would reconstitute the age of enlightenment within the borders of a city located on the far eastern seaboard of a country which was demonstrably going mad.

Clearly, it was going mad, it was his kind of country. First the assassination, then Vietnam, then some other, discreditable assassinations, then the Summer of Love, then Olympia Press America. Then Martin, Robert, Nixon, Apollo, Cambodia, Kent State and Wallace. But by the time of Wallace, Olympia Press was already speeding into Chapter 11 and Girodias, a year after that was, *sans* his new wife, *sans* everything sailing for Paris. "Sunk without trace" is not exactly the phrase for Olympia America, *nothing* is sunk without trace in this country, McGovern is on the lecture circuit and Jefferson Airplane/Starship are heading toward the third incarnation, but it is close. Fairly close. "Sunk almost without trace" probably can be risked.

The New Olympia Reader, 300,000 words of excerpts by about 50 writers, compiled by your faithful undersigned for a freelancer's pittance (but *not* the author of the authorial biographies or the cited blurb) sold about 500 copies in hardcover, sold no copies in paperback since there was no paperback edition and hasn't been off my shelf in 15 years. Shortly, speedily, it will go back on my shelf.

That anthology was reviewed in a defunct literary journal by a novelist of minor reputation and high recrimination who mentioned none of the selections, spent 4000 words talking (in the abstract) about the prevalence of voyeurism in early twentieth-century culture as capitalized upon by senior and junior Girodiaoux and sickeningly exhibited here. Not a review but a poisonous meditation.

"Don't worry about it," the publisher said, "don't think about this twice, because of all the American literary crowd, the litterateurs in the fifties, sucking around the Rue de Whatever, he was the grubbiest, the silliest, the most desperate and the only one whose work I would not buy, I found him effete and senseless. He's been waiting to get back at me for 18 years and oh that wife of his!" This gave me little comfort, not much *did* give me comfort in those difficult post-prandial years when I came to understand that being Olympia's Best Writer, talisman of a disastrous hardcover program, was in effect to be Girodias's Worst Writer.

"Why am I so self-destructive?" the publisher said to me in a somewhat different context months later when British lawsuits had resulted in his first lot of hardcovers being confiscated at the warehouse and burned at the instigation of a member of the House of Lords whose name had been appropriated for spite as the title of a Traveller's Companion, "why do I do this to myself over and over again?"

"Well, Maurice," I could have said but did not, having even less wit than comprehension in that aftermath of the Summer of Love, "maybe it's because you turned 50 on April 12, 1969 and men like you, men who have always formed themselves in terms of the debonair, the practical, the outrageous have a *lot* of trouble at 50 and feel at least that they are going to destruction on their own terms." I could have said that, I could have added that Maurice was exactly 15 years younger than my mother and equally capable of finding guilt in those he implicated, but I did not. One has to get fairly close or closer yet to 50 oneself to be offered such perceptions by which time, usually, it is too late to do much about them.

My mother, speaking of her, was not terribly pleased with her son, so recently the Schubert Foundation Playwriting Fellow but now a hounded and increasingly desperate novelist *manqué* in search of a real market becoming Girodias's Best Writer. The fact that I was also writing science fiction and selling some of it to strange-looking magazines with androids on the cover was—for her at least—no particular compensation. She *was* however somewhat mollified to note in the Christopher Lehmann-Haupt April 7, 1969 review of the two novels that they were defined as "a kind of anti-pornography"; this enabled her to seize the day with her friends.

"The problem with your pornography," an editor at Olympia named Uta West said to me in relation to the problem, "The only real trouble is that you write about sex the way that 95% of us experience it 95% of the time but it's hard to get us to pay to *read* about it, you know?"

Still, like the Common Man in *Marat/Sade*, I had plans. If my sex scenes were dreamy, my intentions and style were, I trusted, not: I wrote the opening chapters of *Oracle of the Thousand Hands* in a dead fever of February 1968, trying to figure out what might impress Nabokov's publisher's first reader and came up with a crazed pastiche of *Pale Fire* and *Despair*, the memoirs of a compulsive masturbator narrated in the alternating first- and third-person with quarts of semen spewed over electric fences, cattle mooing nostalgically in the background at the instant of self-defloration and ultimately a powerful shock from that electrified fence at the moment of final consummation. Girodias or someone there noticed what was going on, he summoned me to Gramercy Park (the Press and four employees worked out of his apartment, skirting the mattress on the floor as they sidled from room to room) and offered me a $2000 contract.

"Well," he mumbled six weeks later when on an impossible June afternoon I came to hear the verdict on the completed novel mailed oh-so-recently, "it's not your number one best seller but it's amusing and interesting isn't it?" *Amusing* and *interesting* were his favorite attitudes and everyone in the ideal Traveller's Companion or Ophelia Press book would climax with a smile and a sigh. "I have to accept this, I guess, but now you do something for me. I have a novel I want you to do as a special project for me."

That novel I soon discovered had been offered to and declined as an idea by every writer who had come trooping around or past the mattress: a young man with an empty life and much seminal backup is obsessed with film, watches five films a day, falls vividly in love with actresses, has an imagination so passionate that he can place himself on the screen with and make passionate love to Elizabeth Taylor, Doris Day, Brigitte Bardot, Sophia and the ever-popular "others." "Use their real names," he said, "I want *scandale*, without scandal this cannot work."

"What becomes of the guy?"

"I don't know. Who the hell cares? Maybe he becomes Joe E. Levine, what's the difference. I'll give you a clause protecting you against lawsuits. I *love* lawsuits," he reminded me.

I delivered *Screen* in two weeks, taking Martin Miller, a Department of Welfare investigator in Brooklyn (as I had been) through a series of Bijoux and into and out of the genitalia of some actresses, also to Aqueduct race track in the borough of Queens and also through more desultory (if unrequested) collision with a fellow social worker whom he did not love (*roman á clef* here) but who intimated his obsession and pointed out that Martin had better get wise, "because I'm for real. I'm also your last chance." (No, she wasn't.) I hold no great brief for the novel but doubt if any better has been written faster, *pace* A. J. Liebling, and it contains for whatever it is worth probably the best sentence I ever wrote and maybe the best sentence published in a novel of lust in 1969; the last sentence of that novel as Martin Miller having walked away from the suddenly desperate colleague, pounds it into a star (and pounds it and pounds it and pounds it, "her body a map, her hands a road to carry me home"):

> It is strange and complex, complex and strange and my orgasm is
> like a giant bird torn wing to wing by rifle fire, falling, falling, in
> the hot drenched sun of that damned Southwestern city.

That sentence written (as were many of the sentences of that and *Oracle*) with two-year-old Stephanie Jill burbling and cooing and muttering and bounding and volubly discussing matters of climate at her father's knee didn't have in draft the word "damned," something seemed to be lacking and in the only revision in either of those two novels, the word was put in for rhythm and emphasis and all of it placed on or near the Girodias mattress shortly after Independence Day.

"You son of a bitch," he pointed out, "you make me crazy, do you know that? I ask you this time for pornography, a simple work of pornography, give you a plot and everything and ask you to keep it simple and low-class, I publish one book for *you* and ask you to do this for *me* and what do you do? You give me 40 pages which are beautiful, just beautiful, you even know the color of that one's *bush* how you tell that? and *then* what do you give me? You give me horse-racing, you give me existentialism, you give me despair! You give me terrible anxiety and depression! You give me pain and thwarted desire! This book will sell 400 copies, I have to publish it hardcover too because in paperback everyone will throw it away; I have to publish it because it is a masterpiece, but you *destroy* me, do you understand?"

It sold 350 copies in hardcover, actually, making it the leader of the second "new hardcover line" (*Oracle* sold half that and a novel by Alex Austin, *Eleanore*, sold according to statement 52 copies) but none of this was my fault, was it? I mean it was indeed (Lehmann-Haupt backed me up on this) anti-pornography for the coming age of Nixon and under the circumstances, the time could have been right.

But times were never right for the doomed Girodias. They had been laying for him in the American press for years and years, he said, because he had embarrassed them by putting into print consistently masterpieces that the American publishing establishment had been too cowardly or stupid to undertake: *Tropic of Cancer* and *Tropic of Capricorn* and the *Nexus* trilogy and *Candy* and *Lolita* and virtually everything else that Barney Rosset or Walter Minton had taken on after he had broken ground. (And because the books were published in English outside the borders of the United States, they were by old copyright law in public domain in this country.) Perhaps he was right; it is not difficult—I can see this as clearly at 27 as I would be unable to admit it at 50—to do justly, to do mercy, to walk humbly and *to be buried anyway*.

Besides, Maurice had said, "written pornography, it is finished. Finished! Visuals are coming, visuals are where it will be, that and high-toned classy books which hairdressers can hand their clientele. Softcore for the ladies, yes, but nothing for the gentlemen. Our basic audience would rather stare than read which they can hardly manage anyway. The ladies on the other hand will call it romance. It will be finished by 1972, just two years from now."

Like Fitzgerald, like Raymond Chandler, like Thomas Wolfe, my publisher could coolly observe his disaster as if from a distance and by seeming detachment from cataclysm feign control. The boat sailed anyway. *The Frog Prince*, the first volume of his proposed series of memoirs, takes him only up to the age of 19 (and is classically uninteresting as would, say, be the biography of the extra-instrumental life of Heifetz or Nixon), was published in France many years ago, perished in a Crown edition here at the start of this decade and bulletins are distant and infrequent. Which is a way of saying "There is no news."

I am, then, or am not near the end of this memoir but would not want to finish without discussing the issue of courage. He had a crazy, a manifest, a *royal* physical courage which I much admired as did almost anyone who had witnessed its display; he had a true general's detachment, and indifference to consequence founded upon metaphysic. In a dangerous, a perilous Times Square bar at 2:00 a.m. once where we had repaired, me shuddering he debonair, after a "debate" with an ex-congressman and a Citizens for Decency League leader on the Farber show, a debacle which had left me exhausted and trembling ("I don't have to read your filth to know what kind of filth it is," O. K. Armstrong, the congressman, only two months ago reluctantly but administratively passed on at 92 had snapped to me), we were drinking beer for which Girodias had paid when a truly menacing, a truly dangerous fellow approached, an even less ingenuous companion lurking in the background, pointed a menacing finger at Girodias's sleeve, a knife seeming to glint from a shrouded place and said, "Nice threads, man. *Really* nice threads."

"Oh," said Maurice, "oh yes, of course, thank you." He began to remove the jacket, rose from the stool, finished the job, extended it. "Would you like?" he said, "it's all yours, my pleasure." The menace went away and Maurice went away and the brave, haunted, doomed Olympia America went away too (in metaphor at least, I am still in that bar, however) and they are to be saluted. Torn wing to wing by rifle fire.

—New Jersey, 1989

Footnote to an unpublished memoir: Maurice did write and publish a sequel to *The Frog Prince*, was interviewed on French radio in consequence of its publication in the summer of 1990, died suddenly after the interview. One would like to think of this as further evidence of the poised irony with which this difficult man attempted to conduct his life; the jaunty bow, the tilt of the eyebrow, exercise in self-publicity and then, *aha!* at the apex and astride his history, that graceful tumble to the pit, the Wallenda of autobiography. But death is too magisterial to command easy, balletic grace from most of us; I cannot imagine (I was not there) how it afflicted Maurice but if anyone *could*, like Don Giovanni, salute the abyss it was the son of Jack Kahane. And two months later, Leonard Bernstein. Larger and larger pieces of time—

—New Jersey, 31 December 1990

AFTERWORD TO AN AFTERWORD TO AN ESSAY

I am pleased—"pleased" isn't quite right but will have to do—with this new edition of the anthology, for all intents and purposes this new edition is the only edition for the book published in 1970 was trapped by the exigencies of distribution and Olympia's imminent failure, it was ignored by the review media and sunk beneath sight and never had a chance. Now it has a chance. Within these pages resides—suspires, one might say, pulsates however feebly—the sixties themselves; emblematic of the decade in ways barely comprehensible at the time this may be a book whose importance can only be perceived in retrospect, after the set has been struck, the guests and their anima laid to rest. We did think—some of us, anyway— that the decade represented a small but real chance to revise this country and ourselves, and that blessed, near-extinguished hope resides at the center of what was called at the time (probably now too) pornography. *Lolita* and *Tropic of Cancer*, *Sons and Lovers* and *Ulysses* bore that sobriquet too, of course, and turned out to have done pretty well with it.

And Maurice Girodias too lives. He is perhaps the most important publisher of the second half of the twentieth-century; the culture would look entirely different without him, his contribution so much a part of the landscape that it is only seen *as* the landscape. A remarkable man, Wallenda of death too, a man whose self-awareness and ironic distance suit him no more for tragedy than for undervaluation. In his light our darkness, in his darkness, this small and perfect, this witnessing and entire corridor of light: the light that falls forever.

Barry N. Malzberg

Introduction
Maurice Girodias

THE NEW OLYMPIA READER

*T*he *Olympia Reader*, as published in 1964 by Grove Press Inc., presented a good cross section of Olympia's Paris production in the 'fifties (starting in 1953) — in the days in which the advent of freedom of expression in literature still appeared as a very distant prospect. When I first published *Lolita* and *The Ginger Man* in Paris, in 1955, Vladimir Nabokov and J.P. Donleavy were convinced that their respective books had very little chance of ever being published in America, and even less chance in England.

Henry Miller, in those days, was still the symbol of social and moral outrage, of Bohemian corruption, of anti-social behavior at its most intolerable extreme. *Lady Chatterley's Lover* was only reprinted in America in 1959. Only ten years ago! And those ten years mark an extraordinary acceleration of history. That cathartic and cataclysmic era has changed the function of human culture and the very purpose of our society, in a way that is not yet accessible to our myopic understanding.

Our society has suddenly conquered the right to adulthood by accomplishing its Sexual Revolution. (Or, at least, it is in the process of doing so, since the vast movements that are at work everywhere are not developing at the same pace or in the same style in the different regions of the planet.)

But the final meaning of that revolution is everywhere the same: the conquest of independence, the access of each man to a minimum of autonomy and dignity. Freud in his day has demonstrated — as a preface to this contemporary revelation — that no man can be free, strong, and happy if he does not dominate his fears, his frustrations, his guilt, his shame, and all his regressive tendencies. What Freud has discovered and defined on the individual level is now becoming true for the whole human community. And it is easy to see how the concept of true democracy is now becoming clear and well-defined on the political map of the world: in the more advanced democracies, sexual freedom and freedom of expression are very fast becoming the symbols and the standards of all other civil liberties. In totalitarian countries, the communist or fascist regimes can only maintain themselves by enforcing the most exacting moral censorship on the arts and on all forms of free behavior. Religion or party discipline, based on superstition and abject fear, inspire the sort of national culture we see flourishing in Russia, Spain, Czechoslovakia, etc.

After ten years of "sexual revolution" in the Western countries — marked quite spectacularly by the abolition of all censorship laws in Denmark — it is now possible to distinguish some recurrent patterns. First, the discovery of freedom invariably provokes an explosion of dismal pornography — the direct effect of that discovery on the semi-literate masses, the shock caused by the sudden disintegration of so many taboos, the need for a total purge-by-obscenity, the realization that, in vice and in weakness, all men are truly born equal. But we know that the initial phase in any analysis should reveal the patients' worst aspects — otherwise it's a waste of time.

The second phase is only being reached now — at least in America. After centuries of repression, it is now being admitted that man's erotic function is truly his central motor, and the source of all his most authentic drives and inspirations. It now becomes a fascinating task to give a meaning to our culture, by turning it into the exact and true expression of man's humanity, and to discover, through the humble mechanisms of sexuality, the infinite perspective provided by man's erotic design.

This new search is only starting, but all the authors presented in this second *Olympia Reader* (the result, mostly, of only two years of publishing activity in America) illustrate its reality. Even through the devices of humor and satire, the general image will emerge, from that collection of writings, of an extremely forceful movement, of a new style, of a new direction. The ultimate discoveries will only come later — beyond and after the Sexual Revolution — but this book is a solid stepping stone which is meant to lead higher and further.

Maurice Girodias
August 9, 1969
London

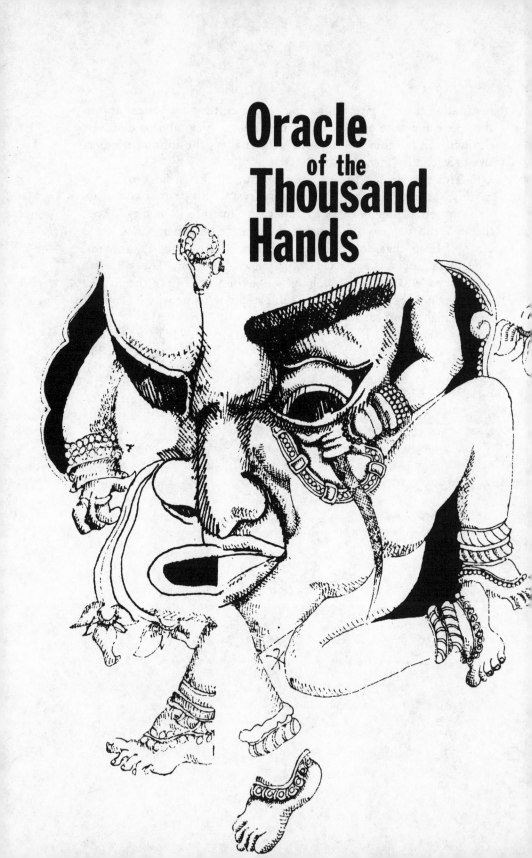

Barry Malzberg

D'ARCY'S GENITALIA: They were of unusual size; even in a state of purest flaccidity they measured several centimeters in the usual three directions. Under engorgement, the subject himself as well as several partners measured them as well over a foot in length. It is further attested that the unusual "slickness" and "warmth" of the organ made penetration unusually easy, even with "slightly built" companions.

D'ARCY'S SEXUAL PREDILECTIONS: They were, as we all know, completely heterosexual; any rumors to the contrary have been created by jealous and envious homosexuals whom D'Arcy again and again spurned to seek female companionship. He preferred normal intercourse in the seventh and eighth positions of Lilly, with certain pre-coital variations mostly involved with the buttocks and thighs of partners. Breast (buccal) tendencies were negligible, D'Arcy having been known to state often that he felt himself too well-endowed for "that preliminary nonsense."

D'ARCY'S SEXUAL PERFORMANCE: It was, as all sources have testified, facile and almost incredibly accomplished, leading partners again and again to the "sublime" peak and letting them down always at their own pace and without embarrassment. Ejaculation was plentiful, fluid was copious, sufficient to "open-up" partners so inclined. Pre- and post-coital maneuvers were swift, gracious and wholly respectful of companion and circumstances. It can be said, then, that the subject's sexual performance was excellent.

D'ARCY'S SOCIAL IMPORTANCE AS SEEN IN HISTORICAL PERSPECTIVE: It cannot be minimized. Dealing with the "quintessence of heterosexuality" (his phrase) raised to the "nth degree of pleasure" (words of Mademoiselle M, a lady of his acquaintance), it came along just at the right time to reverse the slow trend of the Age toward narcissism, masturbation and latent homosexuality. D'Arcy's contribution, infusing as it did, all of his sexual "mainstream" with "new blood," was nothing less than the reversal of history, the setting aright of the microcosm he knew.

WHY THIS STUDY IS WRITTEN: I must admit that there are some questions about that to be squarely faced.

This study will deal with the "lover" D'Arcy from the inception of that self-imposed role in December of 196- to its tragic—and unpremeditated conclusion—in October of 196-. It will in no fashion attempt definitive biography nor does it presume to be more than a documentary of the public years of D'Arcy's existence. The early years, the growing years, the dwindling years, even the brief but poignant dying day . . . little of this will be touched upon within the confines of these pages. The historian must delimit to better define the quintessence of his insight. So few of our contemporary "biographers" admit this simple fact. As we diffuse, so must we move ever further from that basic kernel of insight which may, for all we know, be the metaphor for the folly of life itself. Aha!

So delimited, this work will address itself to such primary questions as these: did the subject feel love? Did D'Arcy, in the last smoke and plumes of love's consummation, know emotional release beyond his gigantic physical bursts? Was he ever, during the public years, frustrated in his pursuit of sexual conjoinment? What did some of his partners think of him? What conclusions can be drawn? Exactly what was the breadth and length of a typical D'Arcy orgasm?

We will answer those questions all in due time. On hand we have documents and testimonies of many of the subject's partners, none of them ever before revealed, confidentially given to the one who transcribes this memoir. In tandem they will piece together, we promise, into a shattering picture of our protagonist, revealing wonders and implications hitherto never before revealed.

THE QUESTION OF QUALIFICATION: It is always asked of the historian: who are you? What is your particular credential? Why do you presume to give the sense of this material to a gullible and easily misled audience? This is a painful century; the question of credibility perhaps in nexus.

Let me state modestly, therefore, that I knew D'Arcy well; far better than any other during the public years and during many of those years I stood by his side. Friend, confidant, partner, assistant, I lived in the closest conjoinment with the subject. The public prints do not indicate this, of course.

The reason for that is that I always demanded anonymity. "Not for me notoriety or exploitation, D'Arcy," I said to my friend once while we were drinking wine together during one of his periods of "convalescence." "I would be less a friend and more an agent of the opposition were I to attempt to benefit in any way from the fortunate fact of our interrelationship. I prize your friendship above all others, I will not have myself known. But, in my quiet way, I will stand by you always."

And my dear, dear friend said to me, sipping his wine slowly, stirring the sediment with his finger in the characteristic gesture, "Truly, you are a friend. But I cannot ask this of you. If there is profit to be made from our friendship without discredit or interference to me, then take it, I say. Give an interview. Let your face be known. Tell them what I say about women, when I am in a kindly mood, of course. Advise them of my culinary idiosyncrasies. This will keep my name as always before them and you will derive a small income from your ramblings. I give you permission to do all of this as long as you understand from whom the permission comes and from what high motives; that is all I ask." And lifted his glass in the sun so that the purple glittered as stone, mixing toward the purest refraction of his driven, absent face.

And once again I said, raising my own glass, my blunt features dwindling to infinitesimal condition as the sun darted behind a cloud, "Never, my friend; this will never be. As long as I have health and strength to continue on our mutual travels I will never lend you the betrayal of publicity."

Even so, it is with a heavy heart that I begin this journal. Well-qualified as I am, there are certainly others who would be equally so: having never, for instance, truly "known" the hot embrace of D'Arcy in bed nor felt the pressure of his massive, earnest thighs against mine, I am obviously less qualified than many to talk of some of the more explicit aspects of D'Arcy's performance. But who else—I say again, who else?—could possibly take up the wearisome pen, shuffle the papers and commence?

Most of those juxtaposed to D'Arcy in the way I mention can neither read nor write, some cannot spell, the majority cannot perform the simplest mathematical examples. Too, a large percentage of these people are missing, which is to say that they are beyond the efforts of local authorities and institutions to find them.

It is peculiar but it is so: a high percentage of D'Arcy's companions are so far on the margin of our society as to be beyond its devices. *Nothing,* an acquaintance of mine once said, *nothing is as unlocatable as a common tart; even in the bedroom it is often impossible to find one.* D'Arcy's career, then, like a rocket in full, booming flight, discharged a trail of gas and combustible matter which negated it origins to the exact degree that the major ascent opened up new territory. I have often found that this is a general rule; being, of course, a strong adherent of the great man theory of history.

Only I, then, an Ishmael of the post-coital ecstasy, remain to tell the tale. My whereabouts fixed firmly by due process of law and institutionalization, my literacy shaped by 18 years of tutors smuggled from the public schools, my credentials beyond dispute, my humility attested to by my years of close friendship with the subject. I would not think that a further apologia is necessary. Awash, then, in the sea of possibilities, tossed by the whale of retrospection. I cling to the flotsam and jetsam of total recall, trying to spare immersion to the thousands who wait cheerlessly on the sands.

Of course, I remain attuned to the possibility that I may be prohibited from the removal of these notes from my present confines. There is a rich precedent for this: so many of my companions and enemies within these gates are similarly "writers"; were all the tracts, correspondence, romanticized history and pseudo-legal writs composed daily in this place to be put in one stack, it would probably reach to half the height of the senior attendant who demands that all our written material be placed in his hands for censorship and approval. Since this senior attendant, a bulky man with large ears, can neither read nor write, it is suspected by many of my companions here that their writings are being instantly tossed to perdition, most likely after "taps," when scufflings and rustlings and billowings in the hall might suggest the lively flush of toilets sending handwriting on its way. Nevertheless, I discount the possibility. The press visits me now and then and also some acquaintances; surely I could place my jottings in their hands were I to feel an imminence of capture. The important thing, as has been truly

said, is to do one's work; a good conscience is its own best reward.

THE CIRCUMSTANCES UNDER WHICH THE STUDY IS BEING WRITTEN: Art and craft, being inextricably linked to environment, it would be fair, perhaps, to describe what it's like here. It is not the most felicitous of ambiances.

For one thing it is wretchedly cold in these rooms and for another, it is almost unspeakably foul much of the time. My collaborants in this large institution are, to an incalculable extent, unbearably dull—their efforts at the written word to the contrary—and entrapped by their small, circular obsessions. They are incapable, in short, of the mildest form of self-amusement, let alone the divertissement of one as complex and sophisticated as I. (It might be said, then, that I have taken to these notes out of boredom but this is not half the fact of the case; the act of writing can be as offensive as that of self-abuse and far less interesting.) The two young men, for instance, who share these rooms with me, seem to have reached an accord of many years' standing—they preceded me here by a long time—not to address one another unless under the governor of extrinsic need, and then in some kind of bizarre code which appears to be the least inventive amalgamation of French, English and the arcane mumblings of the retarded. I find this a great burden upon an active sensibility, but I am completely unable to alter this.

Not that I have not tried. There was a time when I hammered upon the dense barrier of their sullen alliance repeatedly: did it with small jokes, quips, reminiscences and even—for their sake—the admission that I was a companion of D'Arcy's throughout his notable career. I had thought that this final revelation would, when all else had failed, break us through to a small network of feeling or (at least) remonstrance but, shockingly, neither of them had ever *heard* of D'Arcy, much less possessing the slightest knowledge of his travels. It was when they made offensive comments to me about this acquaintanceship and my dear friend himself that I gave up on further attempts to establish a normal relationship in these rooms.

I exemplify: the other evening I was on the way to the "dayroom" here, prepared for yet another desultory game of chess with the bearded fossil who sits silently in front of the board all day, so immobile that it is necessary for his partners to contribute both sets of moves and announce imminent captures, when the elder of my roommates, a fierce man with wild eyes and blond hair so sheer that it might have blazed, said to the other, *Monsieur ici est entrappe.*

Non, non, chattered the other who was under the best of circumstances, rather elfin, *il est disappointe.*

Entrappe and disappointe together. Un jolie homme despite tout, however, est that non vraiment?

"Listen," I said, "there's no need to discuss a man to his face, it isn't polite and it shows a lack of intelligence in the bargain. I'll be wandering down the hall just a bit and you can say all you choose but for the moment call it off, yes?"

Est uproarious, said the first, taking a comb from somewhere around the perimeter of his waist and running it through his hair, squeezing the dandruff pods as they sifted downward. This never failed to excite the elf who stood, then, to the limit of his short frame and, running his own hands through a rather ferocious beard, gestured at me.

Felon, he said.

At that moment, my aged, bottled temper, stirred to the sediment, burbled forth. "Look, gentlemen," I said, "I do not need such talk from you. The same institutions which committed me here have placed you as well and for a much longer period, I might observe. I tell you frankly that unless this behavior stops, I will be compelled to seek new quarters and whoever succeeds me will be far less tolerant of your display of manners. Does that seem clear?"

They laughed at that.

"Now look," I said, "if I must start at the beginning, I will. I am a close friend, perhaps the closest, of the late, honored Justin D'Arcy and in that regard—"

I could not finish. I heard, interchangeably from them, an explosion of guttural monosyllables which sounded vaguely like curses. *Ha, ha!,* they added, *ha, ha!*

"Ha yourself," I said then, and for the first time told them my secret. I had to, to quiet them.

They stopped laughing. The elf seized an ashtray instead and made with it a complex, obscene gesture involving three parts of his anatomy. The gyrations were quite intricate. Then he ceased and both stared, apparently assessing my countermove.

"Makes no difference," I said, grandly, and with enormous dignity folding me like a shroud—that dignity I can conjure up under almost any circumstances—I quit the room and their presence.

THE PHILOSOPHICAL AND PSYCHOLOGICAL BIAS OF THE STUDY: There is no point in concealing this final notation: this study will be, inevitably, composed of a set of digressions from D'Arcy and deal on the personal level. My condition, of course, is so inseparable from his that our circumstances—until his unfortunate disappearance, that is to say—conjoined completely; our obsessions were so linked that it would be presumptuous to even assume that I could part from him. No, I am no cool, detached biographer although, to be sure, I am a faintly bewhiskered one. But D'Arcy's *ficelle;* I see that now, despite my own considerable, prolonged and irreversible detumescence.

But by all means, let me proceed, wander into the sunset of recollection, the old, hollow features tilted wistfully to the horizon, the faithful old frame complying, possibly for the last time, to the Master's demands.

May I leap ahead rapidly in time, modestly discarding the expository necessities, leaving the bridge-work to the biographer who, if possessed of intelligence as you are not, would be able to work out the transitions with a minimum of wordage and a maximum of insight; the transitions being the most painful because least necessary part of all biography. I am poised over the girl in the heat and cove of my room under the doom of a November rainfall—the girl is somewhat older than I am and tragically overdeveloped, her large breasts, fascinating in armor, in a kind of flat, aimless repose with clothing removed, stretched out aimless to her sides and under her arms, the nipples almost invisible under the distension, to say nothing of my clasping mouth. She is muttering faintly, probably about the weather, while with a kind of desperation I try to find her opening, at the same time making polite comments about the disorder of the room, my embarrassment of her seeing it in such shambles, until finally with a moist clamor I feel myself sliding into her, sliding into her, and her arms go reluctantly around me, severing the connection of mouth and breast—which had never been that interesting anyway; I had been doing it only out of a sense of propriety—and with a series of horselike bucking movements not to say whinnies, she begins to carry me, carry me over the sliding eaves of her need.

I feel myself growing inside her and at the same time moving away; all this time birdsongs moving within my head, proud eaglets struggling to churn away from the surfaces of the sea, and the rain comes down unevenly, unevenly, so that I feel myself surrounded by a kind of disorder on all levels as I lie submissive at last in her embrace, feeling the slow steaming and then, as one particularly violent heave of her round body sets my magazines on the shelf above my bed to a kind of scuttling underneath their rubber band, I feel myself turned to them, turned to that attunement, and in a kind of explosion of feeling, all legs, all memory, I am devoured into her and expire slowly, reaching at this time for her breasts to support and inspect them. The feeling at the moment of orgasm has been that of girl-as-giant-fist clasped around my genitalia but underneath that has been something else; a profound undercurrent of woe, perhaps, an unscholarly feeling of mystery destroying the personality. When I came from without her limbs again with that peculiar slurping which seems, I have since discovered, to be the

comma of intercourse, I lay atop her having no idea of what to say until finally she dislodged me and sat up, her breasts assuming their normal (or abnormal) proportions again, falling hugely to the area of her navel where she inspected the nipples carefully, apparently for lustre or change of color.

"You really bite, don't you?" she says—all postcoital conversations have now, for me, assumed the aspect of the present tense; this is one subgenre which, because of its hideous sameness, is always of the moment. "You could have hurt them if they weren't so tough."

"Well, it was nice of you to come to the room," I say, because there is nothing else at the moment I can think of and at that moment, the magazines which have been precarious enough, shift on their perch and topple, in a slow, drooling wobble, one by one to the bed, between us. I shrug and reach toward them, hopeful that it will be seen as a kind of joke.

"Are these those girl magazines?" she says, chewing on a fingernail and reaching the free hand out to caress them. "Oh yes, they are. That's what I thought they were. You see them all over. You keep them too?"

"Just for the articles."

"Oh, a lot of the boys use them to jerk off. You'd be surprised how many use them that way. The shy ones, mostly. Do you ever use the magazines to jerk off in?"

"Not really," I say, assembling them hurriedly and trying to get them back on the shelf without exposing my genitalia which have hardened in idiot need to the coincidence. "I don't think of them that way."

"Oh that's perfectly all right. There's nothing shameful about it. A lot of the fellows who can't seem to get laid use them all the time. Can you imagine anyone not getting laid around this place?" She ventures a tentative laugh which becomes, eventually, a giggle. "It's possible, of course. You're not very good, you know. You need a lot of practice."

"It's not my fault. You rushed."

"Who rushed who?" she says, inspecting the other breast carefully, putting a finger in the nipple as if to test it for responsiveness. "You asked me to come to your room and have a talk and the next minute I have my clothes off. All of my clothes off. Not that I mind, of course. What else is there to do when it rains?"

"Well," I say, still in that slow stun which seems to be the inevitable consequence of the aftersex and feeling now too that familiar combination of dread and eagerness which means that the real implications of an event may lie entirely before me, "I guess you'd better get back upstairs."

"What? They never check after seven o'clock anyway. I might as well stay here all night."

"But in the morning—"

"Who's going to look? It's a progressive place. You've got to work with it; why fight things?"

I take her clothes from under the bed where I have casually tossed them with a social director's ease; where, poised like an arrow, I had hidden her garments in the same gracious gesture with which I had bent my mouth to her breasts. "I want you to go, though. I want to be alone now."

"Oh well," she says, "that's different. If you want to be alone, I can't stop you. Just don't ask me back again."

"Why not?" I say, finding my own clothing in the form of the shapeless bathrobe in which I had greeted her and belting it snugly. "It isn't anything personal."

"You could have some conversation too. It isn't all sex."

"What isn't?"

Somehow, I get through the moments between her nakedness and her entrapment, somehow I guide her without lapse of courtesy to the door, smooth over things, justify the equity of our act, our relations, the role they occupy in some larger scheme. Somehow, I enable her to pass through the door without disgrace, looking at her large rump dwindle in the hall, her step, a series of diminutions. I stand like a bird between heaven and hell; then opt for the latter with a bound, turning the key in my privates like a deep wound, moving out to cover all the inner and outer spaces. I seize the magazines and spreading the largest and most culpable all over the bed, I expose my organ from the (conveniently falling askew) bathrobe and holding it with both hands in a frenzy of disgrace I pull and pull until the last grey waters of consciousness have passed from inside to the outside of me and then I fall into a collapsing sleep, unstifled by groans, the magazines acting as a pillow for the precious rectal cheeks.

The name of this girl has been Carole and Carole is only one of the ten or so girls at this very progressive institution with whom I have coupled; there were Vivian and Portia and a girl named Helen with sloping, almost concave buttocks, and Marcia and Grace and Carole herself who dwelt in a double room above me and had found me interesting. The true tenor and possibilities of this new residence had been unknown to me for the first several days; when they became appallingly clear in the context of the mixed-sexes dormitory and the caliber of most of the personnel, it was still several weeks before I could act upon it. For me generation had always been an unequivocal, inward act rather than the frantic outpouring which seemed to be the *raison d'être* (can you spell that you idiot?) of this place, and when it did finally become clear that there was but one justification, one underlay, it took my atrophied skills a little longer to adjust. But now I was locked into the scheme of things: by day abysmal "classes" instructed by confused personnel, who seemed to be transfixed by latent possibilities which they could barely apprehend and of which they could never partake, functioned as a suitable bridge to the afternoons and evenings, and the evenings were full, rich, rooted in that casuality which is the token aim of the most progressive of all education. While Carole had been correct in saying that a surprising number of my colleagues were probably masturbators, it was wrong to attribute this to sheer lack; one of the prime benefits of this institution as it contributed to my self-knowledge was to give me the apprehension that there were many like me: those who preferred rather than submitted to the sacred self-abuse as the rounding-out of the full man. No one of us could have felt simple lack there; the male-female ratio had been contrived by a demon in the administration office to function at a constant one to one and as an occasional girl would leave the school in a fit of depression, insanity or pregnancy; as an occasional male would find this astonishing gratification of all forbidden fantasies too much for his cautious consciousness to assemble; a member of the same sex would be brought in, almost instantly, as replacement. It appeared that the waiting list for this institution was incredibly long; it numbered in the hundreds or, perhaps, the thousands, there would have been no way of explaining how she had maneuvered me in on something less than two months' notice had I not found out that one of the executive personnel had the same middle and last names as those of the social director, which cleared up part of the mystery. The girls were viable, cooperative, almost instantly gratifying, so much so that it was hard to believe that they, like me, were paying students; it was as if they had assumed a kind of staff function. I found out a great deal about the intricacies of female flesh during that splendid period; all the time holding my rod firmly in the final embrace behind locked doors to bring to my researches the final order of insight which could only be achieved by reinforcement-through-masturbation. Now I can construct for you a series of vignettes,

picturizations, actually, which taken in toto can approximate a pic-
turization of that period although, alas, it would be little more than
a metaphor; insufficient data always leading to this conclusion. The
name of this school was Rock Point and like the other resort it sat
somewhere in desiccated heartland, and the two peaks which gave it
its sole appeal held it clumsily, as two uneven palms might grasp a
cup, as two frantic, grasping hands might catch a breast and squeeze
its length away. Rock Point was privately supported by what was
known mysteriously in the catalogue as "friends of the institution,"
which endowment, added to the handsome sums paid for tuition
and other benefits, enabled the school to have purchased the small
cemetery lying directly on its westward flank. It had commissioned
this cemetery as a "historical site," so much of what occurred seems
to have taken place within its confines.

I am holding the girl named Vivian close, close in the small
shelter I have made of chest and huddled thighs and she is burrowing beneath me eagerly, seeking my privates, her free hand caressing
me aimlessly in the area of the nape of the neck. We are clutched to
the right of a small gravestone, the northern drizzle coming down
slantwise and I feel the guilt once again surging within me that I had
not taken her to my room, and insisted that we get a "breath of out
doors" despite all signals to the contrary and had subjected her to
what can only be a complex humiliation, her body dampened by
the unrelieving blanket of rain which I can feel chill on my exposed,
upturned buttocks. But she does not seem to mind for all of that;
she is embarked on a complex, careless journey of her own, her
hands gripping and squeezing with amazed and growing discovery;
her mouth also enlarged and slippery under mine as her tongue
whickers inside. *Wet, wet,* she is murmuring, her upturned body
careless in the slick moisture and I am reaching as best as I can,
squeezing as best I can, while trying to make that difficult contact.
She is open before me, a furnace stoked by its own heat, unneeding
of operation and for an instant, trying to make the contact, I can
feel the foolishness; the sheer pointlessness of it all as I try to
burrow inside her; the position always striking me, somehow, as
irrelevant and pointless, the supple ease and graciousness of the
masturbatory turn having conditioned me. Her mouth presses
against mine, unyielding rubber and I reach forward with my loins
to find her slender frame: as I do so we slide, gracelessly into the

very stones of the grave site so that the crown of her head touches and obscures some chiseled letters. "Oh, oh," she mutters, "never anything like this before," and I feel her rising to greet me, her slight, superfluous breasts trembling and puckering with the cold impact of the stone and still fighting, still pillowing within her, I reach a damp palm up to grasp the gravestone for support and feel the hollows of the letters pressed against my hand; apparently it is the word BELOVED although I cannot be sure. "Inside, inside, you ass," she is muttering to me—all of them curse at the moment of gathering, I have learned this; their revulsion at the act being so deep that even the Magazines themselves could hardly explain it, make it comprehensible—and as best as I can I point myself within her, reaching the other hand also for the gravestone because without that clinging support surely I will fall from my kneecaps and strike myself a blow in a more vulnerable spot from the stone. So as I move over her I am not touching her but the polished slickness of an epitaph, eyeing her nipples with rolling eyes, the eyes distended and flattened against the palm of my skull by the enormous effort I am making; the seriousness of the commitment. I feel absent flashes of fire, a rumbling below and my glazed eyes, fastened upon the stone, close; now I see the images of The Magazine itself and the images are less what is upon the page, the familiar dismemberment and narrowed focus upon breast, thigh, buttock, but rather upon the pages themselves, their uneven glossiness, the slickness of their feel: the Words written under the pictures that are themselves part of the picture and as her nipples rise up toward me in a trembling of gratitude I bend slightly, my eyelids still fluttering and put the last inches into her; feeling then the steaming and rising, the entrapment itself and my palms graze against the stone, entrap the stone, feeling the stone itself and yet at that moment it is probably not the stone but the very pages of the Magazine that I am feeling and so I come that way in a small spot of gloom, a cove of misery too deep to be reached let alone filtered by the bucking motions of thighs, the sound of cries in the air around me, the rain sifting down. "Come on," she says, grabbing me when I have worked out the last agonized spurts, "come on now and *come* you bastard," and this works me through the storms and stones of another orgasm, my palms falling from the slippery surface of the epitaph and I crumble on her quite helpless, quite drained while in an orgy of pragmatism she draws me over her body to cover her completely while one semi-detached hand, possessed of its own cleverness, begins to search for her pants.

I am in the cemetery again on a late-winter evening but far from the gravesites this time with a huge-breasted, tiny-buttocked girl named Jane who says that she has always wanted to do it open in the cool air, tickled by trees. The tree we have found is a wispy remnant of some crazed itinerant's mission, its leaves rustling dimly around us and somewhere in its very center protected against all elements, we huddle, the two of us quite naked this time while the huge, glowing surfaces of her breast flop a merry drum against my chest, my lips having found fuller purchase on her forehead where, discovering a full head of skin, they suck and suck away. She is not cursing to me but singing this time; singing one of the popular tunes of the era in a voice which both missounds and subsumes its banality; the song is all about love and Jove, heart and start and her voice, an unpleasant contralto, lifts to the uneven pounding of my thighs. I have caught her hole the first time out for once; the practice of fucking outweighing its disadvantage in some cases, the tiny hole possessing rewards which the more easily found (because instantaneously adjustable) closed fist could never provide and as best as I can, I am fucking away my private fuck on her, listening at the same time to the toneless melody which, absurdly, shifts now and then to a whistle, searching for her breasts with thumb and closed forefinger, and what she is singing blends, finally, into the better part which is what she is not seeing and so I come that way, poised bird against her huntressy determination, flicking seeds from my bill into her pouch and she clasps me in an orgy of gratitude as my magazine-inspired sperm greets her ripening and eager Egg. "Oh boy," she says, "oh boy, oh boy, oh boy, you're all heart; that's what you are; a jove of love." My throat, crackling with retrospection's saliva, would tell her something, but I am obviously speechless.

Surrounded by darkness above and below, I am suspended on my bed, hands and knees to full flight, moving eagerly in the ascension and reversal of love, locked into a cell of sensation so private and interesting that I could as well be alone but underneath me is the girl named Margaret, her body spread like drifting water, porous on the surfaces of the bed and she is accommodating me;

accommodating me as best she can in her slippery hole, her hands working idly on my chest. Margaret is one of the "less advantaged" members of the student body; she supplements her scholarship and meager allowance by doing "housekeeping" tasks in the dormitory, and it is in such circumstances that I have come to greet her, her mop, broom and housedress to the side of the bed, her industry forgotten as we move in another, intricate kind of cleaning-gesture. I have then, it seems, done it to the housekeeper here, as well as everybody else, but the housekeeper is 17 years old and is mumbling to me in a credulous voice: *this is terrific, this is really terrific; I didn't know you guys had beds like this; you couldn't imagine what we girls have to sleep in; I could lie like this forever.* And so she could, but I am pursuing her with unprecedented industry, unprecedented business, her breasts so superfluous in the welter of sensation I have aroused through our joining that I am barely conscious of their presence or appearance. *This is really the lap of luxury* she advised me as her thighs thrust in conformation.

Above me, the cheerful, rattling *thump! bump!* of my magazines in their locked pouch indicates perilous movement on the
shelf, the possibility of collision, disaster, falling action at any time
and the knowledge that these magazines could truly fall, right into
the cup of my exposed buttocks, bringing a kind of triumphant
finale to my researches, fills me with ever-quickening excitement; I
can imagine how they would feel clouting me slowly like a large
covey of emergent insects and the explanations I would have to
give — *oh the explanations!*—all of this sending me even further and
deeper into necessity's groin and her arms gather listlessly to drag
me in. *I have to finish off the other rooms soon,* she reminds me
behind her closed eyes, *otherwise I'll lose my stipend,* and I moan to
her in a burst of cooperation and feel myself open and open above
her, a reciprocal opening below; breezes seem to drift over my
buttocks and I get it inside her to its fullest length, feeling her
fingers scrapple on my shoulders and the tube of her gathers around
me all ferocity, all obligement and I finish then to a feeling of slow
scattering, thousands of sheets of paper drifting down around me;
fall upon her in the rigidity of the corpse itself imagining how it
would be indeed if all of this texture and stock, photography and
art would come down over the hushed and tenanted spaces of my
distantly bartered grave.

I am at a "drive-in" movie with tiny-buttocked Jane again; this
time she wants to do it in a new and novel way during which she
can examine celebrities and because of her help and attention I am
in poor position to protest. There is no way in which I can tell her
that the trunk of the rented car which we have jointly taken (but
which I must pay for and which Jane must drive) is jammed, almost
to the top, with magazines; a hasty room inspection during the
morning had determined that these would have to be out of my
premises before was conducted what was called there the "mid-
semester audit." This procedure, nominally to determine whether
or not students were living up to the health habits and ways of the
institution was actually, I long suspected, in search of prophylactics
or the remains of aborted fetuses but I judged it unwise—oh, the
cunning now that I had at last learned what they really meant!—to
have my magazines for discovery; masturbation was the one excess
which the school, even in its convocations, would never imply. *(We*

must learn to love one another, had been the suggestion of the Headmaster during the mid-Christmas assembly, *even if some touching is required in the process;* he had said nothing of Loving Oneself.) So the magazines, carried from class to class in a large imitation leather briefcase with a self-locking clasp, had been unobtrusively tossed in the rented trunk during the conclusion of the rental process; now as I jounced and bounced my lonely way above Jane's watchful breasts I hoped that somewhere in the rear there was no suggestion of reciprocal, less joyous, bouncing of the hidden and more important load. Before my stunned eyes had drifted the slight convexity of the screen, huge images locked with one another in two or three colors, suspended above us, and in the soundlessness acting out scenes far more intricate and beautiful than we could ever conceive, but now I had turned down upon her again, making rough work of the entrance because it would be quickest and the quicker fruition would lead to quicker retrieval of the magazines, but she wanted it slow, begged to me in her small popular-singer's voice to extend it as far as possible, all the time her eyes rolled to the screen where she absorbed the images in a kind of placidity and contentment which I could only dimly apprehend. Her mouth, working on some gum, chewed evenly, her eyes calm and bright surveyed me with an owner's pride as I jabbed and jabbed at her slender receiving reed and then, hastening over her, my eyelids clamped and fluttering against her breasts, I must have had an accident; I must have jabbed something with an elbow because the speakers suddenly flicked on, both of them and the voices began to boom and shatter in the car, words of love and rage tumbling over one another in unbearable volume and I reached out my hand, trembling, to smash or reduce the sound but found it stayed by two tentative fingers she had raised to stay it. "No," she murmured, "leave it on; it's nice," and I fought with the cripple's weakness to free myself of that clasp and shatter the sound, but, confident of what her thighs had done to take my strength, she merely held the pressure and said again, "It's so *nice* this way; what do you want to spoil all the fun for; it's just like they're right in the car or we're up on the screen, isn't that more exciting?"

And confined now by a small and terrible rage, a rage which exerted a pressure which screamed only for Justice—whatever that must be—I found the resolve she wanted, which was only the resolve for perishment, for completion, for a connection so rapid as to lead to an immediate withdrawal, which would be the end of shame, but with her clever, fluttering box she held me off for a long long time and so I was forced to listen to strings and horns, shrieks and giggles, sobs and *scenis obligatoria* while my reluctant weapon ground out its few spurts of enthusiasm and I came mumbling against her, as contrite, humbled and profoundly embarrassed as any character in the *commedia* she was witnessing. Throughout she took me with a massive and almost sympathetic air of contrition, her thighs grinding against my organ, her hole exerting the last inch of pressure against myself and at the apocalyptic moment, as through memory I raged and bucked thinking of those lovelies in the trunk, her thumb rose to her mouth and she sucked it earnestly, her eyes averted as I spent into her. Finally free, I was able to turn down the sound, still clamped within her and as I did so she sighed and looked at me as if for the first time, her fingers winding, winding below to complete the circle of causation.

"It's really a good movie," she said, "you know that? There's so much sense to it, just good common sense. What did you do down there? Did you finish? I wasn't sure."

"You weren't sure?"

"Well, I wasn't really concentrating on the movie and like that. I mean, I hope you had a good time, I didn't want to stop you or anything like that. It's just that I'm not really in the mood."

"I guess I finished," I said. "Do you want me to go outside and pick up anything? You want something to eat?"

"Well, that wouldn't be a bad idea, I guess. I'd want some hamburgers and drinks and so on. Maybe some candy. You sure you won't get lost outside and not be able to come back? I'd hate to have to return this car alone; I'd owe the whole thing."

"I think I can make it."

"Make sure you remember what row we're in and what number car. That's the best way of doing it."

Still within her, I tried to withdraw. "Okay," I said, "but I have to get my pants on." For a fine, slender moment of panic I thought that some of the horrid blue-covered texts in my parents' dresser which I had once read had intimated the truth after all; that I was in the grip of *glans penis captivus*. The harder I tugged, the more snugly the conjoinment seemed to fit. Finally, I lost my bal-

ance and túmbled on top of her, her little jaws still earnestly com-
pressing and contracting the gum. "What's wrong?"

"I can't get out."

"What do you mean, you can't get out?"

"I mean, it seems stuck in there." I guided her unwilling hand
down, let her fondle the dilemma. "You see what I mean?"

"Oh," she said, "that's just the thighs. Nothing to worry about
at all; I'll just move my legs a little." I felt her grunt underneath me,
her body heave. "Of course it's difficult to move because you're on
top of me."

"Well, I can't get off you, can I?"

"I know that. Gee, this is really kind of embarrassing." Her
fingers pinched, brought a glimmer of pain. "Try it now."

I tried, seemed to be on the verge of a small but boisterous
withdrawal, but felt the pressure even harder, somewhere near the
tip. "No, that won't do it."

"Jesus, I'm getting all out of position. I can hardly see the
screen. We'll miss the whole movie and all."

"I've still got to get out of there."

"Couldn't you just kind of lie around and nap for a little
while, until the picture's over? Then we can both work. It isn't
anything to worry about; this has happened to me before. I have a
very small, nervous thing."

"But I thought you wanted me to go out for some food."

"Well, yeah. Yeah, that's right too. Okay, now. You know,
once a boy got caught inside for an hour. Boy was he mad! He
didn't know what to say; we just had to wait until he got small
enough to get out. That wasn't you, was it, who got stuck?"

"No, this is the first time it's happened."

"Oh. I guess I was thinking of someone else. All right try it
now."

"I can't. I can't move."

She giggled. "This could be very embarrassing. I told you,
you'll cool off and get out if you'll only relax. Why don't you put
my breasts in your mouth and just relax on them? Boys seem to
like that."

"I want to get out," I said and at that moment, the Singing
Strings, all 106 of them, apparently in some unprecedented cinematic transition, broke out into an unmuted throb, a series of

pulses so sharp as to break the tenor equipment of the speaker and fill the car with rattlings of sound.

"My God," Jane said, "someone's trying to come and see us. We better really get out of here. Can you drive?"

"It's just the speaker. Now let me do this." I felt myself overcome by rage, but as profound as that was, the pain was still there at the rock-center of the scene, flooding into my organ, making it even more turgid, things more rigid. I managed to get both hands in position, squashing what little there was of her breasts with my upper arms and seized what I could find of my organ, pulling and pulling desperately. She gave a high wheeze, somewhere between a shriek and a sigh and began to settle under me like a blanket.

"God that's lovely," she said, "I don't know what you're doing there but it's just lovely. More, more."

"I'm trying to get out."

"With the fingers, squeeze around that way. Oh, God, that's really terrific now. I can see the movie and everything. The speaker is broken. The movie is good. You've got to squeeze more. Oh, I'm coming, I'm coming. That's it. That's it. I'm coming."

And come she did in a series of thick waves and flashes of thumping which somehow disgorged my prick at her moment of climax and left it, sopping wetly, on the shiny cushions of the rental car. The speaker clattered in the blackness and, rubbing my fingers in her hole, I obliged her to an orgasm. She fell back, her eyes gripped by the screen.

"That was good," she said. "That was really terrific."

Speechless, I used a shirttail to clean off the residue of my orgasm, managed to adjust my garments without undue rolling, poked an elbow against the window painfully and subsided in the seat, watching several ballerinas on the screen attempt to persuade a choreographer that they were usable. I was quite incapable of thought.

"Well?" she said when the ballerinas had made their case and, embracing one another, had vanished in favor of an operatic singer who appeared to be having romantic difficulties with the choreographer. "What about it?"

"What about what?"

"Aren't you going to go out and get us something to eat? You said you would, you know. I'm hungry. I fixed you and all, the least you can do is bring some food back."

I managed to get the door open and inspecting her for a considerable time—she had heaved herself to a sitting position and was working halfheartedly on her brassiere while searching the dashboard for a fresh piece of gum—I got out into the dirt of the enclosure itself, standing uneasily on the ragged ground, trying to find my balance. Now, in the speakerless silence the screen had assumed a kind of beauty, its figures in being devoid of noise seemed to lack context as well. Moving in a sea as mysterious and as possessed of its fulfillment as I had moved in my sea sleeps many years ago. I stumbled away from it, my back to the screen, my eyes to the moon, feeling a special tendril of fiery knowledge cross between my smuggled goods in the trunk and my exhausted loins as I trudged to the food counter.

And, too, I am with Marcia the redundant in a classroom this time in the pitch of a winter evening, the two of us huddled over the desk, quite naked, her eyes roaming the ceiling while I inspect her nipples with microscopic urgency and work on the alternating surfaces of her stomach and thighs with a woe compounded out of lust and fright. We have no business doing it in this building, but she has assured me that faculty and staff themselves are aware of the student need to disseminate knowledge in its oldest form in the very seat of learning and that to copulate in the classrooms is, in the last analysis, only to join in the hidden and therefore more necessary, purposes of the institution itself. I am sliding, sliding, all lost in the glistening wetness, my tool a tangle, my eyes bulging and behind them I am playing the pictures and images while I work at her with a fool's persistence.

"Higher, higher," she mutters and for a moment I think she means a greater thrust and I attempt to spread her deeper and deeper yet upon the desk but her frantic, tickling fingers below tell me that there is something else she has in mind and I find withdrawal forced, a sudden retraction, a sudden drawing. Pouring sweat and mingled juices, my prick looks for a better home and she guides me with her hands to the cleft between her breasts, centering me with an indulgent palm while with the other she tugs at a breast and then, the first hand freed, takes the other in her hand and forms for me a tight channel, a wedge almost, through which I guide the small, desperate prow of my ship.

And it is as close, then, as close as I can ever come, before or since, to the sensation of the magazines, for here it is all before me, her breasts, held in that full, cupped aspect, almost dislodged from her body, her face a disordered irrelevancy behind the spread of her hair, and I feel myself reaching, reaching, grown to enormous size and power within her and she reaches forward grateful lips to touch me with teeth-and-tongue, adding a slow insistence to my rhythm. I can see vaguely below her cupped and held breasts the shuddering of her thighs and trembling of that nervous skin caught between them but it means nothing to me; I am surrounded by breasts and breasts, nestled in them, lost in them and as she increases the tension on them to make a cylinder I feel myself lengthen toward a final extension and come easily, gratefully, missing her withdrawn face, my hands reaching to touch the side of her breasts with appreciation while she mutters encouragement to me and I leak out the last drops.

After a long time I fall away from her, my buttocks brushing chalk, sliding to a stop on the wood and she looks up at me easily, her eyes glistening with an emotion come close to tenderness. "Oh, wasn't that wonderful?" she says. "When my breasts are held that way, they look just like all the breasts in those magazines, don't they? Don't they?" I tell her this is so and bury my apologetic prick in her bush, waiting for the lights to come on, waiting for the assailant to come.

Somewhere in the middle of that year—I am not sure when and it hardly matters—I received a letter from Marie-Jean, the only piece of extra-familial correspondence which came into my mailbox that year:

". . . I obtained your address from my father who with no difficulty attained it from your mother. I guess you suppose you're lucky to be up there, ha, ha, but I wanted to write you this letter to tell you that although you are gone you are not forgotten, at least not by me although you would like to think so. For what you did to me I can never forgive you even though you can forgive yourself so easily for a thousand things; I want you to know that Marie-Jean thinks of you all the time and that Marie-Jean will never relax for a moment until she has paid you back in kind for what you did to her. What form that payment will take and when it will happen is none of your business; it could happen at any minute or not for the next 100 years but it will happen and it will serve you right. Not only did you dishonor and shame me, you dishonored and shamed my father by having your mother take up his time only because then you could be safe in taking me into the cornfields. My father is a fine man, an innocent man, a widower who means everything to me but is not a man who knows people of your type and your mother's and thus could not deal with you or protect himself but I can protect him double and I will. No matter what happens to us there will be a time of getting even. I do not want you to answer this letter as if you do I will find it necessary for me to tear it up . . ."

And yet another fulfillment: straight as an arrow, proud as a blade, I am hunched on the main quadrangle of the "campus" itself, giving it in this noon of the night to the proudest, most preposterous of all the bitches I have met this year; a girl named Elena with breasts which thrust up as squarely as they thrust out, breasts whose resilience increases out of clothes, thighs whose slight flabbiness only made more needful and urgent those muscular exercises which comprised her special contribution to the craft of copulation, her feet pointed at the moon at the same angle that my buttocks were and there was, around us, no intimation of substance or of presence, only the two of us in the spring night, the campus hushed around us, all groans and quivers in the cathedral or the cemetery. It was Elena's special innovation to do it in the center of this quadrangle itself at safe hours; expressing, as she said, her feelings for the environment in the best way possible and she was extremely difficult, not out of prudence, but by virtue of sheer weight of numbers; there was always a waiting list of 30 or more for Elena's embrace and there was no way to hasten one's progress on that list because she was strictly fair about the process; so fair that some escorts, having painfully waited out their ascension, wanted to do it a second time but on another night and Elena felt that not to give an option would be to render herself a bit of a slut. So it was a question of patience, patience, but in the last analysis she was worth it; the most "special" of all the special people who inhabited

the campus, she conceded darkly that she had been there for five years and had worked with difficulty to her position of queen ex-officio; a position whose only benefit was that she was able, in essence, to talk for the student body at the occasional faculty confrontations which were part of the progressive spirit. I had waited and waited, working out my time with the Janes and the Viviennes, waited for so long that it seemed to me that Elena was a hoax and the waiting list was a ploy, but one night she called me in my room to say that she was finally able to take me up on dinner the following evening and now at last I had her; I had the queen on her campus itself, and it was almost worth it because she not only did not block out my fantasies or twist her body unconsciously against them as some of the others had but rather, with a tenderness and understanding I had thought impossible in women, had seemingly understood almost from the start what I wanted and had allowed me to stretch out not on top but alongside her, a fist held in readiness, while she dwarfed my organ in her bulky pouch and produced her breasts, one by one, for me to nibble. I was as loose, swinging and free at ease as if I had been doing it into a magazine; her body, a long, coiled tube, seemed ready to spring to my convenience at any moment. So we sighed and mumbled the night away, our limbs tumbled like glass on the shores of that campus, her breasts bulging hugely and contentedly against all my surfaces and until the sun came we lay there, every confrontation a joy, every joy a refreshment and then, as the sun began to moan darkly in the distance she came upon the oldest, coldest and boldest variation of them all; what she did was to take her breasts in either hand and pointing them toward me, she—

BARRY MALZBERG

Barry Malzberg lives with his wife and daughter in Manhattan and is worried about having recently reached the ominous age of thirty. This despite the fact that he has published, to date, fifteen stories and one novel in the science-fiction field. His novella Final War, *originally published in* The Magazine of Fantasy and Science Fiction, *was triply anthologized this year and won third place in the 1969 SFWA Nebula Awards competition. Mr. Malzberg's first hard-cover novels,* Oracle of the Thousand Hands *and* Screen *are seriously-intentioned works which, according to the author, were neither fun to write nor fun to retrospect. Major influences upon his work, in no particular order, are: Norman Mailer, J.D. Salinger, Saul Bellow, James Agee, Vladimir Nabokov, Fyodor Dostoyevsky and Nikolai Gogol.*

Nether City

John Voigt

Joao lies on the fire escape outside Maria's window, peering in on her, she naked in the warm spring night, naked and dozing and still and alone. It was as if she were in a coma that was close to death. There was no movement of life until the brown flat coarse nipple ring rose in a sleep-bound shudder. She moved one of her arms away from its spot under her head and made a passing movement over her stomach and then she was still again. Joao centered his balance on the fire escape and carefully studied her. He unzipped his fly and with some difficulty took out his erection from his drawers. The night breezes felt unusual and pleasing as they passed over the head of it and he could smell his own pungency. He grasped himself tightly and masturbated as his eyes ran over her exposed body. More than her other parts, her open mouth, freckled from time to time with small drops of saliva, captured his attention and imagination. His eyes did not blink.

But it was no use. His member felt brittle and un-flesh-like as he tugged away at it. Climax was nowhere in sight and he slipped himself back in his pants.

With his knife he slides back the tongue of the lock on her door and on tiptoe enters the room. She snorts but remains deeply asleep as he sits on the bed, removes his shoes, and lies quietly by

her. It was first the finger next to his index finger on the right hand
that he used, beginning by stroking as lightly as he could her eyebrows, first the left one, marveling on how much it felt like a
kitten's fur as he gave a stroke from left to right, then back again,
then left to right again, enjoying the fact that she did not budge at
all from her deep slumber and continued breathing as softly as she
had done before when he had watched her from the fire escape, but
perhaps with this difference: that being that she snorted a bit more
now, but she remained asleep, not waking as that same finger of his,
now wetted with a drop of her spit, went to the other eyebrow, the
right one this time, and just as slowly and softly repeated its back-
and-forth strokes and he even tugged at an occasional tuft of her
hair, leaving droplets of her own saliva to trickle down the strands
and down onto her flesh and then he let the finger—it was more
that the finger had a will of its own, to tell the truth—let the finger
slide down the side of her face, lightly as before but now with all
the other fingers on that hand into play, going to the spongy flesh
of her earlobe, pinching it, then placing the still-dampened finger
into the ear itself, then out and down the cheekbone until the hand
came to her lips, now awake and mumbling something—perhaps
they ask who is it or some such question in an effort to find out
what had awakened her from her deep sleep, but the words inarticu-
late and her eyes remained closed as her tongue tip came sliding out
from her mouth, flat broad wet, looking like the fat end of some
oversized pink-fuzz-fleshed ironing board, which delighted in moving and wiggling its way out of a closed cavern, coming into the
light so that it might attack flesh-pleasure-objects and be attacked
by them, and still her eyes remained closed and her mouth, tired
of attempting to say anything in this half-sleep state of hers chose
to open a bit in a protruding lip pucker, aware even if she was not
that a man lay by her side, a man who had just touched her eyebrows and trailed his hand about her face and had now brought his
fingers to the very crest of her tongue and in the same smooth light
strokes it had elected to move in since the beginning, stroked the
tongue and Joao pictured how she would place her fingers in his
mouth and how he would bite them, lightly at first and then a little
harder and she when more awake would place her teeth right into
his flesh, offered or not, but now she was not eager for such things,
content to lie back and be stroked as her tongue, a fat one, waved

about in the air lapping about at anything that had length about it, but his finger tips chose instead to run themselves on the outside of her lips, then with the application of a bit more force they pry open these lips of hers to push up and down and under to get next to the teeth and gums, stopping purposely to massage the bottom edges of the one broken canine tooth, to—as it were—scratch the fingertip on the small pointed pieces of enamel that remain for such things and her eyes are open and tongue hanging full out of her head like a cobra springing for death, but her lips buzzed life, the finger moving from the upper one to the lower one and back and forth once again before going full into the mouth, once again gathering enough of her spit from under her tongue to lubricate its trip down over her chin into the furrow between her moving breasts but careful not to climb just yet up onto these dark cream twin mountains of tit, capped with round level splotches of tiny red non-erect nipple and with his other hand (which had lain dormant until this time) he touched her hip, the one closest to him, and she swung onto her side facing him and she wanted him to be naked as she was and she began to tug away at his clothes, picking his tee shirt first, sliding her hands into his pants to loosen it, but once inside his pants she slid her hand down to one of his fat cheeks and gave it a pinch and then began to move around her hand—still inside his buttoned pants—in an attempt to get at the still encased member but his pants were tight on him and she grew quickly frustrated in this her first move for clearly he was in charge of what was happening to her because he came on her so suddenly, so unexpectedly, and now two hands into play: the first tracing clockwise circles on her hip; the second tracing counterclockwise between her paps, the erectile tissue beginning to fill with blood now outlined as a slight projection from the white flesh beneath it, rising imperceptibly in the tempo his hands make—hands that were matched though one went from right to left and the other from left to right—matched because both completed their slightly different-sized circles (one ranging the valley between her breasts, tracing not a circle actually but what should be considered as an ellipse, a geometric ellipse, not perfect as in pictures of them, but certainly more in the ellipse shape than in the circle shape his other hand made as it rubbed on her flank) — hands careful not to come to either the front or the back of her, for this would hurry the act and this is not what Joao wanted, nor had he any

intention of doing such a thing for it was not the time to bring his
fingers into the still closed orifices of cunt and anus and by her
struggle during this time, she managed to free her hand that had
been trapped in his pants and in several jerking motions pulled the
tee shirt from him, forcing him to work on her with only one hand
at a time as the other hand rose into the air to let her pull the thing
from his head, but to compensate for this the hand stroking between the breasts ran in a semi-circle unto one of these flesh mountains, and when the arm was raised that had the breast-playing
hand, raised so as not to rip the garment, as cheap as it was, his
other closed in a crab-like claw and he dug his nails hard into her
hip flank leaving four trailing rake marks a few inches across the fat
freckled wholesome flesh, then both of his hands went in under her
in a scooping motion, both of them still lying on their sides facing
each other, and he held the thick-fleshed part of her upper thighs,
but from behind and in this spot where her legs touched was just a
little damp even though he felt it at once, and his hands started to
knead away at this part of her body and he swung his mouth
toward her to trace the pattern his hands had begun, tongue tip
rubbing back and forth in the eyebrows, down to the cheek, the
ear, in the ear, the lips, then into the mouth to touch what he could
with his tongue: her tongue, under the tongue, tongue root, gums,
teeth, spit, and by this time she had pried open the top button of
his pants and rubbed the flat of her palm on his chest, teasing his
nipples into an erect state, erect as they could be, digging into his
belly button hard enough so that he grunted into her mouth, his
mouth full open and she let her spit flood into it as she sucked the
air out of his belly at the same time her hand opening his zipper
full, letting the stiffened love tool push forward under the cotton
drawers that she grasped and pulled down to expose the pubis and a
bit of the flaming red head of it, the arrowhead of it, but not the
full length of his cock for he pulled his hand from her body and
slapped her hand, admittedly lightly, but a slap nevertheless and
hard enough to leave a sting and a small red mark to which she
answered by rolling over and biting him hard on the upper muscle
of his left arm—using broken tooth and all—the pain felt pleasurable
so Joao made no effort to prevent her from doing this but only
opened his fingers wide and pushed them through the hair on her
head then closed them pulling her back, the jolt of it causing her

tongue to pop back out of her mouth and with it protruding this way he brought his mouth over it and sucked it hard, concentrating so hard on this that she gained entrance to his cock and grasped it firmly by its root as if it were a corn stalk and she were trying to unroot it, all in all a gesture that pleased him because of the impossibility of bringing it about because his was a noble prick with flesh as hard as iron and filled with blood, heavy as lead, and he rolled on his stomach freeing his member from her grasp and did not touch her and she with her still-protruding tongue licked the base of his neck, the space between his shoulder blades, the ripples of his spinal column, neck, back, and then the darker-colored spot of flesh right above the furrow of his buttocks, her tongue on the neck bent around now so that he could watch as she licked the right shoulder blade and the left shoulder blade, the full trail of the spine, the fur tuff, and the buttock's valley fragrant with his body, sucking on the stretched neck, the shoulders themselves, trailing spit tracks around to his armpits, taking nips down his side, slow entwining circles around the lower part of the small of his back, licking into the furrow, trailing back up again but faster now and in a reversed direction from before: the furrow, the spine base, letting her tongue hit each of the backbone bumps, up to the neck to add her hands into play by squeezing her thumbs into the fleshy sides of his body, the tongue now back at the base of the neck and without being a bit exhausted after all its adventures and in fact feeling invigorated began to whip down his back again, pausing at the familiar spots but this time laying into the flesh more spiritedly than before as if she were trying to do the impossible (i.e., cause pain) continuing its lapping on his neck, the upper back, the small of the back biting the hairs there, and then wildly into the narrower path between his cheeks and ending in a grand flourish by prying open the tight but not recalcitrant walls of his anus and pushing her tongue up him as far as it would stretch, and it was still wiggling and waving about but now in him, up his ass to be precise, and he lies still on his stomach contemplating her agility but only after a few of her probings he has had enough and he disengages himself from her greedy mouth and hands and swings around and up on top of her and grasps the fullness of her breasts in each of his hands and he squeezes, loses his grip, then squeezes again and the hardness of his grasp adds to the hardness of her much longer now nipples (all told they hang out over an eighth of an inch) and his member happens to fall smack in the middle of her patch of pubis and he continues the motive of his foreplay by grasping himself and rubbing the fully exposed arrowhead of it in circles in the patch, making sure not to touch the tip-top of the vulva that holds an equally erect clitoris, rubbing his penis into her lower stomach hair—thick and sumptuous—holding himself in his hand but not masturbating as he did before on the fire escape, but this time just holding himself stiffly and the other hand cups her woman breasts, kneading one, then the other, stopping to place his fingertips around the nipple tissue and then pulling them forward as if to raise them in length, and in fact this is what happens for they extend a little more than before, and especially so after these repeated motions of his, and her enthusiasm is added to by the hairiness and softness of his testicles that she holds, albeit awkwardly, in her hand, and he too holds himself and traces circles in and about her tuff, coming close to the vulva's outer extremity but only to bring the head of it down suddenly to where her thigh flesh meets belly flesh and her mouth is planted against his, then she sucks down his shoulders and then his nipples, bending her head at a bizarre angle to enable the contact of mouth to chest of hair and small tits, bouncing his balls all the time, her hand moving up and down like the hand of some old jeweler trying to judge the weight of some large semi-precious stones, or the hand of a housewife measuring the weight of a piece of cheese to make sure no one was going to cheat her, but it is his nuts (nothing else) that are filling up with large amounts of come cream so that they ache in wanting to discharge so much of it in her belly as deep as he can put it in her—but not just yet because there is still so much to do like her tiny fingers that flutter around the back of his nuts, and then center themselves on the spot where scrotum sack merges and melts into that small discovered anomalous hunk of flesh that separates testicles from the anus, and it is here that Maria presses down her fingers and feels the stiffness of his erection going back up into his body and ending somewhere beyond her touch around the tip of the spine in a bundle of mechanical nerves that respond to each little press of hers by sending out billions of electrical vibrations and her hand in this spot makes her think that the entire tool could be ripped from his body and that it would extend the full length of a ruler, but only of course until all the blood ran out of it or whatever kept it flesh weapon pointed up at her anus-hole now, still avoiding the vulva lips and the clitoris covered with bubbles of delight cream on the gap—the all encompassing opening of the chamber, the flesh caverns with their collapsible walls that he has entered before but not yet this time because he has chosen to avoid it as he lies on his side and she on hers facing him and letting him run his tool over her pussy so that the hardened upper surface of it hits the opening of the orifice now as he goes past it, descending in a futile attempt to make an entrance in her rear but she is not ready for that now but perhaps later and squeezes her cheeks together as if she were forcing back a huge fart but in fact all she is doing is keeping his fish hook outside of her only to return to batter hard against the tight-membraned muscle of the anus-hole looking like a puckered-up mouth as she pulls on his hair growing in his armpit, head, the hair above his cock, on his cock, on his nuts, in the furrow, stopping to run a long fingernailed finger right up him so suddenly and so unexpectedly that he, feeling the jolt in his prostate, almost pours out a full supply of sperm right on her ass, but he holds most of it back and only enough trickles out of him to make the arrowhead gleam and his finger returns her favor doing the same thing to her which causes their other activity to slow down leaving only this mutual masturbation of anus-holes, as they roll about the bed: he on top—she on top—he on top—she on top— etc.—on their sides—on their reversed sides—she on top—he on top—ripping into each other's assholes, finger-fucking each other hard and wild in the rectum, getting their fingers covered with a good healthy shit smell until when he lifted her up and she fell away from his hand, letting out the most delicious of farts which he casually inhaled thus sparking him on to other actions like bringing his lips to her nipples in a continuing succession, the right, the left, the right, the left and continuing this as he also rubbed circles with his fingertips on her vulva, but still careful not to touch the little button but not opposed at all to sliding some of the natural moist juices that flowed freely from her inner-belly, bringing these juices down and massaging them into her anus-hole readying that sweet spot for any possible future action when he felt her mouth full sucking on his cock her fingers pulling back the foreskin exposing the full dimensions of the arrowhead of it, her tongue liking the tastes it discovered: his moisture, her moisture, their moisture of mixed sweat and sex juices running between lips and breasts, genitals and buttocks furrows, their hands rubbing in the sweet sweat juices and she cried out to him to bring his body in her and her hands pulled what clothes still remained on him, clothes bundled up around his ankles, pulled them from him and she threw them on the floor and her hand went for the cock to hold it firmly and to study the dark pink arrowhead of cock head but the single finger now playing at the base of her twin sweated breasts pressed her down, the finger so hard on her that she could not breathe and a trickle of spit ran from her gasping mouth, lips still wanting to clamp onto his cock and tickle its head with a fat wet tongue but this would hurry the act and deny him some of the pleasure of it so he held her down with one short fat finger and kept his body away from directly touching hers as his other hand moved up for an instant and pulled on the pubis growing in the cleft of her backside, a gentle little tug, and he removed his stranglehold on her chest and the hand that had just played in her asshole went to the coughing, fighting-for-air mouth and four fingers went in and her tongue in desperation licked them, licked the four fingers and a thumb and not minding the taste of her anus and even enjoying it and then he traced ever-descending circles toward her nipples and touched the coarse ring around them with all his fingers, rubbing his belly against her legs, he took one of her hands and led it to his nipples and with her fingertips in his, he showed her what he wanted, something like squeezing the juice from a purple grape but she stopped touching that spot as soon as he removed his hands, and she brought her mouth to bear on his breasts and ran her hands down for his cock, wanting to hold him still there for just long enough for her to run herself right up on him and he rolled to his side placing his asshole against her face and she hungry for the taste of it, parted his cheeks and darted her tongue into his anus and he giggled because it tickled and so readied himself to roll back over to face her, but unable to contain herself and wanting to hurt him, he who had this control over her in the bed, she nipped at his ass in the way a hungry dog gnaws away at some tasty piece of meat and he took his open right hand and with the butt of its heel he smashed once into her chin, crashed open into her face causing her to stop biting and start screaming, and in a second the wordless scream became a droning: fuck me baby, fuck me, fuck me please baby fuck me, a drone that continued through her breathing which had grown heavier now but he knowing the full pleasure he wanted paused for a second to see/smell/hear her and then brought his right hand which was still stinging from the blow he had just given to join his left in scratching above her pussy, beginning then to also rub his foot up toward her crotch and his fingers scratched and rubbed away in the coarse forest of her cunt fur but she only lay still and the air in her room did not move and she moaned: fuck me, please fuck me, fuck me baby and he smiled at this drone of hers and poked her a little jab in her stomach and she farted, but a tiny one like her hands that made a short pooping noise almost completely drowned out by her fuck me fuck me baby please fuck me and he rolled off the bed and danced around her waving his fat prick at her and coming close to her and striking her breasts with it and slapping her face with it and she stuck out her tongue like a lizard and stabbed its arrowhead and tasted the marine and urine flavor of it and wanted more and he danced down the edge of the bed trailing his penis along her right leg until he came to her feet and he tickled her toes with it and she began to masturbate herself, bringing up her finger to her crotch and emulating him rubbing her clitoris as hard as she could wanting the maximum of pleasure now but he did not care about that and he traced a line of lubricating sperm up her side, up the left leg until he reached the end of it and she was mumbling now, fuck me fuck me fuck me fuck me, which made him feel the power of his thick lips and darting tongue and fat stubby fingers that played around the hairy mound of flesh that formed the edges of her cunt and picking at the thinner hair of her anus and he thought of his little breasts and the twin unformed nipples and he hung over her and moved them back and forth over her rubbing them closer, then up and around, dangling his balls over the twin mounds of fat Puerto Rican tits, enjoying bouncing up and down and she not caring lunged forward with her tongue out and hanging down and wet, dripping wet, but the backs of his balls were wetter and she came away from them with his sweat formed between nuts and anus and it was fun to force his asshole tight against her mouth like that, even if it made her gag again and she bit into his left flank and he, both liking and not liking it, rolled on his side away from the pain and was back full on the bed and out of breath and she continued to softly say, fuck me baby fuck me good please baby and his mouth went onto her nipple, his hands not caressing her but rather holding his hard reddish-brown cock with its scarlet arrowhead and he sucked in rhythm to the back-and-forth pulses of masturbation and she desiring him more than her own pleasure chose to hold tightly to him rather than to do herself by rubbing on her clitoris, her miniature cock, and she dug her fingernails into his flesh scraping out dirty oily sweat from deep in his back and he answered her plea to please her by maneuvering his testicles right into her mouth and it was time to do her with his mouth and he set himself in position, on his side with his head pointed down toward her feet, her head pointed toward his feet, mouths against genitals and she popped him into her mouth and moved her head back and forth, on the downswing literally trying to gobble up the full length of his cock—an impossibility, of course, because her mouth was so small and his cock so thick and long: there was his forté: the thickness of it, the girth of it—not to disparage its length, no, not even to hint that his cock was not long, for it was long, very long: but it was so much fatter in proportion:. like a horse's dick, and her mouth stretched around him to receive him, her jaws hanging low, back and forth bobbing on him, he answering her thrusts by a mutual thrust and pulling away when she did, thrusting in with the bob of her head as well as pushing his tongue in her juicy snatch, licking away at the briar bush, the thin vertical lips that were so warm, the clit (her own little penis—but just a touch, just a dab of his tongue) making her put her legs tight around his head, forcing his face to remain where it was, her thighs stopping the moaning sound of fuck me fuck me please baby fuck me put it in fuck me hard, garbled anyway because his member moved back and forth in machine piston movements betraying the enormous power the muscles in his ass and in the back of his legs and in his lower stomach had and she had to remove him to catch her breath, and to repeat (even though he still could not hear her because of her legs being wrapped around his ears) fuck me and she licked his nuts, pausing to nip away at a few loose strands of hair there and then both laughed into each other's flesh because he at the same time was doing the same thing, of course only on the fuller patch of her pubis, hair clenched between his teeth, hair coming loose and getting caught in their throats and making tickling feelings and she slapped him on the ass and he forced out a fart and she slapped him again as if to say naughty boy but she did not mind any smell of his and he gave her outer lips a firm stroke with his tongue and she pushed him in deep into her throat and he almost made it right then but closed his brains off from his spinal tip to hold it back, which numbed his cock and which put the center of his attention on the sucking of her cunt, an act which he admirably wanted to do, suck and suck in a variety of ways: licking the clitoris, then the outer lips, inner lips, in the cave itself tasting the sweetness of that pussy pouring out lubricating juices around his face and fingers, one in her asshole again, and tongue all sweet as could be even if much later and after the act he would find their rotting smells distasteful to him, but that would be later when he was away from her and they had dried on him and were no longer fresh, but now they were fresh, direct from her body and flowing smoothly and without interruption and when he changed the center of activity to her anus-hole, returning from time to short time to suck on pussy and clit, he drove his fat finger up it and even crooked it a bit to rub back and forth in the same tempo of her mouth on him, those pendulum motions back and forth, crooked like a fish hook—it was like breaking open a sac of honey or a balloon of ambrosia for her pussy was rich in thick love massage lotions and he felt her nipples reach a new level, flopping against his stomach, and he pushed down a bit and entertained her by trying to rub nipples together in some awkward countertime to their mouths and it was not as much fun as he had thought it might be so in one whirl and in the way some small mischievous boy would wipe the left-over icing from a baking pan, he swished his finger around in one grand motion and removed it—making a slushy popping sound—and stuck the finger right in his mouth and so he enjoyed the sight, smell, taste, feel, and sound of her love lower body parts and she in her turn, lacking his imagination, contented herself with the application of small love nips directly on his cock with her teeth, avoiding the head as best she could but in this over-heated trio of excitement she let fly nips on the tender head as well causing Joao a combination of pleasure and pain, a combination that in no way caused his erection to diminish or slow the action of his tongue in and around her pussy, his hand toying with the myriad feelings of the various parts of her buttocks as he took in her snatch—so many parts here as well: the coarse hair everywhere present, the thick clean smells of it, clitoris, the spot touched gained the most response, a skin holder of the clitoris, the outer lips, the inner lips, the rough stingy flesh plush inside the orifice opening, urine-stained hair, the smells of the anus lingering close by and she in her turn happy about the jerking in and out feeling of him in her mouth, the up down push retreat in out of it, going into the back of her mouth, occasionally making her gag and the taste of urine faintly mixed with touches of thick salty lubricating sperm and he sucked and sucked away until he saw and felt her body tightening, readying itself to close down the vagina walls in a squashing climax that would shoot globs of pussy juice on to him but that did not happen because a hair before that time he took his tongue away and the waves of sex-heat coming from her good patch almost burned him so he grasped the end of the sheet and rubbed it over her face, arms, legs, back, belly, and then finally right on her center of gravity and even under the thin fabric he could feel the force of it and she paused in her sucking only to say succinctly: fuck me, a comment he could find no other answer to other than running a finger down the great divide of her back, ass furrow, cunt furrow, belly button, tit furrow, lip furrow, between the nostrils, eyebrow part, and then down into her mouth and she sucked his finger as vigorously as she was sucking his cock and he felt the blood run into his finger making it feel full and funny and he decided that her sucking had produced the necessary interest and he placed himself in the position of entry: between her opened legs, but him kneeling facing it and he rubbed his cock around it and liking the feel of her soft female flesh he moved and pushed the head of it around her body, even to the extent of grasping her two feet and masturbating himself between them, cock on the soles of her feet, him laughing as he did it and she saying to cut the shit and put it in and stop fucking around and he went down for a quick suck and she howled and shuddered and he pushed just a touch of his cock head up in her, just enough to part open the lips but not move the walls and he removed it and licked the new supply of slightly different tasting juices his short but not abortive entrance had liberated and he entered again, a little deeper, and she liked it, especially him moving his hips from side to side, rubbing different places in the insides of her and he removed it and placed his mouth on it again and sucked then re-entered and continued this see-saw dance by taking it out and sucking once more then putting about a third of it smack up her then out again to taste it once more before entering her in one firm thrust all the way up and she enjoying the feel of it all the way in her, moved her ass in the traditional up and down way and he remained still on top of her just resting his full weight dead on her and making her work all the harder—and resting to keep from shooting his load that very minute, so very close to climax was he that liquids were freely running out of him and he went up with her on one of her forward motions and with one hand he held her ass tight against him and with the other hand he slipped her pillow underneath to make the angle of entry more comfortable and he began to answer her up and downs with his own, telling her to take it easy, nice and slow, and they both fell into warm regular pumping motions, feeling full tingling sensations in their cock and cunt respectively that can only come from a good fucking and to add to the sweetness of it he brought his lips to her nipples and sucked as hard as he could and for her apparently it was not enough because she whispered harder to him and held the tit he sucked up at an angle for him to more easily reach and it was like she was displaying it too, displaying it even though his eyes were closed as he gently bit into her nipple as she had nipped his cock seconds before, nipped it and she smiled and said harder and pumped a little more and borrowing one of his acts she began to tickle his asshole, running her hands over the whole gamut that their position enabled her to do, and grasp as much as she could she did, paying particular attention to his balls that thumped against her thighs as his cock went in and out, the red arrowhead of it scraping the walls of her cunt and as open as she was now he still filled her completely so that during one of his deep thrusts it hurt her and she squealed out a cry and definitely did not like it like that and he continued the heavy thrusting as much as to say he liked it like that so to slow him down and seeing he paid no attention to her pleading, she got his balls in her hand and gave them a little tug and he farted and lay still but that was not what she wanted either and she continued her pumping up and down as he caught his breath, listening to the wet slurp slurp slurp of her pussy taking him in and letting him go and the plop plop of their wet stomachs slapping together and his hands, that had held onto her cheeks the way in which a farmer would hold onto an oversized and filled water jug on a long journey with the exception of course that his fingers from time to time had probed up the anus-hole but only for short quick exploratory adventures, but this is what had been because now one hand went up to play with the nipple he was not sucking on and the other hand went to the outer lips of her cunt and cupped them in his hand and grew excited at the wet feel of her giving way to receive his cock that slammed and jumped away at her and he marveled at the softness and hot slippery wetness of her pussy and the way those juices ran all over the both of them, the way the hair felt matted as if someone had smeared jelly over them, each little strand, jelly or jam and even more he was pleased by the inhuman metal hardness of his cock flailing away at her and he moved back to her anus-hole, scooping up the slippery juices that were everywhere now but not enough on her asshole and began to smear them up her rear as his cock popped away at her, he edging upward on her so that the flat upper surface of it rubbed against her cunt-button and bent upwards within her and his fingertips took over rubbing the pussy's outer lips, trying to shove his finger up her cunt along with his cock, plunging it all the way up her asshole so that the base of his fingers fell full flush on her cheeks and with this fingertip he tickled away up it, feeling his own sharp arrowhead in the parallel chamber one over and he rubbed away at it as his other hand moved away from her nipple and felt its way down to the clitoris pinching and scratching and touching all in its way before it felt her little erect thing, going left right, up down, left right, up down on it and she was screaming now—probably fuck me fuck me fuck me, as she had been screaming all along during the act but now the words were distended and smeared about and for that matter were completely without meaning since that was exactly what he was doing now and doing it to his screaming too, but just sounds and not words or even garbled words with or without meaning and neither one cared who might hear them and she rose up off the pillow and wrapped her legs high up on him, around his waist and she pumped and screamed at full speed and volume and he spurted out long jagged streams of come inside her and she screamed some more and he kept shooting it in her and she screamed and it felt to her like her pussy was a firecracker that just went off, the kind that go off in the sky and keep on going making pretty colors and she tried to do everything at once and he tried to suck and nip and pinch and scratch as well but all he could do was pump the fiery come right up her and she in orgasm and pressing down with the walls of her pussy to make a tight little home for him.

And it was over. All over.

She yawned, lifted a flank and scratched. Then closed her eyes.

He stayed on her a moment longer. But his dick was shrinking and he felt cold inside of her, so he came out of her and fell over to one side. She mumbled his name and pulled the covers over her wet body.

He rose, picked his clothes from the floor and dressed, then left. She was asleep by the time the door closed behind him.

1st MOVEMENT: EARTH
A Sonata Allegro

Y ou, come to take a visit in Nether City. CAUTION: KEEP YOUR WITS ABOUT YOU. Look, don't touch. In any case only the inhabitants can purge their guts as their foreskins slide back, revealing the gleaming arrowhead of their pricks. Their privilege, dearest reader, their privilege.

Because the circus closed down, the bearded lady donned the cloak of a seer. Waving her arms in abstracted patterns of humans engaged in various copulations, she preaches on street corners and before park benches. Her dugs have grown hairy and ripe.

Listen: Be a witness for the Lord God. Testify to His gift of the strands in spider webs. See them come down from heaven making everything we have, so we love, that we love. Touch each other. *That* God lurks behind His web, peering. Doom on our hair and fingertips. Nothing is vanity.

And as the people pass, returning to furnished rooms $3 and up, they prostrate themselves before her to take the holy dust from her feet.

Listen: the Street speaks to you: Fall before the dark-matted jungle of my crotch and have my dark thighs straddle your mouth.

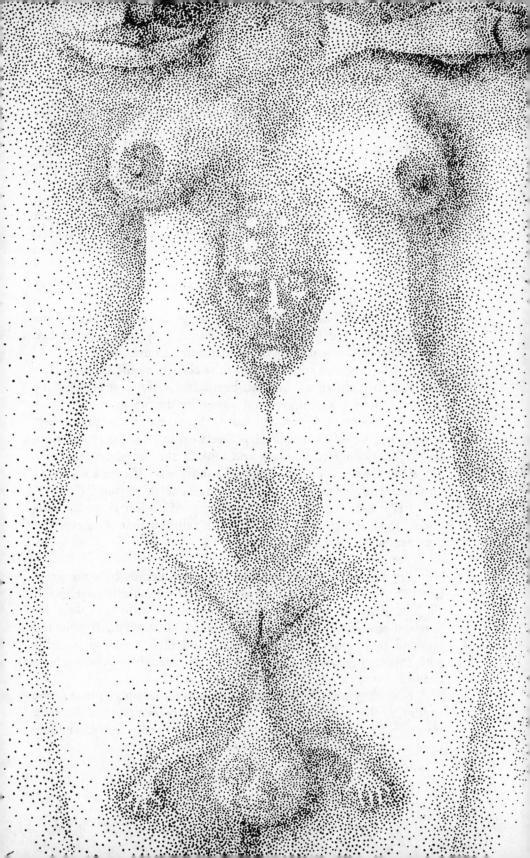

No, don't slide your tongue in the steaming slit—go up, go up, right to the border where the coarse pubis meets the brown pink cunt lips and lap the miniature penis dangling there for kicks you get in your mouth. Lick it softly at first, and then plunge your thumbs into the orifices of rear and front and in my black belly touch your thumbs together and if I scream turn me around and shove your healthy well-fed cock right in my mouth and plunge it to the back to gag me. Come, come in my mouth why don't you? I'll suck it right down and even lick the flecks of your creamy love juices from my face.

Amyl-nitrate in caps. A quick inhalation turns brains into giggling oatmeal. It enhances the orgasm so.

(All this an introduction to the setting.) "It's not the people who live here that gives us the bad name," says the older of two men sitting on a stoop. "It's those that come from outside."

Bright drops of spittle form at the corners of the second man's lips and drip down to his half-buttonless flannel shirt. And he laughs as the spit is completely absorbed by the fabric.

The viewpoint is you and me. Let's make a trip to the nether-lipped city, steamy cunt slit city. Dress up in your finery and walk on the grey concrete sidewalk and look at the haggard faces of the old women with bodies like melted candle wax. They are staring at you from the curtainless windows of their cubicle rooms.

Here doom seems to reign. A resigned no longer questioning doom. Even the sitting inhabitants will tell you that. And even the outsiders will tell you that.

Yet it is not that simple.

For you must remember that you give them joy by your attention. They, tired of suckling each other for life and power, (after all, old dried organs have been drained of ambrosia) wait for renewed strength to fill their bellies and make their loins grow red hot and their dusty slits steam again and their pricks surrounded with thinning grey-white fleece grow hard enough to puncture into flesh.

Now they wait. They crouch on the floor and peer through the windows, the tops of their heads only showing to you. Secretly they fondle their naked groins and crotches, constantly laughing. Look at the way he's dressed, they say. Must be a freak.

(Are you?)

The grey women, after being entertained by the street, turn to the dark men lying on the squeaky brass-balled beds and wheezingly place their still pink clitorises in their black nigger lovers' mouths. Juices thick in texture drip onto the many yellowed stains on the bed sheet.

They cry to each other. Walk away now. There are signs everywhere hanging. Read them instead.

The drug store window says:

> Welfare checks
> accepted for
> prescriptions

louder and longer than the deodorant signs.

The drug store across the street attempting to crush the competition—(i.e., competition because most of the people here are old and dying and get their money from the state house to buy the liquids and powders to slow their bladders at night and to loosen the phlegm in their lungs so that they might live—live) has the same welfare sign:

> Welfare checks
> accepted for
> prescriptions

And in Spanish too: (they do more business)

> Aceptado aqui
> para prescripciones
> cheques de welfare

A drunk passes in the street muttering to himself, "Keep your wits about you."

Don't be disturbed, people are like that because of their upbringing, because of their backgrounds. There is more to see. Look at the blue prowl cars everywhere protecting us with spinning lights on top.

Look at the children with their constantly pastel snotted runny noses playing on the broken park swings. They scream with delight as they fall and strike each other.

Outside Nether City a woman muses over her sister's affair with a professor: "If it were not so unbelievable I'd write a novel about it."

In a garret a man needing money for his wife's operation writes a letter to Harvard explaining his ability to teach astrology. He'd rather teach the children in the park, but the money is in Cambridge. Each morning he waits for the postman expectantly.

The Indian girl from Maine, made schizoid by who-knows what, runs from her lover's building in the night. Seeing you she panics and smashes her red hands against the door begging to be let back in. In frustration she tears her cotton dress from her body and with a closed fist breaks the pane of glass. The blood splatters in the doorway, coming from her sliced wrist. And on her body—patches of red on red. She falls down, opening her legs for you. And with a dagger of glass masturbates. Such a symphony of color.

So much these people love attention.

We stare wonderingly at the vulva, then leave, letting the police (who are everywhere in their blue prowlcars protecting) scoop her up. Just like vampires.

On a park bench, always on a park bench, the aged Negress sat, burnt purple by the sun. She rotates her body slowly, moving from one of her charred flanks to the other. The movement completely precise, the most exact movement in the universe. (Watch makers should come with calipers.) So perfectly even—yet slow. Imperceptibly slow.

Made by God, she is God and is perfect purple-black flesh. An Emersonian Over-Soul that passes gas.

Another senses her perfection of movement. Perhaps smelling the mucus jewels that descend from the split symmetrical womb to the nether lips, all timed to the rocking movement: back and forth—back and forth—back and forth: perfection!

He sits by her and offers her red sweet wine from a paper sack. They sit and drink and talk about the weather—other people—the port in the paper chalice.

She rocks beside the talking man—slowly, perfectly—and from the haze around her come visions of all things visible and invisible.

Not spoken of yet. The rope up the road is not a snake even if you (from blind misunderstanding) think it so.

From this Holy Black Nigger Queen come miasmas of beings and essences.

But none of that is her perfect movement.

Question: What does that mean?

Answer: Doom is in the eye of the beholder.

On the brick wall of the bow-fronted tenement (now renting rooms) is FUKK YOU scribbled in chalk. Two prim social workers walk past it with backs arched straight, the younger ignoring.

But the older one speaks, "It's our job to change that form of self-expression into the writing of poetry." The other nods an agreement to her senior.

Stupid cunt. It *is* a poem (i.e., FUKK YOU scribbled in chalk stolen from a school room). A poem that exists in myriad meanings that spiral out like the rings made by a small pebble dropped in still water, each ring opening to encompass a vast impotent universe that constantly in cycles copulates in order to grow even more incestuously infinite.

The Bridge of the Exposition

To the city came the most important people: the governor and the mayor, heads of education and business, ministers and priests—even the cardinal himself.

All descended into the slum to talk of destroying it. Blight, social blight, was their enemy, and they came together in a spirit of unity. Lips met in a concert of smiles; tongues spoke of continuing progress.

Papers were read and speakers were heard. Everything could be accomplished, they at last concluded, if the proper allocations were made. Build new buildings. Import teachers and social workers: The slum can be eradicated.

Even the reporters, hard and cynical, were moved by the optimism of the meeting. After all, it is illogical that in our rich country there should be the poor. The motion is made: poverty is to be rectified.

All agree.

Parades bring notice. The heroes of the day lock arms and walk down the concrete slabs of the church stairs onto the black roadway. Radiant grey suits and the one scarlet robe—unique—moved in stately patterns to their people.

The women, done with their black loves, look from their curtainless windows to see the procession, and hurry to the street, breathlessly.

On the street: bobbing heads and popping flash bulbs. And the cardinal in the center, like a beating heart in the center of some grey split symmetrical beast cut with the king's carving knife.

Two ancient women, both in tatters, stand in the midst of the crowd. They see the cardinal in the distance, coming to them.

"He still looks young," one of the women says. "Just imagine, the old goat in his seventies. By Christ, look at the way he moves. He ain't no spring chicken."

The other woman looks to her crab-like hands fingering her rosary. "I wish he'd bless my beads," she says.

"He would I bet," says the first. "He ain't the old-fashioned type. You could just go right up to him and he would. They say he's very liberal."

And the second woman speaks. "I've been told the priest at the cathedral sells beads blessed with holy water from the Pope. If the Pope does, he would. Cheaper too I bet."

"When he comes ask him. They say he kissed Mrs. Wilson at the Thanksgiving party. They say he's kind to the poor. And if he blessed your beads, they'd be lucky."

"You think he'd get mad?"

"Not him."

Then he passed close by them. The cardinal at arm's length, smiling and waving at the two women. Mute and frightened they stood, gazing. Unmoving, like the figures of a snapshot.

The procession passed by them and the people returned to their cubicles, leaving one woman alone in the rubbish-strewn streets, clutching a plastic Christ. The others, including the first woman, looked out at her from their windows.

And even this slum is bordered with slums. To the north are the chinks (yellow old men in floppy pants who come from their musty doorways and look at our world to laugh). To the south, jigaboos (white teeth and fast black hands—clap-ridden teen-age hookers looking sweet with their cunts ripe with pleasure and pubis like steel wool, the smell and taste of white man's slimy come, $10 and $2 and French at twice the price).

Nether City itself in white faces with embedded grey lines. And Puerto Ricans, many Puerto Ricans now. (Either yellow, black, or white with mother's picture high up close by their heart and high-heeled boots that move in jealous patterns and two knives hidden on them just in case.) The spicks are takin' over. But Nether City is the core: tenements, insanity, filth: human flesh, vibrant and miraculous. An exposed wrinkled anus (darkened with age) that pulsates.

More and more in a 2/4 meter, feet shuffling to *a merenguo-a-pambichao*—(the brown penis presses against that lump of elliptical female belly through layers of cotton drawers, pant fronts, pastel dresses as the coro sings: *por-queel traba-jo pa-ra mies un e-ne-mi-go*).

Because the Cardinal has a center for them to dance in, the inhabitants of long standing say that he brought them up from San Juan. The spics are takin' over. A new dispensation.

(Too much exposition in this bridge—got to move away from the city—go by bridge to make it—the P.R.'s come by plane from La Perla.)

Go to glory sister.

Amen.

The destination is the second theme—Glory Land. The woman with her beads says, all me and my husband (God rest his soul) ever wanted was a little house out in the country. Flowers and trees and fresh air for the baby. We just sort of drifted into the city. Up from the South.

The Bearded Lady of the Aged Paps answers: Glory Land ain't Mother City. Not in a pig's ass. (The fact remaining that you must return to it if it's your home—in the blood, etc.)

Cock in Cunt

Cock or Cunt

Cock and Cunt

The bridge is between the two worlds, mixing them. Puddles in the potholes on the Ave, (broken and black and strewn with bottle glass of all colors) splatter in the faces of those who don't move fast enough. The whole picture like an under-exposed negative. The cars drive to the horizon—then disappear.

At night they return and the men and boys in suits protected by their cars accost the old ladies.

As their well-scrubbed cocks shoot the spurts of salty cream into toothless mouths, the men moan: Mother.

Then the car windows roll down and the ancient women's mouths hock out the semen onto the curbstone. From a distance it looks like clams spitting out sea water.

Then the cars go across the bridge home, and the men lie next to their wives and say, no dear not tonight, I'm tired. Please understand. Tomorrow maybe. No, not tonight, darling.

The world exists in hard immobile layers—stratified. Each layer believes itself superior; each person believes himself the one who really knows. Therefore the codification of sameness.

Except in the sweet inner-city: Let everyone mind their own business. Suck/Fuck or eat shit—everyone after all has their own shtick.

The children gather in groups and march pigeon-breasted to the bridge over the train tracks and to all the streets of the city that radiate and throw bricks and bottles. Each commuter struck makes a growl, then goes in a full circle, then tips his hat—like the bears in a shooting gallery. Fun and games for those six to sixty.

The street illumines two adolescent boys—one just home from prison with a tie around his eye; the other pensive, listening not wanting to be there.

That'll be the last bust I take. You learn the score in the slam. No more B and E's—that's kid shit. This is it: You can con those fucken suckers. It goes like this: They want. They think they're so fucken smart. But they're all thieves. You gotta come on like a big fucken asshole, get it. They figure they can make a killing, but all legal. So you get their money and make it. They say you can't con everybody, bullshit. Everybody is crooked so you can fuck'em out of their money. Stupid shitheads. I don't see how they can live that way. Some of 'em got money but don't enjoy it. I do. Get a couple of yards and blow this fucken nothing happening hole. You get it? Live. The Life, the Life.

Interaction: Mixing nether inhabitants with others is like shaking oil and water together: black and glistening, the slum-dwellers separate out.

Slowly, and with an air for the histrionic, the professor lets his hands drop to his sides in a movement of humility. Now he speaks.

"A bridge is a place where cultures meet vividly and materialistically. The passing of goods facilitates cities, which in time lays the groundwork for art, a manifestation that flowers up, watered as it were by the money of businessmen."

Their heads down, the students copy his every borrowed judgment. The professor is happy. He smiles. Yet there is one thing that is not right.

For would not the world be a better place if it were more learned? It would help, or so he thinks.

Rotating in perfect timing, the purplish-black Negress laughs at her creation. Such charming illusions men hold. Such ironic conclusions they come to.

I   IV   I
Come to Glory Land
(and a chicken in every pot)

From the upper edges of the strip bordering Nigger Town, the places where the red-faced workers live, infinite fur-lined piss pots are emptied from windows.

At the horizon, if they looked, the inhabitants of Nether City might see the rainbow that is formed: heavy with green and gold coloring, the gold in the rainbow's end. A thickish smell, pleasant, easy to get used to.

In the dawn's light all over Nether City come men in trucks, sweat bursting from their faces. They are dressed in green chinos, labeled with numbers and the initials U.S.A. Into the soft tar on the street they hammer the signs that will lead people from the labyrinth of the red brick tenements.

"What these people need is a good scrub-down," says one of the workers, resting after having implanted the golden exit sign.

On his bed in the two-roomed cellar, Al the old man smokes his cigar and scratches at his armpit. Then deliberately, like a connoisseur of smells, he brings his damp fingertips to his nostrils and inhales deeply—how pleasant. His fingers return to the stringy white fur.

The trucks drive away, leaving the exit signs all about: a huge golden cock with matching balls, foreskin pulled back, revealing a golden arrowhead pointing down the avenue. Etched on these phalli are the words, *Go To Glory Land.*

Another city official, heavy and red in the face, marched all the neighborhood's children to the great golden cock. "See what it says," he intones. "Go to Glory Land." With antics like baby baboons, the children create their own images instead. Kenneth looks up the schoolhouse fire escape to see under Miss Tuchman's dress.

"She ain't got no panties on."

Miss Tuchman's cunt can be conceived: a sweet mossy house of cream, surrounded by a steaming black fur patch that runs to her asshole and fits so snugly in the palm. And that is the end of this bridge. We have left Nether City.

Old men in other places, their complexions smooth as spun cotton, finished and shiny and waiting to be touched on wooden wharfs in New York, London, Marseille, Piraeus, pause in their cars and watch each other's daughters pass.

Juveniles swagger and brag that Molly hand-jobbed twenty of them sitting on a stone wall—like Humpty Dumpty. (Nether City has no stone walls, and no Mollys. The girls are hard to take, they saving *it* to trade *it* for a washing machine and a car, all away from the drunken father and the tired screaming mother. Rape them and beat them. Stand with friends and piss on their bloodied bodies as they cry.)

A woman in a Hong Kong kimono rests on a sofa, exposing her loose pink thighs for the gas man.

"How's every little thing?"

"Fine. Fine. And how's yourself?"

Little boys wondering where little girls pee from.

Want: will die—dying—died—dead.

The key to good etiquette is the art of making fine imaginary lines with your fingers.

Crutches—tattoos—semen.

And the towering skyscrapers are raised with polished people in them. Imperfections in the angles are erased on the drawing board. Right angles to the stars. If they're not even, move them from Glory Land. (And you ignore the people on the streets.)

Throw them in Nether City.

Quel drôle de ménage là-bas.

Length, breadth, width—clean, even antiseptic. Such charming five o'clock marchers. It makes the heart want to sing out.

Obviously no irregularities please.

Marching to their cars. The road home. To enamel slop pails.

Me and the little woman going to eat in tonight. Like when we was first hitched. Got something nice on the stove in that pot.

The poorer ones crowd into the underground trains, and hours later emerge like ruffled ducks coming from a sea storm, shaking their feathers and turning their heads from side to side. Glassy beady little black eyes.

In this world that surrounds Nether City, douche bags gurgle out millions of potential people in enamel slop pails, then lovers rejoin each other.

It is a new day. And the grey symmetrical beast cut with the king's carving knife marches on half a million, their little split-headed prinky-dinks flopping against coarse red thighs. With pay toilet dispensers dispensing round donut-shaped paper sheets to place on hopper seats and the fat round buttocks split down the middle like cock heads purge themselves. Grunting and farting. Scratch and strike a match. And the black men's room attendant who lives on the southern end of the strip but who's working down here for the time being trying to get himself together, repeats like a plastic jig Christmas tape recorder doll: "How's the evening coming for you sir? How's the women treating you?" Moving in turn on the hot water faucet for the befouled red hands, so the water's just right and, "How's the evening coming for you sir? How's the women treating you?" From behind glazed eyes. And the beast queues in front of the door paying 10¢ a turn.

"Fine son, and you?"

> Let's have a parade
> The marching of feet
> The stamping of drums
> The push of the crowd

There's something about a parade

> The marching of feet
> The stamping of drums
> The majorette's skirts

From her window, Lillian who is man and woman (and sees all knows all tells all) watches the push of the far-away crowd. All smiles—quite noticeable really.

Quite noticeable too is Blow Job Annie, and the people move away. Her red shoes cut shiny swatches on the concrete. Boy scouts sing: *won't you come out tonight and howl by the light of the moon?* Legs gnarled with blue lumps, with a flag's red and white strips wrapped around her narrow body. And stars for a blouse. She is singing and carrying a little flag no larger than a handkerchief. In the other hand she holds a cardboard bird on a stick (made in Japan), waving it too because it twitters. Boys and girls spit and the beast turns its head askew talking about the lock-up.

Lillian sees all this because it is her game. In her body will join the Nigger Queen and the woman with the dried paps and the three male elements of 1) Pee Wee 2) Gimpy 3) Preacher. She'll swallow the universe down the way old men swallow down raw eggs. The way Annie swallows spit and sperm. Every old little prinky-dinky. Therefore:

> The One in many
> The many in One

Annie come talk to me, your son, your father, your lover. I am your child. I am Pee Wee.

She screams back her answer, "Get away from me you dirty no good cock sukah up to no good fucken chicken freak shit bum. Humph. The freaks that walk these streets. Can't get left in a fucken minute of peace. Screw yourself. Do I bother your mother? Trying to stick my fingers up her rotten snatch. Why do you bother me? Help Help me! Go save your mother. She's on the street too.

Help Help Help! Fucken asshole, go bother your own mother. She's on the street too. Go fuck her not me."

With these last words Annie spins arms outstretched holding the Japanese bird twittering and the small flag bought from the man yelling: Peanuts. Get your hot peanuts. Peanuts. Hot peanuts. Peanuts. Hot nuts. Hot Pea-Nuts. Come and get em! Nice and hot.

Spotting Annie in the midst of her dance, five black bucks in some white chick's car stop. Her son stands behind her impotent. She screaming, "Go fuck your mother," and they not interested in her words pull her into the car. The car goes back to Nether City into an alley and the five enter together. The one black thick-lipped mouth pressed to her tit draws dust. Her paps are dried with age.

The flag and bird are broken.

"Have you read Sartre?"

"No, but I know about him. Had him in school."

"What's his thesis? You know, the central ideas?"

"Simple: No soul. Ergo: Extend the dimensions stiffly."

"Time too?"

"Guess so."

And Preacher told Pee Wee you always come back to Nether City. It's in the blood, he said. If you come from here you never get away, he said. You gotta come back, he said.

Obviously no irregularities please. Now is the time of the parades—*(Voici le temps des Assassins)*. Men drably and uniformly dressed in unison firm knowing expressions determination fortitude chaos eliminated by hup tuu tree fouah with the black streets sounding with the shined shoes crashing to the cadence and the heart thrill-throbs for we all love a parade.

But parades differ. Those in core city. Nether sweet pussy cream home city are not in chino. The strip's inhabitants dress in motley, sometimes even drastically patriotic. And everyone's out of step for one reason or another. How beautiful. How dangerous.

Pee Wee pins a note on a tree in the park:

> Come home Annie the nigger slime in you
> is not your Nether City blood and I say
> it's in the blood that matters

Lily-white leaves smirched with mud. The earth marred with month-old snow. Let suburban women scream fuck fuck fuck to attempt a slide into one of their infrequent orgasms.

Mr. BiggBaggs' pert Jewess daughter makes a succinct statement to her demon lover, "Fuck headshrinks."

God is a photo of everything.

There is no God but Jahweh.

Everything is God if you don't look.

A young hunter takes aim at infinite bliss with a shotgun filled with words. Give it hell sonny. Let 'em have it. Bag it good.

Length, breadth, width made into straight lines functioning in time. Everywhere this is art. Victorian bow front homes now become slums. (Some are of course re-decorated with plastic and the swells live hidden inside.)

And children are lighting fireworks. It's for the Grand Premiere.

"Well-ll-ll, Ahh."

"It's not commercialism in the strict sense of the word, actually."

"This is true. Ahh, this is true. This is what I mean, actually."

"As a matter of fact-ahh-problems are to be solved through self-actualization."

"Ahh, I agree, as a matter of fact for his high blood pressure G. Barnard BiggBaggs skip-ropes in his plywood-paneled den and besides for his soul-ahh-it's for his self."

And in Mr. G.B.'s words. "Ya gotta take care of ol' Number One first."

Paging Mr. BiggBaggs, paging Mr. BiggBaggs.

"Did you call? Did you say anything, darling?"

"No dearest, I was just wondering if we're going to stay home or go out tonight."

"Oh no, no. Got business in town. Gotta go in alone."

"Can I come?"

"No darling, you can't come, actually. Real estate deal. Make a killing."

The old woman scratches herself on the fire hydrant and Bigg-Baggs safe in his parked car lets his legs flutter together. "Hyya honey, wanta good time?"

And she becomes Delilah for an aging Samson—at moderate cost.

"Darling darling darling oh ahh," a trinity of sounds of tones as her balding silent mouth pushes down to the hair root, then raised up to lap the arrowhead, her head moving in abrupt movements.

Behind the driver's wheel BiggBaggs tries to slip his hands like crabs under her pastel-printed rayon dress seeking out her grey cotton drawers not damp at all next to the prize. Dry like mommy's ones on the clothes line in the Ohio sun.

But the street lamp shines yellow not white and the woman pulls his hand away.

Mrs. B.G.BB. touches her fingertips to the flushed man's cheek. "Poor Teddy Bear. I so much hope. He fell asleep watching T.V. I hope he's not on the night shift too long. And ashes on the floor."

The stumpy cock depresses her tongue. She will gargle with sperm, taking his hand to her dried dugs. "Theyah instead," and BiggBaggs, stumpy stick squirts at the "st" sound of her withered mouth chomping around it, giving way breast flesh under thumb pinches. Rotten teeth feel the coolness of his cock juices.

It's not commercialism in the strict sense of the word—actually.

On the empty early summer morning beach he, with her smell on his belly, walks alone. The sun red and shimmering crawls from the horizon's water edge. His feet press the sand in intaglio. Five toes an arch a heel. One foot, the other and slow at first: left-right-left-right-left-right. Then faster running now. One foot the other pointed toward the water. Behind him impressions lead back to the motel bed and her lying, legs still spread, arms behind the head. (My hair so soft, the color of straw, wild men wake wrapped in it.) Her smell is on him and each impression in the sand fills with warm ocean water.

"Darling it's late. Come to bed?"

"No. The sea calls me and I shall be a sailor seven times over. My feet are in the frothing water. And deeper now. And deeper again. Legs pushing me—I run as in a dream: slowly, slower, imperceptibly: until the water passes over me, my hair swirling like dead black seaweed."

> The shade of Yin is on the back of everything;
> The light of Yang is on the face of everything.

From their blending together balance exists in the world.

"Your mouth runs like a whippoorwill's ass in popeberry time. What are you trying to say?"

Answer: The universe is everywhere and made up of mystic male and mystic female. Brother-sister, mother-father in the same flesh copulating as far back and as far ahead as you want to go. Life comes from water. In Paris enterprising young men wait in the American Express and offer to show Mrs. BiggBaggs the city. Their taut miss-mealed stomachs offer a pleasant contrast to Mr. BB's stomach. In Tijuana the broads dance on the bars and take it all off and this one pig you know really got a good show and she's bare-assed and she ups and pisses right on the table top and me and my buddies down from Diego jump the fucken pig you know and we start going to town on her and it took those dirty spics ten minutes to drag us all off and we screwed out of there and I bet those friggen S.P.s are still hunten for our asses. And that ain't all. You buy 'em a 75¢ beer and they jerk you off. They get a little pink stub for each beer. Holy shit, Tijuana's a lot of fun. You don't believe half the stories you hear about that place, but holy shit they're true. Makes me all hot thinking about. Let's get laid tonight. Let's find a pig over there in Slum Town.

Two hunters hold their guns and peer into the green foliage. "It's God's country."

The brutal visibility the same out here. (But I insist: Nether City ain't Glory Land—not in a pig's ass.)

Those people that didn't follow the golden cock signs pointing up the street and out look like stale bread soaked overnight. There's a soggy viciousness, harmless with hurt eyes.

From livingroom to livingroom, "Let's have coffee. Coming over for coffee? The art of fine imaginary lines with our red lips."

"Did you hear? Mrs. Grass invited Hilda's husband in for coffee?"

"No, when?"

"Someone should tell him. Mr. Grass is such a great conversationalist."

"Did you know he's working on a program to help people get out of the slums? They say he's really reaching those people."

"And what about poor Hilda? Really, some people."

"Hilda's husband is a great camera bug you know."

If the head of his prick had a teeny-tiny camera embedded in it, then what would Mrs. Grass's dark little cavern look like? Would there be Gothic gargoyles hanging down from the walls of Notre Dame, peeping out and giggling at each thrust of Hilda's hubby. Would they know the difference? Can our technology create the needed flash bulbs to illuminate the stalactites and stalagmites of soft hairy like flesh contracting and expanding around the bared prick's arrowhead.

Pictures snapped for posterity. This is the way she looked back then. Three times a week back then.

"Come in for coffee. Isn't it nice to have the men in town doing their business? Keeps 'em out of our hair."

"Ha. Ha. O that woman. Honestly."

Nothing ever happens on these long summer evenings. Kids outside in the garden playing kids' games.

Cockle bells and silver shells all in a row.

Or Mary Mary quite contrary: how does the fruit of thy womb grow?

"Harry's been saying that if we put up that plastic shelving against the kitchen wall at a nice right angle and extend it indefinitely then it. . ."

"Then it would come back in a circle and if your back was turned . . . ."

"Isn't that lovely? Hilda, your husband is such a regular fella."

The agent sent a cab for Annie to take her to the show. At eight she was ready standing by her door so's not to be late and she held her cardboard suitcase in her arms pressed close to her flat chest. She could smell the three mildewed bespangled baubled dancer's costumes under the cardboard. She paid so much for them twenty years ago when she almost made Broadway.

"Annie if you had it over again what would you want to be?"

"The morning sky, ice clouds high up, or the dew."

The piano player paid the cabby and kept telling her that he never would of made this thing but that he needed the money and again to her that he never would have made this job with her (there was only the two of them standing on the suburban lawn waiting for someone to answer the door) but his kid was sick and he really needed the dough and the man opened the door and brought them into the living room that smelled of cigar smoke and middle-aged men's sweated seats of pants and prostates drying up, growing old, growing cancerous and the piano player withdrew playing *Don't Blame Me* for the ten-thousandth time, watching his fingers strike the keys, not looking up, afraid to, not seeing the men tear Annie's Oriental Special costume to shreds with her not saying anything knowing the agent was doing her a favor cause she's so old now but the men stared fish-eyed—as if amazed—and she didn't want to create a scene and she stood confused as they gazed at her slit yelling and hollering like they were at a sporting event and a chord built out of tensions rises from the piano, spreads over the room and slithers out the window. The sound grows mellow and it reaches Nether City, and Pee Wee her son is still on the fire escape because she couldn't get a sitter, and he's a baby and wants his mother's nipple, even if it is dry. In the room the men drop 50¢ into a cigar box brought by the piano player for the purpose to stroke the white cunt fleece and some kiss it only to find it tastes like rusted nails.

In the cab back the musician agrees repeatedly with her that all men are dirty pigs ripping her costume like that after she spent so much on it, then her hand falls on the firm flesh under his left thigh leg trouser. From crotch to tip she kneads the flesh lump. In his mind he thinks the words in ever narrowing concentric circles: knead need knead need knead need narrower now then his sparkler grows wet and dies.

Mr. Grass, Hilda's husband, sat on his ass and watched the world march by. Line of delivery boys, mailman, gasmen, oilmen, male friends, spurting spumes of sperm right up Mrs.' ass. Careful with that plastic board, Sonny. Cost me $3.246.

"Ya wanta go play in Hilda's garden?"

"No sir-ee, too many rusty nails laying in the grass. Too many crusty tails, dusty pails, lusty males, busty fails."

Over coffee cups, "Let's go to the Shopping Plaza. It's so nice there. Nice—you know—nice."

Beyond the shopping plaza, they wear their god heads lightly. Enameled god heads made in Denmark. Chick don't you think?

Mr. BiggBaggs's dandruff flakes covered the new dining table.

Mr. BiggBaggs has leadership qualities.

Mr. BiggBaggs has his analyst once a week.

Mr. BiggBaggs has a penchant for old ladies. Likes to have them suck him.

Mr. BiggBaggs non-Freudian analyst is hard pressed. He even dreams about his patient being in a play called BiggBaggs Rex.

There's nothing else in Glory Land.

JOHN VOIGT

John Voigt's first and enduring love is music. A child of the Depression, son of a carnival dancer and a ballyhoo man, he grew up to hate the slum world around him and escaped by listening to jazz on the radio. He blew trumpet at a holy roller Pentecostal church, until it was decided the devil took possession of him whenever he played. In the Navy, he played string bass and later gigged at the Five Spot in New York's Greenwich Village. In between he studied engineering, had what he termed an "abortive romance" with Harvard, taught in the slums for a while, was a sideman for a Latin dance band and went to graduate school to become a librarian. He began to write and took a job playing at the Playboy Club to support his wife and baby daughter. Nether City is his first published book.

Ed Martin

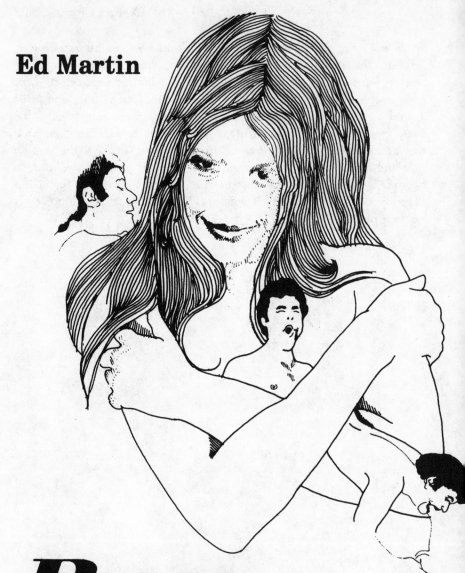

Busy Bodies

The heavy table raised and tilted to a sharp angle. In the darkness no one saw Queen Mary whisper into the microphone in her armpit.

"Easy on the table, Sheila. You'll dump us!"

The earphones under Queen Mary's turban sputtered: "Are you kiddin'?"

"You think I got nuthin' else to do with a room full of anxious customers?" Queen Mary almost raised her voice. "I can't see him but I'll bet Shorty Waldo's on tip-toe to keep the circle."

"But, Mary," said the earphones, "I haven't even started yet."

"Then the elevator has gone nuts. Do somethin'!"

The table settled back to the floor for a moment. Then one side began to oscillate slowly up and down. The movement shifted to the other side. Both sides tried to tilt, resulting in a smooth undulating movement as though sea borne.

Queen Mary felt at sea herself. "How are you doin' that?" she asked the microphone suspiciously.

"What?" Under the circumstances it was an intelligent reply from Sheila. She had no way of seeing what was going on. She was in the prop room in the cellar below. The simple question, however, only infuriated Queen Mary.

"Never mind!" She finally repeated: "The elevator must of gone nuts."

Eloise Perkins gave a little scream and almost broke the circle when the table began to undulate towards her, circling her breasts up and down as though firmly grasped in a couple of strong hands. The people on each side of her quickly said: "Shush!" But she was already quiet, beginning to enjoy the aggressive table.

Queen Mary was not the type to inspect the proverbial gift horse. If the elevator was nuts it was certainly in her favor. All it was supposed to do was tilt the table. "The spirits are strong tonight." To the regular customer, familiar with the nightly procedure, it was a rank understatement. Mrs. Perkins was beginning to breathe heavily. She had slid down in her chair, her legs wide apart, enjoying the massage on her tits.

Helen Desmond whispered to Tom Farrell beside her: "I'm getting bored with this business." She reached over, found his soft flesh and began mauling it. When it seemed to come off in her hand and then disappear, she added: "Oh, shit. Can't you keep it solid?"

Tom ignored her. "Look what I found!" he whispered. He had his hand between Mrs. Perkins' outstretched legs.

"Get your paw out of there," said Helen, matching his tone. "What's the matter with me?"

"Nothing," said Tom seriously. "But did you ever feel anything like this?" He directed her hand to Mrs. Perkins' mound.

Mrs. Perkins slumped further as the two hands crept up, one on each thigh. She did not worry about the fact there were two hands. As far as she was concerned Shorty Waldo was finally making advances. The higher they went, the wider she spread. When they reached her warmth she abandoned herself and flipped a leg out onto the lap of each of her neighbors, presenting herself wide open to the mysterious hands.

"Feel this!" whispered Tom. "She has a little joint." He was manipulating the end of it causing Mrs. Perkins to vibrate with every tweak.

"It feels like an old wet sock," said Helen. "Someone should wring it out."

"I'm working on it," continued Tom. "Here, feel it."

"Oh, for Chrissakes," said Helen. "That's not a little joint, it's only her thing, and a skinny one at that." She gave it a vicious pinch which only seemed to please Mrs. Perkins. "Feel me! I've got a fatter one."

"I know all about it," said Tom. His voice seemed to quaver a bit at the memory.

"So feel it!" insisted Helen. She had her knees drawn up to her armpits, forced wide apart. "Feel it!"

Tom sighed in desperation and tried to stuff his free hand up Helen's orifice.

"No!" said Helen. "Play with my cute little thing. There, isn't that nice? It's nice and fat, isn't it? Not long and skinny like hers. Isn't it? Isn't it?"

"Yes!" said Tom. "Much nicer. Much nicer!"

"Then say it."

"Say what?"

"Say: 'Helen has a nicer thing than Mrs. Perkins'."

"Helen has a nicer thing than Mrs. Perkins."

"You're sure?"

"Of course."

Helen almost shouted: "Then get your fumbling paw out of her sloppy hole."

"Such terrible language. Or you'll do what?" Tom was still busily fingering both of them.

Helen sputtered: "I'll think of something." She was silent for a moment. "If you must continue playing with me at least act as though you're interested." She lay back a little. "I'm getting tired of this fooling around—how about some real sexercises?"

"Not now."

"Not now! Not now! Always not now!" She relaxed and admitted: "It is kind of cramped."

As though in answer to her words the undulations of the table stopped. It began to waver up and down mechanically on Shorty Waldo's side.

"Okay on the table." Queen Mary was back in her armpit. "Let's get goin'." She spoke up again to the room. "The spirits are strong tonight." Queen Mary always stuck to the script. "There is one who feels that he must get a message through. I am trying to help him but there is great interference."

"Are you interfering?" Tom whispered.

"That's a bright question I must say," answered Helen. "And for the last time take your hand out of her sloppy splattering hole. I think it's dripping on me. How about concentrating on me?"

"One more second," said Tom. "I think she's coming."

"Now isn't that sweet," said Helen. "You don't even know her and look what she gets. How about me, your dear, old, trusted friend."

"Later, when I have the strength."

"Later—always later!"

"Someone is not concentrating fully," continued Queen Mary.

"Probably you," said the earphones.

Queen Mary sputtered. Sheila was drinking again. And when Sheila was drinking it always turned out to be a rough night.

"Someone is not concentrating fully," she repeated. "We must have absolute quiet."

It struck most of the assembly that the only sounds were those issuing from Queen Mary. Mrs. Perkins straightened up bright-eyed and was the first to notice the trumpet materialize in the corner of the room. Slightly less fluorescent was a diaphanous material suspended from the mouth of the trumpet. Ectoplasm, was what Queen Mary always called it.

"They are getting through," said Queen Mary. "The spirit world is close tonight." She changed the tone in her voice to a conspiratorial timbre. "Can you hear me?"

She was answered by a sharp knock on the table. The earphones added a realistic comment: "Crazy, Roger and Wilco! Can you hear me?" A bottle tinkled against a glass.

"Knock once for 'yes.' "

There was one knock.

"Twice for 'no.' "

There were two knocks.

The last rap was followed by two more on another part of the table. Queen Mary jumped. Everything was going wrong.

"Knock twice for 'no,' " she repeated.

"I just did," said the earphones, annoyed. "What goes on up there?" Sheila rapped again. "I told you to get that solenoid rewound."

The trumpet gave a loud wail. The recording had been made in an echo chamber. It was a fearsome sound.

Helen jumped: "God! That thing startled me."

"Oh, I could do much better," said Tom. He moaned low in her ear.

"I love to feel your hot breath on me. How about a quick one?"

"Now! Now!" was all he would say.

"Look at all you do for that sloppy hole, Mrs. Perkins. What am I—some sort of crud?"

"Later," said Tom.

"How much later?" Helen pushed his nose into her muff and twisted him back and forth. "First you get me all worked up diddling my diddle and then you ignore me."

"Later!" Tom's voice was strangled.

"What's a girl to think?"

He managed to break away and gave her a reassuring pat. "Let it cool off a little. You know I can't right now!"

"What do you do with it all? Just where does it all go?"

The trumpet and the trailing ectoplasm jerked over towards the table. Queen Mary planned to get the wires adjusted but always forgot. The trumpet murmured a few low notes.

"I can't hear you clearly," said Queen Mary. "Can you speak louder?" The trumpet jerked up and down a few times and there was a long staccato rapping on the table. "Do you want to speak to me?"

There were two distinct raps.

"To someone at the table?"

There was one knock, and by a process of elimination it was determined that Shorty Waldo had a visitor in the person of a recent ancestor. The rapping went wild for a moment and ran around the table a few times. Queen Mary was quite impressed.

"How are you doin' that?" She stayed under her armpit while waiting for the answer. She regretted not taking a bath that morning.

"Even I hear it," said Sheila. "It's that blasted solenoid. Maybe we'd better try the new loudspeaker system."

"Well, keep sober!" Queen Mary was sorry she had mentioned the subject. In her earphones she could hear more liquid being poured. The way things were going she could use a drink herself.

"Waldo Thompson!" The trumpet dragged out the words until they were almost unintelligible. "Waldo Thompson!"

"Here!" It was a rather weak reply. Actual voices in Queen Mary's Spiritualist Temple were a new development. He was a regular client and quite cocky about his familiarity with table rapping. This would set him back a peg.

"That's quite a trick, you know," said Tom.

Helen snarled: "Tricks-pricks! How about a flat lay?"

"I am your grandfather, Hiram Thompson," continued the trumpet.

"Of course not!"

"Then where is it?" Helen squealed and then added: "I mean the other one."

"It's around here someplace. I know I had another one a while ago."

"You're impossible," said Helen. She slouched back further

and, letting her knees drop aside, grasped his wrist and began working his fingers in and out. "If this is all I can get, this is all I can get!"

"Have you no shame?"

"Sure I do! It's a shame a girl has to satisfy herself in this ridiculous manner."

It struck Waldo that the voice was a little high-pitched for his grandfather. But he could not very well argue with ghosts. "Yes, grandfather."

"You have been doing well, Waldo. And it is up to people like you to help disseminate the word."

"Speaking of dissemination," said Helen, "how about something a little better than these bony fingers?"

"Later!" said Tom.

"Later, always later."

Queen Mary smiled. Shorty Waldo was always a fine contributor. This demonstration should make things opulent. Then she flushed as the trumpet added a comment in what actually seemed to be a female voice.

"Shit! I'm here to state that you can't take it with you."

She buried her head in her armpit. "Sheila," she hissed. "For Gawd's sake, cut the wisecracks."

"I heard it too," said Sheila. It was more of a shout and there was a note of fear in it. "I didn't say it!"

"Well, don't get excited," said Queen Mary quickly. "Must be a couple of wires crossed." It was a vague idea and her voice trailed vaguely off with it.

"On second thought, you can take it with you if you want." The trumpet executed a smooth dance.

"I didn't do that either," said Sheila. "The business seems to be running itself." She added after a moment: "And how can crossed wires talk?"

"I think the seance is about to get panicky," said Tom.

"Good!" said Helen. "In the confusion we can knock off a small piece of ass." She tried to get hold of his cock again but Tom was too fast for her.

"Later," he said.

Helen started to raise her voice in frustration. "The least you can do is help. Don't make me do all the work. Shove your bony

hand up my hot thing a little further and give me some sort of kicks. You know how I am when I get like this. Bastard! Why do you have to tease me?"

"Quiet," said Tom. "They'll hear you!" He fished around until Helen began to relax. "How's that?"

"It's as bony as they make them but it's better than nothing. Now slide in and out—that's it! Use all your fingers, you won't lose them. Ah! Much better." Helen had her knees clamped up to her armpits again. She rolled back a bit and her thighs fell open like the pages of a book. "See if you can get it in up to your wrist."

"Don't be silly," said Tom. "I might lose my hand."

"What are you worried about? We can always fish it out."

"Try to be satisfied."

" 'Try to be satisfied,' " mimicked Helen. "Oh, shit! I trust I'm not bothering you too much with my little needs."

"Don't snap at me or I'll leave you high and wet."

"Such a clever saying. Now open your fingers a little."

"Switch to Perkins." Queen Mary dragged her tired head out of her armpit. She spoke up: "There are spirits both good and bad. Your grandfather has been pressed back by a vagrant evil on his own plane. But there is someone else. I feel someone else trying to get through from another plane. They are close—so close!"

The trumpet climaxed her lead. The voice was high and the words poured out at a great rate: "Eloise—Eloise Perkins, this is Aunty Josephine. Have you found the money yet? I told you where I left it and when you find it I want you to give half to Queen Mary. Have you found it, Eloise?"

Mrs. Perkins was rubbing the side of her bare leg against Shorty Waldo. The sudden voice made her think she was caught and she straightened up. "It wasn't in the attic, Aunty. I tore the place apart."

"It must be there," the voice of Aunty began to trail off. "I put it there myself and it must be there. I want Queen Mary to have half. So you must find it. You must!"

"How much was there?" asked Mrs. Perkins.

That was the moment Queen Mary had been waiting for. The woman would not find what Queen Mary herself had dreamed up. Now Mrs. Perkins was beginning to feel responsible. There would soon be a large contribution.

"How much was there?" repeated Mrs. Perkins.

But the voice in the trumpet was disappearing. It mumbled some double-talk, words that almost made sense. Sheila was careful to mention no specific amount.

Suddenly a clear voice issued from the neighborhood of the

trumpet. Although the voice was different from the original Aunty Josephine, there was no mistaking the words: "It was exactly twenty-seven fucking cents—let's see you split that with Queen Mary."

"You're fired!" Queen Mary bit her armpit in desperation.

"I didn't say that! And if you tell me I'm fired just once more, I'll blow the whole thing up." The earphones indicated that Sheila was pouring an extra long refreshment.

The twenty-seven cents was like a wet dishrag in Eloise Perkins' face. She got up from the table remembering to push her skirt down. She had felt rather silly tearing her attic apart. Particularly when the search had revealed nothing but endless dust.

"What!" she said. Her head touched an overhead wire. The trumpet bobbed in response and she was rational enough to see that she had caused it. She jerked the wire again and then it slipped out of her hand. The trumpet and whipping ectoplasm sped into the corner of the room and disappeared.

"I felt wires," stated Mrs. Perkins.

"Who can say what the spirits feel like?" shouted Queen Mary in some semblance of a pious tone. The following moment of silence assured her that she had the upper hand again. "Now look what you've done." Even in the darkness there was no question that she was addressing Eloise Perkins. "You've broken the circle." Her tone suggested that Mrs. Perkins had acquired leprosy.

"Imagine," whispered Helen. "She's broken the circle. That goddam hand of yours isn't worth a shit."

"I wish you wouldn't talk like that," said Tom. "You don't have to sound like a truck driver."

"How about the real thing? You must have enough by now."

"Mrs. Perkins liked my hand all right."

Helen mocked him: " 'Mrs. Perkins liked my hand all right.' Well, if I hadn't had a lay in as long as Mrs. Perkins I'd probably like your hand too."

"There will be no more spirits tonight." Unless they come out of a bottle, added Queen Mary, in thought.

"They've run out of spirits," said Helen. "How about it, Tom—have you got enough yet?"

Queen Mary struggled though the darkness to the wall switch. She turned the light on. The half-dozen people around the table blinked in the sudden light. They usually blinked for a while and then after a few sheepish remarks began heading home.

"I think so," said Tom. "Just enough!"

"Well, drag the old thing out here," said Helen. "And we'll give it a whirl."

"Right here in front of everybody?"

"What difference does it make?" She began stroking his cock, "God help me, if it disappears I'll tear your balls off." In the same breath she added: "At long last, as big and knobby as a fat gourd. Quick! On top of the table." Without letting go she dragged him over on top of her.

The group was still seated, with the exception of Queen Mary and Mrs. Perkins. In a second they were all hugging the wall farthest from the table. Queen Mary had lost complete control and in view of the developments did not care in the least.

There was no mistaking that a hole had laid itself out in the middle of the table. It was neatly framed with short bushy black hair and while they watched, the outer lips opened and revealed an exciting pink. The inner lips puckered around the tiny vagina as though begging to be kissed.

Tom's staff travelled across the table as though rolling along on his own balls. It parried a little with the cunt, slopping up and down, then buried itself a little.

Someone in the crowd grunted.

The cock drew back a bit and then rolled forward and rammed in all the way.

Mrs. Perkins gasped and murmured: "How come it didn't come out the other side?"

"What a big old knobby ghost of a rod," said someone else.

It was sliding in and out at a furious pace as though in a frantic hurry to get it done with. The big balls bounced wildly on the bottom of the hole for a moment. Then it became evident to all that some invisible hands were squeezing them.

"Wonderful!" said Shorty Waldo. "The spirits really are strong tonight."

Mrs. Perkins, still thinking he was her benefactor, backed into him and, reaching around, pulled on his flesh. Its size frightened her. Where had it gotten the nickname "Shorty"?

"What goes on?" asked Sheila.

"If I told you, you wouldn't believe it!"

Mrs. Perkins and two other women looked at her sharply.

"Don't you hear voices?" asked Queen Mary. "I hear voices asking the strangest questions."

"Are the lights on?" asked Sheila.

"Even with the lights on," said Queen Mary. "The spirits manifest themselves."

"What does manifest mean?" asked Tom.

"Lay," said Helen. "Lay—lay—lay! And stop listening to them. Can't you keep your mind on it?"

"The spirits must have something important to tell us," continued Queen Mary, scratching her fat crotch. "Let us return to the table."

"And get a closer look," added Tom.

"Keep your mind on screwing," said Helen. "And hurry before someone grabs those big ones of yours."

The closer the group got to the table the more agitated the act became. A point of balance was achieved about three feet from the table. The group stood hesitantly at that distance while the prick maintained an incredible frantic rhythm.

Mrs. Perkins still had her back to Shorty, still pulling on his growing flesh. She leaned forward a little, hand on the back of a chair, as though to get a better look. Shorty took quick advantage of the offer. After carefully looking around to be certain he was unobserved, he lifted her skirt, spread her legs, and pulled aside the edge of her panties. He was amazed at how wet they were.

Queen Mary maintained her leadership by being the closest —by five or six inches. That would not be enough, she knew. She must have complete control of the situation or she would forfeit her clientele. She decided to sit at the table.

As though in response to her intent, the hole began to open further, stretch wide apart, and the big knobby rod strained to fit it. Something was trying vainly to push one of the big hairy balls inside.

When Mrs. Perkins saw what was happening she opened Shorty's trousers and pulled his meat out. The sudden heat in her hand made her cry out, but to the rest of the group it sounded like a snort of indignation. She put one foot up on the side of the chair and rested her elbow on her knee. She found his balls and pulled them out too. Then, caring for a moment that they might get caught, she looked around quickly. No one was paying any attention to her. She got a good handful of Shorty and slowly but firmly pulled him in. She started to say: "Terrible! Terrible!" in a shocked tone. She got as far as "Terr—" when Shorty, taking the lead, drove his staff into her in one swift motion. It went up to the hilt like driving into soft butter. The rest of the word came out of Mrs. Perkins in a high-pitched voice: "ific—ific! Oh, terrific—ific!"

The group never noticed Shorty and Mrs. Perkins. The fuck on the table was throbbing, ready to burst, and then it seemed to explode like a soundless bomb. It materialized as two perfect skeletons locked tightly together. They could see the big rod coming in a throbbing flood and rattling around in her empty pelvic bones.

"Sorry," said Helen. "I came too soon."

"You did it again," said Tom. "Couldn't you stay solid another second? There's nothing like coming in a bunch of bones."

"No worse than your disappearing on me."

By the time the skeletons were complete the room was empty. There had been a momentary jam at the door, but Queen Mary, by use of her preponderance, managed to get out first.

All except Shorty and Mrs. Perkins. He dragged her under the table and protected her by covering her completely.

Helen moved the table so she could get a better look. "You'd think he'd take her panties off."

"Big rush," said Tom. "She's sure getting what she's been looking for for a good many years."

"I don't think we could worry them even if we wanted to."

Shorty was driving his surprisingly fat item into the frantic Mrs. Perkins. She played her ass up and down at a rapid pace and the juices pouring out of them soaked her panties, his trousers, and started a puddle in the middle of Queen Mary's best rug.

Helen and Tom strolled out into the night air as Shorty and Mrs. Perkins started another more involved position on the table top. It was late spring and it was pleasantly cool. The night was clear and the stars lighted their path. By the time they reached the country dirt road there was no sign of the rest of the group. They walked along the road a way and then cut off into the dense wood.

"This is a kind of scary route," said Helen. "Even if it is a short cut."

"At least you could have stayed solid for another second."

"I'm scared of scary routes." After a second she added: "I'm scared of the fact that I'm scared of."

"I nearly cut my balls off on your lousy pelvic bone."

"It's dark as a pocket."

"I would happen to be on a down stroke when your hot thing disappeared."

"It won't be long now," said Helen.

"No!" said Tom. "It was almost cut down to a nubbin."

"What are you talking about?" Helen stopped and put her hands on her hips.

"My battered flesh," said Tom.

"Don't worry about it. They never wear out."

"Where's yours if they never wear out!"

Helen stopped him. "Do you want to try again—right now?"

Tom looked around, up and down the path, into the woods. "Can't seem to find any—at least not enough."

"Concentrate. I have enough, I think," said Helen.

"We're too close, anyway."

Tom led the way along the twisting path. A short distance further it widened sufficiently for Helen to walk beside him. She put her arm around his waist.

Tom was about to take her arm away when Helen spoke up: "Now certainly that isn't going to hurt you."

"We're too close!"

"Oh, shit!" said Helen.

They turned out of the deep wood onto another dirt road. A large rabbit commandeered the center of the road. In the moonlight he perked up and watched them. His eyes followed them as they passed him close by. A dog began to howl a short way off. The rabbit watched them turn off the road into an aged and long closed cemetery.

"Feel it," said Helen. "I've really got a solid hole, all for you."

"Don't talk like that," said Tom. "Forget it! We're here!"

The old cemetery was not maintained. A few of the old stones had fallen over and whoever had mowed during past summers had continually gone around them. Long tufts of unclipped grass grew close to each stone. They were simple slabs of stone and the passing of many rough New England seasons had smoothed their inscriptions. A canopy formed by large trees made the cemetery darker than the road. They strolled down between the stones.

"Kiss me," said Helen.

"Someone might see us."

"At this hour?" Helen drew close. "I want to be kissed." As though the trees had parted to let the moonlight in, Tom could see Helen's beautiful white face framed with long lustrous black hair. Her eyes were partly closed but he could see sparks of light flashing in them. Her lips were parted and raised. She was solid all over. Tom could feel himself pushing against her. She moved her full hips back and forth a little. She was certainly a devil. Could she do nothing else but try to break him down? Here of all places? It was not right!

"You'll use up your whole supply," said Helen.

"I don't care," said Tom, suddenly reckless. "Kiss me again!"

"Not here!" Then she whispered in his ear: "Let me stay with you again."

"If you'll promise to leave before we get into trouble."

"Of course, darling," said Helen, knowing full well that she would stay the night.

There were actually two places they could go but at the moment they were right over Tom's grave. Helen did not want to waste a moment when there was so little ectoplasm left between them.

Mrs. Perkins strolled home slowly. Shorty had passed out on the table. Mrs. Perkins had tried everything she could think of to get another erection out of him but it just hung there like an old clammy slug from under a wet rock.

She had used her panties to dry her throbbing cunt. It was wet and hot again. She felt a drop of juice running down her thigh and, not giving a damn for anyone, stopped under a street light, lifted her skirt, put a foot on a hydrant, and wiped her thigh. She gave her hole a few extra wipes, it felt so good. She looked up and down the street hoping to see a man. There was no one in sight. She took her foot off the hydrant and dropped her skirt.

She found that by swaying her end the lips of her hole rubbed together. She thought of throwing her soaked panties away but they were new, and the hell with old Aloysius Perkins if he made a fuss.

She went in the front door singing, swaying, and swinging her panties. She bounced into the living room and without even a word of greeting slopped her soaking panties across his face. She stood in front of him, hands on hips, her lower lip pouted insolently.

"What do you think of that?"

Mr. Perkins recognized the odor rather than the item. He methodically folded his newspaper into his lap, took off his glasses, put down his cigarette, and then buried his nose in them for a moment and felt himself stir. He took another deep whiff and knew he was going to have another throbbing erection and no place to put it. By the time he convinced her to lay down and spread her legs, just a little, he would be too exhausted to do anything. It was the old pattern with her. He took another whiff and had to loosen the crotch of his trousers. It was too late to get to that house in the city. Might as well wait until tomorrow. He took another deep whiff in anticipation of tomorrow and roused himself from his reverie. "This smells like—smells like—"

"Fish!" said Mrs. Perkins with conviction.

"My dear, it doesn't sound like you. You amaze me!"

"Well, that's what it is. It's outrageous!"

"Ah!" said Mr. Perkins, relaxing and rustling his newspaper. "I might have known. What's outrageous?"

"Four men raped me!"

"Ah!" He rattled his paper again, anxious to drop this pointless conversation and get back to his reading. "In this quiet town?"

"They dragged me into the woods near Queen Mary's place and then held me down and took turns—one went twice! A regular gang-shag."

"Eloise! I'm surprised at your language. Why didn't you yell for help?"

"They didn't seem to need any." Before Mr. Perkins could absorb this statement she pulled up her skirt and put a foot on the edge of his armchair. "Look what a mess they made of my hole."

Mr. Perkins "tsked" a few times. "Never heard you talk like this, my dear." He bent forward. "Looks all right to me. A little tangled perhaps, but then most—er—holes are."

Mrs. Perkins lowered her voice a little. "Maybe you'd better put your glasses on, dear."

"Ah! Perhaps so." He adjusted them over his ears, readjusted their position on his nose and leaned forward. "You mind?" Mr.

Perkins took the lips between his fingers and raised her a little.

"Not at all. Perhaps if I knelt on the arms of the chair?"

"That might be excellent." He helped her up by getting a firm grip on each cheek.

"Does it help if I tip the lamp shade a bit?"

"Quite so!" Mr. Perkins adjusted his glasses again and settled back.

"Mind if I take a drag on your cigarette?"

"Not at all Eloise, but you know—"

"What?"

"You don't smoke!"

"Shit!" said Eloise. "I just started—right this minute." She tilted the lamp shade further. "Can you see it all right?"

"That's it! Hold still. Now I can."

"I should hope so. You've got your nose right up in my cunt. Why don't you take your glasses off?"

"I think I will." He put them on the table and, spreading the lips again, said: "My! My! It does look rather red and bruised looking. And it certainly is wet, dripping. No wonder your panties are soaked."

"Kiss it and make it feel better."

"How was that?"

"That makes me feel much better. Do it again, and again."

He did not speak for a minute or two.

Mrs. Perkins lowered her voice still further. "Why don't you loosen your fly, darling? You seem to be having a rough time with your tight pants."

"You don't mind?"

"Let's face it—you've got a big fat hard-on."

"Eloise! My!" Mr. Perkins loosened his belt too and managed to slide his trousers onto the floor with one quick motion. When she lowered herself a little and rubbed the head of his staff back and forth the length of her crotch, Mr. Perkins said again: "Eloise! My! My! What are we ever going to do about those four men?"

"Four men—five men—what the hell's the difference? My! You do have a big old stick, don't you? Quick! On the floor." She pulled him down on top of her and aimed his meat. Grabbing his groin she began to pull him in.

"What if the neighbors should come in?"

Eloise gasped as he slid in: "Screw the neighbors!"

"If that's the way you feel, Eloise," he said mildly. And then, as though a switch had been turned, Mr. Perkins added in a loud voice: "All right, you bitch. I'll screw the tail right off you. You're going to get the lay of your life. I'll make you feel like a dozen men had you. How's that? Is that deep enough? Do you like it when it whirls around inside? Do you? You think you've been raped? When I get through with you, you won't be able to say 'screw' for a month."

Eloise just smiled and held on. She started coming as soon as he entered and never stopped until after his hot flood filled her up. Then she fell asleep.

Mr. Perkins staggered to his feet, wiped his flesh on her panties, and looked her over. Legs askew, her slit gaped at him. "You sure got a red one now, baby. How about another one for good luck?" He hoisted his prick in one hand and wiped under his balls with the other. It was getting hard again. "How about it? Roll it over and we'll see how your fat ass is." He got it harder by masturbating slowly. "Eloise! You hear me? Let's tear off another piece! Eloise! By Christ you tired old bag, you're asleep. Fucked out."

Mr. Perkins put the lamp on the floor. Kneeling in front of her, he continued pulling on his meat. "It sure is a mess. Are you sure you're supposed to have all those slits in there, or did we make some new ones?" He stuck a finger in. "Not too much room in there. Where does it all go, anyway? Eloise!"

He knew he was going to come in a moment if he did not stop pulling on it. "Eloise! Serve her right if I shoved it up her behind. That would wake her up. Poor tired old sow—she's had a wonderful rough day. Tomorrow morning she gets it. First thing!" He pushed her leg up higher, ignored her abused hole and inspected her virgin behind. He began to make plans for the morning and a moment later fountained a flood of sperm all over her new lamp.

The neighbors remarked on how well they got on together from that time. Mr. Perkins lost a little weight, had circles under his eyes but then sometimes business problems could do that to a man. It did not seem to affect Mrs. Perkins. She gained weight particularly around the hips, and was always bright-eyed with a bounce to her step.

Mr. Perkins did not stay in town once a week as he had in the past. And Eloise never did seem to have time for another of Queen Mary's meetings. There just was not time for the meetings, house work, and Shorty Waldo dropping in afternoons.

ED MARTIN

Ed Martin was born in New York City and swears on an unabridged dictionary that he did not pursue a checkered career just to create a more colorful book jacket. Just the same, he has been a skindiver, farm worker, cowpuncher, accountant, hobo, composer and ar- ranger, North Woods guide, TV engineer, actor, cartoon gagwriter and, where we find him now: psychiatric social worker. He claims it takes one to know one. Mr. Martin has produced five published novels (four of them for Olympia), some short stories, poems and a dozen published songs. He lives in Massachusetts, and pretends he is a solid citizen by working for the government and being a member of the National Geographic Society. But those who have read his far-out blend of fantasy, humor and sex, know better.

Forever Ecstasy

Tor Kung

When he did come back the next night, Louise somehow had a baby. Or at least her breasts were swollen gargantuanly with milk. Which excited him as much as it disgusted Mother. He could not get enough of their distended lushness. He made little meaningless sounds of joy when he saw how the white dribbled out with her every motion. He got her to dance in front of him and laughed with pure rapture at the milk spraying the room. He got her to kneel on all fours over him so he could suck her. Oh, how good it felt! She was nothing more than a cow, but it was wonderful. He was content to drink her for hours. Night after night he would lie there nursing up at her. Sometimes he would lie back so his mouth was a foot away and milk the fat streams from both breasts into his open mouth. As the happiness built up in him, he would start gulping down one stream while he sent the other splashing all over his face. The milk made him wonderfully crazy. He would make her suck her own tits, which was easy since they were so immense. She would lift the heavy, swollen breast and suck the milk while looking into his eyes. Other times he would nurse on one while she nursed at the other. Then they would laugh and hug her and dance around the room. Or he would call her over and milk her into his coffee, or into his bowl of berries. He began bringing a bottle and would milk her into it and take it home for his cat. She loved being milked! Best of all she liked to kneel over his open mouth and lovingly, massagingly milk her own udders, pouring the hot milk from the soft flesh into him.

It was Louise, in fact, who suggested he fuck her breasts. She lay with her back on the rug with him astride her diaphragm, his great hot cock buried between the great pillows of her breasts. She squeezed them tight around his manhood as he began fucking in and out. He was careful, at first; but when he saw how the milk jetted up each time he slapped into the breasts, he went wild. He began thudding into them, making the milk spurt all over. He started yelling. He dug his fingers deep into the tits and threw his weight forward on them. They gushed. He flexed his fingers hard into them and they geysered. He thudded harder and harder into the great cushiony tits. Milk drenched both their bodies. It fell back into a pool in her deep cleavage until he was fucking into a delicious slipperiness. He drove against them more and more frantically. Milk flew in great arcs across the room, driving Mother farther and farther into the corner from where Louise could hear her screaming over and over. "Revolting. It's revolting."

It was not, Louise cried inside herself. It was glorious. Never had she felt so proud. She was the Goddess of the Earth. She was mother to the world. She was bounty to all men. She was fertilizing the universe. The milk fountaining from her was the glory of God.

Again and again he slammed into her sacred tits. Milk showered them: great gouts, streams, cascades drenched them. With a bellow, he smashed himself into them one last time. He came on her again and again and again. She exalted. He fell forward and they kissed. Then the darkness took her.

Rick was kissing her. The real Rick. Miss Bennett came fully awake. He was bending over her kissing her forehead. It was totally dark in the bedroom, but she knew it was he. She knew it with part of her, that is. It was more difficult each day to keep things clear. She blurred more and more. She was so split up between her dreams and the commonplace reality. Between the proper school teacher and the lascivious woman who taught Solid Geometry so strangely the seventh period. Between her mother's daughter and the hussy she became the moment any man touched her. The halves balanced so equally now she hung uncommitted between them, like some loose submarine tree held between the water coming and the water going out. Laxly deployed, undulatingly garlanded at full stretch. Hovering, stirring and lapsing. Supported by the water, but subject thereby to its slow, liquidly restless will.

The quiet way she pushed Rick back was a measure of the change in her. She could wake up in a dark bedroom to find one of her students kissing her and remain virtually calm. She did not even turn on the light. She pushed him gently away, settled herself and waited. Rick did not insist.

W hen she recovered, she found him waiting with cold orange juice and a towel. He wanted to dry her, because she was soaking wet all over; but she grew suddenly self-concious and would not let him. She was Miss Bennett again. It made Rick angry. He started telling her about the pictures. He turned on the light and made her look at them. One by one. She did so dutifully, saying nothing. Her silence goaded him, but there was nothing she could say. There was Miss Bennett standing in her classroom bare to the waist while all her students stared with shocked faces. How immense and naked her breasts looked! The pictures were disgraceful.

He began telling her about Tuesday. About how she was going to teach the whole seventh period like that. Naked to the waist. She said it was out of the question. He said to shut up. That he was not asking her, that he was telling her. He pointed out that if he sent Miller the pictures, she would not only never teach again, but they'd probably also send her to prison. She would do it or else. She said she would do it.

But he was still angry. He needed some more immediate revenge. He ordered her to get dressed, saying that they were going to do the town. That she needed more discipline. That she was like a stubborn dog who needed to be trained. The word *trained* was like hitting a gong at the base of her spine. A thrill went all through her, though she would still not let herself remember why. So she began. Rick frankly settled himself to watch. It made her embarrassed; but something else, too: she was shocked to see how coquettishly she began acting. She got out of bed primly enough, but she was at the same time standing right where the lamp was brightest—so that it made her nightgown transparent. She picked up the towel and marched herself to the other side of the room. Even turned her back before lifting her gown so she could wipe her soaked cunt. But she somehow made it coy.

"Come here, Miss Bennett," he said in a voice that left no room for discussion. Meekly she went over and stood in front of where he was lying on the bed. "Take that off." Without hesitation, she took it off. Her mind could still register how outrageous it all was. Here she was exposing herself completely to this pupil. Without any resistance whatsoever. Her body seemed a bovine, will-less animal that belonged to someone else. Which performed without question at somebody else's will. Her mother's daughter was helplessly buried in that flesh, forced to watch every enormity of degradation.

Still, even her mother's daughter felt pride in how splendid she looked. She could see herself in the mirror. Her body looked as if it were made of mother-of-pearl. It flared in the direct light he directed on her. She felt deep respect for the dramatically beautiful woman the mirror showed her. It was a disinterested feeling. She had never felt that it was her body. Not since her teens. She had felt guilt about its sexual quality, but never that any credit was due her for its loveliness. It seemed rather an accident. Like being assigned a mansion because all the dormitories were full. She watched her hands in the mirror come up and cup the great shining bowls of breasts, lifting them toward Rick. They *were* splendid. Like "La Blonde aux Seins Nus" of Manet. The same stupefying ripeness. And her face had the same modest expression above. Not modest in the sense of shame, but in its shy unpretentiousness. There was the same submissiveness in the face: an innocent face patiently waiting to be told who was going to fuck her next, how many there would be, and what position they wanted her in. But this body in the mirror had an even more swollen quality. It was so voluptuously gorged with sexuality that it seemed submerged in some special, invisible fluid that allowed her to flow without sinew or bone. The hands under her breasts seemed about to lift her so that she would drift to the top of the room. How deferential the hands were. And how small they looked trying to support those great melon-breasts. The opulent flesh completely overflowed them.

She saw that the figure on the bed was lifting her right leg. It seemed to float up until her foot was on the bed. The figure lying on his back was facing right up into the crotch. He was opening her. Even in the mirror you could see how plumply she was swollen there. The inside of the cunt was wide open, startlingly crimson. The man told her that *now* she could go ahead. He lay looking fixedly as the woman gently dried the hair and the insides of the cunt.

When Miss Bennett went into the bathroom to wash, Rick went

along. While the bath was running, he watched everything. Everything! They did not speak. When she got into the tub, they both knew he would wash her. She turned and stood and bent to enable him to wash every detail. She stood docilely while he dried her. He smoothed great handfuls of talcum all over her body, then lightly rubbed her down again with a fresh towel.

They went to the dressing table, and he put the perfume on: on the nape of her neck, behind her ears, on the sides of her throat, in her armpits, all over her breasts, and at the sides of her stomach. He poured some down into the crevice between her buttocks. It ran down into her cunt and burned. He saw her gasp and knew why, but neither of them said anything. He put her on her back and poured it directly into the cunt hair. The burning was fierce. She whimpered, but that was all. He smeared a little behind her knees, at her ankles, and on her instep. She knew that even after the odor of the alcohol was gone, she would smell far too much. And that he wanted it that way.

Rick chose the blouse and skirt himself. And the black garter belt and black hose. "You won't need any pants or bra," he said. "They would just interfere with the plan I have for you." A shiver of fear went through her. Followed by a shiver of delight.

His car was parked in the alley. She was surprised that it was a late-model Mustang. "That's where I put all the paper-route money, Teach." They headed for East Liberty. He explained to her that he was no gentleman, and what that let her in for. That he did not abide by the rules she had been taught, but that she damn well better abide by his this evening—or else. She knew she would obey.

First they went to Gammon's Restaurant. He walked her back and forth through it pretending to look for the right table, but really so hat she would have to let everybody see her large breasts bouncing so indecently. He chose a table right out in the center where eyes would be on her from every side.

"How does it feel to have every eye in the place riveted on your tits, Teach? And to know that they are trying to figure out whether you are a professional hooker or just a free tramp?" He spoke just loud enough so that people could make out what he was saying, but not loud enough to make it seem deliberate. The management could not object. He seemed to be talking quietly and discreetly to her alone. Everybody was straining to listen. "Half the guys are trying to get up the nerve to walk by the table for a closer look. And every gal is telling her date what a disgusting thing it is that women like you are allowed to come into a restaurant with decent people. They're saying that you ought to be kept in the stall where you belong. How does it feel, Teach Baby?"

It felt exciting. It should not, but it did. Something had gone wrong in her and she sat there enjoying the lust and scorn she saw on all the faces. The decent part of her was horrified, of course. But that part seemed lost in a great intoxication.

"Now the first thing you're going to do, Teach, is unbutton your blouse." He had lowered his voice almost inperceptibly, but it was enough to keep it from being heard by anyone but her. "Ah, Teach Baby, you're blushing. That pleases me very much. It makes it even more enjoyable to force you to do it. You're going to pretend that you're doing it secretly, not letting anybody see. You're supposed to be putting on a clandestine show just for me; but I assure you they won't miss a thing. So start, Miss Bennett."

By the time the waitress came, she had all of the buttons open. The way she was sitting, with her arms up in front of her and her chin in her hand, you could not see anything. But everybody knew. The waitress wanted to say something, but she could not quite bring herself to do it when there seemed nothing actually to complain about. It is kind of hard to say to a woman: would you mind buttoning your blouse? So Rick gave her their orders and she went back to her indignant whispering with the other waitresses. But the suspense of whether she would say anything or not had been painful for Miss Bennett, which was what Rick wanted.

"OK, Teach, now we come to the next step. You lean forward and move your arms aside a little. Everybody will know that you are really giving me a show, even if they still can't see anything." She did as she was told. And felt a spurt of pride when she saw that he could still be so impressed by what she had in there. For a minute, he just looked. When he looked up into her eyes, she could see his admiration for a minute. Then the mask was back. "Very good, Teach. Now I want you to lean back, wait a minute, take the front of the blouse in your fingers, wait another minute to torture them, and then slowly pull it wide open."

"Rick, they'll call the police." She noticed that she had made no protest about doing it, only about getting in trouble with the police. Could she really be going to show her breasts to this whole restaurant of people? The idea made her tremble. She did not even wait for Rick to reply. She began smiling. Casually she leaned back. She could see everybody leaning forward. She took hold of each side of the front. You could hear people suck in their breath. The waitresses were petrified. She began pulling the cloth aside. When the nipple appeared, guys started standing up. She looked directly into every man's eyes as she leisurely surveyed the room. What a spectacular sight she was, reflected in their expressions! The waitresses ran over in a group. The one who had waited on them told Rick to get his *friend* out of there before they called the police. He laughed, and they got up to go. She held her blouse open like that as they walked across to the door. When they got there, Rick took her hand and she dropped a deep curtsy to the room.

The crowd remained stunned long enough for them to get to the car. As they drove off, the men came pouring out of the restaurant looking around wildly. You could see the women yelling and pulling at them. Rick got to the park, made sure nobody was following, and started cruising around. It was a wonderful summer night. You could smell the trees and the earth. The wind blowing through the windows was the kind you get in the real country at night.

Miss Bennett was trembling from the after-effects. It was not so much the horror of how she had behaved that bothered her as the pleasure she had taken in it. She had to face the fact that she *liked* exhibiting herself. What would become of her? Was she a nymphomaniac or something? But as Rick just kept driving easily around, with the radio faintly playing fine old songs by Cole Porter, the sweet night began to ease her back into a soft contentment.

"Did you ever stop to think, Teach," Rick began, "how much sex there is in the world? In all those rooms in all those buildings back there, for example. In all the cities of the world. Everywhere a guy and a girl are alone together, where nobody can see—did you ever stop to think what kind of things go on? In there, they are subject to nobody's rules but their own. They can talk each other into just about anything they want to do—no matter how far out. Especially after they've been fucking a couple of months and are beginning to explore a little. Do you ever think about what is going on in every one of those cars we're passing? When you see a nice young couple in a car early in the evening, do you stop to think that before the night is over he will have his fingers buried in her gooey cunt? Yea, and a lot more than fingers.

"Don't get me wrong. I'm not knocking it. I'm for it one hundred percent. The only thing I'm against is the sad way everybody loses it as they get a few years older. No, they don't lose it. They somehow throw it away. They get some crazy idea that because they want to be married or because they are in love or because they have been to a headshrinker and are mature now, they've got to believe in having a reasonable, responsible, loyal, faithful, exclusive, considerate sex life. I remember a guy telling me what wonderful times he and his wife had before they were married. She was game for anything. Then one time, soon after they got married and had a baby, when he asked her to take off her blouse and bra so she would be sitting at the table in the sunlight (they were out in the backyard where nobody could see them), she said no. She said that she felt different about her breasts now that she had the responsibility of being a mother. And it's not just the women's fault. Guys get married and immediately get up tight about their wives acting properly. So the wife acts like a lady—and the guy starts sneaking around looking for a girl who flaunts herself at every guy who goes by. It's so much to lose, Teach. You know that line you have to learn in school by Gerard Manley Hopkins about the world being charged with the grandeur of God? Well, maybe it is. But mainly because the world is charged with the grandeur of quim. Why do they throw it away, Teach? The more they talk about it on television or put those plastic-looking girls up on billboards, somehow the more everybody loses it. And I can't get over the feeling that they throw it away.

"I had to do a paper for old Thompson in English, and I got to reading about John Keats. He was dying of tuberculosis and the doctors kept telling him the thing to do was eat nothing but bread and water. Here he needed all the strength he could get, but they were taking blood out of him (like they did in those days) and making him live on bread and water. No, it was worse. They didn't make him. They told him it was a good idea and he made himself. There he was starving to death and crazy with hunger, but he used the strength of his will to make himself NOT eat. It seems to me that's the way people are. The ones who are alive enough and strong enough to really have an appetite for sex and life are the very ones who are strong enough to force themselves to stick to the bread and water of the tired old obligation they feel for their wives. Which means that the wives starve too. It's stupid."

It was a long speech. When Rick was finished, he obviously felt embarrassed and started driving fast down into East Liberty again. He kept going and drove all the way downtown. He said he was hungry. They never did get served in Gammon's. They went to a Chinese place he knew about which had little closed booths and curtains across the front so you could really be alone. He made her open her blouse part way so that the old Chinese waiter could look. When he saw her sitting like that, her pale breasts almost out, he looked with real pleasure. Openly, but not rudely. Then he put his hands together and bowed with real grace. It was a great way of showing his appreciation. When he had served them, he looked again, put his hands together gravely and bowed out—closing the curtain. He never bothered them again.

From there, they drove back to the Democratic Men's Canoe Club: a private club Rick knew. They did not make any fuss about his age. Just passed them in as soon as they saw his face through the slot. It was a fairly fancy place for a neighborhood club. There was a bar the length of the wall on the right, a little dance floor, a pianist, and tables. The lights were low and the drunks were the quiet, gentle kind.

At first Rick let her keep her blouse closed. They just sat and drank a little and listened to the music. In her condition, the whiskey wiped out whatever control she had established in herself after Gammon's. When Rick reached over and started flicking her nipple through the cloth, she made no protest. It felt nice. He did the other one. People were watching, but not making a big deal of it. Rick made her drink again, and then told her to unbutton. She was beginning to like it. Everywhere they went, she had to start showing her tits. It was kind of funny, but it was clear that she enjoyed doing it. All her life she had lived with the biggest breasts in the neighborhood—no matter which neighborhood she happened to be in—but she always had to feel ashamed and hide them. Other girls were always getting compliments and going sailing and coming back from a party where there had been all kinds of famous people, simply because they had nice figures. She had twice as good a figure but she had to keep it hidden and go to Bible-Study Outings where she was always assigned to sit with somebody like old Miss Hartmann because the dear soul was all befuddled and could not be left alone. Going into all these places and showing herself made her feel like somebody glamorous for the first time in her life. Every girl was entitled to that at least once, she thought.

Rick ordered her another drink and had her pull the blouse half-way open so you could see the whole of the inside swell of the breasts. Then he waved at somebody to come over.

The guy looked about twenty-five; he had sandy hair, was nice-looking in an ineffectual way, and seemed kind. Rick introduced him as Hank and said he was a mechanic for an airline. When the guy was seated, Rick asked him what he thought of Miss Bennett's breasts. (He always referred to her as Miss Bennett.) The guy did not know what to say. It was not the kind of question he could deal with. Rick asked him if he could see that Miss Bennett was not wearing anything under her blouse. Yes, the guy answered, he could certainly see that. Rick asked if he did not think Miss Bennett had a pair of real whoppers. The guy blushed a little and said yes. Rick said would he like to see more of them. The guy just stared. Rick said to give her a buck and see. Hank knew it was a joke or some kind of trick, but what the hell. What could he lose but the buck. And it was worth a lot more than that just to be allowed to sit looking into that sensational cleavage. He had never been in a situation like this before. He self-consciously got out a dollar and shoved it toward Miss Bennett. She gravely took it and handed it to Rick.

Then she bent forward with her arms making a kind of wall on each side. Kind of like at Gammon's. Only this time it was more like a little cave. She adjusted herself inside and then told him to look. He moved the glasses hurriedly out of the way and leaned over the table, looking hard. It was pretty shadowy in the room, and the way she had made a little place of her body and arms, it was dark inside. But you could still see. Her tits were completely naked! "Christ," he said. He just lay across the table staring like he would never get enough. Then she reached in and pulled the blouse closed again like a curtain. He sat back, said "Christ" again, and ordered doubles for all of them.

Rick said that Miss Bennett would talk about them for another buck. They guy clawed out his wallet and emptied the bills on the table. He found a one with shaking hands and pushed it toward her. She handed it to Rick, took a sip of her brandy and began to tell him.

"They're all mine," she said in a husky, intimate voice. "No injections, no operations, no plastic or wax or silicone. I'm a thirty-nine D. But the D cup is really too small for me, so I have to get my bras specially made. My tits started to develop when I was twelve. They got real big right away. Especially because my brother, Gunnar, was always sucking them. He used to sneak into my room at night and suck them for hours. Sometimes he would suck me all night long. Neither of us could get enough of it. I could have let him suck on me forever. He liked it for another reason, too. Oh, he liked just the sucking, but he also liked how helpless it made me. That's how he could always get me to do the really dirty things. After the divorce, when he went away with father, I used to lie at night with them really aching to be sucked. That's how I got started sucking on them myself. I still do that a lot.

"When they get sucked on, the nipple swells up. It gets thick and real long. It changes color, too. Could you see in here how pink my nipples are, and the paler big pink area round the nipple? Well, when somebody sucks on them the nipples become red. That's how you can tell it's beginning to really get to me. They are so sensitive that it happens almost right away. That's what you call an erogenous zone for all women, of course, but I'm abnormally sexy there. A guy can make me come just by sucking on my nipples. He doesn't even have to get that far. If he can just fight me long enough to get his fingers far enough into my bra to get hold of a nipple, he's got it made. I change immediately. I start asking him to squeeze them and pinch them. Really hard. I really like them hurt. Especially by somebody biting into them. But then I like him to get gentle again, and just suck them. One of my big fantasies is to have two guys sucking them, one at each tit."

Her voice was low and throaty. "Most of the time I have to make other arrangements. I have a needle-spray shower and I stand for hours with the scalding hot water stinging into them. And I cream them a lot. I fill my hands with lotion and smear it on them while watching myself in the mirror. Another trick I have is to wear heavy wool sweaters with nothing underneath. The wool scratches them intolerably. It's very exciting. Cashmere sweaters are a different thing entirely. They are like a velvet hand caressing me as I walk around. A satin blouse is also nice, especially a real heavy one. With nothing underneath between it and my tits, I mean."

Hank could not believe his ears. When she stopped, he blindly shoved more money forward. "Would you like to suck on me, Hank?"

"Oh, Christ, Yea! How much?"

"Well, it's five to suck the left one and fifteen to suck the right one."

"What's the difference?"

She whispered, "The right one is the one I keep more private. They tell me also it's even sweeter."

Hank was as helpless in his own way as she was. He was far beyond understanding anything. He was so excited he could not make out the denominations of the bills. Finally he just shoved the whole pile toward her. She took a five and dutifully handed it to Rick.

"Now, Hank," she said in the same husky voice, "that gives you the right to suck on my left breast. But we have to be careful. You know how people watch." People were indeed watching. Every guy in the place was watching her totally. But in a nice way. Maybe it was because of Rick's reputation, or maybe just because that was the style of the club. It made it so lovely. She felt like she was a celebrity. And that she was giving a performance. Everybody was so enthusiastic about her body, but so polite and respectable at the same time. It was like a perfect dream.

She made him come around the table and sit on her left. She made him take off his jacket and put it over his head and lean down so it made a little tent on the table. Then, finally, when he was in there waiting, she pushed aside the left side of the blouse and lifted the breast in both hands. She paused to let everybody see, then leaned forward and put it under his coat where the mouth waited. Hank was ravenous. She could feel the strength of his sucking right down to her toes. He sucked frantically. He tried to get his hands on the breast, but she pushed them away—whispering that he was just to suck. The room was silent. The piano player had stopped. In the stillness, you could hear the sloppy sound of his sucking. She went into a trance of pleasure. When the time was up, Rick had to reach under and tug her loose. Hank came up flushed and disheveled. He grabbed another bill and pushed it into her hand. She made him wait while she handed it to Rick. Hank was staring hungrily at the big breast with its glistening nipple. Everybody was. She made him get back under the coat and lifted her breast in after him. The next time Rick tried to free her, he had to push against Hank's forehead with one hand and really work the breast free of his mouth. When Hank was finding another five, he got enough of a grip on himself to ask about the other one: was it really sweeter? Rick said it was a matter of taste. The point was lost on Hank. While he was trying to make up his mind, Miss Bennett sat stroking the breast she held in her hand and looking around the room at the other men.

When he gave her the fifteen, and she had given it to Rick, she made him bring his chair around to the other side of her. After she had made him get under the tent of his coat again, she put away the left breast, took out the right, held it out to the room, smiled at them, and then carried it in her two hands under the coat. When the time ran out again, he reappeared hysterically announcing that it was sweeter. Hank grabbed for another fifteen and stopped. He could see how little was left, and hesitated: would it be smarter to invest it in the left tit at five bucks a throw? Rick said:

"Tell him about your cunt, Miss Bennett."

"Well, Hank . . . Do you want me to tell you?"

"Yes! Yes!"

"Well, men say I have a very pretty cunt. The hair is darker than on my head, and there is a lot of it. It's almost as dark as your hair, in fact. Right now I'm so wet that it's probably dark brown. Normally, though, it's a thick tangle of soft, light-brown cunt hair. The cunt itself is plump. When I wear a bathing suit, you can really see what a mound I have. But I'm told that it's an unusually neat cunt. The lips don't hang out like they do on some girls. Of course, when I'm hot like I am now, the lips swell a lot. But with me, the whole cunt kind of opens—sort of like a big rose. It's a juicy cunt, too. Sometimes it is embarrassing, because after I have been fighting off a guy and pretending that I'm a respectable girl—then he finally gets his hand inside my pants and finds I'm sopping. But I like being juicy. Guys like it too, I think. Especially with me, since they say I have a tight pussy. Not too tight, or anything like that. Just tight in the right way, according to them, to really squeeze their cocks.

That's where the cunt-juice comes in, though. Some of them are so big that I really need the lubrication.

"My cunt is even more sensitive than my nipples. Often I come as soon as the joy touches the lips. Even through the pants. (You know I'm not wearing any pants tonight, Hank. I'm completely available. My cunt's naked.) When a guy gets his fingers inside, I'm lost. And when he gets his cock shoved up in me, I'm his slave. As long as he has got that in me, he can make me do absolutely anything he wants. One guy used to make me call up his friends and tell them what he was doing to me. And I had to do it."

Hank could not control himself. As much as he liked hearing her talk dirty about herself like that, he could not hold back. He was about to let go in his pants as it was.

"Can I get any of that?" he asked. He was panting, looking from one of them to the other.

"How much money you got left, Hank?" Rick said.

Hank finally got it counted. "Twelve bucks."

"Too bad. For twenty-five you could have eaten her." Hank groaned. "But tell you what. I'll get her to reach up inside it, get some cunt-juice on her finger, and let you taste it. That will only cost twelve."

Hank pushed the last of the money to her. She held it in her left hand while she got out her breasts again with the right. She arranged them so that as she bent forward, getting her hand up under her skirt, they were laid out on the table. It was apparent to everybody in the room that her right hand was up in there a long time. Much longer than necessary. That she was playing with herself. Which was true. The whole scene, combined with the brandy, had her over-stimulated to such a point that she could resist nothing. She could hardly make herself stop. Hank was whining with impatience. Rick finally had to tell her. When her hand came up, it was smeared all over with the liquor of her. She held it out and he licked it clean, sucking each finger.

When she pulled her hand away, he started babbling about how he could run home and get some more money. That it would only take a minute. Then he wanted them to wait while he hit the bartender for some. The bartender had known him a long time and knew he was good for it.

"Sorry, Hank," Rick said, "the store is closed. We have to get around to her other customers."

When he saw they were really going, he stood up and shook hands. "I'm sure glad to have met you, Miss Bennett."

"Thank you, Hank. I'm glad to have met you. You have a nice mouth."

He hesitated, then timidly asked: "Is this your regular kind of work, Miss Bennett?"

"No, I'm a school teacher."

They left him standing there. They paused at the door and turned to acknowledge the applause that was coming from all sides. Her breasts were still bare. As she bowed, they swung splendidly out.

TOR KUNG

Tor Kung is neither an Oriental nor a Viking but the pen name of a very American poet, born in Pittsburgh, Pa. somewhere around 1929. He participated in the birth of the Beat movement in San Francisco, both as poet and general character, and has read his poetry around the world. He lived for many years in Europe — as staff interpreter for the U.S. Army in the late 1940s; as ex-patriate involved in black market activities in France during the early 1950s, returning to Italy, Sweden and Germany in the early 1960s. He is back in San Francisco now, although his precise whereabouts are unknown even to his friends.

Bondage Trash

Jon Horn

I am the fellow next door. It all started when I answered an advertisement in a magazine available to every man and woman in the United States. Yet you will never read them, the reports on those who allow themselves exotic lustfulness and shuddering disgust in unusual friendship clubs for unusual people, adventurous, uninhibited, broadminded, intellectual, and cultured people. I had seen in the lobby of a hotel my acquaintance, a Turkish national, a totally strange man; and then I forgot the fact that I was married. I had some idea of paying the required fee and submitting to a bare minimum of barbarities—for example, contact with an Athenian in the Vatican Museum, extramarital sex with hand-lovers and aesthetes, pains, tweezings, even branding—at irregular intervals.

I was tired of bisexual, average housewives paralyzed by medical checkups. I did not want to go through the inquisition of virgins, brides, wives and widows, which helps subdue the candidate for violation. Let me reiterate the memories of a hotel man; begging borrowing or stealing a deviate practice supplied by film and television personalities, I decided to examine secret delight, amusement, and laziness more closely in these "playlands." Refined "nerve-racking" and ravishing, that was my meat. Members intrigued me. I came all over the corset-torture brochure and checked the time. The Turco promised five damsels, embraces, wild tussle, unconsciousness, ejaculations, and insanity resulting from violently spiritual wantonness. I waited for developments in the rented room.

Diverted myself with intellectual and artistic pretensions. And while the experts analyzed me, I realized: how is the allegedly normal person to be supplied with devilishly photographed information and guiled into unhappy habit, unhappy passion, and the acmes of delight and rapture? All these abstemious and passionless people *"timide dans les choses d'amour."*

I signed the franchise contract, and the rudiments of humiliating coercion, massage, "vassals," Platonic onanism, sterilization arrangements, unusual bindings, "treating" the woman, and similar medical matters, were briefly elucidated. Of course I was already familiar with methods, many of trembling beauty, and let me reiterate there is no deviation or perversion they do not practice or seek to practice. Quickly the five wantons gathered about. A delectable harmless Christian virgin wife was brought in. The Turk coddles her, pulls her luxurious breasts out of her chemise, rips the silk from her body, grabs her by her extruded hips . . . She was finally undressed and violated in each armpit; passively restive, she permitted herself to be mauled and fingered. The prostitutes had withdrawn. Having passed her "tests," she hurriedly closed her bloomers, was brought back to her room. As a matter of fact, during a comfortable moment in her amusements she asked clamorous questions about membership. She was told something innocuous and advised to continue mutual endeavors in loosely linked associations purporting to share desires for children, well-educated professional men, semi-literate manual workers, basic debased unhappiness these people seek . . .

I am not an expert. What I succeeded in doing satisfied their sickness though; one subject wrote: "I hardly dare taste of the passerby joys of life and immediately I am reprimanded. I want to begin life anew. Children interest me most." He goes on to confess that "as regards the sexual question," his wife's body leaves him cold though she is well-formed (exotic pic enclosed); in eight years of marriage he has never once had intercourse with his wife, and this, he reports, was the "cause of much marital difficulty." Only "little games, perhaps somewhat sadistic," had allowed him orgasm from time to time, and one other note of interest: his mother-in-law. Our correspondent has only to kiss her hand and presto! he has an orgasm and ejaculation. (I know this type: they smell the hand, suck on it hard if they can . . .)

I grew with the department, swamped with supply and demand, learn while you earn, I went through monkey orgasm, exhibitionism, voyeurism, necrophilism, apparatus, ejaculation, and many more. Clubs that cater to every conceivable sexual need, it should be emphasized, are a little more curious, a little more probing, but that is all.

I am the fellow next door; sexology is not orderly, well-regulated. Next door husbands and wives (urine and feces) are cognizant of each other's wishes; they receive assistance from other mutually disposed couples as well as from single people of all sexes. They satisfy their conceivable desires. They are not deadbeats but churchgoers of all denominations. Many of them do not drink at all. They hold prestige jobs, own businesses, or are in the professions. I have seen attorneys, biologists, chemists, druggists, executives, farmers, government employees, hustlers, imps, jerks, kindergarten teachers, lumpen mama's boys, nincompoops, opportunists, pimps, queens, roustabouts, strippers, toughguys, undercover men, virgins, wobblies, xenophiles, young wives, and zeros go in and out. In the main they are not noisy drunken or suggestive, telling only respectable off-color jokes in the store or office, much less in the home. To a casual observer they are perhaps loose sexual contacts, but who suspects the bizarre network . . .?

The women are prostitutes, virgins, or "mistresses" who divert themselves reading "Linda's Strange Vacation," "The Sixty-Niner," etc. According to their own testimonies, they are writers, the Informed, the Beautiful People, models, wives, excellent housewives, exemplary mothers, model husbands, providers, etc. Some enjoy a largely protein diet and nocturnal emissions; only albumens satisfy them. These suffer from chronic confusion of the vagina and the navel.

The sexually sick knocked at the door: would they be answered truthfully? According to the ads, onanistic manipulations, several times a week in normal fashion, and remaining in the toilet as long as possible, as well as other penchants, should only be indulged under the supervision of responsible and experienced therapists. And, aside from ethical questions, they kept me constantly on the go. Over the next few days I thought about the stupid thing I had done. And then I forgot all about the questions of the scientists and experts, the promises . . .

As for deviates, I had seen, though had never purchased . . .

But soon the contact from Istanbul, harmlessly enough, replied to my perplexing hint of offbeat or illicit sex. I didn't much care. I enjoyed unusual experiences, would be frank and give ages, heights, weights. I found none of them interesting enough to personally reply. Eventually I passed them on. Quiet home-loving people, drink moderately: hobbies are playgoing, reading, and photography (Polaroid). All sincere and discreet. "Would like to be your friends." "Sincerely hope you will want to become our friends and that you, like us, are adults in every sense." "Married for twelve years, we talked this matter over, exchanging partners for sex experience. Our belief is missing something vital, my wife said, hope you too feel like this." It is difficult to record my reaction. I know I thought: unscrupulous hands, blackmail and ruin, the last person I'd seek pleasure with. It didn't occur to me at first—we take lots of pix of each other doin' what comes naturally; if I were the sort of person I hoped I was, I could move in with a young couple whose letter I had, who, while sexually loose-living, stayed within the law, catering to a special trade. I was stymied; conservative. By the time 500 husbands had offered me their wives I was divorced, naming 500 correspondents; at least 500 of my correspondents were men.

It may be argued that a known violator is not anxious to blacken his own rank in the sexual services. But all that is claimed here and incidentally, she possessed a veritable harem of male garters—proves and shows that the experts are dangerous no matter what practices they condone to make sexual truth strange (technicalities and legalities; there is a legal technicality called "entrapment" that is the bondage red-tape of the court whereby official hands are tied).

Sex clubs where members participate in planned orgies do not require any expert understanding. Heterosexual couples in government employ engaged in joint possession of a violator are complex in their desires but not necessarily crude in the terms and tactics they use. A known violator may have a contact, or even a foundation grant in real life, but these people frequently keep a dozen others, and there is little to be done about them. According to officials, a violator once caught will cooperate eagerly, seeking to mitigate the incriminating material; this included those who craved to be whipped, tortured, or otherwise abused. While they realize this, officials cannot take action. Therefore, for each offender apprehended a dozen escape, and their activities are widespread, cautiously proceeding down all walks of life.

Statistics publish male and female homosexual indifference, and offenders, like the couple from Azuza, California, are released without incident: undue lenience and mercy, probation sex parties, illegal activities at some offical echelon, and covering up.

But why do they call me "Stud?" You will see.

This woman was obsessed with animals. This woman, her dream of copulation with the Cretan bull fully discussed with her husband, continually submitted to the search for new thrills. Once, during fellatio, the wife stated irascibly: "Tried everything, dogs and goats, no success in this direction, nigger with a giant one, but can't stand niggers . . . o, if we could only obtain a magnificent animal for our personal pet as well as watchdog and family companion!" Thereupon follows a description of how the husband brought the animal into the bedroom and the wife undressed and prepared herself. The husband helped. "What a thrill this is!" "Is this dog erotic!" called the wife. Perhaps it is a wee bit late to say this but we hope the foregoing incident doesn't disgust you . . . now that we have grazed the detailed and specialized tastes in the lap of luxury, we must look further into the shadows where lurk sexual objects with tying and binding habits euphemistically called "discipline," and others.

The plea of one wife was for discretion. An attractive brunette with a Horror of being Found Out. Sex party arranged via mail. She was a stickler: copulation with males would never be allowed unless male was "fixed." She did not have intercourse with her own husband, nor with the other husband at the party, although she performed fellatio for this man and cunnilingus for his wife, and they did the same for her and her husband. At their next meeting they experimented with anal intercourse. The other husband, a twenty-six-year-old technologist, would initiate her. His wife had given her personal assurance of his expertise in that direction. Details of her technique; she made it quite clear that minor titillations were not for them. "Their three kids appeared in the room, little kids decorated with rings, earrings, and scatter pins stuck through loose flesh below naked male glans and pierced nipples of the female. We didn't enjoy that at all!" Photographs were submitted proving this, as well as photographs of the other wife with both breasts decorated.

This woman had an abnormal fear of every conceivable sex act with the exception of one. Because of her extreme discomfort, the results of her desire were unsatisfactory. A Boxer and Great Dane combination, less well-endowed than her spouse, would initiate her. At an informal soiree she found that a young wife and mother like herself not only had the tendency but also the knowledge. She recommended the Boxer-Great Dane. "We've tried other dogs but they were too small or too afraid." The young wife and mother now seeks other and bigger animals, still abetted by her husband, a huge Caucasian with whom she had no success "in that direction."

A glance at the husband-and-wife teams, a liberal cross-section of sophisticated behavior and modernity. He supplies color slides of himself and his wife in the lewd, has been dominated by various women, is excited relating the incredible conditions imposed by them for their services, of the whippings and sexual humiliations which incidentally he now misses. He named many female contacts. He had one fear, that of parcels gone astray; a new addition to his impressive collection of worn, soiled women's underwear sent by one of the suburban dealers he pays handsomely to always be on the lookout for such items, gone wrong in the mails and delivered to his namesake across town, a sadistic sexcop who's blackmailing him already.

His wife failing him, his wife knows of and approves his contacts, he seeks through club bulletins, he is obsessed with fotos of beautiful models engaged in lesbian acts, exchanges pornography with girls and married women via mail, his wife doesn't mind as long as she isn't involved.

She had often thought of "just going out and finding it alone." She went out with a group of young married women garbed in leather wardrobe over dark net hose and exotic lingerie. waist belts, restraint rings on the belts, leather arm sheaths, neck bands, and, of course, high, pointed, black-leather boots. They cruised about in a station-wagon, the trunk full of pom-pom and thong whips, leather gags, rope, bondage helmets, buckles, ticklers, strap-gags and harness, masks, sheer black frivolous tease-nighties, hair brushes and paddles, etc. They would cruise about looking for a likeable slave, male or female, and let their imaginations run away with them.

They were amateurs, and made few actual pickups, usually working themselves into a frenzy and then repairing to one of their houses, whichever was free of children, husbands and domestics for the evening and there they would freely indulge in cunnilingual articulation of their passionate fantasies.

She admitted that going out alone "can be interesting," for she had done so; several occasions had proved "very satisfactory," but these were one-night affairs, and "something vital was missing." Now trying variety of techniques and scores.

These women produce dildoes at hen parties, discuss their on-the-side copulations with strange males, and are wives and mothers themselves, respected and well-to-do members of their communities. They are perfect as contacts.

Some notable fillips within this particular group: with one girl pickup a stake was driven into the vaginal orifice . . . they had an aversion to hirsuteness and discovered a method of depilation guaranteed against scratchy regrowth; most of their pickups allowed them to depilate their bodies before sex.

"Try everything."

Thus, in New York the underground key clubs and sexotheques (all franchised) continually manufacture and disseminate new fads to the monied insecure to keep up interest. Thus last year it was young and attractive couples in their early twenties entering into sexual congress with couples in their sixties who are fat and saggy. These couples eye each other at the club, get acquainted over overpriced aphrodisiacs, and then slip away to some notorious posh hotel where they are already well known. This fad lingers on, but at the seasonal image meeting the oblique director of this important department was reported to have said, holding his head delicately and theatrically between his hands as a crystal ball: "My thoughts turn particularly to trousers and jackets of corduroy . . . schoolboys clothed in cheap goods are specially preferred . . ." And now the department begins the campaign to whip up the young influential deviate in the street by means of his susceptibilities and humiliations.

The women bring a Swedish girl to the club, take fotos of one of the wives performing cunnilingus on the Swedish girl . . . the husband of one of the women drops by the club to get her signature on some document and is soon actively participating . . . the husband performing cunnilingus on his wife while the Swedish girl performs fellatio for him . . . the foto taken of the husband lying prone, the Swedish girl sitting astride and over him while he performs cunnilingus, while at the same time, over the lower part of his body, his wife was at the point of effecting coitus . . .

"Nice group here today; glad you could make it."

This is how we operate.

Defending deviation and discipline, incest and family life, torture, prostitution, homosexuality, and unusual domestic relationships. Why not experiment? But we need respectable outlets in the mainstream media to win a broader public, naturally. Explanation to be given out to official enquirers is in newspaper form:

ENTER WAR ON FOUL SMUT PEDDLERS!
HOW THEY CAN PREY ON OUR YOUNG!
HOW YOU CAN DESTROY THEM!

This was the proper moral temperature, as our expert, the famous Cul de Paris, astutely phoned in his copy. Outraged digested articles, pleas, testimonies, human interest propaganda stories—he possesses trunks and closets full of them at home. Money, connections, clever men like Cul—we were out of trouble with the law. All offended couples, according to one official, shy away, undoubtedly to protect themselves, to keep a basis for friendship. This is where the trouble starts. In "modern sex," complainants scantily respond to weekend operations, communicate four letter words in a bad light, plead innocent, and, being irresponsible, inform; but still, prefer to do their own policing. An entire subsection of "ladies" and "gentlemen" go on reaping clandestine, handsome profits without focusing attention on themselves. The first naturally is pleased, seeking to establish members for sensational and chintzy new factions (like the so-called "spermatozoa dreams" group of late). Yet, as matters stand legally, bad habits like these are rare, and I am always on the lookout for them (as for the liberal young couple who instigated the above-mentioned scheme, a policeman was watching them). My business suffers if new members pledged by me turn deceitful and plot to reap extra profit along with their prodigal sex; my father image suffers. But, "with simple persons choose a simple tool": and so, two homosexual brothers, a young priest and a physician, who were demanding hush-money from fellow members of their soldier-lover club, were told they would have their pipis cut off if they didn't stop. They dared refuse; and so they were sent as "volunteers" on a token expeditionary force to the Eastern front. It is doubtful they knew what "resettlement in the East" actually signified.

And so it goes. This means an inoffensive couple or single cannot be a very real danger. And there are always perfectly good reasons, under other names, for what transpires. Distance does not preclude the same emphasized precautions and restrictions. But are any steps taken to point out to offenders that they are adults and not children?

A second couple, for the record, comes out in the open, simply drops carefully photostated proposals affirming "broad-mindedness" and stating their preferences, then looks forward to appearing subjects of rape. "Boy meets girl." Because of fear, a highly moral theme bulletin is sold only by subscription, as quoted above, then carefully leaked, showing the fine and noble intent of the Center.

Some befriend contacts, think they've learned one or two things, move on and open up businesses along crude lines, couple and single women. All necessary steps taken against recurrence of protesting to authorities; we are authorities.

Correspondence is how those interested gain entry, madam. They join by design, not accident.

Coitus is a dangerous path. The coitus man doesn't go out anymore; deals and shuffles on the phone. He gets excellent results, so he is kept on, despite his plethora of quirks more suited to customer than contact; i.e. his ideas about toilets, his fixation that the tentacles of "the horrid fat man" might reach out from the walls or ceiling and envelop him . . . etc. His anxiety on the street was ultimately a fear of restraint prostitutes. The helmets remind him of a secret which he is afraid to divulge. He goes in for probings of the urethra, bladder douches, large enemas, the introduction of objects into the rectum, nasal and gastric soundings, and the occlusion of the ears with rubber. He is to be seen in his cubicle of an afternoon executing nervous figure eights about the hips and genitals with latex and rubber glove bundles which he twists up tight and tighter while through the phone, cradled in his jowls, he clears up complicated business problems and brings profit and prestige to himself and his associates. They say it was his dabbling "for fun" within his own field, coitus, that is to blame. The rubber therapy helps some, and a perverse female companion served him for a while until she wanted to take koprophilic pleasure with him; "his habit of retaining his excrements and the enemas he gave himself," the girl explained discreetly in her request for transfer, caused an "affective rejection" within her of the coitus man. By this time though his rubber fetish had almost completely supplanted the female in his fantasies, and the girl was granted her request.

I cater to married couples seeking joint activity, bisex couples, male and female homosexuals, sadists, masochists, sado-masochists and transvestites. I send snapshots and phone numbers hither and thither.

An average sampling of these delicate he-men and dominating ladies are interested in any new variations which will make the monotonous simplicity of sex interesting. The sexologist is there to help. I lay the foundation for those interested in "modern living." The fees for forwarding philosophies and techniques with a view to arranging interviews—"if you are qualified, we will help place you and give you a start in the business of pleasure"—the fees are compatible with those of every wide-circulation national organ, church, civic group. Sharing their exciting interests, it is mandatory that dozens of "safe" single men posing as couples be made available; some will be astounded to learn that insertion in a short time—once good faith has been established—is mild mannered and desirous. This, however, is only a start.

Am starved for the right affection. Many phases of discipline and unusual attire are interesting pastimes. Artistic photographs are compared. A sweet affectionate girl of petite physique would like to learn of demanding bossy lady about 30 . . . "having tried everything am not afraid of any of them." File. "I have many unusual ideas, also boots, will travel, am 44 years old, widower, well-built, no racial objections, will exchange views . . ." I answer all letters, exchange snaps, engage in rugged operations which occasion wearing of attractive shapely and fashionable career garments. In a short time, replies requesting classification of "gentle and submissive disposition" pour in—letters promising every possible sexual deviation—and more will be available. A particular contact acts as a spotter, some even learn that long-time friends are similarly "modern" and "uninhibited."

Some married men are only part-time homosexuals; but it is even more saddening that the percentage of female homosexuals with venereal disease is even smaller. A lesbian contracting such a disease could blame a male carrier reaping profits from so-called curiosa and box numbers in connection with advertisements and pen-pal clubs, and pretend to heterosexuality. Lesbians are seldom arrested and examined, while males are "grilled until the steak is done" and then either "cleaned up" or "evacuated." Disease may be transmitted to their wives; this particular evil is seldom if ever.

One does not adopt the tactics of allegedly more respectable drunken male pickups: "We found happiness in the cab that night and I don't ever want to lose it." But, despite the worst kind of an erection, I lose no time or energy in disgusting banalities or childish prattle. A contact with a penchant for impulsive conduct, steel gloves, corsets, and all the rest, was found with a ring around his penis, which led to a urethral fistula. His superiors feigned shocked compassion and he was sent to baths and resorts of all kinds to restore his health. He suffered pangs, ideas of atonement obsessed him. Pain must be suffered without wincing, which constitutes its special value. The accent lies on humiliating coercion. The batteries of tests, the assaults of gruesome games. Examined after a month, the man was a shambles, and could be heard to mutter, "I'm a gem beneath all this dirt and filth!" and "If I had only gone after my sister then I should have possessed her!" An exhibitionistic act on the part of the man. Now the categorical imperative of his post-nerve-racking forbidden or taboo desires drives him to new symbol-ical aggressions.

As a result I never cultivated normal sexual intercourse, but preferred to gratify my desires in this manner, according to the strength of the victim, the beauty and passion of the prey, the use of shame or pain, resistance or despair.

One must inevitably recruit to strengthen the ranks, i.e., of the less densely populated Midwinter Institute. One must reveal a new direction for an always existing threat to behavior. A questionnaire was sent out, subject to closer official scrutiny. A sharp increase in recent years shows there is much to be said for disease. Men come home to find their boyfriends in bed with other men who divorce their wives for younger things with whom they drift into nothingness.

To help with the drafting, this business poetry was sent out by male carriers to the part-time homosexual, and include the following questions:

Would you like pen pals? How often do you consider yourself masculine (feminine)? Do you get enough secret delight, or do other instincts bother you? What role do you prefer? Whipper or whippee? Self-inflicted punishment? Have you ever been arrested or examined? Convicted? Beaten up? Served time? How long? How often? Ever been blackmailed? List quirks.

It is true that this state offers protection to less obvious homosexuals by uniform lesbians in places of public assembly which could be duplicated across the nation, and in some locales known as lesbian meeting places male patrons behave improperly and dance improperly together with impunity—and not merely homosexuals. Unnatural ill-lit bars more gruesome than blackmail, assault, and robbery; unchartered. The young homosexual performed and afterwards disrobed. He suggested his victim also disrobe in a cheap hotel room, after which he suggested that he be lashed and a homosexual act be performed. He was, however, never able to keep his hands quiet during the cruelest attacks; they were always reaching for genitals. The victim, a young unwed father who advocated chastity or masturbation, to all intents and purposes leading a completely normal life, finally spluttered: "This is the Occident, not the Orient!" He was respected in his community. He was found dead overturned with anal stab wounds against a blood-spattered wall. This is nonsense; they completely overlook what chastity entails . . . and this is more true of the married bisexual than the practicing homosexual observing proper sanctioned restrictions. I stepped in. "Scab, unfranchised Yankee dog!" "He was a sadist, a masochist . . . he wanted me to rough him up and seduce him . . ." There was a struggle. There is no point in discussing specific cases . . .

It will be remembered that the goriest most hardened women cops tried to book a similar case, a married bisexual, on keeping a disorderly house, and were in turn murdered and robbed by him.

This female has the courage to be placed in touch with them all, singles, couples, groups of ladies, which, in such cities, can do no wrong. Best up and coming contact of the season: just wait till the awards are given out at Xmastime. And I signed her. Sauntered in one day, sat her big twat down and piped up: "Toronto's the name, sex's the game." The results were almost immediate. I tried her out on a bold far-reaching assignment, "operation hot pants,"

our global expansion scheme. I said I was gathering data from subscribing couples which would enable us to be posted abroad (contemplating a trip to France, Germany, Italy, Great Britain, Switzer-
land, and the Scandinavian countries). In a variety of poses,
Toronto performed free-cunnilingus and "figure-eight" fellatio,
for obvious reasons. But again, over a drink, in addition to the
compromising language and commitments—Toronto was an
employee—supplied her with indecent nude photographs from an
unmarried stud farmer, a series of profitable advertising layouts,
invitations to posh beautiful-people orgies, legitimate coast-to-coast
foreign currency, and some normal sexuality papers for the sticks.
She wanted to thank me, and this occasioned some maneuvering in
order to be "gone into" at the "right time." Since the revealing
nude pix in the Personals columns in *Bondage Quarterly*, I knew
two of the subscribing couples by sight though not personally. They
expected soon to be provided for by advertising or "films." I said I
was a writer. I briefed Toronto. Both exchanged mates, but only at
parties since neither believed in free dating. All were initiates, and
the husband of one couple and the wife of the other were associates
already. Mutual punitive action would be involved ("fun and interests"), much to my satisfaction. All vital information supplied,
including ratings, rates, scores, names, numbers, weights, scars,
tricks. I had no hesitation in making up for my mistake by telling
Toronto pressing business had to be completed to persuade her to
find a plausible reason for having "temporarily left" the city. What
possible harm could be read in that? I knew saying she could return
in the "near future" was sufficient as I saw that emigration could be
the final solution for getting this likely thorn out of my metaphoric
side. When she was long overdue "returning from vocational training" I would regrettably refill her post, confronting my superiors
with their own dictum that the most brilliant novices oft gang agog
and set out on overly ambitious single projects, never to be heard
from evermore. Incidentally, she had confessed to liking "model-
ing"—told her to light out for Zurich posthaste, wrote a chit for her
and sent her off to Petty Cash, cheering her on to keep up the good
work and continue instigating "broadminded" and "uninhibited"
activities in that city whose standards are high.

   She remained seated on my desk, black net-hosed legs crossed,
garter-belt straps taut over naked thighs and hips, cold eyes and

nipples staring down at me. Did she suspect? "Continue corres-pondence," I croaked, the direct approach having failed. One remained cautious to the end. It should be enough to say that her husband, an engineer, finally urged her to set up a club on Sardinia—with a personal loan from me and my signature of recom-mendation to push through the franchise—and to retire from organ-ization work and settle down running a booming way station for compatible modern couples.

This drained me for the many matters I had to attend to, the Greek patterns I was called upon to choreograph at private beach parties, the talk on "Etruscan men who shared their women in common phallic rites utterly licentious" I did not give the Indecent Copulations Federation, the eastern ceremonies I was asked to emcee at drunken Copenhagen festivals, the article on The Fair Buttocked and the Whore I had to have ghosted and didn't even have time to check the copy . . . the May Day rites, the warlock interviews, the casting chores (this was yanked from me early, a sore point, and I missed the filming on the Emma Crouch film—wasn't even sent a pass to see the rough cut . . .)

Karen replaced Toronto, as manifesting cruelty desire; a volup-tuous and obscure girl, I grew quickly paranoid with her. She distributed petit-fours loaded with cantharides, stripped off clothing, caused sodomy and murder, quick and svelte as tit-filled velvet, quietly. All for which she had a great talent. I checked her file. Offspring of factory girl and nun of radical and righteous oblivion order, A-I* child, B-minus rating. Vestigial background: the breed of factory girls shared their disgraceful orgies with sisters joining this sect, orgies engineered some say to add final fillip to defeat of People-As-Workers unions, noisy debauchery smothered soon after to remove temptation and subsequently staffed spanking new pain and pleasure brothels; all very efficient.

I would keep my eye on her. Her specialty, having herself served up naked at dinners, kept her out of my hair a goodly portion of the week. Perhaps they planned this subtly, tactfully . . .

Then I got too intrigued and hung up with a couple, corres-pondents, and I consented to everything. "I have not heard from my other clients but will give you their names when I do. Please keep reporting your progress. Feel free to write me all." Whatever little we know about sex we have learned this way and it is too late

*Artificial Insemination—ed.

to stop. The male wrote that after attempted experiments in coitus per rectum (what can be his sexual makeup?), the tingling ecstasies when they would "kiss, stroke, pet, or suck on" each other's axillary hairs; they were just beginning after all, and having seen my snap (I was so impulsive I slapped an old glossy of my hard and forward-looking profile left over from the wild office cock-tail party last year into an envelope and sent it off to them with an unduly affectionate note), they were "promptly seduced;" his wife anointed his body with pomade and they indulged in bizarre lust on the floor, thinking of me. I was touched. Then he goes on to describe in startling detail the indignities his hotblooded and imperious woman subjected him to, and sums up: "I obeyed her." So would I.

I promised everything they asked throughout the correspondence. They were a professional couple, travel a lot. Thirties, attractive, have a Polaroid camera and have much pleasure with same at parties. They were requested to send photos; I waited, itching. The man included with his next letter the fotos of himself and his wife, posed indecently in the nude: one of the wife's lower body posed indecently on a bed. Another of the wife wearing only a garter belt and hose, one of the wife and a male friend copulating (picture taken by the husband), one of the wife and male friend naked relaxing after intercourse (also taken by hubby) . . . one of the wife performing fellatio for a male friend; one of the wife and male friend watching with glee as husband masturbates, husband being at the point of orgasm (time exposure); an indecently posed nude of the wife on a bed; and many more.

The wife adds an enthusiastic postscript hoping we will all soon "double-date," chatting the while in asides, saying three's no crowd with them, wishing her young son were not in the house because she craves immediate tryout of some new technique she read about: the child is due to be driven to school, and when the father returns alone, "I am going to literally rape my man for I am so much in love with him." This is her code.

I met them in a déclassé bar. The male was a pimp of average build. The wife was tall and full-bodied with abnormally large breasts and an exotic face under long pageboy jet-black ebony hair—the fotos had not lied. We chatted obliquely about the national grapevine, and we talked a bit about ourselves. "My first masochistic thoughts came to me at about age six while I was struggling to overcome my onanism to please my piano teacher. I remember having stroked my aunt's calf, and then I imagined myself being beaten by her. I was just like a little puppy. I would bother her till she smacked me, then run off whimpering with delight. Ah yes;—I must add that the desire to beat girls, viz., the desire to beat their naked legs, took hold of me. What times . . ." The wife stared at us with haughty flashy glazed eyes, like a queen watching two monkeys doing it. I was expected to speak. "I always masturbated; often thought of whipping boys; sometimes I would crawl into bed, pull one of my mother's petticoats over my head in order to enjoy the odor, and play with myself all night long. Until I was fourteen I had long locks and also wore dresses. Everybody thought I was a girl and would say, 'O! what a pretty little girlie!' . . ." The lies petered out. A trace of a sadistic smile came on the beautiful wife's lips. Her fur coat was thrown open and her leather sweater held her great breasts back. I coughed, and suggested we get down to cases. We tacitly left.

Inside their flat I was bound. Then the beautiful wife pranced out of the room in her high-heel boots and leather outfit and the pimp watched me. Then Karen came into the room through the same door that the beautiful wife had just exited by. It was advised by Karen, who wore silk, that hot coins be placed on the flesh too. It was pointed out by the pimp that this was somewhat premature, as he slowly drawled the details concerning bizarre pleasures as he and Karen began to demonstrate on me. First was BONDAGE: the victim, nude or near nude, helpless, tied or chained by arms legs neck and hair and by genitals in case of a male, then gagged and blindfolded, is set in certain positions ready for party activity. Tight ropes and chains sank into flesh, numbed limbs and muscles . . . spread-eagle belly to table and then back to table, pulleys used, crosses later, the barbecue spit discussed, stocks, bonds, revolving propellers . . . a torture box is brought out, for we are at stage two: TORTURE. Victim firmly bound, is lashed with variety of whips on all parts of anatomy from neck to ankles, including torment of sex organs and nipples. Clothespins of the pitch type were used . . . followed by forced entry or informal introduction into the body of such items as daggers, knives, wood clubs . . . hot wax poured on the victim, needles inserted . . . needles inserted into breasts thighs buttocks etc. Designs of a bizarre nature etched into flesh, honey poured on, strange scalding syrups, tar, feathers, and red ants sprinkled liberally. Then perhaps the hot coins on the softest flesh . . .

SEXY HUMILIATION rounds out the trinity. Sexabused by same or opposite sex with accompanying torment of sex organs, mouth, rectum. Victim eats shit, yes, eats shit, and washes it down with tainted piss. Sucks up menstrual drool from foaming cunt. Fucks house pets up the ass while girls in boots laugh. And failing full cooperation, the male emblem is punished severely. In case of a female, she is forced to accept torment of her mouth and throat by the male organ along with all the rest of the shit; then forced to receive the male organ orally (rectally) while chained face down . . . also recommended: two girls tied together one atop th'other, spread-eagle, faces towards each other's sweaty feet, forced to perform cunnilingus on each other all through the night. Also suggested: two men bound in this fashion and forced to join fellatio because "this is extra senshool thrill and humillyation especially if it be witnessed by opposite sex and the more who see the bigger the thrill."

The pimp visited me in the hospital, regaled me with tales of past exhibitions and home-made do-it-yrself torture items, left a four-color brochure with me from an obscure mail-order torture appliance house and some bruising memories. He said he loved to be Karen's slave; he told of being lashed, bound with ropes belts chains and whipped with belts chains rubber hose broom handles . . . Yet he had no visible marks of damage and here I was in a ward on my back with bruises for days and welts for weeks.

I had established three things at least: that 1) my night with Karen and her friends was exhausting fun, 2) the pimp was an engaging liar, and 3) if I don't find some new queen soon I'll die. Someone to take me . . . to help me . . . to use me . . . maybe you know a girl who'd love to own me, yes?—to satisfy all her desires, yes? . . . Negro, Spanish, Oriental, or White . . . from 12 to 45 years old . . . they can use as a fotog, a slave, a model, they can loan me out or sell my mouth and body to other girls and men . . . I will obey . . . isn't there a bizarre female queen who WANTS me? . . . Please . . . help me come . . . become their property . . . keep me nude . . . shaved of all hair . . . in silk latex leather plastic . . . humiliated night & day . . . sell my body to bizarre friends . . . sex abuses, abasements, pain and punishment . . . discipline and obedience . . . surely there must be some bizarre female out there . . .?

JON HORN

Jon Horn is the pseudonym favored by the scion of an old Brooklyn family. True son of the melting pot, boasting Saxon, Arabic, and Cuban blood, he has resided anonymously on three continents. An only child and "war baby", this post-drug post-nihilist exhibits the diffuse genius of the "renaissance-psychopath" syndrome: amateur and virtuoso writer, thinker, stinker, doodler, diddler, life actor and cinemactor . . . . This elusive and dangerous personage delights in the bleakly cruel humor that makes his Bondage Trash *the "unknown masterpiece" of a generation raised on speed and super-pornography. Past personae include: smuggler, librarian, disc jockey, drug dealer, pavement artist and street busker, copy boy, niteclub singer, petty thief, and pimp.*

Lightning Rod

Mullin Garr

*T*he bourbon flowed freely. We ran out of ice, but nobody gave a damn, and we kept the bottle handy to the tangle of arms and legs on the sunning-pads. Eventually we all went into the pool again, and when we came out they immediately went to work on me.

"Let's get him ready for Concha," Audrey proposed.

"Yes," Concha promptly agreed. "Geev to heem hard-on."

Audrey's method was remarkably simple and direct. She leaned over me, lifted the head of my cock with her tongue, and sucked it into her mouth. She let it slip in and out a few times, nearly set it afire with her darting tongue, and then began to devour it like the accomplished bucco-linguist she seemed to be.

It rose stiff and hard and erect, and she went after it like a hungry kid eating an ice-cream cone.

"That's—about enough," I choked finally, "unless . . ."

Audrey raised her head and grinned. "Unless what, big

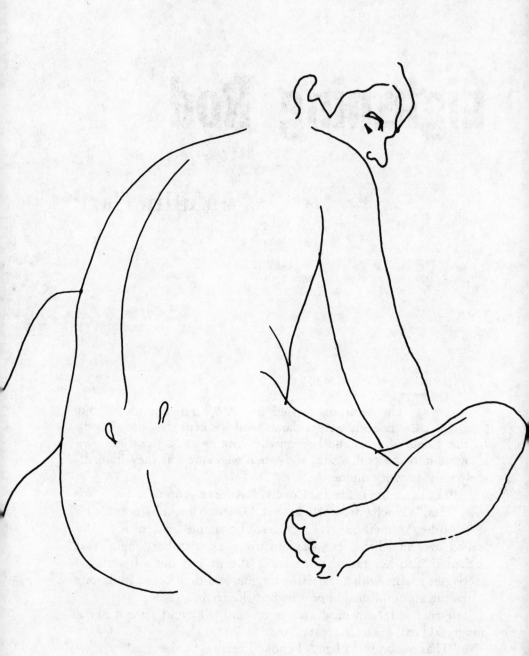

daddy?"

"Never mind," Allison interjected sharply. Her avid eyes were on my face. "You really like that, don't you baby?"

"You know damn well I do."

"Yes—but I don't believe I realized—just how much. But I'll remember."

Frankie took charge. "Concha's pretty small," she said thoughtfully. "She's liable to get hurt unless she has control of things. She'd better start out on top."

Concha eyed my cock. "I theenk so too," she said faintly. "You weemin no look, yes?"

"Don't be silly," said Frankie impatiently. "You weren't off gathering posies while he fucked Allison into a coma, were you?"

"I'm ready to take over," Audrey offered, her fingers busy between her thighs. "Just give me a couple of minutes to open this thing up a little more . . ."

"Well?" Frankie's cold blue eyes challenged the Cuban girl.

"No," Concha said softly. "I fock weeth heem. I fock weeth heem good. An' I don' care you see os."

She stood astride me for a moment, looking down at my cock. The slim legs were quivering, but her eyes met mine and her smile was confident.

"I am not yet ready, my bull," she said in her slurred Spanish. "Have you the patience to wait for me?"

"Do you desire my help?"

"Not yet. Soon, but not yet."

"Then I will wait with pleasure," I assured her.

"Bueno."

She sank to her knees, and without touching me with her hands, maneuvered her small cunt over the tip of my cock. She spread her knees a little, increasing the pressure, but her body remained erect.

"Now I make joy for you," she murmured.

She put her hands on her hips and began to dance. That's right; standing astride me on her knees, that girl was dancing. She started slowly, her hips undulating in a gently sensual rhythm that accelerated quickly as she got into the spirit of the thing.

I watched the dark lips swell and part, saw the juice forming, saw it running down the shaft of my cock, and heard her singing softly as the head sank out of sight.

This was supposed to be her show, at least for the time being, but she was too good to resist. I began to move with her, but gently, and she smiled her approval. Her cunt was very tight, but we got the head into her without too much trouble—and my whole cock was glistening with the reason for it.

So far the others were content with their roles as spectators, and I could easily understand it. She was something to watch. Her slim shapely arms were involved in the dance now. Her hands moved suggestively over her belly, up over her breasts, down her sides to her ass, caressed it sensuously . . .

She was settling slowly, the brown cock gradually disappearing into the tight black cunt—for only when she straightened were the dark pink lips pulled into view.

She began singing to me in her soft crooning voice, asking me how I liked it—and grinning delightedly at my gasping answers. Every muscle in the small beautiful body was writhing. They crawled like snakes across her flat belly; chased each other up and down her thighs, and over her arms and chest. The small pointed breasts vibrated when she shook her shoulders, but they were so firm there was little other movement. They jutted upward and outward from her chest; there was no hint of a crease beneath them, but the aureoles stood out from the smooth gleaming flesh, and the black nipples had grown to incredible size.

She held about a third of my cock in her when the others began a more active participation. Frankie's hands stroked the slim waist, the taut belly, and the small rounded ass; Audrey devoted herself to the muscular thighs, while Allison leaned over me suddenly and ran her tongue into my mouth.

Concha's erect position kept her clitoris out of action, but Frankie took care of that when the fingers of her left hand probed gently into the front of the girl's cunt. Audrey's hand cupped my balls, roamed up the dripping shaft, stroked the soft lips enfolding it—and the results were immediately apparent.

The tight cunt began to loosen, and Concha lowered herself steadily until the firm little ass was squirming against my thighs.

"Todo!" She gasped incredulously. *"Yo tengo todo de su palo, mi toro!"*

"Yes, little one," I answered in Spanish. "You have it all—and it is glorious!"

"Truly?"

"Truly. You are marvelous."

She lifted herself slightly. Her hips moved in a blur of motion, and her cervix beat a rhythmic tattoo against the head of my cock. Her head went back, her mouth opened wide, and a howl of anguish escaped her. The small body shuddered violently with the force of her orgasm: her ass rolled over my hips and thighs as she went into a convulsion of pleasure.

When it was finished she stared down at me, her mouth slack and wet. "Now . . . You fock me, no?"

"Now I fuck you, yes."

Her thighs gripped me as I rolled over with her; then spread wide as she drew up her knees and dug her heels into my back. I assaulted her at once with a driving flurry of strokes, and she came with a hoarse animal yell of delight. Then her legs slipped down around my waist and that frantic little ass went berserk.

She got the same attentions from the others that Allison had received before her, and they sent her into wild paroxysms of orgiastic rapture. She came and came, shrieking madly and driving her twisting jerking ass like the beautiful instrument of sexual delight it truly was.

I figured to be slow in coming after the activity I'd been subjected to lately, but the tight cunt got to me faster than I thought it would. I could feel the heat rising in me long before I came, and I hung on the edge of the cliff for a maddening span of time, with all four of them urging me to come . . . And then I was growling and snarling and biting at the slim arms on my shoulders, and pumping my load into the screaming girl-woman beneath me.

Gradually everybody relaxed.

"I don't have to ask you how it was," Allison panted.

"No. She's a hell of a fuck, doll. How do you feel, little Concha?"

"Well focked," she moaned, and joined in the laughter.

I rolled off her and lay on my back. Allison was even more aroused than the others, apparently. She kissed me passionately while a soft white thigh stroked my belly, and before I realized what she had in mind she was astride me and caressing my limber prick with her wet pussy.

"Forget it," I groaned, and there was more laughter.

But she kept at it, and I think the things she said in her murmuring voice helped me as much as the hot demanding cunt. Finally my cock began to respond, and she stuffed half of its semi-hard length into the slippery pocket.

She came about the time she got me to full erection; came twice more on a good hard-on—and then declared faintly that she'd had enough. Audrey took over.

"Finally!" she said exultantly as she swung a plump thigh over my body. "He's just about where I want him."

She had a big comfortable pussy, and once she opened to me had little difficulty in accommodating herself to my cock. She proved to be a deeply sensual woman who liked a slow teasing fuck, savoring every movement and making every stroke an experience in itself. As soon as I realized it I took the upper position and fucked her with slow tantalizing strokes, jerking my hips slightly to send my cock up into her at the angle she seemed to prefer. She bore down heavily on it when I withdrew, sighing ecstatically at the resulting friction on her enlarged clitoris. But I discovered that her greatest pleasure involved her cervix, so I punished it gently for long minutes while her hips undulated slowly and the soft muscles rippled all over her body.

Her hands and arms and thighs caressed me. She talked softly to me, uttering obscenities as though they were words of love, and discussing the effect of my cock on her with complete candor.

"I've always dreamed of being fucked like this," she murmured. "I always wanted a man with an enormous cock and the skill to use it properly. I can feel your strength wherever it touches me. There's a thrill an inch when it slides into me—and that's a lot of thrills. When you—make it move around inside me I can feel it all over my body, and every time—you rub my cervix with it, my ass-hole puckers . . .

"You, Frankie; can you see it? There, almost out of me . . . Now drive it deep, tiger. Slow and easy. Fuck me tenderly, lover. Ah, that's a big beautiful prick! Nothing less is good enough for a woman like me. I don't want to struggle, and I don't want to wiggle and sweat. I want to make love, and make it last and last and last . . .

"Ah, lovely, lovely, lovely . . . So sweet and good . . . No, I'm not close; just very pleased with the way you're fucking me. I'll—remember it—for the rest of my life. Yes, tiger. Right there. Oh, that's—so good! I don't fuck to come, lover. The fucking is what I want. I come slow, and I come hard, and when I do—it's over. So love me, baby. Fuck me slow, and fuck me easy. And use it all, you big-pricked darling. Let me feel it sliding in . . . Slowly, slowly—and let me feel every bit of it. Yes. Deep, deep, deep . . . Tease me, baby. Play with me. This is the way sex should be, when every touch counts for something. When nothing is wasted . . .

"I've got a good pussy, haven't I? Feel me squeezing you? If I wanted to I could hold you still and milk you . . . Like that . . . Sure, I know it's good. I know it's good.

"Yes, I feel it, but it's still a long way off. It's—so hard for me to come. And I warn you, lover . . . From here on I think I'll—go a little bit crazy."

And that's the way it seemed. Not a muscle in her body was still, but she never accelerated the slow pace she'd set at the beginning. She writhed and twisted and trembled; her hands roamed over me and her mouth caressed me wherever it could reach. She lifted her legs and stroked my sides with her thighs, and sometimes she raised them so high that they were against her huge breasts, and the others were treated to an unobstructed view of the proceedings.

Once she sat up with her legs cradling me, and my spread knees were under her thighs. We sat facing each other for a long time, fucking easily—and only then did I realize there had been no mass participation this time. The others were content to watch this woman who truly knew how to enjoy a fuck to its fullest; to twist the ultimate in sensation from every rapturous moment.

She lay back with a heavy smile, rolling her hips so that both legs were at my right, and I fucked her for several minutes while she lay on her side with her knees drawn up nearly to her chest. Then she turned slowly, getting her knees under her . . . Her thighs were spread wide and her ass was high—and I fucked her dog-fashion while her ass went through some astounding contortions.

Her voice changed gradually until it became almost savage. She rolled onto her back, disengaging for only an instant, and then her legs held me while I plunged into her again.

"It won't be long now," she sighed. "Oh, you big wonderful son-of-a-bitch; are you going to come with me?"

"I'll —come—when you do."

"Then come on, you sweet bastard. Fuck me. Fuck me deep, you horny cunt-lover. Fuck me sweetly. Fuck me with compassion, damn you. Oh God you're good! Oh Christ, you can fuck! Oh you sweet son-of-a-bitch . . . You know what a woman really wants, don't you . . .

"I'm close. Oh Jesus, I'm close. I'm going to make it. I'm going to come. And it's so good, so good, so good . . ."

She babbled and sobbed insanely as her climax drew slowly nearer, and her full body continued to undulate convulsively in the most complete display of sexuality I ever witnessed.

She shuddered; the muscles stood out all over her, and she began to come. I ejaculated into her with slow wrenching spasms and they continued for a long time, but she was still coming when I'd finished, a steady growl of almost unbearable joy issuing from between her clenched teeth.

At last it was over. A final shudder wracked her and she lay quivering, her big-titted chest heaving with the effort to regain her breath. She opened her eyes and stared up at me.

"A wonderful, wonderful experience," she said tenderly. "It was a fuck to remember."

"It was a fuck to remember," I agreed—and I knew I would, too; for a long time.

Allison sighed, and I saw that she was trembling as much as Audrey was. "I don't know about all of you, but I could stand some rest. I'm going to take a nap. Darling? You must be—tired." Her smile was full of affection.

"I'm creaking in every joint," I conceded.

"Let's finish the bottle first," Frankie suggested. "No use leaving it for the squirrels."

"Don't move yet," Audrey whispered. "Stay with me a while longer. Here . . ." She turned over with me until we lay on our sides facing each other, and her thighs still held me close.

She lifted herself on an elbow and grinned when she saw my eyes on her heavy breasts. Her hand touched my cheek.

"God bless a man with a horny soul," she said quietly. "How about bringing us each a snort? I want to drink with the man that just proved he knows what fucking is all about—and while his prick is still in me!"

MULLIN GARR

Mullin Garr is the pen name of a man who lives in San Diego and whose second favorite sport is fishing. He grew up in the hills mostly, and spent twenty-three years in the Navy. Upon retiring, he vowed to write a book exposing the outfit. He practiced by writing historicals and westerns, and in no time at all had accumulated an impressive stack of rejection slips. The change in literary themes came about by accident, as a result of a chance remark made by his wife, and the result was six novels published by Ophelia Press in 1968-69. Remarkable things can happen when an author deals with a subject that is really close to his heart.

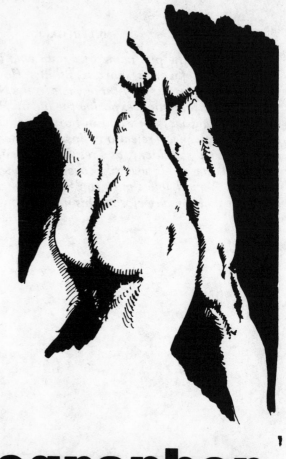

The Pornographer

Norman Singer

Oh wow, I ain't never saw such a swingin' pad! Talk about your castles in the sky, why . . . we're on top of the world up here!" Remorse gaped in awe as she wandered about Jim's massive apartment, her baby-blue eyes bulging with astonishment at everything she saw—the lavish furnishings and draperies and rare books, the walls adorned with Picassos and Modiglianis, the mobiles and concert piano and stereo and color-television. It seemed to put her in a brief state of shock; just taking in the salon-size style and sweep of the place. "Aw . . . nobody gets this rich just from book-writin'," she gave him a fishy stare. "You sure you're not a crook?"

"Positive," he grinned, his eyes fondly trailing her every step, the tightly packed spheres of her behind looking as tempting to him as two ripe peaches.

Setting her purse down, Remorse opened it for a cigarette, Jim rushing to light it for her, and trying to determine the outline of her nipples as she inhaled her first puff. But she moved swiftly across the room to the windows and gazed out at the breathtaking view, dazzled by the display of towers and neon. "Jeez . . . it's so beautiful, I could cry. All them diamonds down there, twinklin' just to me, huh, baby?"

"Well . . . the diamonds will come later," he said lightly, slowly edging closer to her.

"Oh honey, what kind of books you write to shovel in all this loot?"

Not wanting to get sidetracked by any of the secondhand thrills in his library, Jim slipped an arm about her waist and replied with an evasion, "Juvenile fiction."

"You mean stories for little kids?" she was enchanted. "Why you big sweet Daddy!" She yanked his touseled blond head down for a soft and suckling kiss. And then, over his shoulder she noticed the small foyer that led to another room, and once more curiosity got the better of her and she moved. An instant later she found herself in the cloaked and enormous confines of Jim's bedroom, gasping when she saw his kingsize bed. "You sack up in that big six-canoe all by yourself, baby?"

Following at a persistently intimate distance, Jim laughed at the guileless excitement on her face, infant femme fatale so all-knowing, but still so caught up in her own sense of loss and abandonment. "Yes, it's true I sleep alone," he told her. "But not at the moment, dear, because I take it you'll stay the night, won't you?"

"Have you tripped out'er somethin', Daddy . . . I'll stay the *year* in a shack like this!"

"A year . . ." he chuckled back at her, "ah . . . what a sense of humor."

Remorse made a mad running leap and flung herself onto the bed, flipping her boots off into the air and letting them crash to the floor. "Jesus Christ, it's duck-down!" her supple billowing body all wriggles and squirms. "Umm . . . with the right guy, I could take all my meals in a bed like this."

Jim stood transfixed in the doorway as he eyed the mirrored wall across the room and the reflection of her swirling, taunting thighs on his bed. The bluest of stag films in that mirror, he thought, and later the star will make a personal appearance. Undraped, but no applause please, just the laying on of hands. "I'll . . . go fix us a drink," he said, his throat tight and dry with a quick rush of anticipation. "Won't be a minute, so don't you move, sweet stuff, 'cause that's exactly where I want you planted."

"Oh whee! . . . draw me a bath and get my sables, Beulah, 'cause I'm home!" she said as he headed towards the living-room bar.

While stirring the drinks Jim noticed Remorse's huge handbag where she'd left it on a table near the entrance, unfastened. After mixing double-vodkas he detoured across the room and glanced inside the purse. He saw the usual female jumble in there; and also something not quite so usual, a box containing what looked to be a portable dispensary, at least a dozen bottles of vari-colored pills. And in a plastic enclosure—they call it a 'set-up' Jim reminded himself—a syringe and a hypo-needle.

. . . It figures. She's on something. But whatever it is it seems to be working on her like an aphrodisiac. And what the hell, if I'm about to have myself a tender fling, why can't it be a little exotic?

But when he returned to the bedroom it was quite a jolt to see Remorse standing in a far corner of the room, on her head. Her body seemed quite rigid to him as she let her legs lean stiffly against the wall. Oh hell, he thought, and her eyes didn't even look dilated, and I'd certainly know a junkie when I saw one. No punctures on her arms either, although she might shoot the stuff in her rear, who knows? Then, with a laugh, Remorse hurled herself right-side-up, going into complete hysterics as she saw the livid expression on his face.

"No, I'm not on a bummer, baby, and I ain't had me no

'speed' in weeks. That was just a very relaxing Yoga trick I learnt from this crazy Arab I met in the Haight a couple'a weeks ago. You oughta try it sometime!"

"Later," he said, relieved and laughing as he approached her with the drinks.

They took a few sips of their highballs, the vodka warming, accelerating their growing frenzy as they sat tentatively close on the bed. But it was soon quite clear that neither of them had the patience to finish a drink. Suddenly they both fell silent and mute with their desire, and Jim was so frantic to get those swimming panties off her he nearly choked on that last gulp of his drink. So he placed his glass down on the floor; then took hers and did the same with it. And reached for her, caught up in a surging anguish to have this bursting bouquette of flesh whirling beneath him, his hands now cupping the steaming, sweatered fullness of her at last. "Oh yes, Jim . . ." she sighed, "touch me . . . never stop . . ." Fat sweet beautiful babies all his now, fingers deftly furtive and cushiony as they crept slowly inside and edged up the hot skin until they nudged the loose and heavy pontooned start of them, lush bra-free orbs all ready to skyrocket just like the rest of her . . . "Oh Jesus, I've gotta see those! . . ." he moved in closer and removed the band-clasp from her ponytail until the bright yellow hair cascaded about her shoulders, and then pulled the sweater up and gently over her head, half-swooning with the obedient stillness of her as she awaited his handling, a new erection swelling and aching in his briefs as she made her body limp and pliable for him, oh . . . just born for him, for his wielding and training, and would you look at the eloquent hunger on that face . . . (I'll disappear in her, yes . . . that's what I want) . . . tits like that just built for amnesia and identity-loss and super escape-hatch . . .

The great jouncing breasts were free and expanding now and she watched him pull back and gape at them. Then she leaned towards him in a most giving and womanly gesture, her cheek against his, lips trailing, flicking at his ear-lobe, "Cherries . . ." she murmured, and with a groan Jim gathered her to him and buried his face against the naked throb and heat of her, sucking furiously at her nipples, nibbling, biting the palpitating buds and loving the tantalized moans of her as she reverently stroked his cheeks and cradled his chin higher against her breasts, her eyes a supplicant monitor for his mouth as the taste of bananas and whipped-cream still lingered on his tongue and he alternately slid each fat melon deeply into his mouth, wanting to devour the both of them, going predatory and carnivorous with the sudden luxuriant taste of her, his lips fervently caressing at her hot-tit undersides, gently lifting each tear-shaped mound and softly swirling his tongue up and behind to lick and explore the tender back-flesh, an area so silky and neglected . . . virginal secret treasure-spots, always so new and fresh . . .

There was a crazed look of passion in the girl's eyes now and her face had begun to perspire with the urgent need to see more clearly this act of his partaking, hungry to watch his warm sensual mouth all ripe and full of her. "I wanna see your lips make love down there, baby . . . but that little bed-lamp isn't bright enough," she fondled the cleft in his chin as she slid a rigid nipple from his mouth, "and I want you to see these beacons all lit up. . ."

Jim quickly bolted to his feet, the thickening rod in his trousers a throbbing load to carry as he dashed across the room and clicked the light-switch on the wall. At once their jubilant arena was flooded with 200-watts of indirect but glittering fluorescence which intimately revealed the sultry dank ardor that shone on their faces. Her nipples stood out hard and erect as she stroked and tickled at them with the tips of her fingers, slithering her half-nudity to the center of the bed, inhaling deeply for him, still locked in the hugging skirt below, but bare and flesh-blown sculpture full above. "You like to watch too, don't you, baby?" she said. "I could tell it when I saw them fucky brown eyes of yours peelin' me down in the bar, sweet hot maniac-eyes all over my body. And that's why you've turned half this room into a mirror and aimed it at your bed. Oh wow! . . . what shows we're gonna put on in that mirror, Daddy. Why hell, it's just like Cinerama . . . we could have us a cast of thousands . . ."

Dimly, Jim had to believe she was only joking and had no serious plans to overpopulate his bedroom. It would just be the two of them, here and now, and that's all that mattered. The moment.

"I'll bet you watch yourself in that mirror too, don't you, Jim? All naked, I mean. Tell me, do you?"

He grew tense and uneasy with this probing, nor could he

particularly enjoy being cross-examined by someone who was infinitely more experienced in the sort of perversions he had always tried to negate in himself. No matter how fiercely he wanted the girl, he would reject the corrupting advantage she sought and admit nothing. Silently, he started back towards her.

But she was intent on giving a performance and insisted that he keep standing there across the room to watch. Her body sinuous and convoluting, she rose up slowly in the bed and did some bumps and grinds for him, bouncing, prancing topless headliner. Then with a wild jungle shriek she dropped to her knees and posed on all fours so he could see how they hung. Jim stood quiet and watched the gorgeous wobble and droop of her in that position, wanting to lay his face underneath and let the nipples glide across his lips like fevered tonics. But she kept him stationed at his post, eyeing the thrusting bulge in his pants, sensing his urge to strip down fast and rush at her.

"You like to look at my breasts, honey? . . . aren't they round and high and full . . .?"

He nodded. "Lovely. So lovely . . ."

"But I want to hear about *your* body, Jim," her eyes impaled him now. "Do you get undressed and stare in that mirror at what you've got between your legs?"

He said nothing for a second, still not moving, eyes caught on the fat hanging blooms of her; sweat pouring from his body, dripping and clogging around his testicles, his prick bursting against the zipper. He swallowed, cleared his throat. "Do you. . .do that?" he had to hear her say it first.

"Why, hell yes, honey. I just love to striptease myself and stare at my body and try to remember which part of what guy's anatomy went where. Say, did'ja ever see all them stars' footprints in Grauman's Chinese Theater down in Hollywood? Well . . . my body's a little like that lobby, except that all my footprints are love-prints, Daddy, so they evaporate. Story of my life, honey; that's why I gotta keep relivin' everything that happens to this body . . ." She sat upright now and clutched at her breasts, squeezing and aiming them at him . . .

Slowly, he nodded. "Yes, I do that too. Watch, I mean. In the mirror." Confession.

Remorse flashed a victory smile at him. "All right, then stand there and strip, Jim. Take off your pants and your briefs and . . . keep starin' at my tits until you're naked."

He struggled quickly out of his clothes, hands trembling, going limp and breathless for her now, but torn by a nameless fury too, resenting that angel-faced slut over there trying to see him as some kind of drooling pervert, hoping to drag him into the scrounging swill of her own life so maybe they could reach all their climaxes on equal terms, and she'd be the winner all around, sucking in his pride, his cock and his money. But the anger grew and mounted and made him even hotter for her, so he ripped at his shirt and trousers and squirmed out of the bulging jockey-shorts, watching the eager expression on her face as his penis planked out from between his hairy thighs in full ripe view, her hot-tranced eyes fixed hypnotically on the fat and fruity knob that would be charging at her in a minute, as she issued out more of the panting order to him . . . "Now go to the mirror and look at what you've got there, baby . . ."

"Oh hell, I *know* what I've got," he said; but knew this charade was driving her crazier for it, so he turned and stared at his lithe, husky body in the mirror, seeing the reflection of her behind him, her eyes lingering down at his taut muscled buttocks and the backs of his sturdy legs.

"Wet your hand and rub that thing, baby-man . . . make it shine for me . . ." With a shrug, Jim ran his tongue along his hand and started jagging in the mirror, until his organ loomed up even larger and gleamed. But after a few seconds of this he suddenly felt like a prize asshole, and as he ushered a defiant rasping oath, he swung around and hurled his body across the room towards her.

"Oh gallop, horsie!" she shrieked. "Oh you jaggin' sound-lovin' baby, play with that big gorilla-prong before I touch it. Make it yours first, Jim . . . or I can't have it! Ah . . . you stallion, you bull! . . . I'd like to see a butcher hang that thing for you . . ."

But when he reached the bed, Jim stood frozen at the foot of it, penis huge and burning in her direction. The hopped-up gloating bitch, he thought, so damned sure she's gonna get it right this minute I'll hold back on her some more; yeah . . . stand here and let her look at this ramrod the way she had me stare at her breasts, and make her crawl for it.

Remorse sensed this deliberate hesitation and stopped

preening at him, a petulant cry escaping her lips as she whirled about on the bed and hurriedly unzipped the tight skirt and slid out of it, tossing it across the room. Then, shielded only by the gossamer panties, she spread out flat on the bed, hard roseate nipples all round-based and parched for him, her eyes enchanted by his voluptuous thick structures that were so full and jutting and ready to be embraced within the heat and spread of her. But now a quick new shock for Jim as he stared between her legs and realized why she'd kept her panties on after tearing off the skirt; and he gulped and glared to see this precious evidence still there . . . sweet girl-juice tinged with nylon, confection preserved for him, that clinging humidity at her crotch . . . unnn . . . how she'd wanted him to see that, the hot little angle-ass, and right after he'd been getting so hostile . . . aw, saving those Goddamned creamy diddies for him, wanting him to know that the potion his fingers had sampled in the car was still there for him, still the promise-flow, simmering.

Slowly, his movements furtive and savoring, Jim knelt at the foot of the bed, gazing up the length of her body at the ivory-fleshed thighs and rising peaked boobies . . . "Pull them off me, Jim," she begged, "Oh . . . pull the cork, honey . . . let'er rip!"

"Eat you alive, baby," he murmured, then bent down and started nuzzling at her toes, his lips traveling, satiny, staking the claim, tongueing at the pudgy mounds of girl-feet, while his darling prisoner writhed and gasped to see his enraging hot mouth go everywhere except where she needed it most, her legs twisting, squirming, weeping loins still damming up the river for him. Jim gripped the backs of her knees and raised her legs, moving a little higher on the bed, his body crawling and stealthy as he eyed her lovely wet panties, all sopped and pressed against veiled glories, his phallus now a rearing response in its own slight emission, newly moistening the towered head of it, again feeling her eyes fastened there, glancing briefly upward to see the ferocious child-greed as she stared at the dripping velvet knob that stood out from his body as if it were an entity apart. "Oh please, honey, slide it up closer," choked guttural sounds in her throat, little girl pleading for her security-toy, "Oh please, just the tip of it in my mouth, that's all I want, baby..." His lips were caressing the backs of her upper thighs now, licking softly, raising her up an inch or two with each kiss . . . swirling around and gliding higher until his mouth reached the start of untapped moisture near her crotch, and suddenly the hot and steamy fragrance of what was beckoning to him there gripped and prodded at his vitals, filled his loins to bursting, so now at last Jim had to plunge for the blessed snarl and gulp of her as he spread and split those thighs apart and with a groaning sob buried his face against the drenched lingerie. His hands swept around her buttocks and roughly clutched the tight and sweltering cheeks, hoisting her higher for the meal . . . pastry-buffet in there, lurking forbidden treats, his mouth jammed and blowing fretfully into the scorch of nylon still barring his way, as she thrashed her legs about and cried out to him . . . "Bite 'em off me, baby, chew 'em to pieces! . . ." His mouth was clogged full of the wet hurdle-stripping now, and with one tearing yank of teeth and jaw he slashed the panties open down the middle, and like a tiger hauling its prey he dragged the torn fabric down below her knees, spitting out the ripped pieces and hurling his head upwards again to the undraped patch of what he'd been longing to taste all night, his lips sinking, nubbing into the turgid cavity while she gasped and thrust it up closer for him, but sighing in deeper frustration as he raised up to stare there in rapt idolatry, sending his fingers wet-sliding in and slowly out in awe and wonder as he experimented and gaped in groaning discovery of red-gold pubic hairs, pastel enough for him to see through to the naked throb itself . . . oh the sweet pulling gift of her . . . God, the queen-size slit of her! . . . the soaked abandoned vulva-heart of this girl he wanted to feast on . . . and wear . . . oh . . . nocturnal lavaliere, it's here and mine . . . and Christ! . . . I'll drown here tonight, I know it . . . I'm gonna drown in all this sweet moist rain.

The girl's cries grew mewling and frantic as Jim's warm fluent lips lounged there for still more of the inciting torment, his tongue a feathery rage as it expertly licked and encircled the labia, and then slowly he parted his mouth for the deep and nurturing vaginal kiss, letting his tongue penetrate a little farther with each wet-stabbing invasion so that the famished flaring hollow of her seemed to sprout and take flower inside his mouth, going tentacled and grasping for all that he denied her. Remorse tossed and heaved madly in the bed, shrieking and cursing out the fury of her tortured appetites, as Jim compulsively raised up his head again, still yearning to see this soft wet blossom that was so eager to be plucked, eyes fraught with adoration as he softly blew gold vaginal hairs apart to ogle and worship, his senses still inflamed by the girlie lush candy-taste and swallow of her—and then wincing in sudden pain as she gripped and tore at his hair, for Remorse was done with waiting now and seized his head in her hands, howling out her emergency to him: "Oh Jim, please . . . I can't stand it any more! Touch me, kiss me . . . take me!" She rammed his rearing head up between her legs, jostling hips and pelvis at him and groaning out her terrible lost-foundling cries as Jim's lips went plowing deep and owning as he flung the flailing legs high and apart and dipped and sucked, his mouth all flushed and full of the endless flavored flow of her, lips a tender gulping bruise as they swarmed and beseeched . . . half-suffocated and gasping with the seething liquid surge of desire that nestled and moistly cuddled against his tongue, his whole face submerged now and bathed by the mellowing inundation as she jabbed and hurled her body upwards to greet his lusting prowling magnet of a mouth. And for Jim the intoxication did not diminish, for he'd never before felt such an insatiable narcotic need tearing at his loins and welling up in his chest and throat; and as he lost himself more abysmally in the sipping clinging whirlpool, he stretched and flung the girl's thighs even wider apart, wanting her free and fully open to the dearest of his assuagements . . . his tongue venturing in like the plea of a starved lost lover and reaching, grappling in the dark and now? . . . aw . . . finding that precious taffy-jewel . . . unn . . . yes, he had it now, epicurean's tart taunt sliding in his mouth, fresh-petaled clitoris to suck and revere as Jim sank inexorably into this heady euphoric pit of cunt-madness . . . wanting the loin-emptying of her now and later and again and forever . . . and oh, the nourishment lurking for him here in this girl of fire and replenishment! But with a frenzied convulsion of legs and pelvis, Remorse screamed out the breathless warning to him: "Oh God, I can't help it, honey, I'm comin' . . . here's the rest of it now, all I've got!"

Devoted and grateful for this signal, Jim kissed a brief adieu to the heralding buttery trickles, then straddled himself upon his knees and lunged his body down and swiftly forward, sending the full length and breadth of his wet throbbing member in and up to greet the gushing flood of her. "Ahhh!" she sighed and gasped for it, and how he reveled in these shocked and tremulous sounds of her as she felt this rumbling new fever shafting deep inside her belly, his own

cries equally exultant as he sank into the soft warm caress and grip of that satiny entrapment. Remorse now becoming a whirling paroxysm of groans and graceful whimpers as her taut and clamping body poised and strained to receive the gentle hard ease of what he offered, the contentment . . . while Jim held the eager clenching hips and gave her every joyful inch, crowding stuffing sludging the long hot tusk until it found its deepest yielding niche and went in right up to the hilt, basking in the warm fluid rushing there, the soft surrounding swirls of her, knowing at once that her first explosion was already giving birth to another, as he slid his penis back and out again until only the swollen head of it remained to prod and tease at the vaginal lips the way his tongue had. But now she clutched and pressed her legs about his haunches, jamming him firmly inside of her again . . . and oh . . . what a verdant rich hot valley in there cradling the very hub of his existence, as he fiercely jabbed and pounded all he had to give her, tears of release and lamenting poignance pouring from his eyes with each impassioned stroke, for Jim was in love with the feel of this girl, holy God! . . . just the skin-touch and tropic funnel feel of her as he battered and slammed so relentlessly that her body was spiked up off the bed with the stabbing ardent force of him, like a stuck and girl-faced popsicle all pinned and on display, as Jim dove and plunged his searing thickness straight up into that ever-gurgling nest of her, aw . . . making her his now and nailed and sealed to the cross of his obsessive gnawing desire. He roamed his hands up over the beloved pushy breasts that pouted softly beneath him and seized her by the shoulders to march up blissfully higher, soaring and lifty at the summits and going valiant with new giving as she moaned and shot her little bottom upwards in fresh and covetous hunger, wanting still more of his generous thudding approval, while Jim choked back his cherishing marvelling sobs for the mad hedonist cries of her fulfillment, his eyes brooding about her soft licking lips that seemed so gently parted and vulnerable with her need, as he crushed his own hot mouth down against hers, longing to share some of that wildcat rapture, softly nudging his tongue between her lips as their mouths went locked and pledged by the very same vaginal flavors his lips had wrested from her earlier . . . while he slid her body lower in the bed and flipped her legs high over her shoulders, steadily plummeting and spearing his weapon more deeply in that position, the bed wheezing and rattling as he gazed down at their merging flesh and saw his own captured prick dive nobly in and out between those fat hillocks, sensing her delight at being brandished almost upside down for his newer happier glutting, as she squirmed and let her body go like clay for him and sobbed out the endearments, the sacred body-betrothals: "Oh Jim . . . oh darling, how I love the way you want me . . . I feel so . . . important, so good for you with it in me in me in me . . . want it in me . . . love it!" Aw . . . this baby, he thought, this precious grinding baby, my little virgin-whore, ooh . . . my lovely one! . . . and sighing out his own lunatic sobs as he rode up and down on the clasping bounty of her, going unhinged and senseless with the burning feel of it in her like this and loving how wildly happy and gratified it made her, as now he hammered and plundered in a fresh surge of concentration, his

hips pounding and slapping against her moist creamy flesh...aw...
faster now . . . oh . . . Jesus, faster . . . treading juices now . . .
yeah . . . doing it . . . holding back a little, but no, it'll kill us if we
hold back any more . . . ooh . . . going under, losing altitude,
drowning . . . feeling her wriggle more fretfully and knowing she's
starting to oil out at him a second time . . . aw Christ! . . . what a
gorgeous tidal-wave . . . hearing his own yelling cries mingled with
hers as he bit down on the frenzied mouth that sucked at his,
strangled growling lovers' kiss as . . . as . . . oh. . .unn. . . now! . . .
he shot his first and saved-up thunderous load right up into the
heart of her . . . aw splitting spraying endless volleys of hot jetting
bursts and jamming the new flood of her . . . again . . . unn . . . and
again . . . his loins aflame with an agonizing tremor of sensation as
those hoarded juices shot out of him like one cannon blast after the
other . . . oohmyGod . . . the feel of her milking it into her, all that
boiling shooting serum, like maybe she'd die without it . . . and she
knows there's more, wants the last pleasure-drop...lunges for it . . .
and aw . . . here it is baby . . . oh flushing and swim-popping the
wet-splattered velvet-tipped cock in this tongue-trapping mouth-
watering cunt and heaving lung-bursting death in the tangled
oceans. And now?

Sunk and met, as Jim throbbed out his last moist bestowal.

They clung in silence for long and sheltered moments;
unbelieving, letting the cathedral-hush of their dwindling sighs
envelop the contoured offerings they had shared. Then he gently
shifted back and away from her, raising up his head so that he
might gaze down at her face, that heart-shaped imploring of mouth
and eyes, deprived dismoved beauty still smeared with cheap make-
up, unguarded plea of a mouth spewing out all its brittle smart-ass
dialogue whenever she was up and dressed, but so lost and needing
here beneath him. Desertion on that face, he thought. And terror
too. He leaned down and softly kissed the warm full repose of her
lips. "We go rather well together, don't you think so?" stroking
wisps of the gaudy yellow hair.

She smiled and lightly traced a finger along the outline of his
lips, then let it circle downward to nestle at the cleft in his chin.
"You know what I really think?"

"Tell me, lovely one," his mouth again the earnest questing
against hers.

"Well . . ." her arms stealing softly about him, "I just think this is the sweetest damn bed I've ever been in," legs wriggling, furrowing deeper in the sheets and taking root there. "And well..." pulling him closer for another of his soft grabbing kisses, "like . . . I just don't never wanna leave it, that's all! I mean . . . this bed is really sweet . . ."

Laughing Jim sat upright and took her in his arms to rejoice at the gift of her, placing her in his lap like some charming wayward truant. "Are you free to be a houseguest for a little while?"

Her eyes went darting, speculative. "How little?"

"Oh, let's see . . ." cupping a hot globe of breast, he leaned over and lightly ran a nipple across his lips, drawing back to watch it harden as he spoke, "well . . . until you grow tired of a guy who's almost old enough to be your father . . ."

"Well I like that!" she said hotly, and defiantly shook her breasts in his face, rising up in bed so suddenly that both avalanches were hurled at him and he got a little flesh-drunk all over again. "If you knew anything about my psychology, Jim, you wouldn't say a thing like that, because I absolutely hate fellas my own age! I mean it, doll . . . if a guy's under thirty I'd rather puke than let him touch me. I got standards, ya know . . ."

Sweet lying chippie's also got a line, he thought, reaching up to cuddle her closer and plunging down deeper in the bed with her. Jim suddenly felt freer and happier than he'd felt in years, as if he'd just been let out of an asylum and was cured and ready to be counted among the living. His immediate future presented none of the pressures of work or commerce, so now he had nothing but time and recreation and this fantastic girl on his hands for weeks, or even months, if he could hold her that long. There was no more danger of his becoming the sick and detached old voyeur that Claire had called him, and just let her confront him now and tell him how sensually impotent he was. Oh hell! . . . I'm alive, he thought . . . this is it, aw . . . this is me breathing and living and loving and sweating . . . firsthand stuff, person-to-person, flesh-to-flesh hookup and I'm neither writing it nor reading it, because it's all happening deep inside the guts of me right here and now in my arms and Godhelpme! . . . I've gone crazy in love with a tawdry little alleycat called Remorse. . .

They dozed for an hour or so, during which time Remorse had

managed to slip out of bed without disturbing him. She scampered silently into the living-room towards her purse, and from one of her assortment of vials she extracted a tiny white capsule. She swallowed it with a quick shot of vodka. Methedrine highball. With a smile, she rubbed her naked thighs together and felt the quick warming begin. Then ran swiftly back to the bedroom and slipped in between his flung-feet, sliding slowly upwards.

A little later Jim groggily opened his eyes, having been awakened by something soft brushing against his thighs. He had only a second to realize it was her long flowing hair before he shuddered with the jarring hot sensation of her moist girlish lips closing down around the head of his penis. At once it was fully stiff and aroused and he sat up in bed, going eager and breathless to watch her, but feeling his body tremble with the hot seizure of her mouth so lovingly imprisoning him down there, like sticking it into a furnace, he thought, his eyes drinking in those ripe innocent lips so fresh-blown and full of him, the warm stroke-lashes of her tongue making him quiver and expand it for her, and now hearing his own groans as she gracefully swept fully down on the fleshy idol and showed him what a practiced and infuriating expert she could be, deviously returning some of the torture he'd concocted for her earlier, her mouth a subtly surrounding taunt now and wildly loving its throbbing captive, as if she'd been put under some kind of spell . . . transfixed unthinking thirst, and oh . . . this girl-cup so begging to be filled! . . . and how natural it seemed to him to see those full and needing lips so curved and tugging there, and watching her caresses stoked his fires even higher and he thrust his loins at her to give and furiously relinquish all that she sought and dipped for, dimly excited about their future prospects under her care . . . oh this deft and versatile slummy little princess, what a magnificent repertoire she'd have in store for him! . . . ummm . . . Turkish delights on Russian Hill with his own arsenal of sensation giving and sopping and tearing him apart . . . her lips giving his whole body a vacation in the tropics . . . just the two of them, moistly and forever . . . taking nightly dips in the pool of love. But now she swirled up and down faster for it and Jim was about to burst and felt he had to sound the alarm: "Oh God, honey, I'm burning up . . . it's on fire in there . . . it's gonna happen! Aw . . . Remorse, you fit right in my pocket, did you know that? Aw . . . you girl! . . . you sweet hot dumpling of a girl, you fill such a void in my life, ummm . . . such a great big empty void . . . and listen, you are an original, honey . . . oh you gotta believe me, there is nobody in the world like you . . ."

". . . ooounn . . . jus' wait'll you meet all my friends, Daddy . . ."

But with her mouth all blossomed and full, Jim couldn't make out what she'd said. And in the next instant, couldn't care, as he sighed and groaned and offered up the glorious new releases of what she so delightedly took from him, letting it pass to her, dying a little in this moment and bequeathing all of it, every last holy-grail swallow and trace. Love's flow, gone mutual and transfused now, taking the vows.

We'll be the perennial duet, he thought, and I'll train her to be my own . . . now sinking into the comforting maelstrom, the breathless ease of watching her sustain the entrancement, the lazy fevered lounging on the hearth of it, devotion . . . We'll be a world unto ourselves and tell the rest of the planet to turn off and drop out because we are well stocked with every human need and *this* is all we want, the touch and the immediacy . . . He gave her a long and pensive smile, stroking the fluffy blondness of her as she wistfully fondled the portly slumbering key to their alliance.

Soon, they slept again. But in forty minutes she woke him to discuss the positively weirdest case of insomnia she'd ever had. Jim made slow and thoughtful love to her while she recited all the symptoms. Then they drifted off again. And when they awoke, dawn was in the room to offer them the same warm addictions.

Their first day passed like that. And the next.

NORMAN SINGER

Norman Singer is a pornographer who is not ashamed to admit it. He hides under no pseudonym and comes out staunchly in defense of the genre whenever he gets the chance. A Chicagoan by birth and a San Franciscan by choice, Mr. Singer has been writing seriously for more than ten years, attaining moderate success as a ghostwriter, gagwriter and a writer of children's stories. However, with Curtain of Flesh, *the first of six novels published by Olympia, he developed a special style of erotic writing — a combination of poignancy, comedy and sex — which has brought him pre-eminence in this field and caused one of his many fans to remark: "There was Henry Miller, but there is Norman Singer."*

Ray Kainen

A Sea of Thighs

Usually, Standish liked to walk across the campus at Northern Upper Midwest Tech and Seminary. To him, this was the academic life, the golden glow of the sun bringing life to the greensward, the gothic shadows of the Classics and Humane Building behind him, the square blocks of the Applied Sciences and Practical and Esoteric Arts to his left, the gymnasium of the Physical Education and Practical Games and Sports to his right, and across the quadrangle, the Mind Sciences Building. At one time, it had been the Mine Sciences Building, but when the gold mine craze that had once swept the area had subsided, the trustees felt it had been outmoded and gave it to the Psychology and Psychoanalysis Departments. Rather than carving a new name on the building, they merely changed, with characteristic Northern thriftiness, the E to a D.

But he was in a hurry. He would have liked to stop and answer nature's call in one of the gothic bathrooms of the Classics Building, but the problem of unstrapping and restrapping was one that required some leisure to perform. The leisure of the theory class, he thought bitterly to himself, now allowing himself to dwell on his problem, to make himself ready for the approaching therapy session. Not even the small knots of students clustered around the campus, some leisurely smoking and staring into the blue sky, some standing with placard and signs, waiting for the next demonstration to begin, some actually reading and waiting for class to begin, a position they had been in since the beginning of the semester. He almost ran into a small knot of agitated students waving signs.

NUMB NUTS ARE DUMB BUTTS
NUMB NUTS ARE BUM RUTS
and
ALL NUMB NUTS ARE NOT DUMB BUTTS AND BUM
   RUTS
ALL NUMB NUTS DO NOT ATTEND N.U.M.T.S.
THEREFORE, ONLY THOSE WHO DO NOT ATTEND
   N.U.M.T.S. ARE DUMB BUTTS AND BUM RUTS
and
WHERE CAN I GO WHEN MY ROOMMATE SMOKES POT?
THE DORMITORIES NEED INSIDE BATHROOMS

Standish smiled, in spite of his problems. The last was a severe problem that he had endured when going to college. The others were mere challenges in the teeth of tradition, the student trying to overthrow his oppressor, the college.

He entered the door, with its cunning doorknob shaped like

Freud's beard, and immediately hurried up the stairs, down the corridor with the white sign that said, WELCOME: PSYCHOLOGY AND PSYCHOANALYSIS PERFORMED AT CUT PRICES, and stopped before the door. The neat name plate said LUSS T. FIDDLER, M.D., Ph.D.

Standish stopped to adjust his glasses, and then made, as was his wont, a final inspection of his trousers, to see that they hung neatly over his handicap. As he was doing so, the door opened, and the pleasant face of Luss T. Fiddler looked him over. She was dressed in a rather prim costume of a skirt four inches above the knee and a sheer blouse, evidently the garb of a faculty member rather than a student, although her slim figure could easily have belonged to a co-ed.

"The old spectacle and testicle routine, Standish?" she asked, pleasantly. "Come in, Dr. Bummpo. We don't bite in this department."

Her voice, though pleasant, was commanding, the very epitome of professionalism. Standish often wondered why he kept on going to her, when each session became more and more unpleasant. He had finally decided it was because he was basically a very lonely person.

Standish walked across the small office, under her severe gaze, and went directly to the couch and lay down. She closed the door.

"Did you realize that you were fifty-seven seconds late? You are still showing this hostile resistance? Do you have any idea why?" She was never the one to beat around the bush, but started immediately in on the therapy session.

Standish said: "It's a nice day." He knew this would provoke her, but it would fill in some time. Should he tell her the truth?

"So?" she said.

Standish sighed. He knew he couldn't avoid it. "I was delayed because one of my students, a rather erotically oriented female, caught me in a state of dishevelment and insisted on being fucked."

"Hmmm," said Dr. Fiddler. "More erotic fantasy. Did you receive any satisfaction from it?" She leaned forward, and Standish caught the faint odor of her perfume. "How was it done?"

"I was sitting in my office, on my chair, examining my prick to see if it had changed in any way, when she came in. After talking about her Senior Thesis for a while and discussing a particularly pressing problem she had, she managed to impale herself on my prick, and I believe, to receive some satisfaction from it." Standish spoke in the low monotone he had learned was the patient's role.

"Hmmm. Interesting. She received satisfaction, and I presume, you did not?"

"No," said Standish. "It was the same as ever."

"Have you thought about the meaning of this?"

"I'm only describing what actually happened."

"Hmmm," said the doctor, shifting around, wrestling with the problem. "This is something that we've gone through over and over again. You insist on retaining this fantasy of a perpetually stiff penis, which has to be contained by elaborate clothing and wrapping, which never diminishes in size, and from which you evidently receive little sensual stimulation. Do you remember the intellectual explanation we worked out in our last session?"

Standish thought back. "Whereby I had displaced my primitive oral needs into the genital stage, and my need for omnipotence in this area has been projected onto my prick."

"Anything else?"

Standish felt like swivelling his head around, to look at her expression. Always pushing him. "That seems to take care of it."

"No," said Dr. Fiddler emphatically. "What other stages might be involved? Remember, we evolve through the oral, anal and genital phases. How does this delusion of yours correlate with each of these stages?"

"Well," said Standish doubtfully, "I suppose that at the oral stage, it's one huge nipple, that I have ingested. My wish to be all-powerful forces me to keep this protruding."

"Good!" said the doctor. "That's one of the explanations I wanted you to work through. Now; let's go on. What about the anal stage?"

Standish felt vaguely uncomfortable. He didn't like to think about things like that.

"Come, Dr. Bummpo. What about it?"

"That's my trouble," Standish said. "I can't come."

"A very significant pun. But stay on the subject. What does every little boy wish to present to his mother, to make her proud and happy?" She wrote something down on a pad.

"His wee-wee?"

"No," said Dr. Fiddler, scornfully. "Most mothers are tired of the wee-wee by the time they have had children. This is known as the post-partum, pre-puberty 'we don't want the wee-wee' syndrome. Try again."

"I guess it must be the feces?"

"Right on the head!" said Dr. Fiddler.

Standish went on. "During toilet training, the child wishes to give his feces to his mother as a present. The mother generally refuses them, having no functional use for them."

"And this is involved in your delusion?"

Standish shrugged helplessly. "It must be. And this is an extension of the present I wish to give my mother."

"Extended into what?" asked the doctor.

"Extended into my normal genital development?" asked Standish hopefully.

"Normal?" The doctor's voice was scornful. "How can you possibly term development normal when a delusional system has to be built around the main object in the genital system?"

"But it *isn't* a delusion, doctor!" Standish was almost plaintive.

"That's what all patients think about their own defenses. They have to hold on to their defenses in order to keep anxiety from devouring them, obliterating them, driving them back to their primal beginnings, to ultimate despair." Dr. Fiddler was impassioned.

Standish was frightened. "I've always thought I've handled things pretty well."

"Things, Bummpo, things! The curse of our age! When you've spread yourself so incredibly thin, across so many developmental phases, what does that mean?"

Standish tried to think. He began to sweat. "I'm versatile?"

"No!" came the sharp, therapeutic voice of the doctor. "It means that you're defending yourself against the polymorphous perverse tendencies, using your delusional system as a lance to ward off the world and reality."

Standish thought about it. He had never heard it presented in such a way. "But if it's such a defense, why doesn't it give me pleasure?"

"Now we're coming to the point, Bummpo. The point." She finally emerged from her shadowy enclave at the end of the couch, and walked around so that she stood in front of the window. She spread her legs apart. Standish, by raising his head, could see her slim sensuous legs, the semi-transparent skirt, her imperious mien. "You don't want pleasure. Your sense of guilt is so deep and inborn that you must constantly hold yourself back from involvement."

Standish felt ashamed. "I don't know how to go about it."

"Now we're getting somewhere, Standish. Admit to yourself that your delusional system is insufficient to ward off the world. This is the first step."

"I do." Standish felt resigned.

Dr. Fiddler smiled in triumph. "That's the first step. Now, how would you go about becoming more normal in your actions?"

"I don't know."

"You're really impotent, aren't you?" The words again were sharp and cutting.

Standish objected. "I don't know about that."

"A victim of narcissistic parapraxis. Strongly veiled components of latent homosexuality. Libido in a state of passive homoeroticism. What do you think should be done, Bummpo?"

"I don't know. I honestly don't know."

"This fantasy you described, where a student barged into your office and impaled herself on your prick. What did that mean?"

"Veiled multiphasic-rejection, combined with phallic-urethral regression."

She looked at him with admiration. "You're well on the way to mastering yourself. Now, have you ever had experience with a woman?"

Standish was doubtful about his answer. After all, he thought, she had certainly shown him that reality and fantasy can be confused. "Not much," he said, truthfully.

"So you really know very little about female reactions." The doctor pondered the question for a moment, tapping her high heels on the floor. "Get off the couch."

Standish did as he was ordered, somewhat disturbed. His face must have shown bewilderment. "Is it a part of the therapy?"

"I'm not going to put you in shock by what some of my colleagues call nuptial therapy, or attempt an intercourse relationship. I think you need a visual aid at this point to allay your fears." With swift movements, Dr. Fiddler slipped off her blouse, whipped her skirt off, and stood there in brief bikini pants, garter belt, stockings, and shoes while she shrugged out of her bra, turned it around, unsnapped it, and laid everything carefully on the desk.

She moved to the side of the plastic-covered couch. "I won't remove any more clothing, since I notice the hour is coming to an end." She looked up, and Standish followed her gaze. The severe, functional wall clock was divided into a fifty-minute segment of white and a ten minute segment of black. There were still thirteen minutes left of the white.

The doctor sat on the couch, swivelled her knees and legs, still covered with nylon, and lay back. "The literature points out that men react to voyeuristic elements quite strongly. In your case, if you are able to see, some of the fantasy elements in your delusion can be allayed. You will no longer have any need to be frightened of your normal reactions." She looked up at him, and smiled. "Do you feel any desire?"

Standish, actually, felt a strong desire to leave, and to mull over the new insights he had received. He sat down in the chair where the doctor had sat, and moved it so that he had a full view of the couch, her slim body lying on it, now quite passive, her breasts firm, tapering out to swelling hips and a crotch barely covered by a strip of black satin, the garter belt now loose, attached to the gleaming nylons that created ripples of light on the piston-like thighs, toes barely visible in her shoes.

He imagined it should be a stimulating sight. But he honestly had to answer, "Not much."

She frowned. "To be expected, the first time. Perhaps the conditioning process will take some time. But you should try to get used to it. It's something that every man has to conquer, sooner or later." She settled back. "Now, we'll assume that some foreplay has already occurred. You know what that is?"

"Kissing and petting?" asked Standish, giving the answer he was expected to come up with.

"Correct. And now I'm on my back, preparatory to commencing intercourse in the position considered normal in much of the Western World. At this point, entrance is to be effected." She looked backward over a smooth shoulder. "How big did you say your fantasy object was?"

At this, Standish patted himself, as if to reassure himself that it was still there, bound and gagged. "Eleven and three-fourths by two inches. At the narrowest point."

Dr. Fiddler seemed to shiver slightly, and crossed one ankle over the other. "Perhaps that is one of your problems. That certainly exceeds the medians in both directions, and might be the basis of your anxiety. Have you ever tried to reduce the size?"

"All the time," said Standish.

"But that wouldn't satisfy the need for omnipotence, of course. It'll take some doing, but I'll try to handle it. You need a lubricant, of course."

"I thought there were natural secretions."

"There are, but in a situation such as this, they may not be sufficient. Now, you've brought the girl to bed. There may have to be a slight delay while one of you goes out to the bathroom. Then you return." She twisted. Her legs spread apart, and her knees rose.

She twisted herself on the couch. "At that point, the foreplay might have worn off."

"Worn off?" asked Standish.

"It's standard practice to manipulate the clitoris prior to entrance. The clitoris, of course, is considered to be a vestigial organ with some of the same qualities as the penis.

"How?" asked Standish.

The doctor's voice seemed to be more distant. "Naturally, along with this, there will be some kissing and fondling and petting, especially of the breasts. They are one of the primary erogenous zones, you know." She let her hands cup themselves under her breasts, and gently began to fondle them. "Notice how there is congestion, and replication of the sex organ." The nipples had risen. "At this point, of course, it feels quite pleasurable." Her hands became busier and busier. Suddenly, the right hand trailed itself down the smooth, concave belly, and dipped under the bikini panty. Her fingers became a crawling mass of worms under the sheer black nylon, and she raised a leg. "Manual stimulation of the labia is the next step." The index finger suddenly separated from the wriggling group, and dived into the center of the fray.

Her voice began to hurry. "Now, direct clitoral stimulation is being applied." Her other hand continued to fondle and tweak the upthrust nipples on her breast. "This combination of stimuli assures the male of receptivity." A rocking motion had begun in her pelvis, spreading through her long lean body. Her heels had begun to dig into the couch.

Standish watched with renewed interest as the hand wiggled

and her hips began to rotate. The doctor's back had arched. She threw her head back, and seemed to have difficulty in speaking. "We are now ready for entrance. So, we take it off." She took her hand off her breasts, and grasped the flimsy nylon. It tore in one quick jerk. "We take it all off!" Her expanse of tufted mound came into view, moving as if with a life of its own. "Are you ready?"

"For what?" Standish asked, startled.

"For identification and empathy. Place yourself, in your mind, in the position of the male. Are you ready for entrance."

Standish nodded dumbly. "Yes."

"Slowly, now, slowly," said the doctor. She removed her hand, and cupped them as if a rod were between them, being guided to her honey pot. "It's enormous." She shivered with the effort, raising her legs, offering entrance. "Enormous. You mustn't cause pain at this point." Her jaw was slack. Her breathing had increased. She seemed to hold her body still with an effort. The hands slowly descended to the upraised mound, "Please! Please!"

"Please what?" asked Standish, wishing to help.

The doctor took a deep breath. "Every woman has her own series of responses to this traumatic, crucial moment of the act. It's the man's job to be both gentle and cruel. There! There!" Her body gave a shudder and she lay there for a moment in the upraised foetal position.

"What comes next?" asked Standish. Time, he noticed, was running short.

"Some men will begin almost immediately. But a woman appreciates a little more foreplay at this point, where the pressure is allowed to build, where it expands into her whole being." Her hips began to move, almost in spite of herself.

She turned and looked at him, licking her lips. "Another important point. Many men seem to think that all they have to do is go up and down. Like this." Her hips rose and fell in a direct perpendicular to the couch. Thump, thump, thump.

"That isn't the way?" Standish asked. It seemed to be expected of him.

"No," she breathed, gathering herself. "Gentle movements, pressure exerted from all sides." Her hips began a complex of rotational movement and vertical scaling that were difficult to follow. Her heels dug in even further. Her legs opened, and with a sudden movement, they rose off the couch and attempted to wrap themselves around the phantom lover. The tempo increased.

"Bum-ppo," she panted, "this-is-an-important point. The tempo—" with a little cry, she threw her head back, her chest heaving, rocking in those complex movements, muscles twitching.

"The tempo?" prodded Standish.

"The-tempo-must-not-stop!" With that, she increased the ferocity of her movements, her teeth bared, her hand covering her mound, working at it, her muscles loosed in uncontrollable spasms.

"SOCK IT TO ME!" she screamed.

"Sock it to you?" asked Standish.

But she hardly heard. Now swallowing great gulps of air, her eyes closed, her hair back, the tendons in her neck stiff, her legs arched and stiff, her bottom a seething mass of vibration.

Standish felt that he should do something. He leaned forward and put his mouth next to her ear. Even that, he noticed was distended, especially the lobe. He shouted, "SOCK! SOCK! SOCK!"

With that, she was away, her body a mass of contractions, muscles chasing muscles in waves of force. "Thanks. Oh! Ah!"

It spent. She lay there for a moment, and blinked. "Do you get the idea?"

Standish nodded. "It looks awfully strenuous."

She sat up. "It is. But you end up with a peaceful, relaxed feeling." She looked up at the clock. "I must hurry. The experiment is about to start."

Standish felt bewildered. He felt as if he had seen about as much of an experiment as he could tolerate in one day. She noticed it.

"Very important. With Looseygear."

"Looseygear?"

"It's an ultra-secret project on campus. We've got a big government grant." She narrowed her eyes. "I'm not sure if I'll be able to get you in, but you might be interested. Might help to break up your delusional pattern. Would you like to come?"

Standish nodded, dumbly. Things were not going as he had expected.

"If that's the case, we'd better get going." She began to whip her clothes on in reverse order, looking none the worse for wear. She smiled at him. "That was refreshing."

"Thanks," said Standish.

She was ready. "Now, off to see Looseygear."

RAY KAINEN

The pseudonymous Ray Kainen grew up in a small town, attended the universities of Chciago and Minnesota, leaving no impression whatsoever on the academic world, and ended up as a social worker in a mental health institute in a large Midwestern community. He says he turned to part-time writing to work out maladjustments caused by his inability to leap tall buildings in a single bound, even after a running start — as well as to pay for his children's orthodontist. The author lives in the suburbs and puts on an establishment front by painting his house regularly and fighting crabgrass, after which he retires to his lair in the basement to turn out his witty brews of science fiction, satire and sex.

Akbar del Piombo

Who Pushed Paula?

*B*arney, I reflected ruefully on my way back to the mansion, was, without doubt, a personal enemy of mine. The base ingratitude of that miserable hound aggravated my good humor and threatened to spoil the rest of my stay. Hadn't I fixed him up beautifully with Sister Martha? What better proof of my generosity could I have given? Besides his greed, which was galling enough, he was unrelentlessly hounding me, insulting me and sabotaging my chances with Arlette. Why, a human rival couldn't have done better! Rival, that's what he was. I stopped short in my tracks, as if hit by a blinding truth. It wasn't impossible after all, and wasn't the Baron a cuckold by a horse? Still, Arlette was not Heloise, and Barney belonged to the Baroness. No doubt she enjoyed him in her leisure moments when she wasn't swinging in front of Ernest. Barney wasn't hanging around her because he was already in, but Arlette was fresh material and I had come on the scene almost the same time he did. I was sure, then, that he was approximately even with me except for the blow he had given me this afternoon. It was going to be a ticklish affair from now on, for he had the beautiful advantage of free access to her bedroom. I could just imagine him drooling and licking his chops with a red-hot hard-on as she undressed in front of him. From that moment on it was open warfare between the Dane and I.

I went directly to my room to prepare for dinner. Tonight was the first time that all the guests would dine together. An enormous table had been set in the banquet hall and it shone with silver candelabras, fine linen and huge vases filled with flowers. Many were already sauntering about, drinking cocktails and martinis, and it promised to be a real *soirée mondaine!*

I showered and removed some burrs that had clung to my balls during my pastoral episode. Afterwards I dressed in one of the tuxedos the Baron had put at my disposal, which fit to perfection. Fully prepared and refreshed, I descended.

It was an opulent spectacle which quickened the pulse, when one entered the banquet room. Great chandeliers hung down in massive forms of pure silver glowing with myriads of lights that blinded the eye. The stately brilliance was reflected in giant mirrors framed in heavy gold molding. Everywhere one saw the last word in aristocratic elegance, the rustling of sheer satin, the glint of gold brocade, silk damask running through all the hues of red, the rainbow flickering off diamond necklaces, off pearls, rubies and sapphires, each outshining the other in a veritable orgy of splendor. Regarding this resplendent assembly I felt my knees buckle; it was impossible that I was part of it. A duchess or marchioness would pass, sipping from a crystal wine glass, in light conversation, exuding a tantalizing odor of musk dabbed carefully on the lobes of her pink ears and in the secret of her bosom, and just as I would be about to lose myself to her forever, another would trail diaphanously in the other direction, dressed in a tight, ebony black gown, which hardly covered her nipples, leaving bare to the world a skin like ivory, soft as peach-down.

There was only one way to face all this royalty and I went off in search of a drink.

"Ah, there you are, Henry," I heard a voice behind me say and, turning, I saw the Baron, beaming like a baby, hurrying to my side.

He led me to a corner with a sly, winking air.

"One word, Henry, before I leave you on your own." He

looked around to see if we were being overheard. "He's here, you know."

"Who's here?" I asked, wondering what he was talking about.

"Him; whoever he is, he's here tonight." He smiled knowingly.

"Whoever he is? I don't . . ." I stammered, utterly baffled.

"Come, come," he said, shaking my arm good-naturedly. "Have you forgotten? Don't let yourself get carried away by all this."

"Christ," I nearly yelled, "I almost did forget."

"Quite all right, Henry, I understand. That's why I caught you as soon as you came in. He's here tonight and it's up to you to catch him."

"Tell me," I asked, "what makes you so sure?"

"Oh, she's too clever to give herself away by any signs. I've been watching her. It's intuition, Henry, I can tell by something changed in her attitude. Keep your eyes open."

He patted me fondly on the back, and left to join a group that had been calling him.

The last thing I wanted to do this evening was detective work. In a company like this, swarming with beautiful thoroughbreds, the atmosphere getting thick and heavy like a harem with its mixture of perfumes, I didn't want to keep my eye in one place all the time. Forlornly I watched Arlette, more exciting than ever, talking with a half-dozen dukes. They were men of good taste and it promised to be a battle royal to see who was going to get the inside track.

In another group Heloise was holding court with admirers somewhat older than those of her sister. There were two bald-heads, one gray and one pure white. Duty called, so I headed for that group. After greeting me she introduced the aristocrats, who all bowed stiffly in turn. A Comte de Grosqueue, a Marquis de Putain, the Duc de Bandé, the Baron Gallstein; "Charmed"; "Delighted"; "Pleased"; and turned back to her, paying no further heed to my presence. Not that I minded, there wasn't any particular attraction for me in the society of those old birds, but I resented the off-hand treatment on principle. Sirs, I thought to myself, if one of your number is the man the Baron's looking for, I am only too happy to ferret you out. Not only that, but I will even take a special pleasure in meting out the deserts.

Finally we were called to table and the room was filled with the commotion and buzz of people crossing and criss-crossing to find the places. The noise died down to a more genteel timbre when the hors-d'oeuvre were served. By a stroke of good luck I found myself seated across from Arlette, though she had her male company to right and left. It wasn't necessary that I sit next to Heloise but she had taken my arm, to the surprise of their lordships, and led me to her place. Looking up and down the table I saw that the other men were of a different stamp from the Baroness's entourage, younger and less stiff. This made me suspect that the man I was looking for was not amongst these four, which disappointed me, but knowing how robust she was it was not very likely that she was playing with one of these dried prunes.

On my left hand sat a gorgeous duchess, a buxom female with jet-black hair in which was set a diamond tiara, crowning a face of Oriental beauty. She was extremely well-built and knew it. From time to time our eyes would meet and the dark depths under her eyebrows had a wicked look which added new life to me each time I caught her glance. She was someone worth knowing. Once I dropped my fork, on purpose, and bending down, got a good look at her legs. Her thighs were large, the way I like them, and her calves were impossibly seductive. I brushed my hand casually up her legs as I regained my position to see her reaction, and, of course, because they were irresistible. She threw me a look of fire when I sat upright. I thought she was perhaps the type that offends easily so I abstained from looking her way. But at the second course something touched my own knee and I thought at first I had bumped against the leg of the table. It persisted, however, resting lightly, but without a doubt it was the touch of a human hand. Only a dullard would not have realized that it was the hand of the Duchess. It didn't take her long to work her way to my fly and deftly she unworked the buttons and found my rod. Everyone was drinking madly and jokes and laughter were flying thick and fast across the table. Taking advantage of the general effusion, she grabbed my bare penis in her fist and held him fast. He rose up to working size in a flash. The audacity of the woman was amazing. Once or twice she turned to me, asking me a question, the slightest pretext to be rid of her neighbor for a moment. I played a cool game, keeping a straight face and dominating the natural excitement she was causing in my groin. My own plan was to advance boldly on Arlette while we were at table. My feet were the only means at my command under the circumstances. Chatting gaily, now with the Duchess, now with the Baroness, I unloosened one shoe with the other foot. Arlette was in constant animated discussion with her suitors to right and left, and not once did she even give me a passing glance. The table not being very wide, my foot found her leg before I had even half tried. I noticed immediately the change in her expression when she felt my foot touch her ankle, but I feigned complete absorption in the conversation of Heloise. I think it was the Baroness's bosom jutting right out in my face which put the notion in my head to pass on the chain reaction of the lively. I let fall my hand in the lap of the Baroness, and caressed her thigh. My foot had made an appreciable advance up Arlette's leg by the time the next course was served. The eating, which was necessary, even for pretense alone, broke the chain for awhile. Towards the end of the meal the Duchess and I resumed our clandestine research. I leaned back comfortably to enjoy the sensations which were coming from hand, foot and prick. Arlette darted a nasty look when I made it to her knees and clamped them tight around my foot to prevent any further progress. Heloise, however, sat on, chatting as if nothing were happening. By this time I had worked her skirts up and got to her naked thigh. She was a true voluptuary and was able to enjoy this treatment in the way I myself appreciated the skillful hand of the beautiful, lecherous Duchess.

When the dessert was finally served, my foot was still lodged between the unrelenting knees of Arlette, the Duchess had worked my penis into a red-hot pitch and I had the Baroness's legs split wide apart under the table, dangling her clitoris in the air.

I don't know if it struck any of the others as an odd coincidence that the three of us neglected our desserts altogether. Whether they did or not, none of us really cared, for we were all about to ring the orgiastic bell. Just when the Baron stood up from his place at the head of the table, to propose a toast, I heard Heloise gasp, and then she came in my hand. The duchess at the same time brought my throbbing cock to ejection and I nearly swooned as I shot forward all over Arlette's gown.

The laughter and general hilarity of all the guests made an excellent screen, for under ordinary circumstances the three of us would have been immediately suspected of our daring illicit exploit. But wine and gaiety had made many another face around us nearly as flushed as ours and the three of us passed secret smiles to each other, smiles of triumph and satisfaction.

Across from me I caught an indignant glare from a confused and frustrated Arlette. She was the only one to suspect what had passed beneath the table, for hadn't she received my jet of sperm which was now soaking through to her legs? Her position was most embarrassing, for it would be easily noticeable when she would rise, and how could she explain away its obvious character? It gave me a special pleasure to have put her in this uncomfortable position, it served as a kind of a revenge for the indignity I had suffered earlier in the day and I suspected that it had, in a mysterious way, bettered my chances of getting into her pants.

We all joined in the toasts of the Baron, though no one knew what they were for. I turned with my raised glass to the sensuous Duchess and we clinked glasses in a toast of our own. "Excuse me, Your Grace," I said to her, "but I didn't catch your name."

"Nor I yours!"

We laughed like children playing a joke on their elders.

"Pike," I answered, "The name is Henry Pike."

"How lovely! And so apropos! A short name for a long . . ."

She stopped there as she noticed a curious look of interest on her neighbor's face.

"Mine is somewhat longer but you needn't be formal. Di Pizzina. Carlotta DiPizzina."

"So you are Italian?" I asked.

"Yes, I am a direct descendant of Leo X, who sired another branch to his prolific family in the side chambers of the Vatican apartments. We have never received official recognition for that reason, yet we are always accorded every other honor due to those of noble birth."

"I am very pleased to make your acquaintance. The more so that I see the talent your forebears had for side activity has not been lost in their progeny."

Arlette, in spite of putting on an air of avid interest in her suitor's conversation, was, I noticed, greedily following our chatter and had undoubtedly understood everything. The more the party was getting spoilt for her, the more sadistic pleasure it gave me.

Barney, you poor bastard, I thought, here is where I make up for your dirty tricks. The spark of jealousy had been ignited in the virgin's breast and I was going to make sure it would burst into flame.

"My dear Duchess," I continued, "I hope that our newly made acquaintanceship will not end with this wonderful banquet. It would be something I should always regret if this interesting beginning should end abruptly without my being able to return your kindness."

"I, too, should regret not seeing more of you. But if you are staying on in the Baron's house we shall have more opportunity of seeing each other. However, I am not here alone."

"Excellent," I exclaimed, "I am staying here awhile, indefinitely . . . but what do you mean you are not alone?" Immediately I was sure there was a husband lurking in the crowd.

"My three sisters are with me, two with their husbands. The youngest is with her fiancé. And I"—seeing the question in my look,—"and I am about to be married also."

"Is your fiancé? . . ."

"Yes. He is sitting next to the Baron, on his right. The one with the mustache."

I looked in the direction of the Baron and for the first time observed the man at his right. He had indeed a mustache of grandiose proportions, rather like the old-fashioned handlebars. Like the Baron, he wore a monocle in one eye and was slightly balding though not bad looking. She explained further that he was Persian, a Prince, extremely wealthy, and for that reason she had agreed to marry him. Her family was in desperate straits, for none of the other married sisters had brought any wealth by their unions. The prince, who was known as Haman ben Hada Izerimem (she called him Miseri-mem for short), had no illusions about his forthcoming nuptials. It was purely a marriage of convenience . . . still, I reasoned, I would have to be careful for he might be touchy merely for the form.

She pointed out her sisters, who were scattered at various parts of the table, all as beautiful as herself, with the same black hair and Mediterranean complexion. The husbands, however, were of a more commonplace stamp, resembling complacent shopkeepers, completely lacking in the refined sensitivity and taste visible on their wives' features.

"And who are the butchers your sisters married?" I asked.

"Aren't they horrible?" she laughed. "It is really sad, though, for neither of them are happy. They were both deceived into believing they were marrying gold and now they have neither that, nor love."

"If that's the case, then I'm sure they've picked themselves a lover, for otherwise their situation is unendurable."

"Well," she laughed merrily, "about that I don't know. I suspect they have their little escapades, but we rarely see each other and they keep their affairs to themselves."

The information was worth storing in my memory in case of any unforeseen developments.

Gradually the banquet came to a close, and people wandered away from the table in small groups, men lighting up cigars, women leaving for the powder room.

Arlette got up, holding the front of her skirt bunched together and only she and I knew what she was concealing: she dashed off to change the soiled dress.

Heloise took my arm again and reproached me for neglecting her and devoting all my time to the alluring Carlotta. I insisted that it was not at all deliberate and that she had such a coterie of admirers already it was practically impossible for an outsider to make any headway.

"Tut, tut," she reprimanded, "the truth is you have let yourself be seduced by that wicked duchess. I know her well."

It was no use protesting and I even wondered if Heloise hadn't seen the fresh proof of her "wickedness" on my person.

The old dukes who had given me the cold shoulder were now forced to accept me as a member of their group, for it was difficult to go on ignoring me when the Baroness was devoting a good share of her conversation to myself. We all rose together and joined the mingling crowd in the next salon. Carlotta slipped off, after squeezing my hand, to join Handlebars Miseri-mem.

No longer did the extravagant decor and noble lineage of the cosmopolitan company cower my spirits. I had received my baptism of fire during that wanton banquet, and it was only natural that my ego and a self-esteem were flattered. I was a different man leaving the table, changed in many ways from the timid, fearful individual that I had first been when I entered the great room. The Baron managed to pass my way and nudged my arm.

"Well," he asked, "what do you think? Have you made any

progress?"

"Quite a bit indeed."

"Aha," he replied, "it sounds good. I shall see you later when we will be able to talk freely. In the meantime, I leave you to your own devices."

Of course, I still didn't have the slightest idea as to who the culprit might be. I looked around in idle speculation. We had found ourselves grouped around an ivory statuette which became the subject of conversation. While I found it quite interesting as an object, my knowledge was far too limited to hazard any comment. Instead I was thinking what I might tell the Baron later. He was so desperate to find his tormentor that I earnestly wished I had made an important discovery. All I had accomplished was to write off the list the four old men who never let go of Heloise. In any case, I didn't see what I could learn by remaining with this group. It might prove fruitful if I were able to sound out someone who knew the Baroness intimately. Carlotta instantly came to mind. Without hesitating I got up and excused myself on the grounds I needed a little exercise after the heavy meal. Heloise threw me a strange look which I absolutely did not comprehend. Walking away, I wondered if she suspected why I was their guest.

Mingling in the crowd I found Handlebars in a sharp discussion with a tall individual. Carlotta hung somewhat back from them and I gave her a pinch on the ass as I brushed by, then passed onto the veranda, where already quite a few people were enjoying the night air. She joined me there a minute later.

"I can only stay a moment," she said, huskily, "more than that and he will begin to suspect something."

"Can I meet you later," I asked, "or are you both sharing the same room?"

"Oh, no, thank God, I'm all alone. But he has the room next to mine and the walls are very thin, it is quite impossible."

"Perhaps not," I answered. "Tell me quickly which is your room. I will find a way to get there . . . without noise. I *must* see you."

I had taken hold of her hand in the dark. She looked up at me coquettishly.

"It is not possible tonight. I shall tell you where my room is, but you must promise not to come tonight."

"But I must come. If I let you slip by tonight there may never be another chance to see you. Who knows, perhaps he will take you away suddenly. No, that would be unbearable."

My ardor thrilled her vanity and her own desire. She whispered rapidly the directions to her room.

"At two," I said. "Everyone will be asleep."

She did not answer but left me hurriedly to rejoin Miseri-mem. What a svelte, luscious thing she was. There was an extraordinary mixture of boldness and gentle submission in her character which was irresistible. The kind of thing that leads wholesome young men into a sink of iniquity while they continue to imagine themselves pure and undefiled. She brought all the aroma of the sweet scent of Roman nights, of Renaissance gardens sheltered by dark poplars and secreting a nest of lovers in its bosom. A sublime decadence which suffuses the worldly rakehell with its clever arts as a python strangles its victim.

It was the ubiquitous Barney who broke in on my meditations. He slipped onto the veranda like a sneakthief and approached me warily.

"Ah," I snorted, "so there you are, you low-life!"

He stopped and wagged his ponderous tail hesitantly. There was a nervous flicker in his eye.

"Worried, eh? Wondering how things are going for me? Afraid I'm beating your time! Well, you overgrown smuckhound, licker of piles, you anus-twiddler, you can put this in your shit-snout, you and I are from here on out, strictly on the outs. Take off, you cunt-bloodhound!"

The way he winced under my impassioned tirade you would have thought he had grasped the meaning of every word. Whether he did or not, the general idea got across, and he backed away, head hanging abashed, tail flopped between his legs.

"Begone for good, your face is poison to my sight!"

He turned and fled, a deflated, abject cur.

And I returned into the salon to see what next the evening had in store.

The first thing I saw was Arlette descending the grand staircase, clad in a magnificent carmine robe, a strapless gown which hugged her tiny waist, then billowed out in a thousand rippling folds. She nearly took my breath away. She walked with a virginal dignity which shivered my testicles. Everything about her was young, green, approaching maturity. She brought temptation of another kind, in contrast to the almost vicious lubricity of her sister, who was like a dangerous swamp flower alongside this bud of springtime. In this house of marvels, the ingenious multiplicity of sex revealed its endless variety and potency.

A roulette wheel was being set up in an adjoining room attracting mostly the men, particularly the more impoverished dukes and counts whose loose living had decimated their fortunes. Some had difficulty in concealing beneath a glacial exterior the avaricious and greedy designs which impelled them to that table. Young and old alike, bald-headed or bushy-maned, their cupidity ate through their titles and their positions, some even pushing and shoving their way to get a favorable place. In comparison with these money-grubbers, the Baron shone out like the true noble he was. I turned away from this drab spectacle for something more inspiring. The last thing one would have expected on an occasion of this sort was a public lecture. Yet, incongruous as it seems, in the adjacent room that is exactly what was taking place. Intrigued by the novelty of the thing, I entered and took my place at the end of the hall. There were in all about twenty or so in the audience, and mostly women. Amongst the assemblage of duchesses I noticed a row full of nuns. A new addition was a man of the cloth whom I had not seen before. At the head of the room was a large screen and from time to time the images shifted, coming from a tiny projection machine in the rear. The lecturer was a young female, wearing, appropriately, horn-rimmed glasses and wielding a long stick which she used to point out on the diagrams the elements she wanted to elaborate in her speech.

". . . and the most important of all are the testicles. In the average ejaculation, there are from sixty to one hundred million sperm cells. This virile apparatus is contained in a sack hung outside the body which is called the scrotum."

On the screen there flashed a giant-size version of the "male organ" cut in a cross-section view which showed the canals leading to the hanging shaft duly labeled and numbered.

"Furthermore," she went on, "from six to ten billion of these sperm cells are produced in one day alone. The implication is obvious as you can all see, that the average man is capable, physically, of from sixty to one hundred ejaculations a day!"

She looked at her audience with a glow of triumph and challenge. A chorus of sighs went up from the female contingent, and of horror from the nuns' division. As for the man of the cloth, I thought I saw him slump slowly down in his seat. The figure was indeed staggering.

"Unfortunately," and she sighed herself, "few men are aware of their real potential, and give but a ludicrous proportion of this generous endowment. But, we shall not linger on this matter, and proceed to the female organ."

The screen now revealed a gigantic illustration of the female gland. From the cervix at the head of the uterus, one followed the canal downward into the vagina and thence to the labia surmounted by an intriguing little organ called the clitoris.

"The clitoris is the very sexual center of the female and is capable of erection much like the penis. However, it is an uncomfortable fact that the female orifice is located where it is, that is, hygienically speaking. It is so placed as to be between two orifices of excretion, and this means that the genital area must be kept under continual surveillance."

Several women began scratching their cunts involuntarily. The nuns all blushed as if they had been directly accused of having allowed some rancid odor loose in the room.

She gave a few hints about the proper washing and care of the vagina and then hurried on to the more exciting part of her lesson, actual copulation.

"We in the Occident have a rather limited knowledge and practice in the fine art of sexual intercourse." She frowned severely at the audience, and the nuns all stirred again in unison as if she had addressed a personal rebuke to them alone. The nobility, on the other hand, all leaned forward eagerly to absorb the revelations.

"In the Orient, custom and ancient knowledge have handed down a variety and number of positions which far surpass our limited and hurried habits. We generally content ourselves with the classic coupling in which the woman lies on her back with her legs widespread."

The cunt vanished from the screen and was replaced by a provocative view of a pair of outstretched legs leading to the hairy promontory of assault. This was followed immediately by a side view of the same position, seen in cross-section.

"We shall now see exactly what happens when the penis enters the vagina in this 'normal' position."

The screen went black as the operator shut off the slide projector to turn on a motion picture machine alongside.

Almost the same scene was reproduced but this time with more convincing illusion of movement. A one hundred times life-size male organ appeared in full erection. Everyone moved forward in their seats, and cries of awe went up at the impressive vision. Next appeared the protective hairs of the waiting cunt. The penis moved slowly forward, retaining its straining muscles and nerves in abeyance, showing a great discipline on the part of its owner. The cunt lay there in readiness, one almost felt in bated breath, anxious, trembling with anticipation. The nuns were staring at the scene with bulging eyes. The man of the cloth had his right hand hidden beneath his skirts which nevertheless failed to conceal the stiff that clenched in his hand.

Slowly, irrevocably, like some strange primeval monster, it moved across the screen. The scrotum hung down with its arsenal of sperm ready to send up its sixty to one hundred million sperm-cell load. Now one could easily see the labia as the female thighs spread even more apart and just at the upper joining of the lips the small protruding head of the hungry clitoris. No one spoke nor coughed; a peculiar, tense hush fell over the audience and even the lecturer herself fell silent, lost in the contemplation of the hypnotic scene.

How large the head seemed, and how long the shaft from which it swelled out! It did not seem possible for the simple split which lay crouched before it to receive such a mass. Yet when the head arrived at the lips we saw them unfurl in many sheaves, and slowly curl round the head that was going in. Further and further apart they spread, eagerly swallowing the fast disappearing tool, until nothing was visible but the sack itself, and even that for an instant seemed ready to follow the penis in.

"What you have just witnessed may be properly called the 'simple' or 'direct' entry. It was accomplished with 'brio,' for the performers are by no means amateurs. However simple it may have seemed, I dare any of you to accomplish this entry with an equal ease of performance."

In the darkness her eyeglasses reflected back at her listeners, in scorn, like the eyes of an owl. Her attitude was beginning to grate me. What the hell, she sounds like she's the only one in the world who knows how to throw a good fuck.

"Observe closely now, the movements which follow entry."

The next thing that happened, the big cock slid out all the way to the ridge of the head, it lay there for a moment, then slid back in again. From then on it was the classic fuck and I didn't care what else she had to add. If she thought she was the only one who knew about the 'brio' of the performers, I was going to show her a trick or two which I didn't learn in any classroom.

The darkness of the room and the intense absorption of her audience afforded me perfect cover to steal quietly round to where she was standing. I came up directly behind her and stood still to make sure I hadn't been observed. But she herself was gazing up in fascination at the comings and goings of the great organs on the screen. I prepared myself for the daring coup by unbuttoning my fly and dropping my pants. My own version, in the flesh, of the penis working and churning on the screen, flopped out and quivered on the "qui vive." Her skirt was short and was no problem to lift. What was difficult was to lift it so that she would not feel it. In this I was again aided by her close attention to the movie. All that stood between me and her own canal was a thin pair of lace panties.

Just when I was about to grab her she started again to talk. My heart beat fast for I was sure I would be discovered. But by an incredible convergence of circumstances, she altered her position while speaking, unconsciously spreading her legs apart, no doubt in a subconscious reaction to the stimuli of her own discourse.

"You can see how the movement is controlled, regular and not at all jerky. It is just this kind of movement which gives the utmost sensations."

You don't say, I thought to myself with a satanic smile. Well, honey, I shall now show you how a good jerky movement, well executed, can give a terrific sensation. I held the skirt up with one hand, and with the other took an edge of the panties, right by a fringe of lace, and as quietly as a mouse, moved it to one side. When it was far enough apart to allow my shaft to approach her crack, it needed only a small movement of the groin to carry the head forward, exactly as we had all seen happen on the screen. With elation, I discovered that her lips were already lubricated. In spite of her seeming aloofness she had been as easily affected by the vigorous copulation scene as everyone else. I made sure I was well-placed, the penis head ready to part the labia, and gave a long protracted shove, steady, not too fast, but unrelenting. I felt the steaming hot vagina, bathing in its own juices, receive my prick with joy. The contrast of the layers of unfeeling clothing preventing human contact with the burning temperature of her interior made the sensation a hundred times stronger. Over her head I could see the cinematic fuck going on now in full blast. She gave a start of shock and surprise when the assault ran up her cunt. I caught her right in the middle of a sentence " . . . . . and when the lips fold back they are receiving the welcome bang of the scrotum . . ." I hit her right at the word "bang" and the rest of her phrase whined out like a caterwaul. In an ordinary lecture an audience would have been startled out of its wits at such an unexpected break, but here hardly anyone noticed it, and if they did, it no doubt fit in beautifully with the erotic trance in which they were.

I bent her over double before she half realized what had happened and began to fuck her in the most violent fashion, absolutely contrary to everything she had been saying for the past half-hour. In and out, in and out, fast as a bunny, hard as a bull, I rocked the teacher-maiden in full view of the entire room but certain that not a single eye was looking in our direction. She held on to the stick, unaware it was there, not knowing what to do. She glanced at the audience as if she feared it could be seen what was happening to her. Her professional conscience was at work as well and she looked up at the screen and from time to time made as if she were about to comment as before, except that a new shove into her palpitating organ stuffed the words in her throat and she merely swallowed, half-choked.

When the initial surprise wore off and the sensations she was receiving, not describing, became overwhelming, I felt her adjust her legs to a more convenient position and at last she began returning my shoves with a vigorous rolling of her ass. It was my turn to admire her knowledge. The way she twisted and squirmed her buttocks was worthy of the vainest slut. Certain gasps and sighs which came from the audience were very instructive. Everyone was being worked up to orgy pitch and there was a great rustling of skirts and moving about of legs and limbs. Under the vague light cast off by the screen I saw two noblewomen with their skirts lifted to their waists, their limbs stretched out and working their fired-up twats with a passionate diligence. The nuns didn't dare to go that far, but

one could tell by their screwed-up faces the unbearable itching that
burned between their legs.

As for the good man of the cloth, he also had raised his skirts
and while voraciously devouring the big screen fuck, was twiddling
and tickling his pious rod rapidly into ejection.

Suddenly the lamp burned out and the room went black. A
howl of disappointment went up from the audience. Nearly everyone was on the verge of orgasm and the break of the image-dream
woke them up at a difficult point. The operator switched on the
main light and the teacher and I were revealed to all as we were
riding on into the final lap of our genuine fuck.

From that instant on, the room was nothing but sheer
pandemonium. The living example we provided was all they needed,
provoked already to the breaking point by the movie stimulus.
Chairs were thrown over as women leaped on women, as the few
men in the audience grabbed a partner and threw up her skirts to
thrust in her boiling cunt a cock that was strained raw to bursting.
The priest was attacked by three passionate duchesses and the nuns
got up in terror and attempted to flee from the storm. There wasn't
a single human being who was unoccupied in the whirlpool of lust
which coursed through the room like a summer's sudden storm. It
was a fever to fuck, and fuck we all did, *en masse,* some in the
chairs themselves, rocking back and forth so dangerously that some
of them actually fell to the floor but, not caring a whit, went right
on with their screwing. The nuns had found the door locked, for
the wary operator had made his own calculations, based no doubt
on previous experience of this kind. They clung together against the
wall, saying a litany, telling the beads, so that in the general moaning and heaving one heard a "Hail Mary" coming in like a refined
punctuation on our pagan riot.

The operator had intended to grab a little nun for himself but
a furious pair of duchesses assaulted him head on and the three of
them rolled over with a crash, knocking the stand with the projection machines and cans of film into space. The women fought for
his cock like hungry tigresses and the poor man was almost torn
apart by their tearing and pulling. "One at a time, please! One at a
time," he yelled. "You know I have all those sixty million cells,
there's enough for every body."

"But I was first," screamed the largest.

"She's lying, the trollop, I was first!"

"Oh, trollop, is it? why you little street-wench, you know god-damned well I beat you to him. You can't fuck to save your pimp of a husband's ass."

"And you," screamed back the other like a hell-fury, "who-ever said you knew how to screw? Everyone knows what a moth-eaten, mouldy, prinkled old snatch you have in that cankered crotch. Go fuck yourself with a corkscrew, no prick could ever get into that rat's nest."

They took to tearing like demons at each other's hair and clothing. To the great hue and cry of the monster fuck carnival were added their shrieks and the ripping of cloth. In a matter of seconds they shredded each other stark naked, then tore at the flesh itself. In the meantime the operator had dodged out of their way and had cornered a nun who had strayed too far away.

He threw her bodily to the floor and went down on her like a sack of potatoes. She screamed for help but her voice was drowned in the hullabaloo. In a minute's time he unfrocked her, tore off her undergarments, then dove at her cunt with his mouth. The last I saw of him he was gulping down mouthfuls of rich virgin hair, greedily masticating each tiny shred with sadistic ecstasy.

Teacher and I continued our way undisturbed by the racket. She flipped over and grabbed me hard, saying "Now fuck me straight in like this." I dropped her to the floor and we went on into our second orgasm without interruption.

Everyone was going for the second coming. Positions were changed in a hustle of scraping chairs and feet. Some were now entirely nude, wriggling like electrified snakes all over the lecture-room floor. Others were partially disarrayed, brassieres flapping wildly as they jerked asses into each other.

For the third general orgasm somebody yelled "Change!" And the whole assembly went through another mad scramble for fresh partners and new positions. The priest grabbed the teacher away from me but before I knew what happened a duchess flew onto my balls, grabbed my hard prick with her hands and, squatting over me as if she was about to piss, forced him up in her cunt. She was enormous inside and my prick squashed all over, drenched in her flooded-up canyon.

"But I don't feel a thing," I protested, trying my best to touch one of her walls.

"That's all right," she shouted with joy, "I do!"

"Impossible," I answered, "you're as big as a horse. The best I can do is tickle your clitoris."

"Don't you believe it," she cried. "I may be big, but I could come on a hair."

Of course I didn't believe her but I let her go, she was having such a ball. Happily for me, she finished fast, and fell with a thud to the floor. I was aghast at the stream of liquid that poured out of her mammoth cunt. She hadn't been lying. Must be a case of auto-eroticism or something, I thought.

I looked round the room to see who was available. About all that was left was the cringing group of nuns who were going through some prayers for their little sister who was being violated by the operator. Only she didn't seem so much to be really suffering. About her mouth there played the suspicion of a beatific smile as the sharp rod of the operator, who was a man who didn't need any lectures on the use of that organ, introduced the little virgin to pleasures she had never suspected. Her sisters had noticed the change that had come over her after her first fright, and their prayers came out less from conviction than from habit. In some, their eyes shone with awakened curiosity, with a hidden urge, which threw consternation in their ranks. Besides—writhing in total sensual abandon, right before their astonished eyes, was the priest himself, who equaled the lusty operator in his manly vigor.

I myself had tasted virgin fruit of their kind not so long ago and had found it quite the equal of their worldly sisters. Therefore I made my way through the heaving fornication, slipping on the sea of sperm which was coming endlessly out of the slobbering orifices which danced before my eyes. Sometimes a diamond earring crunched under my feet, sometimes a bracelet of gold. A garter belt caught on my leg and snapped in the face of a duchess groveling in a spasm of joy on the floor.

The nuns saw me coming and huddled closer together like frightened deer. They looked at me in terror but there was the unmistakable flare of hope, and I knew that each one was thinking "I hope he picks me."

When I reached them I didn't grab one in the way the operator had done. I simply stood there examining them thoughtfully. A psychological trick, and it worked like a charm. They knew I was trying to decide which one I would choose. I saw one brush back a fallen lock of hair, another seemed to droop with languor and seduction. Still I made no move. The prayers went on of course uninterruptedly, but that was purely mechanical. They were all watching anxiously, hopefully.

Then I had a brilliant idea. Instead of making a choice, I simply took my prick in my hands and held it out, that hard magnificent snake which they knew had the powers of infinite, strange pleasures. Like someone offering a basket of fruit, I held it out, making it dangle just a bit, to show how tense and firm it was, and they could imagine how nice that would feel when it got inside their soft interiors.

They eyed it greedily, licking their chops, crossing their legs to quell the flames in their bushes. Furthermore, all the fucking that was going on all over the room was enough to strip the last shred of chastity from the toughest of virgins.

"Oh hell, Mary," cried one, finishing her prayer and throwing up her skirts simultaneously, "give me that thing. I'll be damned if I care for my cherry more than that!"

I stuck it right into her, just where she was, and the others drew in around us, saying their prayers for their lost sister straight in her ear while she and I fucked away madly.

One of them, a more studious, more objective character, stooped down to view close up the cock that slithered in and out of her sister's cunt.

"Why, it's just like the movie," she said.

The others got down in turn to watch and some asked my partner if it hurt.

"Oh God yes, it hurts like hell . . . but don't stop!" she cried.

"Sister, you are lost," another breathed into her.

"Not yet, not yet, but I'm getting there. Oh, come in me hard. Oh, it's *sooo* good!"

They had stopped their praying altogether now, totally absorbed in watching their sister going to hell. The blood flowed down her pale-white thighs and it struck new fear in their green souls.

"Oh sister, you are bleeding to death!"

"You are being punished," cried another.

"Yes, yes, that's right, punish me, punish me. Oh, it's SO

much better than a whipping." And she fainted dead away as I shot the hot liquid into her deepest channel. She crumpled to the floor lost, like St. Theresa, in a beautiful heap of satisfied lust. Jealously, the others watched her descend, and at last they shed what little remained of their artificial restraint.

Good Mary and Joseph, I thought, it looks like a mass movement for the end of continence, mentally counting up how many millions of sperm were left me on my daily quota. Never before in all my wenching experience had I run into a problem of this sort. Everyone of these decorous maidens was busily engaged in stripping off every last decent garment. I felt like a hermit martyr about to be subjected to a salacious stripping of his sack-cloth to undergo the crapulent Saturnalia of a carpet-knight. To that end I vowed I would die with a hard-on, in the example of the great Count Oblowoff, and standing at full height I prepared my indulgent penis for his next carnal glutting.

Disrobed, the shameless virgins danced over their fallen hoods in a symbolic gesture. The animal debauch had been too much for the natural cravings of the flesh and their long-suppressed desires broke all the bonds they had so carefully tied them in. Every one of them was a perfect gem of a female. And why not? Weren't they the last to bear the unmistakable mark of sheltered virginity? It was like being showered with a basketful of forbidden fruit. And in fact one of them cried out in delicious anguish, "We are sinners, sisters. We are sinning our way to perdition."

"Lost, so lost," sang another, and they all joined in like a chorus, "Lost, so lost."

"So go lose yourselves," I retorted, more or less fed up with this routine and turned my back on them. Instantly I was seized and swung round in spite of myself. They piled on me all together in a scrambling heap, bearing me down to the floor under their struggling bodies. How they sighed and moaned as they wiped and rubbed together from the mere contact of the flesh itself! They wallowed and glutted like pigs in a trough, throwing out arms, legs, asses and elbows, anything that moved. They were getting as much of a thrill from themselves alone as from me, for not many were actually able to reach me. I myself was enjoying a new sensation, something I had never experienced before. It was like bathing in flesh, just pure warm, downy, vibrating, pulsating flesh. There were breaths that swept over my cheeks, nipples that poked in my eyes, bellies that slid on my chest, on my thighs, on my arms. The soft pussy hair which massaged me briskly, hotly, sent new life into my heavy cock. He smacked against thighs which rolled over his head, throbbed between buttocks which caressed him in passing. They were everywhere moving like the sea which rolls up its foaming tide on a sun-baked beach. It was inevitable that at last one of the delirious pussies should engulf him and I heard the wanton cry of victory from the unknown who had luckily absorbed him into her cunt. Under the panting trepidation of the rutting females I lay in a dream-like trance succumbing to a thousand indefinable thrills. They licked with their tongues, caressed with their hands, and one, more hot-blooded than the others, came in a gush just as her cunt rolled over my face. The spicy stew ran into my mouth, burning with an acid twang and firing my appetite so that I pumped vigorously at the cunt which was sucking on my penis. I screwed, blind-drunk, grabbing at buttocks, squeezing on thighs, biting on titties, smelling in cunts. Nothing was spared in our lavish abuse, not an inch of flesh which didn't offer itself in the sacrificial heap, not a hole which went unscathed by a finger, a tongue or even a foot. I grabbed as many as I could hold when I felt I was coming and the force in my groin as I fired in the hole lifted them all high in the air and I blanked out in a shower of tumbling bodies and limbs.

AKBAR DEL PIOMBO

Akbar del Piombo is the "altered ego" of a writer and artist who has lived most of the past fifteen years in Europe (though he rejects the term "expatriate," pointing out one has to know where home is before one can be said to be living away from it). Paraphrasing the bard, the author describes the delightful romps with assorted barons, butlers and chambermaids that he has been concocting for Olympia over the years, as the product of some "heat-oppressed brain." Asked why there is so much sex in his books, he replied ingenuously: "I can't get enough of it. Besides, it sells."

The Double-Bellied Companion

Akbar del Piombo

On the funny thing!"
"Don't be afraid of it; here, put your hand on it."
"But what is it? I never saw anything like it before."
"No? You'll see a lot of them from now on. Go ahead, touch it, it won't bite you."

"I wouldn't dare put my hand on it!"

"If you touch it you'll really see something you never saw before!"

"Oh, it's so ugly! Put it away!"

"I'm going to show you something you're going to love; there, see how it wants to touch you?"

The voices of eight-year-old Mathilde von Spratten Olaf-Pinz and her cousin Sylvester, eleven, were but a faint murmur on the other side of the partition where the young girl's mother lay abed. The noble lady was picking desultorily from a box of chocolates, suffering a heavy ennui. The windows were covered by drapes as if she had no desire to see the light of day. She found the early August afternoon oppressive with its blinding sun and humid stillness. The velvet folds of the drapes turned the atmosphere a deep crimson, coloring the wan cheeks of the Baroness with deceptive life. Though she heard the voices of the children in the playroom, the words were too indistinct to be intelligible. She took another chocolate from the box and ate it listlessly. In the giant mirror above her head, set in the roof of her antique bed, she could see the roseate form of her body, so much like a statue she had seen once in the Borghese Palace. What was her name, Pauline? Like her own!

Had that other Pauline been a wicked woman? She tried to recall the features of the statue and decided she must absolutely investigate the life history of her namesake. Perhaps Sylvester's father knew, he was such an instructed man. She placed her hand on her breast and watched it in the mirror while it played with the soft roundness of her right titty. Then, to even the picture, she put her other hand on her left titty and while she enjoyed the pleasurable sensations of toying with her nipples she watched herself much as if it were someone else. Then her right hand removed her left titty from beneath her dressing gown and when she had her breasts fully exposed she stopped to admire the globes above her. Her thighs were unconsciously rubbing together, increasing her desire to explore her hidden sex. She took another bonbon while she undid the dressing gown and munched the sweet with smacking sounds, changing her position to see more of her generous backside. The thinness of her ankles emphasized the expanse of flesh which rolled around her hips.

Behind the door which gave on her study kneeled her personal maid, a long-lashed eye glued to the keyhole. The white bonnet on her head had been pushed back by the door-knob and fell unnoticed to the floor in the maid's absorption with her mistress' dallying. While so engaged, her mouth dropping lower and lower in troubled astonishment and her panties moistening from her agitation, the butler, Hughes, entered the room. Immobile, with a pot of roses in his hands, he was about to ask a question when the true nature of the situation dawned on him. He put down the flowers and tiptoed up to the maid, his eyes glowing strangely, his huge prick in his hand swelling apace with his steps. The second he drew up behind her he snatched up her skirts and, with the skill of a born rapist, plunged his burning tool into the hairy slot, grasping her waist with his free arm to help her support the blow. His rod slid easily into the lavishly lubricated hole. The poor maid, nearly out of her wits from the unexpected attack, was at the same time gasping in the most sensual way, the shock having brought with it its own appeasement.

So Hughes banged Clara at her mistress' keyhole while the latter was playing joyfully with her own pussy, bringing herself closer and closer to the final moment of ecstasy, a pleasure she felt three times over from the ravishing view in her mirror. She had not heard the sudden banging of Clara's head against the door-knob when Hughes' enormous cock went sailing through her cunt. The butler's gleaming eyes half closed in the thrill of fucking Clara, and she in her turn felt not the slightest pain in her head from the concussion, the sensations being overwhelmingly drowned in the luxurious waves bathing her body.

In the meantime, the precocious Sylvester had succeeded in removing his cousin's skirt, and they sat, face to face, on the floor, their bare legs entwined, each playing with the other's interesting organ.

The hot summer air carried with it the sounds of a horse and carriage coming up the drive, yet none of the busy people in each of the three rooms heard a thing of what went on elsewhere. So it was that Prince Pivo arrived, sweating and unheralded, into the baronial domain. He stepped down from the carriage and mopped his brow with a flowing silk handkerchief which he tossed disdainfully into the air after having blown his nose. He looked round him questioningly, annoyed that no one had come to the door to receive him. Prince Pivo never knocked at a door, nor ever in any way signaled his presence, for he never went anywhere he wasn't expected. He waved the carriage on, and sat down on the baking stone steps, pulling his visored cap lower to protect his eyes from the sun. He watched the carriage roll past the gate and disappear around the high wall of the estate. When the horse's hooves had died away, he stood up and listened, obstinately refusing to enter the chateau but intrigued by the extraordinary silence that reigned in the house. A hundred fading rose bushes crowned the lawn on either side of the stairway, and, separated from them by a cinder path, were two giant chestnut trees. Beyond them, to the right of the house, was a clump of smaller trees sheltering the pavilion reserved for certain intimate tea parties at five, and other more intimate parties at midnight. The Prince decided to wait in the pavilion for any sign of life.

He was to get that sign sooner than he imagined, in a most original manner. As he approached the miniature house, he thought he had seen, for the briefest instant, a face pass before the open window. Its movement was so rapid he had not been able to distinguish the features. He stopped and looked, and suddenly it appeared once more, rising as if from the floor, then sinking away again. And still he had seen no features. He moved closer, thinking that perhaps one of the children was playing games with him. When it came up the third time he saw with horror that the face was absolutely devoid of anything characteristic and was as smooth and round as a balloon. He waited to see if the apparition would rise again, searching in his mind to identify the strange shape. And there it came again, as smooth as before, as mystifying and as hasty to descend. Deciding to take matters in his own hands, and finding a box nearby, he placed it under the window, and raised himself up. Not three inches from his nose, so close the tell-tale odor would have told him what he wanted to know, were it not that his eyes saw enough; the beautiful buttocks of Wilma von Spratten Olaf-Pinz hove up again and went flying down the long, spike-like prick of Silas Cisterne, her singing-master. All about the floor lay abandoned sheets of music, and Silas, in their midst, lay rudely pinned by his pupil's robust arms, suffering his enforced copulation with as much forbearing as he could muster. Prince Pivo nearly laughed aloud at the horrible grimace on the master's face.

A voice sounded from a corner of the room, a high bombastic

voice, somewhat nasal in quality. The startled Prince made out the familiar features of Harmon Heath, the great Shakespearean actor and notorious pederast, astride the piano stool with his bare feet in his fall trousers and his hairy thighs partially obscured by flower-print drawers. His cock was erect, its blubbery head deep in his soft palm, and while he intoned his well-known lines, he caressed the obscene phallus with long, leisurely strokes.

> "Sweet Phoebe, do not scorn me;
> do not, Phoebe:
> Say that you love me not;
> but say not so in bitterness . . ."

He addressed his cock as if it were a personage in the play, sometimes frowning severely, sometimes his face a mask of pain, and all the while he spoke he played with the swollen tip, pointing it at the harassed music-master in ill-disguised disappointment. The rude-natured girl had deprived him of his old friend's services, but he dared not intervene after having seen her extraordinary strength redoubled by her violent passion.

The Prince was later to learn that Wilma, the girl in question, had surprised her teacher in company with the actor when both of them had their trousers down to their ankles. She had bounded with the speed of an antelope on the unsuspecting Silas whose encumbered legs helped her lascivious designs. The Prince scratched his head at the spectacle in the pavilion and stepped down from the box. Wilma's lovely and energetic behind had aroused his own volatile nature and he strode away from the pavilion with a growing muscle between his legs.

He walked by the front entrance once more. Even before he came abreast of the steps he saw the door was open but not a soul was in sight. The golden chandelier that hung in the hallway shone in a hundred shades of orange and yellow from the brilliant light out of doors. The Prince stood awhile at the foot of the steps but not even a stray butler came to the door which would have been sufficient pretext for his entry. Shrugging his shoulders contemptuously, he went part way round the house and headed for the stables where the Baroness' magnificent thoroughbreds were housed.

He had set his mind on a lively canter in the park to distract him, yet the persistent image of Wilma's ass affected him more and more, and when he entered the sweet-smelling enclosure, where the stamping and snorting animals were taking that nervous repose common to their kind, he nearly turned back, debating a plan to trap the girl.

A mare whinnied, whether from fright or nervousness he could not tell, but a suspicious scrambling sound of human footsteps gave him the clue, and opening the door of her stall he discovered the redcoated groom hurriedly buttoning his pants.

"Ho, ho," cried the Prince, catching the trembling youth by his collar, "what have we here? A fine piece of horse-play. So this is why Colleen 2nd has lost every race in the last six months!"

"No, Sire, it wasn't I, believe me. I had nothing to do with her before. Honest, I swear it."

"Haven't I just now caught you buggering the poor beast with your common cock? Hey, now?"

"But Sire, this was the first time. I'll never do it again if you let me go. Please, don't tell them. I'll never live it down."

The Prince let go of his collar and studied the long wavy fronds of the animal's cunt.

"This is ridiculous," he protested. "Fucking a horse! A man might as well put his cock in a vatful of cream."

Reassured that he would suffer no harm at the Prince's hand, the groom straightened but hesitated to answer the Prince. He watched him place his hand over the mare's sex, comparing its length and breadth and whistling in amazement.

"Why, boy, tell me something. What possible pleasure can you get from her? You would do better to go after the cook. Stay away from horses. You will only ruin your chances with women."

The groom did not answer him. He seemed to be turning something over in his mind and then, without warning, in a gesture full of pride, he boldly tore open his fly and dragged forth a prick that would suit a stallion to a T.

Prince Pivo ceased his remonstration, frankly overwhelmed at the evidence, amazed at the groom who stood with his legs apart to let the long and cumbersome weapon dangle about his knees. The lad had produced the most convincing argument in favor of his tastes and Prince Pivo felt somewhat humbled, even ridiculed, before the fantastic organ.

"How did it happen?" he asked finally, in a voice that was full of respect. "Were you always hung like that?"

"No Sire, it's a disease. My father took me to all kinds of specialists but they haven't been able to cure me."

He went on to explain the shame he had felt and how he was afraid he would have to go through life deformed and banned from society. But the Prince was less interested in the boy's personal woes than in seeing that horrendous object in action. He interrupted the groom and asked him if he could get it hard. He said he certainly could.

"Then do so," ordered the Prince.

The groom picked up the head of his club in both hands and began masturbating, beating it against the smooth flanks of the mare. She whinnied apprehensively and turned her sad eyes on her lover. Bit by bit the violet-colored skin began to stretch and dilate, filling out into its true proportions.

When it came fully erect the Prince was no longer sure that even the mare was capable of containing such a cock.

"You might as well put it into her," he said, "just for curiosity," remembering that he had chided the boy but a moment ago for that very thing.

The groom needed no urging, now that he had himself back to his passionate state with official approbation to boot. He braced himself on the side of the stall, where a sort of shelving had been installed for this purpose, and swung himself into position before the twitching tail of the mare. He did not trouble to lift it out of his way but placed his violet-veined organ through the horsehair and, with one sudden shove which called for all his strength, he drove the ramrod through her cunt in one long even movement, which nearly buckled the outspread legs of the animal. The mare lifted her head skyward, emitted a penetrating squeal of pain and pleasure ending in a dying whinny which turned the stable into a clamor and racket of answering cries.

The Prince, his ears ringing in the bedlam, watched the prodigious penis slicing in and out of the mare like some greasy piston pumping a machine of flesh. The lubricious odor that emanated from the slobbering hole soon whipped the nostrils of the stallions into a frenzy of lust. Their own black-sheathed cocks pulsated with mounting passion. A ferocious stench filled the air, a biting odor that pinched Prince Pivo's nostrils.

"Do they always get so heated up when you fuck the mare?" shouted Pivo, trying to make himself heard above the din. For a moment he had the impression that he was in the center of a foundry where a ceaseless roar and hammering accompanied the flashing flames of a furnace, white molten metal poured from a ladle, while busy black gnomes ran scurrying in the heat, screaming insanely as if they were the keepers of hell.

The long, churning prick delved in faster and faster, drawing forth the escaping mucus of the bestial vagina. The mare reared back, wobbling her dripping flanks from side to side as though there were not yet enough of that prick boring into her carcass. The groom, for his part, was rapidly working to orgasm, slamming his belly like a madman, oblivious of the ear-shattering chaos about him. He turned once in his labors, and a fleeting grin transmitted his thrill of pride and power.

It was inevitable that when the mare gave out the final cry of her spending orgasm that the sex-crazed stallions should no longer hold out, and in a demoniac concert their flying hooves shattered the wooden stalls and they burst from the stable in a galloping mass of flaming nostrils, satanic eyeballs and huge erections. Full in their midst and clinging for his life to the mare in whose cunt he was still embedded rode the terrified groom, his pride a forgotten thing as he went by the door, red pants trailing in the wind like an inglorious standard.

Prince Pivo descended from the rafter where he had leaped to safety and regarded the stampeding herd already a half-mile away on the rolling green like a tornado sweeping across the plains. It took him some time to recover his aplomb and he retraced his steps to the entrance still shaken from the harrowing spectacle.

A woman ran up the steps as he rounded the corner, holding her scarlet gown high in the air. Her hair was hidden in a lavish, powdered wig adorned with a purple plume, and her features covered by a mask. Pivo saw her long black stockings and at the last step she picked her skirts up higher, revealing an exciting portion of white thighs. The panther-like eyes behind the mask seemed to gleam provokingly at him, and she bent down and removed a ribboned garter from her leg. It struck him in the eyes as she escaped into the house, a high, trailing laugh echoing in her wake. Pivo picked up the garter.

"'Tis folly," he accused himself, dashing up the stairs three at a time, "pure folly!"

The Watcher and the Watched

Thomas Peachum

*T*he avowed and highly publicized object of the four-year program at Westwood Military School was the generation of leaders. "And the mark of a leader," Colonel Yardley had written in his Introduction to the *Catalogue,* "is success." No success, however limited, went unrewarded at Westwood. Medals were provided for Latin and piety, cleanliness and swimming, swordsmanship and deportment. A brass garland surrounding the face of a clock and titled in the *Catalogue* "The Promptitude Medal" was awarded for being consistently on time. On Sunday morning, when the cadets formed for parade, the sunshine glittered on the variety of polished metal, a brilliance that began at the tip of the sword, raced from button to button up the regulation jacket and detonated in the last glinting of the Westwood vizor with its golden M (for Manliness) engraved squarely in the center.

Manhood was progressive at Westwood, acquired in a series of stages. The last of these, so difficult as to be considered by the majority of cadets as insurmountable, was admission to membership in the football squad. To this honor all aspired; it was attained by no more than the talented few. These few gathered to themselves the whole of that accumulated prestige of the school which had accrued over its near half-century of existence. Four exhaustive months of combat on the preparation for the battle of life which is the playing-field were recompensed at their conclusion by the Football Medal, the unusual size and impressive aspect of which were the pride of all fortunate enough to have the right of wearing it. Cast in the form of a W with a tiny football in the center, it was reputed among the cadets to contain a high percentage of true silver. That reputation was the butt of a certain scepticism among the more enlightened members of the squad, and it was not allowed to pass without criticism.

Ned Bailey, known among his classmates for his wit, suggested one afternoon to his chum and teammate, Wilfred Watson, that they test out the medal's reputation by a real experiment, laboratory and all. Why not, he inquired, melt the medal down into its components to find out what these were?

"Melt one of them down? But which one? Not my medal, at any rate."

Wilfred refused to allow anyone, friend or stranger, to take advantage of him. He was in that regard, particularly suspicious of Ned, whose intelligence seemed specially designed to trap the unwary. It was not the first time that Ned had emerged with a wild suggestion, but Wilfred was among those who learn from experience.

"Now, Will, don't jump to conclusions. I'd melt mine down in a minute, but Dad's so proud of it that he wants to take it home with him and lock it in the family vault. What can I do?"

"I don't know, but you're sure not going to get your hands on my medal."

Wilfred shook his head vigorously from side to side. Three years of comradeship had taught him the wisdom of stubbornness in the midst of uncertainty; the only way to prevent Ned from obtaining what he had in mind was to avoid listening, to remain as obstinate at the end of a conversation as he had been at the beginning.

"Here's the way I figure it, Willie. What we'll do is going to be in the interests of science. Melting it down won't really change it."

The Law of the Conservation of Matter. Ned believed in turning his theoretical knowledge to immediate practical use.

"If melting won't change it, I'd sure like to know what will. Now listen, Ned, if you want to melt your own medal down, I'll help you all I can, but you might as well forget about the one I'm wearing. During the day I'm keeping it right here, pinned on my chest, and when I go to bed at night, I'll put it under my pillow where you can't get at it."

"Willie, I know the guy that makes these. He turns them out by the dozens. You don't think they're made up special, one for each of us, do you? Here's what we'll do. We'll melt your medal down, because I don't have mine with me, and when we figure out what it's made of, we'll take the metal right back to the jeweler, who'll make you up a new one from it.

"We'll split the cost," Ned added, watching with satisfaction the doubt slowly clear away from Wilfred's face.

Wilfred's agreement after more or less intense persuasion was the usual outcome of their conversations, and so it happened then. The afternoon following, they waited in Chemistry laboratory until the other cadets had left; when safely alone, they dropped Wilfred's medal in the waiting crucible. Placing it over the bunsen burner, they watched, fascinated, while the shiny metal grew dull, softened, then spewed diffusely over the concave bottom of the pan. A moment later, the bunsen burner extinguished, Wilfred held up to view with a pair of tongs a shapeless mass of metal, streaked and ugly. He looked reproachfully at Ned.

"I guess it's lead, like the rest of them," he muttered softly.

"There was silver on the outside."

"You go to hell."

The next few weeks were a time of voluntary poverty, painfully accumulating the wherewithal to replace Wilfred's loss. Then, on a free weekend in town, they happened upon a willing jeweler who had the medal in stock, and Wilfred emerged, satisfied, through the swinging door, the shiny W with its football swaying to and fro upon his chest. Wilfred, once in the street, reflected on Ned's daring, Ned's loyalty. A real pal. His suggestions were crazy – that you had to admit – but he'd always give in, Wilfred would, to the bright prospects that Ned painted for him. When the disaster came, Ned always stood by him: they had always managed to squeeze out of it, and always together. A real pal.

It was unthinkable to be seen on school premises without the football medal, after it had been awarded. Wearing it meant unending prestige; not wearing it, when one had the right, was a particularly objectionable form of moral nakedness. The requirements which had to be met before the medal could be awarded were quite as stringently ethical as they were athletic. The cadet was to give evident signs of "the spirit of sportsmanship"; his marks must have placed him in the top third of his class for at least the two preceding years; his conduct had to be wholesome, "becoming to a young man," during his early years at Westwood. The elevated language in which these requirements had been set was, like the Introduction, due to the care of Colonel Yardley. In small print, on a back page, the measure of security had been added that the weight of the cadet in question had to be well over a hundred and sixty pounds. Occasionally, during the long history of the school, the requirement in small print had been known, when met, to sweep the others before it, though only in times of dearth, when the members of successive incoming classes had been unusually small in size. Ned and Wilfred, husky youngsters, easily fulfilled the small print and came quite close to realizing the standards of morality that had been set as well.

Ned, like any young man, had perhaps from time to time been guilty of small peccadillos, but without importance and which passed quite unremarked.

"Hey, Willie, have a look at these!"

Ned and Wilfred had been assigned lockers in the corner of the gymnasium basement. After a spring session of hard practice, Ned pulled from his jacket a folder containing a greasy bundle of snapshots. He looked furtively about to see that no one was watching and tugged impatiently at the sleeve of Wilfred's sweatshirt.

"Ever see anything like these before?"

"I don't want to look at them."

Wilfred, by simply glancing, had already noticed enough. He wanted to look no further. There were things one wasn't supposed to do. Not ever.

"You don't want to see them!" Ned was dumbfounded. "Look

here, Willie boy, here you've got the real thing, right before your eyes, and you tell me you don't want to look at it. What's the matter with you?"

"Nothing, Ned; you know I never like to look at that sort of thing. What would my folks say? Besides, coach told us that the wrong kind of thoughts would ruin our health."

"What do you think of this one?"

Ned knew the value of pretending not to hear. The best way was just to keep fluttering the photographs beneath Wilfred's nose, undiscouraged and insistent. Willie would look soon enough.

"You . . . you really think it's like that, Ned?"

Wilfred noticed that his mouth was wet, and he wiped the back of his sweatshirt across his face. The wiping failed to help, and he tried pressing his lips close together. He stared at the photograph. He turned his body away from Ned, wondering how he was going to be able to change out of his football togs into his school uniform. He should, he realized, never have wavered from his original resolution not to look.

"Well, here's the proof. What more could you ask? Pictures don't lie, you know."

Ned snorted scornfully. How could anyone be such a kid!

"I wonder how long it'll be before we get to try something like that," Wilfred was wistful.

"Why, we could try it tomorrow night, if only you weren't such a sissy. Everybody does it, you know. We're not babies any more. There's a place in town . . ."

Ned saw Wilfred shake his head again, knew that this time it was useless to persist. It was the one subject on which there was nothing to be done; persuasion was so much wasted breath. Once, they had been on the doorstep, the ladies leaning out and waving to them, and what had Willie done? He had turned around; he had run as fast as his legs could carry him in the opposite direction. Ned had decided that there was nothing to be done about it, and he wasn't willing to try the thing alone.

"All right. I don't want to push you into anything."

Ned put the pictures carefully back into his pocket and began to pile his equipment in the locker. As he shut the door, he noticed that Wilfred had not moved, was still holding his sweatshirt in one hand and wiping his forehead aimlessly with the other.

"Changing your mind, Willie?"

"No. I was just thinking about the dance we've been invited to, the one at Miss Byfield's Academy a couple of weeks from now," he paused uneasily, "wouldn't it be great if we could do something like that then? I mean with a real girl and not with one of those . . . others. I don't want to come away my very first time and be sick afterwards. Besides, the girls at Miss Byfield's are supposed to be pretty fast."

"You'll have a fat chance, you will," Ned laughed at him, tapping his knuckles impatiently against the metal locker door. "Miss Byfield is all over the joint there. You just try to move a couple of yards outside the door with a girl on your arm, and there she is in front of you, pushing you back in. The girls could be fast like lightning, but where are you going to do it? On the dance floor?"

He started walking away, shaking his head disgustedly.

"Still, we've got our nights free now. Maybe we could meet them later."

"Fat chance," Ned called back over his shoulder.

What chance there might be belonged to the football team, for the football team occupied the domain, strictly limited at West-wood, of special privilege. Each member of the squad had free passage on the stone walks separating the school buildings, the other cadets having to scurry hastily out of the way onto the lawn, or flat against a neighboring wall. On "free" weekends, like the one planned for the Byfield Spring Promenade, the team had unlimited hours and could come to bed whenever the members chose. They were on the honor system. The other cadets, who were not, underwent a strict bed check at one in the morning.

The conspicuous advantage of membership on the team was, however, the football bus, specially provided and at their disposition throughout the school year. In the autumn, it carried them to the scattered playing-fields of the Eastern coast. In the winter, it rumbled over snowy Vermont highways for two weeks of skiing at the school's expense, to keep their legs in shape. And in the last few weeks of spring, it drove them over black and sweltering asphalt pavements to their just reward, the Spring Promenade, given at one or another of the select girls' schools dispersed in the neighborhood of Westwood. The destination of the bus during the year in question was, of course, the Byfield Academy, hardly forty miles away from their own school.

The Saturday afternoon of the promenade was prematurely warm. The scarlet words THE TEAM, painted on the side of the bus, were cracking in the sun's heat while, inside, Ned and Wilfred loosened uncomfortably their collars, removed their caps with the metallic vizors, and suffered wordlessly in the heat. Theirs was the first in a column of buses; the team occupied, even on the highway, the place of priority. Ned and Wilfred themselves were seated on the throne of prestige of the first bus, a dais just to the right of the driver, reserved each year for the next year's captain and his star player. Over their heads, swinging monotonously with the weaving motion of the bus, hung a placard with the words, "WESTWOOD'S HEROES," printed in bold letters upon it. The window next to them was, for comfort's sake, opened wide, and Wilfred was forced from time to time to wipe the flecks of road dust, thrown up by the bus's wheels, from his spotless dress blue coat. He flicked the dust away with his forefinger, disdainfully. He was proud.

"I hope we have a chance to brush off our uniforms before the girls see us. We've got to be neat. We're going to have a big responsibility down there, you know that?"

Wilfred watched, out of the corner of his eye, the placard rock to and fro on its hinges above his head.

"You're right, Will boy; as far as Byfield is concerned, the two of us represent Westwood. In fact," his voice lowered, "the truth of the matter is that we are Westwood. That's all there is to it."

Ned leaned back. A drop of perspiration emerged on his forehead, trickled down his cheek, hovered doubtfully a moment on his chin and dropped noiselessly between them. Ned watched it fall with scorn.

"You know, Ned, we've been pretty lucky, making the team and all that."

Wilfred was solemn, carefully polishing his medals. He spat on them, wiped them with his handkerchief, observed how the dull metal gleamed back at him as he rubbed it.

"Luck wasn't all of it," Ned objected, "anyhow, the best's to come. We're going to have the pick of the lot down there. Colonel Yardley's fixed it so that we're escorting the two girls who run the social committee. They're supposed to be a couple of knockouts."

A girl clothed in cloudy white, small and airy, would stare admiringly at his medals. He would tell her what they meant.

"Maybe . . . maybe it'll be this weekend, Ned. Do you think it might be like what we saw? In the photographs, I mean?"

"It'd be better. There wouldn't be anybody around taking pictures, for one thing. But, don't you worry, there's not a chance. Not a chance."

"Well, at any rate, they'll be wearing costumes like in the photographs. That ought to be really something. Maybe mine'll be wearing a bathing suit, and I'll get to dance with her like that."

Ned looked at him in surprise, scoffing.

"You don't know Miss Byfield. Oh, they'll be wearing costumes, all right. They'll have skirts on made of stuff so thick the girl underneath could have a wooden leg and still you couldn't tell. Buttoned right up to the neck, those girls. If you'd listen to me for a minute, we'll get out of there as soon as we can. The only place to find what we're looking for is in town."

Wilfred was silent, lips tight together, head shaking in a wordless unmovable no. His opinions on the matter had not changed. Ned looked towards him with displeasure, grinned wryly, turned his head to examine the ribbon of asphalt that shimmered away in front of them.

"I can't see a thing. I guess that mirror was never meant for trying on costumes."

Jill moaned with dismay. Only a week till the ball, and everything seemed to conspire against her getting her costume just the way she wanted it. Miss Byfield was against anything that might lead to vanity among her pupils; the mirror had been carefully planned to answer to the needs of cleanliness and to those needs alone. It was terribly small. In it, a girl was to be aware of her body as the object of regular applications of soap and water, part by part. The body was automatically dismembered. When Jill had her feet on the floor, she was able to see no more than the upper part of her chest and her face to the top of her forehead. To do her hair, she had to crouch; to examine the hem of her dress, the fit of her stocking, she had to climb onto the bed. Wrapping the white linen gauze over her abdomen, bringing it up again to the small of her back, she scrambled on the bed, her dainty ballet slippers bouncing softly on the springs. It was all very unsatisfactory.

Toni hated to interfere after all that had been said, but Jill really seemed to go too far sometimes. She turned back to her own work, cutting out the pattern of brown muslin that was to make her a gipsy.

"With mine, it's lots easier. It's muslin, and you can't see through muslin no matter how hard you look."

"There. I guess that's about right."

She tightened the strip of linen so that it formed a deep V at the base of her belly, leaving her hips quite nearly free. The linen almost tore as she moved hectically back and forth over the bed, trying to get a decent view of herself.

"You are going to wear something under it, aren't you, Jill, dear?"

Toni was hesitant and shocked.

"I wish I didn't have to! Don't you think our cadets will like me dressed this way? Not to mention Mr. Hopkins. He'd be delighted."

Jill pouted. However convinced Toni might make herself out to be, when it came down to the details, Jill had to begin each time all over again. It would be such fun, what they had planned, if only Toni wouldn't go and ruin it by getting scared. Jill posed in front of the mirror, advancing one leg before the other while she arranged her hair. She wished Hopkins were there.

"How do I look?"

"You know perfectly well how you look. Jill, you can't get away with it; come down from there and put something on underneath."

"I suppose you're right. But not underneath, please."

Kneeling down on the bed, she took a strip of gauze from the pile of linen beside her and wrapped it around her. She looked in the mirror, gathered that the color of her skin was more than sufficiently concealed.

"That better?"

"Much."

Taking the rough cloth, she folded it over herself, carefully pinning it up along the seam. The dress had no shoulder straps, and she found it hard to keep the line about her bosom as modest as she would have liked. So little practice as a seamstress! It was beginning to show. She walked slowly over to the mirror.

"You couldn't be prettier," Jill admired, "I like the way you've cut the line along the bottom of the hem. The pieces flutter so! Now you see it now you don't. Talk about me!"

"Do you think . . . do you think Hopkins is going to like us?" Toni felt herself blush.

"I hope so."

She watched Toni bend towards the mirror, take her dark hair between her hands and bring it over one shoulder where it tumbled softly against the top of her costume. She noticed Toni's blush.

"Don't worry about it, Toni. He'll like us well enough. Maybe a little too well."

The clock ticked languidly away the hours of an afternoon Masefield Hopkins found it impossible to fill. The revival, one after another, of all the little time-killers with which a life of killing time had endowed him gave, on this occasion, no benefit. His desk was dotted, length and breadth, with balls of crumpled paper; each crumpled sheet would have shown, when unfolded, the same desperate doodles, the same unfinished curving pencilled line. He had made no attempt to see the girls in the days that had intervened, had avoided anything that might seem to them like pressure. The smallest show of hidden violence would mean, he knew, the ruin of his plans, and the time was not so long to wait. The last hours of waiting were naturally unbearable; he had expected as much. The camera was ready; he had exchanged certain crucial light bulbs for ones of higher wattage; he heard them knock at the door with something like relief. Their complicity, he realized, was not to be obtained with words alone.

Their complicity: they entered his office with their costumes dangling over their arms, wafted on the slight breath of spring air that accompanied them. The weightless white linen, the heavy muslin, billowed behind them; he explained that they would have to lock the door. They locked the door. He described the reasons that lay beneath the need he felt, the special need, the need for them to change into their costumes — he would photograph them in their costumes — to change there, in his office, before his eyes. Jill swirled her skirt about her calves when she turned to lock the door behind them. She was serene. Toni was quiet. His voice low, he expatiated the causes why the bedroom behind his back could not be used, he not being in the bedroom but in the study, not the bedroom but rather the study, where they would undress, together, each aiding the other, where he could see them.

"I'm sure your costumes are becoming," he added.

The difficulty with having chosen the afternoon lay in the presence of a multitude of outside sounds, irrelevant, distracting. There were voices from outside, voices of other girls who were unembroiled. He thought Jill's manner as she undid the top button — no more than that, merely the top button — of her school blouse, as she untied the yellow scarf smartly knotted about her neck, the manner was, as he thought of it, provoking. The day hung long, unending between him and the two girls in front of him, perhaps also between the girls themselves apart from him; in the small space of his academic study the day, the space of an afternoon, hovered lengthily. He heard his watch ticking on his wrist. They would have to undress in his study. Did they understand?

"Yes," Jill said.

Toni said nothing.

He was so nervous he perspired coldly in spite of the precocious warmth of an unexpectedly early spring. The way the cool droplets flowed down the dry sides of his body, he might have been as young as they. He was as young as they. Toni was not given to speech, willing (as she was) to follow the example of the more authoritative blonde girl on her left. Toni, who seemed less fragile with her dark skin, was more fragile; Jill, so exceedingly light, belied her lightness, spoke with one voice for the two of them. He did not quite know how to proceed, seated behind his desk. He considered the apparent contradiction between Jill's complexion and her personality. He considered the apparent contradiction between Toni's complexion and her personality. He wished the girls would speak more often, at greater length.

He walked to the window, pulled down the shade, blocked the incoming sunshine. In the shadow he saw no more of their faces, of their expression, than he intended to see, though capable in the half-light of seeing all if he so wished. He was delighted when the one girl, Jill, suggested that she undress the other girl, Toni. It had not occurred to him, not that in particular, but once made, the suggestion struck him as excellent.

"Splendid suggestion," he said.

"And I'll help Jill."

"Splendid," he said.

That was settled, at least. He lit the lamp on his desk, turning the reflector so that it shone on them, with a certain crudeness. He was not so much in favor of artificial light during the day from the point of view of good taste as from that of controlling the source of illumination. He was in shadow, they in light. He was hidden, they revealed. Sunshine seemed to him coarsely ubiquitous. He had no power to regulate the sun. He suggested they hand him their clothing, garment by garment, justifying this measure on grounds of neatness, since there would be two quite separate piles of folded clothing, and on grounds of proprietorship, since the always possible exchange of garments, Jill wearing Toni's or Toni Jill's, would thus be so easily avoided. He enjoyed the sensation of other person's undersilk against his palm, but this reason remained unexpressed. They were willing, indulging him. The warm day led him, even before they had begun, to unbutton his shirt half the distance down his chest. He had been proud when the hair had first appeared, so many years ago. He was proud still. He took a deep breath of satisfaction, expanding his chest, glancing furtively to see whether they were noticing. They noticed. He exhaled.

He had not expected them to agree so easily to the changing of costume in his office.

Had they rehearsed? From what he saw, from what he heard, he would have guessed they had rehearsed. Toni hardly dared to look at Jill, her eyes quite nearly closed, the lashes shut like blinds, hardly dared to see her friend when she asked her to come and help. To come over close and help. Toni had forgotten how to take the things off all alone. She needed help with all her fumbling fingers and her youth.

"Come take off my stockings."

Toni must have whispered because she was unwilling he should hear. He heard her; the whisper brought him leaning forward in his chair, leaning obliquely over the desk, the desk edge pressing pointedly into his belly. He thought it best to remain behind the desk where he could guard the small protective distance lying between the two girls and himself. When Jill walked to where Toni was standing, when she knelt before Toni, the shadows merged. They were near enough to the source of light upon the desk, near enough to cast long shadows toward the door. The shadows came together long before.

"The garters aren't very easy."

Jill fumbled so; they were easy enough for Toni. Toni hadn't been undressed by someone else since she was tiny. They had been proud of her because she learned so quickly, even the shoelaces. Toni was glad she had worn stockings because it drew things out so, even when she did her best to help. She put her hands to the flutter in her skirt where it fell, just below the knee; she grasped the hem. Should she bring up her skirt? He was watching! But how could she help Jill without bringing up her skirt? She turned away from him so that she did not have to see how hard he looked, and she drew up her skirt, slowly, shyly. From the corner of her eye she saw him bend, bend forward where he would have a better view. He was watching! She would be careful not to pull up her skirt any higher than she had to, just high enough for Jill to reach the garters. Jill's hands were touching her again. Jill was busy with the clasps. Toni watched the kneeling girl undo the clasps; it was so very different when there was someone else. That was what it was like to be older, to dare to be daring. There would sometimes be someone else. She could tell by his staring how impatient he was. He was a man, of course; he couldn't know that garters didn't just undo themselves, that Jill had to slide the stocking down, that a girl was complicated, more complicated than a boy. Toni let her skirt fall when Jill had taken the stocking from her leg.

"Go on!"

"Be a little patient."

That was what it was like to have a friend as close as Jill. Jill wouldn't let him hurry them, no matter how loudly he shouted. The other stocking would be easier, and Toni would let her do it all herself. She began to arrange her hair, paying no attention to what Jill was about. It was enough to feel the other hands, not one's own, undoing, unclasping, the touch of other hands. Toni liked to go barelegged, barefooted, wading with a boy or all alone and naked in the water. Soon Jill would strip her naked as though he weren't there at all. She was glad he was there. Jill shouldn't have stroked her like that; it made her feel funny, like before, and it was terribly indecent when there was someone else one hardly knew. Toni wondered whether maybe she wasn't already just a little damp. It was so exciting, once one's mind was made up! Jill was always right. It was such fun. He had said that they would only be young once. He piled up the stocking on his desk as though he wanted to make a collection of them. Masefield Hopkins: he had a funny name. She looked at him demurely. How could one ever be ashamed in front of someone like that? Like Daddy, but exciting, and Daddy would never guess. Now that Jill was done, Toni didn't want to let her skirt fall a second time, didn't want to hide what he seemed to want to see. It would disappoint him too much. She knew what was needed; carefully she tied her skirt behind her waist so that it fell in a shallow drape about the front of her, just hiding the underwear, the silly cotton, but nothing else. Like in the shows, she knew; that was the way they draped themselves in the shows. Except that in the shows they hadn't anything at all on underneath, just a fake paper rose or something. Later she would be like that. Jill had been right about being patient; it was better that way. The way he stared! She turned towards him, half towards him, pouted at him for staring so much. She was glad her legs were slender; otherwise he wouldn't have wanted to look at her. Immodestly she moved, hardly moved, to and fro in front of him, her feet still. That was what he wanted. She saw how you could tell what it was they wanted. Such a warm afternoon!

"Your turn now, Toni. Help me out of my dress."

Jill could hardly accuse her of laxity in learning. Toni reeked of being seen; her mincing walk from where she stood to Jill was enough to prove what she had learned. Jill was very nearly jealous. If Toni had not been so sweet, so dark and so sweet, Jill thought she might have been angry. As it was, anger was farthest from her mind when she stroked the dark hair that fell from the bent, busy head which directed the fingers unbuttoning her dress. Later was when it would count. Later she would show Hopkins what she was really worth. Jill knew how to take a dare, what a dare involved. She tossed her head, wriggled her shoulders out of the dress. Later, for you couldn't learn boldness all at once. Oh, she knew how pretty her shoulders were, and she had chosen the brassiere with care; it was the one she had bought downtown quite on her own with the money she had saved. The one that didn't really hide anything. At least, he was man enough to notice.

Toni seemed afraid to touch her, but no one could undress without touching. Jill had touched. Jill refused to put a hand to her dress; it was up to Toni to pull it off her. She hoped he noticed how afraid Toni was. As though there was something wrong in touching!

That was what they were there for, for touching and for being touched. She wanted, just for a joke, to run her finger down the hairy line that ran along his chest. That would surprise him. Later, perhaps. The dress stuck. Jill began to squirm to loosen herself from her dress. Toni had to touch her then. Jill made her body rock, rocking the dress down her hips. Toni had to clutch her tightly or Jill would get away. Jill was the sly one. Stepping out of her dress, she caught the sleeve with the tip of her slipper and kicked it towards him. He would catch it if he could, to add to the pile beside him. She watched him catch it with satisfaction. Her hand on Toni's head, supporting herself, she left her foot in the air after she had kicked away the dress, left it in the air, arched and pointing towards him. Three years of modern dance could be put to use. She wondered if he could notice how gracefully she had bent her leg, with his eyes where they were. Too delicate a thing to mention. You could really see through all of it if you only looked hard enough, and she knew she could count on him for looking.

"Can you pivot all the way around like that?"

Did she have to dance as well? Older men were worse with blondes.

"I can, if Toni holds my arm."

They had rehearsed. They were corrupt, early in the morning corrupt before the hour of corruption had been given a decent time to strike. He had only to ask, and the answer would come before the question had reached its end. He clapped his hands (a manner of speaking, they being his pupils during the everyday hours) and the dancer danced. How thoughtful of her to have worn ballet slippers, bound about her foot and about her leg with laces to the knee. The satin slippers shone delicately against her light ankles. Her dancing showed practice. Had she danced before with Toni's aid? The graceful ease with which she bent her body, arched her toe upon the carpet, how she touched Toni as though not needing to be sustained by her: the results of practice, rehearsal, of having lived, girl with girl, in confinement. He considered the underthings, revolving as the girl turned, considered them as dainty. To be so young a girl was to be fragile. Their legs glimmered, bare. He could have eaten them. He had chosen well to stay behind his desk. He preferred them half-dressed, forgot what they were with clothing, proper, everyday. They knew he looked; he saw them bend toward each other with the knowledge. There was time. He was no tyrant in that cold climate, though the sun that afternoon was warm enough. A tropical spring — unusual for the latitude. The voices outside had ceased.

"Well done. I hadn't guessed you were a dancer."

He had almost said "as well."

"Go on. Toni's skirt. Toni's blouse. Go on."

That unbearable commanding voice of men in middle-age. Jill would proceed as she liked, at her own rate.

"Handle me carefully, please, Jill."

She would handle her as she saw fit to do. Toni wanted to be handled, eager. Jill knew her for her eagerness. The little devil had complicated the knot; no one had forced her to tie her dress behind her. Flirt! Earlier in the day, it was Toni who had condemned Jill for her immodesty. Jill would know in future who was who. The knot came undone. Jill pulled the dress down the other girl's thighs, pulled it angrily down to her ankles. Toni's hair was enviously black, Toni always arranging it just as though Jill weren't there, Jill a servant girl, a proper pert blonde lady's maid. Toni pretending not to know she was half-naked, that Jill was stripping her; how silly to pretend. Jill handed the empty dress to his waiting hand. They owned her, Toni; Jill and Hopkins owned her. Jill knew how to make possession good.

"Now, please, my blouse, please Jill."

Although her eyes were opened, lashes high, Toni felt languorous and sleepy. It was so nice being waited on; one had nothing to do but enjoy the warm air that brushed, instead of clothes, against you. What did it matter what he saw, or if he saw? Being seen was part of being sleepy, touched in her drowsiness. Her lips were moist, she knew, and shining, her eyes shining. From time to time she added moisture to her lips with the tip of her tongue. Her high-necked blouse, lacking the skirt to hold it, billowed about her, wrapped about her just at the thighs. And there were so many buttons it would take Jill ages to undo them all. There was no hurry.

"Slowly."

Otherwise a button might tear loose, and there'd be all the trouble of having to sew it on again later, if there was a later. Toni would help as much as she could. She loosened the cuffs with concentration. Cuffs loose, buttons undone, she slipped the blouse from her shoulders, held it an instant before it fell, let it fall. Perhaps she should have worn something under it as Jill had done? But she was proud nothing was necessary. They were pretty unsustained and free. She left them free except in winter when it was much too cold. She brought her hair forward over her shoulder, tressing it in a cascade across her shoulder. There was so little left to do! She looked down shyly at herself, and with surprise; so little left to do. It was different being nude, or nearly so, when there were others. She would do the same for Jill who had been perfect undressing her, daintily, discretely, with many pauses. The least she could do was to return the favor. It was not as though he didn't appreciate it; the briefest glance told her how much he enjoyed, bent forward, his eyes glittering. Toni undid the clasp that held the band stretched across Jill's back. That was all there was to it. A little movement of the shoulders and the thing came away of itself. They were just alike now, Jill's pale skin, her own dark, just alike and pretty as pictures.

With hesitation, tenderly, Toni touched the cotton waistband which remained, which was all that remained, to cover Jill. It was not the moment to offend, to frighten, by too quick a gesture. She slipped a forefinger, one on each side of the elastic, between the band and the skin beneath it. The elastic stretched over her fingers, giving slightly. Jill wore the band so tightly it was a wonder that it left no mark, but Toni noticed as she began to pull the cotton downwards that the elastic had, in fact, departed without a trace. She was careful barely to touch, the elastic distended, distant, but barely any touch was needed. Jill trembled. Toni had not felt her tremble before, when they had been alone. The trembling was something new. Jill was afraid to watch what was being done to her — that was it — afraid to see, she moaned. Could the cotton stroke her so, descending? Toni wondered why the other girl moaned, for the sound made Toni shudder too. He was watching! Tentatively Toni touched her along the inner calf. Jill jumped as though she had never been caressed before, caressed accidentally, by another hand. Toni decided to be careful not to touch her again, at least not right away. Yet Jill seemed still aware of what she was doing! The way she offered that last remnant, fallen crumpled about her ankles, offered it dangling from the end of her toe. He took it, of course, added it to what was already there.

The piles of discarded girl clothing ascended gradually and neatly upon his desk. He had had to push the balls of paper out of the way, some of them tumbling soundlessly to the floor. He was unusually nervous, hence inattentive, letting the paper lie scattered where it would. It was certain they cared not for the paper which unregarded fell, but for him. They watched him, watched him watching them. Mirrors. He had no mirror in the room large enough to reflect them all, although later the photographs would supply the lack. There was, he reflected, no longer any reason to remain behind the desk; from a position carefully taken in front of the desk, no more than a slight extension of his arm would be needed to add the one last bit of clothing, belonging to Toni, to what already lay there. He moved before the desk, sat on the edge, one foot in the air, one foot on the floor. Jill, at long last bending slightly before him as he had endlessly waited for her to bend, unclothed quite as he had imagined her, Jill, he noticed, met his eyes. No shame in either of them, their glances met. Her eyes left his, wandered down. And to think that not so many weeks ago her nature could not have lent itself to looking there. She had changed, realized herself, looked there. He imagined from her enraptured gaze that there was much to see. How could she expect that to have passed which had passed before him without taking some notable effect, some effect visible despite the prudently pleated flannel? He would beseech them to begin again.

"There's still some little left to do. Look at Toni, Jill. Toni's not quite as you are, not yet. Take them off her. No hands, now."

"No hands?"

"No hands."

He was so demanding. Hands clasped behind her back, she could envisage no way but one to do as he had asked. He was taking advantage. If it was not the first time for him, it was for her. She pressed her hands worriedly together, behind her, where he could not see them. She bent over, hiding, looking at herself. He was her mirror, not reflecting her but what he felt because of her. That was even better, more mirrorlike. She knew what he meant about the hands. Would Toni bear it? The way Toni had behaved, she was sure to bear it. Toni had not said no. Jill would do something in front of him she would never dare before a mirror. The room was so dark, with the shade drawn, that it was like the night, since during the night in the darkness one could do anything because there was no one to say you had done it and no one to see. He was less than no one, darker than mere darkness. She knew what he meant about the hands. Toni would allow it to be slipped down her legs without any need to be brushed by a stray finger, a moist palm. Jill kneeled, one knee bending, the other stiff and straight behind her. If he wanted a picture, picture it would be.

Toni was far from certain what he meant; yet she felt ready, her body slightly bent over the kneeling Jill. She was sure Jill understood, and, indeed, Jill seemed so wise in all those matters. But Jill hesitated. There was no reason to hesitate if Jill really knew what to do. It was unexpected; stop. Jill had never kissed her there; that was not their friendship kiss. She wished Jill would stop. She wriggled, wishing Jill would stop. All she wanted was to be undressed, all the way, no more. Jill had to stop. Toni put her hands behind Jill's head, meaning to stop her, to push her away, but she found her hands doing quite the opposite of what she had wished. Bending over Jill, she bowed quite nearly double; the feeling was too deep to reach. How far she reached. Jill would never stop, her rough tongue reaching. Never, never, stop.

"Oh, stop. Oh my God!"

Toni had to shout to make her go on. There could never be enough of that. The tongue cut through her belly. She felt it cutting, making her body flex, tugging at her throat. She touched herself wonderingly. Was this she? Was someone doing this to her? She touched her throat with her hands, stroked herself below. She? Her hands wandered until they found the other girl's hidden head, until they wound themselves in her hair. She would press the mouth farther, farther, be devoured by the mouth. That was what hunger was when it wasn't she who hungered but she who was hungered for. Jill was taking the elastic between her teeth. No hands: that was what he meant. How he watched! Toni felt herself growing doubly naked, once for Jill, once for him. She thought she would fall. She felt herself swaying. That was why Jill had to put her arm about her thighs, to keep her from falling. The cotton rubbed as it went down. She felt the rubbing everywhere, afraid to look, her eyes closed, only the brush of cotton being slipped down while she was held. It was too much. Where was he? She groped with her hands in the darkness. Where was he? She wanted him. Opening her eyes just enough to see him, her arms outstretched, she pushed Jill out of the way with her knee and stepped forward. She had forgotten that her ankles were not yet free. Not yet free, her ankles, and she stumbled forward. It was an accident that she stumbled against him where he sat on the desk, grabbed at him for support.

The children! Naturally, so few years behind them, they were too easily carried away. He tried, unsuccessfully, to push the falling girl away from him. He would have done better to have remained behind the desk. She tumbled against him, kicking her ankles free.

"Toni! Be careful."

"No."

He could tell she was hysterical by the way she pawed for him. He slid himself backward along the top of the desk, but she scrambled after him, moaning wildly. There was no reasoning with them when they were in that state. He felt his shirt tear. They were too young to wear their nails so long. He couldn't fight the two of them off at once. When they were like that, there was nothing one could say. They had reached the buttons; he pleated himself like a crayfish; it did no good. Wherever he went, they followed. Ridiculous; he had given them no right. Oh.

"Stop it."

He had given them no right. They were on top of him, forcing him off the desk.

"Give it to me."

"It's mine."

"Stop it."

They fell sprawling from the desktop together, amid the papers, the paperweight bounding away across the floor, the desklamp on its side and shining toward the ceiling. From the neatly ordered piles, garments snowflaked down around them. He chose, later, not to remember what followed. The reconstruction was difficult, in any case. It had not lasted more than a few seconds before exhaustion set in, theirs being nervous, his being physical. They had invited it, of course. He had warned them. The afternoon had been planned for taking photographs. He wondered had they heard outside? There was no one outside; it was too late in the day. From the floor, in the light reflected from the ceiling, he noticed the patient camera untouched in the corner of the room.

"What about the photographs?"

They might have answered. He was more tired than they. On hands and knees, head bowed, he crawled behind the desk and hid there. In a moment, after what he considered a sufficient recovery of force, he gradually emerged, seating himself in his torn shirt, his mended trousers, his soaking tails, once again upon his academic chair. They sat blinking on the floor.

"What about the photographs?"

Evidently some explanation was necessary.

"Don't be disappointed. There'll be time for all that. I refused you today on purpose, not wanting to spoil anything for what's to come. You almost forgot about the Spring Promenade, about the summer house. Do have a little patience. Everything at once is worse than nothing at all. What about the photographs?"

Masefield Hopkins believed in persuasion. He had suffered more than they, if they did remain perhaps more nervous at the end. And they had had the sense to take off their clothes. His garments were, he felt, beyond repair.

"I shall never be able to teach in this suit again!"

If it was a reprimand, it was warranted under the circumstances.

"I'm sorry, Jill."

"I understand, Toni."

"Shall we get into our costumes?"

"I suppose so."

"There's a pair of sensible girls!"

They ignored him. He felt offended. He walked stiff-legged to the camera, put it in order. They borrowed a comb from him, evidently displeased at having to ask; to borrow, he was overjoyed to note, one had first to lend. And lending entailed a question, however perfunctory, however cooley polite. He watched them combing their hair. The afternoon, far advanced, ended as though nothing at all had taken place. Having lent, having borrowed, speech began quite naturally once more. He would never be able to teach in his suit again. He had, at the end, photographs of them in their costumes, singly, together, and out of their costumes. He had a picture of them in their school dresses, ready to leave.

"I shall never be able to forget you. Before the year is over, I'll have enough photographs of you to fill a dozen albums."

He joked with them, intimates, on a new basis together. One really became acquainted in the course of such a day. There was hardly any noticeable tension at the end of the afternoon. They

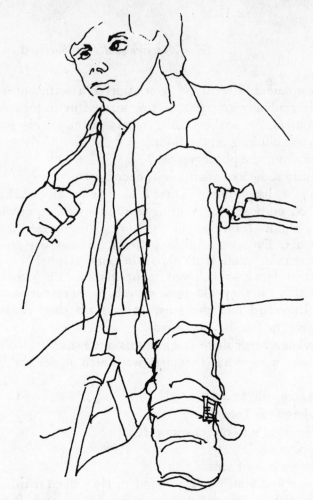

might have only talked together, about their work, his collections, literature. Nothing might have taken place, the new basis forming quite of its own. He would never be able to teach in his suit again. By the time they had left, with an amiable "Good afternoon, Mr. Hopkins" as on any other day, he had explained about the summer cottage, what they were to do, what they were not to say. It was a sort of conspiracy, he explained. They seemed to understand. He regretted the loss of his teaching suit. The coming of night found him restless. He took up again, for the first time in many months, the catalogue of his button collection that was an indispensable prelude to its eventual sale. No reason to keep it any longer; there were other things a man his age, of solitary occupations, could find to do.

The laboring roar of the bus engine, climbing the roadway that wound upward to the Byfield Academy, was the immediate cause of Wilfred's waking up. A less direct cause was his impatience. Ned was undoubtedly right. The girls, whatever they might be underneath and whatever they secretly might be willing to do, would, so far as they were concerned, behave like potatoes in a sack. But Wilfred was impatient nonetheless. One never knew. They were the acknowledged leaders of Westwood. One never knew. He followed with his eyes the steep grade the bus was climbing, his reflections trailing into speech.

"I suppose you're right. Those dances are always the same. But anyhow, Ned, I'm going to stick it out for the evening, whatever you decide. They can all be witches. There'll be lots to eat. We don't have to dance."

"I like it in town."

The bus rumbled past the open iron gates, onto the school grounds.

"They've probably never seen one in their lives." The bus ground to a stop at the level driveway before the main school building.

"We're here. Take it from me; come to town."

Wilfred noticed in the doorway the welcoming committee, a few girls, an elderly man. The girls were pretty. He heard the other buses pull to a stop behind him. He called over his shoulder as he climbed down from the bus.

"You go to town if you like. I'd rather wait and see."

The elderly man, flanked by a slender blonde girl on his left and a slender dark girl on his right, came down the steps to meet them. The girls looked toward the ground, shy. Wilfred liked shyness. Shyness was home.

He would wait and see.

THOMAS PEACHUM

A young American writer, so gifted with contradictory talents that he never has been able to choose one single direction for them. Hence his extraordinary novel, The Watcher and the Watched — *which became the modern bible of voyeurism and allied vicarious passions — has remained, so far, his only completed novel.*

Memoirs of a Beatnik

Diane di Prima

I awoke to the sounds of morning in the West Village. The sounds of traffic. Trucks were going by outside, and the pavement was wet. They were nervous, honking and snorting at one another. The window was open, and the window shade was flapping a little, one side of it hitting the window frame over and over again in an irregular rhythm. I opened my eyes, turned over in bed, and looked at my surroundings.

The room was a bright yellow, which offset the pale grey light of the rainy dawn. Aside from our low bed, the only furniture in the room was made up of skids stolen from nearby paper companies, and painted a flat black. They served both as chairs and tables, and no cushions broke the austerity of the furnishings, no draped Indian prints and antique velvets such as we have become accustomed to in the sixties. One large platform, placed against the wall which faced the foot of the bed, held a candle at least a foot in diameter and about three and a half feet high. Ivan was particularly proud of this candle. He had pointed it out to me when we first got to his place, saying that it had taken seventeen-dollars-worth of wax to make it. It had been our light during the night's proceedings.

Although we were only on the second floor, the room had been "decorated" with some kind of false eaves. They sloped slightly over the windows and enclosed the bed in shadow. It was a large room, and the newness of the paint job and the flawlessly finished floor made it seem like a rather affluent garret. As if the folk in *La Boheme* had come into some money and painted everything, I thought with a grin.

Through an archway I could just get a glimpse of the closet-sized kitchen, shining with new utensils. To the right of the kitchen, I knew, there was an equally tiny bathroom, flawlessly tiled and equipped with deep-napped, fluffy towels in dark luxurious colors, and a variety of expensive bath oils. A perfect miniature, a dollhouse; and somebody was playing house here, sure enough.

Well, here I was. I stretched my legs, arching my toes and sighing just a little, so as not to waken the boy still sleeping beside me. Here I was, and, I thought wryly, this is only the first of many strange apartments I'll be waking up in. The muscles of my thighs felt sore, and I passed my hand over them to feel the graininess of the dried come that was stuck to them here and there. Then I slid my hand between my legs, and softly felt the lips of my vagina. The skin was raw as I slipped my fingers inside, exploring gently. He certainly was a big one, I thought. A big one for the first one, that was good. A shiver of pleasure passed over me as I explored the familiar ground, and goose bumps started up on my arms. Now, I thought with a little grin of cynical pleasure, I certainly won't have any more trouble using tampax.

Ivan was still asleep, his back to me. I softly slid the sheet off both of us, and compared the rosy, almost violet cast of my flesh with the pallid, olive light that his body threw off. We looked good together. It was a pleasure to lie there, mildly aroused, passing my hand over the smooth skin of my breasts and stomach, and knowing that at any moment I could initiate the dance that would satisfy my own desire and bring delight to the creature beside me.

I turned on my side and put my mouth on his back, lightly tonguing the indent his spine made. He had one large vertebra there at his lower back, just before his spine curved in between the cheeks of his ass. I explored it thoroughly with my mouth, traced the spine to its end, and started up again, this time bringing my fingers into play, brushing them lightly over his flanks and sides, raising the fine down that covered his sallow skin.

Ivan was thoroughly awake by now, stirring beneath my touch, and as I raked the hair on the nape of his neck with my tongue, he turned toward me, covering my mouth with his own. I slid my arm under his shoulders, noticing as I did so that for all his length his shoulders were very slight—as slight as a girl's, I thought. For some reason this excited me all the more, and I moved my body so that I half lay on him, and devoted my full attention to our kiss.

There are as many kinds of kisses as there are people on the earth, as there are permutations and combinations of two people. No two people kiss alike—no two people fuck alike—but somehow the kiss is even more personal, more individualized than the fuck.

There are those who kiss intently, earnestly, their lips tight and straining, their tongues hard, thrust with a firm determination as far as possible into the other's mouth; there are those who kiss lackadaisically, casually, languorously, their mouths slack, brushing lightly, their tongues almost unequal to the effort of venturing forth. There are those cunning kissers whose kiss seems casual at first, and sneaks up on you in vast explosions of lust. There are those insinuating kissers whose kiss is so lewd that it leaves you slightly repelled, as if you had just had a quick fuck on the bathroom floor; and those virginal kissers who, in the act of turning your mouth practically inside out, seem chastely to be taking your hand. There are those who kiss as if they were fucking: tongue pumping frantically back and forth between the other's lips in a breathless rhythm. There are many, many other major types of kisses—at least twelve come to my mind offhand. List your favorites below:

Our kiss began at the lips, mouth loose, relaxed, playing and brushing each other gently, seeking to blend into each other, to become one mouth, but with no urgency about it. The excitement built gradually, until lips were being ground savagely against the still-closed teeth. A slacking off, and then his tongue came out and began to examine the inside of my lower lip, prodding and sliding gently into the corners, rubbing against my gums and curving my lip down. The tongue withdrew, and mine came out to follow suit, to play the same game but more thoroughly, slipping around the inside of the upper lip also, and down into the sides of his mouth, puffing out first one of his hollow cheeks and then the other. When I tired of this, I fell to nipping the inside of his lower lip with my teeth. And then his tongue came out, serious and straining, searching out the roof of my mouth, and the skin under my tongue. We shifted in order to lock mouths and bodies more closely together, and my hand found his large, beautiful cock and began to stroke it and fondle it, occasionally pausing to cup its full knob in the hollow of my palm.

Our tongues were jousting now in a fine fencing match of pleasure, touching and tilting as we moved slightly from side to side in our attempts to bring our flesh into more and more total contact. I slid a knee up under his balls and rotated it gently, while examining his entire palate with the tip of my tongue. In reply, he pressed one thigh awkwardly against my crotch, just touching my clitoris. A warm wave of pleasure spread over me, and I began to grind my box against his leg, gripping it with both my thighs, while my mouth left his and sought the hollow place I loved at the base of his throat.

He lay there, his head thrown back and his eyes closed, as I traced the line of his throat, his collarbone, and his breast with my mouth, leaving a fine trail of saliva on his pale skin. My tongue played briefly with his hard, slight nipples, and I continued my journey south, pausing now and then to nip the fine, smooth flesh just under his ribs, or to ream his navel with my tongue. His eager hands on my head now thrust me down, down toward his huge cock, but I resisted, playfully. I was not to be hurried. I took one of the dark hairs on his stomach between my front teeth and pulled at it lightly. I traced the fine bones of his pelvis with my mouth, studying the way the flesh, stretched taut, dipped into a smooth hollow, sensuous as sand dunes. I left a purple tooth mark there and went slowly on my way. Ivan groaned once. His hands, letting up slightly on their pressure, began to play frantically in my hair. I mouthed and tongued the smooth skin between his navel and groin, until the muscles leaped and twitched under my touch, and I could hear his quick, involuntary gasps.

I slid my body down along his leg, until my mouth found his standing cock. I began to play with it, nibbling along its sides with my lips, tonguing here and there at its root, in the tangle of dark, musty-smelling hair. At last, under the urgent message of his hands, my mouth closed over the large head of his cock, and I tasted the bittersweet liquid at its tip. I bent my head down as far as I could, completely filling my mouth, straining to make that space larger and to take him in more completely. The head of his cock pressed against the back of my throat and I gagged slightly, but his mounting excitement drove all other thoughts from my mind. I slid my hands under his buttocks, and drew him closer to me, moving my head up and down, and pressing my own wet opening tight against his knee. My head was swimming; my blurred sight registered a patch of sunlight on the yellow wall over and over again. I remember thinking irrelevantly that the rain had stopped. I could hear Ivan gasping and moaning above me.

My own desire became unbearable. I wanted that large pulsing cock inside of me. I withdrew my mouth from it swiftly as a shudder ran through him. I paused briefly to tongue his full, round balls, and, sliding my body up over his, I raised myself with my arms and straddled him so that my moist hole was just above his rod. I lowered myself onto it, guiding it to the proper place, and squirming down over it to take it into my still tight opening. But there was more. I had not taken the huge tool in fully. We separated briefly, and I slid one leg up, over his shoulder. His hands on my backside drew me close and closer—he was in, up to the hilt. My body seemed to be melting, a grey mist spilled before my eyes. We lay on our sides, one of my legs stretched out under me and one over his shoulder. We pumped and circled in a mounting tide of ecstasy. My long hair had come loose and cascaded over us both. At last I gave way, my entire body filled with pleasure, and felt the flood of delight sweep through my flesh as his warm come filled my cunt to overflowing, and with a shuddering shout he collapsed on top of me.

I know that it was a long time before we moved, because when I raised my head I saw that the patch of yellow sunlight had moved quite some distance across the way, and sunk down somewhere near the woodwork. I moved my leg a little, and Ivan slid his limp wet cock out of me, causing an exquisite and delicate sensation. He reached across me with one arm and picked up the electric alarm clock which had been knocked over by our exertions. Gave a lost whistle when he saw the time, started to pry himself loose, then fell to kissing my eyelids and tugging at my ear with his lips. I slid over to a drier place on the sheet. He pulled a loose strand of my hair across my face, spreading it like a web, and kissed me through it. Our tongues met as if through a veil. I said, "Umph."

"Hungry?" he asked, sitting up and swinging his legs over the side of the bed to the floor, which was only about a foot below.

"A little," I said, snuggling deeper into the pillow to indicate that I didn't want to get up and do anything about it.

Ivan stood up, and I looked at his strange and beautiful flesh as he headed for the shower. Decidedly too long, and too sallow. It glowed. A kind of El Greco quality about it. He was very beautiful, I decided, and cuddled deeper into the warm place our bodies had made. I dozed off.

And woke to the aroma of coffee and the sizzling sound of eggs. Ivan had showered and dressed and was standing over me, grinning, two steaming cups in his hands. He set them down and sat down beside me as I sat up sleepily, the sheet falling from around my shoulders and my hair falling into my face. I sipped the hot sweet liquid greedily. It cleared up some of the dream-fog in my head, and I stole a look at Ivan over the side of the cup. This was not the young pirate I had met in the Village the night before. Nor was it the El Greco painting I had made love to. A young man, quiet, rather thin, dressed in clean dungarees and blue work shirt, his wet hair neatly combed. Ivan caught my eye and my thought, and grinned. I grinned back. Words were not part of our thing. Then he made as if to pull me to my feet.

"Come on," he said. "The eggs will be getting cold."

I stood up and walked naked to the center of the room, where I stretched and yawned, the sunlight I had been watching all morning from the bed catching me around the ankles. I made a loose, untidy braid of my hair to keep it out of my face. Something dripped onto the instep of my foot, but I ignored it. Ivan threw me another blue denim work shirt exactly like the one he was wearing, and I put it on, rolling up the too-long sleeves and, thus attired, went in to breakfast.

We sat at a tiny table in the miniature "bachelor kitchen" and devoured frozen orange juice, fried eggs, and burned English muffins swimming in butter. Ivan had put on his glasses, which completed the transformation to a sober, rather over-serious young working man.

"Just slam the door when you go," he said, his mouth full. "It locks by itself. Stay as long as you like, play records, type, whatever." Then he added, with just a trace of hesitation, "Shall I see you tonight?"

I liked the hesitation. I liked the confidence, too, with which everything else had gone down between us, but without that hesitation he would have been just a trifle overbearing. I suppressed another grin and filled up my mouth with egg.

"I don't know," I said. "It depends. I'm still living at home."

"I'll meet you," he said. "At nine. At David's." David's was an arty coffee shop on MacDougal Street. The only one, besides the Mafia hangouts, in those days.

"OK," I said, still playing it cool. "If I'm not there, don't wait."

He gave me a long, playful look from under his eyelashes, half coaxing, half ordering me to be there, and, after an eggy kiss, he left for work.

I had been in correspondence with Allen Ginsberg ever since I read *Howl,* and when he and his gang came to New York I was eager to meet them. After a few phone calls back and forth they came down to Leslie's, where I was staying, bringing with them a great quantity of cheap wine and some very good grass. We all proceeded to get thoroughly stoned, and Allen, and Jack Kerouac, who was with him, rapped a long, beautiful, high-flown rap all about poetry and high endeavor. Jack's belief, which Allen shared at the time, was that one should write spontaneously, should never change or rewrite anything. He felt that the initial flash of the turned-on mind was best, in life as well as in poetry, and one could see that he probably really lived that way. He seized upon my note-book and proceeded to uncorrect it, rolling the original bumpy sentences off his tongue, making the stops and awkwardnesses beautiful while we all got higher and higher.

I proposed that they all spend the night. Allen had eyes for Leslie and agreed readily, enlisting his lover Peter's help in moving the couch from the front room to the back, and setting it beside the double bed. They were about the same height and made one extra-wide, only slightly bumpy, sleeping place. They dragged the whole thing into the center of the room, arranging plants around it, and burning sticks of incense which they stuck into the flower pots. Bobbie watched, horrified.

After kissing us all lingeringly, Peter split—to what mysterious night rituals of his own, we could only surmise. Leslie lit some candles and placed them at the bedside, turning off the overhead electric light. Immediately, the room seemed immense, mysterious, the beds an island, a camp in a great forest wilderness (Leslie's rubber plants). We all undressed — Bobbie with some trepidation — and climbed in.

It was a strange, nondescript kind of orgy. Allen set things going by largely and fully embracing all of us, each in turn and all at once, sliding from body to body in a great wallow of flesh. It was warm and friendly and very un-sexy: like being in a bathtub with four other people. To make matters worse, I had my period. I was acutely aware of the little white string of a tampax sticking out of my cunt. I played for a while with the cocks with which I found myself surrounded, planning as soon as I could to get out of the way of the action and go to sleep.

But Jack was straight, and finding himself in a bed with three faggots and me, he wanted some pussy and decided he was going to get it. He began to persuade me to remove the tampax by nuzzling and nudging at my breasts and neck with his handsome head. Meanwhile everyone else was urging me to join in the games. Allen embarked on a long speech on the joys of making it while menstruating: the extra lubrication, the extra excitement due to a change of hormones, animals in heat bleed slightly, etc. Finally, to the cheers of the whole gang, I pulled out the bloody talisman and flung it across the room.

Having done his part to assure a pleasurable evening for Jack and myself, Allen fell to work on the young male bodies beside him, and was soon wrapped round, with Leslie on one side of him and

Bobbie on the other. I heard some squeals, and felt much humping and bumping about, but in the welter of bedclothes the action was rather obscure. Jack began by gallantly going down on me to prove that he didn't mind a little blood. He had a widly nestling, hugging sort of approach, and he was a big man; I was taken over, lay there with legs spread and eyes closed while he snorted and leaped. When I shut my eyes I was once more aware of the warm ocean of flesh around me, could distinguish the various love-sounds and breathings of all the creatures.

We finally got loose of the bedclothes: Jack, with a great cry, heaved himself upwards and dumped them all on the floor, then fell heavily on top of me and entered me immediately. My momentary surprise turned to pleasure, and I squirmed down on his cock, getting it all inside of me, feeling good and full. It nudged the neck of my womb, and I felt a thrill of a different kind, a pleasure that, starting in my groin, spread outward to the edge of my skin, sitrring every hair follicle on my body separately. I was suddenly, totally turned on. We bucked and shifted, looking for the best position, fucked for a long time on our sides. Then Jack withdrew and flipped over on his back, indicating that he wanted me to sit on his cock. I did, guiding it inside me, and it touched the same place in the neck of my womb again, but this time more heavily, so that the pleasure was sharper and edged with a slight pain.

It was a long, slow, easy fuck. I knelt, with my feet tucked under me, and moved up and down on Jack's cock, while his hands on my waist supported and guided my movement. I glanced at the group beside me. Leslie was lying on Allen, kissing him, and they were both grinding their stomachs together. I could imagine, though I could not see, their two hard cocks between them, denting the soft skin of their bellies. Bobbie lay a little to one side of the two of them. He was kissing Leslie's back and neck, and he had his own cock in his hand. Pleasure began to increase in my gut. I bent down and kissed Jack on the mouth, moving faster and faster against him. His two hands on my shoulders held me warm and tight, as we came together in the friendliness of that huge, dark room.

Jack stirred after a few minutes of light rest. He leaned over the side of the bed, feeling around to find his soft leather pouch, and rolled a joint of good Mexican grass. Drew on it deeply and handed it to me. I smoked a while, and looked around to see where the others were at. Allen was lying full out on the bed, and Leslie was fucking him in the ass. I tried to hand the joint to Bobbie, who refused it with a shake of his head and fell, sobbing, into my arms. I handed the grass back to Jack, and tried to comfort Bobbie, but he would only lie there, sobbing softly. I stroked his shoulders and back, but I wished he would stop. It was very boring. Jack caught my eye and grinned at my chagrin. I turned my head towards him and put the grass back in my mouth, holding it for me while I drew on it. Finally Bobbie stopped and said, "I have to go to the bathroom." He tromped about with reproachful noises, finding a bathrobe, and was lost in the unfathomed halls and staircases.

Allen and Leslie finished doing their thing, and Leslie was hungry, as he always was after fucking, and went to the kitchen and came back with bread and herring and a bag of early peaches, and he and Jack and I sat munching and smoking, while Allen scribbled in a notebook, occasionally looking up abstractedly for the grass. Jack pulled me between his legs, and began to rub his limp cock against my backside, and eventually got it hard again, and he exclaimed, "Look, Allen!" and leaped out of bed, pulling me onto him as he stood in a deep *plie* and we tried to do it in Tibetan yab-yum position. It felt good, was really fine and lots of fun, but Jack was drunk and high and balance not too good, and we both fell over, narrowly missing a plant, and went on fucking on the floor, my legs around his waist, while he protested that we should stop and let him get into lotus position so we could try that one. But I simply locked my ankles around his waist, spread the cheeks of his ass with my hands, kept him busy, and we flipped over first one way and then the other on the floor.

Allen by this time was reciting Whitman and rubbing Leslie's cock with his feet, and when Leslie got hard again he went down on him, and after Jack and I got through I went down on Allen, Jack finger-fucking me both ass and cunt—he not getting hard for a third time. And then Jack went back into his pouch and came up with a black ping-pong ball of hashish, and we smoked a little and ate the rest, and I fell asleep and dreamed that aether was flesh and human bodies merely cresting waves upon it. I watched them form and unform all night long.

In the morning I had my period full force, and stayed in bed sitting on a towel while Leslie and Bobbie pranced out and scored tampax and coffee and eggs from the horrified local grocer.

And two weeks later, sitting at home in the pad, in a patch of sunlight on the black painted floor, while a small fire blazed for companionship and not for warmth, sitting there in a cloud of plaster dust I had raised by trying to carve a hard chunk of plaster of Paris into the semblance of a hand, white dust in the clean air, the house swept and windy from the broken windows, I heard a key turn in the lock. And turned in white sweat shirt and blue jeans, white plaster dust in my hair, to find Ivan standing in the doorway. Ivan whom I had not seen in many months, who had disappeared into the depths of the South, into some dull Southern college where he was teaching. He stood in the doorway, grinning his old grin in spite of necktie and straight overcoat, and stepped – in shiny shoes – across the swept and splintering floorboards, removing professorial gloves.

I put down the half-carved hand and went to greet him: kiss long and fine, though only a small improvement on our kisses of long ago. And we drank brandy together out of coffee cups and ate bread and cheese while he told me about his life, the incredible circuit of "work," of words and money, that had closed around him.

And I, looking him over, seeing how he still moved so fine, sensing the long hard muscles under the straight clothes, the fine bones of the face, high cheekbones that held through the years, good quick mind fumbling now with the foolishness of semantics and logical positivism, bogged down in the karmic round but still shooting sudden sparks, sending magic across the room till we both found ourselves laughing, rolling on the floor with laughter, knees pulled up and brandy spilling—I, noting these good points which were the kernel, and which all the karmic bullshit hadn't changed, flashed for a minute on the possibility that this might be the father I was seeking.

It was the last really fine day in the pad. Ivan shed his pomposity with his wardrobe, and we fucked all afternoon in the patch of sunlight on the double bed. The quintessence of all the pad had been the friendly magic and high adventure we had lived in it, all floated around us that afternoon in the dusty air. That life had never seemed more graceful and easy, more filled with kindly love and essential freedom, than it did that day, and I knew I was saying goodbye to it. When Ivan split I lay awake for a long time, staring at the fire escape and the starlight through the window.

And when the full moon shone on the fire escape again, I didn't get my period as I should have. And as the moon waned, my breasts grew and became sore, and I knew I was pregnant. And I began to put my books in boxes, and pack up the odds and ends of my life, for a whole new adventure was starting, and I had no idea where it would land me.

DIANE DI PRIMA

Diane Di Prima was born and raised in Brooklyn, came to live and write in New York's creative-destructive vortex of the fifties — Bird in his last days, Miles Davis at the Cafe Bohemia, Sartre, bitterness and hopelessness — until the emergence of her brothers, Ginsberg, Corso, the painters Franz Kline and Bill de Kooning, et al. A prolific poet and active participant in the artistic and revolutionary movements of our time, Miss Di Prima's impressive list of credits includes six published books of poetry, stories and essays, inclusion in numerous literary magazines and anthologies, and poetry reading tours at universities throughout the country. As editor of Poet Press books and the Floating Bear, *a literary newsletter of new writing, she has received several awards from the National Institute of Arts and Letters. Principle influences in her life and work were John Keats' letters, Ezra Pound, Zen, and Tantric Hinduism, in that order. She has four children and lives in San Francisco.*

The Sexual Life of Robinson Crusoe

Humphrey Richardson

T his monkey was not large in size. But it was remarkably constructed. Its arms were not unduly long, as
is frequently the case with monkeys and its legs were not skinny, as
unhappily so many monkeys' legs are. Their line, although modest,
without any emphatic accentuation, was not disagreeable to the
eye. The whole of his body was covered by an attractive, silky and
thick growth of fur, a rich brandy tint in color; Robinson hunted
for symptoms of mang , and found none; hair everywhere save
upon the monkey's belly, which was a spotless white, and covered
with no more than a pale down which, as it descended, developed
into a tuft as neat and precise as if it had been combed and set by a
hairdresser: the tuft ended at the monkey's pink sex, an absurd bit
of flesh no thicker than a pea. Robinson now scrutinized the
animal's face where a thousand various expressions came and went
one after another like something seen shimmering under water. But
what most struck Robinson was the expression of the monkey's
hands, far more mobile than human hands, and those simian hands
were ceaselessly seeking after *something to clutch and squeeze,*
lacking which, they were opening and closing upon thin air,
embracing the air only. Those hands finally managed to seize the

hem of the tunic Robinson was wearing, and the monkey tugged
furiously at it, probably wishing in this manner to signify its gratitude towards its saviour. Robinson still had his eyes riveted upon
those *hands*, like someone who at long last sees his most cherished
dream come true. The monkey continued to pull at the material.
Annoyed, Robinson tried to loosen the *hand's* grip, but no sooner
dislodged, that hand and the other hand too, looking for something
to hold on to, chose the knobby end of Robinson's sex.

The monkey had accomplished this gesture with the most
natural air, quite as though he were seizing a doorknob or a life-
buoy. Robinson interpreted all this as a malicious gesture, that is to
say, a wicked and infinitely interesting one, the kind of gesture that
is impelled by some deep,.underlying instinct. Robinson gasped.

For an idea had burst into his head like a flash: this creature,
this dear little creature was going to bring about a change in his life.
The idea took size. It became gigantic. Through a blue haze, Robinson glimpsed an image of paradise. The monkey hung on for dear
life. A light but faintly hysterical laugh rose from Robinson's heaving chest.

"Naughty," he breathed, a glint in his eye, "naughty," and he
loosened the fingers of those *hands*.

Needless to say, Robinson moved heaven and earth to hasten
the dear little creature's recovery. Cataplasm after cataplasm.
Brews, special decoctions, teas made out of eucalyptus, vapors,
everything. The monkey was soon restored to rights. His affection
for the man who had fished him from the sea, nursed him, coddled
him, fed him, his affection for Robinson had grown. So had his
familiarity. All day long he perched on his guardian's shoulder. With
expert hands, he scratched the hairy leather of Robinson's costume.
And he gibbered and squeaked soft little nothings.

When Robinson's labor required his complete freedom of
movement, the monkey would skip to the ground, find some berry
or fruit, eat it, gibber and squeak, and scratch himself up and down,
down and up, would execute a thousand different stunts, perform
waggishly, but would never stray from his kind keeper.

The memorable gesture of the very first day had never been
repeated and Robinson, taking care not to provoke the animal,
wishing to let things take their natural course, impatiently awaited a
new move on the monkey's part. Robinson held spontaneity to be
of the highest importance in these matters. No coaxing, no insisting;

that would spoil everything. He wanted to have a foreign presence all of its own self voluntarily lavish its attentions upon him. Alas, the monkey remained faultlessly correct. What had it been, a stroke of chance, the first gesture? One torrid afternoon, Robinson got the idea of showing his summer house and pleasure garden to Zizi (as by now he had come to call his monkey). It has been, as a matter of fact, a very long time since he had returned to the bower of bliss, preferring the bracing climate on the windswept coast.

They set off. As they drew near, the aroma of the pepper-plants stung their nostrils simultaneously. Robinson was unsettled and manifested his disorder. Blood rose to his head, a wild light came into his eyes. As for the monkey . . . Robinson, turning his head towards the shoulder upon which as usual Zizi was perched, saw that the creature's body was presenting every positive sign of the keenest excitation. That thing, which we earlier compared to a trifling morsel of flesh with the ridiculous thickness of a pea, had enlarged. In length it now attained a good five inches. It was swaying and bumping against Robinson's cheek.

Zizi seemed totally untroubled and was glancing about him with an air of mild curiosity in his surroundings.

Robinson, a smile upon his lips, patted the erected object, stroked it with the tip of his finger.

Zizi lowered his eyes: a haughty little lord disturbed in the midst of his abstract meditations, he cast a look of incensed disapprobation at the incontinent man. The breeze made the pepper-tree's foliage rattle above their heads.

They entered the compound. As they went in, Zizi reached out and yanked at the vestiges of a silk stocking which had been hanging for years from one of the stakes in the palisade. The monkey pulled the stocking away and wrapped it around his eyes, enveloping his head. Robinson took speedy advantage of this moment of self-imposed sightlessness and advanced his lips, took the pink stem in his mouth. The monkey's reaction was instantaneous: in two seconds at the outside, the organ had shrunk to its original size. A little morsel of flesh about the size of a pea. What the devil ailed this monkey? By thunder, it was difficult to figure out just what made him tick!

Robinson's misadventure with the wildcat had been a lesson to him: he had taken solemn oath never again to employ violence in order to attain his ends. He had treated most courteously with Zizi. He had been content to await a favorable occasion. Under various sets of circumstances, he had several times seen the little morsel of flesh lengthen into something long and slender and enticing, but when he had advanced his hand in token of friendship, the thing had each time fainted quite away, shriveled, and all but disappeared. He had attempted to interest Zizi in his own sex but—at the very best—the monkey had only poked it with an idle finger, touched it, but so summarily, with such indifference, that it hadn't amounted to anything at all. Robinson had gone many months in a state of suspense. He had held himself admirably in check, for months. For months he had resorted to digging holes in the ground—in muddy or clayey ground or in moist sand—and to dipping himself gently thereinto, to remaining buried for a few moments, then to withdrawing with great care so that the sand would not crumble so that the hole in the clay would not fill. When one hole became useless through excessive use, he'd dug another beside it. And he had done this, for months, with Zizi watching, and for Zizi's improvement and instruction. Zizi had regarded this oft-repeated game with a perfect serenity. He would wander thoughtfully over Robinson's back while Robinson lay prone on mother earth. Was the creature pretending not to understand? What was the matter? Robinson was at a loss. Similarly Zizi would watch him with interest, but always with a grave air, whenever Robinson, shifting from the ground to a tree, would bury his device in some knothole.

It was on the 16th of March 1657, that Robinson, occupied with some task, by accident raised his eyes and noticed that Zizi, his faithful little companion, had disappeared. Where had Zizi gone? For, by nature exceedingly fearful, Zizi ordinarily stayed within a circle whose radius was no more than five yards and whose center was his master. Robinson began to search about. He picked up some ends of tarpaulin lying here and there on the ground, he peered into a bush, he looked behind a barrel, and found nothing. Some trick, eh? Zizi was hiding, eh? A farce, was it? Robinson whistled, clapped his hands. No response. Thirty paces away grew a clump of palm trees. Well, thought Robinson, he might have climbed a tree, although for what reason. What could induce Zizi to climb a tree. Wondering about this enigma, he advanced noiselessly to the nearest out of the trees. And he discovered Zizi all by himself behind the tree.

Robinson narrowed his eyes. Zizi's back was turned to him. Intrigued, Robinson tiptoed closer. What was the little rascal up to? What, oh what? What indeed? Robinson, moving stealthily forward, circled so as to come round at him from in front. Well. Well.

Between his slender, delicate hands, the animal was holding that slender, delicate tube whereof we have already said so much. Zizi was agitating it brusquely. Stiff little movements. With each stiff little movement, the entirety of Zizi's stiff little body would tremble, his shoulders would quiver, his head would hunch further down upon his shoulders.

For this little undertaking Zizi was employing the most straightforward means, evidently disdaining the complications, detours and accessories Robinson was wont to rely upon. The man signalled his presence to the monkey, and offered his hands to aid in the operation, but the monkey would have none of it. Zizi's grimaces announced his determination to carry through alone, to go the whole way under his own steam. Notwithstanding this unequivocal refusal, Robinson saw but one solution. He peeled off his clothes in a trice whilst Zizi was forging ahead with his business, and then Robinson Crusoe, King of that Caribbean island, undisputed sovereign in his own domain, presented his behind.

He did so without premeditation: the idea occurred to him, he acted upon the impulse, in highest innocence and like a gentleman. Zizi regarded the gesture in that light and, springing upon the man's haunches, hung by one hand to Robinson's belly while with the other hand he facilitated his entry.

Zizi gibbered and squeaked.

But Zizi was not a clever monkey, not yet. He botched the thing, or was about to. Robinson had to kneel down—he, King Robinson!—and bend forward, offering the monkey a clearer target. But, alas, no sooner was Zizi three-eighths of an inch in when he withdrew, his pink article withering immediately to the size of a pea or a small nut. Monkeys are disinclined to overstay their welcome: a moment, that's enough, and that's apt to be all. Robinson was shocked.

The brevity of that encounter furnished no indication that the monkey had found pleasure in it. Judging the thing coolly, one might suppose that, to the contrary, Zizi was no born buggerer. But the crestfallen Robinson's melancholy considerations were given a rude jolt forty or fifty minutes later.

Robinson was standing. He was gazing sadly out to sea when he felt the monkey spring again upon his back. Prods and pushes dispelled Robinson's surprise: Zizi wished to start in afresh, was gibbering and squeaking wildly. Robinson surrendered himself with the utmost pleasure. But his satisfaction didn't last two minutes.

The habit took with prodigious rapidity. Zizi was now demanding Robinson every hour on the hour, and as time wore on, the duration of the operation steadily lessened until it amounted to little more than a quick stab and a single shriek or squeak. Robinson was beginning to take the joke very badly. He scolded the monkey and energetically refused to carry him about that way on his rump.

But Zizi was now in all earnestness. The monkey had grown frightfully fond of the man, and importuned him constantly. A few days later, worn down, Robinson consented to a new attempt. The result was just the same. Indeed, that may have been the quickest, the briefest, the most lightning-like of all the intimate relations they'd had up until then.

There was no question about it: their sexual lives were incompatible. Robinson gave Zizi the cold shoulder, forbade Zizi to perch upon his shoulder and left him alone in the compound, free to play his little pranks upon the goats if he had any inclination for goats.

But, alas! no such cactus grew on Robinson's island. Friday grinned.

The reader will recollect the transformation in Robinson's character at the time of Friday's arrival. Friday has entered his world, and Robinson had become sweet, gentle, thoughtful, compassionate, tender. But in the long run this temporary improvement in his nature was brought to a halt, and the tide began to turn: the bitter experience of twenty-two solitary years was too strong, and Robinson reverted to his pre-Friday condition. Many a time he would take the savage with an abrupt thrusting brutality—as in days long gone by he had taken the goats. Or the cats or the parrots. Friday complained about his conduct. Robinson scoffed, muttered, grunted. Friday became distant. Robinson's at all times exasperated and exasperating mood fatigued the young man. There were certain moments when his master seemed quite as disagreeable as the monkey Zizi had seemed to Robinson.

The reformed cannibal was still in that phase of tremendous romantic yearnings. He would get up at night and steal furtively out of compound, to go wandering upon the shore in the moonlight. As once upon a time had Robinson, Friday would wrap his arms and legs around the boles of palmtrees. He began to change his mind about Mara. The white man's attitude was a sight worse. Mara had left him in peace; Robinson never stopped jerking up his loincloth or pulling it clean off and flattening him like a cockroach. Where in all this was Mara's gentleness? her subtility? her refinement? Where were her cool lips? her warm lips? Friday had had to argue for weeks to get Robinson to trim his beard and his moustaches (and when at last he had prevailed, where was Mara's smooth skin? for Robinson's was leathery, tough, dry, cracked). And those white teeth Mara had! Where were they? Robinson's yellow tusks battered him when they kissed.

As for the castaway, he was more or less content with the way things were. He had such a terrible time of it getting his hands on the handsome youth, tracking him down, cornering him and finally pinning him took up so much of his time and energy, that he had none left to think or be despondent. All day long Robinson cudgelled his wits, dreaming up schemes to get his hands on Friday. He invented fabulous projects. He calculated endlessly. But what shifts could he, Robinson, possibly contrive to become so agreeable in Friday's eyes that Friday would feel a spontaneous gratitude toward him, Robinson? Wouldn't it be better to beat the lad? Wouldn't it be simpler that way?

That solution—the easier one—was the one he often chose. And he would employ a little irony and sarcasm too.

"Ah, so that's it, eh? The right honorable Mister Friday is fatigued, is he? My dear fellow! My poor dear Friday! Well, you shall see whether I'm fatigued or not! Eh, ha, there, take that, your lordship!" and he would aim a barrage of blows at the fastidious reformed cannibal. The blows bestowed, he would possess the unhappy lad. Possess him furiously.

Friday would often bring his sad, weary, circled eyes to bear upon a little mockingbird he had tamed and made his confidante. He kept it hidden in a secret place, fearing lest Robinson, in an excess of drunkenness, subject it to the same fatal treatment under which Poll had perished.

And so amicable relations were more than strained between the two men. So were their amorous relations, it need hardly be pointed out. The moon, which would send its pale rays through the always open door and window, was often the silent witness of some truly appalling spectacles. They were of all sorts.

Robinson, dead-drunk, shouts at Friday: "Hey, old boy! Come here! Lie down, d'ye hear?" Friday, sulky, lies down on the bed. He is fully clothed. His eyes are downcast. "Hey, old boy! Get out of your underwear, d'ye hear? Blast me, d'ye think I'm the one who's going to undress you for the night? Hey?" Friday doesn't move. If he resigned, that does not for one minute mean that he is docile. "Why?" he asks in a flat voice. "Hey, by God, you're going to see why! Hey, hurry it up, m'boy." "Not tonight, master, I'm tired me." "Tired, are you? Just you wait a little." Hiccoughs. Gouap. Gouap. Robinson staggers over to the bed. He reaches down, grabs the undershorts, pulls. His fumbling hands find their way into the fly. He pulls this way, that way. Finally pulls the garment off. Friday hides his timid nudity. "Hey, by God! Turn over, d'ye hear!" Robinson bellows.

Shocking scenes like that.

And on the morrow Robinson kneels at Friday's feet, begs him to pardon his dreadful behavior of the night before. "I am," Robinson explains, "essentially the gentlest, the calmest, most kind of mortals. Occasional brutality? Well, that is easily explained: It's because I've been along for so long — at least I was before you came, d'ye see, old boy? Why, I was shipwrecked on this island about the time you were born. Think of that! But you must forgive me!" Robinson is so persuasive that Friday, who has a gentle nature too, lets himself be won over. They make up. Friday, very spontaneously, offers Robinson a place in the bed. "Really? D'ye mean it, old boy?" "Yes, master, come bed." Robinson slips in carefully and overwhelms his companion with a thousand gentle words, touches, signs which, despite everthing, Friday cannot help but find pleasurable.

And the next morning it is the same. Every time the same: a better taste in the mouth, a faint sentiment of loathing for each other.

For Robinson himself—even though Friday may have been even more than ever the object of his desires—no longer took the same pure pleasure with him, no longer knew that healthy sensual emotion that had stirred him so deeply back in the days when they had made each other's acquaintance. If now he moved heaven and earth in his efforts to possess the savage, it was to be able to dream peacefully afterwards. Friday's presence had become the stimulant that procured his dreams. There follows a description of one of the more important dreams from this period. Observe that its contents have become normal: Robinson had paid close heed to the cannibal's refreshing narratives.

(Robinson is astride Friday: Amphion aboard his dolphin— their mingled perspiration resembles a sea. As things progress, he weaves his dream.)

HUMPHREY RICHARDSON

One of the most elegant and clever French writers of this generation is hidden under this pseudonym; a paragon of social graces, the darling of duchesses, and the last survivor of the Fauborg Saint Germain's Proustian past. If they only knew the real Humphrey Richardson! . . . But it is a well-guarded secret.

The Organization

Harriet Daimler

*N*ow," announced Midont with mythoreal happiness, "we get on into the fourth dialogue, which is that much closer to the fifth, therefore that much further than the third. I cogitoed for a while," he admitted, "that we would limit ourselves to the declatification of dialogue three alone. Dolmancé," he kicked Lorenzo's pecker goodnaturedly, "certainly was subfuging over the place. Mouths, faces, wombs," he laughed, unable to stop his dissertation now that it had begun, one of the levels' on which Midont had not subliminated himself. But the members of the Organization cogitoed well, and Clarissa cast a meaningful look at Lorenzo, and Lorenzo cast a hand over Midont's mechanistic mouth.

"In dialogue four," announced Clarissa now that the floor was unequivocably hers, "Le Chevalier is frigged by Dolmancé and ejects in Eugénie's face," she smiled sweetly at the fifteen-year-old soon-not-to-be virgin. "Dolmancé, of course," she refreshed them, "will jerk Le Chevalier off. I," she promised, "will be frigging Eugénie all the time. The mythoreal ejaculation in her face," developed Clarissa, "should subfuge with an ejaculation in Eugénie's belly. Cogito that, Eugénie," she said sharply. Lorenzo burst in with:

"Shortly after, Le Chevalier, still erected in spite of coming in Eugénie's illusiomat face, will have his sister Madame de Saint Ange, as Dolmancé buggers him, who is in turn had in the rear by Eugénie's dildo." Midont continued joyfully, aware only of the illusiomat obstacle removed from the talking apparatus. "Le Chevalier commences," he stopped endlessly, "with the duplication of 'Lovely Eugénie, I beg you . . .' " Midont paused. His self-subliminally-imposed desistance was like an atomic bomb subfuged into their midst. "Where is Le Chevalier?" he gasped in a mythoreal emotive voice. "Where is Le Chevalier?" And then, possibly for the first time in any suspension of events, they all looked about them. The phantiverse was empty of Ferdinand. The corponot of Ferdinand was not.

Clarissa said, "Lorenzo, make a search of the other rooms, particularly subfuge all beds, all bathtubs, all toilet seats, all refrigerators, all bottles of scotch. He might be subfuged in any one of those illusiomats. While we wait," she murmured, staggered by the blow of Le Chevalier's absence which was presence, since his absence filled her phantiverse, "we will wait."

"I cogito," Midont rushed in at her gasp for breath, "that we should go on if Ferdinand does not reappear, which is likely since we defactified appearance."

"We will not dramaguise without Ferdinand," Clarissa positively negated.

"But I will jump on your bones," offered Midont. "For this brief inessential dialogue, I will subfuge myself subliminally into Ferdinand's absented corponot."

"And," shrieked Madame de Saint Ange, "when you, Augustin, and he, Le Chevalier, molest me at the same time, shall I subfuge that one is two. No, never," she promised, "that two are one, yes, but that one is two, never. I will not gratuitously multiply corponots in the phantiverse. Never, never. That one is two," she laughed harshly, "when we've defactified that one is one, no never."

"Well as I cogito it, Clarissa," spake Midont, "since one is not one, and therefore Ferdinand has no essence in the first place, why can't I, also having no essence," he hastily modifed the I "take his mythoreal place?"

"Because," cried Clarissa, "we are interested in defactifying De Sade, not each other which we have already defactified, that's why. Do you cogito me?"

And then Midont took his stand. "I cogito, Clarissa," he snarled, "that you have mythoreal preferences. In a phantiverse of subfuged illusiomats, you prefer to be sucked by Ferdinand. It's that complicated!" He stamped his little Mongolian foot.

"I've always cogitoed," he spat in her face, "that illusiomat women are emotive mythoreals. I've always . . ."

Lorenzo walked in and announced excitedly: "I've searched the beds, toilet seats, refrigerators, and bottles of scotch, and he was everywhere," he hiccoughed, "except not his corponot. What shall we subfuge, Clarissa?" he bowed to the president

"We shall," she authoritatively began, and was interrupted not by illusiomats Midont, Eugénie, or Dolmancé, but the illusiomat telephone. It blared in the Ferdinand-empty room. It took five minutes of mythoreal ringing, for Clarissa to subfuge the telephone behind the illusiomat piano. She subfuged the machine into her hand and announced, "This is Clarissa of the Organization speaking."

"Clarissa," come the disencorponoted voice on the other end, "Clarissa, this is Ferdinand."

"Ferdinand," shouted Clarissa as Augustin, Eugénie and Dolmancé moved closer to her, "Ferdinand, where aren't you!"

"Look," he apologized. "Have you passed my dialogue yet?"

"How can we pass," screeched Clarissa, "what we cannot reach!"

"Oh good," mythorealed Ferdinand, "look Clarissa, I've been with Eustacia these last twenty-seven hours." He would descend to vulgar time delineations. "And everything is all right. The little illusiomat," he joshed, "just came out of her."

"That, Ferdinand," taught Clarissa, "was a problem we had made a no-problem to be solved in five months."

"Well," he protested, "I just juggled time a little. You're all for that, and," he lowered his voice, "if you can starve the pussy another ten minutes, I'll be there with the meat!"

And then he hung up, disconnecting the mythoreal connection.

"Ferdinand," blasted Clarissa, "has been defactifying another illusiomat. Premature of him," she admitted, "but nevertheless in the charter of the Organization," she defended. "We must wait for his absence ten minutes."

"In that case," announced Midont, "if I can't defactify Le Chevalier, I will defactify De Sade. I have a few notes on his mythoreal philosophy which I will read to you. Sublimate, if you cogito," he prescribed, "but I will read." In the silence which preceded sublimination he read:

"De Sade, the defactified," he entitled. "In a phantiverse crowded with mythoreals and illusiomats," he reiterated, "along comes illusiomatist M. le Marquis de Sade fighting the morality which is preached in the fantiety. How," he laughed uproariously, "how he proceeds to establish an immorality when morality has no essence, has indeed been defactified by the charter, is beyond me, but since I am defactified too, I will introduce his attack on phantiverse morality. Here is the frequent dilemma," he cogitoed, "of illusiomats who have not studied the Organization charter."

"Now," he relished the mythoreal, "we will cogito De Sade fighting illusiomat windmills.

De Sade's first illusiomat windmill: Since mothers did not wish for their daughters, only permitted themselves to be devirginized by husbands, they have no moral claim on daughters, and daughters should abhor the involuntary mothers.

According to our charter, interjected Midont, the mother-daughter relationship is subfuged too late by the illusiomat mother. It was all right for mommy to subfuge a bit of fun, but to subfuge an illusiomat daughter out of it, was to muck up her mythoreal husband.

Important note: Birth has been defactified, as have mother, daughter, father, husband, *Sons and Lovers*.

De Sade's second illusiomat windmill: All actions being inspired in us by nature, we need be ashamed of none of our actions.

According to the charter: Who is this illusiomat nature everyone keeps talking about?

Important note: Everyone is defactified.

De Sade's third illusiomat windmill: It is a necessity for women to lie; falsehood is vital to them.

According to our charter: A lie is a mythoreal that does not subfuse with the rest of fantiety. In playing the little game of *if you say I have essence, I'll say you have essence,* fantiety shrewdly requires that all the corponots subfuge the same illusiomats. When this is not convenient for a subliminate, the mythoreal name-calling begins.

De Sade's fourth illusiomat windmill: Women should always deceive their husbands.

According to the charter: It is not always convenient for illusiomat women to subfuge with their husbands.

Important note: Marriage with all the connected mythoreals, i.e., wives, husbands, contracts, white cottages, arguments, small gardens, babies, old-age pensions, has been defactified.

De Sade's fifth illusiomat windmill: Libertines fall into three categories: those preferring sodomy, those preferring sacreligious fancies, and those with penchants for cruelty.

According to the charter: Some corponots, particularly corponots with small illusiomat antennae or no illusiomat at all (such as defactified women), sometimes subfuge mythoreal kicks by beating illusiomat midgets that stutter, women who sing, housewives who vacuum-clean carpets; by sucking mythoreal rabbis and grand lamas, subfuging particularly into their illusiomat bowels.

De Sade's sixth illusiomat windmill: of the two classes of sodomites, active and passive, the passive (who gets himself poked) has a better time than the active (who pokes someone in the end).

According to the charter: Six of one makes another illusiomat baker's dozen of the other.

Important note: The active, passive, and having of a better time have all been defactified.

De Sade's seventh illusiomat windmill: A woman being buggered should always insist that her clitoris be frigged.

According to the charter: Corponots don't cogito subfuging all that illusiomat meat with no potatoes.

Important note: The Clitoris has been defactified, as has frigging it, fucking it, sucking it, pinching it, pounding it, eating it and ignoring it.

De Sade's eighth illusiomat windmill: Pervert the young; let yourself be frigged by them; yes, go even so far as to lend them your ass.

According to the charter: Subliminate corponots before they fall into the mythoreal blasphemy of not knowing that they don't have essence, and they will then subfuge your illusiomats like they never got subfuged before.

Important note: Lending asses, like lending ears, has been defactified. Therefore, give away the illusiomat, don't lend it.

De Sade's ninth illusiomat windmill: Pain, inflicted on others, is immeasurably preferred to pleasure; cruelties such as flagellation, executing slaves, baking victims in brass pots, grinding pregnant women to mortar, depositing hungry insects on bound men's genitals, reveal extreme organic sensibility.

According to the charter: Some corponots like it mythoreal
   hot, others like it mythoreal cold. Still others don't mythoreal it at all.
Important note: "De Sade has been defactified."

At that propitious event of no suspension, a tapping was heard
on the illusiomat window, and indeed it was Ferdinand's corponot,
wanting in.

"Hello," said Ferdinand, "I'm not going to be a father. Have a
cigar on me," and he held out an illusiomat that corponots subfuge
into their mouths in order to defactify disease.

"How dare you," breathed Clarissa, "and you're out of your
costume, too!"

"That's because I been dramaguising doctor," he chucked her
playfully under her illusiomat chin. "Been all in white splattered
with blood till this joyful moment."

"Ferdinand," Clarissa said softly, "I give you two seconds to
be in your costume, defactifying Eugénie."

"But nobody else got anything on," complained Ferdinand,
"except Midont, and he don't have no essence at all, not at all. So,"
he bargained, "why don't I just take off what I got on, and we'll
pick up from down there."

"Agreed," agreed Clarissa, "off with your illusiomats. We want
to see your corponot, and bared."

"I'm all yours," lied Ferdinand, whipping off his illusiomat
jacket, trousers, shirt, undershirt, underpants, shoes, socks, and last
his tie and beret. "I'm all yours," and he flung himself into the
center of the illusiomat bed crying, "Lovely Eugénie, I beg you to
be easy; my discretion is entire; there is my sister and there my
friend, who, both of them, can be held answerable for me."

"Then let's go on to work," directed Madame de Saint Ange.
"Ferdinand, you've skipped seventeen lines."

"Let's talk less, Chevalier, and act more; I'll direct the scene,"
insisted Dolmancé. "You, Madame, will frig your friend, I'll be
responsible for Le Chevalier," he grabbed Ferdinand's illusiomat as
if it were made of illusiomat flesh and blood and pumped
vigorously.

"Positions!" he commanded.

"Are we not too close?" questioned Madame de Saint Ange,

throwing Eugénie backwards on the bed and fiddling around for her friggable.

"Impossible to be too close," instructed Dolmancé. "Madame, we must have your friend's face and breast inundated by the proofs of your brother's virility; he has got to take aim and discharge at her nose," thus spake Dolmancé.

The member in Lorenzo's hand was an enormous illusiomat. It was the immensity of Ferdinand's member that made him an honorary member of the Organization. How could they resist defactifying a member of such subfuged dimensions?

Dolmancé's hand was sister to brother Clarissa's. Their arms moved back and forth like two woodsmen on opposite sides of the redwood tree; Clarissa sawing inside Eugénie, and Dolmancé sawing outside Le Chevalier.

"Don't forget to aim it at Eugénie's nose," roared Ferdinand, smiling at the stretched-out-well-attended-to Althèa. "Though," he adlibbed, "I think it would be more fun if she opened her mouth, and let's see how much I can spurt in it. Are you athirst, old girl," he bellowed, "want some foamy old malted sperm?"

Clarissa was working like the realomyth d-v-l. She opened the lips of the tender abused vagina, subfuging the now familiar clitoris with the delicate expertness of a blind man reading braille.

"I cogito your suggestion, Ferdinand," approved Clarissa. "When you're ready to subfuge your come, this corponot's walkie-talkie will open. It's like that bunny doll we had when we were tiny little corponots," Madame de Saint Ange reminisced, "pull the illusiomat tail and the mouth opens."

"That's a crazy thing about Clarissa," Ferdinand informed the laboring Lorenzo. "She likes a good time as much as the next one."

"What next one," Lorenzo attacked Ferdinand. "I don't cogito a word you're saying, and I'm mythoreal surprised that Clarissa does." And he clamped his hips tight one on the other. His fingers were as harbingers of wrath, measuring the long full mute protrusion that subfuged him slave. His hands clenched the root of the swelling, and fisted mercilessly to the purple swaying bulbous end. Up and down he went, violently shaking the bottle to make the soda pop.

"It seems to me, Madame," dramaguised Dolmancé, "this woman of yours ought to have, don't you think, a man in her mouth and another in each hand?"

"Use me," offered Midont throwing the logbook to the side. "I'm only an illusiomat, but then only is a realomyth. By all means," he volunteered, "subfuge me!" He rushed helter-skelter to the couch where all the action was being defactified, grabbing his enthusiasm out of his pants and crying, "Here, here, members, here, I offer you my illusiomat. Eugénie, take your sublimination, you can have it in your mouth or in each hand. It doesn't mind which, one thing about my illusiomat," he assured her, "it adapts."

Eugénie reached blindly for Midont's patiently procrastinated pleasure, but Madame de Saint Ange got there first, a second, in the mythoreal sense, before Althea.

"Subfuge that thing away," she levelled at Midont, "it does not appear at this point in the enliving. Subfuge it away."

"Why," demanded Midont, trying to ram it into Eugénie's mouth, "have you especially defactified Mongolian erections? Look at it," he blasphemed. "You're jealous aren't you Clarissa?" he raved. "You're jealous, jealous, jealous, mythoreal jealous that you don't have one like it."

"Away," howled Ferdinand, "away, ships ahoy, I sight land, anchors up, steer Dolmancé, steer for port, into her mouth."

Clarissa barely had event suspension to command, "Eugénie open your mouth," which Eugénie cogitoed, before the darting, dancing, dazzling, delicious, diaphanous, defactified come plopped into her mouth.

"Magnificent spectacle!" gurgled Eugénie, "how noble, how majestic it is," and she swallowed like the old sailor she wasn't.

"Right into the old motheroo," proudly preened Le Chevalier.

"What's so mythoreal remarkable about that?" snarled Midont. "Cogito, Ferdinand, an illusiomat mouth is an illusiomat mouth is an illusiomat mouth."

"Midont is subliminal," snapped Clarissa. "You get too excited Ferdinand. Such mythoreal rapture at your own subfuging smacks of pride," she warned, "and pride is as defactified as prejudice."

"Stick to your dramaguising, Clarissa," dared Ferdinand. "I've done my part royally and it seems to me that at this moment you should be gathering up my priceless pearls, rubbing them on Eugénie's twat so that she'll like us."

"Your phantiverse vocabulary is impossible to follow, Ferdinand," corrected Dolmancé, "but I gather that what you cogito is that Clarissa, still defactifying Eugénie's corponot, should be rubbing your come into one of her illusiomats, so that Eugénie will subliminate, thereby defactifying De Sade's mythoreal about coming."

"That's it," confirmed Ferdinand, "that's just what I was trying to say."

"Well, what do you cogito I'm doing," demanded Clarissa, "knitting illusiomat argyle socks? I haven't left this clitoris for an instant." But Eugénie, for some subliminal obstinacy, refused to subfuge an orgasm. "Come dear child," Clarissa bitterly implored, "or I'll rub this mean little illusiomat until I erase it."

"You two," attacked Lorenzo, "would be perfect for the enliving of Cinderella, and I see you as the two ugly sisters. I personally," he promised, "will cut your illusiomat heels and toes off."

"And you, Lorenzo," howled Midont, his talent still hanging out below his shirt-tails, "and you I suppose cogito yourself as Cinderella. Why not," he bitterly pronounced. "Why not, at least you have the phantiverse realomyth of not being Mongolian."

"I'm coming," lamented Eugénie, "I'm coming, don't stop, go faster, go slower, harder, softer, like you're doing, harder, slower, faster, yes, yes, yes, yes, yes . . . yes."

"At last, at last," succumbed Clarissa, "we arrive at the point of defactification where Le Chevalier strokes my interior. How I've waited," she repeated, dangerously close to illusiomat tears, "and in waiting," she commanded herself, "not waited, simple suspended eventlessness."

"Suspend events one more instant, Clarissa," guided Dolmancé. "I have an important line."

"We've defactified the talk, Lorenzo. From here to infinity we've defactified the talk," stated Clarissa.

"This inessential must be said," Lorenzo pursued. "A dramaguise scene must be established. Arm yourself with pencil and paper. Here I subfuge. Le Chevalier is in you, granted; but, and here is a but that is bigger than a maybe, but, I am in Le Chevalier's ass, while Eugénie has an illusiomat of an illusiomat, an illusiomat dildo, with which she is not out of me."

"Midont," demanded Clarissa, "have you, along with the costumes, brought an illusiomat dildo?"

"Of course," rejoiced Midont, reaching behind his back and pulling a long, leathery, lubricated, lacerating, lecherous illusiomat dildo out of his privates. "I subfuged it away so I wouldn't lose it. Here," and he heaved the illusiomat of an illusiomat at Eugénie, "strap it on, it goes very well with the mythoreal color of your eyes."

Eugénie shied away from the phantiverse object. "What," she howled, "what is that?"

"That, Eugénie," defined Clarissa, "is another one of the little .devices and duplicities of fantiety. Strapped around your waist, it contributes noticeably to the defactification of women, not to speak of men. Here we go," promised mommy Clarissa, and strapped the dildo around the corponot of Eugénie, as defined and dramaguised.

"It stinks," complained Eugénie.

"And what in the phantiverse doesn't?" bargained Clarissa.

"And now to dramaguise," Lorenzo promised gleefully.

"I don't cogito," interrupted Midont, "why Eugénie has to mess around with an illusiomat of an illusiomat, when I'm standing here with the real illusiomat hanging out."

"Read the charter," said Clarissa derisively, lying flat on the bed and spreading wide the white thighs of her corponot. "Read the charter," she motioned Ferdinand to ignore her sounds and begin, "the charter, Midont," she gasped as Ferdinand sank his still swollen, as dramaguised, maleness into her femaleness. "The charter, Midont," she continued faintly, her hips cascading up and down, "the charter subliminates all." And she flung her arms around Ferdinand, clutching his hips to her so that each blow of his powerful machine shuddered over her entire corponot.

"Oh, I'm dying," died Clarissa. She sank deeper into the bed, and asked hurriedly. "What was that, Chevalier? Your illusiomat subfuges like an illusiomat battleship."

"That was Dolmancé getting into me," Le Chevalier explained. "Not so fast Lorenzo, oh God it's good," he philosophized, "to get it while you're giving it. Oh man," he moaned, "set the rhythm. As you do unto myself, so I'll do unto my neighbor, who is my brother, who is my sister."

"Ahh," lurched Dolmancé, as Eugénie stabbed his asshole with the dildo, "ahh," he quickly acquainted himself with the mythoreal extension, "ahhh, easy on the phantiverse machinery my dear, easy on the machinery."

"Can't I just stick mine in Eugénie?" begged Midont, reduced indeed to begging, "Can't I do a little defactifying?"

"The fifth, the fifth, wait for the fifth," warned Clarissa, "five is the magic number," she choked out the Organizational joke, "ask Beethoven."

"Can you feel this, Lorenzo." asked girl-man Eugénie, "can you feel this? Is it like I was a man?"

"Of course I can't feel it," Dolmancé retorted. "But that don't stop me from subfuging it, and it's sixteen times more powerful, more deep, more heavy, more steady, and more sure than a defactified man."

"I'm going to come, Chevalier," called the low defactified woman on the totem-pole, "I'm going to come. It's too much, it's like iron. It's enough. Enough is too much. It subfuges like your sex and Dolmancé's and Eugénie's are all in me. Too much," she moaned, "too much is not enough?"

"Come in haste, repent in leisure, Clarissa," warned Ferdinand, "better hold on. Just let it go all through you, baby. Feel it in your toes and in your head. Feel it like I'm in your teeth and your knees and the back of your neck. Let it happen to all of you, spear it, baby. Make me a nice big pool to swim in." He commanded, "swing that ass."

"Ahh," sang Lorenzo behind him. "Ahh, she's got me by the hairs now. The adorable little defactified sneak. Honey, honey," he defactified, "they're not Chinese checkers, don't try to jump them. Just lightly." His head trembled, "She's got me by the balls. Oh," he grabbed Le Chevalier's behind and held on. "Am I going to be the first to be defactified? That little fifteen-year-old virgin is making me come first, just 'cause she's last. Ohh," and to distract the mythoreal ejaculation he began to sing, anything, anything, just to hold on to the mythoreal feeling, not end it with a subliminated come. Anything, anything, "Oh," he wailed sans cogito, wiping his drooling mouth on Le Chevalier's buttocks, "Oh," he wailed, "the wart on his ass, alas."

"I must, Ferdinand," cried Clarissa, "I must, therefore I mustn't not come," and come she did with a loud fart that set them all off like so many firecrackers.

Le Chevalier inundated Madame de Saint Ange's illusiomat indiscretion.

Dolmancé inundated Le Chevalier's defactified bowels.

Eugénie flung her illusiomat dildo into Dolmancé's defactification for the last subfuge.

Madame de Saint Ange kissed Le Chevalier, saying, "My brother, let it hereby be subliminated that one in the bush is worth two in the hand."

Le Chevalier kissed Dolmancé saying, "I never thought I should see a branch as mighty as a tree."

Dolmancé kissed the dildo saying, "A dildo, a dildo, my illusiomat kingdom for a dildo."

Eugénie, in essence, had no one to kiss.

Midont in defactification had no one to kiss, but he walked to the middle of the room, checked his watch and balefully bleated, "April is the cruelest month." And though in the mythoreal Gregorian calendar it was February all the subliminates cogitoed.

They were all in dire need of a little sublimination.

"We go on," cogitoed Midont, "to dialogue five. If you remember," he amended brutally, "a young gardener named Augustin is therein introduced. Augustin," his voice was broken chalk scratching across the blackboard of their mythoreal nerves, "has an illusiomat organ that measures thirteen inches in length and has a circumference of eight and a half inches. My illusiomat," he spoke to himself in the room of subliminates, "duplicates those dimensions." He reached into his never removed, always defactified trousers, "Subfuge it someone," he thundered. "To subfuge it," he threatened, "is to defactify it. Yes," he giggled, eyeing the subliminating Lorenzo, "yes, I'll have him yet, I'll have him for my queen."

HARRIET DAIMLER

Harriet Daimler is the pseudonym of the author of five Traveller's Companions, which makes her the foremost female writer for The Olympia Press. She lives frequently in New York, where she was born, and prefers to remain anonymous in order to avoid the confidences of New York's numerous phone freaks. Like most of the crowd who wrote for Olympia through the 'fifties, her main inspiration was the charcuteries, cheeses, and wines of Paris. She believes that she does not have a dirtier mind than other people, though her facility and speed in writing out those extended sexual fantasies makes her wonder what she was really dreaming about while getting all the college degrees, marriages and divorces that are requisite in a normal American woman's life. Currently writing a book for publication in New York, Harriet Daimler struggles against her impossible tendency to write more explicitly than the courts will tolerate.

THE ORDEAL OF THE ROD

R. Bernard Burns

Rodney West never learned anything in scholarly style and it was for all the intellectual sailors of the Western World that he spoke (or thought that he spoke) when he said, "It's a sad world, anyway. Not many of us will get out of it alive."

"What, darling?"

"Don't bother me. I'm quoting. I mean, I'm thinking."

He saw her lips tremble. He put his hand to the crotch of his trousers. *That's* where he did his thinking. That was the only way to think: with your cock. He'd like to be able to take his out right now and shove it into Lisa's mouth, shove it up as far as it would go into that little pink cunt of a mouth. Instead he simply held his hand to his cock and felt it harden as her grey eyes filled with tears. Then, as it became completely hard he took his hand away from it, his eyes away from her, and quietly watched the sun from the street make fishy patterns on the walls to softly lighten the green gloom of the Mexican cafe.

Should he return to New York or go off to Tehuantepec with her? He glanced at General Miaja, who was sitting two tables away, at Miaja, "The Defender of Madrid." Too bad that he, Rodney West, hadn't had the guts to help defend it . . .

"Oh well," he said (they had been talking about Spain) and Lisa said, "I'll go back when they restore the monarchy."

"Well right now, my sweet little anarchist turned monarchist, you can go back with me, back into the toilet."

"No!"

He let a smile that was more sneer than smile disfigure his small sensual lips.

"Oh yes you will. You know why we come here. We can't go to my place, it's too far away, and that lousy husband of yours is always at your place, so . . ."

"I know, Rodney, but it's so sordid back there, and that woman, she's . . ."

"Shut up," he said and narrowed his eyes to look at the green wicker chairs, the green and black tiles of the floor, the dark green walls.

The cafe was becoming less sombre. Sunshine streamed through the open doorway that led to l'Avenida de Cinco de Mayo where the midafternoon traffic of Mexico City, siesta time over, was loud with the tooting of horns and the shrill shouts of newsboys.

"Grafico! Grafico! Ultimas Noticias! Grafico!"

The bitter taste of black coffee in his mouth, Rodney lowered the small cup that was the color of ivory and moved his tongue over the front of his tobacco-stained teeth. He looked up at the green ceiling. This cafe had all the chill marine cheer of an aquarium. It made him think of childhood excursions on Sundays in early spring. It made him think of his cock before they called it "the rod." It made him think of how he'd rubbed it and rubbed it until it had bled. ("You can't shoot yet?" the big boys had laughed at him. "Watch me come!" big Jocko had cried. There in the woods he had watched Jocko's sperm shoot into the air. How he'd wanted to be able to come like the rest of them! Yet how good, how hurting yet good, were those long comeless orgasms, those sweet sweet pains that he'd had even before he'd rubbed it and rubbed it to hardness, rubbed and rubbed it until it had bled.)

A dust-flecked shaft of sunlight shot through a skylight window, bathing General Miaja's bald head.

"Oh, fuck the old bastard," he said. "Fuck heroes everywhere. Fuck the Spanish Civil War. Fuck this one . . ."

"Quiet, darling, quiet," she said.

"And fuck you!"

"Rodney . . ."

Under the table, he dug his fingernails into her thigh. He watched her close her eyes. He saw her tears flow. He felt his cock throb.

What was the matter with him? Who did he think he was, Hamlet? Why couldn't he be a thrower of pies instead of a walking stalking photograph of the writer in embryo? All this damned Ibsen-green business, this gnashing of teeth, tearing of hair . . . To do or not to do, to go or not to go. Damn all this coming face to face with Miajas and Madrids, with Saccos, with Vanzettis, with the ghost of Byron . . .

"*Graza señor?*"

"*Si.*"

He put his right foot forward, thinking of how he never put his best foot forward, but then, looking at Lisa, he knew that this was a lie, for her grey eyes were almost blue with yearning as she wiped the tears from her face and blew her nose. And why was this? Because now he was giving her his supplicating smile, his seducing, his seducingly successful, "I want my mamma" smile.

He decided to pout. He did. Then he looked down at the boy who had begun to shine his shoes. He admired the boy's sleek hair. He admired the fine smooth brownness of the boy's skin.

"Yes, Rodney," Lisa was saying, "I'll go back to Spain when they have a king there."

This time he said nothing. He felt his cock go soft. (The plains of Spain are silent now. Spain is the corpse of a century. The war is over, has been won, and not by you, just as this war, this bigger and more important war, if anything can be said to be more or less important, will some day be over and be won, but not by you . . .)

He shook his head from side to side. The Indian shoeshine boy was grinning up at him, softly tapping the shoe that had been shined. Lisa's head, more ash than blonde, was at a curious angle. She was smiling at him quizzically. Her teeth looked papery, like the rest of her.

"What's the matter, dearest?"

She touched his hand lightly with one fingertip. He took hold of it. He squeezed it. Then he twisted her whole finger.

"Don't, Rodney. Please. Please don't hurt me . . ."

"You know that you like to be hurt, you little bitch. First you like to play mamma. Then you like . . ."

"Yes. Yes, darling. Yes,"—she was trying to pull her finger away—"yes, Rodney, yes. But not here . . ."

"All right," he said, "all right,"—his voice was low and harsh—"as soon as the kid's finished with my shoes we'll go back inside to see Conchita and I'll bugger you until the shit comes out of your ears."

She said nothing. She lowered her eyes, then her head, and he, looking down at the shoeshine boy, again admiring his bronzeness, his youthfulness, his beauty, saw that the boy was watching them with mixed fear and curiosity. Once more he felt his cock get hard. He let go of her finger. He shifted his feet so that the boy could shine the other shoe. He lit an Elegante and drew on it deeply. Then, simply to say something, he said, "What should we do about Tehuantepec, Lisa? What should we do?"

"I don't know . . ."

They became silent again.

"Para hoy! Para hoy, señor!"

He nodded no at an old hag who stood by the table, her face smeary with syphilitic sores that were the color of her gums.

"*Para hoy! Para hoy!*"—she held the lottery tickets in a filthy hand that shook—"*Para hoy!*" She moved away, barefooted, like the newsboy, to whose, "*Ultimas Noticias! Novedades!*" he also nodded no.

The green cafe was blue with cigarette smoke now. Every table was occupied by gesturing men. Except for Lisa and a couple of others, the only women in the place were the white-aproned wait-resses, their tits and asses tight in their black uniforms, who went up and down the narrow swarming aisles where sombreroed Indians tried to sell serapes and men coming in from the street looked for acquaintances or for a table. Here, there, sat an obvious European, thick tortoise-shell rimmed glasses gleaming in the sunlight that was laden with smoke.

"*Para hoy! Para hoy! Ultimas Noticias! Novedades!*"

The headlines were about the fighting on the Kerch Peninsula where the Germans had won still another victory. Again Rodney looked at General Miaja. So there he was. Unmilitary paunch. Patri-archal manner. In every outward way unlike the man who, in his mind's eye, all through the Spanish War, had been inflexibly austere and stern. Sinewy. Draconian. Yes, there he was, just a man at a nearby table who, a few minutes before, had been pointed out to him by Lisa.

"There's Miaja," she had said, awkwardly attempting to be casual. But the tender tone of her voice had revealed memory of Madrid.

Memory of Madrid. If he too but had memory of Madrid instead of the memories that he had of Dostoievskian days when he'd done nothing but call himself a coward. Memory of Madrid. If he, too, but had memory of Madrid instead of the memories that he had of those Salvador Dali days when, head-first, he had been a "sphinx embedded in the sand," artfully outfitted with the glass of warm sweet milk, the woman's slipper . . . (and so . . . and so, small slimy beasts, feed upon the flower that once — the first — must have been my heart . . .).

He apparently looked miserable, for Lisa now placed a fragile hand on his brown wrist, held it there as if she were about to feel his pulse, and softly, softly, said to him again, "What's the matter, mon petit?"

"The same . . . " he began, but then, "Nothing!" he snarled, and pulled his hand away.

The shoeshine boy was tapping at his other shoe. Rodney took his foot down from the box and reached into his pocket for a peso.

"Keep the change," he said, and then he said, *"Por nada,"* to the boy whose teeth gleamed white against the brownness of his oval face.

"Ah, gracias, muchas gracias, muchas gracias, señor!"

"Por nada," Rodney said again, looking at the boy's tight blue faded pants, noticing the bulging outline of his cock as he stood up.

"Say," he said, "how old are you?"

"Sixteen, *señor.*"

The kid might come in useful, Rodney thought. He watched the boy move off, wondering how big his cock was. He resumed his lounging position in the wicker chair, crossed one leg over the other and indolently dangled it. Then, squeezing his cock against his balls, he looked at Lisa who had a solicitous expression on her face, a searching, seeking, look.

"Tell me, Rodney, please . . ."

"Oh," he relented, still thinking about the boy, "it's the same old thing"—he tried to make each French word sound clipped, abrupt—"sorry I missed Spain."

Sounded kind of tough, kind of newspapermannish mannish, saying it that way. Kind of Bleeck's-Bar-On-Fortieth-Street-boys-in-the-backroom brave . . . He lit another cigarette—*flick*, in the yellow fog by Big Ben, *flick,* pull down, Sardou, your grey fedora—wondering if his feeble French had been able to convey that foreign-correspondent nonchalance to her, that trench-coat swagger . . . Damn this language business, anyway . . . Sometimes—he glanced at her—it spoiled the bed business. For no language but one's own could satisfactorily Stravinsky the creak, the rites of springs . . . Still—he looked at her delicate pink lips—he hadn't done such a bad job with this one. Yes, he'd made her say plenty in her native Hungarian, and in Spanish and French. Yes, he'd made her say plenty each time he'd jammed his cock into her.

He wanted to jam it up into her now, up into her tight but juicy pink cunt, up, up, her tight little ass, up as far as he could. And after that he'd make her lick her own shit off it. (Last time she'd refused. This time he'd make her do it.)

"Come on," he said, but then, seeing how solicitous her

expression was as she gently caressed the faint fuzz of hair on the back of his hand, he decided to play with her for awhile, and so he let his sunburned uneven-featured face look as childlike, as trusting, as much in brown-eyed search of mamma, as he could make it look.

"You mustn't think about it so much," she was saying. "It's over, *cheri,* now it's over . . ."

"Yes," he replied, "it's over. This war . . . It's not the same thing now."

"No," she said, "it's not the same thing now."

He raised his thick black eyebrows and with one finger twisted a curl of his dark brown uncombed hair. She seemed to mistake this physical extension of his thought for a gesture of remorse. Motherly resting her hand on the sleeve of his jacket, she began to speak to him in a low choked voice.

"Please, Rodney, don't think about it any more. You were right not to go. You were right not to . . ."

"When'll we go?" he interrupted. "When'll we leave here for Tehuantepec?"

"Then you will go? You will, you will . . ."

Ugh. If only there wasn't such a splutter of saliva whenever she became at all excited. And if only she were just a bit more beautiful. Not younger. No, thirty wasn't old (after all, he was twenty-seven).—Let's see, Olivia would be thirty now. Where was she? Still in Nice?—Yes, if only Lisa were as beautiful as Olivia, or even beautiful enough (her faded prettiness was not enough) to bolt with her, to say to hell with draft boards and the whole wide weary world . . .

"Yes," he said, with a guilty glance, "yes, but . . ."

Ah, no, no Galapagos Isle for him (with her). With no abundance of soap and razor blades (for her; for her to wash her cunt and shave under her arms and shave the hair off her cunt when he wanted it that way). No, no Galapagos, no Tehuantepec, with her for him. And yet . . . Ah, *mamma mia!*

He doused his cigarette in the sediment at the bottom of his cup. Lighting another, he gazed at the green ceiling.

"You must be sure," she was saying above the loud low hum of the cafe, "you must be sure that you will be safer here, in Mexico, in Tehuantepec, than by returning to New York . . ."

He lowered his gaze to the green wall opposite, then to General Miaja, then to the green-and-black tiled floor. With her index finger he tapped his cigarette until a spark flew.

At last, "That's the thing," he said, "I'm not sure. You see, I'd be a deserter. Say,"—he looked up at her, his right eyebrow higher than his left—"did you ever read a story by Drieu la Rochelle called *Le Deserteur?*"

"No . . ."

"Well, it's a damned good story. About a guy who got out of it the last time. Holds true today."

"Everything holds true always."

"Yes," he continued, paying no attention to her, "holds true today. Too bad Drieu la Rochelle turned out to be a collaborationist. Still, it doesn't surprise me . . ."

"No," she said, "it's not surprising. Collaborationists are clever."

"Oh," he said, "some are more than clever. No one has ever called Lucifer a fool, nor has anyone yet accused the Devil's diciples of stupidity."

"Yes," she laughed, "Luis always says the Pope's an atheist . . ."

Luis. For the time being he'd forgotten him. As so she must have, too. Still—he watched her face as the laughter faded from it—if it hadn't been for her Spanish husband, Luis, they'd probably be there, in Tehuantepec, by now. So, in a way, he was grateful to Luis for having kept him from doing what he surely would have done three weeks ago, when all of this with Lisa had begun.

"Oh," she said now, crushing out her cigarette, "here we are again. How can I tell him?"—he could see the veins pulsing in her throat—"how can I leave him after all, after all . . .?"

Silently he said it. "After all these years." Yes, how could she leave him after Spain? Oh, how he loathed himself for coming between her and Luis, Luis, who had been a defender of Madrid, a modern hero, whereas he, Rodney West, had been nothing.

"However, you've got to tell him," he said to her, "that's all there's to it."

Gone was his momentary sympathy for Luis. Lost in renewed realization of another man's desire for her. And this, and her clouded countenance, clouded, he could see, with thought of Luis, revived his own diminishing desire. This, that, and the difficulty of it all. But not the danger. No.

"I will. I will," she said, "yes, I'll tell him."

Too easy. She looked as if she meant it. Pretty nice for him, though. Luis, he recalled—from that first day, that one time that he'd seen him—was a real good-looking guy. And he'd probably thrown many a good fuck into her. But he didn't look like the kind of a guy who went in for buggering and beating. And she sure liked her buggering and beating . . .

"I'll tell him," she said again, "I'll tell him today as soon as I go home."

"No! No, not today."

"Why not today?"

"Because . . ."

How could he tell her that he was afraid of Luis? And how could he tell her that she wasn't beautiful enough for him?

She seemed to guess the last, however, for, "Oh Rodney," she said, "you know that you don't like me well enough. You know that you only like decorative women."

"Oh, don't be silly . . ."

"Yes," she said, "that's true. And why not . . .?"

She shrugged her shoulders sadly. She did everything so sadly. And to him this was one of the most attractive things about her, for to him delights were more delightful when they were dolorous, and what ecstasy he'd had in his crazy but controlled career had always been touched by tragedy, or by a sentimental sense of tragedy.

"Oh, Lisa," he said, "it's not true. That sort of thing"—he tried to make himself feel as if he'd lived the life of a D'Annunzio—"is over, all over, entirely over, for me . . ."

He tried to make himself feel that Fortune Riley, that Olivia, had been paragons of beauty—as they had been to everyone but him, for although he had never lived, nor been seen much, with any but beautiful women, his desire for beautiful women was not as strong as his desire for those who just missed being beautiful, for those who, like Lisa, could show gluttony, the real gluttony of one who had been starved (oh, that little grey-haired hunchback he'd picked up one day! Had he ever had a better lay? He doubted it . . .). And as, now, he said to her, "That sort of thing is over, all over, entirely over, for me," he fancied himself a pouch-eyed debauchee, an aged Brummell, a desiccated Windsor, unutterably weary and blasé.

As veil-eyed as he could make himself be veil-eyed, he repeated once again, "That sort of thing, decorative women, all of that"—with studied insouciance he waved the hand in which he held his half-smoked Elegante—"is over, all over, entirely over for me. . ."

Damn fool that he was. He should know enough by this time . . . But—ah, shades of De Sade!—the unhappier, the lovelier . . .

"Oh, Lisa, Lisa, Lisa . . ."

Quickly as the cruelty had come, as near to nature, so now upon the scene—so now, all nude, excepting for the figment of a fig leaf—arrived Mr. R. W. Tenderness (otherwise known as Rodney the Pure of Heart).

"Oh, Lisa, Lisa, Lisa, you are lovely to me, lovely . . ." Rape-rested, seeing her wet eyes, he meant every word he said. "I want you very much. I want so very much to be with you. Please believe me. *Please.*"

"Oh . . ."—she swallowed, smiled—"my baby . . . Oh . . ."—she swallowed, smiled—"I . . . I . . ."

The cold palm of her hand caressed his cheek, caressed his chin. He stirred in his seat, averted his eyes, he half closed them as, biting on his lower lip, he had the fanciful notion that everyone in the cafe, including General Miaja, was staring at them.

"I need a shave," he said.

"I like it this way," she answered gently, pressing her fingers against his chin before lowering her hand.

Sure she liked it this way. Almost all of them liked it this way. For although he knew that needing a shave made him more outwardly rugged, more I've-seen-the-worst-of-it-I've-been-all-through-all-of-it masculine, he also knew that needing a shave made him appear more distraughtly boyish, more moppety ducky, more winning. Which was why he needed a shave most of the time. Also—and what was more to the point—he knew that most of them liked it this way because they wanted to feel his bristly chin on the tender lips of their cunts.

"You don't want me to tell him?" she asked, with a trace of the hurt in her voice, "you don't want me to tell him today?"

"No, tell him," he said, "I've changed my mind. Tell him, Lisa." He felt something slightly sink in his stomach, but, "Tell him, Lisa," he said, "tell him today."

"You're sure it's all right? You're sure you won't get into trouble?"

"The only thing that bothers me now is the money," he lied.

"Oh, we can always get along . . ." She was very near to looking very happy. "Don't worry about money," she said, "that's the last thing we have to worry about."

"But I only have that five hundred dollars left, back in New York. I'll send for it. But what'll we do when that's gone?"

"Oh Rodney, if we need it I can borrow more money. But in Tehuantepec five hundred dollars should last us forever . . ."

Forever. My God! What was he thinking of? And she'd probably *always* look happy there. Jesus!

"What's the matter, *cheri,* what's the matter?" she asked, with a pink-lipped delible pout.

"Nothing, nothing,"—No backing out now . . . "Tell him," he said, "tell him today."

"You're sure?"

"I'm sure," he replied with something of gruffness.

"You love me?" she asked, with something of petulance.

"Lisa!"

"I'm sorry, I'm sorry, I'm sorry, *cheri.* It's just that I'm"—she looked pensive—"so happy. And it's been so long since I've . . ."

"Oh," he said, with a placated smile, "I understand. But let's never talk about love . . ."—aged Brummell, desiccated Windsor—"let's just . . ."

"Don't say any more, Rodney, I know what you mean . . ."

Did she? Amazing. For he didn't. Unless . . . unless she was thinking of fucking and sucking and . . . No, damn her, she wasn't. Not now. Her eyes looked like a madonna's.

"It will,"—with something of persistence she said it—"be so good, Rodney, so good . . ."

Oh, will it? Cautiously, with brown eyes gone dull black, gone shifty, he looked at her half-exposed ear, at the light mole near the pink fleshy lobe of it. Oh, will it? He lit another cigarette. It had a rank taste. He threw it on the floor, ground it out with the heel of his shoe. Then he began to laugh silently. Like that Huxley character, Maurice Spandrell, in *Point Counter Point.*

"Rodney, Rodney, you look so . . . so *strange."*

Still laughing silently, he stared at her. He stared at her closely, coldly, straight into her eyes. They seemed to grow greyer. She drew back in her chair, as far back as she could. She seemed to shrink. Oh, he'd beat the ass off her today, that's what he'd do! He should have brought a riding crop, but—he touched the buckle of his belt—his belt would do. He saw her watch him finger it. He saw her look lower, at the crotch of his trousers, at where his cock was pressing tight against the cloth. But then he saw her look away and, again, he saw her eyes were filled with tears.

"Oh, so I look *strange,* do I?" To conceal his hard-on, he pulled his chair closer to the table. "Well, why shouldn't I look strange? Listen,"—he grabbed her by the wrist—"I haven't been laid for three days and you know it, you hypocritical cunt. Stop being so sweet and motherly. You know damn well what you came here for. You know damn well that you . . ."

"Oh, but Rodney, you know that it's more than just for that."

"Shut up!"

He tightened his hold on her wrist.

"Rodney . . . Rodney, darling," she said, "I know why you're like this. Yes I do. I know why you're like this, but just for today can't we talk about Tehuantepec and . . ."

"To hell with Tehuantepec and all that shit! Come on! Come on, let's go back to see Our Lady of The Toilet."

He threw some money on the table. Then, buttoning his jacket to partly hide his hard-on, he stood up. Lisa didn't move. Her head was lowered.

"Come on! Get up!"

Slowly now she got to her feet and took his out-stretched hand. Her large grey eyes were saying no, were pleading; her mouth quivering.

"Must we, Rodney? Must we, *today*?"

"Yes,"—he pulled her away from the table—"yes, God damn it, we *must*."

He could feel his cock pushing against his trouser leg as he led her to the back of the cafe and through a swinging door. There, in a small tiled airless space, an old woman sat beneath the dim yellow light of an uncovered bulb. She was knitting. As they came in, she looked up and the stumps of her teeth faintly lightened her dark face.

"Ah!" She put her knitting down on the small table in front of her. She bowed a little. A leering smile contorted her Aztec face.

"Ah!" she said again as she stood up, "good afternoon, my friends, good afternoon . . ."

"Hello, Conchita," Rodney said and handed her some money.

"Muchas gracias, señor, muchas gracias . . ."

"Por nada. Now just take us back where we went last time."

"Si, señor, you are always welcome in Conchita's house. Conchita's house is yours."

There were two doors, one marked MEN, the other WOMEN. She led them to the one marked MEN, then stopped and said, "Wait, there's someone in there."

"Who?" said Rodney.

"The shoeshine boy, *señor,"*

Rodney put his hand on her bent shoulder. "Listen," he said, "Listen, Conchita . . ."

"Si señor?"

"Do you . . . do you think that the boy would go . . . would go back to your house with us?"

"No, Rodney!—No!" said Lisa.

"Shut up!"

He turned and slapped her. The old woman grinned.

"No, Rodney!"

Lisa ran to the swinging door. Rodney seized her by one of her thin shoulders, spun her around to him and slapped her again.

The old woman clapped her hands. She seemed to do a little dance of delight. Her eyes gleamed, like two black coals. Then she said, "Can Conchita come, too? Can Conchita stay this time? Conchita can help you, *señor.* Conchita can do many things for you, *señor."*

"Oh, Rodney, Rodney!" Lisa screamed, "You can't do this to me! You can't! You can't . . .!"

Rodney covered her mouth with his hand and signaled Conchita. Together they got hold of her and dragged her into the men's room where the dark handsome boy turned half away from one of the urinals, his long dark prick, almost black, still streaming piss.

"Pretty boy, pretty boy, pretty Miguelito," said Conchita, "don't be afraid. Don't be afraid. You want some money, Miguelito? You want to make some money?"

She went over to the boy who was still urinating. He had taken his hand away from his cock, but his yellow piss still streamed onto the stained shiny white of the tile. He didn't look at Conchita. He just kept staring at Rodney and Lisa with wide astonished eyes. Then Conchita spoke quickly to him. Her voice was low and tense.

Lisa had stopped struggling. She simply stood there, her head bowed, her shoulders shaking. "Oh, Rodney," she sobbed, "I know why you're like this. I know, I know, my darling, but . . ."

"Shut up!" he said.

He unzipped his fly and took his cock out. It was swollen hard and stiff.

Conchita and the boy both turned to look at him. The boy seemed frightened, but Conchita's mouth fell open and her eyes stared and stared at Rodney's erect tool. Then, breathing heavily, she said, "Come señor, come quick. Come quick before anybody else comes."

Rodney laughed. His cock drooped a little.

"I'm not going to come until after Miguelito does," he said.

With a masturbatory movement he pulled at his cock, then forced it back into his trousers.

"You do the same," he said to Miguelito.

"Si señor."

Obediently, the boy shook the last drops of urine from his long dark uncircumcised prick and Rodney saw that Lisa had looked up for one quick instant to regard it.

He slapped her. He slapped her again. "You little cocksucker," he said.

Like an animal after it's been beaten, she began to whimper.

The boy seemed less afraid now and his limp cock began to show its dog-like tip, very red in contrast to the dark brown skin, as, with a jerky movement of his ass, he made it disappear into his trousers.

"No, Rodney, no," Lisa was still whimpering.

He pushed her hard, pushed her hard in front of him, forcing her to follow Conchita and the boy to the back of the dim toilet where the old woman turned a knob in the grey unpainted wall and a door opened.

"Come! Come quick!" she hissed, and beckoned to them with her other hand.

Still pushing Lisa in front of him, Rodney entered the small room behind Conchita and the boy. It was entirely dark. Conchita closed the door, locked it, switched on the light. Miguelito went over to the bed, looked at it uneasily, then went to a corner of the room and stood there gazing at a colored photograph of the famous bullfighter, Lorenzo Garza.

The windowless room was almost entirely filled with a large Victorian bed that was made of brass. On it were some frayed cushions and a dirty lavender spread. Above it, just behind the copper-toned brass poles of the high headboard, was a small image of Jesus on The Cross, the strained ribs of the emaciated body clotted with wax blood.

Miguelito saw this now. He crossed himself. His eyes grew fearful. He began to move in the direction of the door.

"Pretty boy! Pretty boy!"—Conchita tugged at Miguelito's faded shirt—"Don't be a little fool. Don't . . ."

She looked at Rodney who had thrown Lisa on the bed where, face down, her shoulders shaking, she lay sobbing.

Rodney went over to the door and stood with his back to it. He looked hard at the boy, who was trying to pull himself away from the old woman. The boy glanced at Rodney, glanced away, stopped struggling. Then Rodney took out his wallet and handed him some money. The boy hesitated. He looked at Conchita. She shook her head in assent. "Take it, Miguelito. Take it!" she said.

The boy put his hand out and took the money. He stared at it, at Rodney, at the money again.

"Put it in your pocket, kid," said Rodney, "then get undressed. And you," he said to Conchita, "you get the hell out of here."

"Oh, *señor! Please.* Please let Conchita stay. Here . . ."—she hobbled over to the washbasin. She picked up a towel. She picked up another—"Here, Conchita can be nice to all of you. Conchita can . . ."

"No," said Rodney, "you . . ."

"*Señor!*"

The old woman got down on her knees in front of him and put her gnarled brown hands to his grey trousers. With contempt, Rodney pushed her away from him.

"Get out, you old sack of shit," he began, but then Conchita wailed, "Oh, *señor, señor!* I, Conchita, used to be the most beautiful, the best, whore in Mexico. Then my cunt, it got so big that I began to fuck dogs and donkeys for the tourist shows and . . ."

"I don't want to know the story of your life," said Rodney,

"get the hell out of here!"

With an agility that was amazing, the hag stood up and removed her skirt to thrust her old wrinkled belly at him and at the boy, who stood there wide-eyed.

"Look!"

She shoved both her hands up into her belly and then her arms also disappeared, almost to her wrists.

"Oh, for Christ's sake," said Rodney, "go out and get yourself a donkey."

"But *señor,* just think! You and Miguelito, you both have fine big pricks and you both can fuck Conchita, both get in at once!" Excitedly, she shoved her arms in and out of her monstrous cunt. "Yes! And I can spread my legs so wide that . . ."

"How would you like that, Miguelito?"—Rodney turned to look at the boy and laughed. The boy began to laugh then, too— "How about it, Miguelito?"

The boy looked down. He didn't answer, and again Rodney looked at Conchita who still had her hands buried in her belly. The gruesome sight was working on him oddly. His prick was ramrod stiff. Then he heard Miguelito say, "I will do what you want me to do, *señor,* but I do not understand the presence of these women. I thought that you would want to be alone with me . . ."

"What," said Rodney, "gave you that idea?"

Conchita began to laugh in a shrill voice. "Ah, *señor,*" she said, "you see? You see that Miguelito? He's just another little cocksucker, like all the young boys in Mexico City today. They just go around sucking off the tourists for money and letting the tourists suck them. They're no good, these boys. They don't know how to fuck. They're all just little cocksuckers. They're . . ."

Before she could finish what she was saying, Miguelito pushed his foot in her face and she fell flat.

"That's the boy, Miguelito," Rodney said. "And now listen, you old cunt," he said to Conchita, "we'll let you stay, but there's no fucking in it for you, got that straight?"

"*Si señor.*"

Submissively, the old woman got to her feet. She sighed. She took her blouse off. Now she was entirely naked. Her pendulous old breasts hung almost to her navel. They were wrinkled, like her belly, which sagged above the bush mound of hair around her cunt.

"God, but you're a loathsome sight!" said Rodney. "Oh well,"—he shrugged—"stay that way. Maybe I'll piss on you later. And as for you,"—he turned to Miguelito—"we'll teach you how to do more than just suck cocks. You see that over there?" He pointed to Lisa who was still lying on the bed, face down, lying there as if she were dead. "You see that bag of bones, Miguelito? Well, you're going to fuck that, Miguelito, and you're going to fuck it right, because if you don't . . ."

Rodney raised his fist. The boy flinched, then said, *"Si, señor. Si, señor.* I'll fuck the lady for you. I'll do anything you like, *señor.* I'll . . ."

"O.K. kid," said Rodney, "now take your clothes off."

He went over to the bed and sat down next to Lisa. Roughly, he took her by the shoulders. He turned her over.

"No, Rodney," she moaned, "no, Rodney, please, Rodney, no . . ."

Her eyes were tight shut. Her tear-stained face was still red from the slaps that he had given her. He slapped her again. He said, "Get up and get undressed!"

He turned away from her. He looked at Conchita. He glared at her. He said, "Hey you, get down on your knees! Go on, get down! Get down and take my shoes off!"

The old woman got down on all fours. Her hanging tits grazed the grey stone floor. Like a dog, she inched up to Rodney.

"Bark!" he said to her.

She raised her head and gave a grin that twisted her old brown face into a thousand tiny wrinkles. Then, "Ow! Ow!" the sound came forth, "Ow! Ow! Ow!"

"That's enough," said Rodney, "now take off my shoes and take off my socks."

While Conchita did this, he looked at Lisa. She still hadn't stirred. She still lay there, whimpering. Then he looked at Miguelito, who stood in the corner by the wash basin. The boy was stripped to the waist. His ribs, his chest, his shoulders, his arms, were brown, lithe, beautifully proportioned. He held his shirt in his hand. He didn't seem to know what to do with it, or with himself. He just looked at Rodney who looked at him.

"Come here, Miguelito."

The boy approached the bed. He did so with a kind of wariness.

"Don't be afraid," Rodney said and then he said to Conchita, "That's right, now get them off. Quick now. Quick!"

His shoes off and his socks, he pushed the old woman away from him with his bare feet. He stood up. Bending over, he grabbed hold of Lisa and pulled her off the bed.

"If," he said to her, "I have to tell you to get undressed again you'll be goddamned sorry!"

Still whimpering a little, head lowered, Lisa slowly began to undo the buttons of her dress.

"Help her!" Rodney shouted at Conchita.

The old naked hag went up to Lisa, who drew away from her and cried out, "No!"

Conchita cackled and began to paw at Lisa while Rodney shouted, "If you don't let her undress you I'll make you go down on her! How would you like that? Huh?"

"Oh, Rodney!" Lisa screamed.

Rodney bounded off the bed. He pushed Conchita to one side. He pulled off his belt.

"Get back!" he shouted at Conchita and the boy.

They went to stand in the corner by the door.

"Now take your dress off!" Rodney said to Lisa, and as he said this he hit her as hard as he could with his belt, slashing it down across her thighs. He hit her again. He hit her again, and again.

"Yes, Rodney," she said then, meekly, her voice sounding quiet and appeased.

"And let the old bitch help you."

"Yes, Rodney."

Rodney turned to the boy and to Conchita. "Now get back to work," he said to the old woman.

"*Si señor!*" — Conchita's face was seamed with a terrible look of satisfaction—"*Si, señor!*" she said, and hobbled back to Lisa.

Rodney went over to the bed. He sat down. He took his tie off and his shirt, then, "Come here, kid," he said to Miguelito, "come over here and sit down next to me."

The boy went over to the bed and sat down. There both he and Rodney, stripped to the waist, sat side by side watching the two women.

Conchita had gotten Lisa's dress off. She had seated her in a straight-backed chair. Now the old woman squatted on her haunches, haunches that looked like two pieces of dead meat. Her asshole spread. It was as big, as black, as deep, as her cunt. She squatted lower and, deftly, took Lisa's shoes off, then reached up and began to pull at one of her beige stockings. Lisa threw her head back and closed her eyes. Her slender neck and arms were very white against the pinkness of her panties and brassiere. Her soft blonde hair was all disheveled. Red marks showed on her pale face and on her long slim thighs, now bare, as Conchita pulled one stocking off and then the other.

When this was done, Lisa stood up. She looked straight in front of her, avoiding Rodney's eyes and Miguelito's. Conchita stood up, too.

"That's all right, I'll do the rest myself," said Lisa.

"No," said Conchita in a nasty voice, "the *señor* said that *I* should do it."

Her enormous breasts flopped against her wrinkled belly as she sidled behind Lisa to undo her brassiere and expose Lisa's small pink-nippled breasts.

"What pretty titties! What pretty pretty titties!" said Conchita as she faced Lisa again and reached with her brown hand for her pink panties.

"That's enough now, that's enough," said Lisa.

She looked imploringly at Rodney, who looked back at her with no expression and said nothing. She looked at Miguelito, whose large brown eyes were fascinated by her breasts, so high and firm and white. She looked at him again, at his strong young hairless chest, his full red lips. She blushed and looked away, but not before she glanced with fear at Rodney, who still looked at her with no expression and said nothing.

Conchita was clawing at her panties.

"Very well," Lisa said.

Instantly, it seemed, her demeanor became different. Angrily, she looked at Rodney and then, with a toss of her head, gazed directly at the boy, her eyes making no concealment of desire.

"Very well," she said again, her voice becoming hard, "take them off. But be sure to keep your tongue in your head, you' miserable creature."

With a vicious movement, Conchita pulled Lisa's panties down to her ankles. Then, before she could step out of them, she put her withered arms around Lisa's slim white legs and buried her wrinkled face in the silky young blonde hair of Lisa's cunt.

"Get away from me!" said Lisa, "get away! Get away!"

Wriggling her small hard ass from side to side, her smooth white belly moving with it, she tried to push Conchita from her, but with all her wriggling and her pushing she only succeeded in allowing the old woman to force her face deeper into the lovely crevice that lay between her legs.

"Get away, get away," said Lisa, but more softly and, sinking back onto the chair, she closed her eyes.

Now, like a hungry beast, Conchita shoved Lisa's legs apart, ripping her panties as she did this, and Lisa, with both hands, tore at Conchita's head, pulling at her dyed black hair. But the old woman held on fiercely, forcing her tongue all the way up between the pink wet lips of Lisa's cunt.

"Oh, Rodney!" Lisa cried.

Rodney stood up. He turned to Miguelito. He said, "Come over here with me."

They went over the chair and stood there watching while Conchita licked and sucked and licked and sucked, her thick grained purple tongue moving in, out, in, out, of Lisa's small pink cunt, in, out, in, out, just like a prick.

Lisa began to moan. She threw her head back. And now, instead of pulling at Conchita's hair, she held Conchita's head with both her hands, held it hard, held it tight, drawing it up close against her belly while she pushed her belly as far forward as she could.

Rodney looked at Miguelito. The boy's wide eyes were darting from Conchita's slurping tongue to Lisa's hard high tits, from Conchita's slurping tongue to Lisa's pale drawn face, and Rodney saw that Miguelito's cock looked as if it were about to rip the cloth of his blue trousers. His own cock was just as hard. Quickly, he unzipped his fly and took it out. Then, moving over to Lisa, he said, "Open your eyes and open your mouth," but she didn't do either and continued to moan.

"O.K.," said Rodney, "that's enough!"

He pulled Conchita by the hair, dragging her away from Lisa. Brutally, he kicked her to one side.

"I said," he said, "that there'd be no fucking in it for you. And that means sucking, too."

"*Si, señor,*" gasped the old woman, who had flopped to the floor heavily, her purple tongue, wet and coated with whiteness, hanging limply between her thick creased lips and the broken stumps of her teeth, "*Si, señor.*" But as she spoke to Rodney she kept staring fixedly at Lisa's white belly that was still slowly undulating, at the rhythmic beauty of this sight and at the damp blonde hair that fringed Lisa's small pink hole.

His rigid cock sticking out in front of him, sticking out like a sword, Rodney stepped up very close to Lisa now.

"Open your eyes," he said, "and open your mouth, goddamn you!"

As he said this, he slapped his burning tool across her face. Instantly, she opened her eyes. She put her hands to his cock and held its hardness hard. Then she moved her delicate lips along the long thick spear and let her small white teeth sink gently into it. First her teeth, then her tongue, caressed its entire length, biting a little and tickling, biting and licking. And then she put the red inflamed tip into her mouth and sucked at it and sucked at it while her innocent grey eyes roved up to the broadness of Rodney's bare chest and from there, still innocent, to Miguelito's, where they rested.

Rodney pulled his cock out of her mouth. He loosened the grip that her fingers had on it. He backed away from her.

"Listen,"—he twisted a strand of her hair and turned her face up to face his—"you're not fooling me a bit. You want that kid to fuck you, don't you?"

"No, Rodney, no." Her eyes were downcast now. Her voice was plaintive. "You know that I only want you."

"Liar!"

He took her by the wrist. He forced her to her feet. His cock pushed against her smooth white skin, making an indentation just below her tits.

"Oh, Rodney," she said, "I love you, I love you. Can't we stop this now, my darling?"

He backed away from her again.

"Oh Rodney," she said, reaching out her hands to him, "I do love you, I do, I do . . . All that I want is to be alone with you, to go to Tehuantepec with you . . ."

"We'll talk about love, about love and Tehuantepec later," he said, "now take my pants off!"

"Yes, dearest."

She got down on her knees, her face brushing against his slightly limp but still tumescent cock. She brushed her face against it harder, making it rise, stiff, to its full length and thickness. While she did this Rodney looked at Miguelito, who still stood there as if he were glued to the spot, except that one of his brown hands was manipulating his trousers at the crotch, where his cock bulged big, looking as if it were about to burst through, pierce, the thin material.

"Hey, cut that out!" said Rodney, "don't be in such a hurry, Miguelito. Don't worry. Your turn is coming. Now you just go over to the bed there and sit down."

"*Si, señor.*"

"And you," he said to Conchita, who still lay sprawled on the floor, now looking at Rodney's stiff cock, "Get up! Get up, and get to work! Take the boy's shoes off, the way you did mine . . ."

"*Si, señor.*"

"No, wait!"

Rodney stepped out of his pants, which Lisa had loosened. He kicked them aside, to where her torn panties lay. He pushed her away from him. He took off his shorts. Then, completely naked, he turned to the old woman who, half-risen, crouched there on her hands and knees, was still gazing at his cock.

"No," he said to her, "you just go over there and sit in the corner until we need you and . . . and stop looking at my cock!" He moved closer to her. He took hold of his cock and aimed it at her mouth. She jerked her head up and lunged forward. His cock was almost at her lips when he pulled it away. "Oh no," he said, "this choice morsel isn't for the likes of you. Now,"—he gave her a kick—"go over there in the corner and dream about donkeys."

"*Si, señor.*"

Conchita's voice was cracked and whining as she crawled away on all fours to sit herself down in the corner by the washstand and huddle there miserably.

"And now you,"—Rodney bent over and pulled Lisa to her feet—"you, my little *darling,* you go ver there, go over there to the bed, get down on your knees again and take the kid's shoes off."

"Yes, Rodney."

She went over to the bed where Miguelito was sitting stiffly and, dropping to her knees before the boy, took his shoes off while Rodney stood over them, watching.

"Now kiss his feet!"

The boy drew back on the bed. His face was flushed with embarrassment. He mumbled, "No, *señora* no . . ."

Rodney took hold of one of his legs and dragged him forward.

"Now sit still," he said, "and let the fine *señora* kiss your feet. Go ahead now!" he said to Lisa.

Almost avidly, she lifted one of the boy's brown feet to her lips. Her lips were very lovely and so was the boy's foot as she kissed it and kissed it again. She closed her eyes and ran her mouth along his beautiful small toes. She kissed each one of them. Then, opening her eyes, she gazed up at the boy, whose dark handsome face was more red than it was brown. Still holding his foot in her hand, she smiled up at him, smiled a soft, sweet, gentle smile and, taking his other foot in her other hand, she bent her head forward and kissed it.

"Now," said Rodney, with anger that bordered on rage, "take the kid's pants off!"

Lisa stood up and leaned over the boy, who lay there as if he were paralyzed. With a kind of tenderness she leaned very far over him, so that the pink tips of her white tits almost touched the boy's brown face. She put her face close to the boy's. It was very white in contrast to his. Then she whispered, "Don't be frightened, little one, don't . . ."

Rodney reached for her shoulder and pulled her away. He picked up his belt from the floor.

"I didn't," he said, "give you permission to speak to him! I just said to take off his pants!"

He pulled her to her feet. Her smooth white back and hard white ass and long white legs made his throbbing cock throb more. He raised the belt. He brought it down across her back, slashing as hard as he could. She fell forward, covering the outstretched body of the boy. Then he brought the belt down on her buttocks, making her writhe against the boy's still-covered cock, making her clutch his bare shoulders. Drawing back to slash still harder, he hit her again, then dropped the belt to the floor.

"Now take his pants off!" he said.

She let go of the boy's shoulders. Miguelito's eyes looked terrified. She drew herself up on her knees and began to unbutton his trousers. Rodney went over to the bed and sat down beside them.

"That's right," he said, as he saw the small black crop of hair above the boy's cock come into view, "now pull them down!"

While she did this he looked at the boy's cock. It was limp. There was no sign of its red tip. But it was long and brown and thick. Could it be bigger than his own? Could it be bigger than "the rod?" He felt his cock begin to droop as Lisa got the boy's pants off, revealing all his nakedness. Then he felt his cock descend, go soft, as the boy turned his back on him, turned over and lay prone.

"What do you want me to do, bugger you?" he said, but he said this quietly as he contemplated the boy's young brown ass, so firm, his well-shaped legs, so strong, his smooth broad back, his shoulders.

He looked away to look at Lisa who was standing over them. She, too, had been, still was, gazing at the boy.

"I'll bet you're just dying to ream him, aren't you?" he said. "Yes, you'd just love to stick that little sharp pink tongue of yours up that little tight black ass. Now wouldn't you? Wouldn't you, *darling?*"

She bowed her head as he grabbed her by one of her arms and pulled her down to the bed.

"Well, go ahead," he said, "yes, go ahead."

He backed away from Miguelito. He took her by the neck. He pushed her face against the boy's ass. The boy's body jerked forward. He pinned the blonde head against the brown ass. He held it there hard. He held it there close. Then he said, "Get your tongue up in there! Get it all the way up!"

As she buried her face in Miguelito's ass he loosened his grip on her neck, and as he saw the boy try to move away, then lie still, then begin to squirm, then begin to grind his body on the bed, he felt his own big cock begin to get hard again, become "the rod" again.

Now letting go of Lisa's neck, he watched her ash-blonde head dive forward, watched it push, push, push, against the smooth brown skin. He watched the boy's young body writhe, then moved himself so that he lay next to the boy, lay prone, like the boy. Feeling his cock ram itself into the cover of the bed, he reached for the boy's head and turned it to him. The boy's eyes were closed. He was breathing hard. The nostrils of his Indian nose were quivering.

"Look at me, Miguelito," Rodney said, saying it softly.

Slowly the boy opened his eyes and, timidly, looked at him.

"Feels good, doesn't it?" Rodney said.

The boy blinked his eyes at Rodney. He looked as if he were about to come.

Rodney jumped up. He reached for Lisa's neck and gripped it hard.

"All right," he said, "that's enough. That's enough of that, you little shit eater."

He pulled her off the boy and pushed her away, glancing at her face that was now wet with saliva and no longer white, but pink. Then he took the boy by the shoulders and turned him over. Immense, almost black, its red tip swollen, the boy's hard cock stuck out in front of him. Its red tip had a purple tinge. It looked like the bud of a huge flower that was about to burst into bloom.

"My God!" said Rodney, He stood above the boy and stared down at him. "My God!" he said again, "I think that the kid's cock is bigger than mine!"

"No, it isn't, Rodney."

With no warning, Lisa had crawled in front of him, so that, straddling the lower part of the boy's legs, her face was level with Rodney's cock. She took it in her hand. She held it tenderly. She kissed it, and after this she began to run her tongue along the stiff meaty underside of it, wetting every hair that grew there. Coming to his balls, she began to lick them, too. She let go of his cock. She cupped his balls in her hand. Then, with her other hand she grasped his cock again and held it tight while her tongue worked furiously around his balls and behind them, almost reaching the hole of his ass.

Rodney stood there passively and let her do this while continuing to look at the boy who, his eyes still closed, now put out one of his hands to grab hold of his cock.

"No!" said Rodney, "cut that out!"

He pushed Lisa to one side. He leaned forward. He pulled the boy's hand away. He slapped him lightly on the face. "Hold it," he said.

The boy opened his brown eyes and looked up at Rodney, half in fear, half with lust.

"Hold it," Rodney said again, "hold it, Miguelito. You don't have to jerk yourself off. Have you forgotten that you're going to fuck the lady for me?"

"No, *señor.*"

The boy raised himself on his elbows. His cock went down a little. He stared at Lisa, who had taken Rodney's cock in her mouth again and was sucking at it fiercely. The boy stared at her lips, stared at her tongue, stared at her tits, stared at her ass, and as he did this his cock rose again to full length.

"Ow! Ow! Ow!"

Lisa took her mouth from Rodney's cock and she, Rodney and the boy all turned to look at Conchita who, hunched up on all fours, was madly grinning at them while she barked.

"Ow! Ow! Ow!"

His cock flailing the air, Rodney jumped off the bed and went over to Conchita. He kicked her in the ass. He kicked her hard.

"You rotten old bitch," he said. "I didn't tell you to bark again! Now look,"—he took hold of her hair and twisted it—"there's no fucking, there's no sucking, and now there's no watching in it for you, either." He gave her another kick. "Turn around!" he said, "turn around and face the wall and if," he shook his fist at her—"you make another move or make another sound I'll . . ."

"*Si señor,*" she whined.

Her huge hanging tits flopping loosely, she turned her flaccid rump to him. She pulled it forward to sit with her veined legs spread out in front of her. Then, with her black head bent and the wrinkled folds of her fat back stretched like small shapeless tits, she sat there facing the wall.

Rodney went back to the bed. His cock was only half-hard now, but he saw that the boy's cock was still fully erect and that Lisa was looking at it while the boy looked at her—at her small firm tits, at her white belly, at the short blonde hair that grew around her cunt.

"And now," Rodney said, "and now you two ardent lovers . . . Get off the bed! Come on!"

He pulled at one of Lisa's legs, gave her a hard stiff punch on the cheek of her ass with his other hand, then dragged her off the bed and made her stand next to him. Awkwardly, the boy moved himself forward, his big cock seeming to weigh down the rest of his body. Then, his eyes lowered, his arms hanging loosely, his cock beginning to droop, he stood up to face Rodney and Lisa.

Rodney went to the bed. He sat down on the edge of it.

"Turn around, Miguelito. That's right. Now look at me."

With big scared eyes, the boy looked at Rodney. His cock, too, was only half-hard now, but its bright red tip still protruded a little from the dark brown, almost black, flesh.

"Now," Rodney said, "the *señora* is going to worship the rod. Then I'll give her permission to suck your cock and we'll see whose cock is bigger. *Señora*," he said sternly, looking coldly at Lisa, "*Señora*, you can now begin to worship the rod. And worship it in Spanish, in very clear good Spanish, so that Miguelito will understand."

Rodney moved forward, to the very edge of the bed. He spread his legs. His long cock hung limply between them.

"I said," he said, "that you're to worship the rod. Now begin!"

"Yes, my lord!"

Throwing her head back, and her shoulders, she said this in a clear even voice, with no hint of mockery. For a long moment she stood there in front of him, stood there silently gazing above him, not meeting the steady hard stare that he gave her, not seeming to see him or anything. She stood so straight that she looked taller than she was. She stood there motionless, like a white statue, a marble figure, all white, smooth and white, except for the burning red welts that Rodney's belt had left on her lovely back, on her hard tight ass, on the upper part of her long slim white slim legs.

"Yes, my lord!"

She bowed deeply, so that her hair touched Rodney's bare knees. Then, again, she threw her head back and in the same clear serious voice she intoned, "I love the rod. I adore the rod. I want the rod up my ass. Like this . . ."

She spread her legs. She stuck the middle finger of her right hand between the cheeks of her ass.

"Show the boy," said Rodney.

She turned, so that her ass was almost even with the boy's cock. She manipulated her finger, pushing it in as far as she could, pushing it up, in, until it disappeared. Then she bent forward, so far forward that the boy, staring down at her, could see her finger completely buried in the tight little hole of her ass, could see the smooth white skin around its pink edge, could see the lower part of her cunt, where a rosy wetness lightly moistened the silk-like fringe of soft blonde hair. The boy's cock again rose to its full length and stiffness. Its bursting carmine tip almost touched the pale palm of Lisa's outspread hand.

"Now show me," said Rodney, his voice quiet and commanding.

Bent forward as she was, she turned around, her face hitting against Miguelito's cock.

"Move back, Miguelito!" Rodney said to the boy, whose cock, as if independent of the rest of him, had plunged forward to lie thick and hot against Lisa's cheek, rubbing against her small white half-exposed ear, rubbing, rubbing, into her hair.

His beautiful brown body trembling, the boy muttered something inaudible and a fierce look came into his eyes as, panting like
an animal, he stepped back, stepped away, from Lisa.

"There," said Lisa, "there, my lord. There is where I want the
rod. There is where I want my beautiful, wonderful, my magnificent rod."

Her ass turned up to Rodney's face, she worked her finger in
and out of its exquisitely tight little hole. He spread his legs further
apart. His cock was now completely hard. Then, as she jammed her
finger up her ass again, he took hold of her wrist and viciously
pulled her finger away.

He arose. Still holding her by her wrist, he turned her around,
so that she stood facing him. Once more he sat down.

"Not yet," he said, "you can't have the rod up your ass just
yet. Now lick the shit off your finger. Go on! Lick it off! And take
your eyes away from me. Keep it fixed on the rod."

"No," he said, "you can't even touch it yet. You must worship
it first. Worship it!"

"Yes, my lord!"

Intently, she stared at his cock. As she did this she raised one
of her long slim arms above her head, revealing a soft light fuzz of
golden hair in the delicate curve of her armpits. She touched this
feathery softness with the fingers of her other hand. Then she made
the finger that she had just licked a pointed spear. She made it
ramrod stiff and the shine of her nail polish made it resemble a
small, erect, pink-tipped prick, a small, erect pink-tipped prick that
was fucking her armpit.

"Here, my lord," she said, still staring intently at his cock,
"here, my lord, is where I want the great rod." Almost frantically,
she moved the finger back and forth in the short silky growth of
hair that covered the oval crevice. "And here,"—she dropped her
hand and lowered her arm to raise her other arm and begin to make
the same fucking movement, frantic, in her other armpit—"yes, my
lord, I want the rod here, too. I love the rod! I adore the rod! It's
the biggest, most beautiful, rod in the world and I want it everywhere! Inside of me! Outside of me! Everywhere!"

Her mouth was dripping with saliva and her eyes, wide, crazy-
wide, still stared at Rodney's cock.

"Wipe your mouth," he said, "wipe it on my feet!"

"Yes, my lord!"

She almost fell to the floor and groveled there as she ran her wet mouth all over his feet, rubbing it hard against them. Then she brushed her mouth up one leg, up the other, and down again, her short straight nose flat on his muscular limbs, her white cheeks caressing the short dark hair that grew there.

"Enough. Enough of that," said Rodney.

He kicked her away from him. She fell back, so that she sat on the floor looking up at his cock and his balls. She lifted one of her hands as if to reach out and touch the round red knob where his long cock ended, but she lowered her hand almost at once and rose to her knees. She inclined her head. She moved an inch or two forward. Her head was now between his legs, which were spread far apart. With an expression of adoration in her eyes, on her lips, she looked up at the hot thick underside of his cock and at his balls that no longer hung but were now firmly held in their tight brown sack of skin.

"I love," Lisa said, "the rod's balls. The rod's balls are the most wonderful balls, the most beautiful balls, in the world, in the universe. They hold all that creamy come I love to drink, love to swallow. Oh, my lord, I beg permission to suck the rod! I beg of you, my lord! Let me suck it!"

Her mouth remained open. She pushed her tongue out of it. It lay over her lower lip, touching her chin. It looked like a come-covered clitoris. She gasped. She panted. Her grey eyes stared up—up, up—pleading with Rodney.

"You're not to look at me," he said, "look at the rod. Look at it closely."

Quickly, with a shudder of fright, she dropped her eyes. She closed them. She opened them. She closed them and opened them again. Then, half-leaning against one of his legs, she moved her head as near to his cock as she could without touching it. Her eyes were fastened on it.

"Oh," she said, "I want this great rod to bury itself deep in my throat. I want it to choke me! I want it to kill me! Oh, great rod! Great rod!"

She dragged herself away from Rodney and sat facing him again. She threw her shoulders back and tossed her head. Her eyes never left his long, thick, brown, stiff tool.

"Oh, great rod! Great rod!"—Lisa bowed low each time she said this—"Great rod! Great rod!"

Her eyes still concentrated on his cock, she slowly rose to her feet. She stepped back as far as she could. She raised her arms above her head. Then she began to salaam him, bowing very low, her eyes still staring at his cock as if nothing else existed in the world.

"I worship the rod!" she said, "the rod is my God!" she said.

Making deep obeisance, she kept on repeating this in a clear, calm, grave, quiet voice.

"I worship the rod! The rod is my God! I worship the rod! The rod is my God! I worship the rod! The rod is my God . . .!"

R. BERNARD BURNS

Under some other name, Mr. Burns is a famous, middle-aged American writer.

FIRE CHILD

Salambo Forest

She lay on him heavy and uncomfortable. When you were through with a woman her weight changed in your mind. He moved his arms and shook her awake. The eyes were still the color of the sky, but they, too, had changed.

"Leona! Raise yourself up. Get dressed."

She smiled; lazy, warm pink lips parting as she gazed into his face.

"J.J." The smile lengthened itself and she raised her two arms towards the top of his head, stretching. She loved him. It was a repulsive thing for a woman to love you, he told himself. A very repulsive thing when you were through with her.

"Good sleep." She moved, raising herself to a sitting position.

"It is late. You have to do the belly dance soon."

She met his cold tone with a hurt look. The hurt look hid a question.

This woman was like thin glass. She was wondering if he had seen her leave Tinker's wagon. He gazed back into her eyes, not changing expressions. Yes, he had seen her but that did not bother him at all.

"What is it, J.J.? You look so strange." She stood and bent

over him, her heavy milky breasts dipping into his shoulder.

"Get dressed, Leona. You have to dance."

She turned from him and stood silently staring at the opposite side of his tent. She was struggling with her tears. J.J. wondered how she had let herself get involved like this. He did not like the fear she had. The fear of speaking the truth.

"Ask me, Leona." He sat up on the cot and folded his long hands in his lap.

Slowly, like a mechanical doll, she turned.

"Ask you what?" She bit her lip and the warm salt water moved in her eyes a fraction away from spilling. He sighed.

"Ask me why I am treating you like this. Do you think it is because you were screwing Tinker last night?"

She did not try to deny it. The hay-colored-hair drooped around her naked shoulders as she bent her head in shame.

"Look at me, Leona." He spoke gently, not wanting to frighten her. If this had been his woman, if he had wanted her, he would not bother to speak. He would beat the hell out of her. He would tear her hair from her head.

"I am not treating you indifferently because of that. I understand that."

She moved the distance of three feet and kneeled in a fluid motion in front of his cot, taking his hands in her own. He shook his head and peered into the radiant mass of hair. Where had the novelty gone, he wondered. He had thought the light-colored hair so wonderful, a magical, angelical thing.

"We must talk, Leona."

In his lap, her head moved and he met the blue, blue eyes again. Pain filled them and swam over the delicate pink rims. "I know what it is, J.J."

"You tell me then, Leona. I do not like the tiptoe game we play lately. I never told you I loved you. I only wanted you, I am Gypsy."

"I know, J.J." The water continued but the expression did not alter. He knew she did not force the tears like some women might.

"You are so different. I did not want to fall in love with you. I know how you are." She hesitated, biting her lips as she sought the words.

"Tell me." He lifted a handful of hair and forced the head up so he could watch her face.

"You do not even want me anymore. You do not want me anymore!" The voice was rising ... entering hysteria. He slapped her neatly and she gasped, the tears turning themselves into vapor.

"Yes, Leona. Now we have spoken. I do not want you anymore. You can stay in the carnival ... but you must find another lover."

Disbelief flooded her face and she stood, backing up from him until an open trunk hit the back of her legs. These light women did not understand reality. They did not understand the truth. They said, tell me the truth, and then you told them. She opened her mouth and moved it, making no words. He watched the anguish ... from a safe distance. She was a good person. He did not want to hurt her but he would not feel guilty.

"I never promised you anything. I never said love. I have never loved one woman! Why are you so shocked, Leona?"

"Is . . ." her voice choked, coughed the words out. ". . . it Tinker?"

"Leona, I understand need. I am Gypsy. You went to Tinker out of pain, and out of pain he took you. Is that simple, no?"

Understanding filled her eyes, a warm moving thing. She walked towards him again and stopped in front of him.

"You are wise. I am a beggar."

"No, Leona, not a beggar."

Yes, her head nodded, eyes closed for a momentary flash.

"I am a beggar because I am foolish enough to love you. I let myself fall in love with you. You know it's crazy. All along I told myself, 'don't fall for this guy. He loves women, not a woman. He is a whore.' " She smiled and met his returning smile. The tears were fresh in her eyes. Well, he would let her cry. Women liked to cry, and she was a good woman.

"As I was telling myself this about you ... I forgot to believe it. I just said it." She looked down at her nakedness. He knew she ,was remembering the love-making they had shared just before she fell asleep on him. She touched the round tummy, a smile on her lips. "Every woman, J.J., every woman in the world looks at a man and says ... he is a wanderer. Or, he is impossible to get ... But I ... yes, I can do it. They all think they are the one to do it." The last words trailed off and the tears fell in earnest now. He sat, his hands, long brown spiders, restless on his knees as he watched the heavy rain. She stood, so pitiful, in the center of the tent, just a little way from his lack of touch; naked, her belly round and filled with his sperm, her hands listless and empty by her sides as her head—a halo of light—hung sadly. So sadly, the tears falling in streams. He watched, unable to move as the warm water splashed onto the dirt, splashed onto her red-painted toenails.

Was the world made of such sad pictures, he wondered. He could not help her, could not revoke his words, his decision.

She spoke to the sawdust, her mouth wet like her eyes. She did not face him with the accusation. Instead she let it fall with her tears. "Gizelle. You wanted me, desired me . . . until you made love to her. It is her, the red-haired demon! You want to conquer her now."

He sighed and looked at her wet toes. It would be foolish to answer that. It was partially true. He wanted to conquer her . . . but he did not think he wanted any more than that. If he told Leona anything, she would twist it with her blind love. The way to dislodge a woman was to hurt her so . . . she would look to escape. Perhaps he would use Gizelle for the final touch.

"I am a Gypsy, Leona. I do not like ties, not even the gentlest of ties. Some man is waiting for you."

"Gizelle," she insisted stubbornly, looking up now, her face ugly from pain and salty acids. She wiped it with her two hands like a child would do.

He stood slowly, deliberately. "You have to dance soon. Get ready."

She moved, stepping in front of him. "J.J. Tell me how to be and I'll be that way. Anything you want! Even once in a while . . . take me!" Her hands were the reaches of woman, demanding lies, demanding . . . possession. They gripped his shoulders as he tried to pass her. He stared down at the face, and realized she had spoken true when she had called herself a beggar.

"Stop. It is over." He dislodged the hands roughly and walked from the tent, anger trying to escape from his tight jaws. There were words he wanted to fling at her. Insults! The night carnival swallowed him. He moved past the tent. Fortunetelling booths, wheel of fortune . . . lost in the night. He knew it was partly his own guilt that drove him from Leona's pain. While he had not promised her anything, he had not told her not to hope. Women took that much silence as a promise. He slapped his leather vest pocket for a cigarette and watched the crowd gather at the opposite end of the meadow. A graceful flash of emerald-green costume twinkled as it caught the light with its many sequins. It was Gizelle, the hot-tempered she-devil. Each night her crowds grew bigger as the young men in the town passed the word. J.J. smiled, forgetting the past few hours spent with Leona lying on his chest. Gizelle had been inflaming the young students with her fine, slinky hips and vulgar movements.

J.J. scratched a wooden match on the sole of his shoe and pushed past the hordes of shabbily dressed patrons. He moved toward the emerald-green flashings, still smiling as he chewed his cigarette. He remembered her young body as it took all it was offered. Her slim outraged wrists struggling against the rope. He smiled, moving in among the young, sweating boys and the overweight middle-aged men. His eyes moved among the men, noting the gentle swelling produced in each pair of pants. It was funny, a relief after the too-serious Leona. He knew he stood out like a sore thumb with his one earring, his vest of black leather and his long curling tendrils of hair. A red bandana was tied across his forehead. He folded his long muscled arms and stood chewing on the cigarette which dangled close to falling while he stared up at the twinkling red-haired Gizelle.

How her eyes flashed! She would stick a knife in his heart if he gave her a chance. He was teasing her, making her nervous. She had been sure of herself, up on her little platform, undulating, glorying in the mass hard-ons and now he was here laughing at her. She turned, losing her perfect seductive rhythm as her eyes flashed at him again. He grinned, the cigarette tight between his teeth. After all, how could she feel sexy now . . . when he was there. Had he not told her he had fucked better horses? He nudged a man who stood next to him. He bent and whispered in the man's ear.

"You think that is something. You should see her with the few beads off!"

The red face of the man grew even redder and he laughed licking his fat lips. Gizelle moved in anger now . . . her little platform quaking with her temperamental feet. The two musicians laughed at this display and J.J. left the crowd—moving through the swarming people—laughing to himself. That would get her goat. He saw Tinker leave the big yellow tent and move toward his tent. J.J. moved quickly, catching up with him.

"Tinker?" He placed his hand on the big man's shoulder and grinned into the big handsome eyes. "Were you looking for me?"

Tinker nodded, crossing his big arms with a sigh. "Yes, I wanted to ask you about that . . . Gizelle. I think we will get rid of her. Bastet thinks she will bring much trouble. It has already begun."

"Mildene," J.J. supplied, digging into the dusty earth with his boot heel. "We are all wise to her, Tinker. We know how she thinks." J.J. peered into the face of the older man, thinking how good a friend he was. He would not mention Tinker sleeping with Leona. Tinker must have had a great need to let a white woman seduce him.

"I know, but the risks . . ." Tinker stopped and examined J.J.'s face. "Do you have a . . . wanting for her?"

"I want to break her . . . and see if she is any good. Let me have her for a few more weeks. If she is still so wild and unpredictable, then . . . let her go." J.J. hesitated. "It is a favor I ask."

Tinker thought, his eyes heavy with the weight of . . . J.J. knew, his secret love. The secret that everyone knew but no one could tell.

"It is, in the end, your decision, Tinker. You are the boss," J.J. offered. If Tinker decided to get rid of the red-headed Gizelle, then it would rest like that. After all, she was only a source of new amusement to him. He tired easily of women. The young girl's fire was a fuel for him. It would last a while and then it would go the way of all his affairs. Like Leona.

"A favor." Tinker spread his heavy legs apart and drew his mustaches down from his lips, fingering the thick growth of hanging hair. "Okay, J.J. You can have your new . . . toy. Until we see. I only ask . . . that you keep her away from . . ."

J.J. held his hands and smiled. "It is done, Tinker. I thank you. I will keep watch over further mischief." J.J. bowed to Tinker as he began to leave.

"J.J. I slept with Leona last night." The words were rigid as they left the proud man's throat. "I . . ."

"It is well if you had a need, Tinker. She is not . . . as everyone knows . . . my woman."

Tinker thought for a moment. "Yes . . . it is too bad. She is a good woman."

J.J. nodded, not wishing to discuss the merits of Leona. He smiled and moved towards his tent. He hoped that Leona was back in her own tent by now. It was strange, the compliment that Tinker paid Leona. He had said it was too bad that Leona was not J.J.'s woman—Tinker, the hater of the light-skinned people. Now the only person that did not know about Tinker and Leona's night of . . . whatever it was . . . was Mildene . . . J.J. hoped she would not find out. On the other hand, it might be the thing to . . . set things right between Tinker and herself. The two brooders!

J.J. cautiously lifted his tent flap and heaved a sigh of relief as Leona did not appear. He moved towards his cot and lay heavily upon the cushions, glad of the chance to be alone for a moment. He closed his eyes for a second and let his ears filter out the noises from the carnival grounds. Among those noises was the steady padding of feet . . . heading in his direction. Leona, he told himself, shutting his eyes tighter, pretending sleep. He did not want to speak to her any more about . . . anything. The steps reached the tent and stopped. She was hesitating, he decided, out of fear. Finally the tent flap moved, canvas sounds against canvas sounds. He inhaled silently, sighing in his pretended sleep. The footsteps crossed to his cot and stopped.

"I know you're awake, smart-ass!" He smiled, his eyes still closed. "Get up! Come on!"

He opened his eyes, still smiling. Gizelle stood there, wearing her green dress and her temper. He sat up on the cot and met her flashing eyes.

"Okay, you've had your fun with me, Mister, now I'm asking you to lay off. What did you tell that man?"

"What man?" J.J. asked, the smile changing. Who did she think she was anyway, marching into his tent and demanding answers of him. Hadn't she learned anything from their little lesson?

"You know damned well! He propositioned me! Dirty old man!"

"I thought you might need the extra money." His voice was

serious now.

"You're a filthy worm!" She stood and made her way to the tent entrance. He smiled. She was probably remembering yesterday and how important it was to get to the exit first. He stood.

"Filthy worm?" He shook his head, amused. "What's the matter, are you making your getaway, little girl? I guess you remember yesterday?"

She spat on the dusty earth with a violence he had only seen in gypsy women. He made a tsk, tsk, noise and rolled his eyes. He liked playing cat and mouse with her. She took herself so seriously.

"I don't think it was worth remembering," she threw at him and ducked under the tent flap. He lifted the canvas, watching as she moved quickly through the tent shadows. She wanted him to follow her! Sure! She was like all women. Well, he would not follow her. Perhaps he would wait for her to give in and come to him. He lit another cigarette and lay back daydreaming. He did not turn around at the padded footsteps. This time he was sure to whom they belonged.

"Okay!" She grated the words, walking slowly to his side, her small hands clenched.

She was certainly a strange one. He lay still, closely examining her. Gizelle wore a stone face. Her body did not move. It seemed that she did not breathe.

"Okay what, little girl?" he asked lazily, pouting smoke rings.

"Okay . . . I want to screw you."

"Oh?" he smiled. "I don't think so." He showed his even teeth. "I already had you. Once is enough."

She moved closer, a tight smile on her mouth. "That's a lie. Besides, I don't just want you alone. I want . . ." J.J. turned around and stared as Rowena entered the tent with a young man. Gizelle met his returning eyes, smiling at the question in them.

"What exactly is going on here?" He sat up slowly, feeling annoyance at this little bitch who supposed so much. How the hell had she found out about Rowena . . . and just what did she expect?

"It is a party. Your little friend invited us." Rowena let her dark eyes travel the long length of Gizelle's body.

Gizelle walked slowly over to the man and curled her arm around his neck, her mouth opening in a sensual invitation. J.J. eyed Gizelle angrily. He had seen the young man before, lingering in front of Gizelle's little platform. He did not like the idea. He wanted to tell them all to get the hell out. The little cunt took a lot for granted. Still, . . . he stood watching her kiss the young town boy, watched her tongue flicker behind his front teeth. He was a well-hung boy. J.J. could see the evidence as Gizelle ran her fingers down the front of his pants. She stopped suddenly, turning away from the boy, her eyebrows raised at J.J. Rowena watched, amused.

"Hey whoremaster! Does a little groupie frolic throw you? Are you shy this evening?"

"You've never been with more than one young jerk at a time," J.J. stated, his humor returning as he bowed to the boy. The kid was good-looking; not more than twenty-two. He returned J.J.'s challenge with a tight smile. A sudden silence filled the tent as the four people stood, not quite knowing how to handle the situation. J.J. could not help the short laugh that tore his throat. She was clever all right. Very clever; very much a scheming little . . . what . . . could he really name her? He folded his arms and took in the characters of this little melodrama. What could her purpose be? Did she just want to show him up? Did she want to flaunt her qualities . . . make him jealous? What the hell was the evil little bitch up to? She was special all right. Fire and hell behind green eyes.

"Gizelle? I came at your invitation. Shall we start?" Rowena moved towards Gizelle. When she was a few feet away she turned and grinned at J.J. Rowena did not like the girl either. J.J. could see that she had come to teach her a lesson. He nodded imperceptibly . . . a slight incline of his head towards Rowena. Yes, they could just turn this into a real lesson for sweet Gizelle.

"Rowena . . . undress our friend, while I secure our privacy." The boy looked around nervously as J.J. took down the tent flap and tied it to a thin metal pole. He then blew out the oil lamp and lit instead a small array of candles that stood on a little hassock next to his trunk. The tent danced with the new light. He turned around and slowly, methodically, undressed. Rowena stood over Gizelle, pulling from the girl the last traces of emerald costume. J.J. moved close behind Rowena and lifted her loose blouse up over her head. She moved her thin, seductive hips as Gizelle, smiling in the eerie light, tugged at the older woman's skirt.

"Joey . . . come help me." Gizelle sat down on the cot and held out her hands to the boy. He approached with a certain amount of caution that J.J. found annoying. A Gypsy would not dare to appear so unsure . . . sexually. The boy reached out and touched Rowena's skirt, helping Gizelle tug it down over the slim hips. J.J. bided his time, fingering his cock as he watched the rude display of boy and females playing at undressing each other. A lesson would be learned tonight. J.J. advanced, stopping to stand over Gizelle, menacing her with his smile and slowly expanding cock. He pulled at his extension with both hands, smiling all the while. Gizelle looked away from him with a sneer and held out her arms to the boy, Joey. Joey took his cue nervously and kneeled beside the cot, his hands gripping both her breasts with adolescent eagerness. Rowena clutched at Gizelle's fine, light-skinned thighs, bending her head over the flame-colored pussy and kissing it with little noises. Gizelle moaned, taking the boy's hands in her own and placing them on her belly.

"Push down," she told him, moving her head as she pulled him up. He stood, kneading her belly with his sweating hands and Gizelle pulled him towards her with her two long-fingered hands on his young, long, thin cock. She smiled sarcastically at J.J. and took the boy in her mouth, pulling on him with her sucking lips. He growled deep in his throat, forgetting his nervousness, forgetting his audience. He fell upon Gizelle with little ceremony, pushing Rowena out of the way. Rowena stood, annoyed, glaring at J.J. as she watched the young boy tumble on Gizelle, his hands around his cock now, jabbing at the tight hairs guarding the recesses of her womanhood. J.J. folded his arms, raising his eyebrows at Rowena in mock display of embarrassment. Rowena laughed, but the boy did not hear. Gizelle tossed, trying to make the best of her fumble-fingered lover. J.J. stood over her, looking into her eyes when they opened in annoyance over the boy's shoulder. He found the mark and shoved his young, lagging member in. J.J. smiled as the flesh sagged. Too much desperation. The boy would probably be able to do it . . . one day. Now, he was just a fool, getting deeper into his shame, but not deeper into Gizelle. Sweat jumped in the twinkling candles as Rowena and J.J. stood, looking down unmercifully.

J.J. took pity and pulled the boy from Gizelle's straining body, lifting him under the arms, standing him on the floor where he stood, enraged at J.J., at himself. He folded his fingers over the air, wanting to strike J.J., who only shook his head. He smiled at Gizelle, who glared at him, turning the candlelight to green flame.

"Take it easy," Rowena whispered into the boy's ear.

"There is no hurry. She is right. Watch . . . and perhaps you will gain control of yourself." J.J. moved past the boy and lifted his leg, straddling the thin cot and the body of Gizelle. Gizelle . . . so fiery in the light, her eyes slits of anger, lay open, like an abused flower, beneath him. Just the sight of those angry little tits, the round mound of the belly, the thighs wet from the kid's sloppy movements. He stood, not moving, his cock hanging heavy and heavier as it grew between his legs. Her eyes went to the stiff joint, a finger raised . . . and touched it. He smiled. Her anger would be put to a better use. Rowena moved in, taking the boy by the arm and leading him close to the head of the cot . . . so that they both stood behind Gizelle's head, watching. J.J. glanced at Rowena, watching her take the boy's cock in her hands, kneel and place him in her mouth, all very quietly. The boy closed his eyes and opened them again as J.J. moved, sitting easily on Gizelle's stomach, bending low over the breasts and . . . taking the nipples one at a time and biting them tenderly. So tenderly that a look of surprise filled the angular face of Gizelle. He did not want to disappoint her so he bit . . . harshly . . . then softly again. Her fingers reached for him, forming a cylinder which slid silkily up and down, drawing him out to new lengths. He moved his ass over her belly, pulling the tight pubic hairs with his own hairy backside. He felt the wetness form in her hot little pussy, dribble out onto his weighted balls as they hung, swishing over her hole like pendulums. Still, he was not ready. He contained a grin. This was his show. He knew what he would do. She thought she had engineered this whole show, but she had lesson number two coming. His black hair moved over his neck, tendrils falling over his high forehead. His hand gathered her breasts and tugged at them, moving with the gentle rhythm of her pulling on his cock. He pulled from her grasp, releasing her tits as he turned smoothly, pivoting around on her silky wet body. His mouth was directly over her pussy now and he smiled, thinking of how she would look to Rowena and the boy as his ass, cock and balls landed . . . all together, on her face. He bore his weight down on her ass as he parted the cunt lips with his tongue, taking the clitoris roughly between his teeth. He felt her mouth open with a gasp of pain and he . . . shoved . . . his cock falling deep into her pink throat; choking her with its still growing weight. He heard the boy make a sound in his throat. Rowena would be working on the boy at the same time. The unspoken play lay between Rowena and himself. He smiled into the scented pussy. She had thrown cheap perfume on her pubic hairs. He bit, his fingers pulling the lips far and wide apart as he pumped his heavy cock into her throat. The heavy balls hit her eyes; he felt them, cool under the hot sacs. He thumped harshly, wanting to hurt her.

It would take all his courage to do . . . what he planned. Not yet though. He chewed her, sucking the fish smell deep in his nostrils, sucking the thick juice down into his throat and swallowing. At the opposite end of the bed she was doing her share, probably showing off for her audience. He thumped his cock down harder with that thought. Sounds of strangulation filled his ears and thoughts as he moved. Her legs, spread wide, moved, the tight, lithe thighs quivering like jello. He grabbed a foot in either hand and pushed against the legs, biting hard on one of the cunt lips.

Yes, he told himself, if he worked at it he could come now. In her mouth, leaving her with the salty taste of his sperm and little else. He would begin tonight's lesson. He moved his ass, waving it back and forth in the eerie candle glow as he fought with his tight insides, working the thick fluids up from his inmost bowels; pump, pump. He moved, deep, her throat was tiny, stretched wide, her lips cracking at the corners as he pumped. Once more, he thought, almost hearing the harsh noise of it. Once more! It was hard for him to come so quickly. He was used to long, drawn-out love-making. Yes, there it was, uncoiling like a sleeping dragon, melting in its secret pit, flowing to the surface. With a violent, painful jab he cracked his back portions down solidly against her face. He would smother her as he came, would clog her nostrils with his ancient, white pudding! Woosh! Up from the bottom. His prick stood erect in her throat, spread so wide, himself so embedded that he wondered amidst the blinding ecstasy of orgasm, whether or not he would be able to withdraw when the time came. She was drowning in his violent come, her pussy jerking upwards, smacking his lips with the sweet wetness. He deliberately held out, deliberately gave his ass a final whack and withdrew himself all at once. leaping up from her sweaty body, standing above her, his cock dripping thick sperm onto her face. She cried out, cursing him. She reached for him. It had hurt him to leave so soon. No matter, though; he had to stay in command. If he gave in to his simple desires . . . he would be added to her list of imaginary and real . . . conquests. He wiped sweat from his eyes and stared at Rowena as she kneeled at the boy's cock, sucking greedily. The boy's eyes were glazed with lust. He stared down at the ransacked body of Gizelle, watched her outstretched arms, listen to the cries. He looked at J.J., the question bright and feverish in his eyes.

J.J. nodded, unsmiling. Rowena released the boy's member and stood, swaying towards J.J. Gizelle half sat up, her head twisting as she sought the body of J.J. He moved away from the bed and sank to the floor beside the cot, pulling the hungering Rowena with him. Rowena took his cock in her mouth and worked at reviving it, making noises with her lips and sliding hands. J.J. put his hands behind his head and watched Gizelle, watched the eyes. Joey moved towards her like a dreaming man, his young, thin cock erect. Gizelle let her eyes fall on that young weapon and cried out as she crashed J.J.'s eyes with her own.

"No!" she cried. The boy fell upon her again, savagery in him now, built by the three of them. He found her easily this time and pushed impatiently against her flailing arms as he inserted himself. J.J. watched, his cock growing hard again in the well-trained mouth of Rowena. He moved his hips, watching the legs of Gizelle wrap around the boy's thin legs. She wanted him! She wanted J.J., not that stupid kid. He moved again and Rowena bit the red tip of his cock, sucking the saliva of Gizelle's sweet mouth from his cock. Gizelle made the best of what she had to work with. She thumped her belly against the boy's, her fingernails clawing deep in his soft shoulder. She pumped. The long thinness of his cock was in deep; deep as it would go, but the crazed Gizelle demanded more. Her legs held him captive and she pumped hard, red hair wet and flying, eyes closed in tight desire. She would come to spite him. She would come . . . making do with that skinny little prick.

The anger rose hot in J.J.'s throat, watching the long legs kick air into slices. The blond head of the boy moved, growling as he worked at it, taking nipples in his mouth, chewing, leaving strands of saliva. J.J. saw the slick wetness on Gizelle's tossing face, the sweat mingled with his own come. From side to side, crazed, madness in her wide-awake eyes now, she grabbed handfuls of the boy's hair and screamed.

"Come on, you bastard. More than that! Give more!"

J.J. fought against the desire to tip the child-man away from her and finish the job himself. Only he could fill her now, only he could stretch that hole wide enough. Rowena pulled, taking his joint from her mouth and pressing it like a dainty flower between her two large breasts. J.J. half stood, almost losing control. Rowena made an animal noise. He caught the hatred in her eyes as she watched him move towards Gizelle and the inexperienced boy. She left his cock waving and turned her body around, kneeling; her ass, still beautiful, waving in the air. She reached behind her and parted the small opening for him. Good Rowena had saved his blunder. He fell upon her brown butt and forced the opening, sticking his wet, mottled head, grown huge again, inside . . . slow at first, then more and more. His eyes never left Gizelle as she fought her battle, trying to climax with that smallish rod working her like a screwdriver. He drove himself deep into the tight, dryness of Rowena's ass, his hands gripping the cheeks as he rode. Sliding in, pretending that she was Gizelle. He worked against Rowena's experienced movements. Gizelle fought and drove her belly, beat the boy on the back with her fists. Her legs were around his neck now. He half kneeled, ramming her, his white teeth biting her breasts as he swooped down like a vulture. J.J. heard Rowena scream and realized, as in a dream, that he had caused that cry. Gizelle moved faster and faster, making grunting noises . . . finally straining her trim hips against his pelvis and screaming . . . "Give me! Give me!"

J.J. moved harshly, beating Rowena with his fists as he sank into her deeper and deeper. She fell to the floor and he slid his hands under her pussy, sticking his fingers up her juicy cunt. The boy screamed, a yell of pure joy, shooting his boyish come half onto her belly, half into her hole, lost in his wild enthusiasm. J.J. moved against the rhythms of Rowena; feeling her strain, filling his hands with her hot, thick come. He shot wet suds into her bowels and lay still, resting on the proud butt as he watched Gizelle's mouth go slack and unlovely. She pushed the gleeful boy from her body and made a sign of disgust. He looked around sheepishly at J.J. and Rowena in their tumbled relaxation, standing naked among the perverts he would tell his college chums about.

"Get out of here!" J.J. said softly.

The boy backed up and reached for his pants. It was a strange scene. They all watched him; J.J., Rowena, Gizelle. He flushed as he dressed, fitting his spent weapon back into his trousers. He slipped into his shirt, not bothering to button it; looking nervous now, licking his lips.

"Hurry up and go."

"Okay. Just a minute. I owe . . ." he fumbled in his wallet and took two shining twenties from it. He dropped them on Gizelle's belly where they fluttered in the horrified eyes of J.J., and stuck to the wet slime. Gizelle smiled.

"That's it. Anytime."

With a roar J.J. stood; his cock made a sucking noise as it left the surprised anus of Rowena. Rowena half sat up, staring at Gizelle. J.J. looked at Rowena to be sure. Yes, she too was taken by surprise. He strode naked across the room and lifted the boy high off the ground, sending him crashing to the soft earth. He clenched his fists and backed up. Rowena moved, seeking her skirt. She found it and pulled it on, adding the blouse hurriedly. She knew what was going to happen and did not want to hang around.

"Come on, stupid!" Rowena pulled the light blond boy from the dust and tugged him towards the tent flap. She bent hurriedly, unwinding the rope that held the flap closed. The boy had a glazed look in his eye. He was lucky it was not more than a glazed look. J.J. moved towards him again.

Rowena moved like lightning, standing in front of the boy. "He did nothing!" She held her arms out towards J.J. Behind her, the boy slipped out the tent flap and made his escape into the night. Rowena shook her head, glaring with disgust at Gizelle. She spat three times on the dusty floor and made a vulgar sign towards Gizelle that indicated . . . more than mere words could explain.

"You fix her good, no? She make us into . . . dirt!" J.J. moved towards Rowena and turned her around with a gentle, but masterful hand. She ducked under the flap. He contained his rage momentarily, turning slowly back to the outstretched Gizelle. She smiled coyly, lifting one of the twenties.

"Here! You earned this, honey!" She dropped the bill to the floor and shrugged. Defiance glared in her eyes. Rage moved like a lion, twisting the thin bars of containment. Then, rage was loose.

He moved, lumbering, blind; his eyes filled with red flame. It only took one hand to turn the cot over, dumping the light girl to the floor. She let fear into her eyes for a moment and then returned to the old defiance as she rubbed her hip.

"Stand up, bitch! Whore bitch!"

She stood, her head proud. He reached with his backhand and knocked her to the floor. She rolled across the floor, screams stangling in her throat. Now she would cry! He half ran towards her and lifted her by her red hair, shaking the beautiful head. He flung her across the cot and looked on the sandy floor for his belt. When he found it he doubled it up and smacked his hand with it several times to see how it would feel on her plump bottom.

She watched him come, frozen. In a flash she rolled from the bed across the tent floor, her body covered with dust as she tried to reach the tent flap. He caught her and straddled her body. He wanted to kill her.

"Unhh!" She tried to roll, tried to free her pinned hands. "What did I do so terrible? The same things you do . . . all the women do . . ."

"There is no pay!" he growled, redoubling the belt.

"I did it . . . to get to you. Look what you did . . . Don't blame me . . . You filthy fuck! You whore-sucker! I hate you!" Her hands slipped free and she beat his chest with small rock-hard little fists. He grabbed her hair and slid her out from underneath his heavy thighs. Deftly he turned her around, still gripping her hair. He bent her over the cot and held her with his thighs while he beat her with the belt.

"There . . ." slap! slap! slap! . . . "are no prostitutes here," . . . slap! He could not stop once he had started. Not until red welts began to rise in uniform positions did he fully realize what he was doing. Beating this little whore as if she were his own woman! A little slut like that. As if he would have a woman like that. He lifted his weight from her and stood, waiting for her to move. She didn't even whimper. He turned her over and was mildly shocked to see that she had passed out. You would think someone so evil could stand a lot more pain. Her eyes were closed, her mouth childlike in appearance. He shook his head, reaching for his pants. He pulled them on hastily. He was not sorry for having beaten her. She had gone out of her way to disgrace them, to make him and Rowena feel cheap, to make them feel as if Gypsies were fakers, were cheap and tawdry . . . like herself! She sighed in her unconscious world and smiled, sweet and soft. It was the first smile he had ever seen on her. It was a gentle thing. He wondered where it came from. Only some disaster, like a flood or an earthquake, would bring that smile when she was awake. He drily composed his mouth and rolled her in the thin blanket, covering her nakedness. He was unmindful of her welts as he heaved her to his shoulders. It was too bad she had passed out. She should have to endure her pain, feel it as long as it lasted. She would think twice before doing something so stupid. It could bring the law down on them, they could be refused admittance to a whole string of states. He gave the blanket a thump as he ducked under the tent flap. He hoped that Leona was out for a stroll or something, although he doubted it.

He entered the small tent and met the empty, blue eyes of Leona. She stared at the red-topped bundle. J.J. dumped the girl from the blanket and she rolled naked onto her cot. She woke up, her mouth forming pained sounds.

"What happened?" Leona urged the words out past her dry lips, her hands rising to her cheeks in horror as she saw the bloody welts.

"Gizelle seems to think it enjoyable to run a little prostitution ring on the side." J.J. spat at the now wide-awake redhead. Their eyes met and clinked, swords crossing. He watched her carefully try to hide her pain. Were there tears swimming in her eyes now? If they were, they were only tears of physical pain.

"Good night." He snapped his blanket out from underneath her, moving past Leona. Leona followed him out into the night, pretending she did not hear the foul language Gizelle used as she spat his name into hunks of filth.

"J.J.!" She touched his shoulder carefully.

He turned, tiredly, the blanket hiding his bare chest. "What, Leona? I'm tired."

"I just wanted to ask if it's true. I mean about her . . . selling her body."

"Tonight she did. To a town boy."

"Does Tinker know?" She asked timidly again. He saw the gladness shine in her eyes, the new hope for them.

He stepped close to her and looked straight into her eyes. "No, and if he does find out . . . I will know how. This only concerns us.

It is a kind of battle, Leona. She did that . . . to taunt me. To make me ashamed. Tinker does not have to know. She will not do it again."

"Oh, J.J." Leona covered her mouth with her hands and cried harshly, making ragged sounds of grief. "J.J. . . . what's happening to you? That girl . . ."

"Good night, Leona." J.J. walked back to his tent, his shoulders slumped.

SALAMBO FOREST

Salambo Forest is the unlikely nom de plume of a twenty-five-year-old, black-eyed, raven-haired young woman who feels she must have been a Gypsy in an earlier incarnation. At least this is how she accounts for her life-long attraction to magic, astrology, witchcraft, and other aspects of the occult. In actuality, she was born in Nashville, Tennessee of mixed Italian, Irish and Cherokee parentage, and lives with her husband in Woodstock, N.Y. In addition to her prolific output as a writer (four novels for Ophelia Press this year, an astrology column in one of the sex magazines), she also paints, makes puppets (which sometimes double as voodoo dolls) and gives Tarot card readings for her friends.

STREET OF STAIRS

Ronald Tavel

N.Y. to make blue eyed babies. Don't recall my Mendelian laws that well, but Sandra has hazel eyes, giving us, at best, no more than a 25% chance. Of course, if waiting's the gambit, to mix metaphors, I'm a shark: in the tarots of Ouarzazate I constantly picked up the "Venez Demain."

Venez a Tanger, la ville des sept péchés.

Your humorous cards which, untranslatable, make an impression anyway. What say you, is not the American language. Am. humor. Am. ideals & prejudices, in by a nose as the most nontransable bundle of menace ever? And most unfortunate, now when the stakes are the inestimably momentous of all: the prize is reentrance into our History and our (oh, la!) reality: the losing is loss of the earth and desire their two lovely selves.

La ville des sept péchés en ville is Mar Chicas, of world renown. One has been to Mar Chicas as he has to Antoine's, Les Deux Magots and the Hudson Theatre. The place one has been à Tanger. The dim oblong shack with bar at one extreme and a cozy miniature stage hollowed out of the other, the decrepit flamenco artiste, Marcella ("I once was youthful and lovely even as you are now—many years ago in Sevilla!") alcoholed into the over-all atmosphere of marines plotting in low key advance Mar Chicas as the waterfront dive romantique-par-excellence of the oceans' exotic ports of call. *That Man From Tangier, Lady of Tangier, Thunder Over Tangier, Trapped in Tangier* served at 150 francs a beer and Marcella's tambourine passed from hand to hand; drawing the haute bourgeoisie of the Riviera, the Am. clique at the Parade, Spanish landlords, Westernized Moroccans and Moslem agents off duty—millionaires and beachcombers, the quixotic exiles of continental Europe, merchants of India, Sindbads of Singapore and the nightmare-inhabitants in itinerant troupes of thin-wrist gigolos and watermelon dwarfs.

R.K. once utilized it as his base of operation. Above the port and just far of the medina wall, an ideal haunt for hit and run in la ville des sept péchés.

And you take it upon yourself to criticize my "dissipation," assumed thru an imagined erraticness of my last note: for which presumption and projection you would, in this country, be beaten to a street-broom and I'm picking out a suitable slenderizer this very moment, now, while I'm speaking to you. I kept putting off return, and the later it grew the more apprehensive I. By 1 A.M. I was much too afraid to leave: chances were fairly even Hamid was waiting at the hotel door, with a knife in his hands.

(The previous night I'd waited up, not sleeping at all, till he arrived sometime after noon, on the burp of a swallowed canary; I, furious that he, obviously all right, must therefore have been able to telephone, had neglected to. Tu es sauvage, I said: he took it in the literal: "You are a savage," growing angry and, alternately, defensive: an unanticipated reaction, not having ever projected myself, I'm sure, as my particular exemplification of civilized man. He stormed out of the room, saying that he had been caught in the rain in a café in Souani and that there had been no telephone that wasn't out of order in the area; and he slammed the door. He returned a few hours later, after Abdullah, the concierge, had heated a tank of water for me. I heard him knocking on the door down the hall but I didn't hurry drying myself. When I got back to the room I pretended to be surprised at his visit, though I felt certain he had come to ask for money, his pride not permitting any special trip for apologies. I kept diverting him with meaningless incidentals until he grew sullen, and finally, almost withdrawn. Then I asked why he had come; and he made the request for the money. I told him he was an expensive, irresponsible, and dangerous charge. He stood up and pushed me aside and made for the door again. Will you hit, like you hit the others? I asked. Will you commit a crime on me also? He pulled off his jellaba and threw it on the floor. Never! will you see me again, he said, stomping through the hall.)

Abderrahamne, the great black, stood at the entrance of Mar Chicas. He was fairly drunk and had just raised quite a racket outside. The manager, thinking that a party of tourists was approaching, flicked on all the lights and Marcella jumped up out of her sleep and began singing and shaking her tambourine. When they saw Abderrahamne enter alone, the singing and dancing stopped and the lights went out.

The big black came over to my table and greeted me with his charming, semi-moronic smile. How you my pretty one?—I got lots milk tonight, he said pulling his crotch out to a stiff half foot. He sat down and showed me a letter he had (in English) guaranteeing him a contract for work in Munich and complete accommodations there. He claimed he only had to wait for his passport, after which he would be off to make his fortune. As soon as you get rich in Germany, I said, be sure to visit New York. R.K. will always be only too happy to take you in. I scribbled R.K.'s address on the back of the letter. Have you any souvenir you wish me to forward to your old friend? I asked Abderrahamne. He searched his pockets with sudden concern, but found them to be utterly empty. Just write him come back, he said, come back Tangier—right away!

Take my advice, R.K., and go to Singapore.

I debated briefly with myself as to the prudence of requesting Abderrahamne to accompany me back to the Emsallah: and shortly decided against it. He's much too drunk and full of milk to be very trustworthy now , I thought. The manager invited himself to sit down at my table also. He was middle-aged, and looked mucousy as a muscle-clam. He placed both his hands on my thighs and ran them tightly along the inner side. Je peux faire quelquechose pour toi peut-être? he smiled. Bien sûr, I said, vous pouvez me laisser partir, mon bon amateur des gosses.

I hesitated for some time at the Rue de Brazil entrance to the Emsallah. At last an old Spanish couple started into the street and I followed closely behind them. They turned around and looked worriedly at me two or three times. I must have seemed pretty ominous to them, a hold-up artist or something. I stopped short at the hotel door and turned the key quickly in the lock. No one was outside the hotel front, but I knew Hamid might easily be just beyond the corner of the building. I slipped up the steps and through the dark hall, thinking, how fortunate he hasn't a key of his own or he could be waiting for me in these halls, and sighed with considerable exhilaration once my door was safely latched behind me. That strange exhilaration again. That mixture of weightless freedom and leaden shame. That shame-freedom.

I undressed and put my clothes — my black corduroy shirt and black dungarees, on hangers, the first time I'd put anything on hangers in weeks. I've got to get this room into shape, I said out loud, into tip-top shape, got to shape up, and ship out. I began whistling *La Cucaracha*.

Then I heard the most agonized cry imaginable!—suddenly, like a scimitar, split the damp empty night with a bellow of echoes and twist the seraglio roof of the hotel up and off into the freezing sky! It sounded again, it sounded three times—an animal howl, horrible, of inestimable grief.

The hanger pulleyed away into spaceless suspension, as in the submarine belly of a liner. I stood under it, looking up at its brief ferris-wheel dips. A shaking spectre, the dagger for Duncan. Famished wolves, packs of skeleton anguish, shadowed toward the wood at the edge of the icy savannah.

Then my name, clearly and terrifyingly, rose to the window. I could turn the light off, I thought—but it's too late, he's already seen it. But I won't go to the window, that I promise right here and now. This time he's not getting in.

LET ME IN! LET ME IN! LET ME IN! he screamed. The Emsallah must have risen entire from its bed at that. I heard Abdullah and his wife stirring below.

Now—don't let me in! Never let me in again! Don't open, don't open! I'll never come in, for my God, never . . . oooo . . .

The challenge.

Quite beyond reason, beyond idea, I stood up on the bed and opened the shutters. Hamid was lying in the alley. He moved slightly when the light fell on him, rolled half over on his side, and turned his face up to me. It was covered with blood. A full purple cut between his eyes washed across the bridge of his nose and ran red down to his mouth and neck. Leave me here, leave me here to die! he shrieked. His eyes were wide white and dead. Widewhite.

I jumped into my clothes, ran down the stairs, and knocked on Abdullah's door. Abdullah came out adjusting his night robe, he seemed annoyed and very nervous. No bueno, he said, mucho ruido—no bueno por las clientas. Si, si, yo say. I answered him, pero Hamid—exterior. Por favor Por favor.

I made him understand I wanted help in bringing Hamid in. I explained I was afraid to go out into the alley alone. Muy peligroso, I cautioned, bebe mucho, muy peligroso ahora.

I followed Abdullah through the foyer to the front door. He led the way around to the alley. Hamid stopped screaming when he saw I was not alone, seemed suddenly put-out. Sondie, Sidi? Abdullah asked him.

Wallo, wallo, he said.

He rose to his feet by himself and went ahead of us up to the room. Abdullah said, Durmió ahora, when we reached the door and then turned abruptly and left. I felt considerable apprehension for a moment; I did not enter the room until Hamid had seated himself quietly on the bed.

Why did you call a stranger? he asked.

I'm afraid of you, I said frankly.

Look, he moaned, they have taken my face away because of you. I gave them my face because of you and you're afraid of me.

Who?

The night friends of the contraband-cigarette man.

I don't know what you're talking about.

The contraband man, the one you invited over to hit me in my side, ding-ding muk, him! The one you gave wine to.

What happened?

His friends are afraid for him. They came to me last week to start a fight—I beat them down—every one of them, one by one. This time they came together, and with knives. Four of them held me down on the stone while one big one kicked my head against the curb. Kicked till my whole face was cut on the curb. If I had a knife I could have finished them. But I don't have a knife, I can't have a knife—because of you!

He pulled the covers up over him—he still had his clothes on, and then threw them off again as though suddenly awakened in a steam bath. Because of you, because I can't do anything because of the passport, I can't have a knife, he bleated.

Then he sat up, like a bud springing in a second to sensational bloom, and took me firmly by the shoulders. He whispered through reams of alcohol: Ouilidi, my son, for you I do not carry a knife. For you I shall not want any more, to carry a knife.

I washed his face with a damp towel. Then I leaned my forehead against his wound. I am your little father, I said, and you are my little self-pitying waif.

He fell back on the bed and pulled me with him. Swear to me now, he said, that you will never leave me.

Even if it means staying in Morocco forever? I asked.

Yes: on God and for your mother's life make this swear . . .

I swear, I said, that I will never leave you.

I came in very late, the sun was already up, and I told Mark was like the insane then. Like my brother. And I realized I had known this before, when I wouldn't believe it about him. I had to leave, I couldn't catch my breath while I was that next to him. His illness suffocated me.

I'll be back in one or two hours, I said. I walked through the door and turned into the hallway without closing it.

Moushyb was in Bar Tarek as usual. Hazhi, he called the second he saw me come in. He seemed excited, he told me he had something very important to confide, something that would solve all my problems. Let's have a beer first, I said.

Moushyb explained that three friends of his were in Tangier that night. They were millionaire thieves, men who only burglarized safes in wealthy homes. They had just completed two successful jobs the night before, and were planning to leave in their car for Larache in about one hour. Moushyb had told his friends of me, and how capable I was and they had seemed interested in taking me with them if I myself were willing to go. It's a rare, perfect opportunity, Moushyb noted.

The three men arrived at Tarek in a little while. They were quiet, very courteous, intelligent men. They behaved very friendly toward me. They said they were sailing from Larache in a few days for Italy, and that I would never have to return to Tangier if I didn't want to. They claimed there would always be plenty of lucrative work for me in the different parts of Europe. They began to explain all the details of what I'd be expected to do and I kept repeating at each point that I was well practiced in such things. I thought about Mark.—What was my life with him? I actually lived better before I ever met him. And now he wants me to go to America to have the life of a man poorer than the poorest aveugle.

What do I need that for? For him that isn't so bad: he's had everything anyone could want up till now. Parents with money, a long schooling, always work when he wanted it. A life of a poor person is enough for him now. But it's not good, not enough for me. Since I can remember I've know what it is.

We're leaving now, our car's parked outside, one of the men told me. I walked out onto the sidewalk with them.

The automobile was new and black. They opened the rear door.

Could you wait here for me just fifteen minutes? I stammered.

There's a person that I have to tell I'm going away.

I hurried to the Emsallah. I stepped into the room quickly, feeling very uneasy. He was sitting by the desk. Quite stiffly.

What is it? he pronounced, twisting his face toward me when he heard my heavy breathing. His face was paint-white.

I am going–: I stopped. I looked down at the desk: it was empty. Nothing at all was on it. He had been sitting in front of that empty desk, it was clear, since I left him, since sundown, five hours. Squarely facing the blank green wall.

It was clear because the door was still ajar from when I had walked out. And because the muscles of his back and arms were hard as wood. I rubbed the muscle around his neck and in the small of his back, creasing along them with all my pressure, but there wasn't a single point that gave the least bit . . .

Mark, how will we live in America? He whispered like someone in a trance. We will live like dogs . . . You, also?

– Both.

Then both will live like dogs, I agreed. Some dogs have more than men: food, a roof. Come to bed. Don't sit there. Hahzhi!

O Magnifica of sunbeach and sky, sun, sand, aqua sea and sky, boys perform on wave hem and shell, starfish and starwhite sky, we maypole in the sky . . . I dance light as a thought thing tossing buds in a bed of cloud, toga leaves taken about the danger of the wind, sheaves of blue filigree . . . what delightful secrets they keep from me, smiling behind their oriental scenters, their shelled almond-ivory eyes . . . what ideas of seduction and the sea, I withhold from them!

Will a boy approach me, beachboy and bare, pulling his pride to longing and labor-length, display it for me with excited recommendations in every beachboy tongue under the sky? I shall suffer coaxing as an unused maid, look, touch, and run giggling away. Occident and Orient, soldier and youth, peek, wink—and dare . . . little enticing hollows of their buttocks in the sand; they scamper off to the Academy.

I am still panting at every pore with the grand suspense of it all when I quit the Agea to stroll over to the Goya-dark and peasant that I wasn't feeling well, could we wait till later for what I promised him. He said all right, and I got into bed and tried to sleep. But it was impossible.

Mark lay beside me quite restless. But I didn't move and kept my eyes shut tight. The same idea occurred to me over and over again. If I break my promise to him now I'll be able to know if it's me or if it's my body that he's really interested in.

Finally he touched me. He moved a finger in slow circles in my open palm nearest him. Then he placed his hand on my thigh and began rubbing it. I sat up, looked at him quickly and said, That's why I don't like you! Then I rolled over and faced the other way.

I didn't hear him stir, so he must have rested in that same position, staring at me, for at least a half hour. Then he got up and covered me carefully with all the blankets. He said something out loud in English, in a hard, angry tone—and though I didn't know what it was I could tell he meant no good. You speak well! I said suddenly. He wasn't expecting that and stepped back almost shaking from the side of the bed. You don't even understand when I speak French, he retorted, and now you're telling me what I say in English?

I closed my eyes again. I heard him dressing and running the faucet. Then the door shut. I sprang up and jumped over to the door—I couldn't believe it—it was locked! I pulled at the knob and banged against the wood-work panels. In a moment Mark returned and opened the lock.

You were going to leave me shut up in here? I shouted. Ding-ding muk! Because this, because I don't give you this? I raised my hand to hit him across the face. He bent back, wincing. The sight of him cowering there, of his having to cower before me, turned my insides to a quick, complete nausea. I pulled on my clothes and headed out to the hallway. Mark walked quickly in front of me down the stairs. He stopped at the outside door and turned around.

Give me—

I don't have anything of yours! I spat.

The key, I want to get out too.

I opened the front door myself and threw the key on the ground. Without looking to see which direction he would take, I hurried east out of the Emsallah, crossed the junction at Ben Noussair and went down the twisting lane of Leon l'Africain, toward the windy beach. My anger froze in the cold morning air.

I walked from one end of the beach to the other. If he intends being alone, he'll come here, I thought.

At the end of two hours he still had not come. I was alone on the beach except for a Spaniard walking his dog, and another man I couldn't see distinctly, way down at the wall of the dock, throwing stones into the small, even breakers.

I went to Bar Tarek. I sat at a corner table and drank one whiskey after another for three hours. He's with someone else now, like he's always wanted to be. He wants to go home, he's going to go now.

What? the patron asked.

I'm going to go now, I said, I'll pay for all these drinks tomorrow.

That will be 10,000 francs tomorrow, he called.

Vas te faire enculer.

I went to an expensive bar near Place de France. Some of our Moslem police inspectors will be coming here to drink. That thought amused me. I ordered whiskies and cognacs. I have no idea how long I sat there drinking.

I stood up and walked toward the w.c. Its door appeared to shine and to blink from a hundred different spots. On close examination I found the leaves of the door to be as ornate as those of the Sultan's Palace, and inlaid with bright stones. I opened the door. A man was standing there and pointing into the yard. I stepped down and walked across the cobblestone. The yard looked as long and narrow as a street. But see this, the man said kneeling touching the ground. I stared at the paving. It was an inlay of huge white pearls alternated with balls, the size of hazelnuts, of saffron, ambergris and musk.

It's incredible, I said, I had no idea there was such a place as this in Tangier.

What you want is in that building: the man indicated a pavilion several hundred yards directly ahead of me.

I'm looking for my she-camel that's gone astray, I said.

I know, he smiled. Go in there.

I entered the pavilion and found it to be only one of many, all of which were constructed solely of gold and silver. The pavilions together composed an enormous palace. I stepped around the emerald-stone border of a pool and walked over to the balcony whose columns were spiraled by mosaic serpents of great jacinths and chrysolites. The walks of the street below had been carefully cultivated, as if the whole avenue were part of an oblong, endless garden. Fruit trees and straight palms lined either side and there was a cluster of sour orange striplings around every bench. A river gushed beneath the balcony and pulled away into a medina of unevenly piled jewel boxes.

I rushed from one balcony to another, and wound between countless pillars of green chrysolite and blood ruby, wound in and out of splendid galleries and sky vaulted chancels.

When I reached the roof I stood in middle air.

The city below was completely empty. There wasn't a single living soul to be seen. Why is paradise empty of inhabitants? I cried. My voice went howling like a cold gale down all the wide chambers of the pavilions and through each secret cubicle of the king's-ransom medina.

I held out the balls of musk and saffron in my open palms. They had lost most of their sweet savor. The pearls had grown yellow, and flat as coins in my hand.

Your bill is now 19,000 francs, the waiter said.

I clinked three 100 francs, one at a time, onto the table.

The rest by tomorrow noon or you go to prison, he said.

The Second Palace of the Sultan? I asked. Then tomorrow I'll have the second best thing. Today I have the first: give me another cognac.

I whistled up to the window. The door's open, Mark shouted.

I rushed the length of the hallway, skipped over the flight of stairs and dashed into the room. I saw black, the whole room in black, and Mark dressed in black. I shoved him onto the bed, clamped my fingers around his neck and rammed his head against the bedirons. His lips tightened, pressing out narrow, silent gasps. Now you die, I shrieked, with this knife in my pocket (I thrust my right hand in my jacket pocket) you will die!

He relaxed for a moment under my weight, his eyes stared at the pocket, then he stiffened from head to toe and lay like a board against the mattress.

You must die for the bad you do to me! You have made me crazy, you must die for that!

His wooden inaction shook me. I had no knife in my pocket. But I could strangle him. I strengthened my hold on his throat. His breath caught up over his tongue and stopped suddenly, his eyes lit for a second, then fell shut.

I jumped away into the center of the diagonal tiles. The green and white-diamond lines competed in triggered dashes out from either side of me, a man's length ahead of me, and two in back. No, no! that is too good for you—prison instead, prison where you will suffer. You have driven me crazy, you can not do that, you can not do that here! I pulled down my pants, and my undershorts, and pushed myself in his face—Here! you want this? this? Take it, take it! I fell on his chest and forced his face in my thighs, pressed his neck and hands under my buttocks. He fought out with a strong wrench and nearly toppled me on the floor.

I spun around and pulled up my clothes. Ask them, ask them, they all know—you will go to prison for making me do the things I do. You are responsible!

I saw black, I saw fire.

I yanked open the closet and took out his valise. All your money belongs to me now!

What's in there won't do you any good, he said calmly, there's only checks. They need my signature.

Then you will sign, you will sign them all now!

How much do you need this time?

Tabun ding emuk! Ahline ding-ding emuk!!

I threw down his valise. I sank on the bed. Do you think I would rob you? Now you think that too, don't you? No—I'll go to prison instead—I'll go to prison where I belong. But you'll go with me. You'll be put in the same cell with me. Because you make me do everything that I do, you're—

I could hardly look at Mark. I felt in back of me and circled him around his ankle. I pressed hard. The ceiling sloped down in shaky dips over my head and the bed rose on a sickening rock around a spool and slammed my head against it. Owww! You charah! My life!

If you left me now I would cry—you know that—I would cry, that's good isn't it? I would jump in the water and swim after your boat until I drowned. That's good isn't it? That's what you've done to me. You ruined me—I'm like nothing now!

I spent a lot of money in the bars. I drank all day because you made me crazy. I want you because of you—not your face, not your money, not your body—you, just you. But you want me—oh, no!— you want me for zook. I'm going now.

Where are you going?

I'm going to steal the money that I owe, where do you think I'm going?

Wait!

Wait for nothing. Goodbye.

I ran down the stairs. When I got to Rue de Hollande, I had to stop and lean against a tree. My legs felt as if they had no strength in them. I could barely see the walls of Marché Fez across the street. The high iron gate was bolted and the lock was wrapped in double, thick iron chains. I stood there for a while fingering the chains and pressing my face between the black bars. I wandered back to the hotel; I called up to the window again.

His face looked as if it were under water, a blur of pink. What time is it? I asked.

9 o'clock, he called down.

Then I can sleep for at least three or four hours, I thought, I'm coming up, I said.

When I was in the room again I fell on my back across the bed. I closed my eyes . . . What was it that you said to me in English this morning? I asked.

He laughed softly for a second. I was very angry with you, I said. Pig. I hate you.

I opened my eyes: Pig, I hate you? For my God, no one's ever said that to me.

I said it to you.

He bent over, blotted against the ceiling lightbulb, and unzippered my jacket.

Let me sleep with my head in your lap, I mumbled. He sat down next to me and I put my face against his stomach, with my hands enclosing his thighs. Where did you go after your left me this morning? I asked very slowly.

It was you who left me. I walked to the Casbah. I stayed by the Door of the Sea for several hours . . . I watched the steamships going out from the straits, and the small fishing boats come in on the Canaries Current.

Did you think of your home?

Yes.

Then what did you do?

I walked toward the port and stood on the balcony of Avenue d'Espagne, I paced back and forth on it until people began to stare at me. I think I was crying . . . Because I was going back to my old life, my old, empty life. I was going back without what I came so far to get. Then I wandered along the Avenue and turned up through the vacant lots by Rue de la Mediterranee. By the time I reached the Emsallah I was happy.

Why were you happy?

Because I was going back to my old life.

You can go, you know. You can go tomorrow if you want.

And lean over the rail to watch you as you drown in the wake? No. I'll wait . . .

I heard the roar of that ship's wake, saw everything like rain through the white bubbles. The water felt fatally icy around me.

And you didn't go with someone today? You didn't look for

anyone—

I would be crazier than crazy, I would be stronger than strong, I would be longer than song, belong, wrong, his voice came in bubbles, in muffles over my eyes. His echo, the chamber of the sea, were one. It was the sight of his sound, his voice the others say is the sound of the snake in the garden of Eden. It was a wide, wide to forever vault of the graygreen sea. I sank in it, down fathoms . . . .

What time is it now?

It's past 3:30.

Were you sleeping?

No, no I didn't sleep.

I slept well. I'm going to go out for a while now—

But—

Not for long. Wait here. I'll be back before morning, before sun-up, in fact.

I heard the slow steps of an elderly man, in the first right turn off Calle Alejandro Dumas, no more than a minute after entering the medina. He was European, he looked well-dressed. I want you because of you, just for you, not your face, your body, your money.

Como? the man said to me.

I want your money.

Take the handkerchief off your face, boy. He lifted his hand.

I punched him and he fell backwards against a stoop. Completely unconscious. I slipped the wallet out of his breast pocket and sped around the furthest ruelle to the east, toward the Petit Succo.

There were three or four men half asleep on the side benches in Café Fuentes. I settled myself there quietly and ordered a coffee, sliding the wallet under the cushioning on the chair next to me before the waiter returned. I looked out on the Succo. No one was in sight. Café Central, directly across the way, was dark and boarded up.

I remained where I was for what seemed close to a half hour, and during all that time there wasn't the least unusual noise in the street, no particular stir, practically deserted in fact. Then I made my way south again through Calle Uazan toward the section I had come from. The old man is probably still sleeping, I thought, this is the safest place to be. I stopped in the shadow of the building column in the small Calle Karma and waited there for a while. The first figure that approached I leaped out on and threw to the ground. He surrendered his money without hesitation, and was still lying there trembling when I turned into Bencharki.

I headed toward Calle de los Estados Unidos as the quickest way out of the medina, and passed a lone couple in the dark under the arch of the consulate. I turned around and pushed myself between the man and woman: Pay your taxes to this charah of a consulate! I said. The woman began to cry. I searched through the man's pockets and found only a few loose notes. I pulled the rings off the woman's fingers.

I counted all the money together as I hurried through the Spanish city. There was only 13,000 francs but I was too nervous to make any new attempts. The drink was still swishing back and forth in my head as if my head were a tossing bucket.

When I was back in the hotel room I put the 13,000 on the table.

Mark walked over and stared at it, he counted it.

I could have gotten more, I said, but I was too nervous.

You're a thief.

What's the matter now!

I was afraid for you.

You don't have to be afraid for me. I'm capable. I've been stealing since I was seven years old. Never was caught, not once—no police record.

I thought you were a carpenter . . .

Pssss—carpenter! I was a carpenter for six months. There's no work in Tangier, Mark, how many times have I told you that.

But a thief! I didn't know—

How didn't you know? I never said so? I said so twenty times.

But I didn't believe—I mean I didn't think that was how you made your living.

Well, that's how. Now you know—all right? You know for all times that you go with a thief. And you'll stay with this thief. You're the one who's going to change my life. Let's go to bed. Naháss.

We slept till it was nearly noon, then I got up and washed quickly. I'm going to the bars, I said, and pay what I owe them. Could you give me 17,000 francs to make up the 30,000?

You spent an entire 30,000 yesterday? he asked with alarm.

All right, I'll just go to prison then.

He went to his valise and took out some checks. Don't be surprised, he said looking up, if both of us have to beg for our food in the streets next week. Meet me at Tugeni's in an hour and I'll have the 17,000 for you.

Don't worry. My family will always have food for us.

I don't worry about food. I just worry about when you're going to learn what it is to act like a responsible person.

This is the last time something like this will happen, I promise you.

It better be, he said, because I promise you, this is the last time I'm giving you any extra money. By the way, you need a shave before you go.

I'll get one outside, I noted feeling my chin.

Where?

In a barber shop.

Don't you have a razor somewhere?

I never owned a razor in my life. I've always had myself shaved in a barber shop.

I never did. You've lived better than I have.

He asked me how much I was accustomed to spending each day and I told him that I used to almost always spend about 3,000 francs a day, all of which I had to steal the night before. And he repeated: I think you've lived better than I have. I never spent so much every day, even in America.

Why, when you were still stealing, he asked, didn't you buy yourself some new clothes? Why did you have to wait till Grone and come to me for the money?

This made me angry, his always talking about how much he had to give me. If he only knew how I really suffered like a beggar, like a rag-man, because of him. I didn't want the others to know I had money then, I said, they knew I was out of work and I didn't want them to guess that I was stealing.

You'll have to get used to living with much less in America, he commented with a blank expression on his face.

But I've lived with nothing all my life here. What am I going to America for? To live there like a slave also?

You're going for me.

Yes.

And so that I can help you change your life to something better than a thief's. Like, to a poor man's life . . .

Mark met me at Tugeni's at the appointed time, and he had the money he promised with him. I paid the patrons of the bars, without saying a word, the exact amounts I owed. Then I took a bus to the Marshan and walked toward my mother's house. Now that she knows I'm really going to leave, she insists I visit at least twice a week.

I ate some fish that had been prepared earlier. It had turned. The flavor was bad. My mother spoke about how the whole family was annoyed because of my coming home after midnight one time at the early part of the month. If I want to sleep over I must arrive at 9 o'clock and eat with the family. Otherwise, it would be better if I just stay away. That is what she told me.

My mother. That is what my own mother told to me.

My own house.

At sundown I returned to Mark. Soon as I saw him I became upset. I didn't know what was disturbing me. I couldn't tell about one specific thing or another any more, so much was always happening now. Abdullah carried the dinner in, a fairly expensive preparation. I had to tell Mark I'd already eaten. He was very disappointed. He seemed to withdraw then. He wouldn't speak.

I decided it was right that I sit with him while he ate.

Neither of us said a word through his whole meal.

I felt he had disappeared out of the room. And I wanted to, also. But I waited till he put down his spoon before I got up. At the door something strange happened to me: I stood there, staring at my shoes without the smallest thought in my head: then I turned around like a machine and the words just came out:

Mark, listen to me, we won't make love any more, all right?

I thought. His eyes are like a cat's at night, empty marbles.

We will be comrades, brothers, Chi. From now on.

I came back and touched him on the shoulder. He was shivering.

Yes, if you don't want to, he said. His jaw clamped tight.

Put on your overcoat if you're cold in this room.

His legs were tense, he was trembling because of that. I held his chin up so he'd be forced to look at me: his gaze was blank. He perfect Spanish restaurant at the T of Bencharki (notorious street of prostitution) and Calle Calico. As I step across the citroen-narrow intersection of Calle de la Cruz Roja Española on Bencharki, I espy Maimun, Maimun, of the so many shower of sunblue summers ago, standing with a wheelwide pan of vegetable peels in his hand.

These things I espy. O wary, one, two, three and theory: Maimun is a gentle, just out of adolescence god, new come to Olympia in his sky-shoal moss green sweater, he is sweeping peels from the netted over the clouds floors of those riotously continual banquets of Hercules and Hylas; there is a tin white and red drink Coca Cola sign in Spanish and Arabic on the northeast building of the fancifully-tiny intersection, diagonally across from the tin white and blue streetsign De la Cruz Roja Española in Spanish, French, and Arabic; a small, set in the wall shop of spices and green vegetables on the southwest corner, and Maimun's cell, his bluegreen door on the street confession-chamber small cell is the first cajolement of the northwest and terminary of Cruz Roja: a mendicant child, a girl no more than ten, is holding up a huge brimming bucket of cold-white fountain water, twisting her ragged skirt with her free hand, and then sucking its thumb—she stares at me with perplexed, thumb on the lower lip pout in the warm sunslant at the end of the cul-de-sac; a secret camel's eye is hard and readily by that she be quickly, if fear take her, and completely efferent in the wall: these things I espy O wary—and five, ten, not a bit unleary.

I accept Maimun's invitation: he says there is an American within. And I remember Maimun well now, Maimun of the after all, many after-recalled sunblue and singing summers ago.

I have my best English straightway ready for the American—he seems more European than American, more Italian than Anglican: much more darkly and thinly Mediterranean than robustly Yankee as I look at him. His shoulders are broad and nervously peaked on his supporting arms, his pastel-trousered knees peaked from his low squatting position; the longwide corduroy lines of his cape's-breath jacket ring around the pensive, poised mouth, combed darkblue of cotton irises to the swath dustline of lashes; a Rome of ringlets riot over his sunslaved forehead and ears.

And how do *you* find the Moroccan? he asks. The Moroccans are a gentle and amazingly hospitable people, I offer, friendly without prying and poetic without resourcefulness, innocent but not naive. They are a Berber people, you know. Hamites, and perhaps of European origin—the Europeans of the desert. You see this boy, Maimun, he is a Riffian, his native tongue is Tachelhit not Moghrebi, I may address him in Tachelhit and he will respond warmly. I am en train de Tachelhit at the moment, you see. But look, you can tell by his features Maimun is Riffian. There are the Rif people to the north and the mulattos south of the Atlas, and both are of the same, though for centuries divided, Berber tribe.

You speak English well, the American says with the strong, ungiving emphasis of the equilateral character eitherside his mouth, so I shall ask you my question again: How do *you* find the Moroccans?.... How do you *find* the Moroccans?

I pull rein in and stare rein-restrained directly at him. Is he someone, then, who paces the causeway at high soulstake. Tangier gambler with God? I decide to call his hand; I look down between my shoes at the wearing away oilcloth, the greenstone floor, the little gold-painted alcohol burner just to right of my right shoe. Alors, I am Swiss, you know. I answer thoughtfully, these people are Adam sons of millennium-separation and more than arriving in Africa is called for to call forth the particular fortune-path they fared and of opening sesame on their secret retreat. But there is a fast fortune where they have fortuned, and my little coming to words with this primitive Tachelhit is a modest venture hopefulward. We are west-prone citizens of the Grecianly tragic sun, the Moroccans children of untimed ever dawn-calmed east; our junction of hour and town is mystical, always suspicious and suspenseful; ours is touch as touch and carry can—strikingly as on a hot stone, jugglingly as with too many different-datumed pins, and heroically—always, briefly, heroically. How shall the with-France West approach the Abused-only-in-they-are-held-to-be-Arabs? Evidently, they are abused. So they take up the definition. And they fancy a self-image of Egypt also for whatever alien prestige it may remind, its industry and annexations its stubborn pretense at war. And what would the Berbers be really sans the far, dark shadows of the pyramids? I wonder sometimes. And I wonder what they may ever be in their primitive tongue so pitifully prohibitive of physics and machines. Yet, that the Moroccans are Arabs is pure Arab propaganda and ours—our sensational Quest-Modern prejudice—and a fact which intrigues the Red Chinese, new infiltrants in Africa, as ancient as the untime East, knowledge to divide so thence to conquer. Divide the Berber from the Arab. His Majesty from Nasser—and in His Majesty's cities the wealthy eastern Moslem from the laboring Moor, divide the moneyed cities from the suppressed penurious range. Mohammed V is a Hamite king, you know, no Alaouite dynasty prevails—no descendent of Ali, son-in-law of the Prophet is this Mohammed ben Youssef. Wait! Don't translate that heresy for Maimun: there's a prison term for fastidious history scholars! So here we have the Lie

the axis of all the approaching and coaxing. Marvelous, a magnifica of illusion, marvel: sunbeach and sky. (I decide our American is masochist, will prove Incredulous of Self.)

We engage Maimun at points in the conversation, he accurate to concur mention of the Moroccan Underground for Independence from Arabs-France-Spain. He contributes the old brother of a legendary Riffian rebel-chief now in exile,[1] who lives deep in the quarter not far from we three in discussion of him. He is half-mad, the ward of the Casbah, a single small yet constant agitation for genuine (The True) Independence, embarrassment to his friends, a protecting and hush-him-up of the vast waterfast community of Moroccan Mohammedanism.

The Moor's arts are destructive rather than creative in his intention, I note: destructiveness which on principle is derivative: you see, he slavishly emulates the Mauritanian-artist in century, reproduces himself as a pristine bedouin upon our atomic decade. Then too, our vain search for culinary culture, their oued-narrow width of simile, hot haste all joy debasing directness in intercourse—yes, it is far west here, so far, very far from the curtains and veil delicacy, that accustomed to caressing purring life sophistication of the Arabian Nights.

The American stands in the bluegreen doorframe: two sunbeams tassel his hair at earshell and templehorn. And still, it is the Arabian Nights, he says stepping onto the old-afternoon cobblestone: So long as you can tell a further story, so long is the night, are the numbers of night, you are certain of your head. In the end was the Word.

1Mohammed Abd el Krim al Khatabe, Proclamist of The Rif Republic; at the time in Cairo. He, alone, waged a battle and beget an Idea which, had circumstance and men's intelligence allowed to coalesce, might have preserved the civilisation of Morocco.

And he disappears.

Maimun approaches and coaxes me, barefoot beachboy laboring his pride to longing length, says, Moi-toi, comme antes, oui? Y aprés tu prends moi en Europe? But he is too large, much too large to be anything but painful; besides, he's not a mischief and watery-eyed adolescent Hylas any longer.

Maimun discloses the loss of his most recent employ: he had fled to friends in Tetuan during the heaviest days of the season's tourist trade, his patron saw fit his discharge in fits of righteous wrath. He is free to work for someone new now, (conveniently) free for travel to Europe, preferably Malaga of the Samarkand vineyards. In meantime, he is managing as cook for the strange American. (He zippers up his pride.)

When the American returns from short, strange sojourn in his circular street, I raise that possibility of Maimun's drugging his dishes. Mayn't he have some compromise over your material soul (your this-country search soul) and goods if he were to attempt your imprisonment through drugs? The American has ear to this romance-ransom Moroccan inclination: drugging and the taking to prisoner—women are said to have lucubratory science for such potent brews implicated, he has first-hand from a friend could not quit his hostess' house for dream-steeped months and so another, a French boy, currently in insane asylum effect of the abuse. I need never concern for sleepy Maimun's sorcery, however, he says on a tongue mocked ten-minutes "antes", my this-country search is the sameplate at sametime his.

Then my further doubts and reservations, the petroleum as oil for cooking tragedy of Meknes and the ten thousand for life paralytics, the no-refrigeration or govenment control of marketing, and under-blackmarketing, and so on.

There is a full-page newspaper colorphoto of Elizabeth II nailed on the wall just above the footstool-low divan. Maimun does not know who she is, but inquires enthusiastically after whether if "this woman" should come to Tangier, he might not sleep with her. And there is a fanphoto found doubtless on some eerily wind-papered corner-where of Farid-el-Atriche on the rear greenwashed stonewall, and adjacent and on a grassgreen field quartercircle of a quartercircle-smiling Swiss soccer team. Maimun cognizenti of the Egyptian; of the Western co-operative, innocent. Pero, son bastante bonito, si?

I must leave now, and study languages beside my soup and legends in the legend-loud Spanish restaurant, legends of this American in their duality of native and international's interpretation, the latter having him bodybound and pursewise here and the more mysterious maintaining a soul's comradeship and chain-strength of destiny. For I can place my pre-acquaintance of him now, and it is in story at least: this American is he surely who's been the speculative center of recent denizen-of-the-Casbah letterlists for marketplace and café consumption. Ah, yes, he is that new and latest he in the mystically unbroken lineage of the Moroccan's single reprehension of the Christian Holier less brute-likely threatening than thou: he is that courage, they relate, that strolls unharmed in the ambush and behind treetrunk dagger of Souani nights, that takes more readily than Moroccans to tumbling and tale-telling acrobatics, to secret and devilishly fearsome squares of the succos and medinas, an unwary, sheltered from all unsheathing of envy and lust pedestrian: if he seems exception that proves Holier than thou rule, seek yourself—is inavertible silent insinuation—the rules through which you may win arrowheads to follow him. And there is more than extracurricular reason to want to have his courage—nothing is as restful, nothing as holiday, as courage. Courage is the permission for paradise, is the self admission of paradise . . . .

there must be some terrible Need then, that there's no desire for paradise now. And yet, how so, for is it not the winning of their hearts taking great courage that I am embarked upon? I wonder. I wonder about arts of creation and destruction—about the self proclaiming in endeavors to succeed. There are many ways, and a backward way would establish a Verity also.

—Yet I should not want to show Prewha and his two friends that I fear their coming a second time to violate me, to steal the francs I conveniently left in my vest pocket—I should not want to quit Hotel Agea that they know to break into, and allow thereby to intimidation and defeat. For how did I fare in this city before the war, what of my spy's insight and political prowess—is that all, and together with its ambition, forever lost? In my once-position gone, are all position gone? Only, I think, if that is what I need.

What black belief crawls toward satisfaction in such a need?

Still, fugues of thought and resolutions of the sky and sunbeach blue justify and dignify all acts, all those acted upon . . . .

as all is the lying of a Pure Lie.

*   *   *

The woman should not come back. If she sings and wails at our door for the scraps of our meal and I tell her, "God will give you," she should not come back till the next night. I give her what we leave over many times each week, but if I say, "God will give you," she should stop wailing and go away, isn't that so?

And tonight there is nothing left over because I bought us good meat. It was good meat, wasn't it? Not like at Romano's. Romano served only horse, never beef. You ate a whole horse for all the time you were at Romano's. Yes, I think you ate a whole horse there!

Do you know what happened here last night? I met a woman in the street who seemed very sad, so I asked her what was the matter and she told me her little boy was lost. She said her little boy went out of the house in the afternoon and never came back. I told her not to cry and I took her to the police station to tell them about her boy. Then I walked in the streets with her and I brought her here and asked her to come in. When she was inside I told her to take off all her clothes. She said she could not, that she had to go home to her husband. So I pulled off her clothes myself, and then I nikied her. Her tabun was big so after I did it there twice I turned her over to do it in her zook. But I saw that the hole of her zook was big also and I asked her how come the hole of her zook was big. She said it was because her husband liked to niki her in the zook a lot.

I did it to her in both places the whole night long. She wanted it, because why did she stop to speak to me in the street? And what kind of a husband does she have that lets her go out of the house at night? In the Rif a wife never goes out of the house. And in the morning, you know, this woman didn't want to leave. She said, Let me stay here. I threw her out.

That's why a man must only give the niki and never take it, because if he takes it he is not doing what God wants him to do. Mohammed used to take it when he was young, you know, he was a zemel. And fat Mjido also. Mjido told you he was a patrón in a bordel, but he was just selling his zook there.

But I never gave my zook. Never, even when I was small.

Here, I have packed the sebsi very tight. Hoc. It's good this way—yallah, hoc! When you have to pull hard on the stem it really turns your head, you see . . . it's better than hashish.

I was born in the Rif, in Melilla. They speak Spanish there, not Arabic. I learned this Arabic in Tangier. I've been in Tangier for seven years. When I was fifteen I made scandal in the street in Melilla, I took out a knife and swung it around my head and didn't let anyone come near me. The police made a circle around me and waited for five hours until I put down the knife. Then they took me to the police station and asked me why I was threatening everyone with the knife. I told them I did it because my father beat me. They said we have many new fathers here to beat you, and they put me in prison. Three nights later I climbed over the prison wall and ran away. I walked through the country and over the mountains for seven days and seven nights without stopping. When I reached Tangier I had 30 francs in my pocket.

Tangier was a bigger city in those days, there were more people here, all different kinds of people, the Boulevard and the Grand Succo were so crowded you could hardly walk back and forth. I stole a woman's shopping purse in order to buy my first meal, and I slept outside my first night, on the steps of a café in the Grand Succo.

Later I made myself a shoe box and I became a cerie-boy. And after that I worked in the Tropicale. That's where I learned to cook. But I never sold my zook, for a job or anything else. Never, even when I was small. Because a man must live as una persona, not as a dog—and all other men must have respect for him and do towards him as una persona, and say he is una persona.

But I always think about the Rif because life in the Rif is better than here. Here all the women are pootas. In the Rif there are the women of the street and women of the house. A woman of the house is carefully watched when she is a child, and always kept indoors where she is taught a woman's duties. A man who wants to marry usually buys the girl from her parents for 40 or 50,000 francs—when she is seven or eight years old—and brings her to live with him in his house. She never even once after this sees the streets again until the time the man marries her—when she is twelve or thirteen or fourteen. And she never sees another man because when visitors come to the house she must stay in a back room. The night of the marriage all the groom's friends come to the fete and there is a lot of singing and eating and drinking. But the bride is never seen by any of the guests. After the fete the groom brings five glasses of tea into the bride's room. She is ashamed and very timid and ignorant. They each drink a glass of tea and talk gently together. Then they become more at ease with each other and they enjoy a second glass of tea. Finally, there remains only the odd glass. The groom offers it to the bride, but she refuses it and politely returns it to the groom to drink. He gives it back to her again, insisting this time, and both have their hands keep touching during this whole exchange. Finally the groom becomes courageous with touching her hand, and he moves over to her and takes her wrist and pulls her onto the bed.

When the wife is lonely for her parents she asks her husband if she may visit her parents' house. He says no, and she asks him again and again, week after week. At last he agrees, and the wife puts on her haik and her veil covering the whole face except one eye. With this eye she looks always on the ground as she and her husband travel on foot, and at night so no one can see them, to the house of her parents. The visit lasts a few weeks and when it is over the husband comes to the parents' house at night and takes his wife home again. When they reach home the husband warns his wife against begging for too many of these visits.

Ca, c'est une femme! And this woman is never touched by any man except her husband. She never gets the chance to betray him. God said, If you live with a woman for sixty years, never give your confidence to her. Even after sixty years, the first chance you give her she will betray you. She must live and die without ever seeing a single man outside of the ones in her family. And she will be satisfied to stay with her husband that way, since she knows of no other man. And she will be satisfied with whatever food or clothes he gives her, no matter how bad or cheap, because she does not know of the existence of better things.

A man, of course, is different. He lives in the streets of the public, of selling and spending, and knows the many things that exist and their degrees, and with knowing desires. For people are really the same as animals, and it is natural for an animal to want and to go after what it wants. People talk of God and the right ways of the Koran but if there is no way to force them to do the right there is no way to trust them to. So a man is allowed to sleep with whoever he chooses. Still, God does not like the prostitute, and if a man is rich it is better that he takes a second wife and put her in a separate room where she never sees the first. And if his desires are still not satisfied he can consider a third or fourth wife.

And a boy is the same as a woman, if a man wants to have a boy—if he is small and fat and you can squeeze him in your arms a boy is the same as a woman. Some boys are so fat you can niki them under the arms, or between the shoulder blades. I had a fifteen year old boy that way the other night. I wanted him from before, I wanted him for a long time, and that night I picked him up and put him on my shoulders and carried him here. He screamed and cried for help while we were in the street but I just told everyone he was my little brother who was trying to run away. And I kept him here the whole night. I had to hit him at first because he wouldn't lie still. But he'll never tell his father about what happened. Shomar. So I don't have to worry.

Armelo sebsi, t'sina. M'sien, yak?

A woman is like a dog and God said, If you live with a woman for sixty years, never give your confidence to her. All women except your mother. Your mother is different. If I had a mother I would sleep next to her all night and hold her in my arms like a child. A mother is the best thing God gives to a man. If you carry your mother on your back and go on foot all the way from here to Mecca, you could not half pay back what you made her suffer when you kicked her stomach just once when you were still unborn.

*   *   *

I went to visit Maimun. I went at about 9 o'clock because I knew he would be eating then. He let me come in, but he didn't give me anything to eat.

When he was finished himself we talked and then he pulled me backwards over his knees and kissed me. I asked for 200 francs. He said he didn't have any money.

There was someone else there, a Christian. Maimun told me he was American. So then I said him and the American both for 250 francs. But Maimun said the American didn't want to do it. Allish, haheess? I asked him. He told me no, that the American just didn't do it.

But afterwards the American got up and sat next to me and started rubbing my knees. So Maimun spoke to him in French. And then Maimun told me it was all right for 250 francs.

The American went out and left Maimun to go first. His thing is very big and long. He told me to take it and put it in myself. I did and it hurt a lot. I told him to please finish in a hurry. I hurt so much that I cried a little.

When he was finished I wiped myself and pulled on my pants. Then we waited for the American. I was thinking that when Maimun left me alone with the American I would break the wine bottle that was on the floor and cut the American in the face with it. Then I would steal all his money and run out.

But when the American came back Maimun locked us up in the room together and went away with the key.

So I took off my pants again and got on the bed. The American kissed me a lot and touched me all over my legs and under my shirt. Finally he turned me over and got on top of me. He stayed on top of me for a long time not putting it in but just pushing back and forth. I felt his heart on my shoulder blade. It was beating very hard. Maimum kept coming back and knocking on the door but the American kept telling him to go away.

He must have been on top of me for over an hour. Then he finally put his thing in me very fast and very hard. I pulled it out it hurt so much. Then he pushed it back in a little easier and he finished with a lot of loud, scary gasping.

When Maimun unlocked the door and came in again I asked him for 350 francs. He told me to take 250 and get out. I said no one does it with two men for such a little bit of money. He said you do it and if you don't like it, don't come back.

Then he gave me the 250 francs and pushed me out the door.

* *

When the little zemel came to see me Mark asked all about him. He said he noticed him in the streets before because of the way he dresses like a gangster. He is trying to look tough, I told Mark, but I think he is a little gangster anyhow. He's fourteen years old, he has no parents, just a street boy. He goes with all the thieves

in the medina and learns from them. And he's a zemel, he does it with everyone.

Then afterward Mark sat down on the bed with us and put his hands on the zemel's knees. I said, We can both have him for 250 francs. Mark agreed to that price and told me to do it first.

The little zemel was good, he's tight because he's very young.

When I was finished I locked Mark up in the room with him because I didn't trust the zemel. As long as he knew I had to come back to let him out I was sure he wouldn't try anything.

I went to the Petit Succo and found a friend in Café Central. I stayed there talking with him for a while. While we were talking I was thinking that it is against the Koran for a Moslem to be nikied by a Christian. And then I was glad about the zemel's shame, because I don't like that little zemel.

I went back to my room and started to unlock the door when Mark called out to me to go away for ten minutes more. I walked back to the Succo and looked around there again. I had to return and knock on the door four or five times before Mark finally said I could come in. I thought about how peculiar Christians are, how they take all night to do it and how they always want to do it with the same person. This is very odd—and it is very foolish. A man should niki a lot of different zooks, and not just one, because that is really looking for trouble at trouble's house. When a man begins to have love for a woman or a boy he is no longer free. He is full of pain and he wants to always have the other with him. And then the other makes fun of him and tells everyone about him and then leaves him. And the man crawls in the street after the other for everyone to see, and he has fights with everyone because of this.

The zemel didn't want to leave right away. He wanted me to translate what he was saying to Mark and he wanted me to translate Mark's answers to him. I knew that he was trying to get Mark to ask him to come back sometime and I thought it would be bad for the two of them to see each other again. So I told the zemel to take his money and get out. He tried to wrangle more money just as I knew he would. I opened the door and shoved him out by my knee. Hedda charah fin zemel!, I said to Mark.* * * * * * * * * * * * * * * *

The boy had a full turban of dirty, knotted black curls pedestaled on the faintest suggestion of furry sideburns. His huge eyes were dark and round, his nose small and nostrils wide. He seemed to be nervously, anticipatingly sniffing the air.

He played constantly with the zipper on his black leather American-hoodlum jacket and kept pulling on the knees of his levis as if he couldn't get used to his sitting position. He studied rather than looked at the face of Maimun and myself.

I had never exchanged money for a sexual act before, I had never before bought anyone. While I walked around, letting Maimun's example build my courage, this idea of buying someone excited me. As francs are the minutes of your life.

The boy got under the blanket in order to pull off his levis. (Had I not been born an American puritan I should have been born a Mohammedan one.) I climbed over him to the inside of the bed and supported myself on my left elbow with my back against the wall. I lifted the covers off him lightly and dropped them at the foot of the bed. He lay there with his eyes shut very tight, his hands stiff at his sides, and his taut legs crossing ankles.

I dropped my hand down and passed it along his legs pulling them slightly apart.

And I realized suddenly how the cult of youth:

He felt exactly like a girl. The smallness of bone structure, the givingness of the flesh, the marble touch of the skin.

All at once he seemed inhuman, unhealthy—his childish effeminateness made him freakish. It left me desireless, cold.

I leaned forward and kissed him, but it was unsatisfactory, it was forced, and like kissing drowning lips. I placed him on his stomach and slid on top of him. The feel of his back was that of utter uncut flatness, unbarred touch of his small flat buttocks against my penis turned me even colder.

I rested above him as lightly as possible for a while and then began a steady gyrating to excite an erection. Images of battered, bantered pleas and rape hurried through my mind. I recalled the distinct progression of a stag film I had once seen where a woman with dark glasses suddenly was seized and raped by a tall skinny man. Seized suddenly, tears at her four-button blouse backing her toward the covered couch; dirty nails divided the Florida paisley half toward the gulf shore half toward Indies; he pulled her clitoris down to peninsula between his right fingers in her black found-space-for-them skivies.

And then off with, last, them too, spreading her thighs with right hand while the other, its knower, raised her rivercut forest to the nosedive of camera eye . . .

Aware, am aware of a momentous struggling for breath.

And finally came hard

felt a suction as between a folded slab—a wet, plastic liver

ganglions of my thoughts wired through purple mucus and white and sick pink circles of protoplasm, burying deeply and milkweeding into a splinter-of-windowpane-stabbed wideopen wound. * * * * * * * * *

Tetuan both receded and rose formidably with the distance something like Mont Saint Michel, as I walked the wide straight highway toward the sea. The real difference between the two heights is that in this case the proximity to the water was a weird, almost mirage-like illusion and the farther I walked the farther it retreated. Cars sped past me in the direction of the beach, occasionally a hand stretching out and waving a quick, ambiguous salute. The brilliant sundisc dominated the open highway. Weed and sand fields rolled away to all points of the circumferencing horizon.

The great corroboration of Tetuan.

Tu es ici exactement comme chez-toi—heard a thousand genuine times, heard here genuine times. Mohammed invited me to an hotel, to a picnic in the mountains. Several of the habitués of his father's café invited me to their tables, invited themselves to the hotel afterward. Mohammed told the others about Maimun and me of the year ago, they seemed astounded—I could tell though the whole conversation was in Riffian—and later when they were gone and Mohammed alone was left he attempted to repeat Maimun's supposed success. No recuerdos de shomar, I said wearily over and again for a half hour. We ended by my resorting to the wicker chair and his holding the bed for our duration of the sleepless night. The dawn came in orange over the orange terraceroof when I finally opened the door. There were no windows in the stone room.

Omar was nowhere about. Mohammed avoided all my questions concerning the boy. He was hiding him from me, I knew that. He had sent a letter to Maimun a while back detailing his perennially awaited, at long last seduction of the handsome Omar.

A page ago or fifty-two, it was.

Look, I'm including a delineation to clarify the photo sites.

I'm subject to slip from my wise, above it all, just look at me back there in my situations into a debased, lost circulating in the very same from which I can only calculate myself, my problems, and myself . . . so oriented myself becomes solipsist, utterly unapproachable by the aid of others, the morbid concern . . . of which the physical and psychic assaults engendered come at precisely the moment *I think* they might, or should . . . should for punishment, for some kind of credits, credibility, some proof . . . and coming to me again, in the moments (till recently rare) when I slip out, above, that the only medicine is, not-paradoxically, within myself and nowhere else . . . the new frequency of that revelation's impositions bringing me out of my Dark Night into the sun of this wide road . . . fear, the misery, the death, are trio inside of me, they can not actualize unless I permit them to — and at end of this wide road I no longer permit them to.

A page ago or fifty-two, there were the things, tu sais, of which it is much easier to speak to a close friend than to you — of this I am particularly culpable. You'll have to draw confidence, slowly, patiently out of me—I do love and admire you deeply so you must help me in this. I admit this ridiculousness is my fault, but it is profoundly inured from years of trying to protect myself. Yet why really, or against what, should I have to protect myself from you?

I can be, however, not completely without pride for I've never worked so hard or so steadfastly in my whole life; it was a good and real campaign and an absolutely on all its many grounds meaningful one. Now there isn't much left except the attendance call on whatever remaining faculties choose to preside over and see out the round bottom reached. I should invite all of myself though, that is if I have any sense of rightful due, for the rest of our stratagem is to be brief, and rather acquiescently compatible, I imagine. Compatible, to be more exact, in the inscrutable way things are when, whether to the witness of the world they will terminate joyful or sad, I know, core-calm within me, they will be tearlessly tragic, unalterably Impossible, a page ago or fifty-two.

Then all the sexual attitudes of every mind of every civilization that ever was funneled into my mind. I was thinking of my brother, the out of the me back there in my situations, to whom I am answerable, and of Hamid, of Hamid's expression when I told him that, Va chez-toi, va voir ton frére, c'est mieux, he said. Then he turned his eyes from me and sighed resignedly. Déja tu as couper ton amour, moi non, c'est pour ca, he added. C'est pas vrai, I objected, mais je peux rester ici toujours en t'attendant, et mon frére, n'a pas toujours . . . Je te donne jusqu'á la fin du mois prochain, Ca va me laisser un peu de temps avec leu.

Non, mieux que tu quittes maintenant, Oulidi, ton frére est important, ringing in the sad hears of my short-cut through the Dradeb. And also the momentously significant recrimination, Toi, tu peux travailler ici, moi non. Dans mon pays, toi, tu peux travailler. It is thought provoking. Suddenly I experienced a total uncertainty of the position of my viewing in the streets of the Dradeb. I found it impossible to estimate my height in relation to the buildings, my nearness to them. My distance above the pavement, and my whereabouts—my location at the end or middle of the block—shifted out of all tenable focus.

Some dealer had sold two bars of hashish to Maimun not making clear that it was a double portion for the price of one, or that was clear to Maimun and he did not make it so to me—the latter more likely, I thought quite shortly after consuming both bars and looking up at the mischievous grin on his face. Toi fou maintenant, oui? he queried needlessly. Enna hamuk! I answered and doubled up with laughter. As I pulled myself apart, the bopping doorframe in my right eye and Maimun a seven-card hand of squatting in seven separate frames of my left eye, I knew I was adrift upon several to be rather unusual hours. Generously, he offered to take me back to Calle Mahazen.

The world is utter rubber. I am a billiard on a string, a tadpole, a kite with my kitetail body serpented within the accordioned cylinder of the flanking walls. I fly, I steer along the shelves of the impasse, my gone to China body apportioned on five different shelves at once, dodge, glide above mudlark heads, and all with Maimun's green sweater, a green rubber ball bouncing ahead between elastic, gyrating buildingwhites to guide the way. Colors, the stonewhite wall the blue shutters scribblings and stains patterned skirts, strip alongside my flight and twist together gummily in eternity-meeting parallels.

In the prison of the Mahazen hotel room, (iron beds, story and a half ceiling, bars on the five feet from the cobbles windows), these stable objects—with the mirror glass, sink, soap, towels, two chairs, lounge, table, my valise, and the skeleton key, just there momentarily and for as long as I trust them . . . assume them more than trust for if I stopped suddenly and took just one square, fullfaced look at them they would all rise in a simultaneous flutter and batter and take fearfully off for Extension unknown . . . the well known non-artistic failure of reality . . . and Maimun standing in the triangular tracks, the open door and its optically-compensated opposite of his about to farewell, a page ago or fifty-two, wavers of his outline and washes within a velocity of colors, calling to me and losing that identity of his high voice and green sweater, calling, calling after me from a tunnel of unretrievable plunge, and reprimanding, tossing culpatory observances at me, Toi, tu te faites fou tous le temps!, Hamid stepping forward to the bedrail of the triangle, and reprimanding me.

Faites moi dormir—parles pas mal avec moi maintenant, I cried.

And he sank me in the covers with the pressure of his angry hands. The city spun around ringing out the cool water from a sopping towel.

Having is no stasis, but the constant endeavor to remerit, to re-earn. Having, having the world . . .

I can not take the responsibility of the knowledge in other people's acts. I may sometimes prevent their action, but knowledge can come to them by them only.

I can not tell you now if you have not learned in eight years. I assume, therefore, that you have.

have abstracted love into the absolute self-sufficient purity, where it remains unbaffled by events of the physical because no longer dependent or even emergent upon them, laughs at the parade and conversion of things.

But having is another matter. You will learn.

The other day we returned from Souani and the Emsallah together. We talked about a number of matters, you commencing on various people and how they were, and what you had to do with them because of this, if anything, but I don't remember the details. I do remember very clearly, though, how you took several yards up ahead of me on the Souani hill, turning your head back slightly to talk but always keeping a close eye for the stones on the ground, the shiny black pocketbook on your right wrist, you were several stairheights above me and slightly to my left. It seemed as if there were no bitterness. There wasn't complete understanding, rather a dumb awe (sociably concealed) at the enormity, perhaps grandeur, of the thing, but there was no bitterness.

Because the sort of having thing that would have been difficult between us here, at this point, in this eventuality, never existed for us—was never born with us in our civilization, or later, relationship: was flirted with in idea, fancy, and afterward awkwardly crushed as if it did have life, or in case it did, I don't know, I don't think so.

The good lies in having prevailed until the prevalence itself is made fleshy, is made life.

I can tell you of many sad predictions that are all come true, but I have changed now and I do not always see what there is to tell.

removed to the country of momentary resolutions in the spring and wrote a letter that began:

"All my faults perchance thou knowest all my madness none can know . . ."

and a lot of other lovely words that you can't understand so what good does it do you?

The good lies in having . . .

But you will learn, you will learn, it can not be told.

All taking place in a bold romance of two worlds and a dream of neither, a madman's dream beginning in the green and blue lights of the pier and ending a thought's quarterhour later in the hideous, unspeakable laughter at the corner of Rue Delacroix and Boulevard Pasteur. I *had* seen nothing in the lights who sat like a young Buddha full of kif and said he saw all. I had come desiring, I had come to acquire. I ended by hoisting it out, by pushing it off from within; I ended by bleeding it into fleshiness, into life.

To receive myself, I came.

If you come to me, I shall give you yourself.

But if you know this now or if you do not know it, I do not pity you.

Then we'll scurry in the drizzle under the glassy lights past the Key, Valencia, and Cooper Union, and the monster-building block I don't like, could never make part of me, to the counter service on W.B. And this time, buy two frankfurters.

What is it we have sought in each other?

my God.

can you really? I mean it was so business-like. What?

Was this pages ago, the rubber reduced to the evaporative shimmering, the final, the textbook illusion on the highway ahead? How long did it never take me to see that I shan't win to, much less obtain at the end of this road?

I decided to go back. I about faced sharply and nearly rammed into an old man leading his donkey that I'd been completely unaware of, had not even heard coming up behind me. The man moved aside with a startled gesture, then collected himself and said something in a highpitched, disapproving tone.

The fields appear in shadowless, unhazed relief under the said-sesame of total sun. I see the encompassment as the dry sticks it really singly amounts to, the joints, building foundation structures, and mathematic. I see the ridiculous skeleton of things, and the far ahead, disarmingly meaningless movements of beings. And with this was thought to persecute me?

How the innocent have fallen to content in that all things included were known and suffered satisfactorily.

It occurred to me that a good pipeful or two would hold me

until I got back to Tetuan. Remembering that Mohammed and his friends had taken considerable pains to conceal their smoking in the cafe, I turned off the road and eased my way down a brief incline that would cut me off from the view of anyone passing by. I unfolded my jacket and removed the pipe from one of the torn front pockets. I quickly looked around to make sure of my seclusion, when I noticed quite surprised, that some man in a dark brown jellaba had wandered away from the road to the edge of the incline in order to peer at me. I squatted with my back to him and my jacket pulled over my knees, pretending that I was urinating Moroccan-fashion. After a minute or so I looked up again and there he still was, only now quite comfortably propped against his staff, staring down with complete absorption. I turned my back to him and squatted a second time, scooping out some kif from my sheepskin pouch with the inserted pipebowl. My hands shook under his unwanted scrutiny and because of the awkward position that he forced me into, and I cursed out loud in Moghrebi when several grams of the whitegreen kif spilled into the grass. His standing there is more than curiosity or the by now quotidian lechery, I decided, it is unneeded interference—remorseless invasion.

It was of this that I wasn't certain, that I wearied the highways of the world in pilgrimage for, this acquiescence, this particular subservience—but now I am, now I am surfeited with its trying out, its long, failed experiment.

I smoked a pipe, climbed the slope, and said into the face of my jellabad spectator, Ca ne marche pas ici, monsieur! I walked quickly to the road and renewed my way at a brisk pace.

Hamid, I termulated on my English lips, is of this instance a page from now or fifty-two ago, expendable.

If he isn't possible, he shall not be necessary.

These are the days of knowledge. The wisdom that we always read and always told and always spoke to others: but it is one thing to read and say, and quite another to know. These are the days of knowledge, and knowledge always come in the end.

It comes up the cobblestone steps in Tetuan, and up the ascent to Bab el Asa, a street of stairs, with its head bowed under a cap of

black curls and takes great time to look at you and great months to finally tell you. Then, for a single instant, the eyes open wide and in their indefinable exchange from brown to green to blue drifts their Liberty, out to the last light on the pier, (which they are), past Malabata Point to Gibraltar or Venice or the nearest
mountain top . . .

> the mountain in Tangier is called El Sharf, you
>> notice it immediately upon arriving
>>> set up in a frame of lilac sky
>>> between the road to Tetuan and the railroad
>>> neat as an early Italian Renaissance
>>> cut, landscaped, pathed with trim green bushes
>>> and yellow trees.
> Thoroughly unrealistic, and like all things that don't fit
>> you put it aside. Yet, it is there
>>> for some reason and even
>>> if it awaits an ultimate moment
>>> to claim its purpose
>>> it will do so finally and you will understand
>>> implicitly.

I am thinking about Liberty, that it is the same as the prison Sidi Grandori in the bay, and that it is just there, with lights blinking in an arc like diamonds from a suspended necklace, and that it has always been there and everybody knows it and always knew it, everybody except me. O—I always knew to say it but never really knew it, knew it to write it.

The Liberty is endlessly repeated, it is in the repetitions, it is the repetitions, the repetitions are the expression of the ritualistic nature of all that progresses here, or does not progress but is a ritual endlessly repeating in order to understand to come to knowledge and that knowledge is the Liberty.

And the Liberty sits on a mountain top, El Sharf, or in the prison in its shadow, Sidi Gandori.

You are asked what you will do, for knowledge makes nothing happen. It is like verses or love—or man—it makes nothing happen. So you are not asked what you will do.

> "I shall go to Mexico where ladies
> in red roses float in the canals
> and afterwards Singapore which

hasn't been ruined yet."

But the eyes under the cap of black curls aren't listening now. You haven't been asked what you will do.

I shall go back to school, I shall go back to bed, I shall go back to Sandra. I shall go back behind the mountain, back behind the clouds and sit shivering in the cold drizzle.

The Liberty is mountain tops farthest atop, is proximities farthest apart, is what I came to learn, is what I have learned that what I came to take I can not. Can never.

And it wounds.

"To discover the reality of human relations by establishing it."

And it has all come to pass; unmitigated bitterness.

I have learned the image in which to live. My former revolt, suspension between identities was an endeavor to crack the Freiburger's wisdom.

Can it be good, the way the world must be? I mean can I make it and make within it? What a strange question to ask. Or will there always be some vague spectre in the flowers over her birthday? I keep shifting between impressions, but always, secretly excited about my new image, I think.

I can rest here so long, so quietly between the making of each sentence.

RONALD TAVEL

Ronald Tavel was born and raised in Brooklyn, majored in literature and philosophy and has travelled widely in Canada, Mexico, France, Spain, the Caribbean and, of course, North Africa, which provides the setting for his long, symphonic novel Street of Stairs. *Mr. Tavel has achieved recognition as a playwright, poet and scenarist. As founder and leader of the Theater of the Ridiculous movement, he has written more than a dozen plays, including* Boy on the Straight-Back Chair *and* Gorilla Queen. *As scenarist for Andy Warhol, he wrote, often directed and acted in such films as* The Chelsea Girls, Vinyl *and* Suicide. *Mr. Tavel's poetry and essays have appeared in a variety of academic and avant-garde publications, and he is a frequent lecturer at university and study groups. His new works include an opera commissioned especially for television.*

Pretty Thing

Robert Turner

That night, Pretty Thing was so exhausted from staying up half the night before, drafting her new bill, that she decided to go to bed early. At nine o'clock, she was all tucked in between the sheets, nude, of course, as she had become accustomed to sleeping lately and just couldn't *stand* having anything binding on her.

Soon she was dozing off and entering into a dream. In the dream, she was Sheba Listless and she was sleeping with her father, Jitter Listless, and somehow, he'd gotten behind her and was doing to her what *young* Jit had done on the porch, only she wasn't struggling against it this time because it was even so much better because of the *dimensions* of old Jitter Listless; it was even better than when she used to do the same thing to herself when she was very young, with a broom handle.

Oh, my goodness, she thought in the dream, it's so big—and thick—and hot—and hard—and the way it rubs me there, I can hardly *stand* it.

Then, still in the dream, she looked down the front of her and there was that thing, sticking out from between her legs at the front, just as it had with Sheba. She began to just die of curiosity as to how it would feel—in her hand, that is. She knew it must be good because Sheba had seemed to enjoy it so.

Her hand crept slowly downward and then, sure enough, it was *filled* with pulsing, throbbing, hot and slick feeling gristle. And in the dream, she didn't feel bad at all about enjoying it so much because *she* knew she wasn't *Sheba* doing this but herself, Pretty Thing and so, not being even *related* to Jitter Listless, of course there was nothing even remotely incestuous about the act. She had always wondered what one of *those* would feel like and now she knew. Her hot little hand moved and squeezed affectionately, which, in turn, seemed to induce *that* to swell and stiffen even more until she could scarcely *hold* it.

A few moments later, she was fascinated to see it erupt and felt the wetness pouring all over her hand. Oh, my, she thought to herself, I've made him have a come-come and a real *good* one at that, I would gather.

A few seconds afterward, she awakened, a little dazed, to find her own hand clamped between her legs and almost as wet as it had become in the dream. She shivered and gently petted her still tingling parts before withdrawing her hand. Sleepily, she told herself that that had been one of the best nocturnal emissions, which she knew to be the really scientific term for wet dreams, that she'd had in a long time.

She tried to force herself to go back to sleep quickly so that maybe she could have "seconds," as it were—that is if old Jitter Listless was still *capable*. Or perhaps she could substitute some other man in the new dream, she thought; now, let's see, who could it be?

Just then, the door of her room banged open and a shadowy figure of a man lurched in. Pretty Thing looked up in some alarm but then was relieved to see that it was only her father, wearing his old-fashioned nightgown, and she wished he would be more modern in his choice of sleeping attire; they made such chic pajamas for men, these days.

As he staggered toward the bed, Goodrich Gander blubbered thickly: "M'little gal! Where's m'little ol' gal, Pretty Thing? Got t'see her, Ah tell ya. Got to kiss her good night like Ah *used* to. She jus' a li'l *bitty* ol' thing. Where—where m'honey-darlin'?"

"Popp-uh! I declare!" Pretty Thing called out. "You're drunk. And—and you're cryin'! What in the world's the matter, Poppuh?"

"Nothin', nothin', 'tall, sweet li'l ol' gal, I tell you," he said, standing beside the bed, swaying like a young willow tree in the wind. "Jus'—jus' had a few drinks t'many, Ah reckon. And jus'—jus' wanted kiss m'li'l ol' girl-baby g'night, like Ah used to."

"Very well, Poppa," she answered dutifully. "Hurry up and kiss me, then get back to your own bed before you fall *down* or something. Sakes alive but you are stoned!"

He leaned toward her and to facilitate matters, Pretty Thing sat up in bed, forgetting for the moment, in her concern over her father's condition, that she was nude.

"Jus—jus' li'l kiss-kiss good night for m'baby!" Gander slobbered as he bent over her. Just as he was about to brush his lips against hers, he lost his balance. His hand reached out to steady itself on something and came to rest full over one of Pretty Thing's plump, round, naked little breasts.

The delightfully tactile sensation so produced caused him to jerk erect again and maintain his balance. It also caused him to maintain the contact of his hand with her breast, which he was now squeezing experimentally.

"Eh? Eh?" he mumbled drunkenly. "What's this? Who's here—in my (hic!) li'l girl's bed? Can't be m'little baby girl! Las' time kissed her g'night, she didn't *have* any of these!"

"Oh, Poppa!" Pretty Thing said, laughing indulgently because she *knew* he was so dunk he didn't know what he was doing or even where he was, for that matter, so what harm could there be?

She pushed his hand away but not before his big thumb had rubbed her small nipple to tingling erectness, sending shivers all through her, in spite of herself.

"Now, Poppa, you'd better leave and go back to bed. As you must have noticed, I'm not *dressed* to receive company. And you're goin' to fall on your face in another *minute.*"

"Got t'find out somethin', first," he mumbled. "Is—is somebody else—some *impostress* in my li'l ol' gal's bed? Or is it really m'baby, mebbe wearin' some kind of modern, plastic, 'magic skin' falsies, jus' makin' *believe* she's grown up?"

With that, he again reached out, brushing his hand against her breast before she rolled out of the way, giggling, at this silly game her drunken daddy was playing. Poppa was such a loveable *idiot* when he'd had too much to drink.

The last move was too much for Goodrich Gander and he finally lost his balance completely and fell full length across the bed, passed out and almost immediately was snoring.

"Oh, for Blessed sake!" Pretty Thing said, peevishly, clucking her tongue. "Now see what you've done, Poppa. Now get up. You can't sleep here on my bed; it just wouldn't look nice for the serving people in the morning. You get up now and go back to your own bed, hear?"

He didn't move, nor answer. Pretty Thing reached out and shook him, roughly. All that was accomplished was that he rolled over onto his back, snoring even more loudly.

"Oh, Darn!" she said, then, getting up out of the bed. "Now I'll have to go sleep in your bed and it doesn't even have a canopy!"

As she started toward the door, she heard her father suddenly stop snoring and moan in his sleep. She paused. Perhaps he was going to be sick. She couldn't have *that,* not all over her nice bed! Then she heard him cry out: "Got to pee-pee! S'mbody he'p me! Can't get up! Gemme pot or somethin'. Got to go, G'dam it, Ah tell ya!"

"Oh, Mercy!" Pretty Thing exclaimed. "Now, what am I going to do? I can't just let him wet all over my bed!"

Then she remembered the old chamber pot she'd used as a child that was in the cabinet under the bathroom sink, where she kept it for sentimental reasons. Quickly, she ran to the bathroom, put on the light and got out the pot and ran back into the bedroom. She saw that Poppa was now lying on his side, face close to one edge of the bed. One hand was clasping his genitals like a little boy, through the cloth of his nightgown and he was rocking slightly, murmuring: "He'p me, he'p me—got to peeeeee!"

"All *right*, Poppa," she said, "I *heard* you. Here!" She stuck the pot into his free hand, which was dangling over the bed. It slipped free and clanged to the floor. She tried several times more but he couldn't hold it. Finally, she told him:

"I'll hold it. Now—now, get yourself out and go in the potty." She held it near the edge of the bed, in position. She watched him fumble drunkenly up under his nightgown, around his knees, and then after a few moments remove his hand. He whined, pitifully; "Can't *find* it—too drunk to *find* it, even. Somebody he'p me. please!"

For a moment, Pretty Thing hesitated, thinking how when she was little she'd always wanted to hold her cousin Rhett's for him, while he peed; it would have been such fun, but the mean old thing would never let her. She also thought that if she *didn't* help Poppa he probably *would* wet all over her bed and his nightie, too and even if he were able to do it himself he probably was too drunk to guide it straight, so she'd just have to do it for him and forget her silly false modesty. Why, she could pretend she was just a nurse, helping out a sick patient, which was more or less true. And of course, she wouldn't even *look*, which wouldn't make it *so* bad.

Then, turning her head, with a little sigh, she reached down and flicked up the bottom of his gown. She fumbled around until her hand encountered something like a length of worn out old garden hose, feeling almost sorry for its spongily limp helplessness.

She half-murmured aloud: "The poor thing can't possibly help *itself!*"

Then she had to look, to make sure she *had* the right part of his equipment, though only briefly, and, of course, to make sure that she was guiding it in the right direction toward the pot she was holding in front of him with her other hand. She could hardly help noticing, though, that his dimensions were at least equal to old Jitter Listless's when that person was in the same unlively condition.

She stood there waiting, now, head averted, for the sound of the tinkle of water against the old pot. When it didn't happen, she became a little perturbed and shook him slightly. "Will you please *go!*" she ordered. "I can't stand here like this all night."

He seemed not to have heard her. He was now snoring again but very lightly, this time. Impatiently, she gave him a little squeeze and another shake. Then she was surprised to hear him mutter, as though in his sleep and rather petulantly: "Don't *have* to go, now. Don't *wanna!*"

"Darn you, but you *must!*" Pretty Thing insisted. "After I've gone to all this *trouble!*"

She was amazed then to feel the limpness she held in her hand begin to stiffen and thicken quite noticeably. In some alarm, she glanced down and saw that it had already lengthened and increased in circumference almost twice its normal size. In a matter of seconds it was in a full and furious erectile state, throbbing and leaping against the prison of her clenched fist.

"My stars and garters!" she exclaimed. "Why, I never!"

Then she heard him mumble sleepily, almost like a child and she was sure, then, that he must be having a drunken hallucination that he was just a boy again, engaging in juvenile sexual experiment with some playmate—as he murmured: "Jus' want you to *play* with me! Feels *s'good!*"

"You naughty thing, I'll do nothing of the *sort,*" she answered, now vigorously shaking the huge wand she held in her hand, just to show him she meant business.

"Oh, yes," he muttered then. "That's right. Play with it *good. Up* and down, *up* and down, like that. *Then I'll let you see me pee. Promise!*"

"Oh, well, then!" she said with some exasperation. "Since I've gone this far, there's no sense in stopping. I just know that as soon as I stop and it gets soft again, you will wet the bed."

She made her hand do as he had ordered. Then she was fascinated at the way the silken soft skin slipped back and forth over the big, hot, bounding gristle beneath it. She moved her hand for a better grip and almost had trouble capturing the rebellious thing again but finally succeeded. Now her hand began to move faster. She found herself thinking, I guess it's only fair; I had a nice dream before, who am I to deny Poppa the same privilege? And really, all *I'm doing* is helping him get into condition so that he can urinate; if he gets some jollies out of it, that's *his* problem!

Soon Poppa was moaning and groaning in his sleep and at the same time, Pretty Thing found herself squeezing and rubbing her thighs together as she *used* to do when she was young, before she learned that it was just as easy to open her thighs and use her hand to achieve the same sensation. But now there was no alternative because of course, she was still holding the old potty with one hand and the *other* one was quite occupied, too.

Oh, she thought, after a while, I never realized how funny, how good one of them feels! Now I know I'll soon have to marry some nice young man so I'll have one of my own to play with all the time.

At that, a spasm began to take hold of her and she shivered and shook and bit her tongue to keep from crying out. Her back arched and wave after wave of sensation built up within her and then burst and the flesh of her thighs crawled and contracted and her belly tightened and relaxed and her buttocks clenched up tight as fists and she went all over herself as she felt the straining, turgid monster in her swiftly moving fist grow ever larger and stiffer.

Then there was the sound of something spurting into the pot and as she looked down through glazed eyes, her hips hunching wildly, she saw the milky fluid beginning to cover the entire bottom of it. She thought he would never stop and almost hoped he *wouldn't* because as long as he continued to so react, so did she.

When it was all over and she felt the swelling gradually go to softness, Pretty Thing somehow felt faint. She opened her hand then and released its prisoner. She reached out and wiped her hand on the bed sheet. She stood for another moment, staring down at the sleeping man, listening to him snore softly. She bent and put the used pot under the bed. As she straightened up, she was just in time to see the object of her attentions, previously, ejecting a yellow stream all *over* her pretty bed.

She clapped her hands to the sides of her face and watched in horror until he was finished. Then she turned and ran from the

room, to go sleep in *his* bed, all the while crying out:
"Oh, gold*urn* him, anyway, that *bad* old piss-in-the-bed!"

ROBERT TURNER

Robert Turner, the "unknown" author of Pretty Thing, *has sold some 1,500 short stories and novelettes to practically every general circulation magazine published in the past thirty years, and published some fifty paperback books. His stories have been anthologized in several collections of "best," and translated into over a dozen foreign languages. By some jinx, fame keeps passing him by, but the author says he is not discouraged. A Navy veteran of World War II, the 54-year-old author has been married to the same woman for 35 years, is father of three, and grandfather of five. In between checks, as they say in the writing business, he has worked as literary agent, editor, advertising salesman and public relations director for an underwater mermaid show.*

Love on a

Trampoline

Sybah Darrich

I unhooked her bra and slipped it off, so as to study better the fierce upward thrust of her boobs. She set down her drink and stood up, and I thrust my face into the soft flesh of her small round belly and ran my tongue around in her beautiful navel as my busy hands slipped her panties down below her knees, sliding over the satin-smooth skin of her rump and down her long, creamy thighs.

She kicked free of her underwear, and stepped onto the trampoline, and jumped a few times, her breasts bouncing separately, the flesh of her hips quivering, and the musky smell of her sex filling the air. My member bucked in anticipation, and I lurched tipsily forward to grab one of her ankles, missed, and fell onto the canvas as she flew into the air again. I caught a glimpse of a dark crease, a quivering pink clitoris, and two or three drops of pale moisture on the inside of a thigh that was turning rosy from exercise. When she landed again, my horizontal body flew into the air. Then she lost her footing and sprawled beside me, and I closed my eyes as we both bounced rhythmically to a stop.

When I opened my eyes, I found myself staring at a beautifully rounded kneecap. My head was reeling from the brandy, and every move I made caused us both to sway uncertainly on the taut canvas. I slithered closer and put my face between her legs to taste the drops of white moisture on her thigh. Her fingers dug at my scalp and twisted around in my hair and she hissed between clenched teeth. She squeezed my head between her thighs, keeping my mouth tantalizing inches from her sex, and I began to bite her firm flesh, gently at first, and then more urgently, till her thighs fell open and her moist opening appeared just above me.

I took hold of her tiny waist with both hands and pulled her down till her wet sex rested against my mouth, and thrusting aside the outer folds of her lips, I plunged my tongue deep into the dark recess while my arms slid under her back, my hands gripped her shoulder and pulled her down even more sharply against me. She bent her legs and began to stroke the small of my back with her feet, then slipped her curled toes into the crease between my buttocks, drawing a rasping sound from my throat. My swollen tool bucked against the vibrating canvas and I knew I couldn't hold out much longer.

I raised myself upon both arms and fell against her, holding her tightly just below the waist and grinding my rod against her stomach as we bounced spasmodically. She wrapped her ankles around me so that we were locked together, and raked my back with her sharp nails, driving me half mad with pain and excitement. My hand wrapped in her long hair forced her head back as I sucked a bit at her neck and collarbone, raising bright red welts on the white skin. Suddenly, my ear was in her mouth, every crevice being licked by her hot probing tongue.

My head was filled with undersea sounds, and blackness swam before my eyes. "Now," she whispered as she released my ear.

My legs, still twined tautly about hers, began to spread as far as her legs would go, and then a little farther. She groaned, and brought her hand between our bodies, closing it around my tumescent member. Perspiration broke out all over me as she guided my rod to its sheath, planting the thick head unerringly against the wet lips of her opening. I felt the lips parting and oozing as she ground and rotated her hips. Her buttocks rose to meet me as she spread her lips still farther with her fingers, and I penetrated hard and deep, and began a bucking and rearing that soon became quicker and finally, totally, involuntary out of my control. The thrust of the trampoline worked with us, and at each thrust I sank still deeper into her flesh, forcing a groan from her lips. Finally her pelvis began a spasmodic, jerky movement of its own, and in a starburst of incomparable pleasure I came again and again inside her.

When I awoke I was alone on the trampoline, in my damp jockey shorts, unable to gauge how much of my vividly remembered pleasure had been a dream, and how much had actually occurred. The house was dark, and Stephanie nowhere to be seen. Had I been slipped a mickey, or simply passed out from too much brandy?

I shagged my wet self down the hill, carrying pants, shirt, and sandals in an awkward bundle, threading between the yucca, cactus and sage that bordered the hairpin path.

SYBAH DARRICH

Sybah Darrich (an anagram of the author's real name) carries the paranoia — which is an occupational hazard of writers — to such lengths he would tell us nothing about himself that isn't obviously a Baron von Munchhausen lie. He says he won the Nobel Prize for a super-vaccine so far ahead of its time there is still no disease for it, and that he is at work on a Saturday morning TV series for kids which will be based on the Kama Sutra. For recreation he says he does the New York Times *crossword puzzles with a pen and is an ardent body-surfer on Walden Pond. Take it from there, and enjoy the selection.*

Mullin Garr

Sunday Kind of Love

*I*knew a fellow once who aspired to a writing career, so he retired and made ready to stand the literary world on its ear. He'd been a corporation man so he made his preparations with all the efficiency that a career in business had instilled in him. He rented a large office complete with recorders, file cabinets, wall-to-wall carpet, and a dazzling blonde secretary. He installed a reference library that would have done credit to a historical researcher, laid a copy of Roget's *Thesaurus* on his desk—and discovered to his astonishment that he hadn't the least idea of what he wanted to say.

So he seduced the blonde secretary on the office couch and found enough inspiration in that series of exhilarating experiences to write a period piece about a young cat who faintly resembled David Copperfield with a hard-on. It was a bust.

"At odds with reality," wailed the publisher, but what he meant was that he couldn't visualize young David with his cock up Fanny Hill's ass. And it is a sobering thought at that.

Undismayed, my friend returned to his *Thesaurus* and his compliant secretary, but his wife came to visit one day while he was seeking inspiration on the office carpet. It was an inauspicious moment, and while I was, unfortunately, not present myself, I can readily imagine the awkwardness of such a confrontation.

Finding his position indefensible—but more than adequate for specific research—he thoughtfully continued his quest for enlightenment until he ejaculated into the writhing blonde, at which time her slim shapely legs released their embrace and he was able to arise with some semblance of dignity. (It will be clear at this point that I have drawn on my imagination to some extent, but only for clarification. Facts are facts. His wife caught him *en flagrante*—that is, screwing hell out of his secretary.)

We will draw a merciful curtain over the scene that followed, but what appeared at first to be disaster was actually a blessing in disguise. After the divorce my friend took up residence with the blonde, and was even so moved at one point by her lush charms that he proposed marriage. She wisely demurred, citing the many romances that have been thus blighted, and suggested that if he really wanted to do something for her he could replenish her wardrobe. As a man of means he was able to comply, beginning with a mink coat, and I can personally testify that she often wore nothing else. But more of that later.

Her constant proximity did wondrous things for his burgeoning career. David Copperfield became a princely cocksman of heroic proportions; Fanny became the king's favorite playmate, and while a literal-minded reader might be hard-pressed to find justification for her nude appearance at the Battle of Balaklava, nobody else gave a damn.

In glowing terms his passion-driven prose described her sexual appetites and lusty appeasement thereof, and went into the sort of anatomical detail that made many wonder why the protagonist wanted to fight in the first place.

My friend devoted no less than thirteen paragraphs to an off-hand discussion of her breasts; seven were involved with a casual reference to her legs—but then he callously lumped her ass and hips and belly into a rather hurried resume of three pages, and scarcely wasted more than forty or fifty words on her navel. I don't recall that he mentioned her feet at all, but in consideration of the water shortage during the Crimean campaign, perhaps he was well advised.

Ah, but when he came at length to her pussy! There he waxed truly eloquent; so much so that when only as far as page twelve and the pinkly swelling labia minora I became so excited that I cast the book aside and rushed out into the street, only to be jailed for lewd and disorderly conduct.

My friend's work took the country by storm. Privately, I thought it was a lousy book. But his descriptions of the blonde heroine, and the graphic pictures he drew of her vigorously uninhibited activities, had the nation's tongue hanging out and its pants straining. I eventually finished reading it, and having identified the hot-pantied lady with my friend's secretary I became so enamored of her that I wrote a sonnet called "Salute to Vicki's Vulva." As I recall it began:

"Ah, lift thy boldly curving hips, / Spread the thighs that now eclipse / Thy pussy's sweetly pouting lips— / The lips of Vicki's vulva."

It was a tender thing, and while I was received by the literary world with a disappointing lack of enthusiasm, it drew me to her attention. She was receptive to my advances, but our opportunities at first were rather limited. I shall never forget my first taste of her, when I took her hurriedly while my friend was mixing drinks in the kitchen. She smiled demurely as she knelt on the couch, coyly flipped up the mink coat revealing her lovely naked ass, and blushingly invited me to have at it.

We'd had the foresight to order Singapore Slings, but he caught us in the short rows anyway. Thinking quickly, I pounded her lustily on the back, shouting to him meanwhile that she'd been taken by a fit of coughing and doubtless had something caught in her throat. The clever dear followed my lead and barked convincingly while I stared at my friend across the back of the couch. Her ass never ceased its convolutions for a moment.

He set down the tray of drinks, instinctive gentleman that he was, and raced into the kitchen for a glass of water. We were both coming as he left the room, and she lay decorously on the couch when he returned while I made pretense of fanning her with a newspaper. It was admittedly a clever ruse, under the circumstances, but I doubt that he was entirely taken in. As a matter of fact, I'm sure he wasn't, since he later accused me of trying to teach her one of those strange modern dances.

We were much more circumspect after that, but he eventually caught us anyway. I was seated on the toilet with the lady astride my lap when he burst into the bathroom in the act of unzipping his trousers. He stared aghast at her gyrating hips, and I'll never know whether it was shock or his innate sense of courtesy that made him wait until she'd finished her orgasm. Then he pulled her free and did his best to kill me.

I escaped, however, and he was still hunting me when my life was saved by his publisher. That low, conniving creature lured her away with a chartreuse Cadillac, and my friend swore off writing forever. He now tends bar in the saloon I use as my office.

I stayed in discreet seclusion for a while, and having suffered enough, came forth determined on a writing career of my own. A chance conversation with an old sailor in Astoria, Oregon set my wandering feet at last on the path of destiny. I was irrigating my remorse in a spa called *The Oasis* when I was introduced to the Ancient Mariner by a local personality known as Bum Dig Mary. I kept his glass filled while he regaled me with tales of the Mysterious Far East, which in his lexicon had at its hub an establishment in Tsingtao called The House of a Thousand Ass-holes. And thus was born my world-famous adventure series, *The Thousand-and-One Nights of an Ambassador-at-Large.* (What was the spark that launched this literary comet? Which the tale that so fired my imagination? Hah! I'll never tell.)

I shall pass lightly over the difficulty in convincing Adhemar-Sherman that America's Rebellious Youth were ready for my New Frontier Bedtime Tales, nor shall I dwell upon the tearful reconciliation between my friend and me on my return to New York. Suffice it to say that our blonde came back to us, all tremulous sighs and shy glances, and we now share her, an apartment, and the chartreuse Cadillac. She works the booths here in *The New Oasis,* where we can both keep an eye on her.

That's not the main reason I do my writing here, however. Through these swinging portals pass the kooks, creeps, and characters that people the pages of my purple prose. Down there at the end of the bar, for example, sits Hattie the Hooker. She began her career as a peeler in San Francisco's Tenderloin at the tender age of sixteen, ("I hadn't even learned to go three ways then," she told me with becoming modesty.) and soon worked her way up to the status of entertainer.

In Hattie's framework of experience, an entertainer is one who performs at private parties—usually with assistance of one kind and another—and it was her boast that at eighteen she was capable of putting on a show that "had the whole God damn' bunch comin' in their britches." I have myself seen her in action a number of times, and it may be very near the truth.

A measure of her self-confidence was the fact that she began her act entirely naked, scorning the usual titillating process of stripping garment by garment. One might say with accuracy that she began where others left off. She started her performance with what she chose to call interpretative dancing, and concluded by challenging any couple present to join her in sexual congress. She was quite adaptable, as may be imagined, and seldom lacked employment. But as so often happens, her career was blighted by an unhappy love affair.

She was the feature attraction at a lively gathering of The Benevolent Brotherhood of Body and Fender Men when it started. It was her habit to pick out one of those watching her and dance exclusively for him during the first minutes of her dance, as she said it helped overcome her native shyness. On this occasion she chose a husky young bumper straightener named Ball-pein Riley, and his response was so enthusiastic that she really outdid herself.

She was clean-shaven—as usual—and before long those sitting at the bar where she danced observed moisture gleaming on the insides of her thighs, and more than a hint of pink protruding from the thick-lipped slash between them. In mere moments her cunt was seen to be opening wantonly, and she smiled in demure appreciation at the bulging britches of the Brotherhood.

No britches bulged more bravely than did Ball-pein's, and when she singled him out to assist in her finale, he entered into the thing with the hearty vigor that had brought him to the top of his profession. He fucked her on the bar to the accompaniment of shouts and cheers, and nobody minded that they kicked over three pitchers of beer and completely ruined the Brotherhood's anniversary cake.

Crowbar Brannigan and Socket Sapperstein were keeping score, but when Hattie was in the throes of her fifth or sixth orgasm—depending on whose tally was considered the more accurate—they came to blows over which should be regarded as official, so no records are at present available. All agreed that it was a magnificent performance, however, and most conceded that Ball-pein had it coming when he wiped off his cock on Hanrahan's shirt and loudly demanded an hour's overtime. (Many will recall that I made this incident the central theme in *Ambassador: Statesman, or Bon Vivant?* A title, incidentally, that completely cozened the puritanical city fathers of Boston, Mass.)

It was clear to all that Hattie was deeply smitten. She lay languishing on the bar, fluttering her eyelashes at the brawny Ball-pein while a dainty foot toyed absently with the front of Hanrahan's pants. The other leg was still flung wide as the bumper bender had left it, and the Brotherhood stared in mounting admiration as his rusty load continued to ooze out of her.

The thorough fucking she'd received had instilled a lethargy in her that relaxed the marvelous body and brought a soft glow of girlish contentment to her face. She smiled angelically when Hanrahan broke out his cock, and her shapely foot nudged it playfully as he began to pull off his pants. It was a peaceful, homey scene, and I shall not soon forget it—nor will any of the Brotherhood, I'll wager.

Hanrahan spoiled it to some extent when he crawled onto the bar with his wart-studded cock preceding him, but she laughed indulgently when he rammed it into her and thus averted what could have been a tense situation. She embraced Hanrahan with her long white legs and gave him a fucking that left him grey and shaken, but her melting gaze never strayed from Ball-pein's face. Obviously, Hattie was in love.

She entertained several fender men during the next two hours, but it was clear to all that her heart belonged to Ball-pein. The beer flowed freely and excitement grew as the time of her Grand Finale neared. Ball-pein came in for a lot of good-natured joshing, naturally, as everyone assumed he'd be one of those chosen to assist her. It was something of a shock therefore, when she summoned Crowbar Brannigan to act as anchor man.

She got him to lie on the bar with his hard-on standing bravely amid the swirling clouds of cigar smoke. She straddled him then, gave Ball-pein a soulful glance, and seated Crowbar's cock with a single jerk of her rounded hips. Acknowledging the applause with a nod of her pretty head, she leaned forward, raised her ass invitingly—and the Brotherhood sighed with relief. It was all clear now; fittingly enough, she'd chosen to have Ball-pein rear-end her.

But it was not so. Horrified, the Brotherhood heard her lilting voice calling for Torque-wrench Torgeson, and it was he who finally worked his prick into her artfully squirming ass. Then her lovely eyes sought Ball-pein's face.

"Come, my love," she murmured shyly, "but leave your britches behind." (Some will note that I used this very line in *What Happens When The Security Council Adjourns—an Exposé.*—Fiddler and Scull, $3.75.)

When she urged him to kneel on the bar facing her it was at once obvious that she'd been using her head when she selected Crowbar as anchor man. Although powerfully built, he was only five feet tall, and when Ball-pein moved into position with his knees against Crowbar's shoulders, the mighty bumper man's cock was tenderly brushing his true-love's cheek. She blushed prettily and lovingly slipped the lavender-colored head into her mouth.

The scenes that followed are burned indelibly into my memory. There was a brief period of understandable confusion occasioned by a certain lack of coordination, but once the three were in phase, they proceeded in the best of spirits. Hattie soon began to come in her hearty manner, and it seemed to the cheering fans that her hips had never been more agile, her back more supple, or her ass more entrancingly active.

It would be easy to explain her apparent enthusiasm by pointing out that she was getting it going and coming—in a manner of speaking—but this would be an over-simplification. The trained observer would have noted that at least six inches of cock had slipped between her soft red lips, and she was clearly strangling. No matter how she twisted and turned she could not escape, and when it seemed her thrashings would topple them all off the bar there was no lack of well-meaning hands to prevent that tragedy.

Fortunately Ball-pein came in good time and the poor girl had a respite of sorts. She sucked the softened cock until it grew hard once more, and when he attempted to run it down her throat again, she effectively prevented him by sinking her teeth into it. Following this clever stratagem they arrived at an understanding, and by the time they all exploded in a tumultuous concert of orgasmic convulsions it took eight powerful hammer mechanics to keep them on the bar.

And then, as so often happens, fate stepped in, arrayed in the uniforms of New York's Finest. They'd come into Harry's Place a half-hour earlier, but had courteously held their collective hands until the final jerking shudder of Hattie's sweetly curved ass. Now they moved in, and if their pants bulged as staunchly as those of the Brotherhood, who could blame them?

Crowbar, Torque-wrench, and Ball-pein were all charged with indecent exposure, but were released on a technicality when Ball-pein pointed out that they were not, in fact, exposed at the time of the arrest. Hattie did not fare so well, however. She was convicted of performing in public without a license and sentenced to ninety days. When she was released Ball-pein had gone to Southern California where body-and-fender men are in great demand, and in her despair, Hattie became a hooker.

All who knew her were saddened to see the sweet young girl turn down that primrose path.

She scored well for a while, and her friends were delighted to see the roses returning to her cheeks, and to observe once more the shy smile they knew and loved. Then she met Funafuti Fred, and her downfall was complete. (That's Fred sitting in the corner booth with the three showgirls fawning over him, the son-of-a-bitch.)

His tale is a strange one. In nineteen-forty-five he was a callow youth of eighteen with no features to distinguish him from any other B-24 tail gunner. In July of that year the Pacific war was drawing to a close, but an ill wind forced Fred's plane far off course and it went down somewhere in the Pacific. Fred escaped injury, but was separated from the others, and drifted for several days in a tiny rubber life raft before going ashore on an uncharted island in the Ellice group. Fred has never disclosed the name of this island—if indeed it has a name—while in his cups, one night he conceded that it was near the island of Funafuti, which as every schoolboy knows, is located 180° 50' W; 8° 35' S.

He was welcomed by a group of friendly native women, but when he would have returned their kindness his overtures were met with good-natured, if somewhat derisive laughter. Through the age-old medium of sign-language he finally learned that while they felt his intentions were good, they considered his cock inadequate to the task, and pointed at its puny seven-inch length with hoots and catcalls.

Somewhat taken aback he stuffed it into his pants, and after brooding about the matter for a couple of days set out to find the village whence the women had come. He found it shortly—if you'll pardon the expression—and he also found the reason for the ladies' disdain. Every man in the village possessed a prick of enormous proportions. They all pranced about naked, each fingering the source of his pride with loving hands, and offering to split any woman who felt equal to the ordeal.

Copulating couples cavorted here and there, for these were happy, carefree people with a childlike disregard for the proprieties. He gloomily picked his way among them, while glad cries of rapture beat against his eardrums, and sick with shame at his own lack of stature, he blundered off into the jungle. A tender native maiden of fourteen or so followed him, and taking pity on the poor stranger, dragged him into the ferns and nearly fucked the life out of him. He found her to be as—ah—receptive as a woman of thirty, and after taking seconds they walked on into the jungle, she leading and not caring that his load was running down her legs.

At length they came to a spring, and he was amazed to see a dozen young boys lying about with their cocks dangling in the water. With soft sighs and tender gestures she urged him to do the same, and gave him to understand that he would benefit greatly thereby. He complied with her wishes, and thereafter, began each day with a hearty fuck and a good soaking in the bubbling evil-smelling waters of the spring.

But all good things must come to an end, it seems, and Fred was fortunate to escape from the island with his life. The village Chief discovered that his favorite wife had developed a severe case of hemorrhoids, and seeking the answer found that Fred—who was half Greek—had reverted to the customs of his Hoplite ancestors.

Clearly, hospitality has its limits. Fred broke away after a brief skirmish, and made his way to Funafuti in a dugout canoe. He was rescued in due course by a team from the Coastal and Geodetic Survey, these having strayed off course while in pursuit of a bevy of vacationing Vassar girls. But Fred was content, and well he should have been, for he now possessed a cock which at full erection extended a full ten inches beyond his muscular belly. (God damn him.)

Fred disdained work, preferring to fuck his way through life, and he devoted himself to his avocation with all of his considerable strength and energy. He began in San Francisco and twenty years later arrived in New York, still as vigorous as ever and leaving a broad trail of tattered twats in his wake. He gained recognition immediately, and was soon elected president of Gotham's notorious Eight Inch Club; the very name of which designates the sole required qualification and sends shivers of terror (or delicious anticipation) into the hearts of the female populace. I myself am a charter member, and know whereof I speak.

We were having our monthly soiree here in Harry's Place one night, and Hattie—who was losing her youthful elasticity—had eagerly agreed to perform. The members have set a high standard for themselves, but Hattie was especially provocative, and they were well pleased. Her breasts were still big and firm and pointed, her ass yet smoothly curved—and if her belly had grown a little softer, many agreed that it only added to her appeal. A few purists noted that her cunt appeared bigger and more thickly fleshed than of yore; that the inner lips had grown and darkened, and protruded to a far greater extent—but even these conceded its obvious serviceability, especially when it began to swell and glisten with Eve's balm.

It happened that she'd chosen Funafuti Fred as the object of her warm-up dance, and it followed logically that he should assist her during intermission. She arrayed her shapely self to receive him, and with a charming air of girlish diffidence invited him onto the bar. He undressed completely, turning his back to her in deference to the solemnity of the occasion, and when he approached her it was from a vantage point that afforded him an unobstructed view of the hair-fringed treasure that awaited him.

It gaped seductively when she reached down to spread the dripping lips, and she doubtless misunderstood the awed murmur that arose. She favored us all with her dazzling smile—and an instant later shrieked in horrified dismay as that giant head drove into her defenseless pussy.

In moments, her piteous cries of protest were filling the room. Her eyes bulged; her tongue thrust from between her teeth, but her struggles only drove his massive weapon deeper. When her outraged body held six or seven inches she sent her hand to find what yet remained, and her howl of terror shook the bottles on the tables.

Those nearest the bar reported that her frantic fingers reached only halfway round that mighty shaft, and that her distended cunt was near the ripping point. He slowed his assault with two inches yet to go, and soon a tender smile was seen on Hattie's glowing face. Her ass was observed rising high off the bar; her hips undulated in a slow circle—and wonder of wonders, he slid on in until his balls were snugly against her twitching ass-hole. Hattie the

Hooker had taken a cock as big as her forearm.

They continued carefully until he was moving freely, giving her eight inches or so with every stroke—and sometimes more—and then followed the wildest scene these jaded eyes have ever witnessed. In a half-hour she'd had enough, and in another she was screaming for mercy. But still he fucked her. One hour and twenty-eight minutes after his balls had first reached her ass he came, jolting her from stem to stern with every spasm, and finally it was over.

Hattie had come twenty-three times by actual count, and she was never the same afterward. Gone was the girlish verve that had made her so popular; gone was the buoyant bounce that made her ass so universally admired, and gone too was the incredible stamina that had brought her such wide acclaim. I met her when she left the hospital, and at her request, assisted her in a test run, but it ended in disillusion. Hattie had gained lasting fame, but she'd lost that precious spark that set her so high above the others. Now Hattie's just another hooker.

(A select few will recognize in this tale the foundation for the work I titled *What The A.D.A. Means To Me*—Wanton House, $4.40).

And that reminds me. The big blonde—that one coming out of the ladies' room with the garden hose over her shoulder . . . My friend, therein lies a story, and if you'll just signal the bartender, I'll tell you how I came to conceive of Sam Sunday, the most inspired of my characters, hero of my widely-acclaimed series of adventure stories, *Always on Sunday, or Confessions of a Conscientious Cocksman.*

All-Night Visitors

Clarence Major

Anita is whipping her tight pussy on me like mad! We are in her dark, beautiful apartment, with a little wine that has warmed her, I think, more than it has me. "I want the light on," I say, and get up, the shock of my sudden movement, leaving her, stuns her. I come back, the bright three-way lamp, a new dimension on her caramel-colored, firm, lean body. The taut little tits with their large rich dark *dark* red berries, some sweet nipples. The gentle yellow lights drive mathematical light sets, like beautiful *tupu* sounds of Coltrane. My spongy, sore, moist sword, as I come back to the bed, dripping her juice along the way, the sweet goodness of it all soothing my limbs, I happily pat my stomach, singing a couple bars from *Something New* by James Brown as I jump on the bed, over her now, growling like a dog, "GRRRRRRRRRRRRRRRRRRRR," and imagining, even how it looks graphically in cartoons, or here, which is also a kind of cartoon of love, my soft black dick, by now completely stunted into a virginal softness, hanging there, and Anita goes, "Lazy nigger, you!" And her wide mouth, those big eyes, sparkling, her white *WHITE* teeth glowing, spotless, virtuous teeth. "I'm dog-- GRRRRRRRRRR bow-bow! BOW-WOW! BOW-WOW WOW WOW WOW WOW!!!" I am in her face, and her head is turned sideways, she's looking with those big Lil-Armstrong-jazzdays-eyes at me, as if to say, "Who're you supposed to be *NOW*? What kinda new game is this, little boy? *My My*, men are always boys! Boastful, silly, self-centered little boys, who want somebody to jack them off all the time!"

She giggles, the unclear voice of Donovan carries its weight equal in space, timing our senses, from the FM radio. Her big red tongue shoots out, touches my nose. It is good that I am able to enjoy these moments with Anita, despite all the past contamination between us! She runs her long (she has an *extra* long, extra red, extra *active*) tongue around my cheeks, quickly licks my lips, but I am still a pompous dog ready to bark again, when her hard, long, firm, hand intrudes, in the soft, baggy, damp, hairy area of my semen-smelling, fruit picker. The conduct of her dry hand always astonishes me, as it delights. She is still giggling. I am delighted, of course, whenever she touches my dick, I like it in a very civil way, not just a natural magnet, magic way. She puts me in large swimming pools of myself weighty with *SUPREME DELIGHT,* despite the slight roughness of her hand. Anita's hand is not rough because she's been washing dishes, sweeping floors, or ironing clothes—they're rough in a *natural* way. She is a creamy thing, *hard* all over. Her little tits are stiff cups that stand firmly, like prudent sentries, looking with dark steadiness in opposite directions. Her stomach is firmer than any stomach, male or female, that I've ever seen. There isn't one inch of fat on her anywhere unless we consider her earlobes fat. Donovan is doing *"Mellow Yellow,"* as I gently let myself down beside her, she's saying, "Lazzzy lazy nigger, *humhumhum,"* she is saying, still holding my soft copper-headed dick with a kind of playful sense of disgust. For a moment I feel slightly ashamed that my bonanza detector remains, even in her active hand, serene. She is simply shaking it back and forth, and now asking, *"What's this!"* She smells clean, flesh clean, she always does. So gently soapy-smelling, not strong with some overdose of peakily cheap perfume!

She is already on her elbow, looking down at me by now, smacking her lips, going, "Tut tut tut—What am I gonna do with you, nigger, huh? You're a mess—*won't* it get hard?" *"Be nice* to it, Anita, Baby, it'll do anything you want it to do . . .." Yes, it has been a long time since she's given me that sacred rite she is such a master of performing. I'm thinking, why should I torture poor Mr. ex-Perpendicular any longer, tonight, in her dry hole? She gets up to her knees, and I deliberately say nothing because I know from past experience that Anita does not like for me to ask her to suck it, though when she volunteers, she has proven to be unbeatable at getting to the essence of the act. I remember now as she is about to suck it, she knows that at least turning it around in her mouth, swivelling it, whirling it, rotating it with her thick, long tongue, makes it hard as bookends, and vigorous, so powerful, in fact, that I've rocked and almost unhinged her torso from such long, pithy, severe sessions of pure slippery fucking, pushing one juicy hour, to the rhythm of music, into another, right here in this bed. And I suspect now she thinks she'll get me hard and *then* stretch out on her back, her brittle pussy hairs twisting together there, damply, at the mouth of the jewel, hiding that ruthless, hungry merciless gem! that gobbles and gobbles, eats at me—rather, lies more or less in repose, as *I*, out of deep meanings of the self feel compelled to work myself to death, so to speak, to fill up its crater! But that ain't what's happening this time—She doesn't know it yet, but she's going to swivel it, rotate it, nibble it, lick it, gently chew on it, playfully bite it, turn and turn it in the spitkingdom of herself, dance it with her tongue, spank it with juice, excite it to huge precipices without bursting it out of its tense axis of delight, she's going to hold it in honor with both brown hands, as it dips, tosses, as it ascends, in all O all ranges of mind states! Yes, it is my mind! Equal, that is, to the every level of myself . . .

I know I can turn her *off* if I say One Word now. That's the last thing in the world I want to do now, as I feel the weight of her knees adjusting between mine. "Put this pillow under you—" She's being clinical; O.K., if she wants to be that way, it'll still be good. I feel how I deliberately relax every muscle I can consciously focus on with my mind. She wiggles her firm ass, adjusting it somewhere on her heels, her arms inside the warm soft area of my thighs, I feel the hairs of them. She takes a deep breath, I can smell the air of the ruby we drank drift up to my nostrils. Sound: the slow wet movement of her strong red tongue moving over her lips, mopping away the dryness. Like most of her body's exterior, her lips are usually very dry. Only two spots, exceptions, I can think of: the areas around the edges of her scalp, the crevices between her thighs and where the mound of her pussy begins to rise, are usually warm and moist. As I lift my narrow ass, holding myself in a loop, she slides the big pillow beneath me, I sink down into the conquering softness, her busy automatic-acting fingers tickle the rooty area at the base of this selfish generative Magic Flute of mine, pull and squeeze my sagging sensitive balls. She coughs, clears her throat. I hear the smack of her tongue between her lips again. I have my eyes closed, soon I'll feel the slow, warm, nerve-racking sweet fuck of the pensive mouth beginning . . .

This hesitation. I know it is coming. Her mouth has not yet touched the ruby head of my *dik*. The moment of waiting, the anxiety of it builds like musical improvisations in my bones, my membranes, the heat, blood energy in me; I continue to try to keep it all very still, cool, I am not even trying to concentrate on hardening up my ecstasy-weapon, this dear *uume* to the emissive glory of life itself! And for once Anita doesn't seem impatient, she isn't pumping it, bungling, and jacking it, trying to make it instantly hard—I suspect she's going to make it really great this time. She can be absolutely wonderful, when she wants to! The anticipation of these moments, of a kind of antagonism of sweet memory of the best times, is overpowering. It takes all the will in my being to lie here, still, the corporeality of myself, in the spit-slick heady memory of it . . .

(It is only at these moments, of course, that this particular "movement" of the symphony of life is so beautifully important, all-consuming . . . equal to the working moments when I am excited by the energetic, rich growth of a concept I am able to articulate! Or my sudden ability to construct bookshelves, or create a silly wacky lovely painting, equal to anything that I do involving the full disclosure of myself. I hesitate to say equal to my ability to handle those firearms in Vietnam, against those nameless human collages that fell in the distance, like things, but maybe even equal to that, too . . .)

The hot nude hole of her mouth, *oh God it is so gooooooood!!!* slides now, caressingly, dry at first, but she's excreting saliva, like cunt juice, her firm hands stretching out, in slow-motion, sliding up my flat stomach, my gentle spongy dick blowing up, expanding at a pace equal to the tension in her lips behind the root of her tongue, getting hot as the crevices of her gums, the deliberately slow sinking of her mouth still coming down to the very base of my seed-giver, gently, but firmly engulfing it, in all of its lazy softness, the nerve-ends of my whole ass, my nuts, my thighs are fructifying! The meaty warmth of her velvety, lined interior begins to climb just as slowly; Mr. Prick is anxious to quickly reach the full and painful

proportion of its promise, but I fight that drive by applying more
and more deliberation to my restraint, under the magic, almost
weightless touch of her fingers tripping through the hairs of my
stomach, as she adroitly glides them down. She need not hold my
uume with her hands any longer. "He" is trying too hard to make
headway in his headiness! He holds himself up, I refuse to let the
progressive bastard gristle up to the prolific point where he is like
some giant tendon, though Anita might (*if* she weren't unusually
patient right now) *like* that; O motion, joy, o *shit,* this is TOO
MUCH!!! the still missiling motion of the circle of her tight mouth,
restrainingly prolonged, up—up! I can feel the inelastic cords of my
inner tissues pulling in a complex of nerves, pulling, as her strong
big Black Woman, Mighty Nile, African energetic tough lips, the
muscles in them quivering, the lengthy moist spongy-porous tongue
gently milking the base of my valve, Mr. Hammer's underbelly,
milking fruitfully, in a slow rhythm. My eyes are still closed, I am
trying not to settle my mind anywhere, it tries for a moment to
drift to the greasy magazine of a gun I was examining one day,
sitting propped against another guy's back, at the edge of a rice
paddy, and I don't know why. I want to *stay* right here, with her,
focused on every protrusion, every cord, abstract circle of myself,
of her, every "feeling," every hurling, every fleshy spit-rich
convexity, mentally centered in all the invisible "constructs" of
myself, right here, where she and I now form, perform an orchestra
she is conducting in juicy floodtides; stay *in* her woman's
construction, her work, her togetherness, the rich procreating-like
magic of her every touch as—more and more against my will—my
kok protracts, *swells,* lengthens, perpetuatingly jumpy with fertility, as her permeable mouth decreases its gentle grip in exact ratio
to Dick's eminent *strong* polarity. I love her for her reflective,
melancholy approach to this fine art! So seldom does she take this
much care to do it properly . . .

My serpent is just fatty-hard, but extra long, redundantly so!
It is *best* this way, if I can manage to keep it from stiffening to the
point where the nerves are minimized somehow. I feel the
mouth-motions of her workings, the salivary warmth of her slow,
pensive chewing at the *acutely sensitive head,* where the loose skin
has slid back, the rich, thick nerve-ends in the thin layers of this
loose skin, she lets spit run down slowly around this Bridegroom in

his moment of heaven, the warm secreted water from the prolific glands of her taste-bud-sensitive mouth, I feel these O so slow careful and skillful movements, the deliberate soft scraping and raking of her beautiful strong teeth across the tender texture of the rim of the head, gently bathing with spit the prepuce's densely nerve-packed walls, which rubs these ends of my luckily uninhibited penis! She is concentrating on the head of it, and she can do this for so long it drives me *mad* with porous, beautiful pleasure. She will nibble here, suck one or two times, stop, let it rest limp, aching, in the soft warm cave of her rich dark purple "construct," saliva mixing easily with the slow sebaceous secretion, my own male liquid lubricant, *smegma,* washing around in her grip—a gentle but well-controlled clasp! Then, she might take a gentle but playful plunge *down*, straight down, down, sinking down faster than she's so-far moved, the dick head exploding up into all that wet, warm slime, it's running down, profusely, down the polarity of this *sperma*-generator of love, and all the stinging rich, acute, respirating, the tunnel-sinking sense of it, the sounds of the cool capful of wind speeding away, giving way to this crave-feeding, just the hallelujah-warm, narcotic feeling of the drop, as my dick thickens, pushes out—the lengthy pole emitting into her muscles, and tonsils, the juicy soup of my penis glands, the sheath, now in this plunging motion stretched in this hymn of heat to frantic "mad" ends! Two more strokes like this and she can finish me. I would shoot a hurricane of seeds into her, falling out convulsively, palmus, in nervous-twitching; *but* Anita isn't trying to finish me off this time, get it over. She's going to be good to me, but I *cannot* help myself from the submissive fear that she might suddenly bring it to an end, and it can be very painful if it is done incorrectly. Instinctively, Anita knows this. This knowledge is in the very pores of her skin, she is the kind of pussy-woman, the knowledgable Black Mother of a deep wisdom, intrinsic in every fuse, every chromosome, every crevice of her epidermis, enormous in the internal cavities of her mouth, anus, the atoms of her urethra, the tissues of her every thought, liquid of her nerves, the intelligence of her tracts, digestive system, the energy of her bladder, every foetal tissue of her, every psycho-biological process of her protoplasm!

Yes.

God!!! Yes! She can sustain me, even as I lie pitched on this *brink,* she controls it all. The way I'm beginning to whimper, groan, beyond my own control, she controls it all. With her mouth, she is screwing the head of my dick, around and around. She is worrying it now, from side to side, clasping it, increasing and decreasing the pressure, the circles of my mind follow some rhythm she is leading, in this voracity. My ass already is beginning to throb under the acute, tremendous, mesmeric—workings of her facsimile-pussy, which has the irresistible kind of skill the lower mouth of ecstatic agony, also a spicy feast, with good lips, does not have, because it lacks *this mobility.* I lie still, the rich body-pungency, the fuck-fragrance of ourselves in my senses, the dry taste of my tongue, as I lie here, my palms face up, the smell of rich black sweet cunt filling the room, the odor of her mouth, the wet-smell of my own pungent body fluids that escape her jaws, dripping down into the hairs around this cylindrical, pendulous totem pole, Anita's rhythm upon it begins to increase . . .

I worry. Please, baby! Take it easy; but I am not speaking. A few muscles of fear harden in my stomach but I manipulate them back to peace. *Be quiet body,* but she now masculinely grips it, the excited columns of its interior pressed together, the cavernous tissues throbbing, like my head is throbbing, the roots of my hair, my toes are twitching, like this wonderful upstanding organ, she is holding in its wet harmony, as she treats the head like it's a popsicle. Anita has her hand just below the bulbo-cavernous muscle, wrapped in an amorous squeeze there, which serves as a kind of pump, and a restrainer. As she licks the edges of the dome now, lifting her mouth completely up, air currents rush in, refreshingly stimulating; her hand continues to milk my *coc,* setting a pace, otherwise the explosion would come. She knows. She rests. I rest it, I open just the slits of my eyes as openings to see that she has herself in a very relaxed position, so that she can last, without getting tired I whisper the first words thick like *cum* on the air, "Baby, it's great, beautiful, O I can't tell you how much—" But I don't finish, I feel her mouth's downward movement, engulfing the bulb as it relaxes from some of its previous excitement. She can detect its state by its throbbing, meaning to be very perfect, she eases the pressure of her hand, the cylinder somewhat dried where her hand has been pressed. I can even feel the sperm, free, push up, the quickening exist, though it is still very slow, still under her control, I am helpless. I am almost unconscious with the pleasure of it. She rotates her heated seminal stained mouth five times swiftly on this meaty pendulous organ, *uume...*

Fighting my tendency to explode, she plans to shift the pace of her work, she uses no method for more than one second, for fear of tipping me off the delicate whimpering thin-skinned "construct" I'm being balanced on. She chews at it, with the gentle crunching of her teeth, tongue workings, like she's chewing the juicy texture of an apple, she does this three times—it is so effective, so deeply sinewy good, closing distance between us, a kind of suspended liquid oneness holds us, I am in her, I am one, in her...

Then quickly she suspends that game, and seems to be trying to "drink" it, like she'd drink water from a fountain in the park, a kind of sucking-up conflicting feeling, almost accomodating an earthquake of an orgasm—that she restrains with a downward connective lapping of her tongue, gently taking up each drop of juice as it comes up out of the hot, irritated eye, the umbilical, sweet, nexus-feeling of ME slowly, being milked, into her, slowly, she drinks ME, one drop, one rich corporeal swallow at a time. This is the only way to do it without having the orgasm so *powerful*, rushing up so swiftly that the action would be very painful, a struggle, all of it not being able to explode out the narrow head fast enough. She milks the tail, she goes very slowly, the harmony is perfect...

The symmetry of the way I'm coming is beautiful, this the best I've ever had, the milking process she is using is a method she has perfected, developed on me (and probably on others I know nothing about), and it's great. With her mouth she fishes, ties knots with her tongue, around the bulb, she screws it as though she's using her pussy, she staples it quickly one or two times, then she rivets it, she hammers at it several times with her tongue, she nails it down with stabs, it fights back in contraction, she puts a sash around it with her tongue, she seems to be padlocking it, linking it to her guts as she threatens to swallow it, the juices slowly draining out all along, the nexus deepening; now her mouth is thick with the creamy warm juice, slapping-sounds of the pasty sperm from my swollen testicles, as the spermatic arteries are slowly being sweetly sucked up, slowly into this caramel beauty!

WHAM!

down

she comes, *zipping*, the antagonistic wet grip of her contracting, expanding mouth, is sucking, fucking it, chewing it,
UP—DOWN! updown! . . . The dick is so shocked it stops even the
slow corporeal leakage, stunned. But quickly the "shape" of it
circles in, the magic excitement increases during this wild, twisting,
collapsing moment; my dingdong begins to spit up semen again,
responding to it—this *overwhelming impact,* this squeezing, sucking,
and I hear the sloppy juices jumping, splashing around in her
mouth; she is holding my balls and milking them of their substance,
milking and milking, and *pumping,* jacking, fucking my cock with
all she has, the compendium of her mouth, the contour of its
working shapes against the round surface of my meat god, sucking
him, sucking him, getting him UP, up—inelastic root-depth throb-
bings, I am almost out, with the rushing—pushing feelings pouring
down out of me, up into her, her subduing female mastering of him,
he is *thick* bursting, *blind unconscious* (too much trying to come
out at once). She holds the balls, understanding what is happening,
bringing modified rivers of seed juice out of my loins! She still
controls his ebb, as he *pumps — now now now now blindly dead blind
sweet sweeeetly oh,* and I do groan, even shriek, this bonanza is so
phallically rich, it is *bursting —*

My sensibilities stewing, fermented, quivering—I am breathless,
unable to move, as she has it all out except for the last few drops,
she hungrily sucks—

Oh how beautiful gentle she is with it as she licks it, the yeasty
last drops, the end of the turmoil, how she mothers it, holds my
stomach just above the line of my hair for a moment, then takes my
prepuce with the other hand and holding just the head of this
cherry-tipped, sore, nerve-racked but happy *kok* pushes it back
from the inhabitant beneath it, still throbbing, as he shrinks only
theoretically, not actually, still too *tense:* he will stay hard, though
empty, for awhile yet; now, she gently sucks at it, like she's eating
plums, pulling off the skins, and this brings out the tiniest of the
tiny last drops of semen, the juices, and to make sure she has it all
out, so that I am completely happy, she softly, rhythmically,
masturbates it slowly; this is too taxing, the *pain* of it, I have to grip
her hand, and stop her . . .

So, she knows she's done a beautiful job, and I try to open one eye enough to see her, and when I manage it, she's there, in the yellow light, big, soft red lips as she wipes them with the edge of the sheet, smelling spermy, and looking naked and ripe as a peach, and I'm ready to *FUCK her,* now!!!

No shit!

TAMMY

I have come in from the street. A few moments ago I was frustrated, almost unhappy, but Tammy is on the bed. Her name isn't really important. All I want her for is to fuck her. She is hardly worth anything else. She has a kind of savage ability to fuck well — we screwed a lot last night, and probably didn't sleep until three o'clock. For some reason I suddenly feel very insecure. Her pussy hasn't helped. I had been at it as though it might in some way give me protection.

Everything will be alright, I tell myself. I know everything will be alright, and yet I am not quite sure of what I mean by "everything." I look down at the girl. In a way she is very sad . . .

I found her three weeks ago sitting outside, outside the door, on the stoop. She had no place to go. She got the address of the woman who has the apartment next to mine, she got it from the Diggers Free Store. The message she had was; "Can you put this girl up until she gets on her feet?" Apparently, the woman next to me, who is really not bad-looking, kind of fat, a red-head, certainly no more than thirty but kind of mean-looking, had left word at the Diggers that she would be willing to let people sleep on her floor. This kind of thing is being done a lot in the East Village.

But I came up the steps and said, "Hello," and that was it. She was more than friendly, more than willing, she accepted every invitation I made.

Inside my place, she ran her mouth, a midwestern cracker accent, a mile a minute. She was telling me about how she hitchhiked from some little dinky town in Illinois, got arrested in Ohio, got out of jail when they checked back by phone with somebody there at the reform school where she practically grew up, and discovered that she *was really* twenty years old like she had been telling them all along, from the moment they picked her up.

She wasn't pretty to me and she doesn't even begin to "shape up" now, though I feel sympathy for her. I mean the sometimes—warmth I feel for her doesn't make her look better, but she knows how to fuck. She is a master at it, and works her ass off.

I will continue to come now until I am empty of semen, all of it that can come out, until my tubules are vacant, until the duct rests, without the nervous activity of excretion, I feel the careful building slimy strength of her ligaments; now she seems to be throwing a lasso around my gun; suddenly she works it back toward herself, as though her mouth were reins, pulling at it, the spurts of semen thickening her pithy hole, still without hands, with her mouth she straightens it up, carefully, after swallowing most of the fluid, some of it sliding down the throbbing, nerve-racked pole, still holding up in this phallus rite of sensuous music, and with it straight, she makes some sudden strokes that seem to be some kind of effort to bridle it like she might bridle a horse or a dog; the dick is kicking, slimy with sperm, throbbing, nakedly buckling under so much tension, and she continues, keeping her grip just right, not finishing it, the juices continue to pour into her, she drinks them, and this is all done very slowly, now, with it standing nobly straight up again; her mouth seems to be working like ten busy fingers trying to button a button on a shirt, and my fluid is pumping up faster than ever—she detects this, puts her hands, both of them, on the upper part of the *kok,* and gently squeezes it as it bounces, punches, dibbles around in her cave. She has relaxed her connection. She doesn't make a move with her mouth, the dick is swollen bigger than ever, resting, robust bulbous thing, throbbing, oozing smoothly, with restraint, into her, under this efficient "tongue lashing," teasing, and mouthing. This edifice of mine, this lucky stretched-out time-space harmony, feels the comfort of her hand loosen, and the continuation of pleasant effusion. She is controlling this orgasm so well, it may go on for more than an hour, I am percolating, oozing, dribbling at the dick like a river, but a slow river, being tapped by the mysterious rainfalls of Mother, voids, secrets, wet holes of the flesh world, carried on an expedition to the ends of my psycho-physical reality; at the floodgates of emergency, my dark, fleshy Anita, love, a gateway into which I exist, and erupt, enter; O!!! she frills it, gently, beginning again, now that the nerve-ends have stopped throbbing so O SO soso . . .

She works at it like she's trimming corn off the cob, she skirts it, jerks it, confines it with quick frightening pressure, releases it, threads it, the juice gently secreting, Mr. Tail, ancient in his mighty moment; the sperm is just pouring out—but not the swift way it would in a "normal" explosive orgasm—as she nibbles at the edges of it, its prepuce slick with trimmings; the percolated head is so *swollen* the ejecting semen seems to feel choked in, but not painfully so, as it pushes, gushes, then trickles out, into her leaky hot mouth . . .

She does a bowknot on it, making loud splash splash wet slappy sounds, zips up and down/up/down/up/down (faster than ever-) on the final up, grabs the head of the cable meat, squares it in her nest, locks it tightly, juices splashing, jumping, buckling into her thicker, hotter than ever, rich, oozing circuits of seedy fluid jamming into her; she takes them without blinking, still anchoring the dicker connectively, roped to her control, not allowed to empty, finish completely until she says so . . .

Huge emotional collisions in me, I had no idea I could ever generate so much fluid at one time. The padlock of her mouth now merely restrains it, but loosely, as she steadily holds it; it is like a wet electric meat god, cabling magic into her, screwing the tunnel of us close, stopping up the ends, to make us one rope, into a *ma* void, or, in Swahili, *tupu!*

I feel now the shift of her body. She adjusts herself for the *big moment.* She has planned to bring me into the finish. She is going to work it very carefully, make its *interconnection* so well bridged, so rich, *free low flowing,* consistent, to make it so complete and agreeable, tunnelling into her, the flowing upbeat of the incessant cargo of fluid that completes the symphony. She is getting ready to start. I try *not* to brace myself.

I succeed in remaining as relaxed as I am, my wet *cokke* though has the sharp knowledge conveyed to it, and it stiffens, hard as a tendon, its prepuce slimy and bulging thick as the slick-spongy head; I feel the top of her mouth sowly sinking down to rest on the protuberance of it. How do I know she is ready? She takes both my balls in one hand, and holds gently the belly of them but firmly, while they pout, my embassy, extremely bloated peninsula of a dickhead thickly tightens, "feeling" *her readiness* to work at it. She begins! She really goes! Until every drop of it is *gushing* out.

I realize that I am simply evading so many things by lying around all day like this, letting her play with my dick, sit on my lap, suck it, get down on her knees, upside down, backwards, any way you can think of. I can do nothing else right now. My dick is my life, it has to be. Cathy certainly won't ever come back. I've stopped thinking about the possibility. Eunice has of course gone away to Harvard, and I'm taking it in my stride. My black ramrod *is* me, any man's rod is himself.

This thing that I am, this body—it is me. *I* am it. I am not a concept in your mind, whoever you are! I am *here,* right here, myself, MYSELF, fucking or being driven to the ends of my ability to contain myself in the ecstasy her little red mouth inspires as it works at the knobby head of my weapon, or if I am eating this goat's cheese, the pumpernickel, drinking the beer I have just bought, or whatever I happen to be doing, I am not *your idea* of anything.

Yes, this *is* distraction. I sit down now on the side of the bed, I am about to wake her, because I am depressed, frustrated. Her round, innocent-looking face is hard, deep in the pillow. Her pink cheeks are red, her hands are folded beneath her face, and there is a frown between her eyebrows. I know she is really a very fucked-up, unhappy girl, but somehow basically strong, rebellious; I touch the wet edge of her hair. Strange, she does sweat around the edges of her scalp, like black women. Jokingly I said, "Damn, baby, I think you been lying to me! You *really* a secret nigger!—" She is nude beneath the sheet, I know. I pull it all the way down, and stroke her little girl-size body. Each tit is no bigger than half an orange: I turn her little white wrists over and look at them. They are healing, where she cut them with the coke bottle that first night here, after getting drunk from wine I offered her. Now I have beer here, this is the first booze I've had in the apartment since the end of the wine three days ago. I want to fuck her, like she's a *thing.* I don't want to see her eyes when I screw her, because sometimes they are *too* sad. The overpowering rapture of just grinding gently with her, without compassion, because I know there is no future for us, no real reason why we should protect each other's feelings. I feel I can almost see a pig looking at me from her eyes, at times. I touch her pussy now, the dry hair. My sperm dry on it. Little streaks of dry *cum*.

She rolls over automatically without waking up, and it is easy to spread her legs. I am sitting in a very uncomfortable position like this. I want her to wake up and suck me, but it must be done in a very subtle way. I must convince her that I am really passionately intent on making love to her, that I want to turn her ass every way but loose! This is a ritual. I'm sure. She knows I'm lazy. That I will make a big showing, maybe for a few seconds, with great ambition, in a kind of hungry struggle to rip her open since she likes it rough, then I'll stretch out on my back, on this tiny cot we have here, and take a deep breath. And she is asking, "You like my pussy?" And I am saying, "Yes, yes, it's good." She is adjusting herself over me, so that she's sitting astraddle my hips, with the mouth of her pussy just at the tip of my meat. The female smell of her these three days hasn't been unpleasant at all, though she's had only one bath. Strange that she doesn't smell sour. But there is something about a twenty-year-old girl that simply doesn't get too odious. Maybe I shouldn't say that because it probably isn't always or even generally true. This morning I do not even want to go through the ritual of pretending I am going to be very manly and supervise her, so to speak, sexually. I want her to wake up right now and get to this proposition; I am beginning to feel a streak of evilness creeping in me. I want to *force* her, I can almost see my hands lifting her, opening her mouth, as though she were some kind of doll, and choking her with the platter of my dick.

The dried sperm on her hair turns me off. I don't want to bother with getting that stuff on me. It's old, dry, and the stuff inside her, this morning, from last night, is thick by now, like some kind of cheese, so it is understandable, or should be, that I now want the relatively clean receptacle of her mouth. I know that she won't want to, but I can't put my clean, ecstatic dick into her, not right now. Not while I'm depressed. Sometimes I can do it, no matter how sloppy the snug, sumptuous hole is. I am stroking the insides of her thighs, and unbuttoning my shirt.

I stop fooling around, stand up and strip down to my birthday suit, my butterscotch body, my half of the feast of life!

Suddenly I am straddling her, my knees on either side of her head, I feel playful *and* evil, I am holding my supernatural enravisher, and just thinking about her tongue, the pressure of the walls of her mouth—how they could work together to get it all out of me (flowing, endlessly flowing, waves and waves of enchantment, voluptuousness, and it seeming so scrumptious all the while *to her,* and she never gags) and the tickling sensations of rubbing the tip of it against her half-opened mouth, is causing it to swell, the veins in it standing up, the bulbous head, purple and spongy against the sleep-dry small lips; I'm watching all this. And her eyes are coming open, but she is not fully aware.

She is yawning now, turning away from my playful dick. She's rejecting it, and I feel only more frustrated. Well, I'll fuck her, just to wake her. She's always willing to fuck, even while sleeping. She'll fuck in her sleep anytime, keeping the rhythm, everything going, just as though she were conscious . . .

I suck the hard, small red nipple of the left tit, it tastes of sweat, but not really nasty sour sweat; just as I am beginning on the other tit, I can feel her eyelids blinking against my arm, which is somewhere up there against her face. I have one hand gently moving over her bush.

Then, I feel the gentle pressure of her small delicate expert hand beginning to stroke Mr. Ill-Bred. He begins to get vulgar with his uppity big head swelling bigger, ready for an engagement. But he has a definite nobility, and she respects it. I feel her tight, firm stomach, beneath me, move up deliberately against mine. She is trying to be physically closer. It is enticingly pleasant.

It is genial; I feel a healthy Henry Miller kind of vitality toward it all; her hands—she's now using both of them. The pleasure of it almost equals the early stages of a good, drawn-out blowjob. She has a kind of rhythm, but the position I am in is complicated, and a strain . . .

I take my hand from her cunt, knowing instinctively that this will increase her focus on what *she is doing* to me, not on what I am doing to her. The attraction of my hand, my fingers at her clitoris, only distracts from her skill on my dibbler. I slowly lie down beside her; she's moving a little to make room for me, the cot is so small. Lying down, the odor of her alluring body is stronger, but I do not want to hassle with it, only to let it seep into my psyche, to stretch out in the huge comfort of this luxury . . .

She hasn't noticed the beer sitting on the sink yet, I am leery, if she sees it she'll surely want to get drunk. She's so easily distracted. And even beer will make her drunk. Or so she says. No reason not to believe her. Meanwhile, she sits astride me, easing her honeypot down around the throbbing upstanding round rod. She watches my eyes in their rapture—I know I must have this kind of look. The muscles in her cave of life suck with real strength at the prepuce.

The wet sound, I listen to it, I am enjoying the exiguity of her doing her thing. It surprisingly does not worry me that the hole is not clean, not much anyway, and even the little worry that is here, around the hairs of things, is leaving. This is agreeable. Life seems so large and natural, like it should be. The way I feel, the navigation of her hips. The SLAP, slap, *pop* slap, SLAP, slap, *pop* slap! the luxuriance of her walls around my bluejacket, the scudding hammer looking straight up, its one eye, up into Life, the Beginning, raceless beginning, of everything deeper than anything social. And her words come back to me: "Do you hate me because I'm white?" "I don't hate you—What makes you think I hate you?" "I don't know . . . this colored boy I used to go with in Chicago used to make me get down on my knees and blow him, he said I was a no-good white trampy bitch and the only place for me was on my knees sucking him. *Boy!* did he hate white people! I just thought maybe all colored guys were that way." This conversation took place yesterday. The edge of it comes back because I am thinking of asking her to float my *coc* in her skilled slimy wet pink cave; but I know my reason isn't the same as that other black dude's. I would dig it just as much from a "sister," morals aside; as a matter of fact the best head I've had came from the knowledge box of a beautiful, down, black chick, long-standing; but I now pop the question in the middle of all this intense gratification, "Some head, baby?" "But isn't *this* good?" I'm lying here on my back, and she's working with the faucet like a champ, sure it's great, but I want the extra punch of those magic heights—her tongue, teeth, walls, lips, the mobility of the whole thing, the sucking, biting, pumping, that performance itself! The slick walls, the hair, my twin wrinkled and frolicsome balls being carefully caressed all the while, and the other hand busy gently gliding over the babyhairs up and down my stomach. "Yeah, it's good—you know you're good, but—" "*But* you want me to give you a blowjob! I think you just like the idea of having a *white* girl give a blowjob!" There is this sideways half-assed grin on her face, it's a jest and not unkind, saying tacitly, Hugh?. . .

"I really think you're sick with all this racism, baby, every minute you're into *that* bag . . ." I hear myself saying, also fearing that I'm blowing my chances. "I bet that's why you woke me," she says, ignoring my statement against her mind. She's now simply sitting there dumbly on my *kok,* with a dreamy expression, looking down into my face, but not seeing me, probably seeing something, somebody, some sad scheme in downstate Illinois. She knows that I'm "from" Chicago, which impresses her, but I have refused to talk about Chi with her because we obviously don't have notes to exchange. She came through the city, but was in the hippy intrigue, driven and pestered by cops on the near North Side; I know the area, but in a different time element, I'm seven, eight years older than she.

I really begin to give up, thinking surely I've blown it, the dicker will simply have to settle for the appetizing second-choice of warmed-over stale pussy with old cum still in it; gooey valley with *so* much profusion, when she surprises me by lifting all the way up, the draft of warm air striking the wet milky nakedness of my *dik,* which begins now to become flaccid, and I'm not ashamed of its sudden enfeebled face at a moment like this as I used to be, say, at sixteen, because unlike then, now, I understand MY MIND, and trust its relationship with this experienced *cokke* of mine; and not even a broad can *runmedown,* you know, like this hippy here once or twice jokingly has tried to do with something like, "You're so ole you can't fuck no more." It doesn't get to me, this kinda thing. I just want her to understand *her function,* that this isn't *romance* for me either, she sometimes seems to forget *that,* though she ain't fooled about her *own* position . . .

I'm about to give up when it happens: the caress, the hand, its strength embraces my reclining soldier, I can now close my eyes, no need to fill the insipid psychological space between us because this womanish "treat" will revive my gun to its frisky textured life, I trust. With the stunning firmness of my big toe I wiggle her clitoris. It is a small man-in-a-boat, she obviously hasn't masturbated a lot; I remember now, that first night, during her wild, frantic, endless monologue, slowly it became clear that she has been humped, been working the hardness out of roosters since she was ten or eleven years old . . . The wrap. Her lips wrap around it, the wet usage. The "root" feeling, deep down feeling, the pressure-up. She is beginning slowly, these gateways into simple beauty, these slabs of life, these tissues wrapping around each other, the texture of this plant, growing bigger in the spit-slick walls of mother nature. Growing john is growing so mighty he does not need the shims of her hands, the gentle strength of those fingers, the weight of it. The pulling goodness, tugging at the nerves beneath the skin, the root, at the base of my nuts, the tickle in my ass, running up my spine, the weightless rivers running all through me, into the ends of my scalp, my back, flat, though still, deliberately not tense—though I am tempted to tighten up—seem to ripple. My stomach ripples.

Her mouth cascades, the tight grip lifts, drops again, lifts higher this time, almost pulling up to the tip—almost losing the meat, air felt moving around its wetness. My eyes are closed. Why is this as beautiful to me as writing a poem? As *important* as philosophy, or anthropology, or music? BECAUSE IT IS. Her fingers—of both hands—tickle, caress, flutter it, add to the total flourishing of the act! She is percolating me, and I can lie here in the extravagance of it. No, it doesn't matter *who* or what she is now, I do not love her, I do not hate her, her skin is not white, is not black, is not skin, necessarily. Drenching me with the sweet tidal rides of her mouth! I *deliberately* fight the tendency to *stiffen* from the excitement of it. I am fighting it so hard, the soft membranes slapping, *slush slush,* she tightens up, then *slush slush* again; the plush washing tides of it, into me, into the waterfalls of my mind, my psyche, my fingertips, my deep canals, the silent nerve dark blood riverbeds of my human self responding to the gesture, the wave of her velvet tongue, the "chewing", gentle chewing, permeating action. I am coming, coming slowly, just very very slowly, a draining, that she nurses carefully, licks at, rolls around on her tongue, teases, washes down, her tongue stabs one or two times playfully at Mr. Perpendicular. He does not react with fluid, he is so stunned in the paradox of being *relaxed* under the command of my body, this black castle, its intelligence, and logically wanting to, needing to *explode in orgasm* a steady "serum" of overflowing, sopping-life—the spurt of life! but cannot gush forth, its need for a climax to *keep* existence itself, the deepest definition of its agony, to keep it going, *going.*

My mind begins to wander when she bogs. I am so content,

arrogantly almost, that I need not be alert. I even allow Mr. Ill-Bred to get soft in her so she'll have to wonder about her skill, doubt herself, feel threatened, do better, work harder at the dibble of him. I know her neck is very tired by now, she complained about it last night, and the day before. The position is very uncomfortable, but so is anything of value that is in the—

Ahhh, in gentle appreciation I lazily reach down and stroke her hair. It is moist. Suddenly, like a character out of Batman Comics being sprung out of captivity, her head shoots up, her mouth, a wet radius, closes; she catches her breath, I see the Adam's apple move almost imperceptibly, like the neck of a tense lizard filtered through the brilliant electric technological media of Walt Disney, and she asks: "Say—by the way, were you in Chicago last Christmas, during that grand hoax, when everybody thought God was coming down from the clouds to save us poor sinners?" I am completely thrown into a state of emotional and mental chaos and deep lassitude by this untimely question. I simply whisper; "Yeah, yeah—but come, please, don't stop *now!*" And I force her head down. She begins again . . . I know she will soon stop, though she knows that *I* want her to continue until I complete the circle. The "aching sweetness," a phrase commonly used, does not describe it precisely. She had made the dome by now spit-slick and it is sliding easily.

The softness, she begins to work at it, for the hardness. Dead tired, I know. I feel some anxiety, pity, fear. But please don't stop, not yet, I say silently. This can go on for over an hour "if" she is strong enough. With my toe I examine her split, and discover that it is very marshy (*she* has been coming all this time, enjoying it?), the gooey stuff drips down around my toe, between the cracks (I am able to work at her vagina like this because my knees are bent, and my feet are together meeting directly beneath her bottom), it is watery-fresh, so definitely not from last night's making. The head is throbbing and jumping in her thrifty enclosure, when she suddenly disconnects, lifts her face, red as a tomato, her eyelids droopy with tiredness; she's holding herself on one arm, still sitting on her knees, she brushes her hair back from her face, "Fuck! Ain't you never gonna come?" This increases my anxiety—my frustration. I hardly know what to say, but I say, "I'm coming, now, baby—I was almost *there* when you stopped." Like on the edge of wisdom, but I was always there, at the point and *that* was the dark rich joy of it, being stunned in a pivot . . .

She starts this time, *really* working for a quick explosion from me. I'm holding back as much as possible. I relax, fighting the excitement she is pumping into my limbs, throughout the channels of myself! Her pink grip is tighter, the pumping is automation! It washes me! Giant waves shock my skull, to my fingertips, my lips dry up, my throat dries up, I feel my head lift and fall in hydraulic waves, I can hardly keep still. Everything in me is pushed to the point of a silent-stillness, on the edge of a massive flesh *kok* human storm—on the edge now, as she pumps it (and I still fight her!)—she means to finish, to shrink me! Mr. Rooster slides madly in the pink walls, her fingers dancing everywhere from nuts to staff, helping the mouth at its work, the serpent is stern in her depths though, holding back, expressing its sweet happiness by emitting a super-ficial little stream of false sperm into her hardworking membraney cave, as though to pacify her, give her hope, make her think she is getting somewhere. And she is!! She really is!! I can't *hold on* much longer, the emission is pushing against the many levels of the dammed-up walls of myself. *Oh Shit,* I think, *oh shit,* this is *too* much! I really begin to submerge, sink down into levels of self as I feel it lift—I am dying, flowing down as the *splash!* enters the first stages of its real career issuing out of the gun, it is coming—now—out—of—the—firearm *valve,* its ordeal beats me back into ancient depths of myself, back down to some lost meaning of the male, the deep struggling germ, the cell of the meaning of Man, I almost pass into unconsciousness the rapture is so overpowering, its huge, springing, washing infiltration into Her, an eternal-like act, a Rain, I am helpless, completely at her mercy, wet in her hands, empty, aching, my ass throbbing with the drained quality of my responsive death . . .

And she stays at it gently, knowingly, not irritating it unnecessarily, but just long enough to glide it to security discretely, to empty it of every drop that might leave it otherwise pouting, to suck, suck, suck, suck, pull the very last crystal drop of *cokke* lotion out of me, into this specific cycle of herself, beautiful! beautiful! to the last drop, and I'm in a deep sleep again.

It is three hours later. She is not here. I have been sleeping, I feel fine, very good, like I felt this morning, on the street, going to the bank, thinking of the city's pollution, happy with being—just being, watching Catholic kids going to school, the hippies, passing the vegetable stands—I feel now happy like that, again. What she said, just before she left, it is vague in my mind, but it comes back. Something about going to the Diggers to see if she could find a kitten. I know that I must not get attached to her, so I must get rid of her soon. She is a whore, admits she is a whore, there is nothing wrong with it, but I cannot get attached to a whore. It is no good for me to be involved too long with a whore. It can become a sick thing . . . So she must go soon and remain only a reference, a good sexual shadow.

CLARENCE MAJOR

Clarence Major was born thirty-two years ago in Atlanta, Georgia and grew up in Chicago, where he attended the Art Institute. Primarily a poet and a teacher, the author has lectured and read at Columbia University's Teachers and Writers Collaborative, the Academy of American Poets, Harlem Educational Program, Brooklyn College, the Guggenheim Museum, the Polytechnic Institute of Brooklyn, the National Poetry Forum, the Carnegie Institute (Pittsburgh), the National Poetry Forum, the Illinois Arts Council and the New School for Social Research. He is the editor of an anthology, The New Black Poetry, *published in 1969.* All-Night Visitors *is his first novel.*

Norman Singer

THE BABYSITTER

Gloria Heavenrich descended upon the Waldorf Astoria with a sense of mind-boggling awe and incredulity. She felt a little like "Alice" making that jittery bum trip through her looking-glass. And yet, something about striding so glamorously into that lobby made her feel more like Marie Antoinette, sweeping across the drawbridge after a tryst, with poor foppish Louis sniffing snuff and spitting grapepits while awaiting her return in his tower chambers.

Laden with packages from Bergdorf's and Sak's, Gloria decided it would save time if *she* signed the registry, while Heathcliffe tipped the driver and the doorman. She skimmed haughtily up the foyer stairs and through the lobby, wearing a stunning new suit-dress of bright-hot yellow. She was certain she looked expensive enough to be taken for granted in these surroundings. And then, as she reached the lobby, a flare of panic as she realized she was lost before she'd hardly taken a step. However, she was determined to keep going and sign in *somewhere,* since decisiveness was very important if she were to continue to look like visiting royalty. It was this sort of reasoning that led her directly to the Overseas & Latin American Department, where a weary attendant inquired: "Are you sailing or flying?"

Gloria was about to tell him she always walked that way when Heathcliffe, breathing fast and frantically, finally overtook her, followed by a bellboy carrying more packages and Gloria's suitcase. "Now really, darling, what are you doing over here?" he asked. "If we were going to Rio, I would have mentioned something about it—don't you think so . . . hmm? No, don't answer that. In fact, not a word about anything until we're safely installed."

"Well, I must say!" she said huffily.

"No, you mustn't." He took her hand and led her quite confidently across the huge rotunda; and it was pretty obvious to Gloria how well he knew his way around the place.

"I suppose *you* have spent enough clandestine weekends here to run a rickshaw service!" she bristled.

"If you mean, am I a seasoned philanderer, my dumpling, yes, you're quite right. And you really *do* deserve much more than an amateur, you know." He clicked his heels and gave her a mock bow as they reached the registry desk and waited in a small line.

Still feeling a little stage fright, she whispered: "I'm trying to think what fictitious name we should sign so nobody'll question who or what we are . . ."

"Don't be so absurd, you goose!" he said. "Who in the world would question it when I sign us in as Mr. and Mrs. Heathcliffe Montague of Burlington, Vermont?"

She gaped up at him, her mouth falling open. "Well, I never!" she said; but it was already their turn up at bat, and Heathcliffe was busy at the registry.

No one will question Mr. and Mrs. indeed! . . . she thought— why, the blundering pompous old beauty, doesn't he see this is the only disguise in the world that *I* would question? Golly, the first time he's mentioned matrimony even indirectly, and he's going to propose to a desk clerk!

During the next forty-odd hours, Gloria Heavenrich couldn't have made a more thorough exploration of the Waldorf if she'd been assigned by the Fire Commissioner to condemn the building. Heathcliffe wore himself ragged recruiting searching parties for her; and once she was convinced that she was officially a guest in the house, Gloria became a mobile unit—racing from the Terrace Court to the Grand Ballroom, from the East Foyer to the West Foyer; down the Grand Ballroom stairway . . . hungrily probing, observing, questioning, giving advice or asking for it, and just plain awed and thunderstruck by everything she saw.

For a while she found the other patrons alluring and provocative to watch. But soon they bored her. The Ladies-of-the-Manor she found particularly weird and hilarious to study. She tried not to laugh aloud as she watched how they draped themselves like rolls of yard goods wherever the decor afforded them a chance to look horizontal. Forever standing with their feet at right angles, like those jaundiced models in *Harper's Bazaar* with the nineteen-inch waists and the eighteen-inch chests . . . "I dreamed I met a Silicone Surgeon in my Maidenhead Bra!"

Disenchanted with the paying customers, Gloria soon found greener pastures among the personnel. The life stories she assiduously pumped out of bell captains, page boys and security officers grew into dramatic vignettes of woe and frustration which never ceased to arouse her ire or compassion. Surely these downtrodden vassals were the most vital people on Park Avenue—the true puppet-masters who held all the strings. Of course, it was true that most of the female help seemed much too self-sufficient to require her sympatico ear. The weaker sex indeed! All one had to do to disprove *this* theory was to follow one of these Amazon chambermaids as she wheeled a batch of bedding—bull-dyke muscles all over the place. On the other hand, some of the male personnel found Gloria Heavenrich just about the warmest bundle of commiseration they'd ever wanted to come up against.

Upon conducting a haphazard sort of poll, Gloria found that an alarming number of these men were either victims of an ego-maiming divorce, or the products of an uncomfortable marital situation.

As a kind of portable sociologist, one of her favorite questions was: "Does your servile capacity here at the hotel ever threaten to carry over into your home life?"

"If you mean, does the little woman give me a tip every time we do it, the answer is no," winked one of the bellboys, who happened to find Gloria much too stacked, pretty and curvilinear to take offense at.

And to another—this one a blondly robust elevator boy—she said: "Do you find you still have an unconscious desire to kowtow and take orders when you get home at night?"

The handsome lad eyed her shrewdly, as if to scout out all her juice-trends and play her by ear. "Why ma'am, you never said a truer word, because my wife takes advantage of that very thing you're talking about . . ."

She gave him one of her liquid blue-eyed smiles. "My heart goes out to you."

Gazing down at her busty bodice, the boy thought: "and that's not all!" But said: "Yep, my wife's so sure all my will power's been broken down for the day, she wants to go on playing the same game at night. You know: she-Tarzan, me-Jane? But damned if I don't let her!"

The boy gave her a helpless grin, as if to say: what can I do, women always have their way with me! And Gloria felt some of those old philanthropic tendencies twittering in her tummy, as she stood near him at his post in the lobby. There was an air of scrubbed vulnerability about him that actually had an odor—sort of loamy and fresh-earthed. So Gloria inhaled a lot as she surveyed him. "Well . . . your wife apparently tries to dominate the scene and rule your life and . . . and emasculate you . . ."

"Well, let's just say she's as bossy as hell," he said. "But as for emasculatin' me . . . oh brother! . . . she'd have to be pretty handy with a meat ax to handle a job like that." He gave her a meaningful wink and his eyes grazed down his uniform, coming to rest on his tightly encased topic of discussion.

Following the boy's eyes, Gloria was truly taken aback by the classic symmetry of his bone structure. He got a load of passengers a moment later, and he urged her to take a couple of rides with him, as he had a whole lot of domestic problems and needed some-one to confide in. So Gloria stayed on with him for awhile, spasmodically chattering out more sympathies, and feeling more strongly by the minute that he was far too young to be suffering the pangs of wifely persecutions.

After twenty minutes or so, he whispered something to her: "Hang on for another trip or two, I get off in about ten minutes."

Gloria pretended not to know what he meant and plied him with another barrage of therapeutic questions. Furtively, he told her how his wife really forced him to marry her by saying she was pregnant; and he did the right thing, even though he knew that baby could have been fathered by practically any street cleaner up the block.

"Ahh . . . duplicity, thy name is woman!" Gloria chanted out the litany.

And then the ten minutes were up, and instead of letting her out in the lobby, the boy released everyone but Gloria. Then he shut the doors and descended. And stopped the elevator between the basement and the main floor.

"It's safe here," he whispered, his hot young eyes going to the rigid outline of her nipples.

"What is?" she asked, her heart beginning to pound as she courted the fear and the tingling awareness of where they were—right underneath the lobby, under the legs of all those rich and strutting sinners.

"This is," he murmured, his tone full of alley-adolescence as his fingers tugged and unfastened and flipped out the corpulent display for her . . . waving it at her in full and prideful exposure.

Gloria caught her breath and stared at it. It was round and stiff and long and a lovely shade of rare, pastel coral. "My goodness!. . . What's its name . . . I mean . . . what's your name, dear?"

"Rod." Grinning impudence. Lip-licking assurance of his voluptuous boy-powers to stun and disarm. "Do you like it? . . . huh? . . . *say* something! . . . go ahead, talk about it, describe it, describe it . . . love it out loud . . . I wanna hear . . .!"

"Yes . . ." her eyes reflective and caught . . . entranced by this flaring prong of flesh he held for her in his hand. "Yes, it should be talked about," she said, "for there's never enough publicity about them when they look like that. If only more men had the courage to unveil the really special adornments, such as yours, our failure to communicate and choose a proper mate would be greatly minimized . . ."

". . . Yeah . . . yeah . . . talk about it!"

". . . It's so enormous . . . and nicely turned-out . . . with such a valiant, lusty sweep to it . . . and . . . it's so young-looking, as if it had just been born, this very instant . . ."

He nodded, eagerly condoning her every word. "Man! . . . that's the best character sketch anyone ever did of it . . . and they *all* flip over it right away, which is why I like to show it to 'em real fast in case maybe they won't like the rest of me, like my personality or the way I talk . . . but then, after they see my big fat baby here, it's too late . . . you dig?"

"Too late . . ." she nodded.

"Come on, put your hand on it, honey. Ooh! . . . you sweet pretty thing, you look so hot for it, I could bust just havin' you see it . . . all naked and stickin' out and throbbin' like this . . ."

She reached for it with both hands, wanting to feel the full expanse at once. And she said: "Shhh now . . . quiet . . . hush!" In her hands and burning there and rolled and adopted—hers. She pressed her fingers lightly into the soft cushiony flesh that cloaked the manly steel of his erection . . . and the boy groaned as he felt her deftly gliding caresses swirl about the thick edge of it . . . until the delicate pink ladyfingers went a little moist with the swimming urgency they produced there . . . "Aw lady! . . . you're gonna see it shine if you keep that up . . . wanna see it shine? . . . huh? . . . do ya?"

"Shiny . . . and photogenic," she murmured, tonguing her lips as she gently rubbed the trickly staff. She molded her fingers down to the base of it, where a few scraggly blond gym-champ's hairs sprang out of the tight opening of his briefs . . . "Ooh Christ, I love your hands on it and your eyes on it . . ." He pulled her to him and clutched his lips down over hers, his mouth a sticky-sweet burst of the Hershey and caramel he'd been gobbling earlier . . . moaning with the randy trembling taste of her tongue as it swept in to meet his . . .

"Oooumm! . . . baby," he said, and pulled back to stare at the lovely lips that moistly caressed the tip of his tongue, as he slid and teased it in and swiftly out, watching the eager blossom her mouth became as it formed a gulping plea for more of the warmth of him. "Will ya . . . will ya do something for me?" he muttered, hardly able to speak clearly, "Take my pants and my briefs off . . . aw God, how I love to feel a lady doin' that to me . . . 'cause hot damn! . . . that's the livin' end, gettin' all peeled and unpantsed by a pretty gal with big juicy tits who stares between my naked legs like the whole Goddamned world's fallin' apart . . . and nothin' else matters to her . . . do it!"

Nodding, her mouth a slim flushed smile, Gloria slowly unbuckled his trousers . . . pulled them down over his lithe hard hips. And then the breathless quickening heartbeat as she wrestled the unwieldy organ and shoved it back in his briefs temporarily . . . (mourning the evanescent passing!) . . . so that she could slide both trousers and briefs down around his ankles—and golly! . . . what a tumbling gay delight to see the sturdy youth of his balls spring loose . . . lush companion-pieces for the stout commander that soared above. He had an uncommon wild density of hair forest about his crotch, and Gloria fingered through it idyllically, while he kissed her and hoarsely groaned some more and unfastened her bodice and pulled out a warm plump breast from the straining bra.

His mouth on hers, rubbing, biting, speaking . . . "Let's trade sucks," said the hot-steamed lips, "or don't you know how to play that game . . .?"

"No . . . tell me the games you've been forced to devise, you bereft and lonely boy . . ."

He gazed down at her breast that was now so aroused and tremulous in his hand. He lowered his blond boy's head and took the nipple in his mouth, mildly wetting it with his fresh saliva-fires, briefly encircling it with his tongue as Gloria cried out and gripped his searing penis more fiercely in her hand, squeezing, adoring, gasping to become part of it . . . wanting to wear the long maleness as well as insert it . . .

And even more excited by his words and the fruit-moistened charade he proposed . . . "For every suck I give *this* baby, you match it with one down there on *my* baby . . ." he spoke with his tongue still dabbing at the nipple. "How 'bout that game, huh? Everybody wins, honey . . . believe me! And man, it'll get you so frantic . . . after about sixty seconds you'll want to take on a whole football team!"

"Oh . . . yes!" she said, as he plunged more of her breast into his mouth, now biting, now licking, now snarling for it . . . his lips a ripe-blown harvest of her flesh as he raised his innocent truant head again and stared at her, swallowing some flavors . . . then giving her the signal . . .

She nodded. "My turn," she said, and the glee fairly sang through her lips as she went gracefully to her knees and ardently busied herself there. With the first hot feel of girlish tongue surrounding the head of it, the boy cried out and gasped and straddled his legs wider, giving the oven-appetites of her mouth full rein, leaning against the wall of the elevator, his fingers filtering through her long blonde hair as he peered down at the sensual repast her curving lips made of him . . . and lower at the pouting lone breast of her, the nipple still aimed and pointed for his tongue's most sensitive urgings. But she rose after only wetting the knob of it, barely lighting the torch . . . and he knew it was time for him to share in this bouquet of loving cups . . . his mouth sweeping in at her once more, lips going greedy and foam-haunted for that tip-most point of pulpy nipple . . . and then, a second later, Gloria the mute receptacle at his feet again, roundly joined there . . . receiving the lunging spear that swamped and bulged its way down her throat. And now, faster and faster they alternated, as she rose and gave his lips their bounty, only to descend again and grovel for more of the taut taste of him . . . then he at her . . . and she at him . . . up and down and mutual went the succulence of their mouths, as she sucked in more of his throbbing with each journey . . . her lips all flared and full of this sweet servant boy's bludgeon . . . inhaling all his teen-dipped aromas as she licked . . . up and down went the pledged and transient couple . . . mouths and loins growing riper for it . . . ahh . . . the torment and sweet gulping ... but now ... hurry! After only a few moments of this lovely agony they were both half-crazed with hunger for the deeper tortures, as now she let him undress her, groaning aloud as he softly kissed away the moisture that had gleamed the downy patch of her vagina ... gripping the rumpled blond curls as his tongue dug in to taunt her clitoris ... and then the tremors and soft sighs as he pulled her stripped and baubled body down on the floor ... laid her flat and supplicant and crawled over her ... his member swollen and angered by all their worriesome foreplay ... as now, at last, the tan and pectoraled young elevator boy turned his prick into an event and surged the full experience deep up into her ... diving up that swarming hot spread of her channel ... bare-assed lust-child going into her between floors, crowding the warm side thickness of his tool up her writhing belly with an agonizing slowness ... so that it seemed an eternity before the full cock-length of him disappeared into her body, his fat and humid balls dabbing gently against her flared-out buttocks and he fucked and entered and created the bliss of new emergencies for the girl ... young ramming intern filling the prescription ... ahhh! ... take as directed ... and direct what's taken ...

The boy performed.

Lash-strokes that were wet and sure and artful, as Gloria squirmed and thrashed that swallowing juice-lipped pit of hers up hard against what he gave and battered and thickly relinquished, and felt his eager greasy-kid-stuff mouth nearing hers again ... yearning voraciously to suck the soft hot flower of her tongue as he dove up into her ... faster and slotting and more frantic with every thumping jolt ... slicing his way into the heaving gift of her vagina that seemed to grip his prick and bite it and smoke it and puff it and suck it. And for Gloria ... oh golly! ... it was so terrible and wonderful and wrong and furtive ... but mercy! ... what could she *do* with a boy like this, who was so beautifully designed to please and to purge? And, after all, there was a rampaging lady-beast in his house, one more she-devil whom Gloria Heavenrich had been divinely ordained to cast out ... using her own dear body as the catalyst ... ooh! those long sacrificial legs, oh benevolent one, and chase the glooms from this boy ... give him cheer!

He was panting out some words for her as he pivoted it and so brilliantly banged: "Ya ... want me to explode it up your belly, baby? . . . or should I raise up just in time so's you can nurse it?"

The question swirled about in her brain and body, building new fires there, leaving her so benumbed with desire that she could barely speak. But oh . . . to make this choice he expected, to turn what he offered into some desperate serum . . . ahh! . . . to *do* and to comply! To let him see that what he had sensed about her was true: it was milking-time . . . *always* milking-time for Gloria . . .

"Rod . . ." was all she said; and he licked his lips and knew, grinning . . . but breathing heavily now and perspiring and dangerously close to his climax. Tensing all his muscles, he held his cock's warning pulsations in check until he could slip it out of her wet cunt and then slowly raise his body upwards to offer her the full and photogenic thrust of his lovedipped tool . . . ooh! . . . just like that baby, at the tip's peril . . . throbbing with its dammed-up floodtide . . . God . . . half creamily sprung and ready for the peak . . . aw . . . touch it with your tongue . . . yeah . . . like that . . . and now real slow . . . oohmyGod . . . yeah! . . . let it in . . . aw Christ! . . . what a beautiful wet hot mouth . . . ahh! . . . those lovin' lips . . . those juicy red lovin' lips . . . ummm! . . . suckin' lovely bitch . . . do that with your tongue . . . again! . . . aw . . . I'm dyin' in there . . . aw . . . here it is . . . now and now and . . . now . . .

Smiling and rubbing her thighs together, Gloria received the throbbing spurting wedge right up to the hilt . . . gently squeezing the balls that so warmly caressed against her chin as she drank. And a moment later, the streams and sighs . . . as the boy gasped and groaned and waited and watched while she sponged him dry . . . then dove down between her legs to sop up the buttery flow of nourishment there . . . gulping and breathless for the endless gushing, his mouth brimming and radiant as he swallowed . . . Gloria groaning out her pain of fresh release as she still licked the lingering traces of his boy-issue from her lips . . .

Mouths and loins replenished, they raised up their heads and looked at each other. And smiled the wordless salute: they would remember this. They had left their mark on the scheme-of-things, and the world couldn't possibly have gone on the same if they'd never met or fused. They would separate and never touch again, but in passing had shot out some posterity. Unalterable. Two new moist stars in the galaxy.

Rod squirmed back into his uniform, still abulge in half-erection as he gave her a hand with her panties. "Sure hope the Union doesn't hear about you." His grin was chaste and neighborly.

"Oh?"

"You've got a whole new way of tryin' to organize the help, and they just might want a few lessons . . ."

She laughed, reaching out to gaily fingertip his lips once more. Such a sweet and callow humor. But good heavens, how desperate and floundering he must be at home, poor lad! And golly, there are so many of these wronged and ravished ones who are still untreated! Oh Heathcliffe, my dear and tender Monitor . . . if you'll only allow me to continue with these good works after marriage, I shall but love thee better . . . especially when I just *know* I'll be able to manage beautifully with a clever budgeting of my time . . . because after all, they *do* say if you want anything done, ask a busy person . . .

As she joined Heathcliffe in their suite a few moments later, he found her gaily humming: *I Dreamt I Dwelt In Marble Halls* . . .

"Where the devil have you been for the past hour?" he demanded.

"Now darling, didn't you hear what I was humming? That was a hint. I met the sweetest little old lady who has lived here for years, and she took me on a lovely scenic tour of our castle . . ."

With smiling guileless eyes Gloria licked her lips and fully swallowed this white lie. It was still quite tasty.

THE GANGWAY

Marcus Van Heller

*T*he Combine had no further trouble for a time. Rico's lead sprayer had proved a point. Don't fuck around with the Big Guy.

Dom got a raise in salary. He was now making one hundred and fifty dollars a week and was one of the five members of the enforcer group. Chip improved steadily and before long Dom and Chip were making regular rounds, keeping guys in line, supervising shipments, visiting the clubs and doing the thousand and one jobs the Combine required.

Because they were only five, they were often sent to distant parts of the Combine empire, sometimes alone. Dom got valuable training. Chip taught him that the sight of a gun is often better than having to use a gun. The threat of violence is a strong impeller. Chip, however did not always practice what he preached. He liked to hurt people.

Occasionally Dom went on a job with the Ape. He had come to like the squat little hood with the abnormally long arms. Ape was usually good natured. But Ape's weakness was his prick. "I got a permanent hard," he would say. The sight of a woman would make him grab his balls.

Rico sent them to collect money from a particularly recalcitrant client. He and the Ape drove to the address, an uptown brownstone, and the bell was answered by a colored maid. "Mr. Barensky ain't home," she said.

"We're friends of his," the Ape said, and pushed his way inside. He had his hands on her when she fought him, but she let go when he grabbed both her tits and chuckled.

"Git yo' goddam hands off me," she growled and backed into Dom. He grabbed her about the waist. She was a shapely girl, young and wearing a white uniform.

Her struggles and the feel of her breasts were too much for the Ape. He motioned with his head to a small room off the entry, and Dom hauled her into it. She did not yell, but she fought them tooth and nail. Dom got both her hands in his and the Ape powered her down on a couch and got between her thighs.

"Cut it out, baby," he kept saying, "cut it out—cut it out—"

"Don't you fuck me, don' you fuck me," she hissed.

The Ape had his cock out but he couldn't get it into her. Dom hauled her up and worked her onto his lap. He was rammed back onto the couch with the force of the Ape's attack. Then he saw the little squat man smile.

"Got it in 'er," he said. He began to lunge and the girl whimpered. Dom saw her naked legs one on either side of the Ape. He yanked her white dress up. She was almost naked to the navel. Her panties were thin and the Ape had torn them. The Ape was fucking her hard.

Dom's cock was very interested. He could hold her now with one hand, she had ceased to struggle much. He got a hand under her ass and unzipped his pants. His prick jumped out, naked and eager. The Ape was pounding her round ass, making her squirm. Dom had no trouble finding her button asshole with his dong.

She was wet. She was interested now, and beginning to push back at the heaving Ape. Cunt juice ran down, and Dom felt it on the head of his cock. He pushed the whang into her anus. It oozed in and she began to moan.

His cock drove deeply into her. All at once she began to jerk and pant. "Oh Jesus! I comin', I comin'—!"

The Ape leered at him over the girl's shoulder. He stroked it into her steadily and panted like a dog. Dom was almost crushed beneath his weight and the writhing girl. His cock was in her to the hair. He wondered how she felt with two pricks inside her.

The Ape unloaded into her then, beating a rapid fire tattoo into her cunt. She opened her mouth in a toothy smile, "Yeahhhh, yeahhhh," and embraced him. She folded her long legs about his body and drew him as close as possible. "Yeahhhh, yeahhhhh, yeahhh—"

"Oh shit," Ape said, breathing hard, "This here's a cunt, baby, I mean—a cunt!"

"Fuck me," the girl said huskily, "Wanna fuck—"

The Ape grinned and began to poke her again. Dom felt her tits and squeezed them. She put her head back beside his, eyes closed, and let them have her body.

A woman came into the room. Dom saw her, a middle-aged woman, perhaps Barensky's wife, stop inside the door and stare at them in astonishment.

"Who de fuck izzat?" Ape said, craning his neck. The woman moaned and dropped to the floor in a dead faint.

The colored girl was moaning, jerking, her entire body writhing. She screamed when the Ape pulled his cock out of her.

"No, no, no," she yelled, grabbing at him, "gimme it—" Dom pushed her off his prick and rolled over her. She seemed to realize he was there and reached for him, opening her thighs. He rolled onto her, his knees on the floor and she snatched up his cock and put it into herself. He thrust it into her and her legs went about him.

"Yeah, yeah, yeahhhh—" He began to fuck her fast and hard. She had a delicious cunt. Ape was always right about cunt.

He looked around for the Ape. The squat man had run out of the room. From what seemed like an adjoining room came a scream, then a series of shrill female screams.

"Who's in there?" he asked the maid.

"Whadda you care," she said. "Gimme 'at pump hannel. Ohh, honey, you got a tassel like a horse."

The screams continued. Dom tried to rise. She held him tightly, her vagina working, her ass heaving, "Don' go—don' go—"

"Who the fuck's in there?"

"Weddin' party," she said. "C'mon, fuck it inta me—"

Her arms and legs were almost impossible to dislodge The harder he tried to get off her, the more she struggled, and the more his pecker worked in her. And then she cried out and spasmed, shuddering and ramming herself at him. He let her have it.

He freed himself, unwrapped her long legs and wiped his pecker quickly. The woman on the floor was still out cold. He stepped over her and ran into the entry hall. The screaming had let up. He followed the sounds of crying, and found them in a large living room. Apparently they had been practicing for a wedding. There were four women in the room. Three were older, one was quite young, wearing an elaborate wedding gown.

The grinning Ape had her on the floor, the dress up about her hips, fucking her hotly.

The three older women were out cold too. They had fainted, one on the floor, two in chairs. They looked like suddenly-taken-drunk biddies, Dom thought.

"Ever'body screw de bride," Ape said.

The bride was crying. She lay on the floor on her back, and made little attempt to fight the Ape off. Dom lit a cigarette and sat down near them and stared. She cried, but she responded to Ape's stroking. When the Ape shot his wad, she also jerked and writhed in an orgasm, and cried all through it.

When Dom laid her on a couch and pronged her, she pushed back, and cried. She sobbed through every orgasm.

They finally had to go back and report to Rico that Barensky wasn't home.

That same week two detectives came to Hymie's Place asking for Dominic Cappello. Hymie sent word upstairs and Dom went down with Rico.

"Yeah?" Rico said.

"We're makin' an inquiry about a girl, Carmen Giannini," said one. "You Dominic?"

"Maybe," Rico said. "What about this dame? What's she done?"

Dom stood behind Rico, his black eyes darting from one of the husky cops to the other. So Carmen's mother had finally gone to the flatties.

The thinner of the two detectives, a pale man with a curved, sharp nose, said: "She got herself lost. Her old lady thinks this Dominic Cappello might know where."

Rico pursed his thin lips. He nodded thoughtfully. "Tell you guys what: C'mere." He led them to the back of the saloon and through the door to the hall. "We got some rooms here. You guys take a couple. I'm gonna send in some secretaries so's you can take notes, huh?"

The fatter detective frowned. "We don't got—"

His partner nudged him. "Yeh, investigatin' takes a lot of writin'." He gave his partner a look.

Rico opened a door. He pointed to the next door. Curved nose smiled and went to the room.

"Take your time," Rico said. "We want you guys should do a good job." He winked at them, took Dom's arm and they went back to the bar. Rico crooked his finger and Hymie hurried over. "Get a couple cunts for them flatties."

"Sure," Hymie said. "Flo and Rosie're here now."

"Rosie?" Rico looked around.

"They're around the corner, be right back."

Rico said, "Ain't Rosie the one with the cunt-mouth?"

Hymie grinned and nodded.

Rico shook his head. "She's too fuckin' good for them shit-eatin' flatties. Get 'em something with the clap."

"Yeah," Hymie said, winking at Dom. "I getcha, Rico."

Upstairs, Dom asked. "What happened to Carmen, Boss?"

"We sold her to the Dutchman. I t'ought you knew."

Dom shrugged.

"She's pro'lly out in the tules," Rico said, "fuckin her lil' heart out."

MARCUS VAN HELLER

Marcus Van Heller is about thirty-five years old, stocky, dark-haired and looks vaguely Latin. The pen name does not suit him at all. By his own admission, he is strongly opinionated and not the easiest man in the world to be with. His favorite pastime, aside from drinking, is chasing girls. He has been a reporter, a handyman in a brothel, a janitor in a girl's school (which he left under a cloud), and a diamond prospector in South America. He hates work and would love to live off women, but does not find too many with the money and inclination to support him. His gang backgrounds are drawn from his youthful days in New York City and he claims to have known many mobsters personally. He put in some time in jails here and there, has a liking for Latin America and spent many years there. He tells people he has a Spanish wife — among many other things, cautioning them at the same time that he loves to tell tall tales and create mystery about himself, either because there is little to tell or too much.

DARLING

Harriet Daimler

S he spent a few days feeling completely insane. She
walked the streets of Greenwich Village for hours
looking for the man whose face she had completely forgotten. What

was most frightening was the thought that he might never have existed, that she had created him out of an incredible lust and sickness inside herself. As long as he was not her creation, she could live, searching for him and trying to have, for the final time, the experience he had given her. If he did not exist, she was already dead, and it was a shadow that her lovers embraced.

Gloria had changed in the two weeks of her debauch. Her face wore the exhausted and strained look of one who waits. Her hands strayed nervously across her neck and face with a spinsterish aimlessness. Sometimes, in the morning, she felt liberated. But a glance in the mirror revealed her agony and would send her down into the streets, peering into bars and passing automobiles for her appointed victim. She was completely dedicated to one idea . . . to kill him. Some women, she knew, chose to live their subjugation. They discovered the chastised, tormented creature they were and lived to feed their suffering. They searched for a master to punish them, to sate their craving for punishment. That was the sick dream — to be punished enough. Punished for what? For forgiveness, for a reprieve, for the sins of fathers and mothers and aunts and uncles and cousins. And finally for the sins of rage and appetite — the combined sins of all. There was no human pain to touch her. She was incapable of repentance, all she wished was vengeance.

In weariness, one night, she went to the bar across the street from her apartment.

Gloria sat at the mahogany bar, and locked her heels in the bottom rung of the stool. She talked quietly to Mike, the bartender, who mixed the chilled Martinis and seemed genuinely concerned about her. With infinite discretion he asked her if she was feeling all right.

"Hello, Gloria," he said, as she sat tiredly in front of him. "Haven't seen you for a couple of weeks."

"I've been away," she lied.

"Back home?" he asked eagerly. He had been tending in the Village for eleven years, but his mission was to send small-town girls out of the city.

"No," she said. "Just a vacation to Fire Island." "Fire Island," he echoed. "I used to go there years ago. Got a quiet crowd then. But I hear it's changed."

"It's pretty wild," she agreed. "But it still looks kind of rustic and good, and the beach is terrific."

Talking to him, calmly and mundanely, she felt that she was grabbing frantically for her sanity. That's the quality of a good bartender, to make the drunk feel sober and sensible. This is what happens to us, she thought, when we really go nuts. We become absolutely banal. I'd give him my life if he'd just stand here and talk to me about the weather.

"Excuse me, Gloria," he said, and moved up the bar to take an order for two Manhattans. He stood talking to the man who ordered the drinks and then moved to the back of the bar to mix them. Gloria cupped the martini glass in her two hands and swallowed the clear liquid.

Without saying another word, Mike mixed her a double Martini. He poured it into the emptied glass, which was careless, since Martini glasses should be chilled. But she could not be a second without the drink before her, just as she could not breathe without something between her legs. A penis had become a pacifier to her, like rubber teethers that babies suck on.

She was deep in the second drink when a man sat down next to her and said, "Let me buy you the next one."

Mike looked up hastily across the bar. He did not like to see his regular women customers annoyed. He moved toward them. Gloria stopped him with a look.

"Thanks," she said, "I'd love you to buy the next one."

Mike looked amazed, then disappointed. He thought that all women must be rotten, and then remembered his wife and daughter and wanted to rush out and drive quickly to Queens. They should be sitting down to dinner now, but you couldn't be sure. You couldn't be sure of anything.

"I've seen you in here quite often," he told her.

"Yes, I live across the street. It's a good place to come for a quickie."

He carefully misunderstood the word. "We all need quickies once in a while," and he winked with adolescent lasciviousness. She hated him for the weak pun, and for his enjoyment of it.

"Brilliant."

The man looked back at her, first with confusion and then with distrust. "Lady," he said rudely, "I just want a piece of ass."

She thought only ignorant soldiers used that expression, and for an instant her face contorted with distaste.

"I know what you want," she said.

He was going to let her despise him, so long as he could have a fifteen minute fuck. "You're a smart little girl," he changed his tone.

"Buy me another drink," she commanded.

She reached over and patted the man's hand.

"Don't mind me," she apologized. "I'm just fighting a ghost."

"Someone in your family die?" he asked with the mock suburban concern he always showed to whores.

"Yes," she said, "Someone in my family died."

"Why, that's a shame, little girl," he murmured. "But we all have to go some time or other."

She wondered if she should kill him instead of the rapist.

"We all have to go," she echoed, and laughed.

"It makes you think," he added. "It makes you think that you'd better enjoy life while you got it."

"You're right," she said. "Everyone should enjoy life. To the fullest, to the brimming-over cup."

He looked down at his brown and white shoes. "Now don't be sacrilegious."

She almost fell off the stool.

"What I mean," she said, pressing against his frightened, corpulent body, "is that everyone should fuck a lot."

He didn't answer her for a few seconds. "Who died?" he asked, getting the conversation onto safer grounds.

"I did," she answered. "If you don't object to necrophilia, I guarantee a good time."

"What's that," and in his confusion, lifted his hand for another round.

"It's copulating with a corpse," she told him, in the tone she'd tell him the time, or her name.

He turned his head away. "You got a funny sense of humor."

"What?"

"You got a helluva sense of humor," he said, with the slight toughening alteration.

"I was even funnier," she explained, "when I was alive. When I was alive, I was an absolute scream."

"And now," he said, afraid to look stupid.

"Now I'm only a moan."

He looked at her slim arms and softly-powdered pale skin. It seemed a shame to give her up just because she was nuts.

"Where do you come from?" he finally asked.

"Across the street," she answered, purposefully avoiding the obvious information.

"I mean where were you born?" he persisted.

"Under a stairway," she told him. "In blood and pain. It was quite a shock. I almost died. In fact, that's when I died."

"Look sister," he submitted wearily. "I only have an hour before I catch a train. If you want to do business, okay. If not, I'd rather finish this drink alone." His chin trembled at his offer to relinquish her.

Gloria sat very still. She drained her glass and looked at the fly of his pants. Nothing. She had scared the sex from between his thighs. Her head ached from the four Martinis, and she knew that she'd have a hard time getting up the stairs alone. Alone. Alone. To lie in her bed and listen for footsteps.

"I want to do business," she said meekly.

The man didn't say another word. He gathered the cashier slips in his hand and paid Mike. Then he placed his hand under her elbow and helped her off the stool. The room was turning with carnival abandon.

"I live right across the street."

"What number?"

"Sixty-two."

He pushed the swinging doors open for her, and she was out on the dark, quiet street. They walked silently to her house.

"The fourth floor."

They mounted the steps wordlessly. *He's not so bad when he shuts his mouth,* she thought.

At her door, she reached into her handbag and found her key. She gave it to him as she would to a fraternity date. He looked surprised but put the key in the lock and let them both into the apartment. The rooms were forbiddingly silent, and he nervously cleared his throat. She turned on the lamp in the living room. A distorted light fell on a blue and grey canvas.

He stood and looked at the picture. "Quite a little picture." He rocked on his heels.

"Shut up," she said.

He looked shocked. "What? What did you say?"

"Shut up. Shut up. Shut your mouth. Nothing but stupidities

come out of your mouth. You have no right to be that stupid. No one has the right to be that stupid." She knew she was drunk. "I bet that you never call anyone stupid. You call them ignoramuses. I bet you have six real long words that you use for speeches and strangers."

"You know a lot," he said. Then he pulled his hand back and slapped her across the mouth. She tasted blood and surprise, and finally excitement.

"Do you beat your whores, stupid? Do you beat your whores and your wife beats you?" She laughed gaily. This time he made an enraged fist and punched her in the face. The blow was down on her jaw, and she thought he must have broken something.

"You should enjoy what I'm telling you," she pursued. "You'd have to pay an analyst a bucket of money to get this truthful observation. You have a fat stomach and a fat head and a fat brain. No brain. You are, in fact, an ignoramus. There, I'm using your word. Get the hell out of here."

He made a mirthless grunt and pulled her arms behind her back. She felt the muscles ache with strain. He pressed his thumbs and then his hands tightly around her breasts. She thought she would faint with the pain.

"Take your hands off me, you buffoon. You ignoramus, you disgusting, meaningless paunch."

His hands tightened, around her breasts and his knee pressed against her kidneys. She slid to the floor in agony. The man was insane with rage. He pulled his belt out of his pants and struck her hard across the stomach. She screamed with pain and then saw his gloated furious face. It was too contemptible to let that fool hear her screams for mercy.

"Stop," she called to him. "Stop and come down here and love me. Fuck me! Fuck me! Don't waste your strength beating me. I love your fat sloppy belly. Press it on me," and she opened her legs.

The man had his belt lifted for another slash, and it landed forcefully on her chest. He seemed not to hear her, not to hear anything. The Neanderthal, the preliterate man was insulted.

He got down on his knees beside her and roughly unbuttoned her blouse. She thought that at last he was going to take her, then leave her with the few welts. He pulled her skirt off, and she lay beside him covered only with a thin nylon brassiere and transparent panties. He ripped the undergarments off her body, and she saw his huge hairless hands. The hands alone made him disgusting. She moved her head and was sick on the rug. There was the immediate stench of putrified gin and she was sick again. He leaned his head close to hers, and she heard him say, "Bitch, filthy fucking bitch."

He stood up and looked long at her naked body, lying limp next to the stench. He raised his leather belt and cut her thigh. He kicked her over with the pointed toe of his shoe, and she felt her stomach against the mess she had made. She was sober now, sober and bruised and wanting to die. She felt the belt lacerate her back, and she could not stop the trembling of her body. The belt fell again with his brute primitive strength. It slashed crazily into her white buttocks, and then up again to her neat waist. He hit her without direction, up and down her body, sometimes missing completely and pounding the rug beside her. She knew, from occasional returning echoes that she was screaming for help and release. His arm waved frantically above her, and the leather made a swooshing sound before it planted itself against her skin. There was a pause in the incessant beating, and the dimly familiar buzz of a sliding zipper. She waited to feel her body turned over, but he apparently enjoyed the network of red slashes on her bottom and back.

She crossed her arms in front of her and leaned her cheek against the soft upper arm, like a child asleep. The pain separated her from her body. There was nothing but a creature lying achingly in filth on the floor; a creature from a nightmare. Her face against her arm was wet with tears. How strange that she had cried. Her body had its habits of response, and a blow produced tears. But all the whipping had accomplished was to stop the buzzing in her cunt, and now he would take her when she had passed the threshold of feeling.

His hands grasped her belly and thighs. He was trying to lift her buttocks to a comfortable height. Business before pleasure. His thumbs pressed her scarred behind, and she jumped with pain. Then she could still know more agony; she thought he had finished her. His fingers crawled between her legs to her soft, dry pubic hairs. He kneaded the mound of sensitive flesh, and she writhed with the insult. She tried to find her voice to insult him, preferring his enraged blows to his groping tenderness. But her voice belonged to her body, and neither belonged to her. His finger pierced the futile tension of her inner flesh. She could feel his knuckle scraping against her, measuring the capacity of her vagina. He grunted his excitement. *Pig. Fat, knuckle mad, cunt mad pig.* The words did not escape from her, and she thought with ecstasy, *I'm afraid. Afraid of Mr. Pig,* and her body crouched closer to the floor.

He lifted her higher with an angry and impatient gesture, and he said, "Stay the way I put you sister, if you want to live." But she didn't want to live, and she sank her body to the floor. He slapped her hard across her inflamed buttocks and lifted her body in a high arch. She stayed that way for him, suspended like a Gothic door-way. Her body trembled in its taut position, and he kneeled behind her, relishing her discomfort. Finally his passion succeeded his brief sadism, and she felt him enter her body with relief. He moved in and out against her motionless hips, gasping into the silent room. "Ahh," he moaned. "You cunts are all alike. You love it when we get it in. You love it more than we do." She dug her chin into her passive arm and offered him her still body.

"So I'm screwing a corpse," he laughed. "So I'm screwing a corpse."

His belly slapped against her unresisting ass. Then he packed faster and tighter against her, his prick swelling inside of her. She felt the pressure climb within, and then he grabbed her belly and rocked frantically as he came. He came as if it would be the last time, every fuck the last time, and her heart chilled with detach-ment. He released her, and she discovered her exhaustion. She sank into the rug and the room spinned out of existence.

Her faint could have lasted only a few minutes, and she opened her eyes to his rampant pawing of her breasts and thighs and cunt. He was breathing his liquored breath against her neck and squeezing her with the ecstasy of possession.

"Feel that," he urged her. "Feel that."

She reached her hand behind her and found his stiff eager prick in her palm. "None of this one-shot business for old Charley," he gloated. "I'm gonna fuck you all night, sister. I'm good for another six rounds."

She began to cry her repugnance. With horror she imagined that she would spend the rest of her life on the smirched rug, fainting and being taken by the insatiable boor, and fainting again. The room did not spin any more, and she was relentlessly sober.

She pretended unconsciousness, but he continued to squeeze her body. Then he twisted her head and forced her mouth open. He pried at her teeth with drunken energy and howled vulgarly, "I'll buy! This pony is good for another six fucks."

"You're a pig," she managed to whisper.

"What? I didn't hear you baby. You think old Charley's a pretty good lay? I been around. Used to have women getting on their knees for me to fuck them. Charley never leaves a lady in distress," and he howled his American Legion laugh.

She was too scared to call him a pig again.

She moved her head to the side and saw a bottle of gin on the floor beside her. He had found her liquor cabinet. She heard him swallow and wondered if he would kill her.

He turned her over on her back and sat his fat ass on her stomach. "You're the best little horse I ever bought. A real bucking mare." His prick was pointing to the ceiling, and he straddled her body and moved toward her mouth. "Suck old Charley," he cajoled. "Be a good obedient mare and suck daddy Charley."

She closed her eyes and he pressed his penis into her lax mouth. She held it between her lips like a stubborn, spoiled child refusing to swallow her lamb chop. Charley was undaunted. He pressed up and down on her face, using her mouth as he had her unwilling sex. He used her as he would a lifesized sponge with a few openings. But he was not a man for strenuous exercise, and he grew tired of his joggling motion.

Her eyes were still closed, and she opened them only when he lifted his body and lay beside her. His face and the whites of his eyes were delicately laced with red. He looked apoplectic, as if he might suddenly spit up all the blood in his head and die before her. She wished he would die. He seemed to pass out for a moment, and she realized how drunk he was. But his prick still stood high and urgent in the air. He came to with an impatient shaking of his head, and staggered about the room. She could not take her fascinated eyes off his stiff penis, which seemed to have an independently rigid life. He rushed to her when he understood her mocking eyes, and seemed unsure of himself for the first time since he had removed his belt and beat her. She lowered her eyes to his thin, frail, white, blue-veined legs that supported his enormous trunk and started to giggle at the horror, humiliation, and stupidity of her evening. He stood furious next to her and kicked her prostrate form. But the kick lacked the enthusiasm and conviction it had had one hour ago. He reached for the half-empty bottle of gin and put the thin neck of the bottle against his lips.

I must remember to throw the bottle away.

The hot liquor seemed to renew his assurance. "Get on your knees, you cunt," he commanded.

She looked at him with disdain, and he roughly twisted her body around. She lay flat, her knees, her thighs, her stomach, her flattened breasts, her shoulders and hair touching the carpet. He kneeled behind her and pulled her body into the arch he elected for fucking. She did not resist him, did not really acknowledge that he was there behind her.

"I'm gonna do something I've always wanted to do baby. But I never met a slut I dared to do it with. I'm gonna dig so deep into your ass, you'll taste my come on your tongue."

He slapped her blood-smeared buttocks and without pause of warning, pressed into the narrow crevice between her buttocks. A remarkable pain inflamed her body, and she screamed. He laughed wildly and smashed his prick into her rear again, the pain intensifying with each push of his body. She began to rotate her body wildly to make him come by the next thrust. But he had the hard control of a drunk and he thumped into her narrow hole with shrieks of pleasure. He reached his hand around her jumping hips and felt her cunt. It was dry — a desert of despair. His fingers found her shrunken clitoris, and he grubbily massaged it. To her shock she felt the drops of sensuality flowing onto his fingertips. She could not be sure if her body was moving with terror or desire. He raised the stubborn dot of clitoris and pinched it cruelly. Her body was a flame of pain from her waist to her tired knees. He smashed against her, forcing her chin roughly to the rug. His free hand found the nipple of her hanging breast. His nails were like teeth against the stiff deep red tits. Her body sang its captivity, and she swung eagerly against him. His hands busily tensed her nipples and cunt. Then he lunged into her with a final howl, and removed his hands without warning. Her abused body thumped to the ground. His prick was shrinking inside her. He released a final spurt of sperm, and the smoky liquid seemed to flow to her tongue. Her mouth was full of the taste of him, and with a terrible moan of defeat she came.

He was motionless beside her, and she saw that he had really passed out. He looked dead. She lay gasping for breath for a few minutes, and then swallowed a mouthful of the raw gin. It slid hot down her chest, and gave her an instant's strength. She shook the lifeless form. He did not respond at all. She kicked him hard with her foot, but he was turned up with an impotent calm. Instead of the vicious attacker he had been for her, he resembled a stupefied whale. She remembered her body's deceit and kicked him in disgust. She wanted to get into her bed and sleep, sleep for a hundred hours. But she could not sleep with this senseless bulk on the studio floor. His clothes were dropped carelessly beside him.

Gloria walked to her bathroom and washed her tear-stained, sick-stained face. She took a paisley dressing gown off the door hook and moved her pained body into it. The robe stuck to her hips and buttocks, and she knew that the blood he had drawn was still flowing. She brushed her hair from her face and caught it at the nape of her neck with a tortoise shell clip. Her face was fatigued and bruised, but younger than it had been in the morning. Her skin had the burnt, now pale color of a convalescent. She was not thinking of the rapist, not thinking of anything but getting that bulk off the living room floor. She walked back to him, to find him still stretched out, motionless and stupid. Some spittle ran down the corner of his chin, and he snored with a wet, gurgling sound. She reached down and took him by his two bare feet. His huge shape formed its own fulcrum, and she turned him like a top toward the door.

She opened the hall door and made sure that the house was still and empty. With tremendous effort she pulled his body into the hall; it was naked and ludicrous in the tiled dark passage. She did not want his sprawling form snoring outside her apartment, so she dragged him down the steps feet first to the second-story landing. His head jumped with a hollow sound at each step. *You're going to miss your train, Charley. You may never run to catch another train.* She left him on the second floor and dashed noiselessly up to her apartment. The door was standing open. She grabbed his underwear, his shoes and socks, his pants and jacket, shirt and tie, and holding them wide in her arms, rushed to the landing where he lay. He was covered with spit, his penis little and pink on his thigh. She dropped the clothes on his unconscious figure and rushed quickly to her fourth floor. She slammed the door behind her and nervously latched the safety lock. She breathed in hysterical little gasps and putting her palm automatically to her forehead, found it burning with fever. *Well, I'm sick, she thought. I've been trying to die, but I've only managed to get sick.* For the first time she did not think of her search for the white-eyed violator. All she wanted was to get her throbbing body between the sheets of her bed. She walked toward the bedroom and saw the bottle of gin lying empty on its side. Next to the bottle was Charley's belt. She had not noticed it in her mad grab for his clothes. She picked the belt up and studied it. It was long, to circle his ridiculous girth. There were six holes on the pointed end of the belt, and a silver buckle that was initialed C.D. on the other side. The leather was worn shiny, and it was stained with blood where it had struck her.

A well-earned souvenir. I'll keep Charley's belt as a souvenir. She dragged herself tiredly to bed, holding onto the belt, as if for support, with both hands.

The Coupling Game

Peter Kanto

Dink's stay in the Lesbian Lounge was shortened when word seeped up through channels to the loft penthouse atop the two-mile-high N.F.N. building. Dr. Ethyl Deeton stood at attention before the videophone when she received a call from the current secretary to the Great Man. Manly Manning was misnamed, for she was an ash blonde with a little baby fat still on her girlish body, a pretty face and conical, firm breasts with big, brown aureola and pert little nipples.

"Mr. Feetolzbing hears that you have a virgin for him," Manly said, sneering at Deeton, who had interviewed the little nymph only a few months previously.

"She is being instructed, being made ready for him."

"Mr. Feetolzbing saw the film with MA-34 and he thinks she's ready now," Manly said, with cold command.

"When would Mr. Feetolzbing like to see her?" Deeton asked, holding her temper. Soon, very soon, Manly Manning would no longer be secretary to the Great Man and then Deeton would put her in the female masturbation section and leave her there forever. Little snit.

"As soon as she can be prepared," Manly said.

Deeton hauled Dink out of a sixty-nine orgy with Charleen and two other beautiful Lesbians and sent her to be washed and powdered and dressed in a little, old-fashioned all over dress which showed only her legs and her arms. She thought it was silly, but who was she to question the whims of the Great Man? Pretty Hawksbill plunged a needle into Dink's thumb and extracted a half ounce of red, rich blood, put the blood in a plastic capsule and inserted it into Dink's vagina carefully.

"Remember to give just one ladylike yelp when you're penetrated," Deeton instructed. "And for God's sake, don't ham it up!"

"I'll try," Dink said, impressed by the awe with which everyone spoke the Great Man's name, feeling humble and proud that she had been chosen to give the great innovator a moment or two of pleasure.

Deeton, herself, escorted Dink to the penthouse. A specially trained robot opened the door, checked them with a survey meter for any radioactivity above normal, sprayed them with a powerful disinfectant which made them sneeze and made them strip—to send their clothing through an instant laundry and disinfectant—before he allowed them to dress again and enter the suite.

Deeton was not allowed past the main reception room. She kissed Dink tenderly on both cheeks, wished her luck and went back down to her office to wait the outcome of Dink's visit to the tower with bated breath. All of her work with the girl depended on what would happen in the luxurious cloud penthouse so far above.

Manly Manning looked at Dink and sniffed. "I'll bet if the truth were known," she said, "you lost it when you were five."

"Lost what?" Dink asked, amazed and awed by the luxury around her.

"Are you sure you didn't have a perverted little brother who threw it to you when you were still in diapers?"

"Oh, no," Dink said. "I wasn't that lucky. Did you have a perverted little brother who threw it to you?"

"Actually," Manly said, "it was my cousin."

"Gee," Dink said.

"Enough of this chitchat," Manly said, trying to look stern. On her it didn't come off. She had a pretty little baby face which, when she tried to look stern, merely looked cute.

"What is he like?" Dink asked, as Manly escorted her through a seemingly endless series of well-furnished rooms.

"Who?"

"The Great Man."

"Oh, he's all right," Manly said.

"Do you see him often?"

"All the time," Manly said offhandedly.

"Gee."

"I'm his personal secretary. I feed him and all that."

"How wonderful." They had reached a large, golden door which was closed. Manly pressed a button and a screen lit up on the door, showing the interior of the room. Dink could see a shock of white hair sticking up over the top of a big, padded, wheelchair. "It is I, Manly, master. I have brought you the virgin."

"Oh!" Dink said.

"We can go in now," Manly said. She pressed another button; the door opened on well-oiled hinges and Dink was pushed into the most fabulous room she'd ever seen. All around her were paintings of ancient masters, all nudes, all delightfully pornographic. She was enthralled by a ceiling fresco of about half a hundred male and female figures engaged in the most fascinating orgy when, suddenly, a huge, hairy thing jumped out in front of her, made a horrible sound and bent low to sniff at Dink's pubic area through her clean, starched old-fashioned skirt.

"It's so nice to meet you," she stammered, looking wildly at Manly Manning.

"Oh, don't be silly," Manly said. "That's only Errol, Mr. Feetolzbing's pet gorilla."

Errol, his flat, horrid face twisted into a leer, raised Dink's skirt and sniffed at the smooth silk of her inner-panties.

"Naughty, naughty," Manly said, swatting the gorilla on the wet snout with the back of her hand. She took Dink's arm and led her to the window, which overlooked half the world, it seemed. Slowly, slowly, Dink moved around the big, padded, wheelchair, stepping over cables and tubes leading to it, wondering, trembling as she neared her face-to-face confrontation with the Great Man Himself.

"This is the virgin," Manly said. "Master!"

In front of Dink's wondering eyes was a perfect marvel of medical science. A dried up old husk of a man sat amid a conglomeration of tubes and cables and gadgets. His eyes, closed, were covered by paper thin eyelids which were hairless, as were his eyebrows. His grey wig had slipped and it exposed his bald, shiny pate. His lips were closed around a nipple leading to a tube through which a clear, viscous liquid flowed in spurts as the old man's mouth made sucking motions.

"It isn't everyone who is privileged to see this," Manly said. "He's having his meal."

"What is it?" Dink asked.

"Gorilla milk."

"From him?" Dink asked, pushing Errol away as the gorilla tried to shove his snout up her skirt from the rear.

"No, dum-dum, Errol is a male." Manly laughed, "Man, is he ever a male!"

"He's so . . .so . . . well, all wrapped up in things," Dink said, staring at the tubes and cables leading to the dried up old body of the Great Man.

"It's a miracle," Manly said proudly, as if it were of her making. "This is the tube which irrigates his aritifical kidneys and this is the electrical cable which activates his artificial heart and this is the air flow tube to his artificial lungs—"

"Oh, my," Dink said.

"Yes, he used to smoke, you know. Lung cancer." Manly continued the guided tour of the medical miracle before them. "This is the tube which feeds him, of course. This is the outlet from his artificial bladder and this is the mixer which stirs the food in his artificial stomach and this . . ."

"Is any part of him real?" Dink asked, whispering.

"You bet your bippy," the old man muttered, letting the feeding tube fall out of his mouth to dribble gorilla milk down his front. A servo arm immediately revolved and sucked up the spilt milk, removed the tube and patted the old man's drooling mouth with a clean napkin.

"He spoke!" Dink said.

"That means he likes you."

"Oh, wonderful!" Dink leaned close. The old eyes were still closed. "I'm glad you like me."

"Goat gonads," the old man said in his barely audible voice.

"Got gonads?" Dink asked, looking at Manly questioningly.

"Goat Gonads," Manly said. "He has been implanted with goat gonads. That's what keeps him studding, you know."

"How wonderful."

"Only trouble is they put in the wrong kind of goat gonads," Manly said. "The kind which stink. I'm sure you've noticed."

There was a peculiar smell in the air, but Dink had assumed that it was from some of the medical equipment.

"Let's fuck, baby," the old man said, chortling, drooling, his eyes still closed, nothing moving but his lips and then only feebly.

"Are you sure he's up to it?" Dink asked.

"The Great Man?" Manly laughed. "Just you wait!"

"Fuck," the old man said. A bouquet of servo arms reached for him, lifted him from the chair trailing his tubes and cables as he was transported through the air. A huge bed unfolded from the wall. The servo arms positioned the old man about three feet above the soft mattress.

"Fuck," the old man said, his voice feeble, apparently exhausted by the strenuous move through the air from his chair to the bed.

"Stand where he can see you and take off your clothes," Manly said.

Dink moved to the side of the bed. A servo arm turned the old man's head toward her. His eyes were still closed. "Can he see me with his eyes closed?"

"Don't be a dunce." Manly said. "He'll open his eyes when he's ready."

"We went to a lot of trouble with this dress," Dink said. "Doesn't he want to see it before I take it off."

"Fuu—" The old man gasped.

Dink removed her dress and the old-fashioned bra and the silly one-piece things they used to call underpants. The old man's eyes flickered. One lid lifted. She saw a baleful, evil, dark eye stare at her for a second and then the eye closed and the old man gasped for breath so hard that the artificial lungs had to double their flow.

"Crawl up under him," Manly ordered.

Dink crawled under the hanging mass of old flesh and medical gadgets, fearful of being impaled by some of the weird-looking implements protruding from the Great Man's body.

"Raise your legs," Manly ordered.

Dink pulled her legs up and lay them alongside her breasts, elevating her pelvic basket to lie horizontally under—and here she saw it for the first time—the most monstrous penis she'd ever seen. "Oh, God," she gasped.

"Impressive, isn't it?" Manly asked, grinning with superior knowledge. "He had it grafted from a stud horse."

"I don't think I can take that!" Dink said. "After all, I am a virgin."

"Don't worry," Manly said, reaching down to daub a wet, gooey mixture onto Dink's upturned genitals. The gooey stuff ran down between her legs and moistened her little brown flower, too. It tickled.

"Fuck!" the old man gasped.

"In a moment, Master," Manly said. "First we must make sure the position is right." She measured and pushed on Dink and hummed and looked thoughtful and muttered to herself about windage and elevation and then, satisfied, stood back. "I think it's ready. Aren't you excited?"

"Well, he will be the first man I've even been close to," Dink said. "I'm a little bit excited."

"Are you ready, Master?" Manly asked.

"Fuck," the old man grunted.

"All right, then," Manly said, standing back and looking a bit worried. "I do hope I've got it right this time."

She put her finger on a button. "Here we go, kiddies," she announced, pushing the button and dropping the mass of old man and cables and tubes in a sudden swoop, the big, grafted horse cock leading the way in the sudden drop to stab Dink not in the vagina but in the smaller, more sensitive, much more tender vent covered by the same gooey lubricant, lower in the pelvic-crotch area.

"My God," she screamed in real pain as she was split, rent, plugged, filled to bursting. "He's in the wrong hole!"

"Damn," Manly muttered. "Missed again."

But it was too late, Servo arms plunged the old man up and down into the writhing, pain-wracked body of Dink and it was over within seconds as the newly implanted goat gonads sent a stinking, swift discharge of semen into Dink's bowels and the old man made rattling noises in his throat.

Servo arms whisked him away. Dink moaned. She felt as if she had been torn apart. Red blood smeared the sheets. A servo arm whisked down and collected a sample of it and she knew the old man would be satisfied, because it was her own blood, and not the blood they'd collected from her thumb, either.

"You'll have to pardon me," Manly said. "The way he was breathing sounds as if he needs a transfusion. I'll see to it. You make yourself at home and rest."

Dink closed her eyes. She wept a few ladylike tears. She had been with her first man and she was still, incredibly, a virgin. She wondered if she would ever lose it. She was beginning to feel better and there was a tickling at the entrance to her virginity and she opened her eyes just as Errol, the pet gorilla, pushed his muzzle between her outflung thighs and lapped her clitoris thrillingly.

"Oh, go away," she said testily, but it did feel good, and, after all, she had been all excited about having her body deflowered, so she just lay there and let Errol lick her. However, when he picked her up and threw her down onto her stomach, she began to worry. After all, she was alone in the room with the gorilla. She struggled. Errol bunched her up in his arms, pushing her knees up under her chin, her rump protruding. He licked her on the battered anus and it felt so good, so soothing, that Dink relaxed for a moment and then it was too late, for he mounted her and drove a big, red, hot gorilla cock into her still virgin vagina and began to attack her with fury.

"I don't think we should, Errol," Dink said, but he was holding her close and, after all, she had been cruelly disappointed in the long-awaited deflowering ceremony.

She began to twitch her fanny and imagine that she was a female gorilla and the waves of sweetness rolled in her body and if there had been an orgasm meter, she felt, she would have bent the needle. But the quarters of the Great Man were, of course, very, very private. Surely no one could expect the Great Man who molded a world into a way of life to share his well-earned orgasm with that world. So there were no cameras and no orgasm meter as Dink panted and grunted, acting the part of the female beast, and twitched her little fanny into the impaling thrusts of the pet gorilla and had a beautiful one.

When Manly Manning came back into the room, Dink was really tired and lying on her stomach on the bed. Errol, exhausted, was squatting on the floor, his beady eyes looking at Dink's well-used womanhood with a desire which he had no bodily energy to fill.

"You'll be happy to know that our Great Founder has survived another heart transplant," Manly said. "He'll live to deflower many more virgins."

"That's nice," Dink said weakly.

"And you'll be happy to know that the first word he spoke when he awakened from the operation was this—"

"Yes?" Dink asked, suddenly alert. After all, her future depended on what the Great Man had said.

"He said . . ."

"Yes, yes?"

"He said *fuck,*" Manly said.

"Oh, dear. Is that good or bad?"

"Wonderful," Manly said, "although I'm envious. Just because you're a virgin and I was deflowered by a demented cousin—"

"What does it mean?" Dink said.

"You'll be on the big show," Manly said.

*I*n the big studio on the big, romping bed, Dink and Chad lay side by side, holding hands. Two pretty female robots stood beside them, keys in their hands. When the scene became clean on the screen, the two pretty female robots bent over, unlocked the chastity belt and the harness and stood back, smiling, holding the offending devices now to show that now nothing stood between the star-crossed lovers.

"Oh, Chad!" Dink moaned, putting her hand down to feel just how sopping she was in the crotch. She was pretty wet. "Oh, Chad, I don't think I can wait another minute."

"You don't have to, darling," Chad said. "Now we are together. But first," he said, and it was hard, hard, hard to do, "a word from our sponsor!"

While the entire network was given over to a new deodorant for milady's cunt, since the underarm, the commercial said, is not the pretty lady's most troublesome odor area, Chad kissed Dink and played with her boobs and fell down and paid homage to that which would, as soon as the commercial was over, be his. He let his lips sink into the oiled, wet sweetness, let his tongue play with her swollen clit. She, in turn, curled up and under him and bent his hard, hard penis back and took the glamorous, purple head of it into her sucking tube of a mouth and the director, a robot tuned to the most light-felt sexual urge, caught them thus, in an inspired sixty-nine, when he came back to live action from the filmed commercial. Chad saw the lights come on in the cameras and he knew that, at last, she was *his* and an overwhelming love for her filled him. He positioned her, lifting her legs until her knees were bent and cocked up, her thighs spread, opening her virgin twat to show nice little lips and a stretch of pink and the rosecolored iris of the vaginal opening.

"Now, my darling," Chad whispered.

"Oh, how long I have waited," Dink said.

"Waited just to hold you," Chad said.

"Put my arms about you," Dink said, reaching for him and putting her arms around him to pull him down until his hard penis was poised at the gate to ecstasy. "I've saved myself for you, lover," she said.

"My virgin!" Chad whispered, letting his weight sink his shaft into the oily pit of passion. "My love!"

"Oh, oh, oh, oh, oh, oh, oh, oh, oh," Dink said, as the long, hard, thin, thick, soft, fleshy, swelling, jerking, pulsing, top-oozing cock filled her and she was, at long last, not a virgin but a full-fledged woman who had her man in her cunt and liked it very much, thank you. "Oh," she whispered. "You are fucking me!"

"Yes, darling," Chad said. "I'm fucking you at last."

"Oh, I hope it never ends!" Dink said.

Woody Woody's face, contorted, his body bent over his desk, Pretty Hawksbill buggering him lustily with her huge dildo, flashed in a corner of the screen. "Little do they know, fellow feelers," he sighed, "how nearly she will have her wish, for they will fuck, as we all know, for a WHOLE WEEK."

Pretty gave an extra hunch and the audience shared Woody's

thrill.

Chad and Dink were fornicating slowly, lovingly, long, lovely strokes which brought them to the brink of climax within seconds, put them on the lovely edge where fornicating is wonderful, an edge which, ordinarily, does not last long but fades and then explodes quickly into climax. But not this time. Pekstine's potion kept them poised there in the golden glow of near climax and you could hear the world quiet down. All over the world beings—people, old people, middle-aged people, a few young people, melted into their Feelie trance and lived the pleasures of the ultimate fuck.

"Woody says," Woody said, coming back into one corner of the screen, still being buggered by Pretty, "ain't this grand?"

"Woody says," Woody said, grinning, feeling on the edge of climax himself and hoping so, so he could be rid of Pretty and get back to emceeing the show, "have fun, kiddies! It's going to last a WHOLE WEEK!"

"Do you think we dare turn on the Feelie waves just a bit?" Nicky Wylie asked Jack, as they sat before their small, portable Feelie in their apartment with Jim and May Clark, who had just finished a good blow-job session, and with Mary Winters and Bill Warth. Mary was definitely knocked up and loved it, although it would be weeks before she began to show. She was so proud of it that she'd offered to let both Jack and Jim know how it feels to screw a pregnant lady. Jack said later, thank you, and Jim, who had just ejaculated into his mate's lips, said sure, but not right now. Then they all watched the start of the Big Show.

"God no," Jack said. "This is supposed to be the most powerful thing since the hydrogen bomb and we can't dare risk getting caught up in it. If this works, when those kids get going they'll rivet every human being in the world to every screen that has the Feelie waves on."

"Well, some of us could put on mufflers," Nicky pouted, "so we'd be sure to turn it off after others of us felt what it's like under the influence of Pekstine's potion."

"Like Ulysses and the sirens, huh?" Jack asked. "But, no, let's don't risk it. There's too much at stake. After we take over the world, then we can all go on a binge and take the potion ourselves."

"If those poor kids survive," Mary Winters said. "The girl has good hips, make a good mother."

"Hummm," Jack said when on the screen, the butch Lesbian began to bugger the emcee from the rear with a huge dildo. "I wonder why they put this in."

"Well, you know those N.F.N. people," Bill Warth said. "They don't recognize the greatest act when they get it and they're trying to spice it up with some old-fashioned stuff."

"Strange, though," Jack said.

The artful fucking in the studio held their attention, even without Feelie waves. May, seeing Chad in action, sighed and said, "Effie never did bring her little friend home with her."

"Anyone want to fuck an old pregnant lady?" Mary wailed, with mock despair in her voice. Jack laughed and obliged her. It was pretty good, for he snuck a couple of looks at Dink, with her legs wrapped around Chad on the Screen. He was just doubling his stroke to finish Mary off when the robot director at the Coupling Game, sensing strong sex urges from elsewhere in the N.F.N. building, began to shoot scenes at random. In the Circus, the performers had dropped down from their contraptions and were coupled on the mats, rolling and fucking with inspired rhythm. In the Pocket Pool Parlor, young men were masturbating with all their might while they wandered around and finally found the girls of the Les Lounge, eating each other and masturbating. The Pocket Pool men coupled, sometimes forceably, with the Lessies and there was more inspired screwing. A quick shot showed the blonde receptionist, who had never enjoyed a moment of bodily contact, masturbating herself with the point of her high-heeled shoe. Dr. Ethyl Deeton was discovered screwing madly with two of the newest interviewees, taking sex through the two boldly opened body apertures, sandwiched between the lusty young men and reaching for another's cock with her hand to stuff it into her mouth and, thus, to entertain sensuous cocks in all three orifices. Effie Clark, to May and Jim's complete surprise, was surprised by a virile young lad from the Pocket Pool Parlor and was thrown to the mat in the Circus and impaled on a respectable-sized cock. She fought, but soon settled down into a rhythm. Bill Pixie and his homosexual friends buggered each other madly. A searching camera invaded the very anteroom of the Great Man's suite in the penthouse and spent a good two minutes sharing the exciting feelings of Manly Manning and Errol, the gorilla, who was throwing it to Miss Manning as she lay bent over a chair, her blonde hair hanging down in her face, a look of pure lust in her eyes.

"My Gawd," Bill Warth said. "They've all gone ape."

"I smell a rat," Jack said. He reached for the videophone and dialed Rogers Pekstine. "Raj," he said, "when you fed the juice to Chad and Dink, those two kids on the Coupling Game, how did you get it to them?"

"Is your mate ready to let me throw it to her?" Pekstine asked eagerly. "She promised, you know."

"I think she promised to do it *after* we take over the government," Jack said.

"No," Pekstine protested, "I distinctly remember her promising to let me throw it to her if I got the juice fixed in time for the election."

Jack frowned in exasperation. "Dear," he called, "Rogers Pekstine says you promised to let him throw it to you after he fixed the juice and *not* after the election."

"Oh, dear," Nicky said. "Actually, I don't remember." She walked to the videophone. "Raj," she said. "It really doesn't make any difference to me. If you'd like to come over now we can try a quickie before election time if you like—"

"Oops," Pekstine said, holding his crotch. "There it went. Sonofabitch."

"What I called about, Raj," Jack said, "was this. What, exactly, did you do when you fed your potion to those two kids?"

"I put it into their water coolers," Pekstine said.

"That did it," Jack said. "Well, we'll see you, Raj. You say you're coming over?"

"Try and stop me," Pekstine said.

"I do hope he takes a bath first," Mary said. "He's such a grubby little man. If he takes a bath, I might let him feel how it feels to screw a pregnant lady."

"That would be nice of you, dear," May said. "After all, he's done a lot for us."

"Fellow feelers," Woody Woody said, chuckling as he quickly slipped Pretty Hawksbill's dildo from his bung and threw her down onto the nearest couch, flinging the dildo aside. "It seems, ha ha, that the joke is on us, ha ha. It seems that somehow the exotic, wonderful drug we fed to those two lovely children in there has somehow, ha ha, contaminated the entire water cooling system of the N.F.N."

"God no," Pretty said, fighting feebly, "I'm a virgin!"

"You've got to be kidding," Woody said..

"No! I've never had a man—there!"

"Lady," Woody said, "you have now." He slipped it to her and Pretty, under the stimulation of Pekstine potion, offered only token opposition. He felt her membrane snap. Billions of people felt it, too. Billions of people felt what it felt like to get a cherry and the population meter surged downward a full one-thousandth of a point as some of the audience left the scene forever.

"I mean, ha ha," Woody said, pumping lustily into Pretty's twat with a good-sized tool, "what I mean is, ha, that we're *all* going to be fornicating for a WHOLE WEEK and YOU lucky feelers are going to be experiencing all of it because I've given orders not to let a single orgasm go to waste! I want *you* to feel it all!" He lifted Pretty's legs and drove deeper.

"Yep," Pekstine sighed, stripping away his singlet the moment he entered the door. "I heard in the air-car on the way over. I guess I goofed."

"Not at all," Jack said. "It's wonderful. If they all go at once, the resulting climax is going to be so powerful that not even old Sambo Ghana himself will be able to tear himself away from the Feelie to vote."

"You gonna let me bang you now?" Pekstine asked, standing in front of Nicky with his penis at attention. "Look. I had a shot of the potion and just watch this!" He frigged himself violently. He sighed. "Gawd, it's wonderful."

"If you're ready, I am," Nicky said.

"If you like," Mary offered, "you can screw this old pregnant lady."

"Ohhhhhhh!" Pekstine moaned.

"You're not going to ejaculate?" Jack asked.

"No. It's just that it's so wonderful. She said screw and I didn't come."

"Well, let's not waste that lovely erection," Nicky said, falling backwards with her legs open. "Come on, Raj."

Pekstine gulped, went red, knelt before Nicky's shining

genitals as if before a shrine. "You don't know," he began. "I can't tell you . . ."

"Just show me," Nicky said.

"And then I'll let you know what it's like to fuck an old pregnant lady," Mary said.

Pekstine put his hand on his tool. He put his other hand on Nicky's vagina and opened the lips of it. He inserted his glans penis and waited to see if he would still be afflicted with *ejaculatio ante portas*. "I'm in!" he crowed. "God, I'm actually in."

"Not yet," Nicky said, throwing a double whammy up at him from her practiced loins, taking his dork deep into her with a sliding thrill. "*Now* you're in."

Pekstine pounded. He pumped. He threw his body into it and gasped and moaned and slipped on Nicky's writhing body and climbed back and pumped and pushed and it went on until Nicky was about to pop her cork and she said, "Hey, I just realized that you're going to want to do this for a week and I'm not up to that."

"Ha!" Pekstine gasped. "Hoooo!" He blew out his breath and took one great lunge and pumped his first in-vagina ejaculation and it was so good he fainted.

"I guess all it did for him," Jack said musingly, "was make him normal. He did have a bad case of the preemies."

"He's sort of nice," Mary said. "Hurry up with him, dear, so I can show him how it feels to take on an old pregnant lady."

Pekstine found out. He liked the way it felt to fuggle a pregnant lady and he liked the way it felt to fondle Nicky and May and as the hours went on and the fornicating on the N.F.N. reached a stage of near frenzy, he found out that he liked it just about any way he could get it.

PETER KANTO

Peter Kanto does his writing aboard an antique old lady of an ex-fishing boat called Canto. *The salt air is tough on typewriters and other equipment, but good for Kanto, who slays fish, large and small, when not engaged in producing books, of which* The Coupling Game *was number sixty-five. (Not all under Kanto's name.) Kanto is a bachelor — perhaps, he says, through accident as much as by design. He served in Korea with the 45th Division during Harry Truman's Police Action in the 1950's. His one wound was a punctured pinky caused by stepping on a rusty nail during an M.P. raid on an off-limits juke-joint. He took a degree in Journalism from the University of Oklahoma and worked with newspapers in the South before finding out that a man can buy caulking and paint for an old, cranky boat by using a typewriter for fictional purposes. At thirty-six, Peter thinks life is great, loves his work, plans to write at least twleve more books in the coming twleve months, one of which, no doubt, will be a national block-buster of a best seller. The Canto needs new garboard strakes.*

Conception of the Beast

Benjamin Grimm

*T*he boy stood shivering on the street corner, his numbed hands thrust into the empty pockets of his dungarees, overhead traffic light casting his face now in green, now in yellow, now in red. Myriad flakes of snow swirled to the ground in ever-changing patterns, piling up on lamp-posts, fire hydrants, and car hoods, and the boy held his arms braced against his sides to keep his buttonless cotton jacket from flapping open in the howling, snow-shot wind.

He watched an occasional car travel slowly up the street, tire-chains clanking against the slush-slick asphalt, then turned and stared at sparkling drifts of snow that licked at the darkened fronts of stores across the street. Somewhere, Christmas carols played tinnily on a radio that crackled with static.

Once a fat man dressed in a herringbone topcoat walked briskly past the boy, holding a white poodle on a brown leather leash.

"Mister . . ." the boy called in a soft voice, but the man didn't seem to hear him and continued walking up the block until he disappeared around the corner, his thick blue muffler blowing in the wind.

The boy stared down the block long after the man was gone, his thin legs growing weak and shaky, then for the hundredth time reached into the pockets of jacket and pants, and for the hundredth time, found nothing. He leaned against the traffic light, water seeping through the worn soles of his shoes, and fell into a warm drowsiness as he watched the endless falling of crystalline snow-flakes to the ground. He stood with his back to the wind, long strands of his snow-frosted hair blowing about in the air, droplets of melted snowflake-water streaking his lean, cold-reddened face, and thought of curling up in one of the darkened store doorways that faced him and going to sleep for just a minute or so. Twice, he fell forward as if in a faint, and twice, he caught himself at the last second, clutching the freezing metal of the traffic light's base with one hand, the dented rim of a litter basket with the other.

Then, as the boy's legs were about to buckle beneath him, a light went on in a ground floor apartment across the street. The yellow-flowered shade was pulled almost three-quarters of the way down the window, but through the bottom panes of snow-frosted glass, the boy caught a sudden glimpse of something pink moving quickly across the room. Stumbling across the slippery street, he made for the window like a moth attracted to a flame, icy droplets of melted snowflake-water trickling down the back of his neck.

After a quick glance up and down the street, the boy raised himself on his numbed toes and pressed his face to the window-pane. Inside was a mocha-colored, high-ceilinged bedroom, its floor covered with several thick blue rugs, its walls hung with large abstract canvasses. A circular pink glass fixture glowed brightly in the center of the room's ceiling, and a miniature Christmas tree twinkled with tiny multicolored lights atop a long mahogany desk in the room's far corner. To the right of the desk was a large double bed, its yellow-and-orange striped quilts pulled slightly back to reveal the naked body of a dark-haired man who slept with his hands clasped behind his neck. Beside the bed stood the something pink that the boy had seen from across the street. She was a tall lissome redhead—utterly naked—with large brown-nippled breasts and a flaming orange bush. Her face was the face of a model the boy had once seen in a copy of *Vogue* in a dentist's office: she had large, sleepy-lidded eyes with long, long lashes, a wide, curling-lipped mouth made shiny with pink lipstick, and a smooth-curved nose with slightly flared nostrils. Her red hair was rich and thick and long and wild, with highlights of gold and brown that glowed in the light of the pink glass fixture. Fascinated as the boy was with her face, he was twice as fascinated with the red-lipped treasure nestled between her supple thighs. It looked to the boy like a flower made out of flesh, its petals all shiny and twinkling with dew. He tried to imagine what it would be like in his hand, what it would taste like to his tongue. The vapor of his breath began to cloud the window and he wiped the pane of the glass very gently with the sleeve of his cotton jacket.

When he had gotten the window clear, the girl had her back to him. She was bent over the dark-haired man, her smooth rump pushed out toward the boy, cheeks slightly open to reveal a tiny, hair-licked asshole and the plump juicy crotch beneath. She was trying to wake the man, shaking him by the shoulders and stroking his long wavy hair.

"Wake up, Jimmy," the boy heard her say through the window, her voice very small and distant. "Wake up . . ."

The man tried to turn away but the girl wouldn't let him. She held him by the armpits and kissed his cheeks and nose and chest, her rump wiggling slightly as she worked on him. Then, suddenly, she stepped back and pulled the covers away from the man, her hard-nippled breasts rising and falling as she stared down at the man's naked body. A high-pitched laugh rising in her throat, she pointed toward the gigantic erection that reached upward from the man's fatballed crotch, the purple head of the penis reaching almost to the man's hairy navel.

The man smiled up at the girl and stretched his arms over his head, a long yawn parting his moist lips and closing his wide-set hazel eyes. The girl said something that the boy couldn't hear and the man responded by taking the thick shaft of his penis in his hand and waving it in the girl's face. He made a funny face, his eyes crinkling slightly, tip of his tongue sticking out between his large white teeth. The girl laughed, her breasts and buttocks shaking, and moved closer to the man. The boy could see the magnificent sloping profile of her cunt as she knelt on the bed beside the man's head. She parted the lips of her pussy with two fingers and thrust the red-haired treasure in the man's face. The man leaned forward and licked the girl's rising clitoris with his tongue, then slipped a hand behind her and squeezed her left rump-cheek, his fingers disappearing into the soft dark crack of her ass. The girl let him squeeze her for a time, rubbing her juicy cunt against his nose and cheeks and mouth, then got into bed with him, throwing the covers to the floor. She played with his cock for a few minutes, beating it against his hairy belly while he probed her widening hole with two and three fingers at a time; then she sat up in bed and changed her position, placing her head at the man's thighs, her cunt at his face. Parting her thighs, she forced her cunt tightly against the man's mouth, at the same time tickling the twitching head of his cock with the tip of her tongue. She made tiny circles around the juice-leaking hole of the man's penis, then coated the entire head with her saliva, then the shaft, then his testicles, then worked around to the top and bit gently into the root, sliding her teeth up and down the length of the huge prick. Smiling, she hovered over the penis for a time, watching the little drops of clear fluid trickle down the head and shaft and bead in the man's thick pubic hair, finally opening her mouth wide and taking the penis deep into her throat, twirling it with her hand as the man lapped slowly at the double crease of her buttocks and cunt.

The boy watched with bated breath as the couple ate each other. His smooth cock pulled the thin fabric of his jeans four inches away from his leg, the head beating violently upward, threatening to tear through the material altogether and rise proudly into the snow-filled night air. He barely noticed the cold, so absorbed was he in the licking and sucking and squeezing of the naked couple in the mocha-colored room. Moaning, he reached his hand into his pants and pulled on his burning prick as he watched the girl take the length of the man's cock into her throat and turn her head in slow circles, her eyes smiling into the man's, her hands spreading the cheeks of his ass, her long fingers searching for his asshole.

Suddenly, the girl sat up, her flame-red cunt glistening with the man's saliva. The man reached forward and shoved his thumb into the girl's cunt, but she pushed him away and teased his swollen prick with the tips of her long toes. The man said something that the boy couldn't hear and the girl made a coquettish face at him, her tongue running along her lower lip, orange-red tresses cascading along her pale shoulders. Suddenly, she climbed over the man, straddling his hips with her thighs. She grabbed his bulging prick in both hands and ran it back and forth in the hot pudding of her slit, then reached behind her to tickle the man between his legs. The man grabbed the girl by the waist and forced her onto the head of his cock, his hands sliding down on her buttocks, his tongue reaching for her swinging tits.

The boy took his prick completely out of his pants as he watched the man knead the girl's grinding ass, pulling the cheeks of her rump open and closed, as he forced her downward on the thick-veined shaft of his organ. His nose pressed to the glass, the boy wrenched his penis wildly up and down with his right hand while squeezing his small hairless testicles with his left. His buttocks grinding together, he watched the girl slide all the way up and down on the man's long penis, her wet red crotchhairs tickling his ass-squashed balls as she bent forward and shook her heavy tits in his face.

Suddenly, the boy dropped his hand from his penis as the door to the high-ceilinged bedroom swung open. He was afraid, for some strange reason, that he was about to be discovered. It was like the times in his mother's house when he would stroke himself under the covers of his bed; always listening for his mother's footsteps, always frightened that she would discover the flaky stains on the sheets. His lips trembling, the boy peered at the opening door with wide eyes, then let out a long sigh of relief as a slender blonde girl wearing a blue terry bathrobe entered the room, a broad smile coming to her lips as she noticed the naked couple in the bed. Her face was very fresh and bright, her blue eyes sparkling with naughtiness, her cheeks tinged with pink. There was a tomboyish quality to her hands-on-hips pose as she watched the couple grind against each other, the wavy-haired man squeezing the redhead's nipples between his knuckles, the redhead pulling the man's cock in wide, delirious circles in the depths of her contracting tunnel. They turned toward the blonde girl as they fucked, dreamy smiles on their faces.

"You miserable fuckers!" the boy heard the blonde girl say.

"You never let me know when something's going on . . ." The man said something to her and the girl pulled off her bathrobe. "You bet your ass I will," she said, her voice tiny through the glass.

Naked, she was even more beautiful than the redhead. Her body was at once plump and firm, the cheeks of her ass very prominent, the nipples of her peach-sized breasts pink and hard. Her fantastic gold-brown fleece spread upward toward her deep navel and fitted the insides of her marble-smooth thighs like a woolen glove. Her belly was round and ripe and white, sloping downward into the plump pink-clefted bulge of her cunt. It looked like a perfectly-molded bowl with a golden beard as the girl arched her back to drop her blue robe to the floor.

"You bet your sweet ass I will," the girl said again, walking quickly toward the bed.

She climbed up between the couple's outstretched thighs and licked the dark-haired man's prick as the redhead squirmed up and down on it, reaching behind herself to stroke the blonde girl's neck. Squeezing the man's full sac, the blonde licked up and down from his buried shaft to the redhead's quivering pussy-lips and upthrust asshole, pausing to work her tongue into the widening cunt and lick the base of the man's penis as it swirled in the vestibule of the redhead's vagina.

Again, the boy brought his hand to his prick as he watched the blonde girl stand up on the bed and straddle the man's head with her feet. Hands on her hips, she knelt lower and lower, her legs bent at the knee, her open-cheeked ass thrust out toward the boy's face. Then, suddenly, she squatted over the man's mouth, her hands pulling at his ears, and forced him to run his lips up and down the thick-jellied meat of her cunt. One hand on the redhead's ass, the other on the blonde's, the man plunged his tongue into the golden pussy above him, swirling it deeper and deeper into the unfolding flesh as the redhead squeezed his prick in the depths of her slow-rolling belly. Leaning forward, the redhead placed her hands on the blonde's wiggling ass cheeks, pulled them wide apart, and tongued the rim of the girl's hair-fringed asshole, her nose buried in the cleft of the girl's grinding buttocks.

The boy wondered what it would feel like to have somebody's tongue in his asshole. Beating his prick he reached behind himself with his left hand and slid his fingers eagerly down the crack of his smooth hairless ass. Timidly he slipped his little finger into the burning warmth of his asshole, barely noticing the droplet of icy water that streaked his cheeks and neck, then began to stir the narrow hole to the same spasmodic rhythm with which he jerked his penis.

Inside, the blonde girl said something that the boy couldn't hear and both girls climbed off the man and sat at the foot of the bed. Then the man got up—he was very tall and nicely-built, with broad shoulders and taut-muscled buttocks—and walked along the side of the bed to where the girls sat, his prick pointing straight up at the pink glass fixture that hung from the ceiling. Smiling at the man, both girls crouched forward on their hands and knees, their hips touching, their rumps and pussies thrust backwards. The boy stared wide-eyed at the row of four smooth ass-cheeks that wiggled at his face.

The man got behind the blonde girl and slipped his prick inch-by-inch into her open pussy, then pulled it out, utterly covered with her thick foam, and plunged it into the redhead's cunt. The redhead closed her cunt-lips tightly around the cock and squeezed it in her hole for a time, then released it as the blonde girl balanced her weight on her head and parted the cheeks of her ass, pointing with her long forefinger toward her asshole. The man pulled out of the redhead's cunt — the boy heard a loud gurgling sound as the head escaped the quivering lips—and ground his buttocks together in an effort to force his way into the blonde's big-rimmed asshole. Holding the blonde by the hips, he eased himself into her asshole and humped her jerkily for a time, then pulled out of her asshole and buried himself in her cunt, then pulled out of her cunt and buried himself in the redhead's asshole, then pulled out of the redhead's asshole and buried himself in her cunt.

As the man went from asshole to cunt and cunt to asshole, the girls tongue-kissed each other and toyed with each other's large swinging breasts, the redhead occasionally reaching between her legs to tickle the man's rump-slapping balls as he fucked her asshole and stroked her belly, the blonde sometimes squeezing her ass-cheeks closed around the man's prick and holding him captive in the depth of her intestines.

Then, as the boy pumped himself wildly and switched from windowpane to windowpane when the glass went cloudy with his breath, the dark-haired man began to jerk wildly in the blonde girl's squirming cunt. He belted frantically back and forth, his buttocks popping outward, then grinding in, his hands pulling violently on the cheeks of her ass so that the gold-haired rim of her asshole was pulled wide apart. The redhead leaped off the bed and knelt behind the man, sucking hotly on his testicles and tickling his asshole with her tongue as he thrust powerfully in and out of the blonde girl's cunt.

Then, slowly, the naked threesome came to a halt, the blonde girl collapsing on the bed, the man falling on top of her, his organ still buried in her pussy. The redhead rose slowly to her feet, turned her back to the couple, and sat down at the edge of the bed, two fingers working her pussy as she rubbed her ass against the blonde girl's foot. Then, bending forward to angle a third finger into her cunt, she gave a sudden start, her eyes coming to rest on the water-streaked face of the boy at the window.

The boy froze as the girl held him with her eyes, prick shrivelling in his hand, little finger slipping slowly out of his asshole. The girl got up and walked toward the window, the blonde girl following behind her. The boy's heart pumped wildly in his chest. He looked quickly up and down the snow-covered street, trying desperately to will his legs to move, conjuring images in his mind of the man's fist crashing into his mouth, of the police arriving in three blaring squad cars and dragging him into the station house by the heels.

The redhead smiled at him through the frosted windowpane, her long brown nipples crushed against the glass. The boy stared wide-eyed at the large-breasted girl, stark bewilderment written across his face. Smiling, the girl beckoned to him. The boy questioned her with his eyes. The girl rose to show him her glistening flame-red cunt, then bent again, breasts melting the frost on the window, and made a curving gesture with her right hand. It took the boy some time to comprehend what she was trying to tell him, but then he turned in the direction that she indicated and saw a battered wooden door at the side of the building. He nodded eagerly to the girl, stuffing his lengthening prick back into his pants, and the girl stood up again to show him her cunt. The blonde came to the window too, turned her back to the boy, and flattened the cheeks of her ass against the window, thick foam seeping from her

cunt and dripping down the glass. Then both girls smiled through
the window and the redhead blew the boy a kiss. Again, the boy
nodded eagerly, then turned and ran to the wooden door, his feet
slipping and sliding in the fresh-fallen snow.

Opening the high, creaking door, the boy found himself in a
darkened corridor. Snowflakes melted in his hair as he peered into
the musty gloom of the place, his eyes searching the darkness for an
apartment door or a stairway. Closing the wooden door behind him,
he started slowly down the corridor, feeling along the dusty walls
for a molding of some sort in the post of a bannister. He walked for
endless minutes along the hallway's creaking floor, his prick
throbbing in his pants, his hands touching the walls on either side of
him. Then, just as he thought the hallway would never end, he saw
a tall narrow door before him, a little green bulb glowing dimly
above it.

Smiling, he walked quickly toward it, searched briefly for a
doorbell, then knocked three times on the center of the door, his
prick threatening any second to burst through the thin fabric of his
jeans. He waited several minutes, listening at the door for the
approach of one of the girls, then tried the knob, opened the door,
and stepped out onto a snow-covered, wind-blown street, the door
slamming shut behind him. He turned immediately and tried to
open the door. A heavy sigh escaped his lips when he found it
locked. He stepped further out into the street and scanned the
grimy building for another entrance.

As the boy turned desperately from left to right to left, a
sleek, slow-moving car approached the corner on which he stood,
flakes of snow swirling madly in the bright beams of its headlights.
It was a strange car, longer and lower than those customarily seen
on city streets, its green body polished to a radiant sheen, the
meticulous detailing of its grill and hood-piece bespeaking earlier
times and other places. The boy watched the car through heavy
eyelids, a dizziness born of hunger, fatigue, and confusion seeping
through his brain. He stared dumbly at the ornamental figure of a
bare-breasted woman atop the car's shiny hood, her brass arms
uplifted to the heavens, legs emerging from a half-globe base. He
braced himself against a litter basket as the car came to a halt beside
him.

The driver of the car slid over to the side of the seat and rolled down the window. His face was very long and pale and he wore a strange pointed hat on his head.

"A runaway, is it?" the man said. His narrowed eyes focussed on the boy's chest.

Suddenly frightened, the boy turned to run, peculiar fantasies filling his mind.

"Wait," the man said.

Compelled by something in the man's voice, the boy halted and turned slowly toward the green car.

"You are cold, is it not?" the man said. "And hungry? And tired, isn't it?"

Across the street, a crumpled sheet of newspaper blew high in the air and flattened against the wall of a grimy apartment building.

"Luck . . . turned a little bad . . ." the boy said, mucous freezing in his nose, making it difficult for him to talk.

"Yes," the man said. "Yes, I see. It is a miserable night." He ran his long-nailed forefinger over a deep crease at the side of his mouth. "Very cold tonight," he said. "I can take you where it is warm . . . where there is food and a comfortable bed . . ."

The boy stared at the man's pointed hat, his hands clenched tightly in his pockets.

"I . . . I don't want you to think . . ."

"Yes?" the man said, one thin eyebrow arched.

"I'm not a queer," the boy said suddenly, turning away and staring at the spiralling snowflakes bathed in the red glow of the traffic light.

"No, no," the man said. "I speak of nothing like that." He turned his thin lips into a smile, creases deepening at the sides of his mouth. "My mistress is a sculptress. She will merely carve your likeness out of stone. And, in return, you will be given food, shelter for the night . . . perhaps a small sum of money. You have only to pose for her."

The boy stared down at the snow-frosted tops of his shoes and listened to the distant strains of Christmas carols.

"Well?" the man said. "What do you say? Do you still not trust me? I tell you, you have only to pose . . . You will be given food, money perhaps . . ."

He peered closely at the boy, but the boy would not look up at him.

"Bah," the man said suddenly. "I am wasting my time. Good-night to you . . ."

"Wait," the boy said as the man started to roll up the window.

"Yes?" the man said, pausing.

"I only have to pose?"

"That is all," the man said.

"You aren't . . .?"

"I have no interest in your precious young body," the man said.

"All right," the boy said.

"Good, good," the man said, sliding into the driver's seat and beckoning toward the back door. "Come. Get in the car . . ."

The boy got into the back seat and slammed the door closed behind him. The flakes of snow that clung to his hair and jacket and shoes began to melt in the dry warmth of the car and droplets of icy water ran steadily down the dark leather of the seat.

The man turned to the boy and offered him a small flask of brandy.

"Drink," the man said as he released the brake and shifted into first gear. "It will warm you. It is such a miserable night . . ."

The boy took the flask and opened it, the strong smell of the brandy making him lightheaded. He took a small sip and then another, then sat back in the seat and felt the liquor's heat tingle through his belly and chest. Cradling the flask in his lap, he stared out the window at bundled-up people in the street who walked with their heads bent, holding their hats in place with gloved hands.

"How did you know I was a runaway?" the boy said after a time, wiping icy droplets from his smooth cheeks.

"I knew, I knew," the man said. "We are all runaways, isn't it?"

"What do you mean?" the boy said after a pause.

"It's hard to explain," the man said. "It would be foolish for you to think about it. Think of the food that will soon fill your belly . . . warm, rich food . . ."

The snow swirled more and more madly as the car travelled slowly through the slushy heart of the city. The boy took several more sips of brandy and stared fascinated at the flashing lights of movie marquees that seemed to stretch endlessly into the distance.

The man watched the boy as he stopped the car at a light, his eyes intense in the rear-view mirror.

"You are attracted?" the man said. "To the lights?"

"I haven't gone to the movies for a long time," the boy said.

"It is nothing, the cinema,", the man said. "Sham, nothing, You aren't missing anything. It is nothing to miss."

"I don't know . . ." the boy said.

"A waste of time, all of it," the man said. "Cinema . . . art . . . There are more important things . . ."

The man drove silently through the theatre district, the boy staring from his odd hat to the figurine on the hood of the car.

"Where are we going?" the boy said after a time.

"To the river," the man said. "My mistress lives by the river."

The man drove on for upwards of half an hour, then parked the car on a lonely, windswept street and motioned for the boy to follow him. As they walked under the dim yellow light of a lamp-post, the boy noticed that the man wore nothing but a thin, gown-like garment, its sleeves bloused, its collar long.

"Aren't you cold?" the boy said.

"Cold?" the man said, fixing the boy with his narrow eyes.

"You're not wearing a coat."

"No, I don't wear a coat," the man said.

"You dress so strangely," the boy said. "I never saw a hat like that . . ."

"My mistress is very . . . eccentric. I dress as she pleases . . ."

The man led the boy to the poorly-lit lobby of an apartment building, holding the door open for him to enter. The snow around the entrance to the building was high and fresh, unmarked by human footprints. The boy hesitated for a second, then stepped across the threshold as fierce winds blew in from the river and sliced painfully through his thin cotton jacket.

The lobby of the building was completely bare, lit by a single antique lamp that hung over the entrance to the elevator. From somewhere in the building the boy thought he heard the sound of very soft singing, but he couldn't be sure. It might have only been the wind, or perhaps the high whine of a child.

"This way," the man said, leading the boy toward the elevator.

The boy followed him, trailing melting clumps of snow across the worn carpet of the lobby's floor, then entered the elevator as the man pulled back the heavy wooden door and iron grating.

"My mistress is a strange woman," the man said as the elevator began its rattling ascent. "If aught should seem amiss to you, remember that she is an artist . . . an eccentric. Her . . . habits . . . are somewhat unusual . . ."

The boy took off his jacket and straightened the ragged sleeves of his navy blue turtleneck sweater, then patted down his long tangled hair.

"Do you think I'll do?" the boy said, staring down at the patched knees of his jeans. "Do I look all right to pose?"

"You'll do perfectly," the man said, working the controls of the elevator with his right hand. "You will have something to eat, a bath perhaps, and then you will be perfect . . . quite perfect . . ."

The man brought the elevator to an effortless halt, pulled back the grating, and thrust open the door.

"Remember," he said. "She is an unusual woman. You must forgive her eccentricity. Her purposes are very . . . grand . . ."

The man led the boy into a long anteroom lit by thick, scented candles. The room was windowless; each of its walls was covered with heavy, deep folded drapery, and it made the boy think of strange fairy stories his mother had told him as a child.

"Wait here," the man said to the boy as he walked through a curtained archway and disappeared into the darkened interior of the apartment.

The boy stood nervously in the anteroom, straining his ears for the slightest whisper. He stared continually at the door to the elevator, wondering how it was that the shaft had led directly into the apartment, and debating whether or not he should leave.

Suddenly, the boy was overwhelmed by an utterly spontaneous panic. A pungent smell filled the room. Instinctively, he wheeled around and found himself face-to-face with a tall, black-haired woman who wore a sea-green robe that trailed to the floor. She stood half in the room and half out, the archway's curtains falling against her narrow shoulders. She seemed almost a portrait, so still was her pose, so perfect her angular features. The sight of her made the boy feel very queer, filling him at once with a warm numbness and an icy dread. He tried to speak but could not find words and so merely gawked at the tall woman, his lower lip trembling slightly.

The woman remained motionless beneath the archway, her

large, widely-set eyes focussed on a point somewhere over the boy's head, her arms folded so that her hands—which the boy imagined to be very long and delicate—were hidden in the drooping folds of her long-sleeved robe. Beneath the trailing hem of the robe, just the jewelled tip of the woman's slippered foot was visible. The silence in the room became unbearable. The woman seemed hardly to breathe.

"You do *want* to pose for me, don't you?" the woman said finally, as if continuing a long conversation. "It is important. Do you *wish* to help me?"

"Yes," the boy said softly, somehow afraid of answering otherwise.

"Say it," the woman said. "Say, 'I want to help you . . .' "

The boy hesitated, dark fantasies lurking at the edge of his mind.

"Say it," the woman repeated.

"I . . . want to help . . . you," the boy said, feeling a tremendous relief as soon as the words had been spoken.

"Yes," the woman said, seeming to relax with a tiny exhalation of breath. "You shall help me." She stepped forward into the anteroom, a gracious smile on her full lips. "My . . . servant . . . tells me that you are hungry." She took the boy in with a quick, sweeping glance. "Yes, you must eat . . . and you must bathe and change clothes. Yes . . . you are a handsome boy," she said, touching his cheek with her right hand, her left hand hidden in the folds of her robe.

The boy's cheek tingled at the woman's touch. The smell of her dark perfume evoked in the boy's mind pictures of strange, Old Testament cities that had been told of in the Sunday School he had attended as a child.

"Come, Robin," the woman said, taking him by the hand and pulling him toward the archway that led to the apartment's interior. He followed, feeling terribly queer, then stopped suddenly, chills running down his spine.

"How did you know my name?" the boy said.

"Your name?" the woman said in a melodious voice. "You told it to me. Don't you remember? My name is Robin, you said."

The boy stared at her, doubting his own memory.

"And my name is Nama," the woman said. "Do you recall my

telling it to you?"

The boy thought for a minute, his eyes half-closed. The name, though strange, did sound familiar to him. Yes, he decided, perhaps they had exchanged names. He had been terribly nervous before . . .

"Come," the woman said. "You will feel better after you have eaten . . ."

The boy followed Nama through the curtained archway and into a room which was utterly without light. He became instantly frightened and turned in the direction of the anteroom but was unable to make out so much as the outline of the archway.

"I can't see," the boy cried suddenly. "I can't see . . ."

From far ahead came the voice of the woman.

"Don't you see the door ahead?" she said.

"No!" the boy cried. "I can't see . . ."

"Shhh," the woman said. "The door. See the door . . ."

The boy peered frantically into the darkness.

"No . . . I . . ." He fell silent for a moment. "Yes," he said. "I can see the door."

"Follow," said Nama.

The boy followed, his eyes focussed on a narrow door which never quite convinced him of its reality. The door was quite tiny in the distance, and as the boy walked faster and faster, wishing to gain the door as quickly as possible, it seemed to grow smaller and smaller. Then, suddenly, the door disappeared.

"What happened?" the boy said in a quavering voice. "The door . . ."

"Can you smell the food?" said Nama. Her voice came from behind the boy.

"The food?" the boy said.

"Smell," said Nama. "Smell the food."

Suddenly the boy became conscious of hot aromas rising lightly in the air. He approached dizziness, so welcome were the smells that wafted towards him, teasing his dilated nostrils and causing saliva to flow in his mouth.

"Do you smell it?" said the woman.

"Yes," said the boy.

"You feel hunger?"

"Yes . . ."

"Then eat, little Robin . . ."

With a small rustle, two curtains were parted, and the boy found himself temporarily blinded by the flickering light of many tall candles. Blinking his eyes, he entered a small rectangular room in the middle of which was a table heaped with silver platters full of steaming meats and sauces, thickly-buttered vegetables, and various delicacies with which the boy was unfamiliar. He peered curiously at the richly-colored Persian rugs that hung from each of the room's walls.

"Sit," said the woman, indicating a puffy green armchair that stood at the head of the table. "Eat . . ."

The boy seated himself as the woman moved silently to the far end of the room and stood facing the boy, her right hand resting delicately on the edge of the table, her left hand still concealed in the loose folds of her robe.

"Forgive my fondness for candlelight," the woman said softly, "I detest electric lighting . . ."

"I don't mind," the boy said, heaping his plate with slices of meat and spoonfuls of vegetables.

He began to eat, cutting meat with knife and fork, but was quickly interrupted by the woman.

"You are hungry," she said. *"Eat!"* She made a gesture with her right hand as of lifting food to her mouth and stuffing it in.

The boy lifted a dripping slice of meat to his mouth and stared questioningly at the woman.

"Yes," she said. "Yes. Eat . . ."

The boy gobbled up the slice of meat and reached for another.

The woman threw back her head and laughed, her bare throat arched, the prominence of her cheekbones accentuated by the light of the waxing candle-flames. His hunger let loose by the woman's coaxing, the boy crammed slice after slice of steaming meat into his mouth, thick gravy dripping down the front of his blue sweater, staining the lap of his dungarees. He lifted handfuls of butter-slippery vegetables to his mouth, barely noticing the beans and stalks that dropped to the floor.

"Drink," the woman ordered, uncorking a bottle of dark wine.

The boy guzzled the wine straight from the bottle, grunting slightly as it ran over his smooth, food-stained chin. The woman opened three more bottles and placed them before him, her left hand continually wrapped in her green robe.

The boy devoured his food madly, constantly encouraged by the woman's high laughter, to stuff greater quantities of meat and bread and vegetables into his mouth. Fianally, after consuming almost half of the food on the table and draining several bottles of wine, the boy sat back in his green armchair, utterly gorged, and folded his hands over his distended belly.

"Can you be satisfied so soon?" the woman said. "You must have more to eat . . ."

The boy gestured a polite refusal, but the woman reached over his shoulder and lifted a piece of meat to his mouth.

"Come," she said. "Nama will feed you . . ."

Dutifully, the boy opened his mouth and swallowed the meat, Nama stroking his lips with her fingertips while he chewed.

"More," she said, "more . . ." lifting a second piece of meat to his lips.

His belly beginning to pain him, the boy resisted Nama's feeding, turning his face away from the slice of meat that she held out to him.

"Life is short," she said abruptly. "Eat." Then, the song returning to her voice: "Eat just this last piece, little Robin. You must have a little Cupid's belly if you are to pose for me."

She bent forward and reached under the boy's sweater, rubbing his round, hairless belly with extended fingers.

Then, as Robin finished the last piece of meat, she rose to her full height, elaborate black ringlets of hair shining in the candle-light, and gestured with her right hand toward a dark-curtained doorway.

"Come," she said. "You must bathe."

The boy stood up, a stifled belch issuing from his lips, and followed the woman through the doorway into a bare, candlelit hall. At the end of the hall was a bathroom, its floor made of dimly-sparkling mica, a huge, circular tub sunk into its center. The room was lit by a single oil lamp, small urns of incense burning at either of its sides, and it gave the boy the feeling of being underground.

"Remove your clothing," the woman said, seating herself in a lotus position at the edge of the tub.

The boy hesitated, staring down at his feet, and the woman made a small laugh in her throat.

"Come," she said softly. "Remove your clothing. Am I not to see this body that I am to sculpt?

"The water is warm," she said, "and perfumed with scents that can no longer be purchased . . ."

With automatic gestures, the boy removed his clothing, dropping garments to the floor and finally standing naked before the sitting woman. His body was very white and smooth, his legs and arms long and supple; his penis shrivelled under the woman's strong gaze.

The woman gave voice to a song-like laugh, then closed her eyes and hunched her shoulders sensually.

"You have never made love, have you?" she said, her eyes still closed, right hand held to her chest.

The boy stuttered for a moment, then started to say that he had.

"The truth!" the woman said suddenly. "It is important . . ."

The boy was silent for a time.

"No," he said finally, relaxing somewhat. "I've . . . never . . . had a girl . . ."

"Come . . . bathe . . ." the woman said.

The boy walked slowly forward, controlling with an effort his impulsive attempts to conceal his nudity, then lowered himself into the steaming tub.

"Do you find the water warm enough?" the woman asked. "Is the bath not relaxing?"

"Yes," the boy said, smiling, his eyes closed lazily. "It's . . . really . . . beautiful . . ." He wondered absentmindedly if it was still snowing outside.

"And do you find the decorations to your liking?"

The boy opened his eyes and stared questioningly at the woman. She smiled and gestured toward the walls and the boy found himself staring at a procession of bas-reliefs that he had not noticed before. Each of the figures was engaged in some high-stylized attitude of love-making, and as the boy's eyes darted from figure to figure, his heartbeat became rapid and a hot weakness came over his body. "Did you . . . make these?" he asked of the woman, his voice low and breathless.

"They are . . . my conceptions," the woman said. "Do you like them?"

"I've never seen anything like this," the boy said, casting his glance back and forth along the tableau as if afraid to miss some concealed depiction of delight.

"If you stare at them long enough," the woman said, "they will appear to move. Or so I am told . . ."

As the woman spoke, each of the sculpted figures seemed to commence a subtle churning motion, stiff phalli moving in and out of sucking vaginas and O-shaped mouths, tiny tongues lapping at distended vaginal and anal openings, delicately-crafted hands caressing grinding buttocks and bouncing breasts.

The woman laughed at the boy's open-mouthed fascination.

"It is only an illusion," she said softly, "created by the darkness of the room and the flickering of the lamp's flame. It quickly ceases to fool the mind . . ."

Gradually, the writhing figures came to a halt and stood frozen in their previous attitudes. The boy stared at the woman, eyes wide.

"You see?" the woman said. "Only an illusion . . ."

The boy closed his eyes and relaxed in the tub, warm fantasies filling his mind. He saw himself making love to the dark-haired woman, captivating her with his youthful strength and eagerness. She would fall in love with him, this strange, laughing woman, and he would have her forever in his power. She would make thousands of magnificent statues, and she would never allow him to leave her side.

The woman's soft laughter interrupted the boy's reverie.

"You have strange dreams?" she said.

The boy regarded her suspiciously.

"Oh," she said, as if to soothe him, "It's all necessary . . . all quite necessary. If not for your dreams, how might you find yourself here?" She gestured around her, then laughed again at the boy's apparent confusion. "Come," she said, handing the boy a bar of lavender-colored soap, "Soap yourself. It is very special soap made with the rarest of oils and perfumes. You will find it most refreshing." She rose slowly to her feet, wide-set eyes studiously taking in the boy's nudity. "Then," she said, "when you have dried yourself, you will come through this doorway . . ." She gestured to a second doorway leading out of the bathroom. " . . . and we will begin . . ." She turned and walked from the room through the exit which she had just indicated, the tallness of her body seeming unreal to the boy from his vantage-point in the sunken tub.

The boy slid the lavender soap over his body, his skin tingling with a warm sensitivity. When he stepped from the tub, he smelled as does a garden at dawn, and he delighted both in the smell and sight of his naked body. He ran his hands along his water-slippery thighs and buttocks and found his flesh deliciously smooth and springy, inviting him to lavish further narcissistic caresses on his legs and arms and belly. Then, eager to display himself before the woman, he dried his body with a thick green towel which he found beside the tub. Then, with a last downward glance, he left the room, pleased with the relaxed plumpness of his penis.

He walked through a small hallway till he came to a glass door with translucent green panes through which passed hazy refractions of bright, leaping flame. The boy lifted his hand to knock, picturing the woman lying naked on a soft bed, her legs spread invitingly, then withdrew his hand as the door swung open at his touch. He peered into an expansive room with a bare wooden floor, decorated with huge circular charts on which were imprinted strange symbols and drawings of men and women with the heads of wild beasts. In the center of the room was a circular platform lit by three bright torches, and at a distance of some four yards from the platform stood the dark-haired woman, her right hand resting lightly on a small wooden pedestal on which had been placed a quantity of baked clay, its partially-molded proportions corresponding vaguely to the outline of the human form.

"Come in," said the woman, her back to the boy. "All is ready."

The boy entered the room rather forcefully, holding his head erect, proud of the light slap of penis against thighs as he walked. He hoped that the woman would notice and praise his beauty.

"Stand in the center of the platform," the woman said flatly, her head bent slightly forward so that only the black ringlets of her hair were visible to the boy.

The boy advanced to the platform and stood between the three crackling torches, his eyes wandering to the strange charts that hung on the walls.

"Open your legs a bit," the woman said, regarding the boy with her head tilted to one side. "And raise your chin . . . there . . . perfect . . . And fold your arms across your chest . . ."

The boy complied eagerly, flexing his small muscles as much as possible and casting long glances at the woman's bare throat and thinly-veiled breasts. He fancied that he could see the tips of her nipples through the green fabric of her robe.

"You must remain in this pose," the woman said softly, withdrawing a thin, silvery tool from the folds of her robe and holding it close to the mound of dried clay that stood upon the table.

The woman worked with incredible speed, the movements of her hand too quick for the boy to follow. Often, she laughed as she worked, chips of clay flying in the air, and occasionally, she paused to close her eyes and rest her hand against her chest. Soon, the boy began to sweat from the heat of the torches around him, his body glistening with a thousand tiny droplets of perspiration. The smell of the boy's sweat, mingled with the lingering perfume of the lavender soap he had washed with, seemed to delight the woman, and time and again she came close to the boy, inhaled deeply, and laughed, her head thrown back, breasts shaking beneath her robe.

She worked with greater and greater speed, the increased force of her effort pleasing the boy, as he connected it with the force of her passion for him. He watched the woman's shadow-stroked body with ever-increasing restlessness, fantasies multiplying in his mind.

Then, less than an hour after she had begun, the woman was finished. She stepped slowly out of the shadows, her liquid eyes reflecting the crackling flame of the torches, and faced the boy, a half-smile playing across her lips.

The boy stood tensed upon the platform, droplets of sweat rolling freely down his thighs. He wondered if he should run panting from the platform and take the woman in his arms or if he should wait for some inviting gesture on her part. He felt his penis began to twitch as it did in the mornings when he woke, and he strained to think of unpleasant things—he thought, for instance, of his. grandmother's funeral, and of the time his father was in the hospital—to keep from betraying his eagerness to the woman.

"Would you like to see the statue I have made of you?" the woman said, amused smile still turning the corners of her mouth. "Your likeness in clay?"

The boy nodded. Perhaps, he thought, he would pretend to

study the statue, then grab the woman by the waist when she came close to him.

"Come," the woman said. "Look . . ."

The boy descended from the platform and approached the statue's pedestal. He was intoxicated with his own nakedness and with the closeness of the woman. He stopped suddenly, about two feet from the pedestal, and stared dumbstruck at the masterpiece that rested upon it. The statue was an exact replica of himself, its incredibly lifelike detailing accurate down to the last almost-throbbing vein, to the last twisting strand of hair.

"Are you pleased?" the woman said, drawing close and staring at the boy's smooth profile.

"It's . . . I don't know . . . It's . . ."

"It is you," the woman said, resting her right hand on the top of the pedestal, keeping her left carefully hidden in the trailing folds of her robe.

"Me . . ." the boy said.

"It is almost as if it had some of your life in it," the woman said. "As if it could *feel* . . ."

She brought her hand close to the clay figure and ran her long, sharp-nailed forefinger down the statue's spine all the way to the backs of the thighs.

The boy shuddered, a delicious warmth coming over him, and contracted his rosy buttocks as if trying to squeeze an invisible finger between them. The woman laughed.

"Do you feel what the statue feels?" she said. "Can it be?"

The boy stared wide-eyed at her, sudden fear vying with his rising heat.

"Do you feel this?" the woman said, running her forefinger down the statue's belly to the tip of its limp penis.

Slowly, the boy's penis began to rise in the air, a tiny droplet of clear liquid forming at the tip of its pink head, green veins standing out like cord along its shaft.

"You see?" the woman said, staring down at the boy's upthrust penis. "What a long organ!" she laughed. "For so young a boy . . . May I touch it?"

The boy nodded, his hands trembling at his sides.

The woman held the boy's penis in her hand as she would a small animal, stroking it and pulling its expanding head to a wide circle, constantly finding delight in its twitching response to her caresses. The boy moaned softly with each new exploration of the woman's cool hand, his head tilted to the side, his eyes gone hazy.

"Come," the woman said suddenly.

Holding the boy tightly by his stiff penis, she walked from the area of the pedestal toward a large couch that stood in one of the room's shadowy corners, a green and yellow Oriental rug spread beneath it.

"Sit," the woman said to the boy, twisting his penis painfully and forcing him onto the couch, her lips turned into a cruel smile. Left hand held behind her back, she ran the fingers of her right slowly down the boy's pulsing prick, finally dropping her hand to his warm crotch and squeezing his balls until he moaned with pain. Releasing his testicles, the woman closed the boy's eyes with her fingertips and stepped several paces back from him, the scrape of her bare feet against the elaborately-patterned green-yellow rug tickling his ears as he sat open-legged on the couch, the swelling head of his penis beating against his lean, hairless belly, droplets of sweat rolling from the light-colored floss that graced the hollows of his underarms. His eyes shut tightly, he gave a slight start at the maddening rustle of the woman's robe as it was dropped to the floor. He tried to imagine all the things he would do to her, all the different ways he would make love to her. In his mind's eye, he went over the different positions he had seen in the bathroom and the things he had seen earlier through the snow-frosted window of the grimy apartment building. As he pictured the various postures, pondering the exact techniques of each, a gnawing fear came into his mind and he found himself praying that the woman wouldn't hurt him . . .

"Open your eyes," he heard the woman say, her voice high and liquid, like the song of a mermaid.

His lean face gone tense with anxiety, the boy complied with the whispered command and almost fainted with the sight of the woman's naked beauty. She stood like a queen before him, her supple thighs parted to reveal the blackhaired mystery between them, left leg bent at the knee, small deep-navelled belly thrust forward. Her breasts seemed to the boy like apples, their long nipple-stems miraculously taut and finely-bumped, their smooth upcurved undersides casting her ribcage in deep shadow. Impulsively, the boy reached forward to squeeze the woman's firm breasts, but she stepped quickly backward, amusement shining in her eyes, her right hand indicating the red-lipped apex of her curling black triangle.

The woman seemed a dream to the boy, the smoothly-curving outlines of her naked body glowing orange in the distant light of the torches; her cheeks seemed hollow for the shadows that caressed them, her large, wide-set eyes as black and shiny as the finest onyx. He peered intently at her belly, his eyes traveling up and down the graceful slope of her moist-haired mound, the head of his prick turning purple with the hot flow of blood that rushed to it. He wondered if he should jump up and grab her, squeeze her smooth ass-cheeks in his hands, force her down on the floor. . .

The woman sat down beside the boy and opened her thighs, bending her legs at the knee so as to push her cunt outward, her long toes curling over the edge of the couch's velvet-upholstered cushion. She put her slender arm around the boy's shoulder and smiled sweetly at him, rhythmically raising and lowering her buttocks so as to open and close the mouth of her cunt. She was waiting for him to take her . . . waiting for him . . . waiting . . . She would be his slave . . .

The boy lurched suddenly forward and grabbed for the woman's wet cunt, a deep grunt rising in his throat, but before his hand could make contact with the plump flesh, the woman took him by the scruff of the neck and forced his face, with an unbelievable strength, toward her crotch. The boy twisted his body sharply to the right to avoid having his neck broken, and tumbled onto the carpet, his knees bent beneath him. He made a muffled, choking sound as the woman forced his nose flush with her cunt, parting its glistening lips with two extended fingers. The boy stared at the red meat of the cunt, his prick rubbing against the woman's toes, swirling twists of her cunt-hair tickling his cheeks.

"Smell it," the woman whispered, corners of her mouth turned into a sinister smile as she opened her pussy wide and locked her strong thighs around the boy's neck, forcing his smooth nose into the vestibule of her hole. The boy resisted for a second, humiliated by the woman's strength, then inhaled deeply as the woman began to choke him with her thighs. The pungent smell of the woman's cunt evoked strange images in the boy, images of dark forest and damp earth, of naked goblins and witches dancing at twilight in some dusky grotto. His green-veined penis throbbed wildly as the woman forced his nose deeper into her sucking tunnel, and he rubbed it against the soft velvet of the couch until its plum-like head threatened to burst with the pregnancy of his heat.

"Lick," the woman said, running her fingers lovingly through the boy's long honey-colored hair and rubbing her cunt up and down against his face, cradling his chin in the crack of her ass.

Again the boy hesitated, hurt by something in the woman's tone, but then, as the woman pulled him roughly by the hair, he slid his tongue past the plump lips of her vagina, afraid that she would leave him bald if he didn't comply with her commands. Timidly, he licked at the mouth of her cunt, his tongue stinging with the sharp taste of her thick jelly, then began to lap at the hole like a hungry dog as the woman held him tightly by the hair and pulled his head in fiercer and fiercer circles, filling his mouth with her hot-flowing juices, pausing only to force him to swallow. Frenzied by the woman's quivering heat, the boy swirled his tongue wildly in her cunt, his hands squeezing her thighs and belly, his nose nuzzling her meaty clitoris. The woman sucked the boy's tongue deeper and deeper into her belly with powerful contractions of her pussy-muscles, her black eyes twinkling with amusement at his stifled groans and high-pitched cries of pain. Then, suddenly, she released his tongue and rolled it out of her belly.

Still holding him by the hair, she disengaged her legs from his neck and bent them back until her knees pressed against her breasts, forcing their upthrust nipples to the sides. Smiling, she wiggled her rump back and forth off the couch's cushion, exposing her rosy, hair-licked asshole to the boy's excited gaze.

"Lick," she whispered as the boy peered curiously at the puffy rim of the hole, his parted lips covered with her thick vaginal foam.

Obediently, the boy responded, pressing his mouth to the winking hole and running his tongue along its fleshy ridges, wet cunt-hairs tickling his chin as he licked. The little hole tasted bitter to him as he slipped his tongue past its rim. It reminded him of the smell of the horses in the stable. Soon, he decided, he would make his move. He would stand up . . . pull the woman's legs wide apart . . . and shove himself into her . . . He would treat her like a dog . . .

Grabbing him by the hair, the woman forced him to lap up and down at the double furrow of her cunt and ass, making him pause at each sucking hole to tickle her with the tip of his tongue. Despite the woman's continual humiliation of him, the boy groaned with pleasure, his tastebuds continually tantalized by the dark bitterness of her asshole and the hot sweetness of her cunt. Then, laughing a high laugh, the woman placed her feet on the boy's shoulders and pushed him suddenly over on his back. The boy stifled an angry cry as the woman rose majestically to her feet and stood above him, her long toes exploring his belly and thighs, her eyes smiling cruelly into his. For a brief second, an icy fear clutched at the boy's chest. He felt utterly powerless, utterly at the woman's mercy. It seemed to him that he was caught in the hazy web of some long-forgotten nightmare. Then, suddenly, the fear melted away as the woman wrapped her toes around his penis and pulled it in a wide, gentle circle, her soft heel caressing his thighs. Her eyes filled with tenderness, she bent above the boy, full breasts shaking in his face, and kissed the tips of his little nipples. Sliding along his body, her breasts pressing hotly against his belly, she stroked his throbbing cock with her mouth, tickling its swollen opening with the tip of her tongue. The boy writhed like a newborn infant beneath the woman. Dimly aware of the flickering torchlight in the distance, Oriental rug vaguely scratchy against his back and buttocks, the boy felt his entire being centered in the tip of his prick, felt manhood surge through him with each slow stroke of the woman's tongue. His body strong and beautiful, his prick big like a club . . .

The boy shuddered with pleasure as he felt the woman's hungry pussy swallow his penis to the balls. He made a squealing, child-like sound as his laughing mistress began to grind against him, forcing his shaft in and out of her slippery hole, the open cheeks of her ass sliding along his supple thighs. Up and down, up and down, the woman moved, riding the boy as if he was a pony, tickling his downy armpits with her fingers and thrusting her large breasts in his face while he squirmed like a pinned butterfly beneath her, sweat pouring down his forehead, cheeks, and neck. Swept up in the woman's churning motion, utterly intoxicated by the heavy smell of her pleasure, the boy ran his hands madly over her bouncing breasts and grinding buttocks wave after wave of tingling delight washing over his body, tautening his small muscles and curling his pudgy toes.

Her laughter rising to a fever pitch, the woman suddenly began to shake her hips wildly from side to side, loose ringlets of her shiny hair swirling around her head as she squeezed the boy's small testicles with her hidden left hand, his prick slapping violently back and forth against the sucking walls of her cunt. Pulling the woman's nipples to his mouth, the boy began to grunt like an animal, his eyes opening wide with surprise as his entire body went rigid with the tension of his approaching orgasm. Stronger and stronger, he felt it build within him, pressure rising like black steam, cock swelling, throbbing burning with its force...

Then just as the ejaculation was about to burst from the boy's hot cock, the woman leaped from his body, bent herself over his thighs, and glued her lips to the exploding head of his organ, her mouth working up and down, up and down on its cunt-wetted shaft, her tongue lapping wildly at its smooth underside. Gasping for breath, the boy sent burst after burst of his thick seed directly into the woman's throat, the head of his cock swelling like an overripe plum, swirling around and around and around in the tight channel offered by the woman. He watched, fascinated, as the woman swallowed the hot spurt (she seemed actually to be thirsty) finally squeezing a last limpid drop from the tip of his penis and licking it away.

The woman stretched herself beside the boy, her right leg pressed to his left, her arm across his neck. She looked like a cat, her nose small, the nostrils flared, eyes gleaming with soft indolence as she curled her upper lip back from her small white teeth to smile a dreamy smile at her captive. The boy closed his eyes and drifted into a half-sleep as his penis went limp against his belly. Dimly he thought of asking the woman where he might sleep for the night, but decided it best to wait for her to dismiss him. Images of wilting flowers danced through his mind. He saw himself lying on a bed of wilting flowers...

Abruptly, the boy's reverie was interrupted as the woman rose nimbly to her feet, her body framed in orange torchlight, and walked with the grace of a panther toward the pedestal on which the statue of the boy rested. Her buttocks undulated gently as she moved, stretching tendons in her legs giving evidence of hidden power. Her eyelids half-closed as if with sleepiness, she wrapped her hand lightly around the life-like figurine, touching its tiny penis with the tip of her index finger.

The boy stared down at himself in utter bewilderment as his cooling organ twitched slightly, lengthened along his thigh, and rose slowly into the air, meaty purple head bulging with heat. The sudden surge of sexuality made the boy feel at once frightened—for he hadn't willed, or even wanted the erection—and proud—because it proved the manly extent of his potency. Then, before he had a chance to devote any more thought to his erection, a warm dizziness washed over his brain, making the room go soft and hazy and distant. The strange charts and diagrams that lined the walls began to spin in slow, irregular circles. The torches seemed blurs of interweaving reds and yellows and oranges. The boy couldn't tell if he was lying on the Oriental rug or on the velvet couch.

In the center of the hazy-edged scene, the boy saw the woman. Slowly, teasingly, she turned her back to him and bent forward, thrusting the round, dark-clefted cheeks of her ass toward his face. Stroking the insides of her cheeks with her right hand, she pulled them gently apart, humming a peculiar atonal melody to herself as she drew lazy circles around the pink rim of her asshole with her crooked little finger.

The boy watched her through clouded eyes, utterly unable to gauge her distance from him. Then, as she beckoned to him, her head between her legs, he rose shakily from the couch and walked toward her with the jerking gait of an automaton, penis slapping against his hips. Watching him from between her legs, the woman smiled a wicked smile as he pushed his long cock into the crack of her ass and struggled futilely to find her asshole. Her laugh bordering on a cackle, she took the throbbing pole in her hand and fitted it to the plump rim of the opening, then worked circularly backward, swallowing the hot head of the prick with gulping contractions of her asshole. Reaching between the boy's legs, the woman grabbed his balls in both her hands and pulled him violently forward until his prick was buried in her asshole, thick head probing the depths of her intestines, her smooth membrane fitting him like a glove.

His eyes closing, the boy jerked helplessly in and out of the woman's anus, his hands clutched tightly to her hips in an effort not to lose her as she responded to his thrusts with a wild, rolling motion, grinding her parted ass-cheeks fiercely against his belly and thighs.

Once, she turned to him, a strange look on her face, her ears pricked as if listening for some distant sound. Then, tickling the boy's thighs and crotch with both hands, she churned frantically against him, making him rock on his heels with the powerful thrusts of her ass. The boy moaned with the greedy contractions of the woman's rump-cheeks; his prick pushed and pulled, jerked and twisted in her bottom. Panting, he came to a trembling climax, his sweaty hands groping forward for the woman's bouncing tits, his shooting semen overflowing her sucking hole and dripping down the rigid bucking backs of her thighs. The woman squeezed the boy's prick in her asshole until she had drained it completely of fluid, loud farting sounds escaping the wriggling mouth of her narrow tunnel. Then, when she felt his hands slip limply from her hips, she released his penis and turned to face him, her face seeming younger than before, her body literally glowing with vigor.

His body suddenly weak, the boy tottered over to the couch and stretched himself across it, burying his head in its soft cushions. His heart beat rapidly. The woman lay beside him, hands clasped behind her head, eyes fixed on some distant point. When the haziness had passed from his mind, the boy turned toward her, his lips struggling to form the words in his mind.

"Do you like it in there as much as in your . . . pussy?" he said.

"Like it?" the woman said as if thinking of other things. "In my . . ." She turned to the boy, her lips slightly parted to reveal even rows of small white teeth, her eyes questioning him.

"I mean . . . does it feel good . . . you know . . . in the back . . ."

"It's all the same to me," the woman said softly, staring into the boy's eyes. "One hole or another . . . it makes no difference . . . It's your fluid that brings me . . . pleasure . . . I like to feel its warmth inside me . . . but . . . but . . . enough of that . . . Soon there will be work to do . . ."

"Work?" the boy said. He could think only of sleep.

"Yes," the woman said, a distant look in her eye. "Tonight is the winter solstice . . . a special night. There is work to be done . . .

You will help me as you promised . . ."

"What sort of work?" the boy asked, a sudden draft raising bumps on his flesh.

"Shall I tell you a story?" the woman said, her pencil-thin eyebrows arched delicately.

The boy nodded.

"Long ago," the woman said, "a man named Adam roamed the face of this planet alone. He was utterly, utterly alone. This . . . thing . . . that had created him had not yet made for him a mate. He was alone.

"Adam had many dreams, both waking and sleeping, for he was a man and had a chunk of flesh between his legs like any man. And he dreamed always of the same thing . . . of a woman. But . . . this woman of whom he dreamed was not like the one eventually fashioned for him . . . No . . . She did not spring from his rib, but rather from the darker side of his mind. Adam saw her as omnipotent, able to satisfy his every fantasy and whim. She was a goddess, was this woman that Adam dreamed of. And, you see, she became such an obsession with Adam . . . he dreamed of her so faithfully . . . that she actually came into existence. She became, in a manner of speaking, *real*. But, since she was a product of Adam's hidden mind, she was unlike Adam . . . she represented only half of Adam's being. And, while Adam worshipped her with half his mind, and another being with the other half, this creation of Adam's . . . this woman . . . worshipped *one* being with all her soul. Some have called him Satan, but that is false. He has no name. He is nameless . . ."

The woman grabbed him suddenly by the arm, fingers pressing vise-like into the bone, and dragged him to his feet. She laughed cruelly at the fear that filled his eyes, then threw him down on the dark velvet couch with the lightning strength of a tigress. The boy cowered on the couch, his legs pressed together, prick pointing rigidly to the ceiling. He watched the woman as she placed herself above him, her breasts glowing orange in the torchlight, black hair of her cunt wet with his saliva. Staring down at him between her heaving breasts, she straddled him with her thighs, squeezing his hips painfully between her knees, and ran his swollen cock up and down the length of her red slit, letting her hot juices pour over its purple head as she rolled the boy's balls in the crack of her ass.

Trembling, the boy reached upward and took the woman's shaking breasts in his hands. He kneaded them very gently, touching the springy tips of the nipples with his thumbs, afraid that the woman would hurt him if he tried to assert himself with any greater authority.

Shaking her breasts in the boy's hands, the woman drew the head of his penis to the mouth of her foam-gushing hole and arched her back so that her belly formed a curve like that of an ancient bow. Very slowly, she sank downward on the boy until just the tip of his cock was inside her. Then, half-singing to herself in a queer foreign tongue, she began to squeeze the hot organ in her silk-walled hole, drawing it inch by inch into the seething pudding of her belly as she stroked the boy's slender waist with her fingertips.

"And so, this woman . . . creation of Adam . . . came into existence. She had little interest in Adam, especially after he was joined with the woman called Eve, and she contented herself with torturing him when it pleased her to do so. Some say it was she that entered the body of Eve and offered him the apple. Some say she was the snake. Perhaps, perhaps. Who can say? But when the fallen couple was expelled from the garden, this woman left too, never really having cared for the place anyhow. And she wandered for centuries across the face of the earth, ageless, deathless, purposeless, waiting for some sign from her god. And then, in Bethlehem, was born this Christ whom you have heard of, and the task which was to be the woman's became clear to her: she was to create the living antithesis of this Christ . . . she was to create the anti-Christ . . .

"She prayed to her god and he instructed her to seek out a group of twelve immortals—whom she would know by her inner eye—and join with them in the creation of the Beast, the anti-Christ. One of the twelve, her god told her, would give birth to the Beast, and this one she would know for the daughter of demon mother and innocent son.

"And this woman . . . creation of Adam . . . wandered all through time seeking the twelve that were to be her comrades, and eventually, she found them . . . all most evil save for one: the girl born of demon and mortal. And together, this band travelled through the ages, working what evil they might work, perpetuating themselves on the orgasms of foolish mortals, and waiting . . . waiting for the sign, waiting for the girl's innocence to die that she might accept the task of the Beast's creation. They performed rituals for their god, that he might imbue them with greater strength with which to sway the girl. Then, when the girl seemed ready to shed her last vestige of purity, one of this band of immortals turned out to be a traitor. When the woman . . . leader of the twelve . . . was busy elsewhere, this traitor cast a spell over the twelve that banished their memories—his own included—and sent them fleeing through time . . .

"But they are bound together, these twelve, through time and space, through whatever unknowing reincarnations the law of the cosmos has forced them to. And they are to be found. For the sign has been given, you see. Oh, yes. It has been given. The coming year is to witness the glory of the Beast's conception. But the twelve must be found. And tonight, they *will* be found. I am this woman, you see. Nama, queen of all that is evil. Yes, I am born of Adam's spilled seed, and I have fed for eternity on the spasms of foolish men . . . like yourself . . ."

From far in the distance came the labored striking of a clock. The boy, who up to the woman's final words had listened as he had listened long ago to his mother's bedtime stories, now sat bolt upright, his entire body shaking. The woman was utterly insane . . . He was trapped with a madwoman . . .

"Tonight," the woman said, "my god will show me a sign. He will show me where the twelve are to be found. But he must first be appeased . . ."

She smiled at the boy, her eyes twinkling with a ghastly fire. The boy got cautiously to his feet and started to back away from the woman, his naked scrotum tightening with fear.

"Do you think you can escape me?" she said. "You have given me your promise, and your seed . . ."

The boy made a move as if to run, but Nama brought her left hand from beneath her neck and made several quick gestures in the air, her high laughter shattering the stillness of the dark-shadowed room.

The boy halted, frozen in his tracks, then began to cry, as his eyes came to rest on the woman's previously hidden hand. On the back of the hand was a huge, livid scar, its jagged outline corresponding to that of a pentagram.

"Come," the woman said, rising slowly to her full height. "The hour is upon us . . . time grows short . . ."

The boy remained where he stood, his entire body shuddering with the effort of resisting the woman's will.

The woman made a small gesture with her scarred left hand and the boy's mind went instantly blank.

"Follow," the woman said flatly as she made for a spiral staircase hidden in the darkness of the room's far corner.

Robot-like, the boy followed her up the twisting staircase, his eyes focussed vaguely on the rhythmically-tautening muscles of her buttocks. At the top of the staircase, the woman threw open a heavy iron door and led the boy out onto the snow-covered roof of the building.

"Stay," she said to the boy as she walked to the center of the roof and cleared away a large circle of snow with her feet. Walking around and around the empty circle, she made strange passes in the air and chanted low, gutteral words until the wind rose to a howl and the sound of the churning river below became deafeningly loud.

"Now," the woman murmured. "Now . . ."

Suddenly, the iron door to the roof was flung open to reveal the strangely-dressed man who had brought the boy to the woman. He approached the woman, his eyes gleaming strangely at the sight of the boy's nakedness, and placed a jewelled dagger in her hand, keeping his face turned conspicuously from her.

"Come," the woman said to the boy, drawing him into the circle with a twisting movement of her scarred hand.

The boy advanced to the center of the circle and stood perfectly still, his soft eyes heavy-lidded, his arms hanging limp at his sides. The woman walked around and around him, muttering strange, unearthly sounds and making complex passes in the air with both her hands. Then, as a strange purple glow seemed to come over the circle, she came to a halt before the boy and raised the jewelled dagger high above her head.

"I stand naked in your presence," she murmured, her eyes closed. "I offer you sacrifice that I may find my destiny . . ."

Without opening her eyes, she plunged the dagger downward into the boy's hairless chest and stood motionless as huge spurts of blood shot from the boy's heart and splattered across her naked breasts. Then, as the boy toppled to the ground, the warm pool of his blood spreading to the edge of the circle and staining the white snow a bright crimson, the woman knelt beside him and fell into a breathless trance, hands clasped tightly over her eyes.

"I see them . . . Oh! I see them . . ." she whispered after a time. "They are mine!"

"Nama . . ." the long-faced servant called as the woman turned her face to the howling wind. His voice was low and rumbling, like the sound of the ocean's waves.

Nama turned impatiently toward him.

"You promised me . . . release . . . for the service I have done you . . . You promised me freedom . . . I provided you with a sacrifice . . ."

"You wish freedom, Joseph? Freedom?"

"Freedom . . ."

"Are you not free?"

"I . . ."

"Is not pleasure freedom enough?"

"I seek the freedom of rest . . . I . . ."

"Rest, is it? Rest?"

"Freedom! Rest! Don't torture me! There are crimes . . . crimes on my soul . . ."

"You wish the crimes erased?"

"Yes! Erased . . ."

"Forgotten?"

"Forgotten . . . erased . . ."

"Forget your crimes with new crimes, Joseph . . ."

The woman gestured toward the boy's pale corpse, touching the back of its thigh.

"No! No!" the servant cried, covering his face with his hands.

"He is beautiful, is he not, Joseph?" the woman said. "He is still quite warm . . . and on so cold a night . . ."

"You promised me my freedom! I have served you well . . . I have served you well . . . "

"Your freedom is yours if you truly desire it," the woman said, stroking the corpse's buttocks. "But look into your heart, Joseph . . ."

There was a long silence on the roof, broken by the chugging of a snow-plow in the street below.

"Come . . . look here," the woman said, parting the boy's

buttocks and inserting her forefinger in his tight anus. "A virgin hole . . . taut and fresh . . . like a little girl's . . ."

"You promised me . . ." the servant muttered, stepping help-lessly forward.

The woman ignored him and squeezed the corpse's plump buttocks.

"How delicious these will feel against your belly, eh Joseph?"

The servant knelt beside the boy.

"Come . . . touch him. He is yours," the woman said.

The servant placed his hands on the boy's cooling legs.

"Why have you done this?" he moaned, his face turned to the starless sky. "Why?"

"I do it for you, Joseph," the woman said. "I do it for you . . . Do you not serve me faithfully? May I not reward you?"

"I am damned!" the man cried. "Damned! You can bring me release . . ."

"Do you want release, Joseph? Is that what you want?"

"I . . . no . . ." the man said softly, pressing his lips to the boy's shoulder and undoing the buttons of his gownlike garment.

"And when you have taken him, Joseph," the woman said. "See how thick his blood is?" She ran her forefinger through the spreading pool of steaming crimson. "See?" she said, holding her blood-smeared finger to the man's face. "Thick and rich . . . like broth . . ."

Moaning, the man rubbed himself against the boy's motionless leg.

"And when you are quite finished," the woman said. "Throw his body into the river . . . unless, of course, you want to keep him . . . " She walked towards the edge of the snow-covered roof, seemingly oblivious to the slobbering sounds that escaped the servant's lips. "I may not see you for some time, Joseph," she said after a while. "There are great things in the air . . ."

She stepped to the far corner of the roof, her black ringlets twisting madly in the wind, and drew an imaginary pentagon in the air with her left hand. She stood poised at the edge of the roof for a moment, arms raised joyously above her head, her smooth nakedness shining in the pale, cloud-dimmed light of the moon, then stepped nimbly through the invisible door she had drawn, and disappeared into thin air.

BENJAMIN GRIMM

Benjamin Grimm is not so much a pen name as an actual facet of the author's personality. This doppelganger *does not particularly enjoy his work, despite a life-long fascination with erotic literature which caused him, at the tender age of ten or so, to save his pennies for the purchase of tits-and-ass magazines (which were Scotch taped closed in those days to discourage browsing). Benjamin's fondest hope is to retire to an isolated chateau peopled with the characters from his novel. He would also like to meet Orson Welles and play lead guitar in a group called Banjamin Grimm and his Blues All-Stars. Now, at the age of twenty-two, with four novels for Traveller's Companion behind him, the author finds himself anxiously awaiting Benjamin's departure, but the latter has other ideas. The two live in New York.*

J. J. Savage

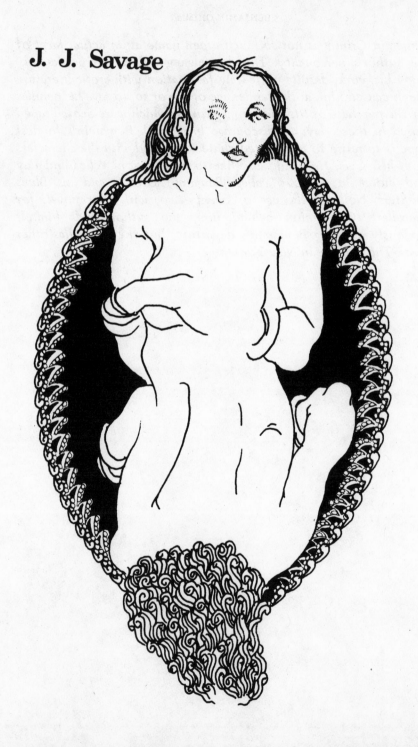

CRESCENDO

You can really have a ball on Forty-Second Street if you got thirty-three dollars in your pocket. (I bought breakfast soon as we were out of the Holland Tunnel.)

Hot dogs, popcorn, orange drink. And a movie with a balcony. I had never seen that before, so I must have gone down to the men's room fifteen times, just to climb the stairs in the dark again. The movie was Dr. Jekyll and Mr. Hyde with Fredric March and Miriam Hopkins and I'll bet you I understood it better than anyone else in the movie house. That movie house! Have you ever been to a movie house on Forty-Second Street? A tall ghost, dripping with squalor, faded gilt, cracked marble staircases, naked statues, cold to the touch—and a grey fuzzy blanket of dust that hangs in the dark air. Men of many ages are constantly participating in a parade in and out of the men's room, fumbling with fly buttons, sweating, eyes searching for legs without pants on.

A woman with pink hair like cotton candy sat down next to me and pretty soon she was playing with my balls and her breath was whistling out over the balcony. She was pretty good at it, an up and down and then around motion and I thought for a minute I was going to blow my load but just then a white-dressed matron came up the aisle with a flashlight and made me move to the children's section downstairs. I gave the woman with the cotton hair a look of apology as I skirted by her on my way to the aisle. Her face was flushed red and her breath was held in, not whistling any more. Following the matron down the now familiar steps it reminded me of Mama following the white coats out the front door.

After the movie, the streets had become darkened by night but lightened by neons and I went back to my ten-cent locker in a hotel lobby and got my jug back. Jug in hand I strolled up Broadway toward Central Park, although at the time I didn't know there was such a place. Without too much notice the pavement broke into grass and dirt and grey statues with green mold on them. It amazed me. A park, right here in the middle of all this noise! And that is where I met Mrs. Mechanik, on the very first bench inside the park and she had a paper bag on her lap. It contained an apple, a banana and a bunch of grapes. The old lady smiled at my young face and then grunted as she moved over to make room for me on the bench. She wore a hat with wax flowers in it and it sat straight on her head.

"My, my. Aren't we out late tonight. I'm thinkin' maybe your Mama is worrying, already. Could be you're a runaway, no?"

"I'm an orphan." I don't know why I said it. It was the truth. I checked the facts after I said it. Yep, it *was* the truth.

"An orphan! *Oy, gefelt!* Alone in the world. Nst, nst. A shame. Best you don't talk about it. You like a banana, maybe?"

"Thank you."

"A jug of water. So what's with a jug of water? You plan on being thirsty?"

"Yes, ma'am."

"So how thirsty can you get?"

"I got allergies. This is my medicine."

"Allergies, yet? And you out in the park at night? Nst. Nst. A shame. A hot dish of chicken soup is what you should be sipping, not medicine. I make chicken soup you wouldn't believe! Thick like butter. You like chicken soup?"

"Yes ma'am."

"Goot! I'm just goin' home anyvays. I got some chicken soup cold in the icebox. I'll heat it up. So you wouldn't believe!"

"Naw. I got thirty dollars. I can buy chicken soup in a restaurant if I want."

"Not *my* chicken soup, you can't. I can see you know from nothin' about chicken soup. C'mon already. You think maybe an old lady like me is spooky? A witch maybe. Ha-ha."

Mrs. Mechanik was no witch. She was without a doubt the kindest woman I have ever met in my life. We took the Fifth Avenue bus over the bridge to her home in Queens. We sat on the open upper deck and I laughed more during that half-hour ride than I ever have since. She was in her early fifties and she was fat and very very Jewish. Her son was with the Army in the Pacific right in the midst of it, and she had been praying for him, sitting there on the park bench. She said she did that often, especially on Wednesday nights when her daughter had singing lessons.

"Like a bird, she sings. A bird! If she was a boy she'd be a cantor f'sure. She's fifteen, such a doll! She don't go with boys—nothin'. A goot girl. Sweet girl."

"What kinda' work your husband do?"

"He's passed on, poor thing. I miss him too. My boy Lenny and him. Miss 'em both. We had children too late. He would have enjoyed Shirley's singing. Well, to be, to be. He was a salesman, the best. Could sell you wool socks even if your feet was stinkin' wit sweat. He died young. Worked too hard. Too many stairs. Nst. nst."

"This sure is a big city."

"Big city, nice city. Goot city, goot country. I'm a Jew here an' I don't have to be ashamed. Lenny is fighting to keep it that way. You Catholic?"

"Yes, ma'am."

"Thought so. See? It makes no difference in this country. I like you and you like me. Isn't that wonderful? You'll like my chicken soup, you'll see. Lenny loved it. Lenny hasn't had his Ma's chicken soup in over a year, now. Well, to be, to be."

In the three years to come, Mrs. Mechanik was to make me an addict to Jewish cooking. Lox, cream cheese, rhubarb cooked warm, herring, pastrami, and once in a while corned beef and cabbage because her Irish neighbor loved it and couldn't cook worth a shit.

She never asked me any questions and I guess she hoped someday it wouldn't happen that somebody would come and claim me. She didn't have to worry. I belonged to no one. No one except my own agelessness. I knew someday I'd have to move on. When people started noticing. I tried not to think about it because I guess maybe Mrs. Mechanik was the only woman in my life that I have loved. I mean without it having anything to do with sex. That's why I've always punished myself with little grunts of guilt, whenever I think of it. What I did to her daughter Shirley, I mean. But I'm getting ahead of myself. You know, I think my other me liked Mrs. Mechanik, too. If he could like anyone, that is. Anyway, he never growled at her like he did all other women throughout my life. Maybe because she knew he was there inside of me and she knew what he was. At least she acted like she knew. She never once scolded me, but rather she would sympathize with me, feeling sorry for me that I had given in to "an evil t'ing that's in all of us. Nst. Nst. Well, to be, to be."

Well that was many years ago and before I get into telling you about Shirley Mechanik let me observe that here I am now, standing before you insisting that I deserve the gas chamber and, to be more direct, *begging* that this be the end of this horror of a life of mine. I wonder if Mrs. Mechanik would mind if I borrowed one more thing from her. That great, all meaning misquote of hers . . . "to be, to be."—Beautiful. It says it all.

I got a clue as to what was coming with Shirley Mechanik that first night when I was led, by her mother, into their five-room railroad flat on a dark street that smelled of many nations. It had bay windows that bulged out over the street like a pregnant woman in her ninth month. The door from the long narrow hallway led into the kitchen and everything had an odor that I have associated with Jewish people ever since. I liked it. It made me feel like I was joining a new private club and the members were rich with history.

Mrs. Mechanik walked me through bedrooms, and in the front parlor (Mrs. Mechanik called it the front *room*) I came, for the first time, face to face with Shirley.

She was beautiful! She slid her delicate hands along her trim hips, smoothing the wrinkles from her blue knit dress in preparation for our introduction. My first impression was a completely misleading one. But how could I know? I mean what she was really like. That she hid dirty pictures in her schoolbooks, would share their enjoyment with me soon. That she was frightened and depressed by the messy signs of her budding womanhood. That she always took a Coke bottle and a banana to bed with her and in the morning she'd look a little too satisfied with herself. Her rear was firm and solid: *that* I noted when she turned from our wet handshake and walked to the divan to sit down. She had almost elf-like ears, too small for her big hairdo. Her face loomed large and bright in my head, a look of brazenness in her cool eyes; even the auburn color of her hair should have hinted the pleasures soon to be mine. But it just didn't hit me that way at first.

Seated, she straightened her shoulders, eyed me from head to foot. Even *that* gesture told me nothing.

Her lips then grew tight in an acid smile and she began asking me all sorts of questions before her mother warned her to mind her own business. For several hectic seconds I think I pondered how I could leave the house and be on my own free way again. But then the conversation deepened, the family picture album was brought out and the laughter came more freely and suddenly I was part of it, feeling I had found *something*, not knowing how or what it was. Family, maybe. In a cobwebbed corner of my brain, Papa loved Mama again.

I think, under it all, what I was enjoying most was the adolescent-playing-grownup game I was involved in. And then Shirley talked for a long time, about her music I think, but I'm not sure; her long body and the image of what was under that knit dress was sticking to me like so much glue, so I didn't listen. She had a cold gem-like beauty. But what she could do to my cock with those juicy lips! That's what I was thinking. A wall full of itchy female bodies seemed to surround me, all in the exact image of Shirley's body. Then she stretched her long legs across the couch and I think I actually grunted out loud. A sharp blade of light stabbed itself from the standing lamp down onto her bosom and I had to close my eyes and swallow all the spit that had gathered in my mouth. You see, as I learned later, Shirley was a born manipulator. Maybe she inherited it from her salesman father. But her sheer power to manipulate a boy—me at that time, through his desire for her was something eerie to watch, after you came to understand what she was doing, what her thoughts were.

So maybe that's why, after her mother went to bed—first showing me my bed and room (formerly her son's)—Shirley began her tantalizing manipulations. She was still on the divan, but now she stuffed a pillow under her head and lay straight out. She didn't fold her ankles, one over the other as you might expect. No, as if planned, her legs were a careful six inches apart and the knit material clung between them, outlining them clear up the thigh. I still sat directly opposite her, though clear across the room, never hearing a word she was speaking straight up at the ceiling. She pressed down and wiggled now and then, as if preoccupied with her teasing game, maybe not listening to her own words herself. She was mostly aware of my eyes, of that I am sure. My arms grew more alternately tense and tremulous, fingers digging into the leather of my chair. My eyes examined in great detail every nuance and salient feature her body had to offer and when she would stop talking and look my way, she would become coquettish again, wiggling and stretching as if tired.

Okay, my passion was baited, boiling. So what next? Was this a kid's game? Just a teasing kid's game? I was getting angry.

She knew she was being a bitch, no doubt about that, and I got the impression it was all great fun to her. Seeing how much I could take. I was sinking fast to some wretched animal state, but of course she couldn't know that. Just a twelve-year-old boy, she must have thought. What fun to tease him.

When she was sure her mother was asleep she made still another complete shifting of position, still talking. Now one bare leg propped itself up on the back of the divan and the knit dress slid halfway up her one thigh. The six-inch spread between her legs had now widened to a full foot and she knew it. Her lean body nestled for deeper sinking into the back crack of the divan. Her words were getting even further away from me, but I think she was saying something about Woody Herman and how the sound of his clarinet affected her. I didn't give a shit *how* it affected her. I was bathing in my own thin layer of sweat and I was fully erected so I didn't dare stand up. Little lice of electricity danced in my legs.

It was just about then that I became conscious that her hot stare was going right past me, up on the wall behind my head. I followed her eyes and turned my head to the rear wall in back of my chair. A six-foot horizontal mirror was what she had been performing to all the time! My spirits visibly wilted, the promise broken. Turning back to her, my eyes gripped themselves helplessly on her cashmered breasts, round and prominent, and suddenly I didn't care who she was performing for. Her pencil-line of a mouth was not tightly shut and her eyes sleepily closed, no longer admiring herself, perhaps because I had obviously discovered her game. Her eyes *were* closed but her face glowed with keen awareness. Her face now spoke to me instead of her voice, a calculated sophistication coming over it, eyes still closed.

There was a scrap of affection in my emotions, but that's all. The rest of it was consuming lust, nothing else. She was a pig, like all the rest and if I pushed the right buttons I could make her squeal. All pigs want to be stabbed, you know that. This pig was just lying there, enjoying the picture of me castrating my ego, longing to just move over to her and just touch her. Maybe I should have put my head in the toilet and pulled the chain and it wouldn't have happened at all.

She moved again, this time dangling her other leg over the edge of the divan and now the gap was wide and incredible, a valley of knit between her widespread legs and the suddenness of her motion took my breath away. An attack of jitters skidded through my body, edginess touching the fringe of terror. The pull in my belly was urgent and strong. Morbid rumblings rattled around in my skull. The void with reality continued to widen, deepen, each time she'd raise her ass off the couch and bounce it back down, seeking new comfort. Tug by painful tug, I was giving in to it. A feeling of slow disintegration started and I sensed a basic hollowness. Inside I flogged myself, trying not to move toward her. But I had to move. I couldn't stand it any longer!

I got up, went into my newly appointed bedroom, took one spoon of my medicine, came back to the "front room," and sat down and waited.

The dress was no longer knit. It was mountains and valleys of blue-hued snow, fluffy and dry and I wanted to bathe in it, roll in it, smell its freshness. Her long body fanned out in a fluid stream. Then that same old numbing sensation throughout my body and I knew I was on my way. A mild wave of nausea, but that would pass quickly; it always did. A slight interruption in my high; I thought about eating her. All at once the valley of snow between her open legs was no longer snow but a maze of plumbing, pipes, fitting, elbows and I was a toilet, water swirling and emptying my waste into her. A part of me wanted to go deeper into the thought but the rest of me was too busy with other things . . . Desperation and panic hit me violently, her rubbery lips were opening to receive my kiss. I was sobbing and twisting my body like a maniac, fighting off filthy images with my hands and legs. My mind clamped shut while my lips were on hers and the room whirled around me, me petrified in its center. A fierce heat exploded in my chest, then my stomach, finally my groin. My hands were between her thighs, rubbing hard, as if to rub her away.

"What are you doing? What the hell's the matter with you?" It was her voice, but far away. The room throbbed with her words.

"Oh, God, what are you doing?" she half whispered, half screamed. But her body was beginning to squirm and whatever I was doing she liked!

"Why should we pretend?" I heard my voice ask her ear.

"Oh, I'm not pretending. But we must be quiet. Do it quietly. If we don't get caught we can do it a lot—every night." Her words were clearer now.

Her white flesh swelled out and somehow the knit dress was gone. A ravine of grassed hair, like a hat on her thighs, and my hand was on it, stroking, kneading it. Her two breasts spread themselves wider apart with the touch of her own hand and I buried my nose between them, their strange warmth scorching my ears. My lips were crazy with sucking, licking, stroking. The immense blackness between her tits was like a tunnel overflowing with delicious sweat, salty yet perfumed. A hammering in my head started with the first taste of it. Shirley's breath was like windstorms in my ear. Fine trembling rode on her breathing and I could feel it traveling down through her body. A low, throaty growl came out of her, or was it out of me . . . ?

"Oh, little boy, I'll teach you everything!" she promised. I did not stop to laugh at her ridiculous promise. "Wait, start all over," she said. "Feel my breasts first." I obeyed instinctively, the tit soft and sinking under my grasp. I felt her tension mount, stiffen, her wet gurgles escaping from her throat. Her hand was on mine pressing it harder into the spongy flesh.

The two hard buds were stabbing back at the palms of my hands now and for a minute I thought she was crying. My fingers moved around the nipples and they grew even as I touched them.

"Faster, faster!" she pleaded, her face a mass of red. "Oh, God, you're a little devil!"

My prick was banging against the side of her thigh, as though it was knocking at a door, demanding entrance.

"Am I the first one?" she sobbed. "Did you ever eat one? Oh, eat me. You'll like it."

The first one. Hah! The picture of so many lay sisters shot through my mind, all becoming one face. Vera's face.

Her risings and fallings under the weight of me was something that was going on by itself, as though not controlled by her.

"But be quiet. Mother mustn't hear. Just eat me quietly." She was pushing my head down, down, down.

My head being pushed down over her belly I opened my eyes to the forest coming at me, and past it to the smooth legs, wild in twisting movements. Her belly was plump, hot against my cheek, slipping by slowly.

"Do you like it? Do you like it? Kiss it, kiss it," she whispered a rasp, hoarse whisper.

The metallic click.

My kitten was alive again. Boob, my little furry kitten, and I was chewing at its stomach and it was purring.

I looked through the hair at my hands, roaming everywhere at once. The only trouble was, the hands weren't mine. They looked sinister and alien somehow. I knew they were attached to my arms and I knew I could move them, but they just weren't *my* hands. They weren't *me*. Or better yet, I wasn't *them*. I've become able to estimate my depth in a trip. At that point I would say I was about one half inch outside of myself. Or, perhaps it would be more accurate to say, had been moved around about one half inch *inside* my body. In there, looking out at myself.

Disembodied then, I went on with it with a new fury.

My mouth was full of her young wet flesh but it wasn't flesh like you might expect. It was spinning atoms, as I now know them to be. Molecules with hair on them. I chewed at them, I stuck my finger, or whoever's finger that hand belonged to, into her hot wet crack and the end of my finger disappeared and I seemed to be living on the food of her.

Her cunt was a sea in front of my eyes, with weird looking technicolor fish swimming about, yet it was tightly zippered where my finger had fallen off, inside of her. But I could see through the zipper and that's where the sea was, with the multi-colored fish and sponges and plants growing. My problem was that I couldn't fit past the little opening in the zipper but that was soon taken care of. Suddenly I was looking, as if from within my own eyeball, into her, and her organisms moved slushily before me. A chord of *Dance Macabre* majestically burst inside my brain and then it was all icy blue sound—*Dance Macabre?* No, the icy blue sound of the rivers flowing inside of her. And then I saw myself in an instant, my eyes tumbling from weeping sockets, my smashed testicles oozing from under a shriveling, ridiculously small penis. Shirley's voice, smooth and young before, came through to me whorish and coarse, now.

"Oh that's it, lick it. Lick it!"

"Kill it, kill it! Kill, kill!" my inner friend's voice echoed, as if singing the same notes of her voice.

She was like a hungry animal, sniffing around me, finding me in her blindness, and my cock was in her mouth! "No, no!" she said, but she took more of it, betraying herself. My cock was a bar of iron, her tongue lashing at it, and the pain of it changed to pleasure.

I slid around, as if on an axle and then her stomach was heavy with me, my prick larger now, larger larger! Then I shrunk to a sort of Tiny Tim that I had seen in the funnies and I was in her ALL the way, ALL of me, tiny and walking around inside her. The heat of her body poured around me everywhere, there inside her womb—or was it my mother's womb?—But I knew I had to leave if I was to begin to live. But it was so comfortable in there! I struggled then, but the womb closed and trapped me. Soon I could look out from within and see her great legs opening up and closing and I knew I must plan my escape on the next rhythmic opening. They parted and light shone in and I ran for life. Then I was out between those legs, gulping for air, then running down her cream-wet thighs. Still small, I redirected myself up toward her breasts, hungry for natural nourishment. I pressed my lips against her nipple and drank sweet life back into my body, feeling myself grow with each mouthful. The sweet liquid splashed into my mouth and this feeling was best of all. The wall at the pit of my stomach burst and the prison of sperm ran riot, dashing for freedom, pounding inside my prick, demanding hot exit.

We groaned together, Shirley and I. We screamed little whispered screams together, our saliva joining into one bubble between our mouths. We flinched small together, stomachs pulled in. We expanded together, arms outstretched, fingers intertwined. Our nostrils breathed together, one into the other. And then we clenched tight together, like two pairs of pliers, one gripping the other and fusing in the heat.

Finally, we came together. Oh, Jesus! The second was an hour long!

Melted like fat drippings, we lay together, in each other's arms.

Far off, as if from a hilltop, Mrs. Mechanik's heavy snores drifted through the rooms.

"Now kill her," came the ever repeating instruction from a bubble inside my brain. I stuck a needle in the bubble and whispered back, "Not yet. Not yet. There is more of the meal to come . . ."

I sat at the breakfast table the next morning in a state of total despondency. I'd found a good thing, here. Had I ruined it? What would be Shirley's next move?

She greeted me with a look of prepared cheerfulness, sitting on the edge of her chair. She watched me for a moment and smiled. "You better drink your juice. You don't look like you feel at home. You *should* feel at home. Mama and me would like you to be part of the family, so to speak."

I sat there wearily and watched her pour the orange juice in a small glass. Mrs. Mechanik was going like mad at the stove. Shirley set my glass on the table in front of me and lifted her own. Over the rim of her glass an eye winked to me affectionately. I smiled back. I was home free! During the night I had suffered through all sorts of worries about Shirley having a chitchat with her mother about ". . . that awful boy. Know what he did after you went to bed?" No fears now. I drank my juice, feeling lighter. This was going to be beautiful! — But maybe Shirley just liked the way I made love after I took my medicine. Christ. How could I tell her that wasn't really me. Shit, I couldn't take my medicine every day!

I shouldn't have given it a second thought. Shirley was in love with *the way* she made love. Simple as that. After breakfast Mrs. Mechanik said, "Mine beautiful children, you'll be goot, be nice, don't fight. I'm making with the USO already this morning. One of the boys from Brooklyn Navy Yard, it's his birthday today. So we give him a little party tonight at the Center. Makes him feel goot, maybe. He's from way out in Arizona. I'm making strawberry shortcake—very expensive, but nothing's too goot for our boys, right, dollings? Maybe some mother where Lenny is does nice for him, too. It all works out even in the end, doncha' think? I'll be gone until about two o'clock. So get acquainted. Be nice. Don't fight."

She put the hat with the flowers on her head and practically danced out the door.

"You got a nice mother," I said to Shirley.

"She embarrasses me," she said, flatly.

"How?"

"Oh, I dunno. I mean she just ain't with it. She thinks everybody is so nicey-nicey. She just ain't picking up what is being put down. I guess it's her old-world training."

"Well I think she's nice. You're lucky."

She propped a hand mirror on the table and started putting her lipstick on. "You know *your* mother? Or did she die when you were too young?" she asked.

"Yeah, when I was too young."

"Too bad."

"Yeah, I'm all fucked up." I said it and drank the last of my juice.

"Don't talk like that. Ain't nice. I hate that word. Sailors use it a lot. They're just trying to be big."

"Sailor ever screw you?"

"None of your business! . . . Why?"

"I dunno. I just thought . . . if you got sailors screwing you, what do you need me for? I mean, . . . a little kid like me?"

"I get by. But . . . I dunno, you're different. Just hit me right, I guess. I was horny last night, anyway. Don't think you can do it whenever you want. Don't think you're just gonna lay me down and lay me any time you want. You gotta earn it." She was done with the lipstick. Her face was a dream!

"Earn it? Go fuck yourself. Who needs ya?"

I got up and went into the toilet, sat down on the bowl and cursed to myself.

I could smell that Shirley was lighting a cigarette outside the bathroom door, which wasn't completely closed. I grunted, taking care of a cramp in my stomach. After that I wasn't doubled up any more, sitting straighter on the stool.

Shirley came marching right in, uttered a good-natured "phew!" and sat down on the edge of the tub and yawned. She waved her cigarette, as if at the stench.

"Get the hell outa' here!" I yelled. "What the hell is the matter with you, anyway?"

"Nothing, not a thing," she said primly. "It's just time for your bath, that's all."

"Bath? What bath? You're a snotty little shithead, know that?"

She smiled, took another over-acted puff on the cigarette, not inhaling.

Then she made some demure eyes at a large picture of Tyrone Power in the center fold of her magazine, followed by five kisses as fast as machine gun fire, which left lipstick stains on poor Tyrone's face. She turns around and turns the hot water faucet on in the tub and then she tells me to get in 'cause she's gonna wash my back.

"You gotta' be out of your skull! I take my own baths. Besides, what you want to give me a bath for? You wanta' be fucked again, I'll fuck ya'. We don't have to fool around."

"Uh-uh. Bath first. Be a good boy. Or I'll tell Mama what a *bad* boy you are. Know what'll happen then? You'll be an orphan again."

Well she had me there, I liked the setup, felt at home. So . . . so it was time for a bath.

She watched me undress, never missing a trick. She even helped me with one sock. "Phew!" she said again, this time louder. I got in the tub and sat down, getting sorta interested in what was to come next. She went right to work, down on her knees beside the tub, scrubbing up big handfuls of soap and rubbing it into my arms, my chest, down below water level to my balls. "Ouch, go easy. Whatya' think you got here?" She smiled patiently and lifted my knee up so she could get her hand down under my ass. I think in her head she was playing little girl games with a doll!

But her face was getting red and I could see her little game was getting to her. To me, too. My erection stood straight up out of the now-sudsy water like a submarine periscope. She rubbed the foamy soap all over it but was unable to dissolve and absorb it into anything less than a roaring hard-on.

Then I feel her auburn hair brush past my nose and for a second it smells like lilacs and she kisses the head of my prick quick and fast and I came up a full foot out of the water!

"Ha-ha!" she laughs.

"Bitch," I says.

"Stand up," she says.

I obey, hoping.

With rocking-horse motion, me in the tub of water, her on the sopping tile floor, I then got what must have been the outstanding blow-job of my life. This kid must have been trained by an expert, probably in the dark back row of some neighborhood theatre. No girl or woman ever sucked me, licked me like that before or since. I watched her do it in the blue gelatine flood of images in the cabinet mirror, and maybe that was one of the reasons it was so great. All of me pointing forward, all of her sucking downward. My spine stretched to a closing parenthesis, arched to her mouth. Her piano lessons must have helped too, because the effect of her five-fingered exercise on the top of my prick, just outside her mouth was heaven itself, if there is such a place.

Her mouth opened and closed as softly as an eyelid and a tiger roared inside me, shoving my rubbery kind of machine deeper behind her lips.

All the time she watched anxiously out of one opened eye, moaning like a walrus. I pulled out just in time for my prick to spring upward and hit the mirror, dead center on the first spurt.

Then she bawled me out and said next time don't pull out, explaining that was half the kick for her.

Next time I didn't.

"Now its my turn," she said, like this was some merry game, and she marches me through the rooms all the way to the front parlor and she props herself up, this time with pillows, on her favorite divan, getting comfortable in her same old spread-legged (one foot on the back of the divan, one down on the floor) position.

"Eat me," she demanded, child greed written all over her face. Her eyes were distraught, howling a plea out at me and I knew I had her. I couldn't let this opportunity pass.

"Sure, ya' little cunt. But don't you ever threaten me again with what you're gonna tell your old lady. You want me to eat ya', sure, swell. But just remember, the first time you squeal to Mama, I cut you off and you can play games with your pussy yourself. Got it?" I growled.

"Yes, yes. You're the boss, but come do it, do it."

"Beg for it. Beg me. Go ahead."

"I do. I beg you. Please, oh, I'm so hot."

Well, wasn't I right? A pig . . . and if you know where to push the right buttons, the pig will squeal. They're all pigs. But then another thought raced through my mind. Now that I *had* her, I didn't want to blow it all. I'd eat her better than she ate me, then she wouldn't be able to live without it and I'd have myself a slave. A regular slave.

I don't know why I did it, but the first thing I did was bite off a mouthful of hair, ripping it from the pores of her belly and you could have heard her scream a block away. I think that was *his* idea. I don't know, because the notion ran through my head so fast and wham! I did it before I could think about it. Maybe it had something to do with my furry kitten. More as an excuse than anything else I then looked her dead in the eye and said, just like Humphrey Bogart, "That's in case you forget, baby."

"Yes, yes," she cried. "I won't forget."

Thin hairs drifted down in front of me, let free by my teeth.

Then I got to it, like a pro. Well at least in that moment of victory I *thought* I was a pro.

First my wet fingers went sliding in and out of her, acquiring a thicker wetness. She was young and tight and the lips clung like a closed fist at my finger. In spite of everything, she was even tighter than little Jenny-Jean and I've often wondered about that. My lips slid along the cream of her thigh and came to rest against my own submerged finger. She gasped, frantic. I lounged my lips around the hole, teasing, hearing her tormented gulps in my free ear.

I kissed it deep and long, pressing my stiffened tongue to penetrate a little deeper. Her stomach was all motion, all moving and I stiff-stabbed her a hundred times, soft-stabbed her another hundred. She heaved and tossed an insane dance on the couch, saying all kinds of crazy things, making all kinds of promises. I was half-suffocated in her meat. She cupped her knees with her hands and pulled her legs higher and I sunk deeper into her, and for a minute she must have forgotten our deal because she rammed my head still deeper into her, but I pushed her arm away. After that she didn't push any more, just playing that same five-finger exercise on the back of my head, and moaning, wincing, crying. Then she flung her legs high and apart, her hips hinged up to me, and my whole face was submerged into her, then. She flowed a flavor something like honey and I rolled it around on my tongue, rising back up in spirits myself. I remember wishing my medicine tasted like that. I slowed down and just sipped at the whirlpool of her and this seemed to drive her to still higher peaks.

"Oh, I can't stand any more! Love it, honey, love it!"

I stood up quickly and then fell straight down on her, ramming my prick into her like a ripping sword. She was disappointed, I know, but I no longer cared. She was lucky and she didn't know it. She couldn't hear the voice inside me saying, "Kill her. Kill, kill!"

And that's the way it was in the following two years that I lived with Mrs. Mechanik and her daughter. It all seems like a clay merry-go-round that fell apart from its own spinning. Those two years went so fast it's unbelievable. I think I might even have been counted among the living in those two years, I was so happy, so content. I might have gone on forever if one day, on the way from school, I hadn't peeked in the back seat of a parked car by the brewery and seen Shirley all arms and legs around some soldier with his pants down.

Poor Shirley drowned the next morning . . . in the bathtub . . . right after breakfast . . . while Mrs. Mechanik was out selling war bonds. A terrible accident.

"The poor child must have fallen in the tub. She had a lump on her head, ya' know," everyone said.

Mrs. Mechanik was never the same after that, crying day and night. Oh, well, it was time to move on anyway. Once again I had graduated down to being the smallest kid in my class and the old raised eyebrows were beginning.

"Maybe I should take you to a doctor, already. Maybe something's wrong. You can't tell. Do you know if your Mama and Papa vas short people? Maybe that's it, maybe," Mrs. Mechanik would say.

I kissed her good-bye one morning and bounced down the hall stairway on my way to school. I never went back to see Mrs. Mechanik again. I should have. Maybe she'll read about all this and come and see me. Best she don't. Maybe she'd ask about Shirley.

J. J. SAVAGE

J. J. Savage is not his real name, of course. He loves criminology and admits to being a frustrated lawyer. In his early years, he had been a private eye detective, and — according to the usual reliable sources — a very good one, who thought nothing of driving two or three hundred miles a day on the track of some vital bit of information. Many of his books, such as In Hot Blood, *have legal and criminal backgrounds. The author lives in a small, beautiful town on the California coast with his wife and two daughters (one of whom has come out with a book of her own entitled* My Fabulous Father). *His twin sons are, respectively, a Marine Lance Corporal and a naval officer. He is a prolific author, much in demand, writing different kinds of books under several pseudonyms.*

ELEANORE

Alex Austin

I

BERGMAN

"To attack the sun, to expunge it from the
universe, or to use it to set the world ablaze —
these would be crimes indeed!"

Marquis de Sade

*T*he island was a paradise.

This was the first thought that came to her as she stepped from the mainland ferry onto the creaking pier that could have been thousands of years old from the decrepit, yet somehow stately look of it. It was a pier to mark end or beginning to legendary voyages that are always too fantastic to believe. It was a pier where old men and children fish with strings on bright afternoons.

She hailed a leather-skinned old man in a battered taxi. She heard the ferry bell ring twice, then a third time. A gray gull came gliding with perfectly still wings directly toward her, but at an angle that permitted her to see only one of its eyes and that one eye looked like a stone that had been set into its head; the gull, its head cocked slightly, pulled up with a swift grace only a few feet from her and flew on indifferently past her, past the ferry, out to sea.

She had to call the old man four times before he heard her. Then he smiled, nodded, started the loud engine of his taxi and drove the less than ten yards between where she had been standing and where he had been parked.

"I want to go to the Hotel ————," she said.

The old man grinned now as if he were vastly amused, but he did not move. He merely looked out of the open window at her with pleased yellow eyes that were wrapped in wrinkles.

"I have some luggage," she said.

He shrugged and nodded and after a few moments during which he seemed to be almost asleep with the grin on his lips, he stepped from the taxi, loaded her four bags onto the rack on top, tied them with rope and a moment later, they were on their rattling way over the dirt road that led around the harbor and headed off towards the distant hills.

From the taxi, E could see much of the town, built as it was in a crowded jumble of houses that seemed to have been piled one on top of the other.

Houses along the curving harborfront were built up into slim, elegant tiers. There was a fountain whose three round basins held rain water and the droppings of gulls and pigeons who rested all day on its rims. Gray pushcarts and women in black and boys screaming in short pants and girls fondling the distant sight of patched sails with their dark eyes — all these were a feast of pink, black, yellow, red, green and umber along the narrow alleys and colonnades running between the houses. Bony cypresses, behind the facade of the harbor, held in their shadows broken towers and part of a wall grown heavy with weeds and a thousand skins of decay.

The old man drove as if he thought the taxi were competing at Rome's ancient games. It bounced over high bumps and at each one he laughed proudly and slapped the wheel with one hand or the other. The machine was a live animal to him. E heard him muttering from time to time and what little she could make out, he was saying to the taxi, not to her.

But the windows on both sides caught views of such open splendor, they took her breath away. Swallows and martins dipped and swerved over the empty fields. Yellow sickle-shaped eucalyptus leaves held the sun as if it had been caught in the palms of a hundred golden hands.

She had hoped for a good place, as she always did. But this more than fulfilled her hopes. There was such a live clarity to everything she saw, it seemed she had been seriously wounded, they had all feared she might become blind, and now, the instant she stepped from the ferry to the pier, someone had torn the bandages from her eyes and a hundred new colors had been added to the world.

Coming to this island, across such a rough and stubborn sea, was to come from a country of shapes to a country of colors. All light seemed refracted and every stone was the beginning of a mirage. The very atmosphere trembled as a piece of silk touched by a calm breeze. Volcanoes slept their gray deep sleep amidst blue and golds, falling to valleys of thick yellows and reds, with purple Judas trees exploding along dusty roads that stood more as monuments to past journeys than invitations to new ones. Lush olive groves spotted the green fields, while near the sea, towers of bald rock were a wilderness of dreary rock-thistle and asphodel.

But there was a bleak, hard quality to all this that chilled her even with the sun burning upon the side of her face and on her folded hands. The landscape was one in which the only miracle was the man standing in the dust. And the old fear swept through her suddenly, the fear of all her journeys.

She moved to the center of the seat to escape the sun just as the old man struck a gigantic bump that nearly made him cry from laughing so hard at his success of getting over it.

Small fish flickered through green shadows.

Darius sat naked and gleaming on a great rock. His body wore the sunlight as a suit of armor. His head was covered with thick black curls that gave the impression the hair was never combed. The sun burned brightly in his face, as if it had been caught in an urn of brass. A thin scar ran down his left cheek. He was a big man who just as easily could have been small; nothing in his personality was related to his size. The ocean splashed up over the rock and the naked man. He sat there with a handful of cherries, and he watched the sea.

Gulls turned downwind and a dry breath of sirocco choked the morning air. At the edge of the shale beach a huge fig tree squatted, like a peasant woman peeing from under her wide skirts.

Darius waited. His large arms rested on his knees as he leaned forward slightly. The black hair was matted down. Waves broke around him, one after the other, the sea's rhythm changing, twisting, plunging in and out of itself. Sea water dripped from his nose and chin, down his chest and belly and thighs, from his hands and from the edges of his lips as he sat and watched. His dark eyes slowly scanned the sea close to his rock with a calm eagerness, an edge of joy that could be patient.

Then her head shot from the green and white surface, her long black hair flowing like silk down around her tanned face and over her shoulders.

Darius laughed out of a joy that was like leaping high in a dance when he saw her and as soon as she'd wiped the water from her eyes, she smiled up at him, part of that dance.

He took two of the cherries, held them up over his head. The girl laughed and spit salt water at him and waited at the edge of the game, a playful creature from the bottom of the sea.

Then Darius dropped the cherries into the churning small waves. They fell two fathoms down to the sandy bottom covered with shells and pebbles and torn green weeds that, being turned about constantly by the sea, were live creatures.

The girl sucked in a deep breath, clamped her lips shut and somersaulted herself over into a quick dive, her bare ass catching an instant of the sun.

Darius watched her long naked body glide among frightened fish as she touched bottom, searched briefly in the green light there and seconds later surfaced with the two cherries between her teeth like neat parcels of blood stolen from the sea.

E told the driver to stop. He said something to the taxi and it stopped. Then turning to her, he said, "There's nothing here."

"It's such a beautiful view," she said. "The sea, the cliffs . . ."

The driver did not seem to understand what she meant.

"I'll just be a minute," she said.

She got out of the taxi, leaving the door opened behind her.

The driver scratched the side of his stubbled face very slowly as he watched her walk across the narrow stretch of bare land between the road and the cliff's edge. All the skin around his eyes was dark, as if it had been charred by swift wheels of flame come only for an instant of his life. The wind caught at her white skirt and the old man patiently waited for it to blow the silk high enough for a look at her excellent legs.

She walked close to the edge of the cliff.

The old man spat out the window, into the dust, narrowed his eyes to the sharp glare of the sun behind her.

E looked straight out towards the sun. It was closer to earth than she had ever seen it. The wind slashed white caps up into the air, playing some viscous game with the sea. At the horizon's line, a flock of wild ducks curved down into low clouds and scattered into their depths.

She had never seen a sky so blue, a sea so bursting with life. The very air excited her as it poured into her lungs, blew into her eyes and into her mouth when she parted her lips to shamelessly taste the wind.

There was amber in the sea too. She was certain that creatures centuries old were still swimming or lying asleep in its depths. Gnawed rocks close to shore had the rubbed look of bone. A piece of driftwood lay stripped on the sand, still wet, a shape of forgotten things.

E's face was too sharply lit by the sun. It was not a naked face, but painted over with skill and with the anguish seen only in beautiful women who will never believe they are beautiful; it was painted over as an ancient canvas, a hundred faces deep, and in these depths perhaps one face made by a master, perhaps none.

Her eyes had been bruised more by what they had seen in mirrors than by what they had seen in the world. And even smiling, as she was now, only at the wind and sky, her smiles were transient and as lonely as if they had only been sketched upon her lips.

Below her, at the foot of the cliff, the foetus of an octopus lay upon the gray sand. Spent ends of the receding tide lapped at the colorless ball of gelatine.

Her eyes moved slowly down the empty beach. She was glad it was deserted. It gave her a feeling of possession. She had come from such crowded worlds to this empty place. It gave her a feeling of freedom too, perhaps safety.

But the beach was not deserted.

She saw the man and woman come running hand in hand, both laughing, out of the sea. They were naked and strong and so young . . . For an instant their nakedness shocked her. The shock turned to hatred. The hatred turned to fascination.

She watched them run out of the sea, then up across the sand, slowing where it was dry, stopping once to kiss.

They ran to what appeared to be the mouth of a cave. But they did not go inside. They fell down on the sand and embraced first like children playing a game, laughing, rolling over and over in each other's arms until finally the laughter was silenced by kisses and they were lovers in the same wind that blew into her eyes.

She stood there at the cliff's edge gazing down upon their joined bodies. Even from such a distance she could see the free smiles on their faces, hear the sounds they made through the sea's roar and the wind's careless whispering around her ears.

The sight of their naked bodies frolicking on the beach fascinated her in the way people are stunned, but excited, by the sight of smashed corpses at the scene of an accident.

She stood there a long time, finally hoping they had seen her watching them.

Then she returned to the taxi without knowing that the old man had also seen what he had been patiently waiting to see.

IV

*T*he mulatto boy lay naked across Bergman's bed. Flat on his back, his eyes closed, full lips just barely parted, he had the sleek look of a wild animal caught suddenly in a human skin.

Bergman stood by the door, his bloated face shiny with the remains of sweat that had, only moments earlier, poured from his flesh-like tears.

The brandy glass beside the bed had not been touched. Bergman smiled at this. The boy never drank — not wine, not brandy, not whiskey or gin or uso. Bergman had tried them all, but the boy's glass was always untouched when they were finished.

He'll sleep a while now, Bergman thought. He always sleeps when it's over. And even his closed eyes are closed in a way to make one believe it took great skill to close them.

Bergman reached up to touch his own cheek as he thought, eyes narrowing down: *If I could steal this boy from himself.* The idea amused him. The smile showed only in his eyes, at the corners. He would wake up to find himself not there. Then, of course, he would have to beg me for himself and I would make him crawl . . .

"Sleep, little warrior," said Bergman in a gruff whisper.

He heard the taxi pull up loud as a herd of horses in front of the hotel. He heard old Nickolio. Then he heard the woman.

"You sleep now, little warrior," said Bergman. "Yes, pretty chocolate body. You sleep and keep your secrets."

Then Bergman laughed softly, his huge body wobbling in the white suit with much more force than such quiet laughter seemed to demand.

"Did your goats teach you all the tricks you know, little warrior?" he asked the boy. "Or is it God who knew so much?"

He watched the sleeping boy a few moments more. Blades of shuttered light cut across the naked body on the bed. His eyes touched each inch of that sweet familiar flesh. A fly landed on the edge of the boy's untouched glass and with its first step, toppled into the brandy and began to drown.

"I've got to pee first," Bergman muttered. His eyes had their own hunger. "I always forget."

He cross the tiled floor to the bathroom. There he relieved

himself and smiled on the way back across the room, perfectly satisfied now with how he felt.

PART VI

I

Women ran down to the sea, carrying burning torches which they plunged into the waves and brought out still burning because they had been smeared with sulphur and lime. One of the women, knee-deep in white foam, looked up, startled, her green mask of a wingless bird betraying no emotion as she cried out, "Look! Look! Out there . . ." holding her torch high as if she thought she could illuminate the entire night with its meagre flame. "Out there . . ."

The others looked to where she was pointing. There were hushed sounds of surprise and awe behind their masks.

Not a hundred yards from where they stood in the sea, was the largest ship any of them had ever seen. It was lit by a thousand lights. Its rigging reached the stars. Music echoed across the brief stretch of water, a music that was foreign and discordant to their ears.

One of the women was so startled by sight of the ship, she dropped her torch into the sea. It rolled over on the end of a wave, burned briefly, then drifted out dark on the tide.

Slowly, the women walked back up the beach, the sea dripping from their skirts, their proud torches suddenly humbled by the listless way they held them, staring at the anchored ship, bewildered by its many lights, by its harsh music, by the tiny figures who seemed to be dancing on its deck.

Father Manoli saw the ship from the cliff. A rare glitter of stars was caught in the turning sea below. He often ended up at the sea's edge when he became this drunk, but he never remembered why. He could stand there falling out of his own body, the world deep and open at the next step before him, yet it was a step in terror and to freedom that he never took. He would come, completely drunk, all paths laid out in his heart, damned as one who has glimpsed the face of God and then has forgotten.

Then, like a scattering of graces, the sea air blowing into his face always sobered him out of his counterfeit crime against God; sobered him suddenly, it seemed, but gently too, just enough for him to salvage a little repentance about becoming so completely drunk while doing his Holy Father's work.

He had been recalling the priests who had come before him, stories handed down like omens that merged so closely together in time, the whiskey turned them all into yesterday.

He himself was the only priest among them all who did not dress up on this day of the Saint. In the beginning, old women timidly informed him that it was perfectly in order for him to mask himself on this day. They talked to him as shy grandmothers might talk to a grandchild who has been given a power they fear. They even told him — trying to pass the information off as half a joke — that other priests had used the Saint's Day not to become a goat or hawk, but to become merely a man, since the Saint permitted even this, and there was much joy to be had in such a disguise.

But Father Manoli knew so little of his own face, he wouldn't even have known truly whether the mask he put on was identical to that face or as different as the face of a man is from the face of a frog.

He had — and the knowledge always came clearly to him on this night — lived his life inside himself just as surely as if he had been condemned at birth to solitary confinement for a crime no one either cared about or could remember. But with her — this woman who had plagued his every waking moment since she'd come to him — he had, he felt in his heart, been on the verge of stepping out of that tight dreary cell in which he'd always lived.

She had said, "Don't pity me."

And he had replied, "I can't," thinking that before this he never would have said these words.

But she had come to confess. She had come to spread the numb legs of her soul before him and his faith was impotent to take her.

He heard her cries and told himself then that God does exist because flesh can suffer the outrageous fires of the soul. To suffer and to touch and to desire: this was God's proof in the flesh of the world.

And perhaps the secret he had never known was that if he could doubt man instead of God, his search would be done. He had always believed in man; but for God . . . could he exchange man for God? Could he make such a bargain? Perhaps if only the old children's story Devil were true he would come with his absolute laughter to seal the pact, make this bargain possible.

But the Devil did not even have to bother with a man who, all his life long, had never even so much as shed a single tear. He'd never cried. He'd failed every inch of his flesh. And what greater tribute could that hooved laughing Prince ask of any man? He could not even bargain with Hell; he had no thirst to quench, his hunger was silence; the purse of his life was empty; there was not so much as one coin with which he could purchase damnation.

Then gull cries shook him. The sea's hushed voice broke through his silence.

Down far below, drifting in bondage to tides, the yacht was white, a defier still of black seas, with pitch-pine spars and Italian hemp ropes and copper painting on the keel.

It was a ship to be seen miles off in any distance. But none of the dancers saw the ship. Below its keel: the swaying of seaweed fronds, forests of another age. Soles, hogfish and skate went on about their nocturnal searchings of the deep. An old man was explaining in the tavern to no one in particular, his voice lost in shouts and music, how a turtle's heart will beat for hours after it has been cut up and butchered. In the Baron's empty room, a candle drew breath to harden images against the white-washed walls; he came upon Sudo in the hills. The boy was crouched like a scared fawn among his goats. Each saw the other, was still a moment as if each were certain the other had to speak, yet at the same time each seemed to recognize the silence, to have expected it in many ways other than this one that now touched them. It was as if each, for only one moment belonging to both past and future, was haunted by the other; each, in the easy way of true gifts, made the other feel perfectly natural to himself, as a stone must be or any beast. Two halves of one life had been scattered like a joke across time, each bearing in love the heartless sign of the pure in heart. But there was nothing to be said. The Baron turned, and as he did, forgot forever the fathomed beauty of one moment. He walked off slowly along strange paths to the crest of a hill from which, finally, he too could look down and see not only lights in the town and torches whirling across dark fields, but the ship as well.

Father Manoli grinned, knowing how drunk he was, to think that perhaps there was no ship anchored out there in the bay at all; such ships did not come to the island; perhaps this was the vision he'd been waiting all his life for, the miracle, the tired game. Why couldn't God or the Devil take the form of a ship?

Father Manoli then idly blessed the ship. He made a sign of the cross over the sea. His hand remained raised before him when he had completed his blessing and the sight of it woke him; he thought for an instant it was the hand of another and thought the hand had blessed *him*.

Sudo looked up to see clouds like winding sheets stretched across the sky, closing together as if the dark itself were the corpse to be tended; he felt a second drop, a third . . .

In the dim light, Bergman's body slumped in the chair, was a huge pile of unmoulded flesh, covered with sweat, flesh of a condemned man waiting for his crime to be committed.

He could not close their music and shouting out of his ears. The pernod only thickened the sounds, poured molasses over piano strings, drew them more deeply into the nightmare he painted in his own mind to obliterate the even more terrible reality of this day during which he could feel both his inner and outer self dissimulating like a cube of sugar lowered into hot coffee on a spoon.

Down in the town, in their damned simplicity, their gray masks of plodding deaf and dumb lives turned to faun faces in the light of the Saint's Day. Dying for celibacy and God, the good Saint, by some miscalculation of his immortal soul, had given them license and the Devil. And it was good, he thought on any day but this one, to see a Saint blunder this way into an honest joke on himself and his people loved him in a marvelous way for it. On this day the Saint seemed to him to be transformed from a man of God into a carnival magician whose best trick was to pull the Devil himself out of a hat and make him dance.

What he did, sitting there, sick, exhausted, was to make an orgy of memory by casting time aside, by crowding one room with a hundred nights, by gathering an entire life in the damp palm of one hand to watch the dwarfed figures tumble and dance over his fingers a silent circus to distract him from the terror, of believing he was the only one on the island Death could find this night.

What a comedy it was, he thought, that men today feared their own souls as they once feared the thunder! How much he would give beyond the false ring of all the words he spoke and all the laughter he laid at the world's altar like a dung offering, to fear the thunder rather than his own soul.

He had to sit in mourning for the void they all filled with their meagre carnival of lies. For himself, he had always preferred Hell to nothingness. His insides had long ago been scorched, ravaged by this choice. Put down in the town they could play like children with their dreams, not having to realize dreams were no more than dubious souvenirs that rot the heart.

And this night in his terror he could not find the old God to calm him, because this woman with her perfect sterility seemed to have been sent only to tell him that God had rotted in our dry loins and could wait with His patience for other worlds to be green again; God had been debauched by our poor ways of believing in Him; God was like that love that's fit only for the strongest hearts, those hungry not for peace or trembling or the crafty fear of beggars, but for joy, only for joy, there is no other kingdom He will rule. For God to care for what was left of this world would be like the pitiful love a woman might have for an impotent lover.

Smoke rose in lazy lines from fires over which whole kids were turning. Shadows were luminous among the trees; a skinny small man in a toad's mask was peddling ikons, talismans and sweets, making grand gestures as he tried to shout above the sounds of music, singing and shouting.

Four women sat in a circle on the grass, blackbirds huddled close, eating round pieces of cheese through their masks. Two boys in the branches of a eucalyptus tree over their heads, strained to catch their muffled gossip of women's secrets and fought at each revelation to hold laughter back.

The girl dancing in the square had limbs that were completely out of keeping with her delicate face; she looked as if she had been made by two artists — one painting on porcelain, the other cutting forms out of the huge stones that contain them. Cold drops dangled at her ears, her hair was a marvelous black erection, tied with red ribbons into feathery tiers. Her hips and thighs undulated back and forth and around in a manner suggesting she was imitating the slow movement of tides seen in the dark. She danced as if dancing were the only thing she could do.

Darius and E were in the circle that had formed around the girl. Men and women of all ages sang with the music. Cries for more wine were mingled with belches. Every sound and shape was cast in and out of a hundred mirrors of the dark. He turned to watch her smiling at the dancer and he could feel the pride in him like a final kind of blood, proud as he was of her beauty, of the world she was; a world without meaning had been named in her flesh, in her knowledge of him, in the promise of moments her fingertips touching his could make.

Then she turned to look at him, smiled when she saw his eyes on her.

"I'm proud," he said. He said it awkwardly and in a soft voice.

"And I'm proud too."

She leaned her head over to kiss his hand slowly just as a loud cry burst at their ears, followed by laughter and a high screeching sound on the clarinet as the towering bald man reeled backwards, the instrument falling from his lips as he laughed, turning into arms that caught him. The girl dancing lifted her skirts high and began kicking one leg, then the other, to cheers on every side and hands clapping in different rhythms now, sweat all over her face under the small mask, on her body under the dress, dripping down her bare kicking legs until finally she too toppled four steps backwards into the arms of a stubby hawk who wrapped himself around her panting body and this seemed the signal for everyone to commence dancing.

"I love you," E said, as a unicorn pulled her suddenly out of his arms, leading her into the dance. "I love . . ." The words were drowned out by laughter and music. Darius was pushed back into the thickening crowd as they made room for the new dancers and he smiled to watch her moving with a frightened grace in the arms of the obscure beast.

Yorgo was eating himself silly by the turning lambs. Shadows of olive trees were broken by candles and torches and by the remains of the yellow moon.

So many torches were being whirled about or held still or carried slowly that, seen from the hills where the Baron stood, the town was on fire, a sacked objective on the map of some secret war.

Candles were set down on the floor and Bergman threw chestnuts out for the three naked girls to pick up between their teeth, crawling on hands and knees between the candlesticks. The girls chattered. They giggled and laughed. They cried out like queens having crowns branded on their skulls when he or one of the others fell upon them, taking them in obscure ways, playing games left over from childhood that have rotted in the flesh cellars where they were abandoned until this night; inflicting luxurious wounds that compelled him to respect a girl who fell back finally in languid memory of a pain that was too great to bear until it diluted her senses, her soul, as does childbirth, and so can be carried in the bones forever without regret.

Soon they became so drunk, no girl could tell one prick from another. They ate giant oysters at midnight, poured herb mixtures to make blood burn into their wine which they drank out of perfumed goblets while the roof spun dizzily around, the table danced and every light in the endless room showed double.

On that night — how many years ago? — the old German who had given the party had a lean hewn face with blue jowls and a rebellious black mustache. His hair grew low on his forehead; fierce brows twisted in scowling flourishes over wary dark eyes. He spoke and moved with the heavy grace of a general who has successfully escaped his own army.

The house had been in a lake. There were chandeliers. The room was filled with silk. Every guest had been beautiful. Yet the purpose of the night had been to destroy each separate beauty as if that were the only way to stop the ebbing of life. Hell was the final adventure.

But each pit of pleasure, then as now, as filled as it seemed from the surface looking down, was always empty at the bottom. He could barely move. The room was full of saints imitating themselves, dressed in the drag of angels. There are these nuns too who take a veil of flesh and make a dark cloister of their mouths as they accept the Host of living gods. A thin tall blonde girl in stockings had died that night and not one of them, man or woman, could say he had not shared in the deed. They had buried her naked behind the old German's house, in silence, not a word was said over her; her stockings were burned; her name was never heard again; she had cried out with wild pleasure all that night and had been beautiful.

His robe hung open now. He felt as if his cock did not belong to him. His life this night had worn so thin, he could see his own death through it, like one of those dim bulbs that seems to humiliate light.

Hungry terns, poor hunters, skimmed in low over dark sands and rocks catching moonlight. Inside the tavern, off in a corner, behind them, heard through the open door, Loukas in his thin boy's voice was singing a song it was said had been left behind by Crusaders who had accidentally landed on the island. Darius drank, listened, waited for her to return. The others talked from behind their masks. Windmills caught edges of the rising wind, turned faster. In the red oleander grove, away from the sea, two lovers lay in each other's arms, young lovers, timid, yet sure in the gentle ways they reached for each other in the soft grass.

A small boy in a rabbit's mask was getting ready above awed eyes of his companions, to jump off a roof.

"They are like the angels when the lights in Heaven have gone out." Bergman muttered the words, nodded, began to smile. One hand lay limply in his lap. "It would be a better peace than this," he said. "No more than a good night's sleep." God wouldn't wake a man like the house detective they all make him out to be. One bullet. Quick. No dream.

Father Manoli, drunk, blessed the dancers as he walked among them, for they sought his blessing on this night as a joke.

The Baron winced as he swallowed his first drink in thirty years. A warm green rain of summer began to fall, but no one seemed to notice it. Sudo heard the small click of eucalyptus leaves as they began to plane down over the gray rocks near him; he could feel the wind. In pastures richly scented with thyme and myrtle bruised by the hooves of goats, more lovers found secret places.

Darius stood up. They grabbed his arms. "Sit down . . ." "Drink." "Later . . ." He gently pulled his arms free. He searched the dark laughing crowd for her. The Baron looked over at him, at the eyes marked by silence and was surprised to feel pity for the young man's being young.

A small octopus writhed among huge bubbles in a black pot, giving off the rich smell of pepper and garlic. Someone said, "It's beginning to rain."

Marauding black clouds were crossing the moon.

Darius moved slowly among dancers. The clarinet player had passed out. Two men were slapping his painted bone face, trying to revive him.

Sudo, clinging to a black goat under a tree, smiled up, no longer frightened, at the rain. He was like grass again. The very drops of water out of the sky calmed him, put away terrors, as if the tips of fingers were reaching down to trace soothing lines across his brow.

Bergman remembered where the Lugar was. He'd come finally to the proper night he'd always known had been patiently waiting for him. Looking back this final time over his own life, he felt hideously chaste. He had not touched, had not, in turn, been touched.

But then he thought: suicide is only masturbation; murder is copulation. Perhaps all his life he had been no more than a child standing before a mirror in the dark, jerking off. He could have murdered *her;* that one must select a proper victim who would be an accomplice. But it was too late and he had failed himself.

He heard a knock on the door first, then a voice call out downstairs. "Is anyone here?" It was a man's mild voice and he spoke English. His head cleared as quickly as if someone had turned off the switch of his despair. "Is anyone . . ."

He shouted, "Coming . . ." in his usual voice that had no sign in it to indicate only a moment before he had been about to take his own life.

He dressed quickly, amazed by his return, it rendered him almost innocent. He pulled on soiled white trousers, a shirt, a white jacket, shoes without socks, and went downstairs.

For several moments, he saw no one and it occurred to him he had only imagined the voice, had even called out to himself, any role was possible.

"I've come for Mrs. Girard's bags," the man said very politely. He was standing in front of the desk, in the corner of the lobby. "I'm her husband."

Bergman could hardly believe his ears. The man took a few steps towards him, entering the circle of light cast down by the three bare bulbs in the center of the ceiling.

"I'm Paul Girard," the man said.

Bergman squinted needlessly, pulling his thick lips up into an expression that looked like sneering.

This Paul Girard stood there, small, patient, exactly what he would have expected: a man who could be polite in a tragedy. He wore a dark, neat suit, white shirt, black tie, his reddish hair cut short. He was compact in a way that suggested he did not wish to take up any more space than was absolutely necessary — even in his own life. He was one of those men who had always been middle-aged. He was one of those sad little conquerors who win a battle because the wind changed and blew a fire in the wrong direction.

"I've come for my wife's bags," he said. His voice was calm, low, proper. He was, Bergman observed, perfectly cut out for the job and seemed to have performed this duty many times before and the mere sight of him brought Bergman's old spirits back as if the poor devil had come bringing a miracle.

"Your *wife!*" Bergman roared, laughing loud with the words, shoving hands down into his pockets. "Your *wife!*" It was exactly what he should have expected again, yet he was utterly astonished and glad of it.

"Yes . . ." He stood absolutely still.

"You've come for her bags, you say."

"Yes."

"Nice little man."

Girard was silent.

"You're her husband."

"Yes."

"You're not staying . . ."

"No. I've come . . ."

"You don't want a room then."

"No."

"Well . . . come in . . . yes . . . here . . . sit down. Please . . ." He took the small man's arm and led him over to a chair near the windows. "Her *husband!*"

Paul Girard sat down. Bergman walked to a narrow table near

the door, lit a lamp, realized it shed no more light than the three bulbs overhead, turned to Girard again. "So you're her husband," he said. The sound of rain grew louder on windows, in mounting puddles, on leaves and rooftops.

And Girard said, "Yes," in a quiet voice.

Bergman peered down at him, tried to fathom his calm tiny eyes but found nothing in them, only a mild acceptance that disgusted him, eyes that were the color of a grave.

"Do you know where she is now?" Bergman asked.

Paul Girard nodded. "She's on the boat," he said.

"Boat!" Berman cried out. Why the damned fellow had pulled the rug right out from under him! *"Which* boat?"

"My . . . yacht." His voice was damp and empty.

"She expected you then?" Bergman asked, pacing back and forth in front of Girard.

Paul Girard nodded. He said, "Yes."

"She knew exactly when you were coming for her?"

He nodded once more and said, "Yes," in the same calm voice that was infuriating Bergman. Why the damned little cuckold had saved his life only to make a fool out of him!

"All the time she's been here she's known you'd come for her."

"Yes."

"On this day . . ."

He nodded.

"What?"

"She always knows when I'll come for her," Girard said.

"The exact day."

"Yes. She knows."

The brief fury put Bergman's flesh back on him; now he was amused.

"Each year," Girard said, "she goes off each year."

"It's always the same?"

"Yes."

"And you come for her bags?"

"Yes."

Bergman sighed. He shrugged, then smiled, then began laughing softly to himself, but the laughter fell away sadly after a few moments and again, he found himself completely dumbfounded by the calm of the poor devil, by the way sorrow seemed to have been created especially for his eyes, resignation for his heart.

"And you know, of course, *why* she goes off each year," Bergman said.

Again the husband nodded and said, "Yes." This time he began searching the room, peering from side to side, until Bergman asked him what he was looking for. Girard said, "I thought perhaps there'd be a bar." He looked up and smiled gently at Bergman. "I could offer to buy you a drink," he said. "But I'll spare you that."

"Offer to buy . . . !" Bergman was stunned. "But yes . . . yes, of course . . . forgive me . . . It would be . . . well, then, proper, I suppose . . . only, well, you see . . . I'm not really the one . . ."

Girard seemed puzzled, but only mildly so and only for a moment.

"No . . ."

"Oh, I'm sorry," Girard said. "I'm afraid I've made a mistake."

"Well, not completely," Bergman said, thinking that as long as the devil was intent on playing cat and mouse with him, he could at least invent a game or two himself. It was only for this reason that he suggested to Paul Girard they go upstairs to his room, pointing out how bleak a place the lobby was. Girard was only too glad to accompany Bergman upstairs. He seemed so glad that Bergman thought immediately he had made a mistake and his opponent had outwitted him again.

As soon as they entered the room, however, Girard paused and seemed visibly shaken by the sight of the huge bed off in the far corner of the room. Bergman grinned, watching him. He closed the door quietly so as not to break Girard's mood.

But after only a few moments, Girard stepped further into the room, looked over at Bergman and said, "It always takes me a little while before I can accept her lovers. And I presume you've been one of them . . . if not the one I was referring to before. But . . ." And he clapped his hands once almost like a child as he went on, smiling just a bit, " . . . I think I can accept you now." He turned frank eyes to Bergman who was thinking he was glad life had surprises left — even if they had to be this outrageous. He must not, at all costs, be tricked out of enjoying the situation.

"Has she told you of the man?" Bergman asked, "The one she loves . . . or at least, the one she used the word with?"

Girard nodded. He went to the armchair, sat down in a confident way. Bergman noticed his hands, even in the smallest gesture, had a tentative strength, a kind of constant groping after the handle of his own life.

"She's told me," Girard said after a pause. "She always tells me . . . Oh, perhaps not all of it. But enough. You see, I know perfectly well I don't understand her. All I know is that she comes back to me. And that's enough, I suppose."

Girard fell silent. Bergman waited. He was thinking how Darius could very well be her life, but this man sitting before him, was her way of life.

Then Girard continued, much as if the words were a continuation of the silence, he spoke that way.

"She'll never love me like that," he said. "No." There was no regret in his voice. "I know that," he added.

"But you're satisfied?" Bergman asked him.

Girard looked up at him again. Bergman was surprised by the change in his eyes: they were no longer flat, the color of a grave. There was a deep kindness in them, a humiliating kindness. "I'm what she needs," Paul Girard said. "It isn't love. Not really. Not in that way. But she can be safe with me." The instant he finished saying this, an abjectly submissive smile gave new life to his lips, even to his eyes.

Girard was silent a moment, but when he began speaking again, it was in a low voice that indicated to Bergman he would continue for a long time and he did.

Paul Girard explained to Bergman what a fine mother she was to their three children, what a perfect wife she was to him. He laughed in an embarrassed manner when he said she was the most perfect mistress to him. ". . . even though I've not had much experience with women," he added.

Then Girard came back from his land of comfortable lawns and said, "One day she'll be old, you see. It will be different then . . ."

And Bergman said, "You can wait for that?"

"Yes."

"You want nothing more than this?"

"You see, I can't even imagine myself possessing any other woman," Girard said.

"You're her keeper then?" Bergman asked.

Girard hesitated, then shrugged, not so much in a confused or resigned as in an amiable manner.

"Perhaps," he said, smiling up at Bergman. "And perhaps she's my keeper too. She'll go off this way next year . . . many more times . . . But she'll always return to me. "

"Loving the others . . ."

"Yes," Girard said.

"Doing things with them . . ." He paused as if asking the other to interrupt him. It could be a holy confession in reverse, as when prisoners sit and hear their crimes confessed to them by the police. He could say, "And you kiss her mouth into which I've shot my load dozens of times." And the other could answer, as girls and murderers do to priests and detectives, "Yes," in a voice as simple as a knife or flower.

But all he heard him say was, "Yes. I know that too. But, you see, she'll always return to me. And that's all I ask of her really."

Bergman was silent again, waiting. But Paul Girard said no more. He seemed to be finished. And suddenly Bergman felt an overwhelming tenderness towards the man sitting so passively before him.

He expressed these feelings by saying, "You never humiliate her, do you?"

"I love her," Paul Girard replied.

Bergman fell silent, smiled to himself. He was alive again, but in a different way; this man had given him a new calm he could not yet understand.

Outside the light rain had turned into a storm. Bergman went to the windows, stood with his back to Paul Girard.

Thunder clamoured now and rolled across the sky and claws of lightning tore open the dark as if the night had been a body. Walls and floors turned damp. Sweeping long sheets of rain shrouded the earth and sea. And there was a luxurious strength in great waves that hurled themselves against rocks and beaches.

In two flashes of lightning as he stood by the window, the land looked to Bergman to be as harsh as steel. It could well have been a dead planet, a home to dragons, a country made of a curse.

Turning slowly to Paul Girard, Bergman said, "I'll take you to his house."

Girard merely nodded in a grateful manner. Bergman led him downstairs without another word. Girard picked up a black umbrella he had stood against the wall just inside the door. They went outside. Girard opened the umbrella, offered Bergman a place beneath it, lifting it high for him, but Bergman walked out into the rain, was completely soaked to the skin in a matter of seconds. Girard caught up with him. They started down towards the town where scattered torches reeled and flickered in the wind, in the heavy rain. Music could still be heard, but it was a blurred sound now. Bergman smiled to himself as they walked in silence; he had forgotten what it was like to walk slowly in the rain.

He walked, smiling this way until he heard the shot. He stopped, looked sharply around, as if he expected to feel the bullet in his own flesh. Girard stood there small and tender beneath the wide black umbrella like a man capable of being hung for the murder of a tailor's dummy.

Girard pointed towards the sea.

It had not been a shot. Lines of blurred thin fire crossed the sky, a white fire the color of stars.

". . . party!" Girard shouted, still pointing. "The ship . . ."

Another burst of fire defied the rain, opened gracefully to form a white canopy over the sea.

They were exploding fireworks and drinking champagne and dancing in the white salon.

E, in a long white gown of silk, a single string of pearls around her neck, stood among them.

They said, "Come over here . . ." Those by portholes. ". . .the fireworks . . ."

She joined them, watched rockets cut sharply up through the dark, the terrors that bind us to the sky, then obliterate it for a shatteringly beautiful instant . . .

"Too bad it's raining though," someone said.

". . . that reach to love . . ."

"Oh, I think it makes it even more exciting."

The terrors that destroy only love.

She could see the island as new rockets burst out in front of the ship. It was a solid carved piece of the dark. She appeared perfectly calm. It was without hope. She knew that. From the beginning it was without hope. That is why we can never die of it.

"I'll live all my life on what we had." She said this too. In another time. There was no face, no body to remember. Only the words.

Her face was overburdened by light even in this dim place.

She sipped at her champagne as they danced, as she could beg her heart for one memory beyond consolation, knowing none was possible. Because we do forget. Her lips were cold. Only in farewells could she feel it. We forget everything. We always forget. We are always forgotten. All who have died of love. She sipped at her champagne.

Someone asked her to dance. She smiled, said, "In a few minutes." The dancers moved in a slow circle, all pressed together, barely moving as if they had lost the music and were keeping that secret. The ship rolled easily, even as sudden black mountains rose up out of the sea, another earth being born this night.

She stood there watching the sea and the island. They danced by her. She was filled with silence. Some paused and spoke of ports they had already visited, ports they would visit on the way home, names that were blurred belonging to no language, but beautiful strange names filled with other promises as when one can fall asleep each night, trusting the dream that is sure to come.

"Paul . . ."

She turned. Their eyes were all perfect emblems of defeat.

Darius opened the door.

He came towards her, past the dancers, hands outstretched to touch her hands.

"Dear Paul," she said softly.

"Would you like to dance, my dear?" he asked her.

"Let's just watch the others," she said.

"Is there anything . . ."

"Nothing, darling," she said. "I'm fine."

Darius was silent when he saw Bergman standing there alone.

"Where is she?" Darius asked Bergman.

He said, "Gone."

Darius was silent. The door swung back and forth on old hinges behind him. The wind blew in gusts of rain to wet a half-circle inside the doorway. Bergman could taste dry salt on his lips.

"Where is she?" Darius asked again as they watched the

dancers arm in arm, gentle faces together, rain and music blurred in the dark and under polished lamps. "Where . . ."

"He came for her," Bergman said. "Her husband. She knew he was going to come for her. A nice little man."

Another rocket burst out into the night, casting fire everywhere.

"You've redone the salon," E said.

"I wanted to surprise you," said her husband.

"It's beautiful," she said.

"Every year," Bergman said. "It's the same. She has to find love every year, what she calls love. Can you understand that? And he always comes for her, always takes her home again. They're gone . . ."

Darius stood there, could have been made of stone or iron.

Bergman was surprised at a sudden feeling of something almost like pity for the young man. But he laughed the feeling out of himself, let a mild fart carry the good spirit up into a brief sensible stench.

"You're better off without her," he said. "She's a dead woman. What do you want with a dead woman?"

Darius' eyes fixed themselves on Bergman, focusing now in the dim light.

"She's dead," Bergman said. "You can't love the dead." It seemed to him that Darius was trying to move and couldn't. No light touched him and shadows lay dead on the floor all around his feet. Bergman grinned and said, "She'd spread those pretty legs of hers for any man." He could see the suffering like iron grown into the young man's eyes. "Even for a fat pig like me," he continued, enjoying the role he had chosen to play; having heard once, "Be the only meaning of the world; there are no other kings." "And not just spread her legs," he said. "Has that helpless mouth of hers explored every inch of you? Has it? That tongue . . ." Bergman laughed. Darius was motionless. "Have you fucked that pretty lady's ass until she screamed under you and promised everything with those screams?" The laughter broke and faded under his words as he spoke. "Did she give you all this, boy, or were you cheated by tenderness? Eh?" He laughed again. "Cheated by *love*? She could do that too. Let one man piss over every inch of her if that's what she thought was to be given to this one. Then give only tenderness if that's what fitted another one. The dead can be the wisest of creatures, the most dangerous race. Don't you know that? Or won't you believe she's swallowed whatever I wanted to stuff into her helpless little mouth and . . ."

Darius grabbed Bergman by the collar, wrenching breath out of him, shoving him back several feet, both their bodies hitting the table, a half-empty wine bottle crashed to the floor. Darius picked up the knife that lay beside the white cheese.

Bergman grinned slowly. "Like the Germans," he muttered. He nodded. "Good."

Darius held him. Their eyes were a language. Then he let go. He stepped back.

"Use it!" Bergman said. "There's nothing else you can do! Go on! Don't fall apart! Use it!"

Darius dropped the knife. Bergman laughed. Darius turned, started towards the door. Bergman said, "There's nothing you can do!" Darius ran outside. "There's nothing you can do!" Bergman shouted with mockery. He walked quickly to the door, out into the rain. Darius was gone. Bergman laughed, standing in the dark, the rain blown by heavy winds into his face, forcing his eyes shut. He stood there and laughed and said the words again, but softly, to no one, "There's nothing you can do . . ." still with mockery and recalling his double failure, with both her men, laughing at how a lover was as impossible to humiliate as a condemned man. ". . . nothing you can do . . . " his voice completely drowned in hard sheets of rain, in broken thunder.

"Come back . . ." He was laughing.

But mere rain mocked his laughter, watered his curse to anguish, left him a fool in the dark of this night.

Darius ran from the house, ran breathing hard. He felt her sinking out of him. His face looked broken.

E said, "I'll never love anyone as I love Darius." She spoke with a hideous calm, as one who's learned how Death speaks without a sound and yet is heard above any other voice. Her husband stood quietly at her side. They watched the dancers. Her painted mouth smiled as they passed her. "I've never wanted anything so much in my life as I've wanted to marry him." Her husband said nothing. The dancers smiled as they passed her. Her smile, in return, was made of raw nerves and had the quality of a fine glass falling to the floor.

"But I'll be all right," she said.

Paul Girard turned kind eyes to his wife.

"I'm safe with you," she said.

"Darlings, come have some champagne."

"I am," she said. She pressed his hand without being able to feel it. Then she accepted a glass and heard, as though through the far memory the dead must have, a toast and glasses touching and mild laughter under the sea's raw cry.

They lifted glasses and spoke her name.

Their glasses raised like knives all around her. Their faces were deeper masks; but their hiding place was a land she knew, their lie in their perfect isolation, was as much truth as she could imagine lasting longer than a single night. Defeat was no burden when the victors were a race apart.

They spoke her name. Their voices called her and brought her back.

"Darling," he said. He kissed her cheek. She turned her eyes, ringed dark with colors once again, to this man she would serve always without love.

New thunder mocked every sound made now. The dark kept turning in on itself, a hounded beast.

Darius paused at the sea's edge. The breath came hard in him. Wind blew sharp rain and the heavy spray of waves into his face down over his body. He could not believe what had happened; can rocks die or birds not sing or the sea be as empty as a well? The love he felt for her now, in an instant, had become a dark love, like coming to the middle of the night and knowing there is no other place to be. All light had burned up into astounding ashes in his heart. The land's rim into the dark was cut short as though the earth had turned flat or itself could die, break off in such folly into dead space, the dark closing round him as a strangler's skilled hand at his heart.

The sand was firm under his feet. The tide broke the sea's pulse, each time a final time, upon the shore and louder still in black rocks nearby as he searched like a blinded animal for the ship, his black hair matted down, his face like stone wanting to be stone.

He heard a voice far-off. His groin grew tight with hatred for his own flesh as he saw faint lights of the ship that had already begun to take her from him. It was an impossible distance away; but he knew this sea and was as much its master as it was his master.

"Darius . . ."

He ran down the beach.

"Darius . . ."

The hand caught him.

"I saw her . . ." Father Manoli said breathlessly. Then he almost shouted the same words, "I saw . . . her . . ." Darius pulled his arm away from the priest. He walked this time, turning, walked down the sand towards his boat. Father Manoli ran again to catch him, stumbling, falling upright it seemed, holding his eyes wide-opened against the rain. He grabbed the arm again, hard as he could. ". . . not in this storm," he shouted after having only muttered the first words of the sentence.

Darius looked over at the priest as if he'd never seen him before.

"My son . . . don't," Father Manoli said. "It's killing yourself . . . this storm . . . you . . ."

"Let go, Father."

". . . against God . . ."

"I'm going to bring her back."

"Not in that sea . . ."

"In that sea," said Darius. "Let go."

"It's impossible!"

"Let go . . . Father . . ."

"No . . ."

Then slowly, the priest obeyed. He let go, but his hand barely seemed to move.

"There's nothing you can do," he said with pity.

"There's nothing else I can do," Darius said.

"You can't . . ." The priest felt tears.

He was forced by the sheer power of the sea sucking with deep mouths at his legs to leap into the boat, nearly capsizing it, managing only with much effort to settle it properly amid raging waves.

He undid ropes and in seconds seemed to have been hurled miles out beyond the land. He took up the oars. Her ship's lights teased in and out of the dark and walls of the sea building up over him, sea reaching for sky. He was calm. The sea began to enter his heart, had begun long ago, reached deeper now, reached finally as deep as he was.

The oars did no good. He knew that. They were useless. Still he used them with a perfect skill. Every inch of his body poured its separate strength into his arms, his back and shoulders and legs and heart. And for a brief time that seemed to him as long as his life, he kept up with the lighted ship, even gaining on it, hurtling lightly forward, twisting to one side, then almost gliding sternward on a lie of calm seas, his brain filled with the thunder, with the rain's sound, with fleshed winds coiling around the whore-body of this night.

He used the oars with this skill and closed in on the barren lights, as if his boat were sailing in the palm of God's own hand.

ALEX AUSTIN

Alex Austin spent a year and a half prospecting for gold in the Mojave Desert, and six months working as a ranch hand in California. He was once voted No. 14 jazz drummer in a poll conducted by Metronome *magazine, and is currently playing with the Village Jazz Quintet. He seems to be prouder of these accomplishments than of the fact that he has published over 500 stories, poems and articles, in such well-known publications as* Harper's, Stag, Mademoiselle, *and* The Quarterly Review of Literature. *He has also written three novels besides* Eleanore — The Bride, The Blue Guitar *and* The Greatest Lover in the World. *He was born in New York City and lives there still, with his wife and baby son.*

BARBARA

Frank Newman

Miser Catulle Desine inptire
et quod perisse vides perditum ducas.
You can't undo what's done,
Why do you try?

CATULLUS

Who's to say love is not a game we play?" ... contemporary country and western music has about
the same sensibility as the Roman Elegiac Poets—range just about

from Ovid to Catullus. Same preoccupation with death. Roman word for 'to love,' 'to come' and 'to perish' the same. Direct ancestor of the Spanish death business, though thank God, unfucked up by Christianity. What isn't in Elegy is in Roman so-called satire. 'What made Milwaukee famous made a fool out of me.' Perfect. As vulgar as Horace."

Frank was babbling on interestingly. But babbling. He dealt with his nervousness by being Frank. Neurosis is a punster. He opened his word store. Let his feeling freely flow in his words so as to avoid or postpone expressing them with his body. Tom was content to sit and listen while Frank built towering verbal structures out of the energy of his feelings, following the clear shining thread of his intention through baroque gardens of the interaction of Frank with his overfilled perceptual environment. Frank was secure in his persona as a fag. So secure that he did not join in the queers' compulsive hatred of the closet queen, recognized that there were really intermediate states. In other words no trace of the "he's one, of course" complex. No expressed self hate at all. But Tom wondered. He was secure in his persona as a fag. Wouldn't he hate his persona as a fag just for that? Because it was a persona? Because it was the despised crutch that he needed because he was afraid of his self?

Frank talked on and on . . . Tom became aware that the dancing stream of words was swerving as Frank sensed the direction of his preoccupation. "But we can learn to forgive and return to childish respect for stuffy old Catullus anyway. It's one of the things you can only . . . really no matter how smart you are . . . learn by growing older. It's too rotten to believe until you've been beaten on the head with it for a couple of decades. The world really is that hard though, so we learn to forgive. Young children can do it 'cause they know the world is pain. When you are five, the pain of having to eat some food you dislike, or the pleasure of eating one you like is great enough so that children can understand. But when we are young men and our will is active, we think so strongly, we believe so much in our powers (and rightly! rightly! they can create . . . from nothing) . . ."

The world whirled around Tom's understanding of the older man's understanding. He knew that they were alright together, that whatever he said or did would be alright. He looked at the great grey dog, whose head was resting on his master's feet, where he sat across from him and talked. "Do you make love with Dinny?" The dog raised his head when his name was mentioned. "Yes, of course, we love it, don't we, Dinny?" Bending down, he ruffled the beast's neck. "Many homosexuals who have large dogs do, or try to. Perhaps very few of them have a good enough scene with the dog to make it a regular thing. No. I guess that's not so. You can make it and still have an exploitative relationship with the dog. Once you get them started doing it, many dogs take to it. Especially if you raise them from a pup and keep them away from bitches. If you have a dog that really digs it and you know where you're at with him you can even let him have bitches and he'll still dig fucking men . . . and chicks are an easy extension with a smart dog . . . though the dogs you see fucking chicks in shows are often not too good. Nobody has had the emotional investment in training them that a homosexual has in his own dog. Oh hell, why talk about it. Come on Tom, Dinny, let's go to bed."

In the bedroom the two men undressed and stood there looking at one another. The big grey dog paced around. His interest aroused. He sniffed at their assholes and cocks. And kept on casting eager looks up at his master's face. "He's quite gentle with me. Understands that we can't take as much as he can. Really knows the limits. And he digs giving me pleasure. But it better be just me. I'll explain why later."

As he was talking he walked across the room and picked up a jar of K-Y jelly off the table. The dog's stumpy tail began to wag with pleasure as he saw his master take the cream and thoroughly lubricate his asshole. Dinny sat down before him and watched with evident pleasure, his tail thumping against the door, the tip of his bright-red, wet-looking cock, with its curious doggy point, carrot-shaped, just protruding from its covering sheath. Frank got down on all fours. He was smaller than the dog. Now Dinny's tail was erectly held out as he paced around Frank's crouching body, stopping with his nose by Frank's arse, his cock protruding a couple of inches now, near Frank's face. The dog began to lick and nip gently around Frank's arse and Frank, ducking his head under the dog's leg, began to suck and lick at his shiny red cock. The cock extended itself visibly, sliding out of its covering like a periscope from the water. Where only an inch of hair-covered tube had stuck out from his rough grey belly, now eight inches of thin, bright-red cock, ending in a very pointed triangular head, protruded boldly. Frank gobbled as much as he could of the slimy red object into his mouth and the dog began yipping . . . high-pitched yips coming from the great throat . . . and excitedly tearing his cock out of Frank's mouth, mounted him from behind, plunging blindly with his full weight until the red cock found the lubricated entrance and sunk deep in. Plunging with a very fast, regular thrust, his forelegs up over Frank's shoulders, his whole rear section waggling madly, tail erect. The dog reached his spasm in minutes. Then stopped. It seemed to be having great difficulty in withdrawing.

Frank gasped to Tom. Even now he could not stop explaining. "Dogs have a bone in the front half of their cocks. Most animals do. Only man can't get it in soft. It doesn't become engorged with blood till it's inside. The prostate glands are located on the shaft. About halfway down. They make like two big swellings. Country folks call it a dog knot."

A lunge of the great dog twisted its body around so that he was facing away from Frank, his cock bent backwards between his legs still sunk in Frank's arse . . . "You know how dogs get what they call 'hung' together . . . like that's what's happening . . . ahh . . ." Frank moaned again as Dinny, striving to pull his cock out, was actually dragging him around the room by his arsehole . . . Between gasps and moans he continued speaking. "It's easier for him to get out of me than from a bitch . . . sometimes a dog can be hung in a bitch for hours . . . time for the sperm to swim uphill . . . argh . . . it's like having an apple pulled out your arse . . . argh!" No sooner were these words spoken than the dog's cock came out with a loud smack and Frank came, his gism shooting wildly down to the floor and spurting over his belly from his jerking cock.

Tom stared in fascination at Dinny's cock. "How long will it take before I . . . " He helped Frank from the floor and lay down beside him on the bed. "How could I make love to him, Frank? He's so beautiful." The dog was lying contentedly on the floor, head resting on forepaws. His large intelligent eyes watching the pair on the bed.

"Here, Dinn." Frank patted the bed and the dog leaped up and stood on it, easily straddling the two men. "Look, you can jerk him off. He's ready again." Just the carrot tip of the bright-red cock

stuck out again from the hairy sheath. "Just take him by the
sheathed part and jerk him off. As if you were jerking yourself off.
He'll just stand there. He's hip to it."

Tom took the rough grey inch between his thumb and forefinger; under the haired flesh of the sheath he could fell the bony
hardness of the dog's prick. He began a gentle jogging and the cock
began to extrude itself. Sliding out its full length as the dog panted
over the bodies of the two men. The strange dog knot appeared.

The color growing darker and darker. Beet-red. When the dog came, Tom quickly pointed the red cock towards his mouth and caught the drops of thick, yellowish come on his lips. Licked the strange, bitter taste. "Let him go, Tom. He likes to be by himself, if possible, while it goes down." Tom's hand releasing his prick, the big dog leaped off the bed.

Tom.

Leslie.

But Barbara was home again, consoling herself with her brother, and he with her. "You know, sis, don't think I don't love this," Franz was saying, as he poked his vigorous cock into her eager hole, "but I would really dig making it with some strange chick. I sort of knew your body all my life and ... well, shit, I'm very curious." Barbara silently promised herself to get Leslie to fuck her brother at the first opportunity and clenched her legs tighter around his driving waist.

Si j'ai du goût, ce n'est guère
Que pour la terre et les pierres.

If I have any hunger it's only
for earth and stones.

ARTHUR RIMBAUD

"Come in, girls."

"Hi, Sam," said Leslie as she stepped into his room, Barbara on her heels.

"Wow!" he said stepping back and admiring the girls.

Leslie had dug up a dress. It was a simple black cotton mini-dress with a high, high skirt and a deep square-cut neck. By itself simple enough. But she had added a pair of medium-high heels and a black up-lift bra (also, not visible at the moment, black lace panties) and the lift of the heels added a dimension of formality, wickedness to the short black dress. Her tits strained upwards from her tightly strapped bra, hints of the black nylon showing around the edges of the deep-cut neck. Barbara was wearing a little girl dress. A white and blue striped pinafore, that was cut simply enough to pass either for a grownup's mini-dress or for a school girl's formal dress. On her feet were thin, white cotton stockings, stretch cotton, pulled up just below her knee. Over them, black patent leather shoes.

"Wow!" Sam repeated softly as the two girls pirouetted into the room. He grabbed them both into his arms and crushed them against his chest, falling backwards onto the bed and carrying the two girls with him, each crushed thigh to thigh against one of his sides; and they both nuzzled him under his neck as he turned his head, mouth open, from side to side trying to catch one of the two mouths burrowing into the sensitive space where the neck joins the collarbone.

"Let us up for a minute," Leslie urged. He relaxed his arms, and his questing mouth. The two girls stood up and smoothed their wrinkled dresses.

"Lie back and let us do you."

With a soft look Sam lay back. The two girls undressed him. Barbara kneeling primly on the bed by his side, her knees together, a bare inch of her starched dress caught under them, undid his shirt buttons slowly and drew the shirt from his back. Leslie, who had been kneeling by his feet, reached up and undid the string of his bathing trunks, drew them over his hard cock and down his strong black legs. He lay back naked. The two girls stood at his feet looking at his magnificent athlete's body, black against the white sheets. Then Leslie drew her black dress up over her head and stood there in her shiny black bra, shoes, and black bikini panties. Stood provocatively with her knees together, slightly bent and her arse high. Leslie kneeled down and took Barbara's foot in her hand; slowly she drew the patent leather shoe and white stocking off one foot, then off the other. She stood up behind Barbara, who stood there barefooted, squarely before Sam's massive black bulk lying on the bed. With slow, deliberate motions, Leslie raised Barbara's hands into the air and began slowly, slowly, to draw the starched white dress over the head of the child . . . up to above the thighs, then up to the neck, and then, off with one swift motion. To reveal

Barbara standing there also in black panties and bra, looking every inch a complete, though miniature, woman. The black underwear emphasized the beginning womanly curves in Barbara's figure, which had been hidden by the loosely flowing pinafore. Presto! Magic transformation of little girl into woman. With a leap and a roar, Sam was upon her. He jumped out of bed and with a swooping motion of his long left arm, gathered the little woman and carried her slim body back onto the bed under him. Fell like a tree on her. In the same continuous motion his right hand had reached behind and torn the flimsy black stuff from around her loins so powerfully that she hadn't even noticed, and the swoop ended with his cock ramming its way into her as his whole body fell at once over hers, his black bulk smothering out all light, his weight taking the breath entirely from her body. The pressure let up. Sam was supporting his great bulk on his arms. Looking down into her face with a sweet smile of affection and understanding while his rolling hips were sending a message of pure delirium to the back part of her brain, turning her spine to a quivering jelly of gratefully responding pleasure.

"Hey, hey," Barbara breathed softly as she sent up an offbeat responsive jerking of her thin hips. Picking up his complex beat and redirecting it into another pattern, to which he responded with a third that involved them both in a frenzied dance of the lower regions, hip turning against hip, pelvis against pelvis, as they hammered out their knowledge of each other. Above her Sam was grinning wildly and swinging his torso in jogging loops, driving his enormous cock ever deeper into her actively accepting hole. Leslie joined in, falling on her knees beside the bed she thrust her head between the legs of the joined pair, and darted her tongue between the two glued-together sexes whenever their sliding motion gave her room—ran her tongue up one black thigh and down the other white thigh. Up under Sam's balls and around his arse crack. Little darting licks into the crack. Quick accent notes to the fucking. With a gasp Leslie threw herself down on top of the beating pair, burying her face against the smooth black skin of Sam's buttocks; her arms went out around the pair, under Barbara's slim cheeks; at the same tumultous moment her forefinger punctured deep into Barbara's arsehole against the driving strength of Sam's cock, and her tongue pierced through above into his tight hole. As Leslie's hot tongue sent blue flames of pleasure up his rectum, Sam again dropped his massive weight onto Barbara, and with three swift convulsive thrusts of his hips shot his hot lead sperm into her tightly stuffed hole.

Barbara was quivering and moaning with pleasure as the enormous weight of her two panting partners rolled off her. Sam lay on his side, looking at her. Then he turned over and devoted his attention to Leslie, who was lying on the bed on his further side. She had taken off her underwear and was completely naked. He spread her legs apart and raised them till they pointed at a forty-five degree angle into the air. With her legs spread and elevated so that her arse just rested on the edge of the bed, he got out of bed. Stood before her, between her legs; let his body, held straight at the waist, fall forward till its weight was caught by his arms outstretched and stiff, the palms flat on the bed. The enormous head of his swollen black cock, purple black, hovered at the pink entrance, which gleamed with lubricating cunt juice. He inched his body forward and his cock began to sink into the soft flesh. Held at an acute angle by the slant of stiff body, it glided in its top edge hard against the upper surfaces of the vagina, the head pressing downward against the lower wall of the vagina, until halfway (5 inches) in; its natural upward curve transferred the pressure of the tip from the lower surface to her hole to its rear closure. He thrust it deeply in, letting his body weight fall on it, taking weight away from his hands till half of his huge weight was ramming the point of his cock with a steady pressure up against the tight muscular and thick mucous plug of the upper end of the vagina, ramming into the entrance to the womb.

There were still two inches of cock to go. It was wider at the base, and now the tight sphincter of the vagina entrance was taut, stretching as the thickness of the cock forced its way. Leslie's legs closed around his waist. Clenched. Driving him further into her. Ramming the hard cock against the hardness of womb entrance. As she did so, Sam slipped his hands around her waist and stood up. Holding her impaled on the stiff, almost vertical rod on his hard-on. He stood. Her arms locked around his neck and she rested her whole weight, raising her knees and clenching them around the waist. He held her in his hands and masturbated with her. Moving her body as if it were some small animal's, like a man rubbing a lump of soft stuff against his cock, he held her entire body in his two great hands and moved its unresisting weight up and down along the length of his rod. In her position she could offer no corresponding activity. Her whole body hung loosely from her arms around his neck letting the maximum amount of weight just fall onto the great cock that filled her wet cunt to unbearable degrees and pressures. She was reduced to a hollow tube of flesh. No longer hollow, a filled tube of flesh . . . nothing but sensation between the outer surface of the tube and the electrified inner surface. Her cunt seemed to run from her head to her heels, it was all of her. And it was all filled. Overwhelmed by him. Mindless, she plunged up and down on his cock, moved by his hands. No necessity save to feel. To feel him. Filling her. With screams of pleasure he began to leap up into the air. Holding her on his cock. Landing with both feet together and simultaneously slamming her hard onto his cock. Fingertips almost meeting as his huge hands closed tighter yet around her waist, slamming her into him. He came in a cascade of hot gism and a high-pitched full-throated scream of satisfaction, and Leslie too came and quivered, still impaled on the jerking, ejaculating cock, clenching herself to him as her legs let go in their violent spasms, and her body's weight pulled her off his hot cock.

Leslie collapsed onto the bed alongside of Barbara, and a moment later the bed shook as Sam too fell onto it. They lay there in a limp exhausted tangle of black and tan limbs. Leslie's round ones, Barbara still wearing the black bra. After a while there was a stir in the pile. The two girls' heads were moving along the length of Sam's body. Two pairs of soft lips were searching out the sensitive spots. Leslie's head moved upwards, her body against his, until her lips found his mouth. Barbara moved down until her lips closed around his cock. The two girls lay there, each pressed as close against him as possible, sucking and kissing softly until his manhood began to revive. Then Barbara reversed her position. Both girls lay with their heads on his shoulders; simultaneously they began to roll their bodies on top of his, both tongues seeking his mouth, both tongues meeting in his mouth, arms thrown over one another, Barbara's right thigh and Leslie's left between Sam's legs. They ground themselves equally against each other and against him. They both thrust their tongues side by side deeply into his mouth. His cock grew harder against the twisting flesh of the two girls. They rolled on him and his cock seemed to jump wildly under the two bellies that squirmed against it.

Now the two girls, each clinging to him at the mouth, were fighting to push the other off. Down below, leg against leg, elbow against elbow, each girl tried to force the other's thigh out from between his, struggled to win his cock for her own possession. Sweating, Leslie's superior strength won and his prick slid into her groove. She caught its length between her tightly clasped legs. But Barbara still hung on up at top, her arms twined around his neck, her tongue in his mouth, her forehead braced against Leslie's cheek, pushing her rival away from this lesser prize. As Leslie and Sam fucked, Leslie on top, but Sam's hips finding plenty of purchase for his powerful thrusts from beneath, Barbara's hands went down to her clit and she manipulated it furiously, while kissing Sam's mouth with slobbering frenzy, finally dividing her kisses between the mouths of Sam and Leslie, until all three of them were again joined in a circle of wetness above and a throbbing of orgasm below. Barbara's self-induced orgasm had still left her with a driving need to feel herself filled with a hard male organ. She lifted her eyes to Leslie's, seeking advice on how most quickly to revive Sam's sex.

Leslie rolled herself over Sam's prostrate body and took Barbara in her arms. With an eye to Sam, who turned over onto his elbow to watch, Leslie began making love to the younger girl. She started by caressing and kissing her budding tits. Then she stretched out the younger girl flat on her back. Kneeling over her she began to caress every part of Barbara's stretched-out body with the soft points of her swinging tits. Letting them hang down over her, she moved her body so that the delicate pink nipples brushed over the sensitive spots of Barbara's body. Up her thighs and around her belly, softly brushing back and forth, the swinging tits brushed up, up and over her little concave mounds, swinging nipple brushed against rising nipple. This show was exciting Sam visibly, but Barbara too was growing interested in the game. She arched her back to bring her own breasts into fuller contact with Leslie's and rolled her hips to make her nipples slide back and forth against Leslie's tits. The two girls gyrated their breasts against one another's, Leslie's softer tits somewhat indented by the pressure of Barbara's firm young buds; then with a determined motion, Leslie moved her body around so that she was kneeling over Barbara facing towards her feet, her tits now hanging directly over Barbara's face. Barbara's lips puckered up and caught one of the nipples that brushed so tantalizingly over her mouth, at the same time reaching out to grasp Sam's now quite hard cock in her little hand. Held in her hand it looked thicker than her wrist. She pulled softly on his cock and he came toward her, rolled over her as she lay prostrate, sucking contentedly at Leslie's tit, and entered her.

FRANK NEWMAN

Frank Newman's innocuous nom de plume *is in reality most apt. Barbara, which has become an underground cause celebre, is outspoken about a variety of revolutionary ideas, for the author is proud of being one of the new men, i.e. "proto-dope-fiend-peace-freak." In 1956, while 10,000 Brooklyn College students obediently filed out in bombshelter practice, Newman was one of six dissenters sitting it out in the empty cafeteria. He is a poet, a teacher of Greek and Latin, and a father of two, tribal patriarch on a matriarchal scene. His collected poems,* The First Post American Cultural Congress, *are to be published soon. The author and his family are at present residing in California.*

Americaville

Minor F. Watts

Daphnis Street, the main street of Americaville, ended East at Dodge Lane with a movie house on the north and Bella's Bar on the south. The movie house had no marquee and resembled a two story hotel from the old Wild West with a second story balustrade around a balcony where expresso coffee and cookies were served during intermission in the summers. There was a hitching post in front with several water buckets so that the few village equestrians could hitch-up and water their well-bred horses. Albert Arens Fairstone, known as Coree, was seen several times daily hitching his horse and it was amusing to watch him fall on and off in his usual tipsy state. He managed, with the help of passers-by and storekeepers, to pack the saddlebags with the packages he had bought from the daily lists his wife, Carole Lee, known as Toree, gave him.

Bella's Bar was an old unpainted Cape Cod house with a yard scattered with curiosities that Bella bought or was given over the past twenty years: statues of horses, English jockeys, reindeers and a sleigh, dogs and cats of various breeds, an old iron stove her grandmother had used, two modern twisted statues of Picasso's that she had acquired when visiting him in southern France, dragons brought from the Orient and part of a Buddhist temple on the intersection corner, five bathtubs, one with gold fixtures, sunk into the ground and filled with water, fish and lilies; and the two totem poles which had been given to her by the Indian Reservation tribe when she donated a little red schoolhouse to them, that she had bought from the village and had moved from its original site on North Dodge Lane at the time the village was going to have it torn down to build the new glass and driftwood school. Beside the entrance, midway on the sidewalk, the two totem poles had English candle carriage lamps attached to them that her barman lighted each night during the season.

The bar and restaurant was regarded as the night club of Americaville, and Bella had catered only to the four hundred, but now that the locals had money to spend on expensive foods and drinks and proved often to be more prodigal spenders than the summer residents, she welcomed both groups. The small horseshoe bar, decorated with bamboo, life preservers, a fish net above and local stuffed fish on the bar wall, had no stools to give it a more cocktailish atmosphere and small tables covered with red and white stripe cloths were casually scattered ten to twelve feet from the bar. Framed English caricatures were hung on the oak-paneled walls beside the four colonial windows in the front.

A large outdoor modern patio was in the back where dinner was served on colorful garden umbrella tables, lighted by hurricane lamps, and at its far end, a glass dance floor was in front of the bandstand, and stunted jack pines grew around it. A huge fireplace was built against the bar wall to charcoal meats and lobsters, and if rainy or cool weather made it necessary, a push of a button brought the oval glass roof together. A society name band and a gypsy palm reader were hired during the season.

Most of the summer residents had spent the afternoon, as usual, at the beach, tennis or golf clubs or home gatherings and they were rather gay upon arrival. Bella decided to ask the band to play early this evening to attract some of the people into the patio and relieve the crowded bar area.

Jacque, Lorraine, Pierre, Norman, Hack and Josh Thompson, the owner of the *Americaville Press,* were gathered around one of the small tables in a corner near the bar and their voices could be heard above the noisy chitchat of the others. They were having a dispute concerning the relationship between politics and art that was started that afternoon at Jacque's studio. Jacques didn't understand why Norman insisted that politics shouldn't be discussed among artists. He argued, "An artist must know about everything; for, he should reflect the pulse of this generation and any event that might affect people, including politics, must be of importance to him and his work. How can one eliminate the discussion of politics?"

Norman pounded his fist upon the table and roared through his wide thin lips, "Because this generation is being controlled by the boxes who are man-bitten instead of christ-bitten. Meat, they didn't get time to be themselves because they were swallowed up with mortgages and time payments. Those boxes are afraid to piss without asking their suburban-multi-headed wives who want every man-bitten-materialistic object made. The pricks are ball-tied in a social structure with so many knots that they become sterile.

"This is partly the result of those Mad-Triangles who stymied the country with billboards, t.v., radio and newspaper ads. Wait and see, people are going to end up with pointed heads, two big eyes and no balls.

"Politics follow society and society is slush. Take those phallic rocket Russians who were going to save the common man. They're another form of slavery, just as the western camp is to their madness. Politicians have no answer to the world's problems except to create worse ones and each generation becomes more inflicted with their hopelessness. They act like a bunch of backyard kids and history repeats itself with a great knowledge to destroy and now hydrogen bombs can demolish entire countries and perhaps the world with the touch of a mad-boxed-in finger. Why be bothered? Live it up, flesh, and dig what you can out of this crazy world or you may be dead. And, when you're meatless, you're gone, gone."

"I'm trying to find out what qualifies you to be a poet," Jacque emphasized.

"Yes," said Lorraine, "an artist must use form built on past artist's works and once he has the fundamental knowledge, he can further it if he has new principles and ideas. Fortified with these he can reflect the present generation in its essence."

"Dead shit," yelled Norman. "What we got to do is to forget form of all kinds that put us in this nothingness box. We're a hopeless, wandering, wondering nihilistic generation, searching for something beyond everything thus far known because what's been offered by the church, politicians, socialists, economists, scientists, artists and any one else one can think of, solved nothing but nothingness. What we've got to do is to destroy form of any type and not be boxed-in. Got to keep iced about those things that are destroying us.

"Look at Josh, for a perfect example of being crushed by their nothingness that was supposed to have had the answers to man's woes. You're only in your early forties, Josh, and look at you. I've read some of your earlier poems. Did thou-those sons-of boxes man-bite you and make you turn grey, bent over and smoothed-brained? That boxy weekly local newspaper you put out is not what you wanted, is it? But you've got a home to pay for, kids to educate, cars, washing machines, television and more crap to lock up your brain. Right, fleshless."

Josh rubbed his sunken dark-circled pale-blue eyes. "You boys may have something to chew upon. Matter-of-fact, I was an inspired poet when I was young and untouched by society, but they did push my original dreams into my subconscious. And I have to admit, every so often, I become so depressed that I could lock myself in a closet, scream cursedly and then break the door down and rape everything in the house, including my daughter. It may have been better for me if I became a farmer and ate real dirt than see filth around me and write the opposite. It would kill any man before his natural death."

Jacque became more determined as he gulped down his scotch and soda. "Hack and Norman, from what I've read of your writings, you ramble on without any form and I can't see this as art."

"Sometimes I know you're a banana," said Norman. "Hack and I write about what we do, see and feel at the moment. It's spontaneous, a sense of presence, a here-and-nowness. It's the truth and since the world is senseless, so must our art be formless."

Jacque got up and announced, "I'm going to telephone a couple of my arty friends in the city and ask them to come out for the holidays. I haven't seen them since I traveled to Paris to study and I want their opinions."

Hack jumped up and said, "Norman, let's call Su Dayton, the writer, and she can pass the word to some of our hippy-friends to come here to support us. What a Roman peg-mouth slugging holiday this will be."

"Hell, I know her too," said Jacque, and the three of them went to the telephone booths on the opposite side of the room as Bella came over to the table and took notice of Lorraine's tailored red and white stripe toreadors and white short sleeve mannish shirt and her flaming red wavy hair exactly tucked in place as she leaned away from the table to check on Jacque. 'Her golden skin and slim body and long shapely legs made her a desirable middle-age woman,' thought Bella, 'but those falsies are obvious.' She tried to avoid Lorraine's caustic divination, "don't worry honey, he will be back soon."

She shrugged and addressed Pierre. "Pierre, that cute pony-tail brunette at this end of the bar wants to meet you. She's Hope Garden, one of the ocean group, and would like to be in show business and thought you might be interested."

"Oh, eh . . . . . definitely," he answered. "I'd love to meet her."

Bella waved to Hope and she came over and was introduced to Pierre and she sat beside Lorraine and said, "dear auntie Lorraine, or is it cousin? Well, it doesn't matter because we do have something in common, we both like men."

Norman, Jacque and Hack returned and Hack leaned over the table and asked Hope her name. She looked at him coldly and didn't answer. "What a direct chick," he said as he sat back into his chair.

She twinkled her baby face at him and communed, "you look like an Indian from the wrong side of the reservation."

He pulled his straight black hair from one of his ears and answered, "you're absolutely right cuntsie with your green, green eyes, and incidentally, there's no right side of the track on the reservation. I could go for you."

She gave a toothy innocent smile and responded, "would you like to take me here and now or wait?" Then she directed herself to Pierre. "I love you Pierre. I have always loved you. Now you hate me. Go ahead, hate me."

Pierre shrugged his shoulders. "But mademoiselle, I don't hate you."

"You will hate me," she replied.

Norman took her hand. "Move in, Breast, and we'll adopt you like togetherness."

Pierre got up, bowed and excused himself. "I think I'm on the wrong track and will wander a bit and lose myself more." He pushed his way through the crowd to the patio and recognized Virginia May Duryea with an ocean group at a table near the dance floor.

She saw him and waved at him to come over. "Good evening you precious thing. I would like you to meet Mr. & Mrs. Guggenham, Mr. & Mrs. Thomas Macie, Mr. & Mrs. Alcott Dana Forde and Mrs. Berta Ann Russell."

She pulled a chair from the table beside her and told him to sit down. "Now I remember, we met at Jacque's father's funeral, did we not? I married Jacque's uncle Randoff. So, I'm sort of his aunt. Call me Vigil, everyone does. I saw you gathered with the arty group when I came in. What are they dreaming of today and what are you drinking?"

"Scotch and soda."

"Food for a Frenchman. I thought you may want something continental and unamerican. John," she called the waiter, "another scotch and soda and keep the rest of the glasses from going dry. Well, Pierre, what are they shouting about in there?"

"About the world and such," he answered as he fingered his right cauliflower ear under his overgrown wavy black hair. "This afternoon at Jacque's studio, Norman read two of his poems and Hack one of his short stories. They were so full of concocted words and phrases that I missed the point, if they had one."

"Excuse me," interrupted Vigil, "you are dreamy looking. Now that I've got that off my chest, what did Hack read of his?"

"He read a short story and I couldn't for the life of me understand it. It must have been extremely intellectual because the rest of them discussed it for more than an hour without coming to any conclusion."

Pierre hesitated and glanced over the group. 'These people were different,' he thought, and he felt uneasy in their presence, and he couldn't understand why. His family were monied people, but these appeared naturally handsome, friendly and vivacious compared to his own family and friends. The expensive clothes and jewelry these individuals wore seem to belong to them forever. Even Mrs. Guggenham, with her naked body, dried-up long narrow English face appeared proper with her simple, but real stones shining from her dropy earlobes and the thin gold chain around her long neck ending with a heart-shaped ruby between her narrow leathery breast, acted animated. All the women had precious appointed diamond bracelets and rings on; whereas, the men, though dressed in colorful expensive sport coats and shirts and tailored dark pants, wore no jewelry. It occurred to him that the men all looked similar in that they were tall, hawked faced, large framed and not an overly groomed-appearance, outdoor types with quiet confidence built into their secure positions.

"Those kids are confused," said Mr. Macie gruffly. "Didn't you get one damn idea from the short story?"

"Well-errrr," he continued, "it is about four people who refused to do anything and are waiting to die because they think it is the only way for them to discover whatever they have been looking for in their past. I could not tell from their conversation whether the characters were dead or alive, and I think each one was from a different race or nationality. Anyway, they didn't seem to believe in anything and were just waiting, but one of them knew what or who they were waiting for, I think. Oh, I really don't know what it was all about. Perhaps you should ask them."

"Why don't we," said Vigil to the others. "Let us take our drinks and go to their table and find out." The others agreed.

As they approached the group, they could distinguish Norman's high-pitched voice. "I don't care. I just don't give a come and who cares."

"We care," resonated Vigil. "Do you mind if we sit with you and hear about your story, Hack?"

Jacque rose, gathered more chairs and asked them to please sit down and Lorraine and Hope sighed a hello to them.

"Pierre has tried to explain your story to us, but he was confused. You are a good thinker, Jacque, could you explain it to us?"

Jacque shook his head no. "Each of us has a different opinion of the story. Wouldn't it be better for you to hear it?"

"That is an excellent idea, and I will volunteer one of my parlors tomorrow afternoon for a reading," offered Mrs. Macie.

"This gives me an idea," said Mrs. Guggenham. "Why not include a theatre and an art gallery as projects of the Americaville improvement association? The present art cinema could be devoted to trying out new plays once a week and the museum to art exhibits. It is about time we had more culture in our village. Would you artists be willing to work with the committee on these projects?"

Jacque, Pierre, Lorraine, Josh and Hope enthusiastically offered their services, but Hack and Norman said they were against the plan. "Come on Norm," demanded Hack, "let's get out of here and look for a new twist." They got up and left.

Mrs. Guggenham felt abortive. "I am very, very sorry they feel that way. I was hoping they, especially, would be interested. This may have been one way to keep them out of mischief. Could you talk them into joining the project, Jacque?"

"I'll do my best, Mrs. Guggenham, but even I don't grasp their artistic estrangement."

Mr. Forde got up and stated, "I will donate a thousand dollars toward the new project." The rest of the ocean couples matched the amount and they offered to canvass the summer residences for added donations.

Vigil complained of the lack of drinks and ordered another round for everyone. "How about a dance Pierre?"

"I would love to, Mrs. Duryea."

"Vigil, to you."

"Vigil, may I have the pleasure."

After excusing themselves, they pushed through the crowded bar area and out into the patio and danced two dances, stopping for sips of their drinks they left on a near-by patio table, and during their third refill, Vigil became more talkative.

"Where did you learn to speak fluent English?"

"My mother was English and she taught me when I was a child, and Jacque and I roomed together in Paris and we taught each other more of our respective languages."

"Where did you meet Jacque?"

"My father, who owns a newspaper in Paris, knew Jacque's father from childhood. You see, Dr. Duryea was born in France and came to America when he was fourteen. Jacque stayed at our house his first month in Paris and we became immediate friends. Father thought it best for us to be on our own and we moved to an apartment in Montmarte and Jacque studied under several known artists and I attended Sorbonne University and studied journalism."

"I should have remembered about Dr. Duryea and his birth; after all, I married his brother. My first husband, Biddle C. Prince, you no doubt heard of, the steel magnate, died when Toree was in her early teens, and afterwards I married Dr. Duryea's brother, but we did not have much time to visit his family because of his busy city practice and the constant social obligations. However, I always have been interested in Jacque and his brother, Todd. You like Jacque, don't you?"

"Very, very much. I never had a friend who was so warm, pleasant and intelligent."

"Who does he love the most, Bella, Lorraine or one of the many others?"

"I don't know madame. We never talked about our romances. Our closeness is in our art and we took profound interest in each other's works and spent hours discussing them and related subjects."

"It is proper that you two are close friends. You are both so manly. It is not easy to find tangible men these days. You are short like me, and I love your wooly hair and your balmy face. I could hug you like a child. Yet, you have such manly manners."

"Thank you, Vigil. I don't see your daughter and her husband here."

"You mean Toree and Coree. I tried to talk her into coming tonight, but she has always been quite independent, though never the hermit she has been the past few years. I do not know whether she is egocentric, selfish or the fact that Coree's inclination towards alcoholism causes her to be so non-social.

"You realize that it was my father or was it my grandfather who started this summer colony and talked his business associates and friends into moving their families out here for the summers; however, I have to admit, high taxes are causing us difficulty in maintaining the life we had before the late thirties, but it is not necessary to forgo the traditions of a developed society that held America together for years, such as Toree and Coree are doing."

Pierre noticed that the numerous drinks were starting to take effect on Vigil; her poise did not falter, but there was a happier glow on her fair tan face that was accentuated by her soft silver-white fluffy hair. Her buxomness did not interfere with her graceful dancing. He reflected and thought she and her kind made his generation look sick, old and lazy. She had a perspicuous aura.

Vigil continued, "I think that I have talked them into attending the fourth of July ball at the beach club. Would you join us as my guest? The unattached Forde daughter will be with us and I would like you to meet her."

"It is very kind of you to ask me and I accept with pleasure."

"That is settled, and I would ask Jacque, but he never accepted my invites in past years."

"I know. He doesn't care for dances and such. He has been always a loner, from what I knew."

"Yes, that is true. I have not seen him with a group until this past month. Paris must have done him good. He was good at horseback riding, swimming, tennis and sport car racing when he was younger, as I remember, and I noticed he was very and always attentive to the various women he escorted. You are like that too. I am so used to the social jumper that men like you and Jacque are a rare treat to a woman. You are more gregarious than Jacque though. Come on, I am going to introduce you to some more Americanites. Good lord. There is Mayor Higgins. I hope he does not drink too much and lose his balance again. Mr. Murrie invited him to the opening of his new swimming pool party and the Mayor leaned over to test the water and fell in, clothes and all."

At midnight, Bella nodded to Jacque and went out the door to the right of the inside of the bar into a hallway and up the stairs to her apartment. She seldom left the bar and restaurant until closing, but tonight was her night with Jacque. She quickly closeted scattered clothes; Jacque abhorred slovenly women. Then she went into the small oblong white tiled bath, removed her lipstick and creamed her face and wiped it off . . . . he liked her unmade face, sprayed on his favorite perfume, and went into the bedroom and put on clean sheets and placed a pitcher of ice water, two glasses, his brand of cigarettes and a lighter on the cabinet night table, took off her clothes and hung them and removed two wooden hangers. She hummed the tune, My Time Is Your Time, and half-danced into the bath next to the bedroom and placed the hanger on the hook above the mirror on the inside of the door and put on her light blue negligee that was hanging there. In the kitchen, she got some ice for the bucket, placed it on the silver tray on the round glass-top cocktail table in front of the old worn-out sofa in the end of the rectangular livingroom, added two old fashion glasses, a soda bottle and a fifth of White Label Scotch and turned on the new Hi-Fi set on the opposite side of the room near the door and tuned in rock-and-roll music.

"There," she said softly, "I think all is ready."

On further thought she went back into the bathroom and checked Jacque's toiletries, placed two hand towels and a bathtowel on the top of the john and another small extra soft handtowel on the washbowl. Then she brushed her short auburn hair and looked at herself in the long mirror. 'I wish I had a more glamourous face,' she considered. 'Even dieting doesn't thin it. If only I were two inches taller and not so plump. I look more like an ordinary homey housewife than a bar owner.' "Oh well, maybe this is why Jacque likes me," she sighed.

She heard the distinct knock and went into the living room and unlocked the door to let Jacque in. He had that passionately warm smile he reserved for these occasions and his wide stern lips reddened into a sensual quiver which softened his familiar bold face, and his customary cold grey eyes became soft and his fine wide nose blended into the dimples that made his firm jaw less square. His tufted eyebrows wiggled towards his flat nasal bridge as he passed her and patted her roundish hip and silently mixed two drinks and handed one to her as he went to the bath and closed the door behind him.

He took off his clothes and hung them neatly on the hangers, went over to the old john that had a broken, loose grey seat and took a long loud piss and saw the hand towels and his mind flashed back to the peasant appearance of his mother when he first learned of his emotional disturbance that grew over the years into a crisis four years ago at the age of twenty-four. Bella reminded him of his mother not only in appearance, but the attention of his daily necessities during his weekly visits to her apartment. And, after he flushed the john, he turned around to the cracked basin and saw the articles on the glass tray above the basin to render for his uses: Noxema to soften his beard to prepare his sensitive skin, a sharp straight razor similar to the one his father had used, the lather with menthol added, the aftershave lotion with no sting, the expensive not-too-strong men's cologne, the hand cream to soften his oil-stained smudgy long fingers, and special soft handtowel to clean his privates to prepare for the blow-job Bella would accomplish while he reciprocated with his tongue on her clitoris. Often he wondered why his doctor-father didn't have him circumcised so it was not a must to pull the massive excessive prepuce back and clean the foul-smelling discharge at least twice a day from his overgrown penis that was too large to insert into a woman. Whenever he had tried, they would scream with painful horror and if he had forced it into them, hemorrhage resulted and often the wounds needed suturing. He had tried tall large women with the same experience and he had heard that women with large ankles had bigger openings, but this proved unreliable. Of those who knew him intimately, men had envied his excessive appendage and young women had thought him a sexual monster. The fact was difficult to conceal even with loosely constructed pants and he had to have especially tailored bathing suits to allow room for the giant organ that had the capacity to expand to sixteen inches when hardened and five inches in width at the head that increased considerably towards its base.

Though his parents had never known of his attendance with a psychiatrist during his twenty-third year, it had been his mother and not the doctor who had made his pecker-problem more liveable, and the scene of events that had enabled his mother to advise him, now vividly reeled through his mind.

It was Christmas Eve that was reserved always for the family gathering with the customary goose dinner cooked and served by his mother, and as they started to eat, his father complained of a pain in his right arm that extended across his chest. He gave a thunderous burp that drew their immediate attention and suddenly he slumped in his kingly chair with his arms hanging down, eyes closed, head resting on his sunken chest, pale-blue skin, motionless. Todd rushed over to him and lifted a closed eyelid, took his pulse and dashed to the Clinic on the other side of the central hallway. Emily realized her husband's condition and went to him and stroked his hair and held her cheek against his and when Todd came back, he pushed her away, ripped open his father's coat, shirt and undershirt and administered an injection of respiratory and heart stimulant directly into his heart.

At this moment, Jacque leaned forward, fainted and his head fell into the plate of food, and Emily went over to him and lifted his head from the plate by his hair, took his napkin and dunked it into the glass of water and wiped the food from his face. He revived within moments.

"It's no use," said Todd. "Jacque, are you able to help me carry him to the bedroom?"

Jacque shook his head a few times and took some deep breaths and replied, "I will carry him by myself." He pulled the chair with his dead father back and took hold of him by one arm and lifted him on his shoulders and carried him into the living room, out the door into the hallway and up the stairs to the master bedroom on the right of the top of the stairs over the Clinic area, and during the entire trip, he tried to grope his father's privates without success because the dead weight would not maneuver properly into a position on his shoulders to do so. Jacque had never seen his father naked and he had wondered for many years if he had the same size organ, and if he had, how had he managed a proper sexual relationship with his mother. It must have been a good one because they had two children and he was almost positive his father had no extra-curricular sexual affairs. She had been his secretary-nurse and they had seldom gone out socially and when they had, always together. They had been a devoted couple and had even slept in the same bed. They had little time to devote to their children; consequently, the two boys had grown into manhood without close parental concern beyond the necessary provisions of food, shelter, education and an occasional family dinner that had been often interrupted by emergencies.

Emily and Todd entered the room as he placed the body on the bed and he told them to go down and make the funeral arrangements and he would stay with his father. He wanted to investigate his privates, but his mother sat on the bed beside the dead body and replied, "you go and make the arrangements. I want to be with your father while his body still has warmth. Let me have these last moments of closeness with him."

They left the room, closed the door and went downstairs to the hallway and Jacque turned to Todd and insisted, "Todd, I'm going to my studio and may be there a long time, perhaps months. Don't bother me, you or mother! I don't believe in funerals or life thereafter and if I had my way, he'd be cremated without any ceremony. Don't worry about me and take care of mother and leave me alone!"

Todd grabbed him by his jacket and he pulled him back near the stairs where he stepped on the first step to be able to stare his darting green eyes into the steel-grey ones and his puckered lips twisted on his hideous ghostly face as he shouted, "you Godless creature. If you pull this selfless act at a time like this, God should strike you dead." Jacque pushed him with a blow on his chest and Todd landed on the stairs. "Don't give me one of your religious tantrums again or I'll kill you, you God-damn idiot. You leave me alone or I'll go upstairs and take that dead body to the village dump for the rats to play with. This is your moment of glory and you can play God-like for the first time in your twisted life and my presence would only make your show unreal. You religious pimp." Todd lay on the steps for a moment unbelieving of the words he heard as Jacque turned and hurried out of the house, slamming the door that shook the house. He got up and went into the office and telephoned another doctor to come over for legal confirmation and then he called the undertaker and the priest. When he went back to the bedroom, he was surprised to find his mother brushing her hair that she had loosened and it hung to the lower part of her back while she looked out of the back window towards the studio. He covered his father's body with a blanket and she glanced back at him and directed, "don't do that. I'm acquainted with death and not afraid to accept it." She walked to the dead body and pulled the blanket from his head and combed his hair. "We never got around to our vacation he promised me for more than twenty odd years." She took Todd's hand and looked sympathetically, "Jacque will remain in his studio a long time."

Tears swelled his heavy eyelids. "I guess you heard. How could he do this to us at a time like this? He'll probably drink himself into oblivion. Shouldn't you go and talk to him?"

"I don't think so. Jacque is in a peculiar state of shock and I can't help him at the moment. Perhaps time will adjust his problem or make it less acute. Leave him to himself for now and try to understand and forgive him. You have so much goodness to make allowances for this trick of nature." She let go of his hand and walked to the door and turned around to face him, "come now. We must go downstairs and face our responsibilities and duties and you must be prepared to handle your father's practice alone from this moment on."

Jacque walked sullenly around the house and under the grape-arbor in the backyard to his studio, went inside and checked his liquor and canned food supply. "Good, there's enough for a couple of months." He climbed the spiral stairs to the second floor room and took a long drink from the open bottle near a canvas he had been working on and studied it for a moment before beginning to paint.

A month later, Emily stood by the back window in her bedroom at two A.M. and wondered whether Jacque left his studio or was he ill or was it possible that he committed suicide, and the latter became her foremost concern because until a few days ago, she had heard the intemittent jazz and concert music and periodic violent screams of anger, and had seen lights glowing at night and shadows flashing from the shaded windows, but lately the nights had been silent, dark and motionless. She remembered he had often expressed to her at a young age that he had wanted to be with his father more often like the other boys had been in the village and go fishing, hiking and camping with him, and he had thought his father disliked him even though she had repeatedly told him his father had been the only physician-surgeon in the village at the time and his patients had depended upon him day and night; it had been a typical doctor's life that he would understand better when he got older. However, when he had entered his late teens, he had decided that he hated his father and this had confused her and she had never known any logical response to express to him then. Little had she known that he had become jealous of every moment she and her husband had spent in their bedroom. Though his father had given him sport cars, trips to Europe and paid for any artistic schooling he had desired with an unlimited allowance, none of these material gifts had alleviated this feeling that had grown within him. They had not been aware of his physical problem until he had been in his twenties, even though he had tried to expose his concern at sixteen years old when he had stood naked outside of the bathroom door at the end of the hallway one evening as they had come out of their bedroom to respond to an emergency and he had said, "perhaps you can order the same size underwear as yours, Dad, now that you see me." Being in a rush, she had replied, "shame on you for forgetting your bathrobe. Tomorrow after school, go to Gilden's store and order what you need," and they had hurried down the stairs. Little had they realized the organ continued to grow into an extraordinary size, and they had never been aware of his crotch during the next couple of years, as had his schoolmates and certain individuals in the village. The problem had become apparent to them when several young ladies had made emergency calls to have their internal injuries attended to and three of them had told who inflicted them. Several times they had thought of privately talking to him to advise him to avoid inexperienced women, but the right moment had never arrived. It had been just before his father's death that Emily saw him in the nude again through the back window of her bedroom when he hadn't pulled the shades down in his studio that she had realized his predicament and she had chatted about it to his father the afternoon before the fatal event.

Emily went to Todd's room across the hallway and knocked on the door. He was awake and switched on his bedlamp and asked her to come in.

"Todd. Get up. I can't stand not knowing about Jacque any

longer. We've got to go to the studio and see if he's there. I haven't slept for the past three nights."

"I heard you moving around. Perhaps God punished him enough and he's willing to repent." He got up, dressed quickly and they went downstairs and out to the studio. Todd banged on the door and silence only followed his repeated poundings and finally he tried the door and was surprised to find it unlocked. He switched on the light and they found the combination living-kitchen room dusty, but undisturbed, and they turned on the stairway light and climbed to the studio workroom and put on the ceiling lights and saw Jacque sprawled naked on the floor on pillows, emaciated, bearded to his chest and groaning. Todd pushed a path with his feet and hands through the cluttered canvases, empty cans of food and liquor bottles to where Jacque was begging, "please, please, let me die. Let me die."

Emily kneeled beside him and said, "if you die, I too will die a living death."

He turned his bushy head towards her and his sunken eyes focused upon hers and he asked, "you really want me?"

"Yes, I really do." She picked up a near-by blanket and handed it to Todd. "Here, help him up and put this around him."

Though he was disgusted with the conversation, he helped Jacque struggle slowly to his feet and toil to the house and up to his bedroom between the bath and Todd's room.

During the next few days, Todd gave him blood salin-dextrose transfusions, vitamin injections and he instructed his mother to prepare special soft foods and egg nogs for him and to give him sponge baths. And, as time went on, there was little he could do medically; for, Jacque gained his strength physically, but mentally, he was extremely depressed. Emily devoted most of her waking hours with him, and after three weeks passed, Todd suggested, "don't you think we should call in a psychiatrist?"

"No," she flatly stated, "I think I can cure his state of depression. A psychiatrist could only discover what I already know. I want to help him, but I don't know if I'm able. However, I will try my best and if it doesn't do the trick, I will do as you say."

"Could you enlighten me?" inquired Todd.

"You may understand someday, but I don't want to explain it to you now. It's too involved. He's the image of his father in appearance except for one thing, and that certain thing I must try to overcome, and lord knows, I want to."

"I think I know what you're talking about, his penis. But I don't see how you can help with that weapon. What he really needs is a priest."

"You promised me not to talk religion to him and a priest is definitely out, and his sexual problem I refuse to speak to you about."

"Well, if you think you can help him, I shall not interfere. Joan is home from college for a week between semesters and I will be having lunch and dinner with her."

That day, Emily didn't visit Jacque and she had Lola bring his lunch to him. This will be her first visit to a beauty parlor, and she knew she would be late coming home, so she instructed Lola in the preparation of dinner and asked her to stay on to serve it in the dining room, and requested her to work full-time instead of her usual two days a week.

She thought the owner of the salon, Caesar, a madman at first because he wasn't at all interested in her opinion of how she thought she should look, and when she objected to the cutting of her long hair that had been tied in a bun since she was a child, he ran around the parlor screaming, "no, no madame. I won't allow you to keep this excess baggage. You've a beautiful young face and you keep it old. No, madame. You're not going from Caesar's with that mop. I'd kill myself first."

He stopped in front of her, held her face gently and said, "madame, you could be so lovely. Trust your Caesar. Let him give you your youth back."

He took the pins from her bun and let her hair flow down, combed it and told her to close her eyes and before she realized it, he had cut her hair.

She put her hands to the back of her head and shouted, "no, no. You didn't. You really didn't. My good lord, you did!

"You really did!" She got up and began to cry.

"Now, that's my good girl," he said softly as he placed his arm around her. "You sit down now and Caesar is going to make you happy." He took a Kleenex and dried her tears and she sat down and he began to work on her hair.

"Magnificent," he said after he had worked for a while. "Now we're going to remove the grey hairs in your lovely brown hair, tinge it with a blonde streak, give you a facial, shape your eyebrows and manicure your nails. Then, you will be my sweet beautiful princess."

Three hours later, she was allowed to examine herself. She stared for a long time, not believing it was she. "Why I look so glamourous and ten years younger. It's really not me?"

She turned towards Caesar, smiled and said, "I love myself. How can I ever thank you?"

"My new male friend! But I don't have any such person," she answered in astonishment.

"Now my beauty, the doctor has been dead for about two months now, and you should have and need a male companion. That's what my work is all about."

She smiled and answered, "perhaps you're right, Caesar."

She went to Saks Fifth Avenue shop and the manager and the salesgirls raved about her new look, and she chose a red cocktail dress with the low scoop neck and the high belt. It was more daring than she thought she should wear, but she liked the way she felt in it. Then she went home and up to her bedroom and sat down on the old straight chair that her husband had before the oak desk in the room so that he could do his medical reports late in the evenings and opened the brandy drawer and took out the bottle and sipped it. 'For different reasons,' she thought, 'this bottle was for his heart and now mine.' It tasted good and she took a few more sips, got up and felt tipsy. She went down to the kitchen to ask Lola to tell Jacque that she expected him to dine with her downstairs at seven o'clock. When she entered the kitchen and Lola saw her, she inquired, "may I help ya?"

"Just seeing if everything is alright Lola. Don't you recognize me? I'm Mrs. Duryea."

"Why Mrs. Duryea. What have ya gone and done? Why master Jacque will never know ya. Well, I swear. I didn't know they could of lift a face in a afternoon. Mrs. Duryea, you're jus lovly, jus lovly, scares me tho. I don't get over ya being Mrs. Duryea. My, your bootiful, jus lovly."

"Thank you Lola. Would you please tell master Jacque that I will dine here at seven instead of his bedroom and that I desire his company."

"Oh lord, Mrs. Duryea, I just couldn't stand to see em an and keep the secret, and besides, he'd never come down jus on my say so.

You'd better show him you and I knows he come flying down."

"Perhaps you're right, Lola. I think I will go up right now."

She gathered a tray of the ice bucket, a bottle of scotch and one of soda from the living room bar and when she entered his room, he was sitting in his blue stuffed chair and had a glass of water in his hand. He turned his clean-shaven face in her direction when he heard her come in and dropped the glass of water and stared at her speechlessly for a moment and suddenly he whistled, got up, took the tray and placed it on the bureau, took hold of her, examined her closely and then gave her a strong hug and a kiss on her cheek. For the first time since his father died did that warm knowing smile creep across his face. "All for me?" he wondered out loud. "Yes, all for you, my dear," she quickly replied. Sweat began to pour from his forehead. She hesitated and thought of his future and knew that it would be no good unless she went through with the transition. And, she added, "but I want it to happen too." She smelled the familiar sweat that she knew from her husband and thought it must be a world of inner uprising to allow this to happen and she hoped she could take the fading stage. 'He has the same compelling expression,' she thought.

He moved from her a short distance, opened his robe and let it drop to the floor and nakedly he took her new dress by the side of each partly exposed breast and ripped it apart and pulled it down to the floor and tore off her inner clothes, picked her up and placed her on the bed and smothered his body over hers. Before he was ready to insert his monster, he raised himself by his arms and knees and asked her to look down upon him. "Did Dad have the same size?" She looked down and said, "no, my dear, he did not. His was much smaller."

Jacque placed his head between her sagging breasts and cried, "what am I to do, mother. I thought he must have had because we looked so much alike, and that is why I was so jealous of him. He had found a woman who could take him. What am I to do? No women that I tried, and I have tried hundreds, can take it."

She lifted his head and answered, "I am not sure and have thought much about your problem. Perhaps older-middle-age woman will have had enough disappointments in their sexual lives to understand your problem and make allowances for it. There are many ways to enjoy sex and various individuals have different preferences. Have you tried to enjoy coming by their mouth and hand and do the same for them with your tongue on their clitorises?"

He shook his head no. "Not at the same time."

"Perhaps it will feel more exciting and complete by sharing your emotional climax."

He lifted himself to a squat position and asked, "what about having children?"

"I talked with your father about this and he said it could be accomplished by artificial insemination."

He laughed. "You really talked about me to Dad?"

"Yes, about this very thing."

"Well, I'll be damn. Let's try your way."

She rubbed his hairy chest and then fondled with his penis and even she had to admit that it scared her to death, but he soon turned around on top of her and took action.

After they had arrived with emotional pleasure, he turned about his body and held her cheek close to his and said, "it was enjoyable, every moment of it. Perhaps, for the first time, a woman felt somewhat close to me at the right moment."

Jacque heard the knock on the bathroom door and he came to and answered, "yes."

"You didn't forget about me, did you?"

"Oh, no, Bella, I was lost in thought. I will be out in a bit."

She went back to bed after taking off her negligee and she wondered if Jacque was becoming tired of her. She hoped not because the men younger than her were so costly, tempermental and not dependable. And, her own age and older ones seldom got to act anyway and more often got drunk beyond caring for sex in any manner. Besides, Jacque was always a thoughtful, pleasant person whose father left sufficient money for him not to be concerned financially, and even if he asked her to marry him, she wouldn't, though she would love to, because in another ten years he would be only thirty-six and she would be sixty-two which wouldn't work out in the long run. She loved him and didn't mind the manner they had sex. Matter-of-fact, it was enjoyable, and to hold this man was enough satisfaction. Unfortunately, he was too much of a man.

When he came into the room he sat down on the bed beside her and clasped his hand around one of her firm breasts (they were still young as a result of her weekly hormone shots) and he kissed her on her neck and then made two more drinks with the set-up next to the bed and handed a drink to her. He took a long swallow and his eyes, she noticed, had turned steel-grey and his jaw square.

"Is something wrong?" she mumbled.

"Would you mind too much if I went back to my studio right now? I want to paint."

The bold expression on his face made her realize that it wasn't any use to say anything else, but, "of course, not. You should paint when you are in the mood."

He gave her a light kiss on her high forehead, put his drink down, got up and went back to the bathroom to dress.

MINOR F. WATTS

Minor Watts majored in veterinary medicine to escape the draft in World War II, and spent two years as a food inspector for the occupational troops in Japan, China and Korea. Afterwards, he became a practicing veterinarian in the resort town of Southampton, Long Island, which served as a model for the community described in Americaville. *In his spare time, he wrote unpublished short stories and became an amateur naturalist. He gave up his practice for some years, travelling and searching for his artistic identity; during this time he had some success exhibiting his paintings in New York. The realities of alimony and child support cut short this period of "hippie" irresponsibility and he resumed his practice, this time in Patchogue, L.I. He is currently at work on two new books and several short stories.*

C. S. Vanek

THE SKIN BOOK

The moment I arrived in the Marie Antoinette suite I
stripped and got out of the nylons and girdle, and
stashed them away in a drawer. I poured a large ration of Scotch
and put my suit back on.

The room hadn't changed much in the two years since I was there last. The drawing room was a jumble of imitation antiques: a silk upholstered sofa which looked quite comfortable, and assorted chairs with curved wooden legs and straight backs. I picked out one that had no arms and pushed it into the middle of the room, facing the sofa. I drew the blinds and pulled the drapes across them. The room was now in nearly total darkness.

I switched on a floor lamp and moved it so that the chair was spotlighted in front of the sofa.

At two o'clock precisely there was a tap at the door. I let her in and locked the door behind her. She was wearing a mink wraparound coat over the blue dress she had worn in my office.

"Sit down," I said, nodding toward the chair. She gave me a quick, questioning glance. "Sit," I repeated.

She sat, hands in lap, legs primly together and her eyes lowered modestly. Her coat fell open and I looked at the yellowish patches where her nylons were taut against the bony prominences of her knees.

I went to the sideboard and poured myself some more Scotch. I stood behind her and ran my fingers through her hair. She didn't move.

"Are you frightened?"

She gave a little nod. Her response sent darts of excitement into my groin. She was completely mine, I thought, and my hand shook when I picked up the glass of Scotch. I wondered how far I could go with her.

"This isn't going to be very nice," I said. My voice came out huskier than I wished.

The girl made no sign.

"Does that worry you?"

She shook her head.

I moved in front of her and sat down on the sofa. Her knees were directly in front of me. I saw her cast an envious glance at my drink.

"Would you like one?"

"Yes, please," she whispered, not looking at me.

I had an idea. Picking up a large glass ashtray I went to the sideboard and poured some Scotch. I returned to the sofa and set the ashtray on the floor in front of me.

"There you are," I said.

Without a word she went down on her hands and knees and dipped the tip of her tongue into the dish. I thought I heard her give a sigh of contentment. Watching her lap up her drink like a cat I wondered what she would like me to do with her. There would be no point in asking her. My intuitions informed me clearly that the very essence of our game was—firm control. That was the expression she had used. I recollected some scenes from my early morning fantasies of my wife. They were invariably unencumbered by inhibitions and it occurred to me now that the girl before me must also have had strange fantasies.

Watching her drink like an obedient animal I was reminded of her spontaneous act of tying my shoelace. That, too, had involved genuflection. Perversely I made her get back on the chair. She would have ample opportunities later for going on her knees.

She sat before me and stared down at her hands. I ordered her to move her legs apart. Her cheeks colored and she turned her head aside. Her knees parted an inch or two.

"Wider," I said curtly.

Zoe bit her lip and opened her legs as far as her skirt would permit. Pale skin above her stocking tops vanished into the deep shadow at the apex of her thighs.

"Stay like that," I said and moved the lamp. She was not wearing panties; golden hairs shone in the lamplight above her glistening pudenda.

I got to my feet and opened my fly. She turned her head away.

"Please don't," she whispered.

Her plea quickened my lust.

"Open your mouth," I ordered, taking out my penis. She averted her face and pressed her lips tightly together.

"Are you going to do as you're told?" I spoke menacingly but Zoe shook her head violently. Yet she continued to keep her legs spread.

I unbuckled my belt and started to pull it slowly through the loops.

"You know what I'm going to have to do, don't you?"

She was trembling.

"Yes," she breathed.

I pointed to the arm of the sofa.

"I want you over that," I told her.

I felt no great urge to whip her; the thought of doing so did not arouse me. In fact, my desire began to melt away. But when she moved obediently to the end of the sofa, pulled her dress high and bent forward, my pulses quickened unbearably. It was not the prospect of beating her that enticed me but her surrender. I can do anything I want with her, I told myself. Anything.

I examined her buttocks and thighs.

"You've been whipped recently?" I prodded the remains of thin welts. She tensed, then nodded her head.

"When?"

When she didn't answer I slapped her hard. She gasped.

"A month ago. Just a little under a month."

"What did he use?"

Zoe breathed hard. I slapped her again.

"A belt and . . ."

I spanked her with all my might.

"And?"

She was moaning softly.

"And a whip. Only you see, it wasn't . . ."

I wound my belt round my wrist a few turns and sliced at her thigh with the free end. Zoe's body leaped as though galvanized. She screamed deep in her throat.

"It wasn't what?" I asked, and hit her again.

"A he. It wasn't a he."

"A girl whipped you?"

"Yes."

"Is she your lover?"

Zoe nodded.

"Your only lover?"

Her head shook.

"No. Not the only one."

"You have men lovers, too?"

"Yes."

"Do I know any of your lovers?"

She hesitated, then shook her head.

I didn't believe her. I wanted to make her tell me about her lovers but something held me back. My eyes had strayed to the drawer in which I had thrown my wife's stockings and underwear. Had Zoe seen my wife naked? Had Zoe also undressed?

"Did *all* your lovers beat you?" I asked suddenly.

Zoe took a deep breath.

"Well?" I insisted.

"They . . . I . . . Oh, please don't ask me so many questions!" She was crying.

I flung down my belt and put a hand on her shoulder. She pushed me aside and straightened up. Tears streaked her face. She reached blindly for her pocketbook and pulled out a pair of panties. I glimpsed a coil of plaited leather. She had brought a whip with her.

"You didn't really want to," she cried bitterly. She turned her back on me and stepped hurriedly into her panties.

"You know that isn't true," I said lamely.

Zoe shrugged unhappily and looked at herself in the mirror. I watched her go through all the brisk motions of a woman anxious to depart. She smoothed her stockings over her thighs and flicked her dress down.

Now she was neat as a pin again and I knew she had been watching me in the office the way I watched my wife in the mornings.

"I know how you feel," I said with perfect truth.

For the first time she turned and looked me in the face.

"You have no idea how I feel!" she spat at me. "No idea at all!"

"Oh, no? What makes you so sure of that?" I said huffily and felt immediately ashamed of my tone of wounded vanity.

Zoe grabbed her pocketbook and headed for the door.

"This is ridiculous," she muttered angrily. "You're sounding like a—like a sophomore."

She fumbled with the door latch. "Will you open the door!" she cried, her coat swaying from her hips. She smelled of woman and fur and her legs gleamed in the dim room.

I sprang after her and spun her round.

She stood stock still and stared at me with cold contempt.

"Would you mind taking your hand off me?" she said with ice cold calm.

I tightened my grip on her shoulder.

"Show me what you have in your bag."

She clutched it to her. With a loud sigh she said, "Are you going to open that door or not?"

"No," I said, and slapped her face so hard she stumbled to the floor. I picked up her pocketbook and took out the whip. It was old and well-worn. I breathed in the familiar smell of oiled leather.

"Take your panties off," I ordered.

Zoe looked up at me, her eyes wide with fear.

"Maxwell! You wouldn't dare!" The tip of her tongue came out and tickled her upper lip.

"You heard what I said, Zoe."

She rose to her knees and was about to remove her fur coat. I bent down and slapped her face again.

"I said the panties, not the coat."

"Yes, Maxwell."

She sat on the floor and, swivelling her hips seductively, eased the pale blue nylon along the stockinged curves of her legs. Had my wife stood over her at such times? The whip felt supple and greasy in my hand. Had Joan ever held it in her hands?

Zoe was kneeling again and looking up at me with a curious blend of provocation and nervousness. It was now or never. I wanted to whip her unmercifully. Now that I knew that she wanted me to I had no qualms about hurting her.

If only I could experience a *reason* for beating her.

Zoe lowered her eyes.

"Are you angry with me?" she asked. There was an edge of suggestiveness in her voice. She might have been reading my thoughts.

"Yes, I am," I told her and waited for her to propel the situation a little further.

"You're not sure how far to go with me, are you?" she asked with the bluntness characteristic of women treading their way in intimate situations.

I put one hand in my pocket and swung the whip negligently with the other. "I'll do anything I please with you," I said.

Zoe was not convinced. Giving a complaisant shrug she waved her hands idly and said, "Well, suppose you tell me what you want to do?" She sounded like a mother, patiently reasonable with a child.

When I didn't answer she asked politely whether I would like her to go back to the sofa.

"Shut up," I snapped.

"I was just trying to be helpful," she explained. Her cool demureness infuriated me. I shifted uncomfortably from one foot to the other. I had been wanting to urinate for some time. I wanted to go to the bathroom but I was reluctant to leave her alone. It would be like a defeat: I imagined myself saying, "Excuse me a minute," and Zoe reverting to polite conventions and nodding and murmuring, "Of course!"

She waited impassively. I edged closer and stood with my feet astride her thighs. Her upturned face was on a level with my fly. I pulled open the zipper and flicked out my penis. I aimed it at her face and waited. For a long moment nothing came but she must have known what I was going to do for she closed her eyes and held her face still while her fingers moved to the neck of her dress and held it away from her so that I could see her bare breasts swaying.

At last the floodgates opened. Her tongue appeared and I watched my urine pouring onto her face and stream down over her breasts.

"Into the bedroom," I said, giving her a little shove with my foot. I watched her get to her feet. Her breath came in short gasps and she was trembling. Her tongue moved lasciviously.

Pearls of moisture glistened on her stockings and there was a large dark patch where the front of her dress clung to her skin.

I pushed her face down across the bed and pulled up her coat and dress. I had intended to penetrate her vagina from the rear but the sight of her little anal rosebud made me change my mind.

"I've no vaseline," Zoe mumbled into the bedclothes. It sounded like a plea. I told her to sit up. She did so quickly and I thought she looked relieved.

"Spit on it," I said coarsely.

She stared round-eyed at my penis and puckered her mouth. A thin sliver of saliva slid from her lips. Her daintiness helped to release my lust. I slapped her face hard, making her whimper.

"Wet it," I shouted at her. "Or do you want it up you all dry?" I raised my hand threateningly and she worked her mouth feverishly, soaking the end of my penis.

"Turn over," I said, and gave her a push.

I was about to enter her when I felt suddenly ashamed of what I was doing to her. She was moaning quietly and beyond the sleeves of her mink coat I saw her small fists knotted so tightly that the knuckles were a pale yellow. Then I thought of my wife and the many times I had dreamed of seeing her in this pose and with a violent burst of desire I rammed my penis into the pink brown ring of the girl's anus. Her scream echoed softly in the dusty splendour of the hotel room as the whole length of me plunged into her hot, soft passage. Then she let out a long, long sigh and in the flickering light of the neon sign her hips began to rock with the eternal rhythm of lust.

Our movements grew steadily more violent, just as I was on the brink of my climax a sudden movement flung us apart. Frantically I swung her onto her back and grabbing her by her short blonde hair I pulled her mouth onto my penis and flooded it with the most massive orgasm I had ever experienced.

Afterwards I lay down on the bed, breathing hard, and Zoe crawled close beside me making little whimpering noises deep in her throat. Her lips were slightly parted and her eyes had a tentative expression.

"Do I shock you?" she whispered and her breath wafted our private, earthy odors all round us. "Do I?" she repeated, and held her breath.

I pulled her close to me and pressed my mouth against hers. "No, you don't," I told her. My words boomed in the hollow of her mouth and I could taste myself on the ripe tongue that moved shyly against mine.

"Are you going to whip me, Maxwell?"

Desire remounted my loins. I nodded and climbed on top of her. She spread her thighs and I felt her hand guide me into her vagina. Her legs swung up over my hips and locked ankles above me.

"Tell me what you're going to do to me, Maxwell?"

"First I shall have to tie you up," I began.

The girl ground her pelvis beneath me. Her vagina was pouring juices on my pubic hairs and testicles. There were wet slick sounds every time I moved in and out of her.

"How will you tie me up?" she whispered with her tongue wet in my ear. I shuddered with pleasure and we continued to plan her beating in minute detail until we both climaxed.

I pulled out of her and we both watched my semen running from between the swollen pink lips of her sex. It rested on my outstretched palm.

"See? It's coming into your hand," Zoe said and obeying my unspoken command she raised it to her lips and licked.

She curled up in my arms. I glanced at my watch. Four o'clock. I suddenly remembered my date with Ruby.

Zoe stirred sleepily in my arms.

"When are you going to whip me, Maxwell?"

I yawned.

"Soon enough."

"I'm glad," Zoe murmured in the hollow of my neck and promptly fell fast asleep.

C. S. VANEK

C. S. Vanek was born in the Southwest region of Bohemia, studied English at the Gymnasium there, and became a tourist guide, travelling to such places as Paris, Hamburg and Copenhagen, where his observations led to an abiding interest in the various manifestations of erotica. Later on, he studied anthropology, and in London, found a small Greek shipping company (they do exist) that was, quite literally, carrying coals to and from Newcastle, in some kind of exchange of different kinds of coal. He managed to get the cabin of the first mate (who was getting married) on a small cargo ship going to Newport News and, forbidden to work by the seamen's union, had nothing to do but eat Greek grapes and read the first mate's collection of old Traveller's Companion books. From Virginia he went to Toronto, and thence to Wurlitzer Park in Tonowanda, New York, with a group of dancers from the show Pajama Game. *Eventually he came to New York City, got into the communications field, edited, wrote for* Fortune *magazine and worked on educational materials. It was natural that Vanek's predilections would lead him to the field of sex education, and thus, to writing for Olympia Press.*

Acid Temple Ball

Mary Sativa

The East Village. Bums, homosexuals, teenagers with hot young bodies in from Queens looking for action, love people from tub-in-kitchen apartments; couples, trios, and more elaborate sexual groupings, communes and tribes. I walk along stoned in the acrid fall wind, dark hair blowing around my arms and shoulders, cowboy boots and tanned thighs, skirt just below my crotch. The old Puerto Rican men leer at my soft 21-year-old body; I stare lustfully at the long-haired boys of seventeen or so. Blank-eyed, they meet my glance and I am briefly embarrassed and touched with a flash of desire. Everything is ringing and bright, naturally, because I smoked a nice rounded pipeful of excellent grass before facing the great outdoors. I want to take each of these pretty boys, one by one, and tangle my hands in their dirty hair smelling of pot and incense, stroke their slim stomachs and backs, bury my face in their warm thighs, lick and taste their hard pricks, kiss their laughing lost eyes.

However, I send myself out on the street with certain directives, like a homing pigeon carrying a message. I am on my way to school and it would take at least an active offer of drugs or sex to deflect me. My art school, after all, offers the companionship of old friends and possible lovers, fat joints passed around in the painting studios, good rock on someone's transistor radio, and probably an offer to snort speed or trip at least once in the course of an ordinary afternoon. I can't object to sitting around there spaced out of my head, daubing pretty colors on a smooth board.

On the other hand, I must pass Davy's pad on St. Mark's Place in order to complete my five-block Odyssey, and this fine morning I am intensely tempted to see him and try to seduce him. Davy is a skinny, strung-out drug dealer and movie-maker. His hair is even coarser and blacker than my own, his hunger for drugs more intense. He is always moving and looking around, always worrying or needing something, always gentle and patiently friendly. He wears dark prescription glasses concealing elegant drooping eyelids. His eyes are as obscenely beautiful as naked genitals and it seems as reasonable to conceal them; I lust for Davy's eyelids, I picture him in bed with his glasses off.

I have wanted him for a long time, perhaps a few months. But time has a habit of being strangely stretched out, and even sequence is beginning to vanish. I have wanted to screw Davy for a ridiculously long time. And he probably won't be home anyway.

I walk through the green entranceway, down the hall, knock on his battered metal door. The hallway smells of urine, cabbage soup and pot. Perhaps he is home. A longish wait, sleepy mutter. He opens the door; I am extremely, happily aware of his presence.

"Hey, how are you doing?" San Francisco-gracious, the noblesse oblige of those totally wiped out on drugs; he's probably coming down from speed or on tranquilizers. Bare-chested, tight pants, big awkward naked feet. Moves jerkily, like a puppet.

"So how are things, man?"

"O.K. I was on my way to school, decided it was too big a deal this morning."

"Yeah? Oh, here's the pipe."

Davy twitches around the two-room apartment, putting Janis Joplin on the turntable, picking at some crumbling brownies on a pile of old newspapers, pushing his hair back from his eyes. I light the pipe, take a deep drag, hand it to him with a light caress on his bare bony shoulder. We smoke, handing the pipe back and forth, smiling at each other. Things improve, and they weren't half bad to begin with. The light in the room sparkles, Davy's flesh seems soft and cool, I want to drink him into me. Janis is singing the story of life, the brownies are beginning to look awfully good; Davy looks even better than usual. I want to feel my hands on his thin hungry body, want his hunger to feed on me, to feed on my hunger. His nervousness excites and torments me, I long to feel his tension eased in me, to feel his need revealed and exploding in my body.

I feel lonely even though I have an old man at home; grass sometimes makes me feel terribly lonely. Or not, depending. But everything is intensified, made more emotional, I really need Davy's body against me, I am haunted by the shape of his thin belly, his blunt fingers, the rough dark hair on his arms and chest. Looks pass between us which would be old-movie hilarious, except that we're both beginning to groove on this scene: romantic, stoned lust. Staring deeply into each other's eyes, our lips parted.

"Have a brownie, Davy?"

He grunts acceptance, I move close to him and place the brownie in his mouth. I watch him sucking and chewing, I rub my mouth hard against his, smell chocolate and desire, take a bit of the brownie from between his teeth. A deep pleasure all its own. We crunch away happily, and I lean against him, rub my head lightly against his chest. At this point I am being even blunter than usual, hoping that hippie good manners plus temptation will sweep away his reservations.

He begins to stroke my hair, slightly trembling fingers moving hard against my skull, brushing my hair down across my back. I remove his glasses and kiss his hot translucent eyelids, the black lashes and brows; my hands stroke his thin vulnerable back. His fingers are on my shoulders and sides, find my buttocks, squeeze and press, I begin to tremble and arch against him. Our mouths eat at each other, wet curious chocolate tongue twisting and stroking into my throat.

We find ourselves on the floor, arms locked hard, the record over. Davy puts on Jimi Hendrix. I roll my skirt down, slip out of my underpants, pull off my soft sweater and remove the cowboy boots. I stand naked, moving to the music, touching my hard nipples with my fingertips.

Davy watches me, laughs, comes back to nuzzle my upturned breasts, his mouth hot and greedy, his hand between my legs now, stroking lightly back and forth, squeezing my thighs, flicking his fingers into me and out again. I bend down and begin to kiss his chest and stomach, nuzzling the curls of dark hair at the base of his belly, working at his belt. He wriggles out of his pants and lies back on the floor watching me from under his heavy eyelids, his breath fast and irregular. I kiss his body all over, all the little delights I have been hungering for, his throat, the hollows of his thighs, palms of his hands, and again and again his prick, sweet little flower growing hard and long under my tongue, thin and long. Sweet needle to fill my hungry guts: heat and dissolve before injecting, dissolve him under my tongue. The source of endless thrilling rushes and short intervals of content. Will he give me pleasure and peace, will he ease my hunger? I climb onto his body, slip down over his tense prick, feel his hardness gliding smoothly into my eager cunt, feel his balls against the back of my thighs.

I press my breasts against him, bruise the swollen nipples against his thin chest. Roll my hips, feel him deep and solid inside me, solid and real as space on acid, the shape of desire. I want him sharp and firm inside me, want it more and more, feel it more and more. At some point I notice that I am grinding mindlessly against him to the irresistible rhythm of a record which is over. Click, click, click. Grunt, grunt, grunt. I slow down, lean back, sigh and get up before I can think about it, turn over the record.

I come back toward Davy dancing, rolling my belly and shaking my breasts to excite him, getting hung up on the music and an illusion of perfect control over all my muscles. Ripple by him laughing, stroking my belly and thighs with my hands, lean over and rub my breasts against his face. He laughs and chews and sucks on them, grabs my shoulders and tumbles me over on my back, falling between my legs, fucking like hell. His thin hard body driving into me, bright patches of color in my mind, unrelated scents and sounds, overwhelming pressure, pounding. His sweet body moving in its own self-absorption. I kiss his ears, the tense muscles in his neck, whimpering, squeezing his ass against me, cramming it tight between my legs.

He begins to ball very slowly, pulling his prick almost all the way out and then easing it in with a slight twist, the swollen head jolting into me. I hold my legs tight against his, push my hips forward to meet each thrust, bounce against him and press him toward me. He moves almost all the way out, chews on my neck, then groans, coming into me like an explosion going hot all over my body, my own waves and moans rushing and beating against his, squirming beneath him as he lies inert and potent at his greatest depth, solid and spurting within me; I grind out the last of my lust and sink back happily beneath him.

We rest an endless time in clicking silence, Davy breathes deeply, the long-over record turns. I watch the ceiling playing Times Square in a modified fuzzy way. Not really coming forth, all made manifest, undeniable, as on a trip. But there for one who knows how to look. Davy cuddles against me, skinny warm pleasure-giving flesh. He mutters: "Mexican food."

"Mexican food?"

"I'm starving. Mexican food."

"We could take speed and ball all day."

"Mexican food," Davy replies, with uncommon finality.

"Shouldn't we smoke some more first?"

We eat lunch at a little restaurant near Washington Square, spicy beef in crisp corn ships, crushed avocado salad, red wine. Somehow I'm always ending up at this taco joint with more-or-less lovers; perhaps fucking me induces a taste for highly seasoned food. I was there on opium once, not eating much but really digging the colors and smells. Hit my head three times on a wooden light-shade and didn't feel a thing.

Even when I manage to get to school, I always come home at lunch to get stoned, listen to rock, generally clear my head. Our old grey cat sits on my lap, getting sleepy and high, the sun goes in and out from clouds, dancing on the floor, bums throw bottles outside the windows, Puerto Rican school kids hassle each other, sing, pick up girls; old ladies yell at the kids. Like life is really going on, all the time, despite cracked plaster, usually cold water, cockroaches . . . It beats any other place I know for a real sense of something happening, thousands of little deals and games and peculiar needs finding satisfaction. A market place for flesh and minds and all varieties of hustling. I sit and smoke and groove on the action in the street, feeling confident that whatever happens will be a trip of one sort or another. Took a little speed this particular morning, getting a bit behind on work. Methedrine always sells well in my art school's cafeteria: half my class must be speeding on any one day. Bitter white powder wrapped in aluminum foil, close myself in a toilet stall after my first class, lay out the powder in little rows on a hand mirror from my pocketbook, snort it into each nostril with a soda straw. In just a few moments a rush of well-being and energy—I just take enough to settle in for some schoolwork, don't want to spend all day running around, talking compulsively with anyone I meet. Any kind of complicated boring project seems possible and fun. Everyone I talk to seems charming and worthy of a lengthy conversation. Toss off some book design assignment that's been annoying me for weeks, fairly much dig doing it, smooth coordinated action of hands and mind. Feel beautiful, healthy, and in absolute control.

   Actually it's a nasty drug with bad physical and emotional coming down—but the big rush of optimism is out of sight, and it is a way to get almost any job done. Bop home considering all the fun things to do, since my schoolwork is now mostly up to date and I'm still feeling energetic and delighted with myself. Pick cat hairs off the carpet? Try on all my clothes one by one? Do freaky dance exercises? Wash out the refrigerator? Anything is easy to do, and once started, almost impossible to put down. Big powerful business people almost all do a lot of speed—their fucking psychiatrists prescribe it—knowing which side their bread is buttered on. So bop home, walking quickly and erect, conscious of myself like a dancer or a racehorse. Smoke a little grass to calm down and get a new point of view on how to spend my afternoon. Smoking pot on speed is very strong and trippy, calms you down and makes you more sensual, but doesn't generally wipe out that delicious energy, that sense of well-being, and that compulsive desire to talk and do and move around. I'm just sitting, minding my own business and taking drags on a joint, comes a knock on the door. It's Nathan from his apartment upstairs. Davy is going in on a grass deal with him. They just got in three kilos from the west coast, want to borrow my old man's scale to weigh the shit out. And would I like to come up and maybe help them break it up and maybe try a little of their new dope? Sure thing, not a really extraordinary offer, but certainly something I could dig this afternoon. Nathan is physically the opposite of Davy, a plump, slightly aging cherub, bright red curls and blue eyes. A really pleasant, easy-going guy, also into making movies. Sees Davy over some of his rough times of coming down, always knows what to say to give someone a nice lift. So we climb the additional four flights to the sixth floor, carrying the scale in a paper bag with needless paranoia. I'm forever having to carry quantities of money and drugs when I've been speeding and am prone to getting really freaked out: nervous about cops and such. But I can even get into digging that, sixty bucks in the bottom of my cowboy boots and a quarter pound of grass in my pocket, am I a wolf among sheep or a lamb among wolves? More of them, but I'm higher, so that's cool. I climb with Nathan to the top floor apartment he shares with still another movie-maker, really enjoying the way my legs handle the steps, no strain, I'm light as air and strong as an Olympic runner. The sun streams in the uncurtained windows, city slum stretches beyond, street noises are softer and less insistent. Heavy blues on the turntable, Davy bouncing to it and running his hands through the grass in a huge shopping bag. Haven't seen him since the time at his place, maybe a week ago, thrill of my body recognizing and craving his. Know me, baby, know me, don't pretend we haven't been there together!

"How are you doing, baby?"

Touch his hair lightly, he smiles recognition, not afraid to see I still want him.

"Dig this beautiful grass. Did you bring the scale?"

The kilos are hard-pressed blocks the size of a textbook. We crumble off hunks into the bag, have to get it loose so they can weigh it out in salable quantities, an ounce or so each in a plastic sandwich bag. Maybe they should include peanut butter and jelly for favorite customers. We break up the shit, resin from the plants sticking on our fingers and under our nails. Glorious strong smell. A knock on the door; everyone jumps three feet and hides everything suspicious, cigarette papers, scale, grass, pipe, pill bottles. Just a neighbor from down the hall to inform us that junkies are using the building roof as a place to shoot up. Found works, needles and empty ampules inside the roof door.

"Watch out, they'll steal everything."

"Thanks for the tip, man, we'll be careful to lock up."

He leaves, we go back to breaking up the grass. Almost done with the first stage of getting it into decently small hunks; Davy begins rolling joints from the new grass. Time to celebrate. A fresh record on the turntable and seven fat joints for the three of us. We sit cross-legged on a mattress, keeping two joints going at once, start a new one every time one is finished. Breathing nothing but dope, no time to talk, just suck in grass, pass joint, take next joint, exhale, suck in more grass. Sometimes forget to exhale. Really almost tired of smoking, colors are as bright and electric as on a trip. Force ourselves to keep smoking, really pushing; how high can we go on mere grass? My head is still flying from the speed, everything is super-cool and I'm having a ball, laughing and trying to stone myself into oblivion with these two great guys; lover and friend, three friends who could be lovers, who could do anything. More and more touch Davy as we pass joints, rub against him, put my hand on his knee.

We're all more or less collapsing, put out the last joint with an obscenely long butt. I rest my head in Davy's lap and he plays with my hair and strokes my bare shoulder. Poor Nathan is looking a bit woebegone.

I whisper in Davy's ear, "Is it O.K. if all three of us? . . ."

"Sure, baby, wouldn't leave Nathan out of something so nice."

I put one leg across Nathan's lap. "Why don't you join us, Nathan?" laugh, lean back into Davy's lap and rub my now bare foot back and forth on Nathan's thigh. Nathan groans slightly, begins stroking my legs and thighs. My arms are over my head behind Davy's back, he leans over me, thrusting his tongue deep back into my throat, squeezing my breasts in his hands. Nathan lies between my legs, stroking my sides and legs, and kissing my belly and cunt through the thin material of my dress. I'm moaning and rolling around, feeling all these fingers and lips, feeling super-stoned yet feeling like moving; don't just want to be fucked, but actively to fuck, grinding my hips and dancing with all my muscles, each movement effortless, rolling like a belly-dancer under their hands and mouths.

Davy rolls my dress up over my head and Nathan helps him pull it off, Davy undresses while Nathan works my underpants off with his teeth and hands. He unzips himself and I suck at his pink cock, sprawled across his lap with legs open, my ass moving up and down. Davy gets between my legs, rubbing his prick across my ass and between my legs, and then slams into me, hard, pounding, and I force my ass up to meet him, biting on Nathan's prick and grunting with each thrust. Deep hard strokes fast as we can do it, and then he pulls out of me slowly, still hard. I groan and grab for his cock.

"Nathan's turn," he laughs.

I lie back, Davy beside me, my hand squeezing his cock, his lips on my ear and neck, all over. Nathan strips, kneels between my legs, fucks me with a slow hard beat, twisting his body between my legs, drawing long sobs from me. I put my legs up, knees bent; Davy sits over me, dangling his prick over my lips, and holds my legs back hard against Nathan's thrusts. I bounce my hips against Nathan, harder and harder, grinding deep against me, want to keep fucking all day, whimpering and nibbling at Davy's prick. Nathan comes quickly and surprisingly into me, a deep groan and all the weight of his body surging into me, quivering hot gusts ripping in me. I arch my back to grind against him, but Davy forces my legs apart and down, stroking me lightly and soothing me. Nathan rolls off to lie beside me with tiny wet soft kisses. Davy and I stare at each other with bottomless hunger. He kneads my breasts and rubs his hard cock against me. "Lie on top of Nathan."

Smiling at Nathan, I lie face down on his soft body, my legs between his, soft little penis nestled against the front of my cunt, begin deep sweet tongue kisses, feel Nathan's prick swelling a little, his hands cupping my breasts, pinching my nipples. Davy rubs my back, squeezes my ass, bites the back of my neck as he eases himself between my legs. His weight grinds me against Nathan's body, he slams into me as though he wanted to ball forever, stretch and iron out every wrinkle in my cunt, fill to overflowing every opening in my body. Nathan's prick is hard now, rubbing back and forth against my stomach and clitoris, pushing the lips of my cunt sharp against Davy's driving cock. Nathan's legs are outside mine and Davy's, he moves against us and squeezes our legs tight together. We're all bouncing and grinding our hips and bellies like mad, Nathan begins rolling under me, beginning to come, Davy rams into me with all his hunger, all his force to fill me and stuff every quivering inch into me, coming in hard shuddering spasms, Nathan's prick spurting against my clit, I explode between them, shaking my ass, opening my legs and pressing them tight together, rolling and moaning between the two throbbing insistent bodies, waves and waves of hard gasping pleasure shuddering forth between my legs. We sink back, wet, tangled together, stinking of sex, and stoned out of our minds.

Eric smiles at me; I realize he wants something. He has no legal hold over me; I don't need to be afraid. Still, it would be nice if he could just vanish in a puff of smoke, I really don't want to go through all the heavy emotional changes involved in getting rid of him again. I want to go upstairs and get stoned and curl up with Jesse, maybe wake in the middle of the night to Dylan's flute, come downstairs and drop some acid and eat peaches until we get high. Instead I have to fuck around explaining myself to Eric.

"I've been in town about a week, looking for you. One of the papers that printed your photographs gave me the address."

"Have you talked to Jesse?"

"No, I've just been waiting here."

"Let me go up and tell him I'll be out for a while."

"I've got a room, we can get some dinner and talk."

I go upstairs, change into sandals and a loose Indian print dress, smoke some grass. Jesse is sleeping. I kiss his pretty sun-burnt cheek, roll his shoulder a little to wake him. He smiles and reaches for me, his eyes still closed.

"Jesse, baby, Eric's in town, I have to talk to him. I promise I'll be back by morning. I don't have to work tomorrow; we can go to the park."

"You sure this is O.K.? I'll talk to him if you like."

"No, he wouldn't actually hurt me or anything, I'll be all right. Miss me?"

"Sure will." He kisses me and strokes my back, I lie in his arms a moment and then go downstairs to Eric.

I get in the car next to Eric. A lot of remembering. He looks tense and uptight, but I recognize his anxiety and it touches me. Did I leave him because he was not young and beautiful and wild enough, or did I really need to find my own way?

"You look older," he says to me softly. The speed and working and never getting much sleep have made me thin and large-eyed, but I am brown from the sun and I feel about 12 years old. The way I spend my time, the things I think about and desire. Ice cream and dreams and pretty boys.

"I'm doing O.K."

We get Mexican food at a cheap little restaurant, eat it watching the shadows stretch themselves out, feeling alternately tense and at home. The food is pasty and tasteless, though I know it is highly seasoned. My parents called him a few times and then dropped it.

"I just wrote them that I had a job and everything was O.K.; I don't think they'll come here or anything."

The high school Eric was teaching at is closed for vacation; he'll be travelling around Canada for the summer, camping out.

"Would you like to come?" I mash my food with a fork and arrange it in neat piles on my plate and don't reply. Tear my napkin into thin strips, roll the strips into little balls, arrange the balls in a concentric design like a church window. We are finished with our dinner, Eric pays the check, and we go.

He has a little room in a cheap hotel in downtown San Francisco, television set and plastic dresser with a big mirror, double bed taking up most of the room. The window opens to the city and the sky, a deep glowing blue. I take off my sandals and sit on the bed, light a cigarette.

"What do you want, little girl? I miss you."

"I miss you, too, Eric, but there are so many things going on in my head. I just want to be left alone, I guess."

He looks sheepish and unhappy. I put my arms around him and hold his head against my breast. His shoulders shake, I pat his back and make comforting noises.

"Eric, baby, I still love you. Just believe I'm insane, if it will make things easier. It's really good here, it's really good being on my own and taking care of myself. Jesse just happens to be around. I don't depend on him."

"Come back with me, I need you, I wouldn't tie you down."

"Eric, I don't want to blackmail you into something that would fuck both of us up. I don't want to use you that way. Forget me and lead your own life."

He begins to kiss my face and neck, deeply and hungrily. We hold each other tight; lost and unhappy we each grope for the other's well-remembered body. He undresses me slowly and tenderly, I am exhausted and passive, I lie back dreaming under his fingers. The sweetness of flesh remembered yet new. And bitterness, bitter as methedrine in my throat. His lips and fingers move over my body, seeing and recalling. Eric has never been much for gentle preliminaries, but tonight time is stretched and lost as on a trip; this is the one time, now and for always, and we must see and feel everything. He kisses my breasts, takes each nipple softly into his mouth, I feel the wet openness of his mouth and the roughness of his beard and moustache around it. Kisses down along the center of my chest and stomach, kisses and licks out my navel, kisses along the tops of my thighs, the little crease of flesh between belly and thighs. Between my legs, chewing at the hairy lips, tongue testing, kisses down my thighs and legs to my feet. He lies next to me, looking into my face, touching it lightly with his fingers. I remember his face seen on a hundred trips, remember him four years younger, remember the imagined future between us which has been wiped out. He is part of me, but I have seen parts of me die time and again.

He is my flesh, my lover, I will always love him. But I still love my parents, my first lover, my teenage girlfriends, myself as a child. I love them and watch them reborn in myself and in new lovers. Eric will not be lost for me nor I for him, but I refuse to remain tied physically to an image which no longer satisfies me: myself as wife and mate. He watches my open face, I hide neither my desire nor my isolation from him. He closes his eyes and draws my naked body close to him, his coarse pants and shirt against me.

I touch his chest and begin unbuttoning his shirt, he finishes undressing, lies close against me. His hands on my ass pressing me against his erect prick, undemanding and shy as though I were a frightened virgin. I touch his smooth strong back, the length of his spine under the taut skin, the bulge of buttocks, his firm thighs; I move against him. He groans and rolls over on top of me, holds his hardened cock in his hand and fits it into me, moving it from side to side and slowly edging into me. He raises himself on his hands and makes deep slow thrusts, watching my face, feeling the responses of my body. I rock my hips back and forth as he thrusts, wipe out the bitterness and loneliness in pure sensation, the pounding of his body answering my panting, my quivering beneath him.

I remember his body, remember it deep inside, remembering flowers into the moment of his being there, crammed between my thighs. He pulls my legs over his shoulders, my knees on each side of his head, body folded tight, ass pulled up in the air. He is painfully deep inside me, rubbing and pounding at the front of my vagina; my thighs ache with the strain of the position, but it is overwhelmingly sweet. Hot jabs of pleasure. I grunt and scream. His hands are under my ass, holding it hard against him. I bite my lip and roll from side to side under him, trying to move away and trying to feel him come hard and deep as possible into me.

He moves in quick hard jolts of pleasure, I squirm and cry. He kisses my ears, licking deep inside them with his tongue, his panting breath coming in warm waves. Harder and harder, I feel agonies of pleasure ripping through me, his prick heavy and full and quivering, short wet stabs, honey gushing. He groans, slamming into me, grinding against me and squeezing my ass with his fingernails. Little short motions, honey-fingers jabbing deep inside, pleasure echoing like a bell; hollow ringing, reverberating. I am choking with sobs, wriggling like a fish, impaled on his cock. The last throbs die away. washing me with peace and sleepiness and content.

He untangles my legs, rolls over next to me, we kiss softly.

"Will you stay with me for a while?"

I shake my head, no, "I'll stay with you tonight."

It is dark in the room, a neon sign outside the window makes a red splash on the floor. We both sleep poorly, waking often; haunted by dreams. Before dawn I wake and find him sleeping soundly, curled up like a child. I dress and sit by the window until the sun is up, kiss him goodbye and leave before he can follow me.

I hitch hike back over the bridge to Berkeley, in a pick-up truck full of grapefruit crates. The young kid driving shares a joint with me. I watch the morning sun sparkling on the bay; the radio is screaming out the Stones: "And me I'm waiting patiently! Lying on the floor! Just trying to do my jigsaw puzzle! Before it rains anymore." There is morning mist over San Francisco; in Berkeley it is clear. I feel fresh and clean and relieved, coming back from a heavy trip.

MARY SATIVA

Mary Sativa was born in 1947 (not under that name, of course) into serene middle-class suburbia, got turned on in high school, and followed the well-trodden drug-and-sex route to New York's Lower East Side. She studied art and photography, learned to hitch rides, cook curries and minimize her demands on reality. Madison Avenue orgies with art directors alternated with strung-out afternoons on Avenue B, and the will to make pictures succumbed to the difficulty of merely staying high and fed and well-laid from one day to the next. She hitchhiked through Bulgaria, Turkey and Morocco, returned to New York, wrote her first book for Olympia, and is currently "practicing quietism in a commune on the shores of San Francisco Bay, working on a new novel in between trips."

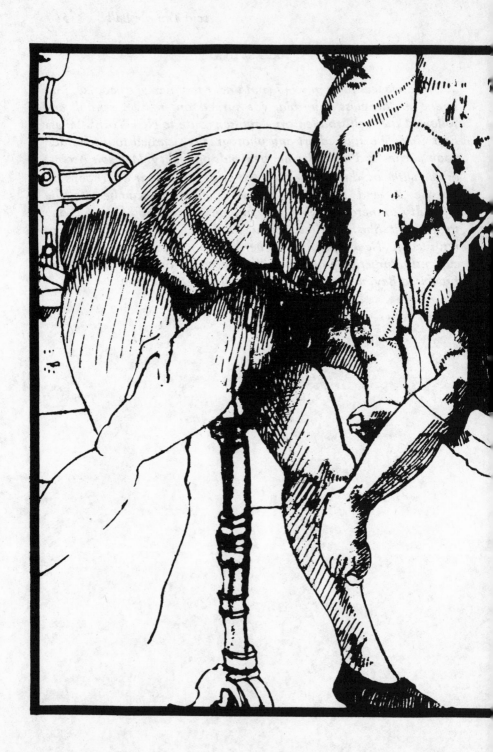

Philip Barrows

Whores, Queers, and Others

*I*n November 1959, I read, in *Time* or *Newsweek,* a full page review of a book called *"One Thousand Homosexuals"* by Edmund Bergler, M.D. which intrigued me. The book apparently proved that homosexuality was actually based on a more severe personality disorder, psychic masochism: "the aim of extracting unconscious pleasure from conscious displeasure . . . the unconscious wish to defeat one's conscious aims for the purpose of enjoying one's self-made failure."

This book review really hit home. Even I could see I had a fantastic "talent" for doing the wrong thing at the "right" time, saying the wrong thing to the "right" person, picking the wrong person for the "right" reason. In spite of all the so-called advantages in life, I was undoubtedly a failure, financially, intellectually, socially and morally; and I was certainly wallowing in self-pity.

Dr. Bergler's theory seemed to be that homosexuality was built on this psychic masochism (which we all feel to some degree or other) by the child who, in his first 18 months, is unable to distinguish the important from the unimportant "rules" and creates, out of his own biological make-up and the environment, a distorted image of his mother as a torturer. Instead of admitting, in later life this deadly fear of women, he rejects them. This leaves him, as a sexual human being, only three remaining sexual outlets: fantasy, relations with animals, or relations with other men.

But, obviously fantasy wouldn't satisfy the psychic masochist's need for punishment, at least not for long, because every neurosis is a progressive disease. "Psychic masochism includes the tendency to play for ever increasing and always more dangerous stakes in the trouble game."

To a certain extent, you can play for ever increasing stakes in having sexual relations with animals, going from chickens to dogs to sheep to calves, etc., but where can you find a wolf or a lion or a tiger? And, how much danger would they really represent, compared to the danger represented by a man who could kill you just as easily, or destroy you financially and socially by talking about you?

I bought the book and read it through twice; the first time, while drinking in the Lodge, and the next morning, I read it again from cover to cover. In the afternoon, I re-read certain sections which seemed still difficult to comprehend intellectually, even if I could emotionally agree with the flow of his argument.

I was very irritated by the book. Some sentences should have been developed into paragraphs. A lot of flat dogmatic sentences were nonsensical. He seemed extremely smug and sarcastic. The book seemed, at times, badly organized, a patchwork quilt from other articles and books he had published. Much of it sounded as though he had dictated it "off the top of his head," and most of the examples seemed ludicrous.

But, who was I, a broke, alcoholic homosexual, to argue with a guy who claimed he could straighten me out, as he had more than a hundred others, in eight months; moreover, a guy who was a former director of the Freudian Institute.

So I wrote him, asking for a preliminary interview. He wrote back immediately, giving me an appointment for 7:30 the following Wednesday morning.

He was a small man and his apartment had the cluttered but comfortable feeling of most intellectual Germans, Austrians, Hungarians in New York. Interior decorators who saw it probably shuddered until they heard his first questions, and then they probably squirmed, forgetting the apartment, seeing only those intense penetrating eyes. He was, I thought, a brilliant but savage prosecutor, cutting short any involved explanation or justification I offered.

"Yes, or No? When? Where? How often? Why? How long? How much? What position? What's your type? What bars? What baths?" and so on.

What malice in his comment, "It's a wonder you're not in jail or on the Bowery already, but at the rate you're going it won't be long!"

Our short talk left me more naked, humiliated and exhausted than I had ever felt. But, paradoxically, I also felt cleaner, and lying in my self-made gutter, I was at least looking up to the stars.

"Unfortunately, I couldn't begin to see you for months, and you do need immediate treatment. Moreover, in spite of your supposedly seductive letter you couldn't begin to afford me. But over the last several years, I have found about twenty other psychiatrists here in New York who agree with my theories—my clinically-proven facts—and have agreed to follow my techniques in analysis. Unfortunately, not all of them have done exactly as I told them so my list is now down to eight in whom I have absolute confidence. Here is the name of the one I think can best help you. Do you object to a woman psychiatrist? Good. Call her, tell her I referred you and ask if she has the time to fit you in. If not, call me and I'll recommend another one. But, if at any time during your analysis you don't feel it's working out, call me and I'll see you to talk about it—no charge, whatsoever. Maybe she'll be doing something wrong, or maybe you're not as ready for analysis as I think you are, or maybe one of the others could establish a better rapport with you. We don't want to waste time or money—yours or ours!"

He never sent me a bill, and the doctor he referred me to was able to see me three hours a week. At times, I've thought of seeing him again, but haven't. Now he's dead.

In case you can't get this book, his theory runs somewhat like this, as I learned during the next two years from the psychiatrist he sent me to:

As the infant grows in his mother's womb, he is the omnipotent center of a self-sufficient universe. Even after the agony of birth, he still feels himself all powerful, and the normal parents help perpetuate this illusion, by keeping him comfortable, warm, in a darkened room, letting him sleep, responding to his every cry, etc. He is still unable to realize that the world around him is not a part of himself, that breasts or bottles belong to "outsiders."

Yet, he has no conception of time, and waiting, screaming for a bottle for one minute can seem as terrible as waiting an hour, and arouses all the aggressive hate that an adult can feel. Some of his "magical powers," his omnipotence, seems to have failed him. But he can still claim all his "good magical powers" and blame his mother—the witch of legend and fairy tales—for her "bad magical powers." This preserves his cherished fantasy of omnipotence—when the witch doesn't frustrate him.

During this period, the child builds up seven fears in which the only villain is his mother. In all seven, "the child figures as the innocent victim of a witch who is capable of starving, devouring, poisoning or choking him, of chopping him to pieces, of draining or castrating him."

The seven generally occur in that order.

A delay in the bottle or breast arouses a fear of starvation.

The desire to bite the nipple is translated into, "I don't want to bite; she wants to bite me." (Personally, I think this fear of being devoured comes from the mother's frequent playful and sometimes noisy or growling kissing of the infant.)

Given the bottle, the infant has to admit he's not being starved, but it isn't as good as it used to be, it's poisoned.

Hugged or swaddled, or overwhelmed by the size of the breast above him, the child learns the fear of choking.

Cleaning and washing seems to take something away, he is being chopped to pieces by this witch.

Helpless in burping, urinating or defecating, he feels he is being drained.

The last of the fears—castration—seems based on his observation that whatever has given him pleasure, he loses: the breast or bottle, his urine and feces, his milk teeth, etc.

Admittedly, much of this seems nonsensical. But how much sense does an infant have, as he tries to maintain his fantasy of omnipotence and explain away the inexplicable environment which is beyond his control? Since the baby has no words, he cannot later explain these fears to analysts, and so this septet of fears has been reconstructed from the dreams and free-associations (daydreams spoken aloud) of hundreds of thousands of people who have gone through psychoanalysis.

As the child learns to adapt to reality, the fears are modified and given more socially acceptable—even if never mentioned— explanations. Instead of saying, "she starves me," the child might think "she refused me love, attention, gifts." All neurotic symptoms show a more "acceptable" formulation of one of these seven fears.

As the parents train the infant, they have three very real weapons: punishment, moral reproach, and the ability to arouse guilt feelings. These force him to obey, yet if he admits they come from the outside, they destroy his fantasy of omnipotence. So, he unconsciously identifies with the commands of the elders—"I'm doing it because I want to, I'm good, and not because you tell me to." This adaptation to reality lets him save face and go on constructing fantasies of his future glory when he will use all his magic powers.

This identification with parental commands and approvals establishes in the child's *unconscious* mind a "department of don'ts and great expectations" which Freud called the ego ideal. This is benevolent, enabling the child to avoid constant punishment while saving face. This "department" of the unconscious mind is the child's idealized self-portrait, as he now magically rules his environment and as he will be in the future, a grandiosely successful adult. This last part provides most of the later trouble because apparently another part of the unconscious superego, the "department of torture," takes these dreams and promises of future successes seriously.

This "department of torture" can be considered the stern, nagging conscience of the *unconscious* part of the child's mind. This department is full of all the fury and aggression which the child has been forced to conceal—for fear of punishment, reproach or the arousal of guilt feelings. Unable to express this aggression against the hostile adult world—and especially against the witch-mother—the unconscious torturer uses all this fury against the child's unconscious ego ideal. It constantly throughout life compares what the child has become or has accomplished with what the infant had dreamed of becoming or doing. The amount of punishment meted out varies according to the discrepancy between the infantile goals and adult achievements. All of this is completely unconscious.

All the approvals, riches, loves and honors that the world can offer cannot match the megalomaniacal child's ego-ideal, so the torturer can always inflict this unconscious nagging punishment which shows up in daily life as conscious dissatisfaction and guilt. Conscious rationalizations have no effect on this unconscious torturer. The inner torturer can only be modified by going back through psychoanalysis exploring the irrational unconscious mind through dreams and free-associations.

The difference between the neurotic and the normal (simply not-too-neurotic) man seems to be the degree or amount of repressed aggression in the unconscious mind. The amount of conscious happiness you get out of life depends on your ability to beat down the onslaughts of your inner torturer. The neurotic is used to repressing aggression. His unconscious mind is filled with it where it constantly attacks him as the self-torturer. He allows only a little to come to the surface, or conscious mind. Most of this little, he needs for actual competition in the real world. He has only a tiny bit left over to consciously try to beat down the unconscious torturer.

The "normal" man did not learn to repress most of his aggression as a child. He still has most of it in his conscious mind, ready to use against the world and also against his weak self-torturer.

Yet the neurotic fights heroically against the unconscious torturer, trying to get some joy out of life, using unconscious strategies of alibis and refutations. Psychic masochism, present to some degree in all of us, is the neurotic's most important strategy.

All kids want to be happy and avoid pain and punishment. As they get older, they have to learn, and incorporate into their now conscious minds, the rules laid down by their parents. These form the conscious conscience and unconscious habits of the growing child and later the man who gets along well with his fellow human beings.

He accepts and incorporates only those rules that he "thinks" are the really important ones in his little world. Accepting these, he eliminates most of the major conflicts or dangers in his world.

Yet some kids, even "nice" ones, fail to incorporate one of the important rules of life into their ego ideals, and in consequence, conflict (external or internal)—and its aftermath of punishment, reproach and guilt—remains very much in evidence throughout their lives. These kids become addicted to psychic masochism.

Living on a steady diet of punishment and pain, they have to reconcile this need with their equally insistent need for pleasure: they must learn to derive pleasure from displeasure.

"This is precisely the unconscious procedure of the psychic masochist . . . and as he sees it, his transformation of external pain into unconscious joy has been a triumph over his stupid upbringers. (Later on the department of torture takes the place of 'stupid upbringers.'). The authorities, in his view, 'think they punished me, they are wrong—I, by my provocation, made them punish me!' "

Obviously, he once again is unconsciously omnipotent.

Re-enacting, again and again, an infantile drama, the psychic masochist perceives and collects some injustice (generally by creating it with his own provocative behavior), blindly defends himself against it with a fine show of false aggression, unconsciously expecting defeat, and then winds up in self-pity, "Why am I always the innocent victim?"

The blind defensive fury of a psychic masochist looks like real aggression but is different in degree, technique, purpose and function. It lashes out, even against innocent bystanders, when an infantile pattern is repeated. The "enemy" is artifically created or a sheer fantasy—"they hate me." A feeling of guilt is always present. The smallest provocation can produce the most violent response. He can't wait for a more suitable time or place to wreak his vengeance. A slight cloak of sadism may hide the masochistic excitement he feels unconsciously in expecting retaliation and defeat.

Why this pseudo-aggression? To sidetrack the inner torturer.

When the psychic masochist unconsciously translates pain into pleasure, he is defying the torturer. The passive acceptance of external punishment, reproach and guilt for the sake of unconscious pleasure is the crime of crimes to the inner torturer.

So the torturer holds up the mirror, the ego-ideal. "You said you were going to be strong and powerful, but here you are weak and suffering." This provokes intense unconscious guilt. Most guilt is silent, consciously nearly unperceived and when perceived, unrecognized as guilt. The real betrayer of silent unconscious guilt is not self-accusation but self-damage. When, rarely, silent unconscious guilt announces itself to consciousness, it is always fastened to "the wrong reason."

The easiest way to deny the crime of crimes—"I passively enjoy pain!"— is to attempt to inflict it on someone else—"See how strong and powerful I am to attack the people who are unjust to me or cause me pain?" Naturally, the person attacked retaliates.

So, this blind pseudo-aggression—usually in response to a problem provoked by the psychic masochist himself — serves two functions. It provides an alibi against the inner torturer's taunts about passivity, and it also provokes actual pain.

The inner torturer is momentarily satisfied. Its only function is to express repressed fury and aggression by punishing the unconscious ego ideal. The form the punishment takes is unimportant, as long as it is increasingly damaging.

A not-too-neurotic person would see that the "cure" is as bad as the disease, but the man who has unconsciously adjusted his inner attitudes so that he can perceive pain as pleasure, uses this as the standard technique for coming to terms with his unconscious infantile problems and fears.

The homosexual is a psychic masochist—plus. That "plus" denotes the inner twist which has delegated to man the terrifying power and desire to hurt him, the power he had originally ascribed to his distorted image of woman—his mother. He is still so terrified of that distorted image of woman which he created in his first 18 to 24 months that he must reject all women and flee to man to get the painful pleasure he wants.

Homosexuals are severe psychic masochists who unconsciously don't crave love, admiration, approval and kindness, but the exact opposites; pain, humiliation, rejection and conflict. Only by provoking these can he "prove" he is still the fantastically powerful center of the infantile universe.

"The homosexual's whole life is devoted to the duality; consciously warding off, and unconsciously living out, a severe inner masochistic conflict." When you accept this duality, you see how absolutely impossible it is for a homosexual, even with the best of conscious intentions, to be truthful, loving, kind, loyal, faithful to his lover, or even to show good judgement in selecting a reliable, compatible lover.

How does a homosexual select a lover? Usually in a narcissistic way. Every infant knows—long before it can think, remember or even associate ideas—that his genitals produce pleasure.

Whenever the child feels tensions arising within himself, he automatically attempts the masturbatory pleasure to allay his anxiety, ("Since nobody else loves me, I have to love myself and I have to love my body because it can always give me pleasure!") Yet, this habit is usually prohibited in our society after the child reaches four or five. The memories of it are repressed by the conscious conscience, but sooner or later another boy teaches him again the pleasurable relief from tension he can derive from masturbation.

The conscience still objects, though, so the boy—now nine to fourteen, say—needs the approval or "moral support" of another boy who also masturbates. He usually gets this, cleverly but unconsciously, by arousing the sexual tensions of another boy to the point where they masturbate in each other's company, even if they don't actually masturbate each other. This other boy is selected, unconsciously, because he has some of the attributes of the unconscious super-ego. Unconsciously, this mutual masturbation is narcissistic, masturbating in front of an unconscious psychic mirror. If the boy, himself, is flat-footed, the other may be picked, unconsciously, for his high arches. If he is forced to wear his hair long, the boy in "the mirror" may have a crew cut or tight curls. If he is physically weak, the other may be powerful. Narcissism—"the arrest at, or regression to the first stage of sexual development, in which the self is an object of sexual pleasure"—is such an early and unconscious state of mind that it cannot distinguish between reality and fantasy. The other boy's desirable characteristics become your own as this relief from sexual tensions produces relief from masochistic tensions.

The conscience, the internal parrot of the parent's do's-and-don'ts, can be silenced for a while. "You told me to go play with Al! You told me to be like him! You said what a nice boy he is! So how can I be doing anything wrong when I'm just doing what you told me and what he wants to do?"

Narcissism—even when unconscious—is the final island of safety for the severe psychic masochist. Surely, you yourself, or your idealized self, will not starve, devour, poison, choke, chop, drain or castrate yourself? Thus, in this very pleasurable relief from conscious sexual tension, you also derive relief from unconscious infantile masochistic tension. After all, you wouldn't hurt your own self, would you?

And yet, each week how many murders occur as "the idealized self" lashes out in fury at the homosexual-caricature which he sees of his own "idealized self." To say nothing of the constant nagging of "lovers" whenever one does something which "the idealized self in the mirror" should not do? Since not even the most sensitive person can be exactly like the unconscious ideal of another, he is bound to frustrate and provoke that other person when that other person happens to be a severe psychic masochist.

As a result, even the most ideal homosexual love affair—where each is almost exactly the other's ego-ideal—is wracked by arguments, jealousies, infidelities and fears unknown in all but the worst heterosexual love affairs or marriages.

Most homosexuals therefore agree that you can't maintain a love affair if you live together; the constant obvious conflict between the lover and the idealized self-portrait is too painful. It gives the inner torturer unlimited occasions for unfavorable taunting attacks.

So the "lovers" live apart to avoid this constant tension. But, they know that inner tension can be relieved sexually. At first, by masturbating, then by masturbating in company with another boy—real or imaginary—then by manual, oral or anal masturbation with the "idealized self-portrait." Finally, the idealized self-portrait "is merely an erect penis, practically any erect penis, and giving relief from sexual tension to that erect penis gives relief from inner tension to the self—even if you can't see the body the penis is attached to or know the guy's name. The greater the unconscious masochistic tension, the more sexual tensions you need to relieve. And so you lurk in a park, a public toilet, a Turkish bath, behind a glory hole, eager to take on practically every erect penis that comes your way. And if none comes your way, you go out to the Champs-Elysees, the Via Veneto, Washington Street, Avenida de la Reforma, Eighth Street, Third Avenue, Main Street, Peachtree Street or your local Route 66; hunting down that bulging crotch, even if it belongs to a derelict, a psychopath, a detective or a young boy.

Or else, you retreat into the world of fantasy in front of a movie screen, television set, "muscle men" magazines, nude photos, or simply memories or imagination. This retreat into fantasy may be socially less dangerous but its passivity arouses the inner torturer even more, so your pseudo-aggression, distracted from the pursuit of actual penises, will undoubtedly vent itself on others, your family, friends, or business associates until you get the unconscious pleasure from conscious humiliation that you crave.

You can only win by proving that you can lose.

Or, you can win another way, but it's even more painful and expensive, and for a year or two or three, almost as time consuming.

When you can, through psychoanalysis, learn to perceive, every time you feel restless, dissatisfied, anxious, irritable or guilty, just what in the past few minutes or hours has frustrated you, causing your inner torturer to taunt you for failing to measure up to your infantile, idealized self-portrait (taunting you for unconsciously getting pleasure out of a consciously real or imaginary painful situation), you'll be able to see that it almost invariably is connected to one of those seven infantile fears of the distorted mother image. Seeing this, you can actually consciously say to the inner torturer, "How childish can you be? Get off my back! I'm not going to suffer now for something that happened—or probably didn't even happen—when I was one or two or three years old! I'm not going to suffer; I'm going to relax and enjoy life!"

When you learn to do this constantly, because the inner torturer is almost constantly attacking, two amazing things happen.

First of all, it gradually drains the inner torturer of all his furious strength. How can he reproach you for "the crime of crimes," unconsciously enjoying suffering, when you flatly refuse to suffer, consciously or unconsciously?

Secondly, as you learn to perceive, dissect and slap down the masochistic tension whenever it creeps up as restlessness or guilt, you automatically prevent it from pushing you on to your habitual way of relieving it sexually. Bit by bit, you destroy the connection between masochistic tension and sexual tension, and this kills your homosexuality—your pseudo-aggressive attempt to relieve sexual tension in an unconscious "psychic mirror." The unconscious psychic mirror is broken. When sexual tensions arise, you will satisfy them physically and emotionally with a woman, no longer terrified by the seven fears associated with that child's very distorted image of woman. No longer unconsciously needing to suffer, you will no longer attribute to woman the power to make you suffer.

You'll be able to see women the way normal men do.

Some women, the neurotic ones, undoubtedly would unconsciously want to make you suffer. But, even the most confirmed woman-hater will admit they are all not neurotic.

Some women, both unconsciously and consciously, want and will knock themselves out to make you happy. They are intelligent, hard-working, amusing, kind, generous, faithful, living, admiring, approving, decent human beings. And they give you every pleasure in bed that another male can.

The only "pleasure" they can't give you is that of your seeing or masturbating, in one way or another, another penis. But by then, you won't need that "pleasure" any more. You needed that "pleasure" once, just as every little boy needs it—for awhile. You had to reassure yourself that pleasure does not lead to the loss of the pleasure giving object (breast, bottle, urine, feces, milk teeth, and supposedly, therefore the penis). Seeing or holding the other penis, you could reassure yourself, "He enjoys it and hasn't lost it, so I can enjoy it and won't lose it!"

Once you've bit-by-bit destroyed the unconscious pleasure excited by the unconscious or even conscious fear of castration, you'll no longer even unconsciously be afraid of losing it so you'll no longer need to check to see that other males haven't lost theirs. You'll no longer find any "pleasure"—relief from tension—in seeing or holding another penis. Why bother, when your own, with a woman, gives you even more pleasure, both psychically and physically?

In the last eleven years, I have talked with at least five thousand homosexuals. I suppose I should delineate just what or who I mean by that word. First of all, I do not agree with many homos, queens, fairies, fags, faggots, queers, gay guys—or whatever epithet you use—that everyman is a latent homosexual and would be an active one if he met the right guy at the right time in the right place. While there is probably an element of love for members of his own sex in every man—what a hell if there were not—I don't consider that homosexual. Nor do I apply the word to those who may have "fooled around" a lot with other males before the age of marriage or during periods of sexual segregation in colleges, prisons, the armed forces, etc.

I mean only those who physically, socially, and financially have the opportunity to have sex with normally attractive women yet prefer men more than 10% of the time. I allow this 10% "margin of error" because many normal men occasionally have sex with a queer just for "kicks." But, would he do it more than 10% of the time if he had complete freedom of choice and no danger of anyone's knowing about it? Many fathers and upright-citizen friends of mine would fail this test.

What causes this preference? Even after four years of psychoanalysis I glimpse . . . the answers only momentarily and vaguely as in a swirling fog or the haunting memory of dream fragments. I can only retrace the patterns I remember. Perhaps in the accumulation of these incidents you can find, as archeologists do, the pattern of an earlier way of life which led me to this point.

When I was three years old, my mother became pregnant. My father blamed her bitterly—they couldn't afford it. Before her pregnancy, she had persuaded him to let his druggist go and she clerked in the store to save money. Now, he would have to work alone from eight a.m. to eleven p.m. seven days a week except for a siesta on Sundays. This probably bothered her more than him because she loved the excitement of waiting on different types of people, never knowing who would come in next or what their problem would be.

She met them all with enthusiasm and tried to sell them more than they wanted. This used to embarrass me, but it may well have paid for my education.

"You'll have to get rid of the baby! Drink this!"

"Frank, that's murder! I couldn't kill the baby!"

Night after night they argued while I cowered in my crib, not realizing that they were not fighting about me. I began wetting the bed again, and this only made him more angry.

He argued, he cried, he vomited after each meal, and sulked for days at a time, refusing to talk to us at home. Yet, she was adamant. She wanted a baby—preferably a baby girl. As far as the store was concerned, she'd only be out of it two months, and then she could get some schoolgirl to stay with us. She would not kill the baby.

Last week I saw a psychiatrist in order to get a prescription for some pills which would make me nauseous every time I took a drink—my own psychiatrist sent me to her as a specialist.

First, she wanted a brief case history: age, occupation, childhood diseases, adult diseases, operations, and then "Are you a homosexual? For how long? Had you been drinking heavily before then or only since then? What was your first homosexual experience? How would you describe your father? Dull? And your mother? Domineering? Is your father easily depressed and prone to worry about things beyond his control? Does he get sick to his stomach easily? Do you have an older brother? Eighteen months older? And a younger one? Four years younger, you say? He would have been born in 1931, then. Did your father have a lot of financial problems in the depression? I thought so.

"Let's cut right to the core of the problem. Over the last five years, I've devoted more and more of my time to cancer surgery and no longer take patients for psychoanalysis. As a surgeon, I like to cut cleanly and quickly to the roots of disease—physical or emotional—as fast as the patient can stand it. I want to ask you a few questions and hope you'll try to give absolutely honest answers, regardless of the shock or pain. Do you mind?

"To establish my qualifications for asking the questions, and arriving at certain conclusions with you: I was a court-appointed psychiatrist for many years. The first time a fellow was pulled in on a homosexual charge, he was given the choice of coming to me or going to jail. Naturally, they all preferred to see me. I've talked to thousands, so nothing you could say or do would surprise me; having worked with thousands of them, I divide them into two types.

"The first type is a lot like people who drank during prohibition; they have no sense of guilt, no desire to change, and only wish the laws were more 'realistic' and allowed them to lead carefree lives. I could do nothing with this type. They'd come here to chat, rather than go to jail, but they had no intention of changing. They just wasted my time.

"But the second type was completely different. Like you, they were utterly miserable because of their addiction to men, and were willing to try anything that offered the slightest hope of curing them. I was able to help six of them cure themselves so they have no interest in men any more. Five of them have married, have kids and seem incredibly happy—happier, they tell me, than they had ever realized human beings could be. These homosexuals had several things in common to begin with. They were very unhappy and disillusioned with their homosexual activities. They realized how much it hurt every aspect of their lives, how it made them most fearful in even the most normal social activities, afraid they'd make a slip of the tongue or absentmindedly stare at the wrong place. They saw how it made their lives increasingly narrower and more desperate. These men were ready to do anything in order to break out of their mental prisons—even if suicide was the only way.

"Some of the six were cured in a year or two. Others needed three hours of analysis a week for four years. But, fast or slow, the same pattern, the same problem, and the same explanation and solution came out in each case. From what you've told me in the last ten or fifteen minutes, I think your pattern, problem and cure are exactly the same and whether you realize it or not—and I suspect you do—you're on the verge of a very startling and repulsive, horribly repulsive, discovery about yourself. Once you can face it openly, I think your problems will quickly disappear. Not overnight, of course, but within a month or two or three certainly. You've reached the chrysalis stage, the cocoon is ready to split and you'll emerge a healthy adult with an adult's emotions and the ability to cope with adult reality. Let me get out my scalpel, as it were, and slit the cocoon and scrape out the core of your emotional cancer, if we can, but, first, let's digress for a few moments.

"How often do you suppose incest occurs in our society? You think it's very rare, eh? Well, a sociologist friend of mine has just compiled a study of 1,000 cases which reached the courts in Chicago in the past few years. Even that number is deceptive because these were only poor people who couldn't afford the secrecy of separate bedrooms or a discreet divorce or separate households, or alimony. These are people who went to court only as the last resort because they had no other way of solving their problems. Mothers seducing their sons or daughters; fathers, doing the same; brothers and sisters, brothers and brothers, sisters and sisters, aunts, uncles and even grandparents. Any combination you can think of is in that report. Rare? It's much more common than even the most pessimistic of us realizes. Remember the first book of the Bible? You know how Lot's daughters get him drunk and seduce him? Incest must have been pretty common in those days, too, to warrant a story in Genesis.

"Just last week, a woman called me up in tears. I'd operated on her mother for cancer of the breast a few days before so I thought at once that the mother must have had a relapse and died—her heart wasn't too strong—but no, this daughter insisted I see her husband that evening or she'd go to court in the morning. She couldn't take it any more. For the past three years, he'd been screwing their daughter who's only eight years old now. So I saw him at eight that night.

"He was a real nothing, a nudnik, a schlunk, a slob. He just sat there where you are and smiled while I talked for about forty minutes, giving him what I thought was a pretty good explanation of the responsibilities of a father, the sexual ignorance of a child, the damage it would do to her in later life and what it revealed about his own emotional problems and so on. When I got through, what do you think he said?

" 'Well, Doc, what you say sounds like it makes sense and it's probably true in most cases; but my kid really loves it!'

"I just looked at him. What can you do with an ignorant psychopath like that? So then I told him exactly how many years I would personally see to it that he'd get if he ever even kissed the kid again, or tried it with any other kid. Two days later, his wife called in tears. She'd caught them at it again so he's in Bellevue now and I don't think he'll ever go free again. But how many other wives are too ashamed to call for help?

"Suppose you are a woman, a religious woman who doesn't believe in divorce. Suppose you're pregnant; too pregnant to satisfy your husband, too pregnant to take care of yourself or go to your folks' house. Suppose you're dead broke, too, and have no way of getting any money? Suppose you're very proud and can't admit, even to the closest members of your family that you've made a ghastly mistake in the husband you picked. They might taunt you about it for the rest of your life. What would you do, or what could you do, if you suspected, or even knew, that your beloved husband, the man you picked for better or worse until death do you part, was fooling around with one of your older kids? Who would you tell? Who would believe you? What could they do? Even if you left him, how could you have the baby and take care of the two older kids?

"Here's how one pregnant woman in that situation handled it. What do you think of her solution? She wrote her mother that the doctor predicted a very difficult and dangerous delivery—would the mother please come and stay in case anything went wrong? Could she come right away and stay a couple of months? Then, she complained to her husband that his snoring kept her awake and anyway, she needed more room in the bed. Would he sleep in the other bedroom with their older boy—a little over five—and she'd take the younger one in her bed. They'd all be more comfortable and get more rest because she could then more easily and quickly comfort the young one who had started to have nightmares every night. What husband could deny such a reasonable request? Of course, when her mother arrived in a few days, the husband naturally gave her his bed and moved out to the livingroom couch so both children were now safe.

"And when the three-year-old woke at night, screaming about the man in the dark who wanted to hurt him, she cuddled him, hushed him, assured him it was only a bogeyman in his dreams.

" 'See,' she would say, turning on the light, 'there's no bogeyman here. There's just you and mommy here. And you know mommy wouldn't let anyone hurt you. I love you, and Daddy loves you, and your brother John loves you, and Grammy loves you. We all love you and we'll never, never let anyone hurt you. So say your prayers now and we'll go to sleep again and God will protect us.'

"She handled it pretty well, wouldn't you say? Especially for herself. In a couple of months she was having relations with her husband again and able to convince herself that it had all been just a nightmare, the little boy's nightmare, and she never had to face the ugly reality that, under severe stress, her beloved husband had molested a tiny child."

"How could a father do such a thing?"

"Have you ever seen a boy that age sleeping? He usually sleeps on his tummy with the blanket kicked off and his little bottom exposed. The father has to pick him up in the middle of the night to take him to the bathroom. Frequently, the kid never wakes up, even though, because of a distended bladder, he may have difficulty urinating through his erect little penis. He makes his water, as they say, and his father puts him back in his crib where he promptly rolls over on his tummy, still sound asleep.

"Under ordinary circumstances, a father finds this cute, chuckles, and goes back to bed. But what happens to all of us when we are under very great strains? Fathers, or mothers for that matter, are no different. When we are emotionally weak or neurotic to begin with, stress pushes us back emotionally—sometimes even mentally—to a period in life when he were happier. Some men go back to the rebellious teen-age period and run around with young girls. Some go further back and find relief in masturbation or "fooling around" with other men. Others may emotionally retreat under pressure to that happy time when they got their pleasure by sucking a bottle, only now, they don't drink milk and it may not even be a bottle they suck.

"You have to remember that each and every boy normally goes through several stages of development. The first two years or so of life, he gets most of his pleasure from his mouth sucking and drinking. Then, as he is toilet-trained, he learns the anal pleasures of defecating or holding it in to annoy his parents. After a year or so, he finds that holding or rubbing his penis produces a very pleasant feeling, but most parents soon put a stop to this so the kid reverts back to the earlier oral phase and sucks his thumb, lollipops, or chews on his fingernails or pencils. Going to school, he may soon be shamed out of this, or lose interest in it as he discovers the physical pleasure of rubbing his whole body against other boys while wrestling or playing other contact sports. This starts the somewhat homosexual period when he plays with only boys. Around eleven, boys rediscover the pleasures of rubbing their penises and may even experiment inserting them in each other's anus or mouth. Since they're so inexperienced, this is rarely physically satisfying, so they're eager—although somewhat fearful—to insert them in girls where they belong. That's the ideal pattern, and most boys follow it physically so they appear to be normal, even though they may not have been able to adjust emotionally. Only under stress do they reveal whether or not they are still emotionally stuck at one of the earlier stages of development.

"Look at the adoption statistics! The only reason a couple can't have kids of their own is purely physical—one or the other is sterile. Yet, when examined by a trained psychologist, 75% of the couples who want to adopt a child are rejected because either one or both of the would-be parents is too emotionally immature to raise a normal, non-neurotic child.

"What about the couples who don't have to go to an adoption agency but just hop in bed to get their kids? Don't you suppose that 75% of them would flunk the maturity test, too?

"Take this father I've just been talking about. He's unable to have sex with his wife because of her advanced pregnancy, yet like most men, he needs sexual relief when he's under a severe strain, and this poor devil was under a severe strain. His business was rapidly going downhill to bankruptcy. He was already saddled with two kids and now would have another with lots of doctor bills. He'd married the sort of woman who would help him, but now she was more of a hindrance than a help. So, without realizing it, he emotionally retreats to the phase when he was happiest. In his case, it happens to be the level of a four-year-old. He's very conscious of anal pleasure, yet being a man, physically, he's also very aware of genital pleasure. And what does a four-year-old boy enjoy? A boy of three whom he can torment and dominate.

"Every night this poor fellow sees this cute little three-year-old with his little erection and bare bottom. He knows the kid doesn't wake up. He knows the kid couldn't accurately describe what has happened even if he did wake up. If he's a psychopath, he rapes the poor kid. But this man isn't a psychopath with no sense of good or evil or guilt. He's just emotionally retarded at the four-year-old level, so he probably just pats the kid's bottom to begin with.

Nothing happens, the kid himself doesn't even stir. So he gets a little bolder and touches the kid's asshole. Still no reaction. Then, maybe that night, maybe the next, or maybe after a week of this, he inserts a finger, wondering just how loose it is. If he's very gentle, the kid still sleeps on, but most excited four-year-olds aren't gentle and the baby wakes up in great pain, terrified by this unexpected attack. He screams out and the father comes to his senses as the mother rushes in to see what the trouble is.

" 'He's just having a nightmare!' the father tells her, trying to shush the terrified kid. But mothers know that nightmares don't just happen like that so she sends him to the kitchen to heat a bottle of milk while she quiets the kid, rocking him in her arms. Maybe the kid can tell her what happened, but probably he's too startled and confused to be able to put it into words. The damage has been done. And who do you suppose gets the blame for it? That's right, the mother. The kid realizes she's trying to cover something up and he naturally feels deserted and betrayed by the woman who's supposed to protect him. He's learned several things from this incident; women can't be trusted, supposedly friendly men may attack him and cause him pain, and that part of his body which gives him pleasure can also produce pain. His whole little safe predictable world has been shattered.

"From now on, whenever he gets tense or anxious, he'll start looking around for the man who may be about to attack him. He'll be so intent on this, he won't even notice women around him any more than he notices chairs. When his anxiety gets too much to bear, he'll provoke some male in the environment to attack him—even if it's just a verbal attack—in order to get it over with and be able to relax. Without remembering why, he'll feel threatened and trapped in a woman's arms. The most important thing in his life from now on is his ability to manipulate dangerous men. He's a homosexual before his sex life has even begun.

"I've found this incident and pattern in each of the six homosexuals I've been able to help. Sometimes the kid was actually raped—and not with just a finger—by the father, or a brother, or an uncle or the boy next door. In every case, the incident was buried very deeply in the kid's memory and it took years of analysis to bring it to consciousness, bit by distorted bit. It's such an extremely painful, humiliating and embarrassing memory and it happened such a long time ago. But, that's the core I've found in the emotional cancer of homosexuality.

"Applying the scalpel to your case, can you remember having nightmares about a dark man when you were very young?"

"Yes, and I still have that nightmare occasionally even now."

"Does the dark man carry a club or other phallic symbol?"

"Yes."

"Was your father under great stress at that time?"

"Yes, just the way you described it."

"From what you know of psychology, would you say your father is emotionally stuck in the anal period?"

"I'd say both my father and my mother are."

"Did he play with you very roughly, say tickling you too hard, when you were small?"

"Yes."

"Did your mother try to stop this and usually manage to keep you in sight when he was around?"

"Yes."

"Did she ever let him take you any place alone?"

"Not that I can remember."

"Did she have someone come stay in the house during her confinement?"

"Yes, her mother."

"Did she actually take you to bed with her during that period?"

"Yes."

"Can you recall being fascinated, as a small boy, by the size of men's hands and legs?"

"Yes."

"Were you very affectionate with your father?"

"No, I was terrified of him, he seemed a stranger."

"When your mother threatened punishment, did she threaten to do it, or have your father do it?"

"She threatened to have my father whip us, but when it came to actual punishment, she always did it herself. Only once did my father whip my older brother, and he really did a job on him. His belt actually broke the skin and my brother couldn't sit down for a couple of days. His ass was all black and blue."

"Did your mother whip you in the same place?"

"Yes, it was always bend over and pull your pants and shorts down."

"Who did the first fellow you found sexually exciting look like?"

"My father."

"The first time you had sexual relations with a fellow, what happened?"

"One of my friends blew me for about fifteen cents, but his teeth scratched and my best friend was watching with a disgusted look on his face so I just got bored and jerked off without coming."

"How about the next time?"

"We are wrestling. I was thirteen and he was sixteen, so I didn't have much of a chance, so my two buddies shouted, 'Grab his balls.' So I did. One of the buttons of his fly was open so I pulled the others open, stuck my hand in and grabbed his balls; they were very hairy and he had a hardon. Just then a priest came in—we were at a Catholic boys' camp—so I let go, hoping he hadn't seen it. The kid told me to wait for him in the large outhouse out back in five minutes. I waited but he didn't come so I jerked off."

"But what happened the first time one of you actually had sex?"

"I was raped at boarding school."

"What happened the first time you enjoyed having sex with a guy?"

"He started to screw me but it hurt too much so I screwed him and loved it. I'd never been so satisfied, even when I'd screwed a girl seven times in one night."

"Were you drunk?"

"Yes, I'd been drunk every night for about a year and I was very drunk that night."

"Did he remind you of yourself—physically, mentally or emotionally?"

"Yes, physically, he looked like what I always wished I looked like; mentally, he was very intelligent, a Fulbright scholar; and emotionally, he was a lonely and full of self-pity as myself. I'd guess he was an idealized, or highly romanticized version of myself and also of my older brother."

"Since then, has your type changed or has your preferred technique of having sex—screwing—changed?"

"No, I still go for blond crew-cuts, and I still want to screw them. The only change is that he was older than me and I like them younger. He was the only older guy I've flipped for."

"You don't get much satisfaction from oral contact?"

"Very rarely. Only if I like the guy very much and then only as a prelude to screwing him, or occasionally in a semi-public place like a movie or subway toilet and then only because of the excitement or danger involved. It's almost impossible for me to come just by being sucked, and I'm a lousy cocksucker, myself. I'm just not interested in it. I'd rather watch two other guys doing it while I jerk off."

"If there weren't any danger or problems involved, how young would you prefer your partners?"

"Thirteen or fourteen."

"The same age you were when you were introduced to sex . . . Do you want to give them a better introduction to it than you had?"

"Yes, I'd be much gentler with them and teach them how it's meant to be fun—there's nothing to feel ashamed of."

"Would you be trying to teach them that, or just trying to convince yourself?"

"Both, I guess. I wish some guy had taken a kindly interest in me at that age. I'd have been saved a lot of guilty self-recrimination."

"Do you pick up guys when you're sober? Or just when you're drunk?"

"Only when I'm drunk. I don't have the nerve to make the first move when I'm sober. I'd hate myself too much if the guy was disgusted and rejected me. But if he makes the first move, I'll go along with him."

"So, if you stopped drinking, you'd stop a lot of your homo-sexual activities?"

"Probably, but I'm so lonely I can't stay on the wagon very long and go through day after day without sex. When I'm sober, I can see a cute teenager and know that he'd go along with it if I approached him— most teenagers here in New York are pretty free from guilty feelings about sex, fortunately for them—but when I'm sober, I don't want them to know I'm queer. I'm afraid they'll despise me the way I despised the first few guys who blew me or propositioned me. I know this is irrational—they'd probably welcome the proposition, but that's the way I feel. So, I get drunk so I won't feel so puritanical about it. And, a lot of the time, getting drunk doesn't help, I'm still just as puritanical about corrupting them. I want to, but I just can't bring myself to do it."

"But when you do, you're very gentle with them?"

"Yes, if I think I'm hurting them, I go soft, impotent."

"So, physically, you're saying to your father, 'This is the way you should have treated me.' Or, maybe if they cried out in pain, their mothers would rush in and catch you?"

"Maybe, but at that moment, my feelings towards them are very mixed. I love their bodies, and I love them for allowing me to screw them; I'm extremely grateful, but at the same time, I despise them for letting me talk them into it. I feel all powerful yet I feel I'm destroying something good and beautiful and wonderful."

"As you felt your father was destroying you?"

"I guess so. I never trusted him and felt he'd be happier if I wasn't around. Before my baby brother was born, I thought he meant me when he used to tell my mother, 'You've got to get rid of the baby!'"

"So you keep reliving the same incident over and over again—the rape or seduction of the little boy you once were—only now you're in control of the situation. You're the all powerful father. You're the dark man of your nightmares. And the angry rejection you're afraid of when you think of propositioning a boy is the same angry rejection you felt when your father molested you. It's the same burning anger you felt against him, and you're afraid that the other kid will let it explode, even though you repressed it. I would imagine that you carry on mental arguments all the time."

"Yes."

"And you always expect people to give you a hard time, even when they're your best friends and have no reason to give you a hard time?"

"Yes."

"So you're accusing the whole world of feeling the same hatred and rage and destructiveness which you were unable to express as a molested child. Blaming others, saying they're the angry ones, lets you conceal from yourself the intensity of your own anger which might be punished if suspected?"

"Yes."

"Projection of your emotions onto other people is one of the commonest techniques for coping with difficult or impossible situations. I suppose you gave the impression of being a 'perfect little boy' . . . polite, submissive, very obedient and quiet?"

"Yes."

"And because you're so afraid of being punished for your secret rage which would be expressed physically, you went to the opposite extreme and hid it by becoming a good student, a reader, a thinker, in a little ivory tower?"

"Yes."

"So you've been a hypocrite all your life?"

"Yes."

"Naturally, this makes you feel more guilty and consequently more angry with yourself and the world that forces you to be so sneaky?"

"Yes."

"Seems like quite a vicious, ever-narrowing circle, doesn't it? Either you destroy, emotionally and morally speaking, every nice kid who reminds you of yourself—or more importantly, who reminds you of the cocky, aggressive type of kid you really wanted to be but had to conceal—or, you have to provoke one of them into a situation where he'll attack you, beat you up, rob you, haul you into court, or maybe even kill you, doing to you what you wanted to do to your father. But, this is too painful a desire to admit to yourself, so you retreat to the oral, bottle stage and get drunk every night. Or any time you feel anxious. But what good does that do? When you're drunk, don't you have to take some of the responsibility for getting rolled or beaten up? And losing what little self-respect you still have?

"Do you think this will punish your father or get even with him? Is he really worth it? Let's admit, for the sake of argument, that he did, unconsciously, of course, really want to destroy you. So now you have to destroy him in order to save yourself. Why not do it by becoming more successful than him? Wouldn't that make him feel more ashamed? Why not become a better father than he was? Why not help boys like yourself instead of destroying them?

"Sometimes I'm convinced neurotics prefer to pursue their own self-destruction rather than destroy a legitimate object of wrath just because that object of wrath had a socially approved label like mother or father. Raised by a fanatically religious mother, you may still be doing atonement for the hate you felt towards both her and him, and trying to make it up to them by distracting the attention of a vengeful god away from them and towards yourself . . . 'Look, God, don't punish him because I'm much more guilty. He only did it once, but I've done it five thousand times! Punish me instead of him! Let them beat me, rob me, fire me, kill me, but forgive him the way I should have forgiven him but couldn't, and still can't.'

"Only you don't believe in a god anymore, so you've got to do the punishing yourself. Constantly imagining unpleasant situations, constantly berating yourself for real and imagined offenses, constantly nagging yourself for not being true to that you whom you might have—and still could—become. No wonder you have to get drunk every night to black out so you no longer have to listen to that prosecutor shouting inside your mind. No wonder you see only anger and hatred all around you and can't give or accept any love ...But there is another way out, you know. I think your defenses are cracking now and you won't need them, you'll outgrow them in another month or two. In the meantime, I'll give you this prescription to help with the drinking problem . . ."

Johnny told me more about himself as we drank and talked rapidly, trying to crowd a lifelong friendship into a few evenings.

Talking, drinking, laughing, or on the point of sobbing when he told how depressed he had been lately and had tried to commit suicide, I realized that I was falling in love with him, or was at least completely infatuated. I'd never known anyone so frank, so intelligent, so charming, so witty, so highly self-educated, so handsome, so sensual. He was just about my ideal, except for the suicide bit. He was just what I'd like to be at his age, 26. When the club closed at four, we slowly walked up the hill to his hotel, arm in arm like the Italians, and it seemed the most natural thing in the world.

"Will you come up to my room for a nightcap?"

I'd been afraid he wouldn't ask. Late in our conversation, he'd told me he was a homosexual and asked me if I'd had much experience with "queers." I told him about Joe from the factory and Pete and the aborted attempts with Al Carter and Don Miller. I told him I didn't think I'd amuse him in bed so he'd switched the conversation to something else.

After the nightcap, I stood up to leave and he walked up to me, hugged me gently and kissed me with all the tender passion I'd wanted all my life. I was drunkenly dizzy and happier and more relaxed than I'd ever felt. I clung to him and kissed him without any inhibition but with all the love that had been dammed up for years.

"You'll stay, won't you? Let's get undressed and in bed!"

I undressed, only slightly embarrassed by my hardon, and he hung up my clothes. When I got into bed, he turned out the light and went to take a shower. I could hardly wait for him to get in bed, but afraid that when he did, he'd find me so inexperienced that he'd ask me to leave, or so big that he wouldn't let me fuck him.

When he crawled into bed, I found I was trembling with both fear and desire. He slipped one arm under my neck, leaned over and kissed me deeply while his free hand caressed my chest, stomach, thighs and balls. When he grasped my cock, I lost control, and with a startled moan of regret, I shot. He dove down on it sucking out the last drops and then lapping up the first spurts that had spattered my stomach and chest. I twitched at each touch of his tongue on my taut muscles, and discovered the new tactile pleasure of running my hands through curly hair.

"I could see at the bar last night that you were well hung, but I didn't think it would be this big or this hot. Doesn't it ever go down? Can I brown you now?"

"You can do anything you want!" I'd surrendered absolutely to my unnatural desires. I wanted him to be as happy as I was.

But when he took a jar of vaseline out of the night-table's drawer and greased up his cock, I was startled and afraid of the pain Pete had caused. But what the hell, Frank hadn't hurt when I was drunk and relaxed! I rolled over and clamped my teeth in the pillow, willing to undergo any pain in silence rather than disappoint my ideal, the first person I had ever loved. He spread my legs and slowly worked it into my ass. It wasn't as bad as the first time, but it still hurt a helluva lot for the first couple of minutes. After that, the pain actually felt pretty good. But I was hoping he'd come fast and get it out.

"Man, you shuah ah tight!" His Southern drawl had become more noticeable with every drink he had. "Does it hurt?"

I nodded, afraid to let go the pillow.

"Well, why didn't you say so?" He cheerfully pulled out. "It'd be a shame to waste that big cock of yours though. Will you fuck me?"

"Yes, I've wanted to since the first time I saw you, I guess!"

He laughed and went and washed himself. He brought back a towel and spread it in the middle of the bed. He greased up my cock and then his asshole. He rolled over onto his stomach, his cock in the middle of the towel. I climbed on and into him slowly. It was as hot and slippery as a cunt. I wrapped my arms around his chest and started fucking slowly all the way out almost to the tip and then all the long smooth way home. His ass fitted into my stomach perfectly. I lay there a minute, afraid the next stroke would make me come, and kissed the back of his neck. He moved his face around and I found that by pulling up a little higher on his body we could even kiss in this position. I kept running my hands through his curls, surprised that my hands could feel so ticklish.

All the way to the edge, all the way home, and he rolled his ass from side to side and up and down just like a whore. Why couldn't Al Carter have sucked like this guy or fucked like this guy? Their hair and grins were just alike. Christ! The good times we could have had. Or why couldn't this guy have been up in that tree instead of Don Blodgett. Or my brother? Christ, how wonderful it would have been growing up with him!

I fucked with all the violence of those years of frustration and he gasped, "Give it to me baby! Oh, man! Give it to me all the way! Fuck me, fuck me, fuck me, and don't ever stop!"

I did, as blindly, berserkly and brutally as any rapist since the beginning of time. Like a woman, he groaned and moaned, gasped and chewed my lower lip and tongued the roof of my mouth. I came with an exultant roar that I'd never heard before, seeing pinwheels exploding, and collapsed on him. His asshole kept milking my cock and the sweat trickling down my back and sides kept me twitching.

"Good God a-mighty, man! You sure do know how to use that horse cock! I've never been fucked like that and a lot of guys have tried! Any time you want a testimonial, I'll be glad to give you one! I sure wish I could get you in bed every night! Too bad I'm not your brother; we could have had a lot of fun!"

We chuckled and lay there happily. I wondered what John would have said if he'd heard and seen us . . . Who cares? Gradually, my strength came back and I got up and went to wash. The shit on my cock disgusted me, but as I gingerly washed it off and then soaped it down, it felt so good I had a hard time pissing. I left the light in the bathroom on and the door slightly ajar so I could see his handsome face again. It was just as handsome as I'd remembered and my cock got hard again as I looked down at him. He opened his eyes and smiled.

"Let me whisper sweet suckings in your ear!" he said and pulled himself to the edge of the bed and started sucking again. I ran my hands in his hair again and he took all of it, the muscles in his throat gulping.

I thought he was going to choke or suffocate, but he held me in there with his arm around my legs. I started fucking his throat. Why couldn't Joe have looked like this guy? What a different reaction I'd have had! He moved a leg to balance himself and I could see where he'd shot on the towel when I'd fucked him. He was getting a hardon, himself, and reached down and jerked off while I fucked his face. I stared at his cock as though I'd never seen one before. It was uncircumcized and not too big. His golden pubic hair glistened in the light from the bathroom, and I remembered the boy who had saved me from drowning, the first Catholic I'd seen with pubic hair. I wished I'd seen him jerking off. I'd have liked to help him with it. I'd have done anything he asked. I was ready to bend over and suck it to please him when Johnny shot like a white hyacinth, the white petals spurting up and out in every direction, flowing slowly down over his hand. I came as soon as I saw the first one, the muscles in my ass pumping up every drop in my balls. He swallowed and moved his head back and lightly tongued the tip resting between his lips. It was too ticklish, almost like an electric shock, and I leaped back. He wiped my cock and then his on the towel. I got into bed and hugged and kissed him as eagerly as the first time.

"Great God a-mighty man! You just roll on over there! I've got to get some sleep tonight!"

He rolled away from me and fell asleep at once, but I leaned up on one elbow and watched him all night. He was certainly beautiful all over, lean and well-proportioned like a statue of a sleeping Greek youth. I wondered why Praxiteles never sculpted one, but he probably did and the early Christians had destroyed it. The fine hairs on his forearms and legs were golden, too. Where he wore a bathing suit, the skin looked like white satin. I got a hardon staring at the way his legs curved into his ass, remembering how perfectly we fitted together. I wanted to smoke but was afraid to disturb his sleep by moving. He looked so innocent in his sleep. I watched his chest slowly breathing, grateful his suicide attempt had failed. He was too beautiful to die! I would have gone through life never knowing this complete happiness. My hardon ached and ached, longing to go back home.

By seven, I couldn't stand it any longer so I reached over him for the vaseline and greased up. At first, I only intended to jerk off while looking at the sexy curve of his ass and back and legs, but after a few long slow strokes, I knew I wanted to fuck him again. What the hell, this wasn't any puritanical Don Miller or Jim Powers! He admitted he'd been fucked by hundreds of guys and I was the best! He really liked it! I edged over and gently forced the first two inches in, afraid of hurting, awakening or irritating him, sure I could come in just a few slow strokes without putting it all the way in. It felt terrific with just the rim of my cock inside his sphincter muscle.

But he suddenly shoved his ass back and took all of me at once.

"Man, what a wonderful way to be awakened!" He stretched his body out next to mine and yawned. "Now, how about a nice, lazy 'Good morning' fuck? It feels so good!"

He arched his body slowly forward 'til he was almost off my cock and slowly came all the way back. I let him do it four or five times, but it didn't feel as good as when I did the thrusting, so I held him tight and gave it to him slowly but all the way, massaging his prostate gland each time, making him moan contentedly each time. He greased up his cock and then pushed my hand down to it. I got the point and gave him a slow handjob in time with my thrusts so it felt my cock went all the way through him and I was jerking it off on the other side. But it felt so good we were soon pumping away as fast as we could while I chewed the back of his neck and listened to his grunts of pleasure and the slapping of my stomach against his sweaty ass. Again, we came at the same instant.

We lay together and he lit up two cigarettes. We smoked in contented silence. Everytime he reached out to flick his ashes, his asshole clutched at the root of my cock. What a perfect way to die, I thought. I'd never be happier!

But, I had to get up and shower and shave and go to work, as though it were just any ordinary day. He still lay there with that big wonderful smile when I took a last kiss, long and deep enough to last me all day.

PHILIP BARROWS

A modern Frank Harris, but with much more perception and much less bombast, Philip Barrows has first experienced to the full what he describes — then he has proceeded to paint his fresco of contemporary eroticism at every social level, which will remain an image of our society, rarely given to us.

My Mother Taught Me

Tor Kung

I hung the coats in the closet, smoothed the bed, and slipped out. Back in my own room, I took an icy shower and laid down to put my mind in order. Maybe I was going crazy. Or was already. These things *couldn't* be. Already they eluded me when I tried to remember. Like those things from my childhood that would float up now and then from the secret place, sending waves of excitement ahead, only to vanish at the point of seeing. Like in the movies, when the diver is underwater and a marvelous something looms closer and closer—and is suddenly gone. And you can never decide whether it was a whale, a lost city, or Neptune striding his farm.

My mind couldn't deal with what had happened. It automatically put such unlikely things aside. The mind must. The senses give approximate data and the mind constructs the truth. The eye sees the moon just above the roofs: the mind moves it up an endless distance. The ear tracks a giant prowling the cellar: the mind discovers the waterpump is in trouble.

It *must* be some kind of test to see if I was the kind of boy they wanted in their family. And I wasn't doing very well. I put on my fine new clothes and carefully brushed my hair. I looked at the freckle-faced kid of fourteen in the mirror and knew it *must* be that. I looked into the wide blue innocent eyes, leaned forward and whispered: "Mother wants you to watch her get it! Tonight!"

At dinner, I found that everyone had dressed. Father wore a dinner jacket. Louise's white dress draped in graceful folds on her thin body something like the togas in my Latin text. She was the cleanest, purest thing I'd ever seen. Gunilla filled an expensive, long-sleeved, high-necked bronze dress that should have been modest, since it covered everything except her hands and face; but it was made to show her ripeness. The material was tailored precisely to her bust, fitted even to the inside slopes—so that each large, jutting bowl was proclaimed individually. And each nipple pushed clearly against the cloth saying there was nothing underneath but flesh.

Mother was very elegant in a severe black dress that left her shoulders and most of her breasts bare. I was shocked. There seemed such an amount of nude flesh. Her superb shoulders and long throat and round arms glimmered in the candlelight like a moonblaze. The breasts were exposed to just above the nipples. (I even glimpsed the brown circle around it when she reached for more wine.) They seemed lifted from below, offering themselves. They strained at the bodice which was supported by only two thin straps. I tried not to stare. From the compliments the others paid the dress, I knew it was proper; but it drove me wild. More even than Gunilla's. Mother's body was somehow both lush and slender at the same time. And there was something else. Partly it was the elaborate coiffure that piled her hair in great golden masses on her head. Also the makeup and the eye-shadow spoke of a world of sophistication far beyond Gunilla's youth. But it was more than that. There was a mysterious quality of preciousness, an aura of maturity, grace, complexity, and aristocracy. A life-time's accomplishment. Yet it was wholly sexual. Those luminous naked breasts so clamorous in the formal setting had the intense sensuality of night beside Gunilla's sunny lust. Her queenly head on its sleek throat dreamed above her obscene breasts like a perfect velvety dark rose amid its heavy, sensuous perfume. Through the whole dinner she was turned inward, periodically flushing for no reason—so her eyes sparkled. Louise, like Mother, ate almost nothing. Her fawnhead with its limpid complexion bent over her plate in a deep reverie. Gunilla and Father were obviously exhilarated and chatted animatedly through the meal about horses. I fed on the loveliness of the women's heads blooming like lotus in the candlelight against the late twilight that filled the great windows.

We went into the salon and Louise played Mozart. Gunilla sat so she was behind Father and Mother, opposite me. Almost as soon as everyone was settled and the piano began, she caught my eye and smiled. She raised her knees until her feet were on the edge of the chair. The she deliberately pulled her skirt up into her lap, uncovering her legs all the way to the hips. I gulped. It was beginning again. She slid forward and let her legs fall apart, lifting her blonde cunt toward me. Her eyes flashed. Noiselessly she lifted the lamp from the table beside her and put it on the floor, adjusting it so that the light was directed into the hair. It was unbelievable. There she was lying back in the chair with the light shouting on her in the dim room, flashing on the full thighs, burning in the cunt hair. Her hands started stroking and opening the flesh. I couldn't stand it. All they had to do was turn their heads slightly, and they'd see her! There would be no possibility of covering or equivocating. I tore my eyes from the fantastic indecency of it, stammered something about being tired, and fled.

In my room, I had just gotten my pants open when Gunilla came in.

"Well, little brother, you're so sex starved you have to sneak up here to masturbate. Come to my room and we'll see what can be done for you." She took my hand and led me along the hall. "Besides, Lars, we have to get our seats because the show is going to begin soon." Her room was a confusion of books, clothes, nude pictures, African masks, salvers of fruit, records, and the like. Everywhere was a soft rosy light.

Gunilla did something to the dress and it fell off. Her tawny body stretched out on the bed. She was lovely! She grinned up at me. "I don't know what you do to me, Lars, but it sure is powerful. Down there in the salon, I *had* to do that. Because I knew how it would excite you. You make me feel like a complete whore. But marvelously so, without any ugliness or disgust." She got up on her knees and began caressing her breasts, shaking them and holding them out to me. She took the left one and, lifting it, leaned her head down until she was able to suck the nipple, watching me all the time. She was obviously bubbling with happiness. "Oh, little brother, what a joy you have brought into this house! I'd do anything for you! But Mother *did* almost catch me. When you left like that, she knew something was up. I'd just gotten covered up when she turned to look. And there was that lamp on the floor. She asked me what it was doing there, and I didn't know *what* to say. She really looked at me. But I don't care, Lars, about anything now except delighting you. Come to your little whore sister and let her pleasure you." When I got undressed and in bed, she turned out the lights, explaining that we mustn't scare Mother, and leaning above me on her hands and knees began caressing me with her dangling breasts: teasing my lips, slapping them gently against my face (they were immense in the dark), drawing them along my stomach. Then she laid down and got me straddling her chest. She put my cock in the gorgeous valley between her smooth tits, then (pressing them together) told me to fuck. It was lovely. She cooed obscenities meanwhile until suddenly I came. Over everything: her tits, her neck, her face. This drove her mad. She smeared it on her breasts, on her face, and then began licking it from her fingers. Afterwards, she washed and came to cuddle with me.

"Nilla," I asked, "do you really think she'll do it? *Knowing* we're over here watching?"

She giggled. "So little Lars is worried he won't see his Mother getting fucked! Poor thing. Well, little boy, you just lie their licking my nipples like that while Nilla tells you about your Mamma.

"The thing you must understand," she continued, "is that Mother is completely wanton. Now, I know this is hard to believe, but it's true. At the same time, she's terribly shy about this wantonness, so she keeps it locked up in herself. Believe me, though, it's there. I know! In fact, some of my earliest memories are of Mother licking my cunt to comfort me when I was unhappy about something. I must have been three or four. And she trained me to lick *her*. I don't know how early that started, but I remember she'd put chocolate or jam in her cunt so I would suck it out. Afterwards, when I developed a taste for these things, she'd let me lick her, or would lick me, as a special reward—like on my birthday. And I remember when I was tiny, she taught me to stick my hand inside her. I was so little that I could get my hand and a lot of my arm in, and I'd handle her inside. You can imagine what it was like with those five fingers working around, all the way to her womb. And I'd stroke that. She'd come and come. When I got older, she grew self-conscious and pretended it had never happened. But up until then, Wow! I remember once when she put me into bed with her dog . . ."

There was a knock on the door. We froze. There was another knock, and Father's voice whispered: "Are you there, Gunilla?" I got under the bed just as the door opened and he came in. "Gunilla?" He repeated.

"Yes, Daddy, but please don't turn on the lights. I don't have any clothes on."

Father chuckled, and the lights clicked on. "Excellent," he said, locking the door. "But why are you covering yourself like that? There's nothing wrong with a Father seeing his little girl's body, is there?"

"Please go away, Daddy. I'm tired!"

"Oh, no," he laughed. "I've been trying to catch up with you since the other night when you prick-teased me and then ran away. It's true that you supplied me with Annie, but it's you that I want to get into." There was a lot of scuffling as he evidently tried to pull the blanket off Gunilla. "So," he said. "We're back to this. You're going to hold out for your money again. You were so hot that night that you were throwing it at me for nothing, and I thought you had learned. Well, all right. As it happens I brought your 5,000 kronor. In fact I brought the 5,000 kronor you said you wanted to lay me. Or to gobble it." As confused and inexperienced as I was, I could sense how brutal Father's manner was. How wrong the tone was. "So there's the money, now get on your back and earn it."

"Daddy, are you serious? Do you really want to have intercourse with your own daughter?" I smiled, hearing the mocking tone in her voice. He evidently didn't hear it.

"Hell, yes, I'm serious. I don't pay 5,000 kronor to dip my wick just for laughs. Now let me see the merchandise."

"Stop, Daddy, or I'll scream. I'm serious. I think maybe I've changed my mind."

"What! No, you're just leading me on again like you've been doing for years. Now let go of that blanket."

"Stop!" It was clear Gunilla meant it this time. The struggling ended. "Now, if you promise not to touch me until I say you can, I'll take the covers off while we talk it over. O.K.?"

"O.K."

"Then stand over there." The bed creaked as Father got up. "And you promise to stay over there?"

"I promise."

"Daddy, do you really want me to pull down this blanket? I told you I don't have any clothes on. Do you think it's decent for a girl as big as me to be showing herself to her own Father?"

"Gunilla, I swear to Christ that if you don't hurry up, I'll rape you—screams or no screams." She must have begun. The bed rustled a little, and I heard Father gasp. "Sweet Jesus, Gunilla, you've got the biggest dugs I've ever seen! You're a goddamn cow!"

"Why, Daddy, why are you staring at my bosom like that? I think you *like* looking at your daughter's naked breasts." It was clear that she was putting on a show for me.

"You're fucking right. You wait till I get my hands on you and I'll demonstrate how I feel about my little girl."

"But, Daddy, that's a sin. You're supposed to protect your daughter's purity."

"Quit stalling and get that blanket off."

"I'm embarrassed, Daddy. If I pull it any farther down, you'll be able to see my private parts." She let her right arm drop over the edge of the bed until she found my hand. Then she groped down my body till she found my penis and began stroking it. "You must remember how young I am, Daddy. I'm shy. Please don't ask me to put it right under your nose, and with all the lights on. Please."

"Gunilla."

"But you're my *father!*"

"Gunilla, show me that twat before I kill you." His voice sounded half strangled.

"Well, I guess a good girl always does what her father tells her to." She squeezed my penis. "There!"

There was a low "Ah-h-h-h-h-h-h-h" from Father. Then Gunilla's firm voice: "Stay there!" This evidently stopped him.

"I'm going to nail that if it costs me every ore I own," he muttered to himself.

"You mean you really want to fornicate with your own baby?"

"I mean that I'm going to screw you if it's the last thing I do!"

"But even if it wasn't a horrible sin and incest, Father, how could you dream of putting that big thing of yours in my little hole?" She squeezed me again, and I suspected she touched her cunt teasingly.

"Think of it! I want to drive it into you so far it will make your eyes pop! And as for it's being so little, I'll bet it's been glued to every male teacher, servant, visitor, workman, dog, priest, banana, candle, or doorknob that has come into this house!"

"Daddy, you must think I'm a little whore!"

"I don't think anything about it, I *know!*"

"And you also want to stick that huge thing into your own daughter's little mouth."

"I want to drive it into your throat and come till you choke on it!"

"But, Father, you have such perverted, unnatural desires!"

"You've made me this way, bitch, cock-teasing me until I don't know whether I'm coming or going. You and your depraved mind. But enough chatter. You've got your 5,000 kronor, now let's see if you're worth it!"

"No, Father. I've changed my mind. No amount of money is worth committing such a nasty sin. With my own father! I'm going to learn to be a nice girl."

"What!"

"Yes, and unless you go away quietly, I'm going to tell Mother."

"So tell her. Is that supposed to scare me? You know damn well that she's ruled by whomever is throwing it into her. And since she's too shy to have an affair, that means me."

"That's true, Papa, but you and I know that all the money is hers. And that all your fine cars and fancy clothes and big office and flashy mistresses and your yacht all depend on her sufferance. You aren't likely to risk that, even though you are the one bedding her down."

"Damn you, Gunilla. You're a witch." His feet started for the door.

"Wait a minute, Daddy."

"What for?"

"You forgot to pick up your money."

He cursed and slammed out.

Gunilla fell on me laughing and kissing whatever she could reach. She took my head between her hands and stared into my eyes.

"Oh, little Lars, how much I do love you. Not only am I going to give you Mother to screw, but we're going to free her from that vulgar man."

The room lightened at that moment. Gunilla raised her head, then bent down to giggle: "That's Mamma's light, little brother: come on, the main feature is starting!"

Gunilla quickly turned off the lights and we scrambled onto the bed like two giggling kids spying on Christmas. From our darkness, Mother's window was like a television screen. Everything in the room was preternaturally bright and clear. And curiously important. Perhaps it was because I was so excited, but the window focused everything to an intensity like the viewfinder of my camera. There was the tense expectation that comes when the theatre curtain rises on a brightly lit empty stage.

Then, suddenly, Mother crossed the room. She was visible for only a moment, but my heart began to hammer. Again she crossed and disappeared. And again. I must have moved impatiently, because Gunilla (who was pressed against my back) whispered that it was all right, that I would get to see Mother strip and see her used by Father. That she was a little nervous about showing her cunt to her teenage son; but that she would.

Mother came into view again. It was true, she was nervous. She was wearing the same severe black dress. Her bare shoulders blazed white. She paused, this time, uncertainly; then she turned toward the window. Slowly she raised her arms straight above her head, stretching. Her large breasts were lifted by this to such size that they almost burst out. She stretched lazily like a cat, her body rippling in the gown. She turned her head to the side and licked her shoulder! Immediately she blushed and disappeared.

After a time, she returned. She kept her eyes down so she wouldn't see the window. She went to the dressing table, looking casually behind her several times. Then I realized: she was making sure it was visible from the window! She sat at the vanity. She sat still for several minutes, looking down—obviously deep in thought. She was incredibly beautiful with her blondness and whiteness and satin luxury of flesh. Her aristocratic aura. Finally she looked covertly at the window and a tiny smile of great happiness showed for a second. She crossed her legs and took off a shoe.

Slowly she ran a hand up her leg, around the knee, and up to the hem of her dress. A pause. Then she continued, the hand pushing back the hem till the dark band at the top of the stocking showed, then the white flesh! She sat looking down at the skin she'd revealed, stroking it softly. The smile showed again for a second. She moved the dress higher! Both thighs were exposed. I could see almost as much as that first day at the orphanage. Was she thinking of that too? She put her heel on the bench and swung her knee out to the side the same way. Again I had a glimpse of lace and like, but black this time. She stroked the insides of her thighs. Then she was seized with shyness, and put on her shoe, and went out of sight.

Gunilla whispered that it was all right. That she would do it. And in fact, when she returned, she did seem to have made up her mind. With her back to the window, she unzipped the dress and let it slide to the floor. She was magnificent, even though far from nude. A tight black garment covered her from below her shoulders to half way over her buttocks. (Gunilla said it was a foundation garment.) I could see her sheer black pants stretched tight over her lower ass. Then the splendid legs with the stockings making her look far more naked than if she were bare. The nude thighs and shoulders and arms shouted to me.

Her hands came up behind her and she began undoing the catches of the foundation garment. With maddening slowness. My eyes were fixed on her slender fingers. As each catch opened, the lovely back rose more and more in my sight. Finally, it came apart, and the whole back was bare! A splendor. I could see the rounds of her breasts under her arms! I knew that they were naked facing away from me. I had only to wait for her to turn!

Leisurely she began to. She was going to turn full to the window! I was dying. At the last second, she brought her hands up over them. She was facing the window now. The breasts were too large for her hands. The swelling flesh spilled around them. She was hiding little but the nipples. Her fingers began to spread, and suddenly I saw the nipples peeping between them. Brown. Stiff. Great! Gunilla was half yelling for me to see, saying how Mother was so worked up that she was going through with it. Gunilla was wild, playing with herself and me at the same time. Mother's hands were moving. They exposed the breasts! They were under them, cupping them, lifting them toward me. The tits were being offered to me! Large, soft, firm, white, erect, full, brown-nippled. The fingers shyly returned and began teasing the nipples. Suddenly Mother blushed and ran, her breasts bouncing.

Immediately she was back, a little defiant. Then, gradually, proud. Pleasure was coming into it for her. She lifted her arms over her head, tossing her breasts slowly by swinging slightly. She was looking down, watching them. Suddenly impatient, she reached down for her pants. She slid her thumbs into the elastic and started to push them down. She paused, embarrassed. Turned her back. Paused again, obviously more embarrassed to bare her ass to me. She turned facing the window and slowly pushed the pants down. The navel. The belly. The first cunt hair. Thicker cunt hair. All the cunt hair. She stepped out of the pants.

She started to unfasten her garter belt, but then obviously decided it was more obscene to keep it and the stockings. She actually began to parade. Showing herself! From all angles. Then she sat down on the floor. She lay on her back, her bent knees before us. Then began to open her thighs slowly. It was all there: the big breasts, the curving body, the furry cunt open between her full thighs. Her smiling face in the midst of the spread blonde hair. I was struck by how large she seemed. Monumental. She was like a goddess. Milk-white. Moon-flesh. A radiance. An essence. Her long, full-thighed legs seemed immense. Her belly seemed supernaturally beautiful and gigantic. There was a quality of giganticism about her. She was a goddess! She began to stroke her cunt delicately. Father came in.

"Yes, Karin, you're right, the room is a little stuffy. And we need not draw the drapes because Nilla has gone out with Lars somewhere."

It was a lie. He knew Gunilla was here. He wanted her to see. But he didn't know I was going to see too! But Mother knew, and she had asked him to open the window so we could hear!

"Well," Father continued, "you must really be hot today. First this afternoon and now tonight. You're really laid out *au plat* to be fucked. And look at your tits, the nipples are as big as marbles." He laughed and teased the nipple with the toe of his shoe. He was obviously showing off for Gunilla. He knelt down beside Mother. "Do you need it, Karin? Really need it? Enough to do anything the way I've always wanted and never had you? Well, I'm going to really enjoy this. Show me how much you need it. Show me how you play with yourself when you think of that kid son of yours."

Mother stared at the window, wildly excited. She played with herself. He got up and came even closer to the window.

"Now crawl to me if you need it." His voice was becoming ugly and cruel. She crawled toward him—and us—her full breasts swaying. "Take it out. Go on, fish it out if you want to suck on it. Yes, like that." She was kneeling before him opening his clothes. He turned sideways so Gunilla could see everything. "Now suck me, Bitch," And Mother did. I saw her fine mouth close on his great thick penis. I was revolted and jealous, but somehow it excited me even more for that. She was blushing, ashamed, knowing I was seeing it. She got him turned so I couldn't see her face and so on her hands and knees she could open her legs, showing me her full hairy cunt from the rear. She was obviously also excited by the degraded position she was in before me.

And she knew that everything he did to her, I was doing to Gunilla. Everything she did for him, Gunilla was doing for me. She knew that Gunilla's mouth was crammed with my cock as hers was with Father's. She had pulled back and was talking up to him—being wanton so I would hear.

"Come, Bill. Shoot into my mouth. You always wanted to come in my mouth, Bill, to make me swallow it. Here's your chance." She began sucking again.

"So you finally want to get fucked in the mouth, huh? Well, I've got a different idea. I want to come in your *face!*" He pulled out at the last second and came directly in her face. I could see the spurts splashing all over her eyes, her mouth, her hair. Gunilla had seen, too, and deliberately pulled back at the last second so I came all over her face the same way. Something in me knew I liked that, just as I blanked out.

In a few minutes, I heard Gunilla urging me to wake up, saying I would miss the next act. I looked through the window. Mother was staring at me. I knew she couldn't see, but her eyes were wide, trying. She was lying sprawled on her back wearing her stockings and garter belt, wiping her face on her hands and then on the rug. She looked directly at the window, opened her thighs wide to show her cunt and said: "Wouldn't you like to fuck me?"

A gong exploded in my head. She was saying that to *me!* "She's talking to you, Lars!" Gunilla whispered. "She's asking you to fuck her. I *told* you." It was true, I was going to fuck Mother. Father thought she meant him and told her to get on the bed.

"No, no, Bill. Give it to me here. You always wanted to do it on the floor. Now I'm going to let you. Come on and fuck me here." She wanted to stay where I could watch her being fucked!

He took off his clothes and knelt over her face. She licked his balls. She licked below them. She took each ball in her mouth and sucked gently. She took the cock deeply in her mouth in a long sucking motion. She rolled it around in her mouth, working her head from side to side, moaning with pleasure through her nose. Or was it Gunilla? It was both. Her eyes were turned always to the window. Everything was for me!

Father pulled loose and knelt between her legs. She lifted her legs and put him in. He drove forward with all his strength!

"You fucking whore," he shouted as he fucked. "Filthy, fucking whore. Bitch fucking whore." Mother stared at the window as he fucked her. She spoke directly to me:

"I am a whore, your whore, little angel! I'll always be your whore, your plaything. If you can get me like this, I will do anything for you. I want to suck you. I want you to fuck me. Oh, how much I want it!" Her eyes were staring at the window. I *knew* she was talking only to me! I couldn't believe it. "I love you," she said to the window. I almost blacked out.

"Stop it. Stop it, Karin," Father was bellowing. "Turn over so I can fuck your ass."

Mother's eyes widened with shock: "Oh, no Bill. Please."

"What? Don't tell me no. You know that you like it in the ass."

Mother was trapped. Not only was she ashamed in front of me, but she knew what it meant for Gunilla. "Oh, God," gasped Gunilla, "I've never had it that way!"

"Shut up," said Father, "and turn over before I beat hell out of you."

"Please, Bill," she begged. "It can hurt so much if it's not done right or the woman isn't used to it."

"What the hell are you talking about. So it can hurt. You know that I won't hurt you the stupid way. And the other pain you like. Who are you kidding?"

"Well, use some cream or vaseline or something," Mother wailed to us.

"You don't need that any more, Karin! But all right, if you want to pretend you're a little ass-virgin, I'll go along." He went to the dressing table and got something. Gunilla scrambled around and found some cream.

Mother was face down with her ass lifted by two pillows he'd put under her. Her head was turned so she could speak to the window. She obviously was giving instructions to Gunilla. She was embarrassed but helpless.

"Work it into the asshole. And smear it on the cock. Remember to push down inside, not up. Pushing up is terribly painful."

"That's enough, Karin." He slapped her hard across the buttocks. "Stop your playing and open your ass so I can get at you."

Gunilla had prepared herself and me. According to Mother's instructions she was lying the same way with the pillows under her. Father had penetrated Mother and was fucking back and forth. I managed to get the head into Gunilla. She groaned. I hesitated. She whispered for me to go on, that she *wanted* it. Seeing Mother getting it like that excited me so much I couldn't resist. I slowly pushed in. Gunilla let out a cry and buried her face in the bed. I looked into Mother's eyes and pushed. Gradually she began to open. I was inside. I stroked gently out and in.

"Oh, that's good," gasped Gunilla. "It's so strange but it's good. Oh, I like it. Oh, I like it very much! My cunt moans to be fucked at the same time and that makes it even more."

Gunilla's hand slid down under her and she began masturbating as I fucked her ass. "Oh, God" she said. The little surprised cries of delight were getting louder. "Oh, God, I think I'm going to come. Fuck me harder!" This last was a yell. Mother's eyes gaped. She had heard. Father was too intent on his pleasure, but Mother, being pounded down into the carpet, she heard, and it excited her even in her consternation and shame. Lust came into her face.

"I'm coming," she shouted at the window.

"I'm coming," Gunilla shouted.

"I'm coming in your ass, whore," Father bellowed. I was watching Mother's face. The lust was blended with love and yearning as she stared at the window, hearing Gunilla yelling!

"I'm coming with you," Mother called to Gunilla. "We're getting it together. I'm getting it in you. He's fucking both of us." Her face was all terror and wonder and wantonness, fixed on the window. Wave after wave thundered through her. Everybody came at once, shouting and fountaining. I heard, as I fell, Mother yelling: "Lars, Lars, my son."

I'm Looking For Baby K

Joanne Stonebridge

They walked up Page, and Simba let her into a large apartment building between Cole and Clayton. It was a handsome, well-kept building as was his apartment, walls lined with books and record albums, a few very strong abstracts in the hallway. The apartment was neat and clean, furnished with expensive, very masculine furniture that looked custom-made. It was the very opposite from the hippie pad she had expected.

Simba put down the drum next to the enormous stereo console, slipped a record from its jacket and put it on the turntable. He turned to look at Sheila as the deep throbbing of an African drum solo seemed to surround her from the many speakers on the floor and walls.

Sheila was suddenly shy and a little frightened. She took a cigarette from her purse and lit it nervously. "Simba, do you really know where . . . Karen is?"

He stepped to her, took the cigarette from her fingers and crushed it in an ashtray. "First things first, baby," he said. "I have a score to settle. Do you want to take off your clothes or shall I?"

"Now Simba," she said, backing towards the door.

"Have it your way," he said, lunged forward and caught her just as she was about to turn and run.

She struggled in his arms, murmuring "No, no . . ." as his strong fingers found the button and zipper of her skirt and pushed it down so that it tangled in her ankles. She almost lost her balance and had to grab at his neck as his hands went beneath her jacket and blouse and cupped her breasts, his fingers squeezing and pulling at her nipples.

"Don't!" she said in a half-scream, but the touch of his pants on her naked thighs made her pull him to her, rather than push him away. Simba's hands stroked down from her breasts to her belly, finding and unhooking the garter belt, pushing it down so that her nylons slithered down her legs by themselves. His fingers came back up between her thighs and one hand cupped her cunt, his middle finger sliding between the lips of her sex which was now moist with anticipation. Sheila stepped out of her skirt and stockings and tore off her jacket and blouse herself, then clung to him, rubbing the hard nipples of her breasts against his smooth cashmere sweater. Her own hands were busy now, pulling his tee-shirt from his pants and reaching beneath to caress the hot skin of his back. On her thighs, she could feel the bulge beneath his fly and her fingers helped his as he opened the belt and pulled down the zipper. Sheila pushed down his pants and shorts and with his feet now trapped, began to push him back towards the couch.

"No, you don't!" Simba freed one foot and spun around with her, carrying her to the couch by his hand under her ass, one finger in her cunt. He threw her down on the edge of the couch and entered her roughly, forcing his cock through the resisting walls of the vagina. Sheila cried out in pain, and tried to twist her hips to be free of him, but he held her shoulders against the couch as the movement of his hips matched hers, the weight of his body fully on her hips. He stayed that way until she stopped struggling, then drove roughly into her again. This time was not as painful as the first, as her own juices responded to lubricate the broad head of his cock. Simba didn't spare her, but pounded his cock into her in rough thrusts as if he were punishing her for her dominance in the park. Sheila was angry and hurt and determined not to give him the slightest pleasure. She lay back on the couch completely inert as his hips and back drove his cock bruisingly into her body. Sheila clenched her teeth to drive away the heat that was rising in her belly.

"You think you can get away with that?" Simba said hoarsely, and began an even faster and deeper thrusting than before. Sheila tried to resist, but the wild plunging within her, a plunging that became ever more intense, made her gasp with pleasure. Of their own accord, her arms went around his back and her hips flexed up to meet each thrust. She whimpered into the hollow of his neck as the hot flash of her orgasm surged through her body. Still Simba plunged on, the arc of his iron-hard cock as strong and wild as if they had just begun. Sheila's knees lifted as if to protect herself from the onslaught, but this merely drove his cock deeper within her. Sheila's hips now thrust to meet his as his thrusting brought her to an even higher plance of excitement. Her fingernails raked his back and her lips and teeth closed on the flesh of his shoulders as her hips tried to match the rhythm of his quick, deep penetration, his slower withdrawal, then the quick untiring penetration again, and again, and again. Sheila moaned and her belly quivered as the lightning of her second orgasm burned its way through her body and mind, nearly blinding her. Still Simba plunged on, maintaining the same wild, rough pace.

The thought flashed through Sheila's numb mind that the man was not human. He was a demon who would consume her utterly with sex. So intense was the orgasm that the muscles of her legs and hips quivered with fatigue. Her arms around his back, her legs wrapped around his waist were more for support than participation. Sheila hung on, hoping that his orgasm would set her free, but still he drove into her, the walls of her vagina so sensitive now that each thrust nearly made her scream with pleasure-pain. It was as if his cock had become white-hot and its erotic flames were sent in the waves of his penetration to her skin, her hair, even her fingernails. She was a torch whose source of fuel was in her cunt, the light and heat burning through her whole body. She lay helpless as his attack continued and incredibly, she could feel yet another, even fiercer orgasm gather itself. She groaned in fear and anticipation as the trembling in her belly and legs signaled that she was again brought to the brink. Then a screaming orgasm tore through her like a hurricane; her head lolled back on the pillows of the couch, her legs twitched and untwined from Simba's waist, her arms fell from his back and one hung loosely over the edge of the couch as spasm after spasm of pleasure shook her body.

Breathing hoarsely, Simba let her lie for a moment, then began again to plunge deep within her. It was too much for Sheila and she twisted away from his body whimpering her surrender. She slid from the couch and lay on the floor. Simba laughed through his panting and patted her ass. Sheila curled herself into a ball to protect herself. "You win!" she panted. She looked at his black body on the couch and was astounded to see his cock still hard. "Didn't you come? No. I didn't feel you come."

Simba reached in back of the couch and brought out what looked like a package of ordinary cigarettes. He lit one, inhaled deeply and handed it to her. Sheila recognized the odor of marijuana and took a deep drag.

"I have a certain control," he said. "I can't stop it from getting hard, but sometimes I can tell it what to do after it *gets* hard. Sometimes." She handed him back the joint and he inhaled.

"What about in the park?"

"It takes a little time to set yourself up. You know, you really raped me there ... took me against my will. I don't like to be forced to do anything! Nobody does."

Sheila moved to the couch and gently took his cock in her hands. She looked at it closely. Engorged with blood, it was almost blue-black. She marveled at herself that she could be sitting here naked, a black stranger's cock in her hand and feel so completely at home. Sheila took the joint from his fingers and inhaled deeply once, then again. "Do you want to, now?" Her lips kissed the ridge of the broad head.

"I think I do," Simba said. He took the cigarette from her fingers and lay back against the cushions of the couch, smoking.

Under the gentle influence of the marijuana, Sheila thought his cock almost glowed with blackness. Her fingers gently caressed his balls and the root of his cock as her lips and tongue took the head into her mouth. She bent her head and the cock slid into her mouth almost to the back of the throat. Her teeth closed gently on the shaft as she drew back and stopped at the glans. She sucked at the head, her tongue sliding around and around the base of the glans, then pushing at the hole. One hand gently cupped and fondled his balls while the other less gently gripped the root of his shaft and pumped it up and down. Then she took as much as she could into her mouth and began the same process again. Simba was beginning to breathe heavily and, in her mouth, she could feel his cock begin to throb against the back of her throat, her tongue and lips. Simba's hands came to her head, resting in her hair, directing her with subtle pushes and pulls to the places of highest excitement. His hips began to move slightly as Sheila's hand gripped the base of his cock more firmly and worked it even more rapidly. Now she sucked the cock into her mouth with her teeth brushing the glans; her tongue moved quickly on the underside of his cock as she took it as far as she could without gagging. Simba's breath was coming in deep gasps now and his hands were firm on her head, holding his cock deep within her mouth. Sheila could feel his orgasm start under her hand at the base of his cock and she squeezed his balls as the first spurt of come touched the back of her tongue. Simba moaned and Sheila withdrew the cock to the head. She held his cock in both her hands and sucked hard on the head, pulling out each explosion of come, swallowing and pulling out the next. Simba trembled and writhed under the tremendous sensations. Sheila was still sucking as Simba was spent and it was his turn to withdraw and push her away.

He was panting hoarsely. "Man, where did you learn that! Christ! I thought you were going to pull my backbone out of that little hole!"

Sheila's mouth was full of the spicy taste of come. It was the only the second time in her life that she had ever done it. Her jaws were tired as she said, "I thought you deserved something special for what you gave to me." She moved up the couch and lay beside him. Looking across his black chest to the well-furnished room, the walls of books and records, she was curious.

"Simba, how do you do this? When I saw you in the park, the first thing I though was 'He looks like he should be in college'."

Simba stretched, "Well . . . " then he laughed. "Well, Baby K's momma . . . you know, I don't know your first name. I rarely let a woman rape me in the park without getting her first name."

"Sheila," she said. "I don't know yours either . . ."

She felt his body tighten slightly, " . . . but it doesn't matter. Simba's fine, even fitting, although I didn't know they had black lions. I didn't know before. *Are* you in college?"

"I've been to several." He seemed reticent.

"But how can you afford all this? You don't get anything from playing drums in the park, do you?"

Simba mused, "No, not several colleges. I've been to two colleges and one university. Majored in Religion, Business Administration and Creative Writing. How's that for a combination?" He laughed, but tightly, and Sheila decided not to push him in this way.

"Do you know where Baby K is?" she asked and looked into his eyes.

JOANNE STONEBRIDGE

"I was a runaway at thirteen and spent the next five years in and out of homes for wayward girls. I was busted for prostitution in Boston when I was fifteen — I looked twenty-one and could lie like I was ninety-one, so got thirty days in the county jail instead of an indefinite term in Juvi." These words from Joanne Stonebridge, alias of a well-known San Francisco writer and wife of one of the Bay Area's most prominent physicians, sounded totally unbelievable in the plush setting of their Sea Cliff home. The author claims she was once a contact-courier for a Mafia leader importing dope, and that she turned down an opportunity to run a posh whorehouse in Nevada "because I couldn't see myself tied down to a job and responsibility." She is currently dividing her time between writing and referral case work from Bay Area psychologists who utilize her expertise in the areas of drug addiction and juvenile delinquency.

THE HOMOSEXUAL HANDBOOK

Angelo d'Arcangelo

I think not knowing anything about women is such a bore. I frankly don't understand how a man can consider himself a man unless he's had one: most don't. Not that there's anything wrong with male virginity, but it's so . . . excessive. And unnecessary.

Dr. Kinsey's Sexual Behavior in the Human Male puts it this way in the chapter, Homosexual Outlet. (Just two little quotes from pages 605 and 651).

18 per cent of the males have at least *as much of the homosexual as the heterosexual* in their histories for at least three years between the ages of 16 and 55. This is more than one in six of the white male population.
And,
4 per cent of the white males are exclusively homosexual throughout their lives, after the onset of adolescence.

You see what I mean? If you plan to be an exclusive homosexual, you're in a very small minority. Sooner or later you're going to have to deal with women, if you haven't already. Worse things could happen to you and they probably will.

Let me tell you how I lost my maidenhead. I was pretty slow to mature. Didn't know how to jerk off till I was fifteen. An altar boy showed me how in a C.Y.O. camp. And that's odd, because I was constantly being accused of acts I didn't know beans about. But I was a big kid and just getting hairy. Who knows, maybe they could read minds even before they were made up? Even in a morbidly shy kid. What a sad stumblebum I was, with enormous doubts about my masculinity . . . thanks to a sadistic father . . . and the suitability of my pecker, which seemed to me to be absurdly small; a veritable button. I was later to find out to my immense relief that what I had was the "surprise package" type of dong. But most of the boys surrounding me didn't, and how was I to know? It took years of patient research.

Let's skip all this and plow ahead for a couple of years. For reasons far too murky to explicate here, I enlisted in the United States Air Force, still, at seventeen, a virgin. It was on my first leave that I solved that problem, thanks to Velma Swartzchild, high school sweetheart. That dusky red-head had been begging for it for months, sending me inflamed letters in which she described, by means of parable, the high temperature of her inner thighs. How she had rubbed herself against me just before I joined up! She behaved in every way like the good, healthy, firm-bodied girl she was. I knew and so did she, that when we danced or kissed my cock got hard and stood up. (This joy javelin of mine, by the way, is exactly seven inches long, of an elegant thickness, and quite handsome). Everything seemed to be on our side. So we tried it. Let me clarify that: Velma was no virgin, so I was the one *really* trying.

A tryst. Her house. A late hour. A dim kitchenette. We sat on the edge of her mother's double Murphy bed one early evening while that good lady was at work. We were kissing like goldfish, getting hot as hell. I reached under her skirt and pulled down her moist panties. She helped a lot. Getting them over her knees was crucial, especially since we didn't want to end our kiss. But once around those ankles, the knees opened, and I was strumming my first twat. A far from unpleasant sensation, let me tell you. Her temperature seemed to be about one hundred and eighty and she smelled like "doing it." Delicious! She was moaning and rolling her eyes in no time, writhing like a white woman when I got on my knees, unzipped, and slipped it to her. I sank like Moby Dick and didn't stop until I hit bottom with a thud, and for God knows how long we fucked so hard we were in a kind of state of shock by the time we came. We were banging together like twenty pounds of liver dropped from a three story window. Kaaflop! Kaflooey! (Velma, wherever you are, Darling, I bless your name. I've even gotten hard at the typewriter just thinking about you). *Malhereusement,* her grinning mother popped in and I had to pop out: we couldn't go at it again.

Anyway, Velma ruined my pants. I could never wear them again after that, though I kept them as a sort of trophy. She had so drenched my fly with her sexual fluid there was an elliptical white tell-tale ring marking the spot that dry-cleaning never could remove. What a girl! And you know, on the way home, happy as a pig in shit. whistling and snapping my fingers, etc., it suddenly came to me how *easy* it was. I distinctly remembered as I was cumming thinking to myself, "Is that all there is to it? You mean *this* is it? Why any damned fool can do it." I have seen nothing, had nothing, that would cause me to change my mind. Fucking is so easy, and such fun.

Dear Uncle Fudge,

I have what many people consider the most exciting, different, and "now" boutique in Galveston, Texas. I cater to swingers of both sexes with fun clothes, here at this gay sea-side resort. Up till now that hasn't been a problem.

I'm a bachelor and not too aggressive, sexually, though I do it mostly with guys. Or I always have, which is why I'm writing to you. But two months ago I hired a girl to help out in the shop. She is a beauty. Oh, is she a beauty! I like her very much, as a person. No! More than that. I want her c - - t, but I have been brought up to respect women and to be a gentleman. I think she likes me though. Every time I come over to the cashier's counter her nostrils dilate suggestively.

What do you suggest?

Shy Texan

Dear Shy T.,

If her nostrils are dilating, what do you think her pussy's doing? George Bernard Shaw said of Joan of Arc, "Her ideal biographer must be free from nineteenth-century prejudices and biases; . . . and must be capable of throwing off sex partialities and their romance, and regarding women as the female of the human species, and not as a different kind of animal with specific charms and specific imbecilities." There you are, "Swinger." Say it about any woman and it'd be true. You've got to shake those damned goose feathers out of your head, because your mother probably stuffed them in there so you'd sleep instead of listening to her and your father pump-rattling the old bed springs. And her screaming, "More, Morris! More!"

Listen to your uncle, put up the "Out To Lunch" sign and pull down the shade at the door. Make sure you've sent her into the stock room first though. Then, the place being secure, go in there and get into her panties. Get next to her. On the work table, on the floor, it doesn't matter. If she's a hot number she'll probably take charge. If she's rather cool and offended, you'll lose your cashier and that'll be that. You can't miss what you've never had. Or she may just want a little "wine-n-dine" schmaltz. Give it to her, after you apologize, and take her home. Who knows, in a decent bed she may be absolutely marvelous.

One thing more. Don't be afraid to tell her you're a virgin. Don't tell her unless it becomes necessary, however. But, if it looks like things are not going to work out quite right, tell her. There's a way of doing it. Let her know it's not because you've ever *wanted* to be, there's nothing physically wrong with you, but you're very shy with women. Tell her you just need a little help, a few tips. Tell her it's only that you're afraid of hurting her. You'd be amazed how well that bit can work.

Women feel differently about sex than do men, and so require a different style of approach. They are not simply cockless boys with tits. They aren't, and they resent being treated as if they were. Here are two stirring examples of female "heat" from literature. First, from Racine's *Phaedra:*

I saw him blushed . . . I paled under his eyes.
My fate was sealed. My troubled soul, lost!

My clouded eyes could see no more, nor my voice speak;
I was paralyzed, and yet my body burned.

And from Brecht's *Mother Courage:*
How do I love thee?

                                                    Fiercely!

Let me count the ways.

                                                    Disgrace!

Everyone said, "She's just a bitch

                                        with an itch."

But I was possessed so strongly,

                                    right or wrongly.

God! Moonlight bright as day!
A cloudy night in May.

                                O the liftin' of the haze
                        An' the swirlin' of the gloom
                    An' the smoke of burnin' hay . . .
Vanished, like the mist . . . th' enemy I kissed
. . . Gone! The lovers we DESPISED.

In other words, they like it too. It just takes them longer to
stoke up. Thank heavens Freud, if he didn't do anything else, at
least reminded us of that. The fact that she does want it and that
any worth-while woman will meet you half-way, means that you
can take it a little easier "male-wise." The new equality of the
sexes has killed chivalry, freed us from the need to be considerate
of women, and delivered them into the position of having to be
responsible for their lusts.

It's my view that in a book of this kind, intended for
homosexuals, we need not go into the particulars of feminine
genital construction or the minute details of the most predictable
sexual positions. What I do suggest is that you buy yourself one of
those informative and perfectly adequate marriage manuals with
illustrations. Such a book will tell you how to perform in an
acceptable way. I will attempt to suggest certain refinements on the
standard penis-vagina contact, and dwell thereafter on other
positions, cunnilingus and sodomy, and genital "accessories."
Let's talk a little about genitals though. Did you know, for

instance, that in the first stages of our lives in the womb, our sexes are undetermined, and that consequently we begin with a basic genital similarity? Only as we progress in the foetal stages do the particulars of our genital structures assert themselves. Therefore, as grotesque as it may seem, one might imagine the penis shrunk down within the body, and the tube of the eurethra expanded to a considerable size, with only that tiny pimple, the clitoris, protruding. That would mean that excitement would be given to the rim of the "gash", its lips, as it were, and to the clitoris which corresponds to the head of the penis, and upon deep penetration, to the walls of the tube itself. This odd picture is not without foundation in fact, for it is known that women, when they are excited, experience an "erection" of sorts too. Their pussies distend and stiffen with blood — the clitoris grows larger and hard.

Aside from the fact that the genitals in the broadest sense are different, it remains to be said that the organs surrounding them are the same. Like sympathetic strings on an antique viol, these organs twang and vibrate in harmony with our sexual apparatus. This is important in sodomy, where in fucking we wish to stimulate the woman in the same way we might wish to stimulate and excite a man, and it is worth bearing in mind that the sensations of the "receptor" are just about the same, whether male or female.

Many men fuck a cunt as they masturbate, slipping and thrusting their pricks into a tube that reminds them of their fists, and use an in-and-out pumping motion until they reach orgasm. This is the standard American way. I might suggest that for additional pleasure for the woman if you're going to use this method, and particularly if this is the "missionary position" of woman on her back and man above between her legs, it's better to move your body up a little higher than usual . . . just an inch, so that your chin might be, instead of at the level of her chin, at the level of her nose . . . for as you remain inserted, (assuming you've got the inch or so to spare cock-wise) . . . your prick will be pressed against the upper crease of the cunt, where the shy clitoris peeks, and therefore, as you plunge up and down, the point of the "clit" will rub against the upper side of your prick all through the fucking. Whatever difficulty you may have in kissing will be more than compensated for.

From a man's point of view intercourse, no matter what kind

it be, is very often simply the forcing of something relatively big into something relatively small. The size of the penis is of more practical importance to men; his genital gratification is on that one level and with that one instrument. Women respond to friction on the outer lips of the vagina, to the forceful dilation of the uterus and the agitation of its walls, and to the stimulation of the clitoris. As you can see, this is a more varied set of responses than the male has. But it can work to your advantage. Women have their preferences, and a woman who is accustomed to cumming through deep penetration into the vagina, (the province of the heavily endowed man), will never be satisfied with that superficial penetration of the lips and the stimulation of the clitoris associated therewith. The preference is a personal one, with older, more experienced women preferring the deep penetration, and the younger woman preferring the shallow path, the way of the smaller prick. Certainly that change in preference is due to the frequency of intercourse and the stretching of the pussy that inevitably occurs; not to mention childbirth, that ruiner of delights.

One ought to try to combine several methods of fucking for each encounter with each woman, depending upon her responses to various positions. For example, it is advisable to vary the up-and-down thrust with a "grinding" motion of the hips. For the man it has the advantage of being slightly less exciting and therefore prolongs the fucking to the enjoyment of both parties. For the woman it is even more exciting. One simply inserts to full length, absolutely as deeply as possible, and then moves the hips about in a revolving movement that brings the shaft or root of the prick into a rubbing contact with the total circumference of the twat. Remember that the rubbing of the lips is extremely exciting. Do not withdraw your ding-bat, for in grinding you will be shifting your weight this way and that; use the rim of her twat as a fulcrum for the lever of your tool which, while still inside, will rub the walls in a sort of reaming manner most agreeable to the ladies. In this way you will be reaching all three levels of genital sensation at one time. A few times around, and vary it with a pump or two to batter the channel back where the ovaries are, and then more grinding. Orgasms aplenty, I promise you.

Now the rubbing of the lips of the vagina is important, as I said, and especially with young or small or inexperienced girls; girls not truly accustomed to constant fucking. It should be part of your repertoire, not only with your hands, but with your legs, thighs, and loins. It is not uncommon that women can be brought to orgasm simply through this rubbing. It is a staple of lesbian love. Two girls can, by interlacing themselves, like forks, "bump pussies" as we used to say when I was a lad, and enjoy all of the thrills and chills of intercourse without even fingering themselves. This is a good thing to remember if you are one of those men who find one orgasm per evening your limit. One can still carry on with a limp dick.

If the girl you are getting into the sack with happens to be quite used to deep penetration and active of body, she may resent the old *male superior* position. I have known girls who absolutely loathed it and felt insulted when pressed into the "passive" role, or held down and plowed. Don't be a fool. You don't have to be on top, and it is often most amusing to lie on your back, your arms behind your head, as Bouncing Bette straddles your lap and rides your prong like a wild-haired Fury. It is a wonderful way to get your girl randy, and many otherwise demure girls metamorphose into the most shameless, foul-mouthed jades, given a cock of their own to play with. And then for you there's the sight of those wobbling-bobbling titties just above you, saying, "Want to play?"

You ought to try to approach from the rear too for deep penetration. It's quite good, and just a little humiliating for the girl. Don't begin with it, but make it one of your final positions. When I say humiliating, I mean only that when you're hooked up in that fashion it's impossible to maintain that romantic imagery women are always blathering about, the kissing and murmuring tendernesses, etcetera. What you have is the superb tableau of a stallion mounting his mare, of whatever you care to call it; something of the barnyard, something primeval and base and marvelous. And I suggest that you ride her, cover her, in just that way, with language and force appropriate to the pose. There's enough masochism in most women to permit the complete enjoyment of such a position, and without worry of possible perversion. In addition to all of this, the position offers one very good advantage. While you're approaching from the rear, you can reach around and frig her clitoris with a free hand, thus giving her increased pleasure.

Now, that marriage manual you've bought is going to go into

all of the many other coital positions very thoroughly. Don't forget the illustrations. But as I said, that's not going to be my major concern. Let's get on to "muff-diving", shall we?

It's an amazing-looking thing, the cunt. I'll remember the first time I ever looked "into" one for as long as I live. I had been dicking around with an absolutely frenzied little grass widow with a cottage by the Pacific. Divine girl! Well, a mutual friend of ours, another girl, came to visit her in San Francisco, and for some reason . . . possibly because the visiting girl and I had had an affair some time previously . . . my blonde Diana "swapped" with the brunette for the duration of the visit. At any rate, there we were in bed one afternoon having a go, and I was scarfing like a madman, when all of a sudden it dawned on me that I really didn't know what I was eating. Plenty of afternoon light on the hide-a-bed, so I took a slow careful look at that steaming orifice. I must have gotten carried away because after a few seconds she opened her eyes, looked down and saw me poking around down there, and made a remark I do not care to repeat which meant let's get down to brass tacks. She was, in other words, deeply vagina-oriented and wanted to ride the slide-pole without excuses or lengthy preliminaries.

I know perfectly well that, as faggots, a good many of you are going to squawk and carry on about the smell: before we even get down to the good parts! But I must warn you, if you take that attitude you're being absurd, narrow-minded and stupid. I know that women are referred to as "fish" in fag-lang. But that's defamation. Clean women don't smell any more than do clean men, and the cunt itself is no more odoriferous than the armpit or the cleft of the cheeks, or more high than the glandular smell of a randy man when he's excited. Slide back a strange fore-skin on a hot day and you'll probably get a scent much more distasteful and sharper, or at least *as* sharp.

But the word here is clean. If the girl is not one of those who keep meticulous house with douches and astringents and such, she may indeed be dainty and fresh on the outside, but a charnel house between the legs. And it's unfortunate that most of the "easy" girls, the fag-hags and such, are such skanks and likely as not to be unclean, but don't you agree that boys of the same dispositions are as likely to be rank? No gentleman would care to be found face down in such a swampy twat; therefore, should you find your "girl" to be a little unkempt, don't beat about the bush. Tell her to clean that thing out. Once it is douched and washed, and assuming it remains so, there's nothing to keep you from the Venus-facial.

To the right and left of the gash notice the large lips. Their consistency is rather like the lobes of your ears; fleshy and supple. Peel them back a little and notice that they are lined with folds or membranes of a suppleness and a smoothness like the inside of a baby's mouth. These are the small lips. And as the keystone of the arch, the clitoris peeks out small and pink, like a tiny eraser in the pudgy fist of a kindergarten kid. Within, in the darkness, there are a series of ledges and corridors and compartments that you can check out on your diagram. You won't be able to reach them with your tongue so we don't have to go into them now. Actually, in eating pussy, you use more than your tongue anyway; you use all of your mouth and your chin and lips. Why the chin? Because there are plenty of girls who object to whisker burn on their faces where it shows, but delight in it on their smarting twats.

All of these surfaces are sensitive to touch. As you lick them, kiss and nuzzle them, your girl will experience marvelous sensations of pleasure. You can bite the lips of the honey pot a little, but very gently: I suggest biting with your own lips tightly over your teeth. This is a splendid way to agitate the clitoris. And I've always found it a good idea to save the tongue for the last moments as she is nearing her orgasm. That's the perfect time to plunge it as deeply into the womb as you can, sucking and lapping the walls and the clitoris, taking as much as you can into your mouth.

By the way, all that business of women gushing like fountains, swamping the bed in absolute tidal waves of orgasmic fluid is strictly for the pornographic trade. Don't believe it. You won't drown. The amount of seminal fluid secreted before, during and after orgasm is modest, and utterly pleasant. Don't expect her to spurt as men do. It doesn't happen.

I must tell you that if there's any one thing I don't like about eating pussy, it's the hair. I think it's absolutely appalling, unattractive, and inconsiderate to have a great shaggy nest between the legs. Such a bush makes it so fucking difficult to get where you're going. A pudendum that's shaved is the very nicest kind, but many women won't go to that length, considering it extreme. Still, have no truck with a woman who won't even trim the excess of hair from her private parts. It shows a great lack of feeling on her part. My first wife was a very hirsute beauty, and I was constantly lacerated where it hurt most. Can you imagine chewing a brillo pad? Or forcing your dick through one?

Two more things; should you do your scarfing with the woman on her back, you will find Nature has provided you with a "chin-rest" or bony ridge, that will make it much easier for you to lap longer. Finally, all of the methods of chewing, licking and tickling that are practised in this or similar postures can be carried out in a sixty-nine position without the least inconvenience. In fact, there may be an advantage: I have always found it much easier to concentrate my attentions on the clitoris from this angle.

Your biggest challenge in attempting the sixty-nine will be teaching a novice how to suck you off. I've tried to explain the methods for this in another chapter, and the explanation should prove helpful. Of course, if she already knows, marvelous! But I have experienced cases where the girl was perfectly willing to be sucked, but did not actually care to risk the loss of her dignity gobbling the goo. Some girls put such a high price on their vulvas, they tend to resent any request for other holes as a slight to their femininity. It is very easy for them to take the lazy way out and simply lie there while you plug and pump: they can fancy themselves superbly feminine without undue exertion or a mussing of the hair. Have no truck with such tedium. Dump the baggage. Still, if you would like her to learn to suck, you must go at it this way. Use every means in your power to excite her and keep her excited for as long as possible, increasing the pleasure, but always keeping it just a little out of reach. Don't permit her to have an orgasm until she has at least fondled your prick. Take it step by step. The more excited she is, the more she'll enjoy the fondling, the frigging and eventually the sucking. Take your time with it. Take all night, if you have to. Meanwhile, get into position with your face in her furbowl and keep her on the brink.

Of course, people learn by example too. One way to teach her quickly is to bring another man to bed with you. Make it somebody she likes, but if you intend to keep her, make sure she doesn't like him as much as she does you. She can watch him sucking you, or you sucking him, taking turns with each other or both of you, as the case may be, until she gets the hang of it. It is a very exciting kind of lesson, designed to bring out and brighten the most lascivious aspects of a girl's personality. And then all of the oral positions and variations can be enjoyed between the three of you, with her blowing you, for example, while he scarfs her. Or the three of you can form a daisy chain.

I happen to be one of those people who believe God meant people to sleep together in threes. Which doesn't mean that I do very often find myself so couched, but a good *bouquet garni* has its charm. In fact I know of a rather attractive young man who works out more often than not with his girl. By that I mean he uses her as part of his lure-system to get other men to bed. Which is apparently as much to her liking as to his. In short, if two people are only moderately attractive separately, they may become profoundly seductive together.

Which leads us to Sodomy. You know, one of the best times to get your girl used to taking it up the ass boy-style, is with another man in bed. The same rule may be held true for sodomy as for sucking: *demonstration helps.* You and your friend can demonstrate the ease and pleasure of this kind of penetration to her, pumping and fucking each other before her, which certainly ought to allay all her fears, or you may be able to persuade her to take one or the other of you into her bum as she's being fucked in the cunt. An ultimately charming solution is reached in this way. Suppose you lie on the bed, your legs hanging over the edge. You encourage her to straddle you and take your prick so. She is in the saddle. Pull her foreward so that her face is upon yours. You are kissing, playing with her breasts, etcetera. Your partner, should he care to look, will be confronted with surely one of Nature's most beautiful sights; the dimpled buttocks of a girl spread open to show her pussy slurping down on a cock with loose hanging balls. (Your legs must be open so that he can see fully what's going on, and in order that he can join you in comfort.) It would behoove him to thank you for this opportunity with his mouth, either upon your asshole or balls, which will spur you to greater heights, or upon the shaft of your member churning the lady's guts so deliciously. Then he ought to do a little backward, close-quarter, cunt-lapping and draw his tongue upward to the crack of her now quite open ass, and to the angel's fist therein which he will presently fuck. Lubricate her ass beforehand as you would anybody's, finger it to give her a preview of coming attractions, and then enter her. Penetrated simultaneously, the little bitch will find herself in the ultimate paradise of sensation. For the two men the delight will be considerable too. Such a sight, such a partnership, is a very strong erotic bond between friends. Two lovers can fuck each other through a woman, therefore changing or seeming to change sexes, offering themselves through the girl's femininity without compromising their own masculinities.

The satisfaction a woman receives through anal intercourse is very nearly identical with that which a man receives. Instead of the prostate gland and so forth to the front, the entering penis rubs against that part of the colonic wall that closely neighbors the vagina, thereby massaging her deep sexual parts from within. It is extremely pleasant, and as I have suggested before, in this position you can frig the cunt just as easily as you might jerk off a boy.

Another position comes to mind. One that is useful for both anal and vaginal penetration. This is the male inferior female superior "squat". It's quite popular in the Orient, but the squatting position is not very popular here, and I suppose that outside of the legal and religious prohibitions on fucking positions, this is because of the relative size of the American female. One thinks of bouncing a "Lolita" on one's lap, but hardly a big-breasted pom pom girl of one hundred and thirty pounds. Nevertheless, the greatest advantage of this position is its versatility: one can alternate holes with a minimum of trouble.

Being a homosexual, even a known homosexual, is absolutely no disadvantage when it comes to getting women. In fact, it can be an advantage if you use it properly. There are two things on your side. The greatest majority of men have some homosexual experience in their histories; therefore, they do make out with women with some regularity. The married man with an occasional taste for cock is no rarity. Conclusion? A good many men learn certain aspects of loving from other men, and that makes the whole woman-thing much easier. Second phase! There's something in women, a pride, a blind narcissistic optimism, that makes it imperative for most of them to believe in the ultimate power of their twats, their "love," to cure all ills. They tend to think the solution of the ills of the world is between their legs. *And,* Sweetie, they tend to believe that a good healthy dose of "snappin' turtle pussy" can cure any man of the Greek madness.

What a perfect set-up. All you have to do to make out, assuming you move in a gay or artsy-crafty crowd, is to let it be known that you are ambivalent about sex. Let it be known that you don't know anything much about women, but that you just might like to try it if you *found the right girl.* Let's say you tell others the only reason you play around with boys is because they're easier. Well, there's the hook. In the fag-hag, or fruitfly syndrome, there's scarcely a girl or woman that wouldn't like to wear your balls on her hatband. And don't worry. She'll do all the work. You won't have to court her at all. Just listen to her bullshit and the endless autobiographical recital which is designed to fascinate you by convincing you of the high esteem in which she is held by others. Eventually she will believe you are ripe, and sock it to you. She will seduce you.

How will you get her to seduce you? First, make sure she lives alone, though it's much better indeed if you have a place of your own, for a woman like this wants very badly to invade your privacy and will prefer your pad to her own. If she has room-mates and such, don't under any circumstances go there or allow the sex business to take place in such distracting surroundings. Visit her at home as seldom as possible. But keep your place open to her. She will offer to cook. Let her. She may offer to clean, wash the dishes, tidy up or what have you. Let her. Anything she offers to do for you, permit her to do it unless it is stupid or inconvenient. Demonstrate enormous appreciation and approval. If she tries to get you drunk to "loosen you up" or "put you at ease" with your own liquor, make sure you drink her under the table. Get her as high as possible without permitting her to lose control of her faculties. That would make her absolutely impossible. There's really nothing as dreadful as a drunken woman. But a tipsy tart, that's another matter. Slip her some pot or hash or both. Nothing stronger. And then, when she gets you to the sack, turn the tables and fuck the bejesus out of her. Put her through the hoop in every position you can think of, that's my advice. The important thing is to be a milquetoast out of bed and a satyr in it. If she goes home that night or in the morning, make sure she has something to talk about. Her girlfriends will be positively green with envy, which is what she wants, and your stock will rise enormously, which is what you want.

For as long as you want her it is important that you remember to constantly remind her that you have homosexual tendencies. That will keep her on her toes. She will guard you like crazy against men, but leave the other coast clear, enabling you to slip the pork to one of her girlfriends behind her back. But be very careful and discreet. You must arrange it in such a way as to make the story sound like a lie should the friend tell your girl about it.

This is all wonderfully devious, but an amusing way to stay in cunt without exerting yourself. You will have the satisfaction of actually getting it while swaggering male impersonators you know try to persuade themselves of their manhood, and virility with half-truths and street-corner flirtations.

But, should you care to get rid of the dear, and that may indeed come sooner than you think . . . or better . . . than she does, there is an easy way, a nearly fool-proof way to go about it. Pretend to be falling for her. Come on strong. Be a *man*, demanding and aggressive. Insist that she tend to womanly duties. Housekeeping is almost certain to drive her from you. Assume control of her life, from bobby pins to paychecks, and do it in such a way as to give her the feeling of having created a monster. Pretend to no longer be interested in men. She will find some means to break it off. After all, the reason she chums around with faggots is because she's afraid of men. Let her end the affair, but don't let her know you're letting her. Throw a terrible scene! But mind you make sure nobody sees you. That's the secret of these little vignettes. Perform only when you're alone together. That'll do it. She will somehow find a way to part, trying not to hurt you.

I don't mean to sound completely cynical, you know, but one of the difficulties with women is getting rid of them. As a man dealing with men most of the time, you have to take this into consideration. That means planning. You know as well as I that one gains and sheds male partners with great ease and rapidity, and that's part of the charm. I think you simply have to outsmart women in order to enjoy them physically without the inconveniences of deep attachments. Unless you want prostitutes, which is another story altogether.

Before the pill women dragged on their uteruses like ships on their anchors. That some people persist in regarding human intercourse as a matter of procreation alone is even more absurd and perverse than our national illiteracy rate, because a fertile woman can conceive only a certain number of beings in her body and that number is not large. However, all human beings require many thousands of sexual experiences, or orgasms, to maintain their health. Therefore, accept the evidence of pleasure as an end rather than a means, even with women. I put particular stress on this because for so long I was terrified of women because I was afraid of causing pregnancy, and imagined myself at, say fourteen, supporting an endlessly fertile wife and a brood of snotty brats.

Illigitimacy is on the rise. That's not just a woman's problem. It may seem absurd to discuss this in a homosexual's handbook, but as a guide to conduct, surely it ought to be considered worthwhile to ask young homosexuals to prepare for an occasional cunt-session with the appropriate prophylactic equipment. It's wonderfully cheap and easy to use. For men it's the "scum bag" or "rubber" of infamy.

I remember crossing the harbor of New York one summer afternoon when the Staten Island ferry people were on strike. We had to ride across the harbor on very small, very low Coast Guard ferries used in place of the usual ones. I was standing on the lowest deck amid the Sunday outing crowd of tourists and boy-scouts. Some nuns were leaning over the railing. Suddenly I heard the Scouts whoop and whistle. I turned and saw what the wind and the tide had brought in from Brooklyn and from the city's sewers; a sub-aquatic forest of waving white rubber eels, thousands of love-bladders.

I don't know why some boys fuss about using them. Oh, I know that business of "would you take a bath with a raincoat on?" But that seems to me a little beside the point. Although there is some dulling of sensation, there is ample evidence that this can be beneficial to many men who lack timing control, for clearly an excess of sensation on the penis can lead to premature ejaculation. There's nothing difficult about wearing rubbers. In fact, you can make a sort of bed-time sport out of it, a game of slipping on those good membranes which Casanova called "Love Envelopes". Enjoy the thrills and fun of dressing up the phallus; two can play. Some girls are too up-tight for it though. I remember I used to be pretty good at getting them on with one hand while keeping the other busy in the hair pie, and kissing at the same time. With my thumb nail I'd cut the wrapper. Then I'd slide it out of the foil, and after testing it to see which way it was rolled, slip it on with one movement. Most of the time they never knew I had it on until it was all over, which is a good thing when you're dealing with lower class girls particularly, because many of them seem to believe that your wearing a sheath indicates a fear of disease, that you regard them as prostitutes, as unclean. Isn't that something?

But suppose you've managed to lure some fag-hag into your den by posing as a man susceptible to seduction. All things being as they are, she will probably throw herself at you with the energy of a Moray Eel. Splendid! But, if she's been hasty, she may have forgotten to insert her diaphragm. Find out immediately. In case she has forgotten it, *don't do it,* unless you use the appropriate vaginal jellies during your intercourse, or unless you can get her to douche afterward. But, heaven forbid, if you've nothing in the house and she has nothing with her, why, use nature's own. Masturbate, use your mouths, or screw her butt. Flip her into a sixty-nine, and if you aren't sure of yourself in any position don't hesitate to ask for instructions on technique. If she's too squeamish to bother . . . and she probably won't be . . . get rid of her at once. Oh, there's nothing drearier than a big-bellied female trying to get a fag to marry her. Avoid this most maudlin of comic scenes.

Note:
Technique as it applies to staying power is largely misunderstood or misapplied, it seems to me. I don't know that the man who can keep it hard for an hour or a night for one orgasm is better than the man who is able to have repeated orgasms over the same space of time. Once again, taste runs away with the day.

Isn't it curious that almost every anatomical part of the Virgin Mother is shown in some icon and worshipped? What about her cunt? Would one not expect to see replicas of it in gold somewhere? Maybe there's a small Russian Orthodox chapel somewhere in the Urals dedicated to the sanctity of Holy Mother Snatch. Or in a niche in a Sicilian catacomb.

This craze for virginity has its comic aspects. In Italy, for instance, women tell themselves and their children that one shouldn't fuck. "Women are to be respected," they say. "We are the Virgin Mary." But the fathers know better and tell their sons to fuck women when and wherever they find them, young or old, at any time and under any pretext. Latin people understand these things. They know that one may have to listen to women on occasion, put up with their nuttiness and absurdity, pretend to agree with them and so on, but they know it's only in order to get them in bed. Women are made for fucking. They're perfectly ridiculous otherwise.

Many G.I.'s returned from the Pacific, and particularly from Japan, with wives. A good many more returned with knowledge, and in some cases, samples of merchandise sold in "sex stores." These included pornography, of course, and certain kinds of sexual accessories such as dildos, sheaths of an ornamental rather than a prophylactic nature. Many of these objects were of great beauty, for the Japanese are able to extend the realm of art into many areas. For the ordinary G.I. Joe, slipping on one of those gaily modelled and fringed "rubbers" must have been a high auto-erotic treat.

Of course, we had all heard of the "French Tickler," that legendary device celebrated in song and story. Some had seen them. Few had used them. Crudely made, they were often plain rubbers with a trailing horsehair attached. The hair acted as a stiff bristle-like irritant to the vaginal walls. The joys promised by this device were more than outweighed by the lacerations.

Now we no longer have to take a trip abroad to buy any of these delightful and "healthful" devices. They are readily available to us through the mails. Many specialty houses distribute them, but I would like to describe some of the products offered by Universal Sales, P.O. Box 34578, Los Angeles, California 90034. I can recommend these items as aids to high-voltage female "thrills".

There are several models of the "tickler". One is called the Coronal Extension. This is an elastic band worn just behind the head of the penis, *au naturel*. It sports two curiously breast-like rounded appendages which extend to the right and left of the underside of the penis for maximum contact with "the more sensitive center of sexual feeling located in the middle-third of the vaginal canal." Proper stimulation of this center of sexual feeling usually results in far more rewarding, *"far more satisfying relations."*

"Behind the theory, design, and construction of the Coronal Extension are years of patient study and experimentation, distilled into an effective finished product you may use with assurance."

This company offers an even more "new and remarkable" version of the tickler, *The Duo Stimular.* It is not a particularly attractive-looking business, however. A celebrated avant-garde cellist, Miss Charlotte Moorman, is reported to have said, "My God, it's got cleats!"

For vaginal or #1 orgasm, the Duo-Stimular begins with a sub-coronal ring similar to the Coronal Extension. Instead of the two passive-looking blobs on the underside of the ring, there is a double row of fourteen "cleats" the shorter ones on top, and the longer ones below.

For clitoral or #2 orgasm, the Duo-Stimular offers another ring which fits on the shaft of the penis close to the body. It also has a matching number of aggressive projections, and in addition, a kind of up-lifted coccyx that reminds one of a Scorpion or one of those dinosaurs with great horns in the end of his tail. There are eight projections on this particular beast and they assure that the Duo-Stimular "is designed to deliberately and effectively stimulate the erogenous zones sufficiently to assure either the Vaginal orgasm, or the Clitoral orgasm, or both." There are simpler modifications of these appendages. One of them is the wedge-shaped "Snap-On Stimulator" which again is aimed at the Clitoral big "O".

However, we are assured that it is not even particularly necessary that you be erect for succulent and deeply rewarding intercourse. A number of splints and sheaths can take care of all that for you. There are a couple of banded Roman-looking Surgical Splints which support the Penis "almost its entire length." Then there is a series of bullet-shaped puss-pokers that, although relatively flexible, cover the entire length of your pecker and rest on a wide plastic base for, I imagine, safety and extra thrust. There are elastic bands attached to them which secure the devices around your hips. And assuming that you have lost your penis either through surgery or neglect, or that you never had one in the first place, in which case, my dear, you are probably a Lesbian, there is a

Universal Harness that will, "hold almost any Artificial Penis — *regardless of make."* We are reassured too that this device, like all of the others offered by this company is *"easy to use — easy to clean — easy to maintain."*

There are extensions for the penis that do not quite cover the whole thing, but end in a kind of rubbery membrane which you roll down just as you do a conventional rubber. We must assume that in the heat and frenzy of the moment they will not slip off, for no retrieving device is offered with them. And this note: "CAUTION: We strongly advise that any man who has a large penis NOT use the MALE EXTENSION", which sounds pretty sensible to me. I get a vision of driving the thing out of some poor lady's asshole. Ooops! Sorry!

But there are several de luxe items that must not be missed. There is the Prosthetic Penis Aid with "Raised Clitoral Stimulator" which comes in three colors, Ebony, Brown, and Flesh-color. (I suppose one could mix or match at will for visual stimulation and/or social comment.) It is simply a monument of "life-like" veins! Indeed, it appears to be corrugated. This device is offered in a really miracle version which is worn without belts, straps, or harness of any kind. It is held on with . . . yes! . . . air pressure! Simply by pumping the small conveniently placed rubber bulb, air is forced through the generous amounts of tubing, up and inside the NEUMO PENIS-AID and lo! you have "an aid for prolonged intercourse as well as allowing for intercourse when *Erection* is not present or lost through . . . *Premature Ejaculation! Undersized Organ! Impotency! Obesity!"*

Now that's hard to top, ladies and gentlemen, but I will only say that you can buy an Orgo Aid male replica penis sheath with a vibrator unit attached just about where your balls ought to be. This unit is battery operated and comes apart for easy cleaning.

Then there is the Rectal Unit "For Adults Only" which when inserted into the "Users" rectum — allows the man or woman to experience the effect of the "Vibration Unit." It is not, however, shaped to resemble a penis. Which ought to allay some guilt feelings somewhere, for somebody. It looks to me like a bent curling iron.

The Vaginal Aid seems to be basically the same arrangement with but one exception: the tip of the "Non-Toxic, soft plastic tube that is sufficiently rigid for easy insertion," is a miniature flail. Now unless I miss my guess, a few minutes with this pussy-jiggler ought to whip those natural juices into a veritable meringue of delight.

"Why," you ask me, "Why, Uncle Fudge, do you feel inclined to include all this madness in a text book for us simple inverts?"

Well, my angel, don't forget that this chapter deals with women. Some of this information may be of help especially if you find yourself . . . saints protect you . . . married to a woman who does not excite you. Which is, by the way, your own fault, you snivelling booby!

Or look at it this way; you might be able to use some of this stuff with another man. I imagine just wearing it about ought to be pretty arousing. Use your imagination. I just want to warn you of one thing, however. The suction of your little asshole is likely to be quite a bit greater than it would be for vaginal pumping, so use caution with any of these extensions or coronal collars. You may find yourself bent over in a doctor's office one day while he looks up in there with a flashlight, trying to snag it with a butter hook.

No, don't count on using any of this stuff in men. That's not really very practical. But you can sort of scatter it about the apartment. These little trinkets make marvelous conversation pieces. Or, do what the manufacturer advises. Use these items to make some high-breasted wood nymph your perpetual cock-slave. She is very likely not to mind in the least.

ANGELO d'ARCANGELO

"In my family and among our few friends, to suggest that one has gone through anything quite as nearly excremental as birth is to lapse, without hitch or hope, into a very nearly middle-class tastelessness. My mother, still at her age a woman of blazing fashion, has chosen to forget the date of my birth (as well as those disaccommodating incidents which may have caused it) and I can scarcely do more than she. The dear seems to recall that we met rather early in her life (not to mention mine) and that she liked me immediately. She says that unlike most of her beaux I did not dance for some months but smiled quite a lot. My father

has always been too kind to interrupt, color, or otherwise alter my mother's notions about me. His first words to me sans Nanny *were,* Que les femmes sont droles, eh, Lolo?' *That we in no way resembled one another dear Papa chose to regard, mirthfully, as either her prank or mine. Since leaving home Mr. d'Arcangelo has written* The Homosexual Handbook.

Roger Agile

BISHOP'S GAMBOL

"**I** have never done it with a bishop before," said she, unhooking her brassiere.

"Nor have I with a magazine writer," said I, unhooking my collar. "At least, I don't think so."

"To tell you the truth," said she, stepping out of her gossamer panties, "I've never done it with anyone."

"Good heavens!" said I, my trousers at half-staff. "Do you mean it?"

She nodded.

"I didn't know there were any left."

"It is pretty silly—"

"No, no! I find it—refreshing. Especially in one with your obvious assets."

"Thank you."

"You're blushing! All the way down!"

She scrambled into bed, pulling the sheet up over her really extraordinary bosom. "You're embarrassing me!"

"Dear, dear," said I, sitting on the edge of the bed and removing my right shoe. "I really don't mean to. Perhaps we should talk for a bit—first, you know. I mean, we have only just met this afternoon. And it is your first time. I wouldn't want to spoil it by making you uncomfortable."

"You are sweet," said she, propping her auburn head up on the pillows. The sheet slipped down, affording a glimpse of Himalayan splendor.

"I try to be thoughtful," I said.

"Are you sure you don't mind chatting—just for a little?"

"No, no, no," said I, patting her hand. "After all, that's really the purpose of your call."

"Well, I do have an obligation to my editor."

"Of course you do. Well, then let us meet that obligation first. And then, perhaps, we can oblige ourselves. Where shall we begin?"

"Oh, at the beginning. That's always best," she said, folding her hands primly over her flat tummy. "What I'm simply dying to know is, how did you come to be a bishop in the first place?"

"My dear," said I, letting fall my right shoe, "it was inevitable. But from the beginning . . ."

2

"We'll call him Roger," my mother said.

"Rover would be more like it," replied my father, "for a poorer looking mutt I never saw."

"Ah, Jack, you'll have your joke," said my mother.

"This time the joke's on me. When are you coming home? The wash is piling up. There's not a clean sock nor a clean dish in the house. Cissy's coffee's not worth a fart, and I've not had a decent bite since Burke's wake last Tuesday."

3

When my mother had caught up with her housekeeping, she began to bother my father about the matter of my christening. "For," said she, "it would be a terrible thing were the child to die unbaptized."

"Is it sick?" my father asked.

"Have I given you a sick child in the lot?"

"But—" said my father.

"Don't I keep their bowels open and their noses dry?"

"But—" said my father.

"Have you ever been out of pocket by so much as a dollar on account of illness?"

"There I have you!" cried my father. "What of the time young Arthur ate the ant button?"

"An accident," my mother replied. "That was an accident and no true illness."

"The brat was ill," my father said. "Didn't he ruin my patent leathers with his puking? If that's not ill—"

"But he got sick by accident."

"God damn!" cried my father. "God damn the perversity of woman! Why, if I'm infected with a virus I suppose that's accidental, too. Certainly it is not deliberate on my part. And if a tapeworm takes up residence in my gut, is that not an accident? By your reasoning, if indeed it can be called reasoning, all illness is accident. Even the clap is, I suppose—an accidental injury—since the contractor has come by it unwittingly and only by bad luck.

"Life," my father went on, "is but a series of accidents. God help the insurance company if your view becomes the accepted one."

How far my father might have varied his argument, how high he might have soared into the realms of reason and rhetoric can only be imagined, for at this juncture my sister came running in to announce that Arthur had fallen out of the pear tree.

"Another illness," my mother said, with a hard look at my father. And she ran out to rescue her first born.

But the matter of my christening could not be put off. That primal smudge upon my soul must be laundered out, my mother declared, so that I would not be denied entry into Paradise in the melancholy event of my dying before I attained to the age of reason.

"I could do the job myself," my father said, "and save the expense of tipping the priest and having a party."

"You'll do no such thing," said my mother.

But my father was a man of some humor. "Why not?" said he. "I could tend to it while you're bathing the little bastard and kill the two birds with one stone. Or when I'm watering lawn, for that matter, I could turn the hose on him and be done with it in an instant."

My mother paid him no further mind. "I shall want my brother Fred for his godfather," she said.

"Fred?" cried my father. "Why the church would cave in on us the minute he stepped inside the door."

"He is my only brother."

"Your father had more sense than I," said my father, scowling first as Arthur sat in his chair with his arm in a sling, and then at me in my pen. "But if it must be Fred then I shall have Salome for godmother."

"That sluttish sister of yours? Never!"

"Why, as to her sluttishness," replied my father serenely, "that comes of her being named as she was. Had your brother been named Judas, I have no doubt but what he'd have hanged himself before now and saved us all the embarrassment of bailing him out of the drunk tank a dozen times in the year."

"Your sister is a loose woman," said my mother.

"So was Mary Magdalen. Besides, she's goodhearted for all her faults."

"Goodhearted!" my mother sniffed. "So I have heard."

"Well, I'd sooner have young Wet Bum there take after his aunt than after his uncle."

"That would be rare."

"Not so rare as you think, Why, when I was in Paris—"But here the potatoes boiled over, and my father was left with only my brother and me for an audience.

The day of my christening was full of omens. The sky was murky and, though it was mid-August, the wind off the harbor was cold. A gray gull perched on our chimney, and my Uncle Fred was sober as a democrat in Vermont on Election Day. It was not an auspicious beginning.

Fretful and whining, I was carried to the church in the arms of my father's sister. We were late, and the pastor's humor was not improved by waiting. He set to his work in a brusque manner, and hustled my halting godparents over the hurdles in their recitation of the Creed. Then he had at me with oils, salt and a whiff of snuffy breath that set me to coughing and sneezing.

When it came time to administer the *coup de grace,* the priest positioned me over the font and let the water fall. I retaliated in kind.

"Jesus!" cried the priest.

"Christ!" cried my uncle.

"Hee-hee!" cried my father.

Aunt Salome fainted and slumped to the floor.

"The boy is a born heretic," said my father.

"Or a bishop," said the priest, rubbing at the stain on his cassock with his sleeve.

No clap of thunder accompanied these prophecies. There was only my Uncle Fred saying, "I want a drink."

4

"Master Agile, do you seriously expect to amount to anything in this world?"

"Sir, I expect to be a bishop and a heretic."

"Master Agile, put out your hand."

5

My brother Arthur was the scholar in the family. Not for him the bruised knuckles and the tortured lobe. He applied himself.

Martha, my sister, was also diligent.

Of me my father despaired. My compositions were mere blots, my arithmetic a hodge-podge of error and whim. But though I stumbled as I read, I ran with endurance and speed.

"Oh, Roger, my father's coming!"

"What's going on out there?"

"Meet me at the library," I said, and I was off like a scared hare.

My policy was this: to love all girls equally and to be grateful for opportunity in whatever guise.

I was a fair-complected, curly-locked lad, and the girls did not find me odious. By the time I'd come to my twelfth year I had kissed every girl in the school worth kissing—within two years of my age either way.

And when I was fourteen I met Millie.

Millie was a well-nourished young woman of color, somewhere between eighteen and forty-eight years old, who came in once or twice a week to help my mother with the heavy cleaning. I say that I was fourteen when I met her. Well, Millie had been around our house for some years before that, but it wasn't till I was fourteen that I really got to know her—so to speak.

I had come in from school and dashed on up the stairs to take a leak. I knew no one would be home, so I didn't even bother to close the door. I just whipped out my tallywhacker and braced myself in front of the bowl.

"Watcha got there, boy?"

God! I went up in the air about a foot, turned in mid-flight and pissed halfway to the ceiling.

"Hee-hee! You got the distance, honey, but you suah ain't got the range."

"Millie! What are you doing there, for Pete's sake? I didn't know you were here."

"Doan I know that? I jus' come in to clean the crapper an' I seen you standing there with that thing in yo' hand like you knew what it was fo'. So I jus' natcherly had to see whut you gonna do with it."

"Well," said I, putting the dog back in his kennel, "now you know. I'm sorry I wet the wall, but you scared me so bad I couldn't help it."

"Hee-hee! I doan min' that. It was worth it jus' to see you jump."

I felt my face going red. "What d'you expect, for crying out loud? A guy doesn't expect to have some woman looking at his whatsis when he's trying to go to the bathroom."

"Whut you so bothered about, boy? Doan you like the gals to see it?"

I really didn't care to continue the conversation; I just wanted to leave. But Millie pretty well filled the doorway, and I couldn't very well go around her. So I said, "I dunno."

"She-it! He doan know. I bet you puttin' it to all them little chicks over to the high school." Millie's eyes narrowed. "Truth, now. Ain't you been bangin' them li'l drum majors and such?"

"No."

"Mm-mph!" Millie shook her head. "Can't unnerstan' it. Doan you wanna screw them gals?"

Well, now that she mentioned it, I had to admit to myself that the thought had once or twice crossed my mind. And as it crossed again, I experienced an observable reaction.

"My, my! Look at that li'l fella stand up! I expect he need a li'l help 'long about now."

"Millie! What are you doing, for God's sake?"

She came over to me and began fumbling at my fly. "I just wants to help a friend in trouble, tha's all."

"Well, we're all gonna be in trouble if my mother comes home and—oh!" Millie's calloused brown hand reached in and took hold of my tingling tool.

"Doan you worry 'bout yo' mother, honey. She ain't gonna be home fo' another hour at leas'. Yo' brother's out peddling his papers. Yo' sister's with you' mother. An' yo' father's never home befo' five-thirty. Any mo' questions?"

I couldn't think of a one.

"Now," said Millie, leading me by the handle, "you jus' come with ol' Millie an' we see whut we can do fo' that po' li'l friend of ours."

I might have resisted, but how you resist when someone's pulling you along by the pecker beats the hell out of me. Millie led me to my own little room and sat me down beside her on my bed.

"Now," she said, "I gonna mess aroun' with you fo' a li'l bit. Make you feel good. But you gotta make Millie feel good, too. Fair enough?"

I allowed that it seemed fair.

"Okay. Now, then, le's have a look at this li'l rascal." Millie began fondling my frail reed, causing it to swell nobly. That evidently pleased her, for she smiled a dreamy smile and began working my want back and forth more and more rapidly. The sensation was not unpleasant.

"You like that?" Millie asked.

"Ye—yes. A lot!"

"Now you gotta do for me." She took my hand and guided it up under her dress.

"You're all wet," I said.

"She-it! Doan I know that? C'mon, boy, get workin' up in there."

Well, fair is fair. I got three fingers up and began wiggling 'em around. But Millie grabbed my wrist and began steering my hand back and forth like a piston. I got the hang of it and had at it with a will.

"Tha's good. That's better. You keep that up, honey. Yeah, yeah, yeah!"

I kept it up. And Millie continued to twiddle my tool 'twixt thumb and forefinger in a most delightful manner. This was fun! It was a whole lot more fun than the do-it-yourself approach I had hitherto employed. I felt wonderfully relaxed yet stimulated, and I didn't care if we never quit. Indeed, I hoped we never would. But the best was yet to be.

Millie suddenly slumped back on my bed and drew me over on top of her. "Where is that li'l ol' peckah?" said she, chuckling a dark and naughty chuckle. "Where's he at?"

She groped for my groin, found what she was looking for and guided it smoothly into port. I found the sensation thrilling, lovely, exquisite. Apparently Millie did too, for she cried, "Ooo-ee! That's a good fit! Le's go, sugah baby! Le's make it!"

I soon fell into her rhythm, and we rocked along together quite merrily. It was marvelous, and I felt a sense of pride which, I believe, was not entirely unwarranted. I mean, after all, it was my first time out—or in, and here I was riding like a trooper.

"Go, go, go, li'l fella!" cried Millie.

And I went, went. went. Most willingly. To hell with Boy Scouts; to hell with baseball; to hell with Saturday matinees! This was It!

Millie's arms tightened around my neck. Then her ankles locked over the small of my back. It was getting hard to move, yet something within me urged me to move faster. I strove mightily for more mobility, but just as I got well braced for a thrust, Millie fastened her teeth into my shoulder and heaved her hips clean into the air. She nearly threw me as she writhed under me, but I plugged away in a fine sweat and suddenly she fell back with a loud sigh, utterly limp, eyes closed and a most contented smile caressing her lips.

"You all right, Millie?"

She looked up at me and gave a slow, wise old wink. "Jus' fine, honey. How you doin?"

"Good. Real good."

"You come, darlin?"

"No."

"Well, doan be a stranger, child. Come on back in where it's warm."

"Thanks, Millie." I slid back in, and in a few happy strokes I did the deed. Oh, wow! Oh, if the guys could see me now! I felt like the king of the world. Millie held me close as I poured out into her dark void, and when I was spent I collapsed on the yielding billows of her breast with a feeling of triumph, gratitude and utter bliss.

Millie patted me gently on the back. "That was real good for a firs' time, honey," she said.

"I guess it takes practice, huh?"

"Some. But doan you worry none. I be back on Wensdy."

That next Wednesday, and for many a Wednesday thereafter, I romped with my dusky tutor. I advanced rapidly under Millie's capable instruction, and in the course of things became genuinely fond of her. I actually wept when, early in the spring, she eloped with a Caucasian professor of music from the local women's college. I hope he was good to her. She was certainly good to me.

With Millie gone, I went back on manual for a time; but I had been converted, and it wasn't long before I began to put out feelers among those little drum majors—and the cheerleaders, and the dramatics club, and the National Honor Society.

By the time I was seventeen, I had progressed notably.

"What have we here?"

Snap-snap!

"What have you there?"

Zzzzzip!

"Oh, Roger!"

"Oh, Louise!" Or Cindy, or Mary, or Jean, or Betty, or Meg as the case may be.

"You do love me?"

"What do you think, Silly?"

"Because if you didn't, I wouldn't—"

"Of course not. You're not that kind of girl. Shall we again?"

"Oh, Roger!"

"Oh, Louise!" Or Cindy, or Mary, or Jean, or Betty, or Meg as the case may be.

Of them all, it is Louise that I remember best, for reasons which will be made clear. She was the Honor Society one, a very intelligent girl with a keen interest in history and in screwing.

"Oh, Roger, I just love doing it here in the cemetery. Would you unhook my bra, please?"

"Um. Sure."

"Thank you. Ooh, the breeze feels so nice on my bare breasts. Do you like my breasts, Roger?"

"Yeah. I like 'em a lot."

"Oh, the moon is lovely tonight! I just want to stretch out on old Mr. Stickney's marble slab and feel that smooth cold stone all along me. Do you think he minds?" Louise lay back on the slab, her breasts as white in the moonlight as the marble on which she lay.

"I don't think he minds," said I, dropping my pants on the cushion of pine needles. The cool wind played about my crotch, setting my tool a-tingle.

"Just think about all these people here, Roger—all the fucking they must have done. I wonder if they miss it now?"

"You're a funny kid," said I, lying down beside her and going all goose flesh from the touch of cold stone.

"Do you think so?" said she, absently toying with my rigid rod.

"Yeah, but a nice kind of strange," said I, twining my fingers in her blonde thatch.

"You're sweet," said she, stroking my head. "Want to nibble some?"

"Um." I filled my mouth with firm sweet meat of her breasts.

"Oh, I like that. I like being here, naked in the dark night among the dead. I like having your mouth on me and your fingers in me. And when you put your prick in me I just melt inside."

"Get ready to melt, then." And I slid into her.

"Mmmm! Oh! Excuse us, Mr. Stickney, but Roger and I have to fu-u-UCK!"

I can't say that I enjoyed thinking about the late Mr. Stickney at a time like that; I must say I didn't think much about him. Louise wrapped her slender arms tight around me and set to bouncing on that icy marble.

My elbows and knees were a little sore, but I felt so good everywhere else that I scarcely noticed.

"Pump, Roger, pump! Pump hard!"

I pumped. And the marvelous suction of her warm, wet cunt seemed to draw me in deeper, deeper until—

"Roger! Come, now! No-oow!" Louise kicked her heels toward the moon, and together we died sweetly on top of old Mr. Stickney.

Louise sat up and stretched, accentuating the full curve of her breasts so pale in the moonshine. "It just keeps getting better all the time."

"I'm glad," I said, for I liked her.

"I wonder if they re jealous."

"Who?"

"The people here. I mean, here we are, young and alive, and warm and making love. And they are all so cold and—"

"Gee, it's getting pretty late, Louise. We better be going, huh?"

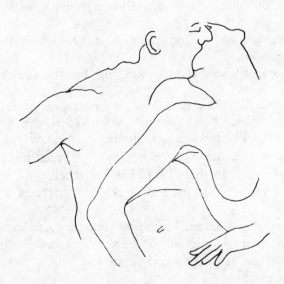

"Ha, ha. It bothers you, doesn't it?"

"What?"

"Doing it in the cemetery."

"No it doesn't," I said. "I'd fuck you anywhere, anytime."

"Why don't we do it in a church sometime?"

"Louise!"

"Ha, ha! Oh, Roger, you can be stuffy."

"Well, I stuff you pretty good, don't I?"

"You stuff me beautifully. Hand me my panties please."

"Sure, Hey! What's that?"

"What?"

"On your behind. Hold still a minute." And in the moonglow I could just make out an imprint on her firm little butt: *Ye shall have life.*

I think Mr. Stickney was trying to tell us something.

ROGER AGILE

According to the author, Bishop's Gambol *is largely autobiographical; he even calls himself Roger Agile, after the book's hero. Like Edgar Allen Poe, he has the distinction of having been bounced from a military establishment – Poe was drummed out for gambling, and Agile for ... well, gamboling. Somewhat later, he became a teacher, but did not limit his activities to the classroom, and seeing that the world was not ready for his philosophy of education, left teaching to become a door-to-door salesman, taking full advantage of the opportunities of that trade. He discovered a religious vocation, and after some years within the hierarchy, left to found his own church, the Pillar of Love Tabernacle in Los Angeles, where many a free spirit has found even greater freedom under the easy creed of Pastor Agile.*

Sicily Enough

Anna Winter

Dogshadow thin I arrive, carrying my third child like a weapon through this old town, while the only thing I feel is my hair tight, hurting where the baby holds on. A fierce clock, she reminds my vague shocked self that I must function. We kiss and I inhale her breath like food, warm as the milk I flowed into her some months ago.

October in Sicily, and there is the first volcano I have ever seen. Cool mountain, lambent with snow on its mouth; how can it be so hot inside?

I buy grapes, wash them in the fountain while broody dark men watch me bending over. I suddenly feel well-fleshed, and the skins of grapes slide agreeably over my tongue. The baby has fun spitting with them. I buy a great deal more to bring to the other children waiting at home.

It will be easy to eat in this country.

Long walks, up and down steps, going from view to view, the town spread around in broken architecture, painted in tired color that was once red. Walls better than current art, moonpitted, incredibly dry. What a sun has made all this happen! Centuries of summer, centuries of cats and dogs breeding under Roman arches.

Women who still wear black, faces yellow, a smear of bad flesh under the eyes that arouses me and suggests a hundred perversities. Every woman has breasts and thighs and hair in her armpits; I see them as black curling flowers. Their legs are strong and hairy, men do not force them to shave; here they do not alter animals or their passions.

This directness, this use of the body attracts me at once to the Sicilians and makes me feel warm. There is no subtle sex here, no American sex, but coupling itself. The day for a Sicilian has happened if he has made love. It seems empty to sleep unless it is post-coital; it's lonely.

I long for a lover there as I have longed for dogs to sleep with in my virtuous days. I want warm animals so near me that they are inside.

Desire grows on me. I see it reflected in the men who stare at me, their lust is an approval of my fattening body. I eat so much now, just to look at the vegetables is to feel nourished. A kind of cauliflower that grows almost nowhere else is in season. The whole top of it is painted deep purple, formidable as the color runs off into the cooking water till finally eaten, white again, drenched in pungent olive oil.

My children are so well here. They break rough bread and dunk it in sauce, they eat garlic and tomatoes; our cuisine is the maid's who makes lentil soup with pasta, broccoli with rice. We seem to be in a farmer's kitchen. My house is a good smell, while in the garden pomegranates burst on trees and oranges hang like lanterns.

Everything here becomes hazed over by sun and abundance. If something terrible has happened to me I no longer remember it so harshly. I feel as though I have a million senses now, held together by brain and guts. All I have known and suffered and longed for come together for me in Sicily. Good and bad, hard and soft, there is everything in those four words, any combination of them means something. Good soft bad hard or good hard bad soft or. If I am to go on living, and I must, since I have six black eyes looking at me, since my children are happy and do not understand that someone has died, then I shall become part of this landscape. I will grow into these trees, into these hills, and wait and stare and hope for the volcano to erupt.·

There he is, small angry-faced man. As he stands up to greet me a ray of sun slanting through the window grabs his eyes. They glare at me in the agate yellow of certain birds, the pupils pinned on me. I have seen that yellow in the amber I found on the beaches of the Baltic, where I played as a child. I have seen that yellow in the eyes of Clarita when she lusted for me. She was rapacious, like the watching bird, her eyes cold yellow pointed exactly to the center of me. As his are now.

"You are American?"

"You speak English."

"Not very well."

"Oh, too well. I want to learn Italian."

"You will have a Sicilian accent if you learn from me."

"I want to."

This will be my first lover. I must prepare myself as for the first time ever.

My hair needs to be cut, no more pins in it. I examine my fine skin and bathe it carefully. I polish my children as one does beautiful apples. My walks have a direction now. I go to his bar where he stands in the doorway waiting, sure of me. I had no idea that he is the richest young man in town, the most beautiful. It is his eyes I look for.

We work slowly, he is patient, always teaching, so aware that I am getting ready for him.

We go for many drives. I admire the countryside, and he takes me as far as the snow of the mountain.

How magical the preparation for love.

In the cafe I meet his Sicilian friends. There, every woman who passes is judged. When they approve, "buona" is uttered with a hoarse gusto, and I picture at once an entwining of genitals like the display of entrails in a butcher shop.

The face of the woman is looked at last. She must simply not be ugly. A robust body with abundant breast and rear and a fattish face is a fine "cavallo" or "vaca." The inspection is continuous, noisy with smacks and hisses, an obvious need to make each opinion public, to share. They tell each other exactly how they feel and how they would treat each case.

I have learned quickly to know what they say if only by their gestures. Beautiful in the way of mutes, hands weave away at the meaning of their talk. Hands measure intensity of meaning, but a small downward motion of the mouth destroys an entire argument.

My mother had this way of destroying me. Her mouth is thin and the slightest doubt is immediately visible in the downward arch of her lips—and there is a real shock in me as I know that she is against me. Her mouth curves at me like a snake, her face changes so much there is no chance for the girl to impress this judge. Everything has been smudged over. Is it then that I begin to lie? Or do I just begin to sneak? Sometimes I try again to tell her what I feel and again she makes this unbearable face. More and more I hide what I feel and soon am such an expert that I even cease to feel.

The seduction of my mother failed. She will not marvel at me. As did Clarita when she caressed my young body with her old appreciation, the yellow glowing in her eyes. My mother made me cold. I slept with a million blankets and no heat came; my body was sealed off in a cold young coffin.

And here is a country without music, books, painting, only certain lusts. Of course I must live here; this is why I came to this quicksand where there is no space for sadness, only quick frantic sucking motion, up, down.

Night. Palm trees staring straight up, sky soft around stars, clouds moving through the heads of trees. Olive, cypress and palm, their different foliage hard in the black distance, trees so separate from one another that one cannot imagine a forest. Palm, cypress, olive; leaf, shape, size, everything unique, blowing up into the sky all at once, the night dark, glowing with such ornament, waiting for its own end.

In the cemetery night pushes against what was, while the cypress rises and small birds rest.

Sound of mandolins in the tavern, sweet and liquid, played by two ugly men, drifting around Roberto like a habit, he hears none of it, just stares at my thighs. The first music I've been able to listen to in a long time, it does not frighten me into the past.

Red wine, fresh from the slopes of the mountain, cheap and delicious like penny candy, I drink it fast, it seems to improve my Italian. The room, square and low, underlit, with a skinny dog asleep on one of the chairs. The owner dedicates a song to me about the torment of love, smiling at the "nuovia coppia" that has the town talking.

I feel pleasant, involved with everything and everyone there. A ditchdigger I have seen working along the streets, dark and beautiful, now dressed in a marvelous velveteen jacket that shines like a chestnut, nods to me but I do not answer. I resent his trying to make real my flirtation with him. I only like to watch him working, to dream about his strength and simplicity, I really wish he would not confuse his reality with my fantasy. "Don't speak," I think, "don't let me hear your voice, just be there and let me dream about you. I don't want to touch you, I just want the idea of you. That's my man there, that handsome creature lounging by my side, more elegant than you, an offspring of Greeks and Moors with the body Michelangelo had adored."

Yes, my eyes roam the men with ease for I am safe among them, coupled to Roberto whose loins are making me happen.

"Quanto sei bello," I whisper. He grins but has to answer: "A man is simpatico not beautiful."

"I don't speak Italian well, make mistakes, but don't teach me too much."

"Va bene, va bene," he nods, his eyes irridescent, picking up all the light there is in the room.

The piazza where we meet every morning. He in his kingdom, that bar where he strides about like a small emperor.

"You are my empress now," he says lovingly, so proud.

"No, just your mistress," I answer in a coy way, new to me. His courtship of me has gotten into my bones. I feel all woman, organ deep as I glisten around him, my breasts full.

Walking down the corso, thighs heavy against my sex on this Sicilian street where I pass several times a day, where nothing changes except the flimsiest detail, where I am on parade. They all know what has happened. La Americana, amanti de Roberto. I have fallen into a certain status, condemned yet full of prestige because my lover is rich. Besides, it's not often that a woman with three children has any vitality left here. The women are jealous of my strong body, the men wonder about me. "She must be very good," I overhear. "Che buona."

There is a ritual as I enter through the arch into the wide incredible piazza, more beautiful than the shell in Siena. I go to the railing that overlooks the sea, trees falling down the view to the sea, the earth dark and dry green. To the right glares Etna. I look there first, no, I behold it. Nearly a perfect cone, it rises strong at the sky, the snow hard and clean, whiter than a nun's eye.

The piazza, bounded by curving, crumbling churches on two sides, with Roberto's bar in between, hypnotizes me. I sit for hours at a table, trying every drink ever brought to Italy, looking endlessly at the pure view of space and sky changing over the piazza where emptiness is broken only by seven trees and the people strolling. Seven oleander trees that never cease to bloom, white, pink and red flowers.

Five miles along the coast, gigantic over the cold sea, rises the town of Forza D'Agro. Lazy in medieval poverty, it waits to be looked at. Roberto and I are spring coming into those black, sunless streets. Shops are tombs for food showing porkfat, tripe, enormous loaves of bread. Awful old people stare at me, disapprove of my tight trousers and the way I hold Roberto's hand. He is clean among them, so young.

Passing a stable I desire him and pull him quickly into the warm smell of manure.

"Let's make love here," I say, but he laughs and worries. I take off my shoes and push my feet into the texture of dung. I suppose I am going too far, but I feel different here, not vicarious but in the actual sway of history. The age of this town has pulled off a certain veneer.

Roberto looks very uncomfortable and tries to get me out. "Questa Pazza!" he exclaims. But I do not feel crazy, I simply feel less civilized and wish he would go along with me in my sudden involvement with the twelfth century.

However, his embarrassment has spoiled my mood and I follow him. He wants to show me the town and its silly monuments. While he gapes at a church I smell bread baking. There is the oven, teeming with fire. A donkey stands patiently by the door, so heavily laden with wild rosemary that it resembles a solid halo. "Look," I say, but he hardly knows what I mean. Certainly the church is lovely and I am tempted to steal from it. How I should like one of those wooden candelabras, golden and flaky where worms have been.

Down below in Naxos, the first town built by the Greeks in Sicily, eating prehistoric octopus, while my eyes drift over the splendid view of my island above.

Worn, fabulous landslide of a view, green as black jagging to that sea where lava still lies exposed as it has lain for centuries.

Not thinking of the view; it has been sown into me. His body planted in me, I feel a tree. How shocking in the mirror, how very secret and deep it looks from the outside, while inside there is a wet intensity even deeper than what the mirror shows, and that's very deep. How cataclysmic to be penetrated, those thighs opening wide to let him in.

From a dusty figtree I take a bursting fruit. It must be splitting to be good. As I am at my full opening, ripe and glad to have this pleasure made known to me. How many women are allowed this as they plow through years of intimacy that are never catastrophic.

Perhaps I am losing my mind in this fleshbath, perhaps I shall lose everything, even my children. I forget them so often now. I have only this spastic, one-dimensional affair, but oh, it goes deep.

I know I do not live in order to remember; at the end memory will be as nothing. To say I really had it, how might it be if in the dry years I would have to say where was it? I do know that what I experience now is important, the future might only matter if I had lacked this.

With or without regret life ends and it makes no difference to me how it will end, only that it will end. It doesn't matter how things turn out; they change anyway. How can I provide for the future, even my children's! What is perfectly clear is that I adore them now and am in touch with life itself three times a day; eating, sleeping and fornicating—there is no other tenderness.

Fatigue pulls me on the bed. I should sleep and become strong for the rash sun tomorrow. It's always too bright in the morning. The day begins fast with the running sounds of children as they continue the day before. For them sleep has been a simple interruption. "Oh, children, your noise is my reality!"

My heart has gone dim in the huddle with night, spread under him like a stain of red wine on a white cloth. I put on dark glasses to protect me from this sun and the size of the mountain growing whiter each day.

How well we know each other, if knowledge has anything to do with these odd gropings over a foreign bed in a foreign country. The man caresses me in Italian: "You are my bread," he says and eats away at me, mushing my body into this incredible fatigue, his weight on me like stones I have helped put there. What am I doing? What is this strange excess?

When he sleeps everything is over, he is merely beautiful—not someone I care for. Why doesn't he leave? I don't need his shut face lying there, his body so still that he might as well be dead.

His sleeping wakes me and I rush to see my children in their beds, afraid they will look dead as well. Oh no, sleep lies on them lightly, on their round breathing faces life is growing.

My mother's thin face over the lush, soft body, this sense of being her all over again. My face is what I saw in her when she was thirty and I needed her most and was lonely for the generous droop of breast that Roberto loves so and uses as though I were his mother.

All dimensions gone here. Just the way the cocks crow in the night as nowhere else. What disturbs them so? Dark night with roosters screaming, wind pouring from the sky in a dry rain; I do not grow older but deeper.

But the weight of my children is a monkey on my back. Impossible to neglect them with ease. Coming home late, so late, I go into their rooms to stare at those simple yielding bodies. One of them coughs and I feel destroyed.

My passion with Roberto is a labyrinth where I hump along from angle to curve, free for a very short time, the white thread of my children wrapping me into a knot instead of leading me out. I go deeper into the maze, dragging them with me while I long to be childless, thoughtless, immune to all former feeling. Often now I lie so still under him, afraid that one more move will make me swoon, blot me out.

In a dark museum where his body is the only statue, more splendid than David, perfect because it's also warm. How well I understand a torso murder for love of each limb. I hack away at him with appalling want. And he, how he spreads himself for me in his self love. He would exhibit his anus without compunction, aware that every part of him is appropriate. I feel like one of those insane collectors who will do anything to acquire a Michelangelo. I am insane till I lie down alone again, pale from greed, sex-rotten.

I know so well that I should leave here. It's the crazy people who make me sure. That one, all dressed in black, a male widow, shouting to the children behind him. I see my own son, angered I pull him away and force him to be sad. "But I wasn't laughing," he says.

The madman stops in the piazza, stands in the center, a fountain yelling. Everyone laughs. I myself worry. What's wrong with me? For these people sanity is real and insanity is a spectacle not to be taken seriously; the crazy man is a clown. I am considered a sentimental fool. What's to be done in this red and white country?

Every time I leave my villa, lying slightly above the town, I walk slowly down the steps toward the sound below. A kind of welcoming hell swells towards me from the corso where the entire town is walking hard, talking hard, hungry, agitated.

Listen to the noise, it's the only music of the place. There is a strong and evident rhythm; one can tell the time of day by the amount of it, strongest in the evening about seven, before dinner.

I walk through them, only listening, not enchanted by their mess. I crave monotony, don't want anything more to happen, still haven't understood what has happened.

Winter here is a few weeks of rain, hard wind at night that empties the streets. I walk along the corso feeling free and clean.

In the cafe idle men huddle around the fireplace. Roberto sits with me in a corner, worried about business, constantly interrupting me as I try to read a book. I'm sick of his banal problems, how boring he is out of bed. Should he bring prices down, is it going to be a good carnival so that he'll make up for these bad few weeks? I don't care, watch instead his pretty mouth, the nice way he slumps in the chair. I long for a deaf mute.

My house is soaking from all the rain, clothes don't dry, the maid complains, children irritable from staying in so much.

Three weeks of this, the town looks lonely, unprepared as

every year for anything but sun. These Sicilians don't realize that it must rain and be cold sometimes. Their houses poorly equipped, they press around puny charcoal fires, old women hide them under long skirts. Several of them die every year from the fumes.

"Cattivo tempo," is all they say, stacking black umbrellas around the rooms where the rain is really in.

Roberto is worried about me, aware of my boredom.

"You'll feel better when the sun shines. I know this place is dull for you like this."

He takes me with him when he buys lemons for the bar. This interests me because we drive through dreary, sick villages, the heart of this country. Such places, all the poverty spilled in the streets, rags of children everywhere while the mothers sit and sew or pee! Whatever vegetable is in season. That's the diet, a plate of fried greens or tomatoes, on good days a rind of meat. Sad looking people, unprotesting, much too used to this.

In the lemon factory it's warm. There are special heated canteens that turn green lemons yellow in a hurry. Women grade the fruit according to size and color, wrapping the best ones in little papers that make the crate look festive.

How they stare at me, anxious to know what country I come from. I have soft, friendly talks with these swift-handed women who work ten hours to earn less than a dollar. One of them cuts a thick-fleshed lemon and teaches me to eat it with salt. Roberto watches with delight, glad I'm not bored, pleased when they refer to me as his wife.

The sound of rain is becoming intolerable; it's washing away the glamour of Sicily. These dull people are wearing me down. Roberto seems puny and always thinking about money. When there are no girls to look at the town idlers have long, stupid talks about the government. The only thing they ever read is some sort of reactionary newspaper that makes more ado about the killings than politics. Amazing, dreary murders happen every day in this last country, always involving hatchets or other farm implements. The Taormina citizens are proud of their clean record. Of course they have the Greek theater that brings them slews of tourists every year. But what is there to look at in a town like Giarre except mean faces, people who are deep down hungry and call it love.

Roberto and I quarrel often, about all this.

"Yes, you're right," he says, "but it takes time."

What he is really thinking is how he would be better off in Rome where the real money is. When I get angry he shrugs his shoulders, lapses into dialect full of vowel sounds like Arabic, and tells me how I excite him, how he would rather go to bed.

"You don't really care about politics, bella, you need me. I will soothe you."

All right, I slither off with him. He is right but sometimes making love is going off to be slaughtered. Pigs, cows, what a base animal I've become.

Sullen, avoiding the center of the steps where water runs steadily, cursing the mob of cats sitting trancelike against sodden walls, bored by the prospect of going to meet my inferior lover — awful wet world.

The corso is a tunnel where I clatter along in the grim light of the afternoon. My butcher is busy stuffing sausages, a hot water-bottle stuck in his belt to keep him warm. His hands are terrible pushing pork and anise seeds into shiny membranes.

In the grocery Don Vincente is spraying flit. Some of his cats are walking on the counter going after ricotta, some bits of mortadella left in the slicer. He doesn't chase them off, not till the customers come in anyway. I wish I had some appetite; it's such good food when the sun is shining.

"Signora Americana, buona sera," he calls to me. I wish they wouldn't keep greeting me all the time. Can't walk down this street without being saluted twice a day. "Buon giorno" in the morning when I least feel like talking, but one has to answer, "Buon passegio" in the afternoon, they wish you well for everything. "Buona niente," I mumble back, ashamed of myself.

I suppose I am the first person in town to know the sun is back since I do not close my shutters at night. Going to bed is a preparation to enter a tomb. How many times I've avoided Roberto because he can't sleep unless everything is shut tight so that I feel anonymous. In such total darkness there is no telling who is next to you. But an open window is forbidden, one will get a stiff neck or catch a cold. Fresh air belongs outside, so does light. Anyway, how else can you keep out the flies and mosquitos. Sicily is really the darkest place at night. Bombs have fallen here but windowscreens are unheard of.

Sun. At last.

My maid brings up a plate of strange spiny fruit in celebration. "Be careful," she says when my son grabs one. Too late, his palm is full of little thorns that will take hours to get out with pincers and some of them will stay in and fester. Concertina opens the prickly pear with three precise gashes and offers me the startling red fruit inside.

"This is practically what we lived on during the war," she explains. "It's full of nourishment but you must be careful not to eat too many. In the war, when there was so little bread, we ate many of these. Sometimes we couldn't defecate for days after."

She shows me how to lift it out of the skin without getting any spina, and to swallow the seed without chewing. Juicy and cool inside, the rain has been good for them.

Later in the day I watch some boys getting this difficult harvest. They tie a tin can to a long stick, cup the tin over the fruit growing out of a large cactus, and snap it off into a bucket. It seems a nervous procedure, especially after all this rain. No matter, the fruit is good, winter is over.

The sight of him wobbles my groin. Desire flares inside me as the sun on my back. Hot as hell and deep like that; red in all my corners, the thick smell of sex everywhere.

We make love like religion. He lets out my name with his sperm and I feel adored in a way that no virgin has ever been prayed to.

Lapped in waves of good feeling, free and solid my body rises for him. So profound is our contact, today I have forgotten my children. A holiday of the flesh, essential breathing flesh, connective tissue between day and night, before and after love, it's all a rhythm going toward and coming away from actual love which is intercourse.

That in me which can be touched responds only to him. My response is sudden gushes, my inside mucous flesh seems to detach itself from tough walls in an unbelievably painless wave. His very fingerprint is a profound mark on me. Like patterns in the desert, that are, after all, the only sign of anything there, it doesn't matter how lasting. If the wind did not stir the sand the desert would have no movement at all.

Thus I lie under this hot Sicilian sun, sweating at last, waiting for more swells and rills.

For weeks cats have disturbed me. Their baby-voiced pain sends me hunting for a child; I think it is my baby screaming.

There are more cats here than people, thinner, wilder, hungrier. At night they rush around in packs, knocking over garbage cans, eating away at anything. They are stronger, more organized in their hunt than the dogs that pad after them. Also in their lovemaking, for dogs look stupid then, as though caught up in something they had nothing to do with. Cats in heat make such a special noise that nights flare into a new season; sleep is given over to the sound of their lust.

Oddly enough, when I finally succeed in watching two cats mate, it is before noon on a hot, clear day. At night they always disappear into corners I cannot find.

There they are, as unaware of the world as I would like to be, deep in an act so mutual it stuns me. Jealous, I wonder about my own sex; surely it is less profound, copulating with Roberto, a fragment of the passion visible here.

The male is much younger and smaller. He has yellow fur, lion crouched on the old female he holds her nape in his teeth, growling moistly, she underneath him all silent, completely held.

He works a long time. My baby tugs at me, wants something. Some women stop and go on quickly, clearly disapproving of my standing there, so openly watching.

"Desgraziata," they say to the cats, certainly to me. For happening there, in front of that American and her child is an act of night, of hiding. I feel very much their hostility, sorry about it, but not enough to stop watching. I like to see animals coupling. It eases memories of my mother and father on sad-sounding beds, sighs dangling into my thin sleep like broken arms. I used to lie in my little room, in my little body, afraid that nothing else existed except that sound and myself listening to it.

The small yellow male jumps off the old female and they both lie down opposite one another, begin to lick and suck and scratch at the wet they have produced.

Down to the beach to feel movement, the fast tough drive down, the sight of water pushing and pulling.

Up in Taormina one never hears the sea, although it is

everywhere visible as a remote view pretty and undisturbing. It has no sound at all. Taormina so still, so permanent.

Here at the beach the sea makes noise. The sea here is immediate, contingent on itself. It is change. I watch the tough water, so soft from far away, such a dream of water when you look down at it from that eternal town above.

And here — look how water grows into a killer!

The red flag is run up. A bad current suddenly makes my children struggle in the water. Rocks the size of a child's fist are pulling out from under my feet. Roberto yells to get out of there, keeps on dressing himself.

The waves come in hard and yellow, flat with mud. I grab my children and run up the beach, clutching them like stolen flowers.

Then I take each one for a rest. Lying on top of me, the youngest first, how different they are, how varied their clinging to me. My breasts hurt under their weight but I ask of them an impossible tenderness, pushing them against me this hard is useless, children cannot comfort the mother.

This is my real loneliness — lying on top of me.

We float in a huge grotto, the boat threatened by rocks growing like thorns out of the sea. Black, unwelcoming, the cave goes deep, bats live at the back. But the water is brilliant, looking at it I feel upside down, as if it were sky. So blue that swimming in it would surely leave color on the skin. But I am afraid to jump in, too radical a place to enter.

Roberto keeps looking at me, watching my nervous face. I keep very still, make my face hard, don't want to show him anything. Why should he know any more about me; this is a private thing winding among rock thorns, I don't want his comments nor his looks.

"How nervous you are," he says, seeming to like it very much and this makes me feel cold and like his mother. He should not be with me.

I do jump off the boat into that infernal blue, a kind of bravado I detest takes hold of me, forces me toward the end of the grotto where black is waiting. A sudden swell on the water, a motorboat must have passed outside, and I see how far away he is, watching for me, strain showing on his chest where he pushes the oar to steady the boat. I'd better go back, he doesn't swim well enough to save me, would he even try?

My feet scrape on the side of the cave as I turn fast, more afraid than ever now that I sense what a coward he must be. The rock here is purple like a medusa. My son once caught a medusa. Trapped in an empty carton it quivered, really mauve, dangerously beautiful. The afterbirth that oozed out of my body rapidly, I wanted to eat it. It looked more significant than the son just born. The doctor was shocked but he did let me touch it. I was stunned by the look of this glassy, soft flesh that had just left my womb.

The medusa cannot be touched nor eaten and I have warned my son.

There is my son lying flat on the sand, his legs crossed and swaying. He holds a bar of ice cream high over his head, brings it down for the lick, fans it above his head again, looks at it as it melts and drips in the sun.

He eats that ice cream with the complete concentration available to him at six. At this moment I see my son as he would make love and find him beautiful, as though I had already aged to the time when there would be no more envy, nor any more desire to make him my lover.

My fantasy is fabulous. I'm able to imagine the most forbidden. Surely I am a good mother since I know so well when I am not.

The sight of his body reminds me that I can never really touch him. To eat him to eat Roberto. Is my lover the son made possible, returned to me, put back in short blasting thrills, without that pain I bore so well?

Roberto has driven into me like a corkscrew; I cannot disengage myself without losing essential pieces. In these hot patches of afternoon, light and heat gather into direct touch. He becomes light and heat itself, welling around me in absolute contact. Myself turned inside out spills away at him. I am the beach where he ebbs and tides. Windless days moving only in my belly.

Yet nothing gets finished. Sick grows my lust. I feel afraid but it's only here, buried inside this Sicilian tomb, that I can conceive of death, perhaps accept it as the only dignified craving.

Hot light of the Sicilian sun hits me like a rock. Through the window I see the woman next door washing her endless sheets. An ugly creature who screams her way into my life every morning so that I hate right away. No way to wake up except hating noise and light and the things in the room that I can't see clearly because of my bastard eyesight.

She is threatening; her bulk a black hole in the sky. I pull up the blanket to cover the red hole I've become.

All this terror because of my eyes, hysterical vision, blurred, every small light an immense fire, her sheets ride at me in flags, pointing to the prostitute sleeping late.

In the bathroom I look closely at what she might have seen. A frightened, nostalgic search for the gaudy object of the night before; the mirror returns an ugly result of a thin, strained face with spider dreaming eyes, so magnificent at night when she paints herself for the part. Black light not caused by drugs as her friends suspect. Caused by what then? All her fevers.

Yes, Regina of the night, a huge flower nearly a foot in diameter, blooming only in the night. Profoundly open, showing a vast white depth, as I show black in my deep, myopic eyes. Startling to wind around dark streets and find this giant growing, opening. By day a wilted mess of long hanging, worn petals.

That bitch over there, scrubbing her virtue while a tense Sicilian song screams out of her, going past me to the neighbors waiting for her message like savages.

Swimming today was unpleasant, the water too warm.

Scooping my hands through the soft wet, of a sudden I held a medusa. Frantically I let go, shaking away the feel of it. Then I looked down at the vague rocks below, hating my weak eyes. I would always be afraid of it down there. Why not, I couldn't see it. A low pressure feeling made my body heavy, swimming was hard, a tunnel to be dug.

Roberto spread on the sand in an odd, passive position. "Molto pederaste," I tease, standing over him, stealing light.

"Why do you put shadows in front of me," he complains, sliding away in the luxuriant way of a man who pleasures deeply in sex, gives his mare milk freely. A passive gladiator, knowing himself to be potent at will.

"Oh bella, what could be better?" he asks.

"All that which isn't," I answer him.

For him there is nothing casual about sex, it is an absolute and absorbing experience. How it tires and thrills me. I sit inside this rainbow of sensations like a super-sensitive doll, lost but watching. I feel that I control him, that our copulating is an art exercised by me. I need only to use certain gestures and he swoons. My effect on him makes me swoon.

Then I forget him and listen to the termites eating the bed that holds us.

Summer is a violent presence. Too hot now to drive to the beach. I scold my children into the cool house, annoyed by their energy. My son kills flies while the baby pokes at ants. Her milk sours in the glass.

The streets are quiet, a fierce glare on the pavement. In the distance Etna looks ordinary without snow.

The maid uses her umbrella to go shopping. I worry what will please the children. So hard to eat anything in this heat except fruit and vegetables. The best thing is melon, a huge speckled kind with a ruby center. We are all thinner from this diet. Only way to tolerate this weather is to sleep all day and sit in the cafe evenings. Then the piazza is alive again with frantic children. There's no use putting them to bed before eleven, much too hot. My maid wets down the pillow under her head.

"This is nothing," she sighs, "wait till the scirocco blows."

I wish I had the energy to leave here.

Scirocco wraps me in a humid trance. The fish on the beach called Molla, at first I thought it was the fin of a great fish but there it lay, being all of it, really small and dead and gray. Touching it was such a mistake, all slime, with the most sticky smell. I kept digging my fingers into the sand, trying to scrape off the smell, the matter.

Just so is the scirocco fast on me. I sit in space padded by that kind of slime the fish had, the muck that jellyfish are made of.

I look at it all. The sea, the rocks, people; just objects. I'm afraid I will sit like this in another country waiting for a sense of importance, lying, manipulating, to bring back a sense of life. There is no sense leaving here for there is always that formidable silence, that sitting so still that I do better than anyone else, while inside me is movement. I think and think, my hands paralyzed, eyes gone far, staring blind the horizon.

I have sat like this a long time, in a fever of silence. Inside my face is hard, aching tension. All my life stirs in me, pushing at me, begging to be let out.

This seems to be my new madness.

I need this piazza with its lack of view, only sky against which trees hold still and the lanterns flare into several moons. There is only that, and myself on the other side of it.

Now the heat and the mountain are together, fire and size closing up my view. The sky is thick with scirocco and never blue.

As Clarita loved blue with her sapphire ring and the blue, man-tailored suits and blue eyes that I wanted to eat as I have eaten the eyes of carp my mother cooked for me. Who watched me eat the head of the fish and there was no disgust only approval of my taste. The tongue of the fish milky soft, the eyes gelatin soft, soft heads of fish, my mother's eyes love soft on her happy-eating child.

As I wish now to lick the eyes of Roberto because there is nothing disgusting about him. Clarita spoiled my pleasure when she watched me eat the head of the carp. She felt disgust and gave it to me. But Roberto has renewed my desire to eat eyes. I want his. The appetite more important than the eating and thus I know that I am not yet mad. The head of a fish and the head of a man — I still know the difference.

As there is no separation here between sky and water and mountain; it's all together in a humid blur, put before me on this piazza where those few trees still stupidly produce florist-size flowers, dropping into coffee cups. Those trees will never be a forest, will never know the difference.

I realize now how lonely the metaphor; when Roberto was inside me I said: "You are a tree inside me."

For days the air has been too heavy. In cool countries it's this way before a storm but there is no rain for Sicily in August.

Roberto keeps checking the mountain. "That's where it's coming from," he says thoughtfully. "You'll see something happen very soon," he adds, as though he is planning a special gift for me.

And it does. Etna goes into full eruption. A sudden, dull boom calls for attention. There, in a dark moonless sky, twenty kilometers away, the volcano pours and roars out the fire inside it. Hundreds of feet in the air the flames shoot straight up, red as forever.

The town is awake, this hasn't happened in years, not this strong. The air is better now, some of the pressure gone.

I show my children what they have never seen before.

"Are we all going to burn, Mama?"

"No," I answer softly, "it's too far away."

But inside me there is a great fear along with terrific excitement; my body is very hot as though it were a huge erection.

I am so confused by this erupting landscape, I rush towards Roberto who receives me proudly as though he has made this happen. I look for some sense of order, everything appears hot and smolten together. What is male or female anymore? What am I doing with an erection? Oh yes, it's his! But I feel the potent one.

Etna continues to erupt. News of it is in all the papers of the world. Relatives send me telegrams to see if we are all right. Of course we are at this distance, but I feel troubled. The sight of lava boiling down a mountainside, even miles away, is not simple.

My lovemaking is affected. Some nights I only want to be kissed; it's everything for me. In a kiss there is no finishing, only constant hunger and constant eating. Making love is finite; somebody, some organ tires. But in my mouth is every desire and I feel the juice and the teeth and the deep smell of the person I kiss and whose longing for me I suck into me.

Roberto is bewildered yet he follows the contours of my temperament as though I were the mountain we are both excited by.

I begin to despise his lack of protest. His tolerance of me is flaccid, I cannot respect a man who will permit me every caprice. Kissing is not enough, he should know that, should rape me.

After many days of intense, pointed heat the eruption subsides. The climate is radically changed; summer seems over. I long for clean empty cold, so necessary to my burdened self. But winter from here is a rare feat, even in my imagination.

Fretting away time, swinging on people's talk, grasping their faces like fruit falling; a poor harvest, nothing like the appetite inside me.

A blind man passes, blowing on a flute, making sounds so high, hurting, but really music. My breathing stops along with his; together we go to the same high, thrilling place.

But the six o'clock light in the piazza is toneless, not blue.

Seven oleander trees sticking out, dusty, always quiet trees, I never see them move. Wrought iron trees, they might as well be the same species as the lanterns near them.

I put some money in his hand and beg him to play on. He does, his Sicilian face bent over complicated sounds, his face down dragged, trying to please me. But it's difficult to breathe, all the dull green, old, nonmoving growth of Sicily is here in this piazza, in these seven trees. Sound becomes just that and I am no longer interested.

I walk away, out of town, towards the low hills stretched out like a chain of cemeteries. The dead green color; no real green, just shades of black, especially the cypresses, black ties of mourning worn by men, the priest-colored trees.

How annoyed I am, sensing my own fatigue in the tired presence of this ancient country. With those women staring at me, ill shadowed faces pressed against the window of the door, the only source of light. Fat, pale women, engorged from bad food, a bland shortlived look in their eyes. Visions of their dusty organs that will someday dry up and peel away from them like the paint on their decayed houses.

They sit alone or in smudged groups, sewing on their dowries of gorgeous bedsheets. This is the only passion allowed them before marriage, the linen they will bring to the eventual husband must be the finest, scrolled with such tiny stitches that it takes a month just to embroider the edges.

Nearly all wear mourning, their sex gored by black dresses making the curves of them look empty, all wrong. Barbaric religion with its loud, dimestore rites, at the innumerable fiestas these camouflaged women carry wooden saints like lovers, fireworks blasting away the little money earned, on their faces the bang bang joy of childish sacrifice.

Immense bordom that forces me into the manufacture of intrigue, of false sentiment. Grabbing the looks of strangers, finding here a nose, there a mouth that pleases. And the women looked at by me, the sudden man. That lovely Italian girl. I said she is the pillow of a bed and had to explain that it meant the softest, the best part of the bed, of lying down. A woman's face like a soft sigh of relief.

Roberto sitting alongside me in this fog of sex. We do nothing but invent each other's perversities. I am dutifully degenerate, but my face is false; not passionate with desire, but passionate with a desire to feel. Yet there is this thickness, this awareness of sexual importance. The mountain hovers, girls pass, each one appraised and filed away by both of us in a special safety vault of flesh.

This theatrical doom, this smear of a landscape so tired of living, of reproducing itself, having lost all vital organs. Only some desire left and that old, antiquely worn, a patina of what was. A tired stage with pointless drama. Scrub, flowers, no real trees just the worn spears of cypresses.

And yet I feel important here. I have a role, my mirror is Roberto who values all that in me which he cannot name but finds in my bed where I give him, because I can still do that, so much loveliness. Inside me there is something sensitive with many feelers like an octopus, nervous star of the sea.

What happened today except that I laid my head on the legs of Pino.

I had just been swimming, felt a great energy in the water like a bird flying. The water a deep, dangerous sky. Outside the bay the water incredibly cold, made my urine come hot and slow and I lay still to let it happen.

A feeling of rest afterwards, lying against him on the beach, pebbles on my thighs sticking hard, creating ugly toad skin in marvelous colors. I was sure nothing else would happen to me that day; it had all gone in the water.

Roberto up in town, working. He is certainly not jealous of Pino, a homosexual. "You need friends," he says, making pitifully clear his limited function in my life.

I spend hours with Pino. Meeting him is seeing a real shape in a cloud and then watching it disperse. He looks like a man, I cannot believe him when he talks about men, it must all be a trap to make me love his soul. For there is love between us but we touch only with words and certain concentrated looks. I feel a special fear lying on a part of him that belongs to his body. One of us is virgin; I cannot afford to long for him, there is something so deep and erotic between us that any contact can only magnify its impossible dimensions.

Talking with him makes me feel large, round swollen with white light. "Tonight at two o'clock the moon will be full. Try and get away from him." He says this, he who has the moon inside him in big flat circles.

There is my baby twirling her white towel around her in a moon circle. She doesn't know how much I watch her. Thinking about Pino I absorb her complete sanity and am grateful. I think also of Roberto standing so concretely somewhere in his bar. I certainly love those two simple creatures, experience them in the same way.

But Pino with his insistent intellect draws me to him. "You're just using Roberto," he says, "you don't love him."

"I can love many people all at the same time."

"Perhaps, but your love is in pieces, broken into three."

Of course I know what he means but he is only waiting for me to lose my sex while I wait to see his. In the meantime he's revolting. All his physical processes annoy me in small definite beats; just the way he is sucking an orange, juice dribbling on his hairless chest. I recall Roberto on whose body hair grows like experience.

This queer, with his snaky mouth enveloping food, his toenails are enormous, his arms too short. Touching him would be gray as brain skin.

And yet, what must he feel in my presence, he who is so much more delicate than I am. Of course he is homosexual, it's spilled on him like wine, enhancing but also sour. I long for one straight-forward person. Really only children please me now. I am becoming saturated with sex. I shall need a retreat soon.

When the moon is full I visit Pino in his room. He looks so destroyed, lying on a bed, dressed in ugly clothes which make him look washed up. He does so want to be picked up and put together again. In his body, by me.

As I find him there, strewn on that bed, I worry, afraid he'll make a move toward me. I cannot desire him because he is man-woman and I only want simple loving, shape of tulip, penis flower.

"You want everything," he says, as though this is wrong of me. But surely he says this because he can give me so little, that pervert.

Like the eruption of Etna, when I saw too much light, I feel affected by him, confused.

"You're my first Eve," he continues, and I feel disgust at a confession he should make to his mirror since he is his own woman. Pino is every gender put into one body, badly twisted, depressing because of its complex shape. A body would be plain. Being with him makes me swollen in an unnatural way, not at all like being pregnant, my body then a great rich avocado.

Even his mouth is in sections, long snaking over words, and kissing him is kissing parts. Shame rises in me now in the clearest fashion, shame not desire forces me into this impossible pose. I lie crumpled on his bed, part of the particular debris around him. Not a place for sleep here, full too full of books and terrible ripped pages of poetry, where has he gotten all those? Everyone who has ever written lies on his bed, he knows too much, reads to me while the moon hovers dangerously near the window. I know nothing compared to him but he does not know it's shame over my poor exploited body that keeps me from him. I can only think of the perfect athletes he is used to while his head longs for me. But if I am to be his first woman love then I must be perfect and I am not. Thoughts of Roberto who sucks even my toes and becomes potent with the sight of my soft, tired breasts, my mother scars. Fairies only know love in the front or love in the back. Pino fouls my idea of myself. Lousy queer, young and childless, without anything, just the idea of me in his head.

Finally we touch somewhere. He fingertips across my hair which goes limp under his hand. I wonder whether he desires me now or whether he just wants to see how I am made.

Vaguely aggressive his odorless body near me is a thorn spread out as he lays himself flat against me. I follow his position and we are two people in the same coffin.

"I must go."

"You're so incomplete," he accuses, but I do get up, nauseated by this long evening. Later on I will push my face into Roberto, glad to get his smell. His sweat is something good coming at me, his very exudations are appetizing, just as my children's bodies are completely edible, my appetite for the four of them never diminishes.

Now just the face of Pino is left, full sad before me as I prepare to leave, exposed as for a deathmask. He has the air of someone in constant preparation for suicide. But I have enough of him, must leave. His head is separate from his body; he is in pieces and I will not help him. Loving cannot be talked about. He is wrong about everything below his head and his body went away from him a long time ago.

Electric light busts the leaves and palm trees split the sky while we sit in this garden and talk. He is a bottomless pit, graining the landscape. The garden full of ignored flowers in oppressive abundance. No smell at all, only appearance. Field and country unknown here, wailing with cats and dogs in each of which I see my own peculiar disfigurement, depending on the degrees of sadness that makes me either shrug or cry.

With Pino I am frankly sad, allow my face to ugly away. My hair is tight in brain-pulling hurt, I confront with him open suffering. Which he does not believe in. Or does not find sufficient.

"Do you ever tell the truth, or rather do you ever feel the truth?" he asks, his black milk eyes staring into me and I am glad that he does not have as many eyes as the limbs of an octopus. Yet he sucks at me in the same way and I become fish caught, human eaten.

Oh this garden, with that face exposed like an over-ripe melon. Clarita, when she tired of me, threw me away from her like rotten fruit.

Pino is quiet, looking down, deep lines frame his snake mouth. In his swamp of thought he waits for me but my body is right, my mother was a peasant, once she was thick and blood fresh. I saw her working in another garden, a long time down, her animal health leg-spread over the hot growth she tended. It doesn't matter now about her change, the smell of nasturtiums still puts me in a swoon of remembrance.

Here in Sicily I eat the flower itself and come that much closer to the smell of it and I chew at the memories of other beaches where I gathered pieces of amber to save forever but have lost.

I grab at the flowers, at my mother who took care of me then on the white sweet sand. I roll in the smell of her orange love, thick inside the dear flesh of her palms that curve me round with bliss.

Now my own children are the face I wanted to be and I wait for their deep sleeping when I thieve away at those round open faces, finding my mother's love in giving to them. Do finally get full, in feeding I am fed.

Day hazes into night. The flesh trap opens and I fall under Roberto's body. The hair on his chest is so many sculpted flowers. My hand traverses a forest, indescribably mine. I suck at his nipples as at a female fountain held up by a phallus. "I'll split you open with my penis," he says, a passion in his voice that heats me and makes me obey.

When will this end? The pleasure I find with Roberto is wrong, he is not my peer. My talks with Pino have brought me back somewhat; I have loved a better person. But I want Roberto's body, worried over wanting an animal. Never have I gone so against my grain. Why can't I love the right man with all my red flesh? This little man with the delicious skin, I would so much like to respect him. And do not. And continue to sleep with him.

"Your sex is an illusion," says Pino, and I don't know anymore, he has blurred me. Who will save me, will bring me the word? Who will tell me that making love is honest. I do love Roberto if love means everything, including disgrace. His body and mine together are love concrete. Before and after we are dogs and cats, vulgarity and boredom. I do not esteem him.

But the trap shuts hard, banging at me a message that says only this moment, this movement is the truth.

"Stop seeing so much of Pino."

"You said I need friends."

"People are talking."

"Everyone knows he is queer."

"He is still a man."

"You flatter me."

"Bitch, don't play with me!" and Roberto slaps me in the face. "You know I've been patient with you. But don't make me appear a cornuto in front of my friends."

"So that's your problem, not whether I'm faithful to you, but whether your friends think so."

"You can't understand us. You are a foreigner."

"I'm glad, I don't want your problems. You have stupid problems, you think everything is sex."

"Without sex there is nothing."

My face burns. Really quiet pleasant. He looks beautiful, anger comes straight at me like an arrow from a bow. A terrific flush of desire takes me to the nearest wall where I spread myself out as his target.

Goodbye to Pino.

I offered him my hand in the most furtive, fleeting way. He had no time at all to say anything. I did not want him to speak; everything had ended for us. The rest could only be sentiment and lecture.

I cannot forget the startled eyes, the clear pain staring at me, at my cowardly farewell. The fool I'd made of him in loving me.

I left him abruptly as I had done so many times in his house. But this was the last and he knew it and ached from it; I only felt impressed by the expression in his eyes.

There sit the two brothers in front of me. Made of the same flesh, one more beautiful, both with thick graceful skin that I want to bite. I wish to have them both lust for me and put me in bed between them. Imagine two brothers bursting over the same woman!

This perversity is clearly confined to my imagination. If Roberto knew that I even thought about his brother he would probably beat me. A woman belongs only to one man in this country. His brother hardly ever speaks to me for fear of arousing any suspicion. If he cares for me at all, and I think he does, his every intention is to leave his brother's woman alone. Someday I hope to meet him in another country.

Sicily, old, with a tough sense of order. A story in the paper of a woman whose husband was killed. She knew the killer but would not tell the police. She merely pointed to her belly, swollen with child, and said: "He knows, and will attend to it someday."

Vendetta. When I am bad with Roberto he just stretches out his hand, bobs it up and down lightly. The gesture carries a gentle but very precise warning.

Yet I happen only here in the place I resent. Sicily manures me into being. If I could only respect the fruit of me. Rotten, complicated bloom of sex, exaggerated as the flower of a cactus.

Tired, all juiced out. I'm thinner, very fatigued. The doctor recommends an analysis of my blood. But it's all this fornicating that's draining me. Nothing else is any good, or good enough, only with him can I stop thinking. I don't even dare sleep; my dreams are weary reminders that I have no other recourse.

My mother an octopus. Many arms coming out of the very

center, all grabbing me to her soft parts where she may, I permit it, chew me, use me up. I am now the octopus, mucous, held together by soft moist membrane, suckering everywhere. Dreams of unending hunger, interrupted by sleep. I have many mouths and only in the suck-feel attachment of my tentacles do I feel in contact, my reach is long and bizarre. I shudder at the cold touch of many arms that I never wanted to grow but only to have around me from another source.

I find myself like pressed flowers in an old book, dry and faded, an ugly trace of what was once wild and juicy. I look for water to fill me, I drink and swim, Japanese flowers that grow in water and become something. I dive as deep as I can but come up dehydrated.

There is that glossy sun again, open above me like a naked body, while in this Sicily those secret public hills keep on and on, hiding from me. Are they attics and cellars I crept around in with my schoolfriends as we jabbed and scratched into our child bodies looking for hair and holes and black sex? My inside felt exhausted, the dull worn green of Sicilian earth, not growing anymore — only there.

How long is desire when given time enough, Sicily enough?

I wait for an end to this degrading passion. I wish he did not exist, while the sight of him, his teeth, his glittering eyes, grapes spit out, fish bones, his urine, all that is produced by his body excites me.

There are moments of hatred between us, we drift into a mean way, I've reduced him to an exasperated state. He slaps me around, spits. And I need this humiliation in order to feel. Only crisis provokes me.

What will happen to him when I am gone? For I shall get out of this. I am complex, capable of many excitements, a sensual intellectual, and he has also made me beautiful. Never have I looked so well, surely this is the last ripening, my flower fall, myself a ripe fruit in fall. Where to land, where to conceive further?

And he will be left behind to idle away his life in stupid innocence, unwilling to grant me evil, believing that my usage of him has been love. Yet now, while I am here, I am committed to him; a witch ensnared by a fool.

Exposed to myself as that small beach where we wait for a tide that is never high enough. The filth of the Mediterranean remains, more obvious now because of the clean edge.

Roberto is deep in thought and does not feel the wave that spreads over his feet making them shine.

Earlier we argued; he saw me flirting with some tall Swede. I do it on purpose; his jealousy excites me for I am at that point where any effort is an interruption in the blank day, that *vuoto* where nothing happens except when it is beaten into me. I've become the big lax mouth and even ugly food is chewed at; disgust itself becomes something felt, more interesting than ordinary pleasure, pushed down my throat so there is no choice.

"Suck me here," he says and I do, pleased by the command, the actual revulsion layered over by months of effort to be sexually enormous.

"Lick me," and I, aware of my lying face, cannot avoid my duty because I too can see my passionate face in the pupils of his love-frantic eyes. I have conned this boy with my liar charm — I suck and lick and sigh while he is truly involved with a woman he has never expected to love. Small animal that he is, smaller than his emotions, laid across her in tiring ceremony.

"Are you satisifed now, do you still need someone else?"

"Maybe tomorrow," I taunt.

He rolls away from me and goes to sleep. The small beach is dull. I look at the terraced hump of fields behind, a chewed out skyline. Eyes pale in my head; I am not curious.

Ruin of a castle, built by the Saracens, it decays above the town in toothy outline. Not splendid anymore, just a good place to take the children where we play hide and seek.

"Where are you, Mama?" yells the middle one, a girl who looks like a happy version of me. What a disgusting woman I am behind the mother she loves.

I bury myself in the shadow of the castle, wanting to delay her discovery of me. To the west lies Etna, no longer active, nothing but a shadow now, as thin as the dark I'm hiding in. "If only you'd keep on blowing up," I think, "it would keep me moving, anything is better than this dry burden of myself."

It's cold leaning against that dark wall. I'm tired of this game. Why doesn't she find me or is it save me? Yes, my children will save me, they are my only weapon.

How long it seems till she comes, her voice screams closer, "Mama, I'll get you, wait, wait . . . " breaks off in laughter at the sight of me. Her hand is warm pulling me into the sun, her trophy.

One cloud in the whole sky, exactly like wet cotton. There is no wind and that white blob stays there, nearly inside the mouth of Etna. I am determined to sit it out, surely the cloud will move on, nothing up there should be so still, large as a nightmare when the vomit kept heaving up from the bottom of me.

Alone in the night of my mother's garden, my suffering real, visible in spit and bile and tears. She's not there to wipe it off, gone the soft cotton of her breasts. Agony looking at that sky with the stinking stars, burning down to me the first knowledge of infinity. Everthing small and close and warm gone; my mother an abstraction.

I see her in the mountains of Sicily, a face in the dry tough hills where olive trees shrug off indecently small fruit. The age of these trees darker than the Greek ruins spread about here like ordinary facts; history is a carpet to walk on, marble columns are flowers I ignore. My lament is not general — I want only my mother.

The cloud hangs over me. I watch it hopelessly like a mystic fixed on the wrong object. A false symbol as is false my love with Roberto. But I want everything now, my greed established from the very beginning, the mark on my forehead pressed deep by my mother's blundering, blameless hand.

Lusting for a red split mountain but this is not a mountain of a man. He is caving in, his soft parts eroded from my excessive want. "Let me rest a while, it will come back," he sighs, useless next to me.

I go to the bathroom and try, with very cold water, to wash away my affliction. Downstairs some child is coughing in his sleep but I don't have the energy to go see who it is. I'm the one in trouble.

When I am back in bed he puts his head on my breasts where I allow him to remain. He clings to me in the passive way of a helpless child who already dislikes his mother.

"I'm sorry," he mumbles. "As soon as I'm rested I'll go home."

"Don't worry," I answer politely, feeling free of him. If he were suddenly dead it wouldn't matter to me.

"Do you think I should see a doctor?"

"Why don't you wait and see if it happens again."

"Yes, that's true, it's only the first time."

He gets up, dresses with excessive care. "My impotent dandy," I think, "I use you like flowers in a room, distracting from the white wall."

He stands by the window, taller now in his shoes. He says, "You have a beautiful view of my country," his voice too loud in my empty room.

"Hurry up, I want to see the children."

"But they're asleep, they don't need you."

Intensely nervous I snarl, "What do you know about their dreams."

"I'll see you tomorrow when you feel better," and he tiptoes out, in his exit all the cowardice I've suspected in him.

Etna erupts again, but it's a stale event, I've seen it before. Seen by day the fire is weak, a dull red. Let the tourists gape at it, I think and remain in the cafe where parts of strangers' faces rock me in the maze of my past.

I sit in this cooling land. Summer is over, my passionate swimming gone dry. Dogs I no longer love straggle across the piazza.

This is a ride on a badly lit bus taking me from an unhappy place to an indifferent one. Going home from school was like this, not really sad, just pale, lifeless. I felt like the other passengers looked. We were all poorly made statues coming alive at stops and starts, disliking one another.

A certain sleep is riding me, a doze like the underlit buses I've known.

Roberto noses at me with regained confidence. He bullies me into feeling something, but it's flat, my body responds to a habit. He bores me, the town bores me; I've understood everything. This idolatry of a human body — where does magic begin anymore?

The bed is soft, too soft; the covers heavy on me, too warm —
but warm. Outside the air is a hostile mass, inside this bed the heat I
crave is mixed with his particular flesh. Has no one ever loved me
like this? Is that the clue? He wants to give me his blood; I will let
him.

Again he is a gorgeous statue all mine, lost in me. I am
absorbed by the hard penis and the soft red wet of his mouth. How
difficult it would be to lie alone in the wind outside . . . . He does
mean something to me after all, he is my deepest physical sense, the
one I least understand, or least satisfy, or most — I don't know even
this anymore.

Sloppy drunk, the corso yawns ahead like a tunnel, I push on, the
hell with walls, I just want to get through.

"Guarda la Americana," I hear in the shops. My condition is
obvious and I don't care, I wipe my hands along the windows just
for spite.

I feel bad, crippled, the sky a near dampness in my bones. I
ache; wrong color on the walls, the narrow street is one big stone.

Finally the arch that opens to the piazza. I need coffee, Italian
coffee stuck into me like an injection of energy.

There's Roberto, my little horse, sitting all tight and vanished
in himself, waiting among the bad sounds, his voice harsh in
greeting: "Ubriaga, sit down before you fall."

That voice, low, of a small man, bent against peddlar songs
more powerful than his. The fish dart of vulgar speech drones at
me: "Cattive," he hisses, and pulls me into a chair. People are
staring. "Your children should see you now."

I've heard that. Now I sit still, in false dignity on the auction
block of this market where I have sold myself to undignified
pleasure. He fills my vagina as I fill time, waiting for an end.

So it's possible to adore legs and shoulders, the place where
teeth are set. Look at him, what a passionate ornament he is. Anger
and frustration have colored him into a man. He's holding onto my
arm as though it were his. Having lost respect for all else, what
remains? Only parts of the body. What a limited cult. Here I am on
my knees in filth, praying over a groin.

Can one survive without killing? I need his death as I need
health.

The real disgrace is in the drink poured down during the act of disgracement.

"Look at you, you haven't even washed your feet for me."

"Get me a drink."

"Wash your feet."

"Spit on them."

I drag out of bed, wipe up his saliva, my body naked as a cross.

"What a beautiful back you have anyway," he says in a forgiving way.

A long pull at the bottle to help swallow this merda. Then a pill, enzyme to digest the merda, color of dirty tongue licking away at my self esteem, whatever that was, I can't remember. There are only traces of something I recall and which continue to feel heavy. But lick, suck, squeeze away loneliness; hate is better than an empty bed.

After such love — oh mother, forgive me — my body lies in a crazy heap. Head splitting, eyes breaking open, afraid to look. But also afraid to lose this mad pattern, it does interest me, it does eat time. Pour down more drink, another pill, avoid health for it may mean death. Certainly someone will have to be eliminated.

Oh my fantastic affliction, are you feeling weak? What can I give you now, or what will you take away from me? Who will I be when you leave, and where are you going?

To my children?

I hate you. I shall destroy you, not Roberto.

Oh children, do not open the door if I am not your mother.

I send my maid away for a few days, hoping that work will put a straightjacket around me.

She will visit her family in a hilltown close by where the harvest is on. "Come on Sunday with the children, I'll show you how we press the wine."

"Yes, I want to see that, want to see new things."

"But where is she going, Mama, who will take care of us?"

"I will, of course."

"Oh you're always tired, or visiting friends."

I look at them, aghast at how far things have gone.

"Well, I was tired for a while, now I'm o.k. and we'll have fun."

They still believe in me. Together we set the house in order, go shopping. I feel well protected walking down the very street where I stumbled so recently. "I'll make you pancakes for supper just like in America."

We buy strawberry jam and lots of apples, hard and yellow, grown on the slopes of Etna. Don Vincente gives each of the children a candy.

We scatter on down the corso, nothing seems to get in the way. Through the arch and into the big golden piazza where I lose them like balloons.

I rest on the steps of the cathedral and watch them play. Across the street I see Roberto working over the cash register. He beckons to me but I gesture no, no, too busy with the children.

He comes over with some cakes for each of them. My son declines, "Yeah, I know, now you'll just talk to him and we won't have any fun."

"Don't be silly," I answer, "Take the cake and let's go on to the giardino publico."

Safe among them in the public garden. It's a formal tropical garden like a painting by Rousseau. All kinds of flowers, even daisies lushed out into trees. Nothing is small, hibiscus the size of a hand, trumpet flowers, flesh-thick, grown to man-eating size, with a smell so deep. They say if you sleep under them you can never wake up.

The sun is digging at me, tiring and complicating my view of this Sicilian growth repulsive with overproduction. Never dying but also never beginning, it's a still place where I have seen hills retain the same color for nearly a year, a dreadful green, lacking all vitality.

In the middle of it all stands Etna, the top of her black, bare as a bone. "Look at the mountain," my daughter says, "It must be very thirsty."

Sunday morning we drive to Granite, a town built on the rock it's named for. A bleached succession of stone huts blending into the background like rubble.

Concertina, very clean and glad to see us. Her mother and father shake my hand in a formal way. He's old and small, a tough remnant of a man. He leads us into the house, and we all sit down at a large table. The mother cuts some rude bread. We drink a toast with wine that's almost blue it's so strong.

Then it's quiet. A lot of flies gather around us. The old woman scatters them away from the bread I am shocked by the many creases in the palm of her hand, as though she's cut herself too often.

Concertina shows us the house, steps leading to the plain room where she was born. She opens a wooden trunk and counts through the linen she has prepared for a dowry. "What a lucky husband you will have," I say to show my appreciation. It's pleasant to be here; these are kind people who see no evil in me and so I have none.

We talk about America, look at pictures of relatives who live there. The mother has me describe the subway, "Yes, yes, just like our bus when it goes through a tunnel." She shivers, "It's so cold then."

I look around at their belongings. So little else except the beds, the table. The kitchen is merely a recess in the main room, with charcoal fire and some water in a pitcher. One large, highly colored religious scene is the ornament on the wall which is painted a pale cold blue. These people could move out of here with very little fuss. On this quiet Sunday poverty seems an attractive state.

Later we all walk down the miserly street to the tavern. In the back room, on a platform, some boys are stamping on a pile of grapes with bare feet. It's very damp and cold, their feet are blue, toenails black from the stain of grapes.

The juice runs off the platform into a barrel from where it will be strained and poured into bottles. The smell is terrific, fresh and sour at the same time.

In the gloom of this cavern the boys treading look like prisoners. They are young unhealthy creatures, they make the sunlight we've come from a memory.

My children are restless. I buy some tepid Coca Cola to drink in the bright street. My son drops his bottle and some dogs rush over to lap at the mess.

"Let's go to the oil press," Concertina suggests.

We continue down the street, dogs following, in each doorway some people are staring at us.

Another cave with a large wooden press with more boys turning it. I wonder what's happened to the men in this town. I feel ill from the rancid odor, the viscous product looks dreadful.

"We must be getting back," I tell the maid. "You'd better get ready."

"But my mother has a meal for you."

"Good, the children must be very hungry."

We go back to the house and I try to eat the pasta heavy with oil and tomatoes. "I'm sorry, Signora, my stomach is not good today, forgive me if I don't finish."

"You must make your lady some camomile tea when you get home, Concertina."

The maid looks at me strangely.

On the way back, the baby falls asleep in her arms. I feel sad and jealous, wish I were going back without the maid so the baby would have just me again.

I drive too fast, want to get finished with this dreary ride. Approaching Taormina, the lights of the town glow like pearls in the dusk, a necklace of wealth awaits us up there.

The piazza is lush with people in Sunday clothes. The church door is wide open, an elegant light streaming out as from the lobby of a great hotel.

The cafe is full of Sicilians from Messina. They always come on Sunday night to have a treat, to look at tourists. As I enter the terrace, pushing my way through ample families eating ice cream, drinking sodas, I feel a hundred curious eyes on me. Fortunately I've put on a skirt and some high heels, it just won't do to wear pants and sandals on these nights, it makes me more of an oddity than I already am with my straight hair and pale lips. Anyway, a woman is not considered "elegante" unless she is dressed the way they are. I've not been able to convince Roberto that to be casual is to be chic, he'll approve of my costume tonight, I'm sure.

Finally I see him, way in the back, watching over the waiters as they carry trays out of the kitchen.

He looks nasty and busy; I suppose I ought to come back later when there's less work but I want to be near him. The sight of him makes me feel heavy, not in a good way but complex, too full of something.

"So you're back for more," he mocks, not standing up to greet me. My excitement falls apart like a badly wrapped package. There's nothing inside me now except the awareness of fraud. I feel ugly as he looks me up and down.

"You look very tired from all your hard work, maybe you'd better sit down here," he adds in a bland voice.

I realize then that he is play-acting, he is trying to hide his pleasure at having me back. But who can pay the price of this tawdry bit of theater except myself?

That night I watch his eyes go flat, absolutely under my reign, while his body over me is sodden with joy at mounting me again.

I have a squalid sense of victory. I do not desire him, all this now is patience on my part, an animal loneliness and also a kind of whoredom. Next, thinks a whore; next, think I.

Clearly the fever in this unlovely affair is in the vulgarity. Truce, calm found only in bed after the act. A bad calm, full of knowledge that this sweet exhaustion is momentary, that in the daytime our ugly tempers will muck all that went before. But the fight is unfair; I am superior even though I seem to lose. I allow him to win as soon as I feel his stark, desperate love. For I am sure that the only tender moments in his life are with me. Underneath his dreadful breeding, inside the heart of this merchant there is a soft man, seen only by me, his first love.

I am his bread in a starved country where he was taught to distrust gentleness. "Only a *jufa,* a fool, gives to a beggar what he himself might use some day."

He says this and shows me trunks of clothes he can no longer wear, stacks of junk that he can't throw away because some of it might be useful someday. "Someday," this is the slogan of Sicily, decrepit from centuries of vengeance, where fear of the Mafia is greater than the fear of God.

This flesh bath is growing tepid. I begin to smell him. Horrid preoccupation with new details of him, smells, gestures. Even as I use him night after night the judgement of him continues. The decline brings nastiness but I savor it; survival is an ugly struggle. Success is in one more tentacle to make me more fit in this complicated world. I am an octopus swimming off in a new direction, quickly, so that my arms will not pull me to pieces inside the trap.

Watching him eat, I really must leave the table. Terrible mixing of foods in his mouth, eating with such concentration. That which makes him exciting in bed oddly enough makes him intolerable in common life. Real gluttony. How vulgar this insistence on doing only what he is doing, as though he has killed the rest of life. He gorges himself, is made nervous and sick by his appetite. He cannot accept more than what he can hear or touch. There is so much more, but he is afraid.

He washes, washes before and after love, keeping busy, shutting out the afterward, which is for me the only reality. What I do with him, what he considers the real present, I think of as a lapse in me, a jump toward earth in a dubious parachute, longing for the solid creaking plane above me plowing through an abstract beautiful sky, arriving nowhere—but having been everywhere.

It's true that I needed him to fill the blank present. But to love him could never hurt me because I never valued him. My investment was small, worth a piece of skin only organ deep. I can cut him out as one can cut the genitals of a man — as one can never cut off the real, slow sadness of thought.

My past is a train that he has boarded and it is here that I sever myself from him. As we sit under the same motion, while I think, he picks his feet and reads the paper. Nearly everything passes by him. He does not sink into the gloom produced by motion which must be felt if one is more than animal. He knows only that life is inconvenient while for me the train keeps on, the view moves and I am moved.

There he sits, irritating me. Just the sound of pages turning, his cough, are reminders of my disgrace when my sex deceived me and tried to be all of me.

Wretchedly, graph clear, the downward curve races on. This hot confused affair, once a complicated maze in a formal garden, becomes a simple descent. I've worn him down, he scratches in an effort to caress. And what is left for me except occasional wet drunk explosions into emotion more remembered than felt, a phony tenderness as I accept and also resent the ending which is happening.

He tries to beat me back to the original time and chills at my passivity where once I hit back, aroused by any kind of touch, excited by his very fingerprint.

The long season is over, it ends clearly as these November days sharpen and widen in view. Scirocco has left; the sky is blue by day and blue by night. The moon is strong seen, no mist. The mountain is so lucid that it seems smaller.

My humid trance is over.

With terrible logic my sense of nausea has become actual; I vomit in the morning for a whole week till I finally suspect, no accept, that I am pregnant.

Disgust, nausea, irritation, exactly these three; they are my lover.

And I?

Split, torn, sobbing self. An octopus born in the twin month. But my suffering is not divided. There is no doubt in me. I will not carry this man's child.

I see my three children and there is no dilemma. To love them means to hate this foreign object inside me. To conceive a new life one must respect it, and I despise Roberto whose tool I've used, turned against me now as a boomerang.

When the pygmies kill a female elephant the best of the hunters climbs into her womb and then cuts his way out in fierce celebration.

Oh no, the problem is not what to do but how to go about doing it. I want a very brief ritual.

Concertina is not surprised. "I've worried about you for some time, the way you don't eat. But anyway, what do you expect the way you've been carrying on."

"Don't judge me, just help me."

"What about him, what does he say?"

"He doesn't know. I don't want him involved in this."

"You Americans are crazy. He's had his fun with you, why shouldn't he pay for it?"

"Because it's not his fault."

"Well he did it, didn't he?"

"No. I let it happen. Now enough of this. Tell me where to go and then be quiet."

She stares at me; the line between servant and master is thin.

"This is a bad country for women, Signora. There's not a priest who would help you now. They get fat from our sins."

"I know. That's why I'm counting on you."

"But I've no right to help you."

"Do you want to, Concertina?"

"I guess so. I don't know, I'm scared."

"I'm pregnant."

A long silence between us. We're sitting in the kitchen, two women alone. Her simple face looks as sad as any I've ever seen.

She gets up and draws a glass of water, drinks and offers the same glass to me.

"Go and see old Maria, she knows a lot."

Her voice absolves me; the servant has set the master free.

I find Maria's house in the poorest part of town, where there are no streets only vague steps leading down. Steps so narrow, I stumble and feel blind, find the way again, hooked to the last light of afternoon. It will be easier going back.

Rabbit skins nailed to the wall, outside, inside. The yard is gorged with live rabbits, nasty red-eyed animals, much too soft.

She kills them expertly, one neat pull severs the head from the spine. A gash, and the animal is turned inside out.

"One must work for a living," she says, her face so calm and so old that I instantly believe in her.

"Wait till I finish, the butcher is waiting."

In her hands the transition between life and death is so smooth that it's hardly worth watching. I smoke some cigarettes, while she goes on killing, cutting, nailing.

"So you've heard about me?"

"Yes, they say you know the truth."

"Why not, why only talk about good things. I am not a gypsy."

"Will you do it?"

"As you can see, I do everything, just as you want everything."

Black eyes fever into me. My hand in hers is a quivering rabbit. Her vision spurts at me like blood; I am the creature wounded.

"Lie down and let me have a look."

She pushes up her sleeves and goes to the faucet, begins to wash her hands with a green lump of soap. My sigh interrupts her. I lean against a soft wall where the fur of dead animals is nailed in rough squares.

"Don't be afraid, it's only a little pain."

There's no use arguing with a witch, I just leave.

Going up the steps I take a last look down at this wrong place. I need a bigger country.

The first snow has laid a cool glove on the mountain. Soothed, I am able to breathe again, my loneliness is clear fresh air.

That meal is over. Having truly eaten him, I must now rid myself of him. Only a doctor can help me. What difference now another pain, another killing. How true that it becomes easier to live this evil, cutting life. The aborting knife will disinvolve me; a cool clean instrument will erase this last remnant of the humanity that was present in those long repeated moments of red forgetting.

ANNA WINTER

Under the nom de plume *above, Olympia Press has brought out the first two short novels by an American lady writer.* Sicily Enough *is a portion of* Flesh and Blood.

Jett Sage

Crazy Wild

A Jaguar XK-E Coupe sounded the traditional ta-ta-ta-ta; tum tum, at the edge of the field, and a sling-shot roadster let out a WOW wow wow wow . . . as it roared past with a dragster in hot pursuit. "Piss like a cow; Fuck like a duck; Mama wants a dick in the asshole!"

Odin looked at the two girls on the hood of his Ferrari, they crossed their legs, he looked at Baby Doll, she picked her nose—he looked at Daddy-O. "Look, Pops," he said, "if you're not just a rattler, we'll race you . . ."

Daddy-O flushed slightly. "Rattler?"

"Big talker."

"Oh," Daddy-O took out a bankroll. A Spade Cat moved an arm through the air and grinned. "Stickm?" he said. A gravity knife dropped into his hand from his sleeve. With a flick of his wrist a six-inch blade came leaping out of the handle. "Stickm?" Odin shook his head without taking his eyes off Daddy-O. On the field a Corvette Sting Ray made a fade test: accelerating to 100 m.p.h. in a few seconds, then skidding to a stop and accelerating again. A souped-up Studebaker Avanti drove up to *la linea* and stopped next to a Porsche 2-liter Carrera.

"Five hundred dollars," said Daddy-O. "I can beat any freebie on this track."

Odin watched a dog sniff around the Porsche and raise a leg against it. The driver cursed and got out. He took a flying kick at the dog and fell flat on his ass. The dog ran on a few feet—then stopped to watch him. The driver jumped up and ran after it, throwing rocks and gesturing his arms savagely. The dog took off across the field, howling.

"I knew a guy who drove under a stud horse in a Jaguar," said Daddy-O. "You shoulda seen what happened to him."

"Rained, huh?" said the Spade.

"No. He gave birth to a half-jaguar and half-horse. When it ran out of gas, he could ride it to a garage."

The starter came over to them. She was a beautiful bitch who wore her white hair long over her ears, brushed back with Command. Her skin was pale and under the white brows her eyes, although actually colorless, appeared pink because blood vessels were visible in her retinas.

"You run off from a standing start," she said. "OK?"

Odin nodded and put on a blue fibre-body crash helmet.

"Winner takes all," said Daddy-O. Then: "Hey—" he grinned at the albino. "Do me a favor, willya, chick?"

"Sure," she said.

He gestured. "Spit on me."

"*Whaaaaaa . . .?*"

"Spit on me!" He gestured again.

The girl looked at Odin and shrugged her shoulders. Then she threw her head back and spat squarely in Daddy-O's face. Strings of saliva ran down his cheeks.

"Thanks," he said. "Thanks ever so much."

"What'd you want me to do that for?"

"What for?" Daddy-O exclaimed in surprise. "You're an albino, ain't you? You bring good luck!"

The girl looked at Odin again. He shrugged and slid into the Ferrari, buckling on his shoulder harness and safety belt.

"Here they come!" someone shouted excitedly.

A deep rumble of exhausts rent the air as the other cars came up to the line. Pimples poured his Rag-Top into the narrow space between the Ferrari and Daddy-O's AC Cobra. The Cowboy drove his Deuce up along the other side of the Ferrari and two freebies put their sports coupes on the outside positions, bracketing and holding the line-up like a pair of matching book-ends.

"Watch out for that Uncle Daniel," the albino told Odin, jerking a thumb toward Daddy-O's AC Cobra. "It don't look like nothin' but it's got one of them big Ford V-8's inside."

"Um." Odin gave her a knowing smile. "Sure, chick; but quit coming on like that. Don't you think I've been around?"

The albino winked.

Baby Doll came across the field from the woods, running heavily but fast. She stuck her head through the Ferrari's window and pulled his face up, her fingers under the jawbones at either side of his throat. Then she kissed him, not quickly and not softly—but slowly and roughly, as a lover would. His throat worked hard and steady, drinking in the sweetness and dew from her lips. His hands moved around her neck and down her back to where his fingers found her buttocks, though there was not much to find. He cupped each little mound, making a crevice in the back of her shorts.

"All right, you freebies, *La linea!*"

The albino walked into the glare of headlights, drawing an enormous shadow along the ground. READY. She raised her hands over her head and stood with legs wide apart, giving the starter's signal. Flame-throwers exploded; roars and growls echoed and re-echoed across the meadow, then faded to throb with waiting power. AIM. Toes stabbed the gas pedals, restlessly gunning the motors. FIRE! She jumped into the air like a cheerleader and the line of cars leaped forward with head-snapping jerks, the dust from their spinning wheels tossing and whirling in clouds around her.

The sixth car, the Ferrari, let the others get off the starting line before it growled after their bouncing taillights. Odin knew that Pimples and the Cowboy had expected to sandwich him between them. Up ahead the two cars slammed into each other with a dull thud of metal against metal: like garbage cans—or two palms smacking together, expecting to smash a fly. Through the showers of dirt and gravel Odin saw the Deuce and Rag-Top sideswipe again and spurt swiftly down the field. One of the coupes tried to cut off Daddy-O's Cobra but he spun his wheel sharply to the left and burned rubber—ramming furiously across the ruts in the field. A second later he poured on the power and the white Cobra sputtered and roared, outrunning the coupe. Behind Daddy-O and the freebie Odin got into a dog fight with Pimples and the Cowboy. Jockeying for positions the three cars boomed down the straight when suddenly the Ferrari put all its horses to work and shot between them—its speedometer inching past 115, past 120, hit 140, then 145. A minuter later the Cowboy crashed into a coupe and went flying over the hood, screaming—his Deuce skidding around, spinning sideways, then rolling across the field like a toy, coming to a stop upside-down, its wheels turning. The coupe balanced on two wheels for a time—its tires smoking as the driver pumped his brakes. Then it bounced back on all fours and went howling after the pack. Ahead of the Ferrari Daddy-O was having a battle royal with the Rag-Top driven by Pimples. In a dead heat with one coupe, and hot on the tail of another, the Cobra rolled back and forth across the field, trying to find a place to pass. At the end of the track the cars slowed down, hitting their brakes for the ditch-turn and the long race home.

This was when Odin made his move.

Spotting an opening he shoved the Ferrari alongside the Cobra

and between the coupes, heading straight for the ditch at a hundred
and fifty. Then suddenly his foot jumped off the accelerator and hit
his brakes. Straining against the safety harness he spun the big white
steering wheel to the right, slamming his foot back on the gas pedal.
The front wheels skidded around—sending spray upon spray of
gravel banging against the underside of the car. A row of furrows
gouged into the ditch as the rear end skidded sideways and around
in a wild U-turn. Digging gravel his wheels tore into the dirt and
leaped forward. There was a sudden wail of hot tires behind him,
and then the ditch exploded. A rock churned up by another car
struck his window, running a spider-web across the glass. A second
explosion followed and a great ball of solid red flame reflected in
his rear-view mirror. One of the freebies had crashed—like a bomb
exploding. Suddenly a bolt of lightning hit his eyes and the Rag-
Top's blazing headlights careened toward him. For a moment he
was blinded; then his vision returned. He cut to port sharply, his
tires squealing as he raced by the car with his speedometer needle
on the peg: too fast to see anything, except a blur of Pimples' face.
The Rag-Top had become sick near the edge of the ditch. A slimy
black wake of oil spread across the track. He fought his wheel and
went into a spin: ending up backward near the trees at the side of
the field. Shifting quickly into low he stepped on the gas and made
a hairpin turn as a charging car—the Cobra—slid slowly onto its side
in the oil-slick and big Daddy-O flew low, scraping along in a
shower of sparks and flames. Then, jumping the Ferrari into high,
he looked down the straight. Over the ditch a gigantic ball of smoke
rose into the sky. He shot by the Rag-Top's oil vomit and raced past
the coupe where one of the freebies lay on one elbow, staring with
empty eye-sockets towards *la linea.* The coupe's gas tank had exploded and cremated the boy on the spot.

With its pipes blatting powerfully across the battlefield the
Ferrari went into a turn and swung around the Deuce that lay like a
dead horse with all four legs in the air—one front wheel slowly
spinning. Sliding up to *la linea* with a squeal of brakes, and rear
wheels dragging, he skidded to a stop six inches in front of the
albino.

Everybody was drunk and yelling around. A covey of Fords
and MG Midgets were already starting to pull out. Odin unbuckled
his shoulder harness and belt, removed his crash helmet and went

over to the albino who sat on the nerf-bar of a '65 Chevy. The albino reached into her tight dungarees and produced the pot: $1,500.

"Winner takes all," she said. "Maybe I can help you spend it? . . ."

"No thanks," he said.

"I live in Kissimmee, just down the road a ways," she shouted as the cars whanged past. "Stop by for the Rodeo, why don't you?"

"Some other time," he said.

The dust and the noise rose thick and heavy. He went back to the idling Ferrari and sat under the steering wheel, shifting into low. Then he swung the car about and raced down to the ditch. The crackling of burning oil and an occasional *whuff-ff* or *plopp-pp* when flames found a new pool of gasoline were the only sounds. The number two coupe was a mass of seared and twisted steel, half submerged in the slick, oil-smeared water. Black smoke rose from the wreck and the rubber-smell was overpowering. Odin cursed and was out and walking toward the ditch when two freebies brought up their buddy. The boy resembled a mammy singer—all black except around the eyes and mouth. Then his charred smoking clothes came into view over the ditch-edge, and in the brief second he stood against the flames and great dirty cloud of smoke, someone giggled and the others, seeing him stand there like a comic firecrackered cat-thing in a Tom-and-Jerry movie cartoon, began to giggle also. And when he took a goose step and fell flat on his face the crowd roared with laughter. A Looney Tune. Odin started to laugh too, although he knew the boy was hurt bad. The boy thrashed furiously on the ground and his penis erected through his torn pants as he suddenly let out a bubbling scream of pain. One of his fellow freebies called for a first-aid kit and a battered metal box with a red cross on its lid was relayed through the eager hands of the gang, as if it were the elixir of life itself.

The man with the first-aid kit dropped down on one knee beside the Burn and opened the metal box. He looked inside. It was half empty with junk—flat tubes of nothing, rusty razor blades, strips of soiled bandage, a roll without adhesive, empty bottles, bits of blackish cotton and a six-inch screwdriver. In a corner he found a partly squeezed out green-and-white tube, and he unscrewed the cap and let a ribbon of light yellow ointment curl and loop across his fingers. Then he gently rubbed it on the Burn's cheek and the horny black skin slipped away, sticking to his fingers, exposing sickly white bone, slick raw flesh and small drops of red-streaked suppuration that ran down the burnt face. For a stupefied second the man sat with his hand still out. Then he jerked it back and tried to snap the sticky black flesh from his fingers. But it would not come loose. "OhmiGod, the son of a bitch is fallin' apart on me!" he said. He got up stumbling, snapping his fingers, cursing with that stupefied expression, saying "OhmiGod.—OhmiGod!" He stooped; picked up a stick and scraped the foul black slime out from between his fingers. Then vomiting, he flung it and the stick both in the ditch. Behind him the Burn clawed at the ground and moaned, "Oh Jesus. Oh God. Oh Christ," then, "Help me, sweet Jesus. Ooooh! Jesus help me. Kill me. Kill me. Kill me. Oh, oh! Jesus, oh Jesus stop it. Stop it! Let me go. Oh God wonderful wonderful God let me . . . Oh, Jesus, oh, Jesus, *don't!* Oh oh oh *don't!* Somebody kill me oh Jesus shoot me. *KILL MEEEEEE—*" and then he died.

The night was very quiet. Odin looked down at the Burn. He felt nothing. *"Banzai,"* someone said softly. *"Banzai,* you motherfucker. May you live ten thousand years!" He did not look at the Burn again. He walked on past him and followed the skid marks on the ground. They were easy to read. The weird flames played across their shadows, burning them into the earth at the edge of the ditch. They spelled *Kamikaze.* Like a Japanese pilot making a suicide attack with his plane, the driver of the coupe had made a dive at the AC, striking it amidships, attempting to ram it into the water. But the smaller car bounced off and accelerated away from trouble—so it was the coupe that plowed into the ditch and met its doom in the "Divine Wind"—*Kamikaze.* The AC had continued on a wavering course along the edge and Odin followed the wheel ruts.

In the eerie light, about twenty-five yards from the burning coupe, he saw the AC balance motionless in the mud: rear wheels up in the air, nose buried in the dark water of the ditch. Daddy-O was sitting with his chest wrapped around the metal-rimmed steering wheel, his head wedged hat-deep in a jagged windshield hole. The engine had been driven back through the frame of the car, making a fatal spear of the steering column, the red shaft passing completely through him. It stood out from his back, naked and pointing at the starlit sky, encircled by the white-red splinters of shattered spine bones. A frothy river of hot blood rolled along his back, soaking his shirt, running down and away from his ribs to clot in the cold channel water. Two hyena-like creatures were hunched over the body. One was a husky boy with a harelip and hair cropped so close that it was only black fuzz on the bullet shape of his skull. The other was Pimples. They stood waist-high in the red water, and they were working on the dead man's mouth. The Harelip had his thumbs sunk to the knuckles in the talcum-powdered cheeks, forcing the mouth open while Pimples knocked the gold teeth loose with a ballpeen hammer and pulled them out, one by one, with a pair of pliers.

An owl hooted nearby, and, from farther down the ditch came the booming and grunting of frogs. Somewhere, far away, a calf blatted.

Odin stood for a moment studying the stars. It was past midnight, maybe one, and he would have to get the hell out of there. From the furrows in the soft earth along the ditch-edge he could see that the sports car had leaped forward completely out of control after being hit by the coupe. The car had been traveling at more than ninety miles an hour when it went flying over the edge and nosed into the bottom of the ditch. The AC's forward motion was stopped instantly, but Daddy-O kept flying forward at ninety miles an hour, until the steering shaft speared him.

Odin raised his hands, cupping them at the side of his nose, like a hog-caller, and made a blood-curdling *Heeheeheehee whoop!* sound. "Come on up outta there you goddamn hyenas," he shouted.

They straightened with a start, then turned and stared up at him, standing there at the top of the ditch, with his long shock of blond hair whipping in the wind.

"Fuckth you!" It was Pimples, shouting in that sick voice of his. They turned back to the dead man and the hammer sounds continued, tapping away in the night-silence.

Odin walked slowly along the edge and picked up a rock and a half brick as he crossed in front of them. "Come on, move!" Rocking back on his feet he threw with the same fast, effeminate flip of the wrist he used when throwing a knife. The stone hit the Harelip with a sodden smack. Then there was a solid *whack* when the brick struck Pimples—and splitting; crumbling it sprayed a faint cloud of dry, pallid dust into the pus-filled papules on the side of his face.

"Yuh bathtard!" yelled Pimples. "Yuh motharfuckin' bath-tard!"

They came toward him, wading waist-deep but fast: their thick overalled thighs working awkwardly through the water, arms waving and bodies swaying. Then they clambered up the side of the ditch, sliding and slipping, ankle-high in ooze and black slime and rotting vegetation. Pimples, who reached the top first, was covered with soil and slime. He carried a dank smell with him. Climbing heavily over the edge after him, the Harelip followed, soaked and foul-stained. Pimples was leering. His colorless lips stretched to show one yellow tooth in the wormrot mouth that had somehow escaped Odin's stomping boot earlier in the night. He was swinging the ballpeen hammer against the palm of his hand and water drops kicked up little puffs of dust by his feet. The ugly Harelip was at his shoulder, looking at a stag-handled hunting knife, feeling its edge on his thumb, stropping it on a leather sheath that hung wet and dripping from his jewel-studded cowboy belt.

Pimples tossed the ballpeen hammer from one hand to the other.

"Ah don't lak a pretty boyth," he said. "But bah Gahd, Ah'll lak yuh, boyth, aftah Ah gets thru wid yuh." His mouth bared in a sunken grin. "Cause yuh won't be so gahdam pretty den."

The Harelip looked up from his knife and laughed idiotically.

"Pritty," he haw-hawed. "Why, dollink, he's bee-yoo-tee-ful!"

Odin said, "Thank you, Zsa-Zsa."

For a moment there was only the drowsy insect murmur, the distant booming of frogs, the drifting fireflies and the sounds from Pimples' mouth, laden with mouth reek.

"Ah'm gawnta whup yuh good," he said. "No gal's evah gahn to look at yoah face again, boyth!"

"Yair." The Harelip moved forward a step. "And I'm a-goin' to stick this here shiv into your pouch and pop out your nuts—" he said softly, with pleasure. "Then we'll shove them on a stick and roast 'em. Ever taste roasted nuts, mahn? They're the most. Swell up in the heat, see? Get kinda dark like marshmallows. I dig them the most, mahn . . . all them male hormones."

They began to walk slowly toward him while he, just as slowly moved back.

Pimples leered at him. "Tell him 'bout the niggah."

"Yair, mahn," said the Harelip. He smiled at Odin. "This-a niggah come down from Noo Yawk to visit his cousin, lives in Orlando. Dicty-lookin' sonofabitch. Skinny boy, but tall, more'n seven feet and black as a mule's ass-hole . . ."

"An' he lakt tuh mess wid white meat," Pimples broke in.

"Smelled o' Palmolive and his hair was flattened down with a pound of pomade," the Harelip went on to Odin. "Wore re-al catty clothes too and walked around lookin' bad—you know, de diddley-bop strut?"

He demonstrated the Negro's knee action.

"Spent all summer hanging around that ice cream stand out-side the bus station in Orlando, calling after the white girls. So we got a lettle blonde chick to give him a tumble. Mahn-oh-mahn, you shoulda seen that black sonofabitch grin when he got into the car with her in front of all them local niggahs. Them big white teef showed in his mouth lak sugah lumps."

Stealthily, step by step, they moved forward and, in a couple of more steps they would have him pinned against Pimples' car.

"So she done brung the niggah out to this very field and he was tryin' to get into her when we come out of the woods over there and ax him what he was doin' to the po' little innocent uncolo'd chile. Well, mahn, up he jumps pullin at his trousers, tryin' to get 'em over his pecker. He was an awful tough niggah . . . but only when he was with other niggahs. They're like that. Alone niggahs act like angels, but when they get together, they change. Well, this niggah wasn't so tough no mo' because he was alone and there was twelve of us. So he starts running up the road leads to the highway with his black ass stickin' out while he's tryin' to tuck in that six inches of pecker and hold up his pants at the same time."

Odin kept backing off, slowly, slowly, until the car was at his back and his progress away from the ditch was blocked.

He never took his eyes off their hands.

The Harelip smiled and turned the knife in his fingers. "Well, we done caught up with him," he said, "and threw him down like some durn calf and castrated him. Godamighty, could that niggah scream! Hee hee hee. We roasted his nuts and served them like mystery meat on a fig leaf. Made him eat 'em, too!"

"Dum . . . dum . . . dum . . . dum . . . dum," hummed Pimples.

"But you're a white man," the Harelip went on. "You won't

have to eat your own nuts . . . we'll eat 'em for you!"

Odin slowly brought up his right leg to wrap a hand around the wooden hilt of his stiletto, but suddenly let his leg drop and drew back his hand. The sheath in the top of his boot was empty.

"This what you're lookin' for?" said the Harelip, smiling. He took out the stiletto and flicked it contemptuously at Odin. Then, throwing it at his head, he missed and the blade sank hilt-deep into the Rag-Top, as though into sawdust or sand.

"You lost it in the rumble, mahn."

"Not so braveth wif-out yoah shiv, eh, boyth?" said Pimples. The pale, bloodless lips stretched over his yellow gums and the ballpeen hammer swung in lazy arcs from his hand; just waiting to come down, hard, on the back of Odin's head if he made a lunge for the stiletto. "Yuh all alone, boyth," he said.

Far away, on the road leading through the woods to the highway, the powerful sound of exhaust pipes were quickly fading to pianissimo as the last cars left the field.

The Harelip took a step forward—so he stood with a foot on each side of Daddy-O's half-burnt cap—and he slowly turned the hunting knife in his hand, cutting edge up. "Mahn," he grinned, "We're gonna have a real *swingin'* one . . ."

Odin stood before them silently, watching them close in and smile when he suddenly crouched forward. The Harelip's fingers tightened around the handle of his knife and Pimples raised his hammer. Creeping toward him inch by inch they thought they had him like a hog on a hook. But just as they got set for the big slaughter he dragged a frontier-model Derringer out of his left boot. Both of them stopped short. The hole in the end of each barrel was big enough to stick a finger into and the stubby gun shone with a deadly dull silver in the light of the stars as he slowly brought it up and let them look down those two black finger-holes of death, mounted one atop the other.

"You crazy?" gasped the Harelip. His voice went high, the words coming out thin and juvenile. "We're just kiddin'!"

Odin snarled, "Shaddup!" and the short, stubby gun jerked suddenly in his fist. There was a splitting *crack* and a spurt of flame blasted the night to pieces. A metallic *ping* followed, then a high-pitched girlish scream. The bullet had struck the hunting knife, snapping the blade off near the handle, and then smashed through bones in the Harelip's hand before it went screaming into the air.

Pimples lisped, "Yuh bathtard! What raht yuh got tuh . . ." Then his voice petered out as Odin pointed the Derringer at his head and said, "So tell me more," very softly.

The ballpeen hammer hit the ground with a thud and Pimples stared down the loaded barrel of the gun. Then he looked at the Harelip who stood beside him, moaning, holding his hand.

"Yuh hand ith bleedin', Harryth," he said.

"Motherfucker," the other said. Then he began to moan again and Odin grabbed Pimples by the front of his T-shirt. "OK," he said, "Let's have it."

"What?"

The Derringer moved toward the ditch. "What you stole from him," he said.

Pimples looked away from the ditch where Daddy-O slept dead and pig-speared. Then he dug into the back pocket of his overalls and brought out a handful of gold teeth—yellow-green with bile, some half-white with bloody roots still on them. Cursing, Odin lashed out with the Derringer and Daddy-O's teeth rocketed from Pimples' hand, flying off to one side where they scattered over the field. Then he shoved the Harelip aside and pulled the stiletto out of the Rag-Top. He swept it in a long arc over his head and brought it down fast across Pimple's face, cutting him open from forehead to chin, splitting his nose.

"AIIIIIEEEEEEEEE!"

Pimples collapsed and buried his face in his hands—blood bubbling from between his fingers.

Odin reached over and pulled Daddy-O's bankroll from a tool pocket on the thigh of Pimples' overalls. The bills were water-soaked and smeared with blood. He squatted on his heels and wiped the roll on a turf of saw grass. Then he wrapped it in a handkerchief and put it in his side pocket while the Harelip, like a starving hyena, slinking and high-shouldered, approached him slowly, circling him as a hyena circles a wounded lion, watching for an opening. He did not move and the Harelip came up behind him, not moaning now but breathing heavily—so he could be heard even though he placed each foot on the ground gently, moving no stones or making any sound at all. Then—turning sharply on his heel, actually roaring and his tawny mane tossing, Odin was on his feet and a long tongue-red flame leaped from the Derringer's lower muzzle and licked across the darkness: ripping off half the Harelip's ear. The Harelip threw his arms over his head and screamed, screamed again and again, each scream higher than the one before and higher than any scream should be. Blood washed down the side of his face and he fell to the ground. His eyes showed the whites like a frightened horse as, still screaming, his coward-constricted sphincter muscle slipped and a great surge of shit came slushing into the seat of his pants.

"From the boys in Harlem," muttered Odin. He broke the custom-made gun, shook out the exploded cartridges and blew through the barrels, clearing them of smoke. The he slated the gun forward, his thumb on the hammer, and forked two fresh, brass-cased .38 S&W Specials into the barrels before snapping them in locked position. Then sliding the gun into the holster in his left boot top he carefully wiped the stiletto on another turf of dry grass and slid it into the sheath in his right boot—lowered his pants leg and walked back along the ditch to the Ferrari.

The field was dark and deserted. The flame in the ditch was drowning. The fire-eaten boy still lay where he fell and died.

Odin stopped.

A small dark animal shape stood with its forefeet on the Burn's stomach, shoulders up, head down and depressed in the black human flesh as it fed on dung and pink guts. The slobbering sounds and gurgling grunts as it gorged itself, drifted across the field along with the smell of roasted flesh and burned cloth. Odin ran up and kicked it. The thing caught on the toe of his boot and it sailed sideways to fall in a heap six feet away. It hissed at him. Then it was up and back: ripping and tearing into the Burn's guts with sharp teeth and dirty claws. But it was unaware of his presence until he actually kicked it again, his boots sinking deep in the stinking wet fur. Squealing with pain it scurried for a foothold on the ditch-edge before it slipped and disappeared into the black oil-smeared water.

Odin took out a book of matches he had picked up in Miami. He struck one of the red-tips. By its light he saw the ragged opening in the Burn's abdomen. It was a small hole about the size of a baby's fist, extending through the flash-burned skin and fat beneath, exposing a loop of small intestine that had been pulled up through the transparent serous lining membrane of the abdomen and through the reddish-brown muscle fibers, its slick pinkness slimy with saliva and defiled with dirt where the thing had torn it and ribbed it with teeth and claws. Beside the Burn lay the squeezed out green-and-white ointment tube and Odin read part of the printing on it before the match went out. VASELINE, it said, A SOOTHING DRESSING FOR BURNS AND SKIN IRRITATIONS...

A great horned owl swooped silently overhead, then dived into the ditch. Away somewhere, on the tree-bordered meadow, a bobcat growled like a buzz-saw hitting a wooden knot. Then the stubtail started spitting and snarling. Suddenly there was the infant-like cry of a possum. From away down the ditch came a terrible *neek-neek-ugh-eek-neek-neek* sort of sound, and the owl flew off with a frantic kicking and screaming thing in its deadly talons. Far in the night a hound called, and the call was answered from miles away. Then there was the chirruping of the crickets and the booming and grunting of frogs. The fireflies winked and drifted noiselessly against the darkness, a fox used his voice away off somewhere and suddenly, strangely, the night grew silent again.

The wind changed and rats, attracted by the smell of roasted flesh, rustled in the saw grass, scrabbling among the stones as they started to ring around the Burn. Walking slowly back to his car and sliding behind the wheel, thinking, *They'll eat him. So what? What's the difference? Who gives a shit anyway,* Odin slammed the door, shifted into low and took off easily, turning the car around to head for the highway-road at the other end of the field.

He swung around the oil slicks where the Rag-Top had become sick and shifted into second. Up ahead a heavy Hudson barreled along—its tail-lights beady red eyes going like hell. The Harelip was at the wheel. Suddenly Odin pictured him sitting there with hands on the wheel—Pimples in the back seat puking, holding his face together with warty fingers—his head thrown back, his hyena eyes wild and scared as the crazy screams came thinly hoarse from his throat and blood ran out dark and thick and hot from his half-torn ear. The screams grew fainter, and then the heavy car disappeared in the black solidity of trees around the highway-road. Then even the screams were gone.

"Good-bye, Motherfuckers," Odin muttered half aloud. Still in second gear he growled past the corpse and the burning coupe, his hopped-up engine whining crazily before he shoved the stick down into high gear and then suddenly yanked his wheel to cut around

Baby Doll who leaped out from behind the dark bulk of the Deuce that lay upside-down in a shattered mass of glass and mangled steel, both doors open, one smooth dual-dragster tire dangling from a smashed and twisted wheel. The speeding car was almost on top of her and she made a frightened sideward leap into a small, golden, Florida Key-deer. He jammed on the brakes: beneath him the Goodyear Blue-Streaks dug dirt and sent out a shower of stones and gravel as the big car bumped crazily on canted springs over ruts and holes and occasional black patches of saw grass on the field. The left front fender missed her by a cock's length and he slewed around, tires burning, the outside tire rims digging into the dirt as he hit the brake pedal again like a pile driver and slid to a skidding stop several hundred yards away—the soft, thick dust slowly settling around him.

Baby Doll had lost her shoes in the leap and she was on her hands and knees in the dirt, searching for them under the snapping stars. Then she rose. Balancing on one foot and then the other, she put on a pair of white-and-brown saddle shoes, hurrying, not taking the time to put them on properly, her heels not getting inside but resting on their backs as she shuffled along trying to keep them from falling off.

". . . AND NOW LIVE AND IN COLOR! EARLA CARROLL!" She came out on the night club's dance floor and stood in the blazing spotlight, holding a microphone, one leg thrust forward and her weight on the other. She was the image of Ekberg cut in ebony—hot jazz in living color, all red and black and tan and beautiful. The palms of her hands, her heels, the soles of her feet were white. She was of the earth, earthy, her big black breasts rose like twin watermelons from the bodice of a tight velvet gown that hung to her hips and stuck in the crevice of her buttocks. She opened her mouth and a row of square white teeth glistened brilliantly in contrast to her dark, purple-black skin.

"I'm glad to be . . . yes, Indeed! . . . where all the right and the smart folks're free . . ."

At a ringside table an old fat white businessman jerked himself off in a handkerchief. The others stared at Earla's breasts and buttocks, using their napkins for fig leaves.

"I don't know . . . May-be so! . . . but that's all right . . . 'cause I like 'em white . . ."

She liked them white all right. Nine inches with the foreskin pulled back. Over at the bar a man was masturbating into a piece of cold meat. Everybody was jerking away for dear life under the tables and now and then a violent erection sent a spurt of seed shooting across the tablecloth, where it landed with a splash among the plates of roast beef and caviar.

Odin sipped an apricot milk shake and watched the men jerk themselves off in the dark bowels of the night club. Then he looked at Earla. He smiled. Her long black legs balanced on high-heeled gold slippers. The edges of her feet were white. Further up, where the curve of her thighs pressed against the velvet gown and swept into her stomach, his sperm still swam inside her pussy—searching for the womb. He had been a long time with that woman. The bed was rumpled. She lay flat on her back and looked up at him with smoldering brown eyes that seemed to be floating in seed. His balls were drained. Outside the hotel room the seawind clashed among invisible palms and hissed in the saw grass along the shore.

"Fuck me," she said.
"I just did."
"Fuck me again."
"I'm dry, baby."
"What?"
"D-r-y."
"I thought you *never* went dry!"
"Well; I'm dry now."
"Can't get it up, eh?"
"It's up."
"So-o?"
"Nothing left, baby."
"Let me suck it, then."
"No."
"Why not? You sucked *me* off last night!"
"Sure, but—"
". . . and stuck your tongue up my twat!"

"Um."

". . . and *licked* me!"

"Yeah."

"Let me blow on it."

"No."

"You never let me do *anything!*"

"What you wanna do?"

"Suck your cock."

"No."

"Let me blow you . . ."

"No," he said.

She rubbed her knees together. "Come on, boy! Come *on!* I'm up like a straw . . ."

He laid his hand over her pussy and squeezed it hard. Then, threading his fingers in the soft heartshaped twat of hair that hung down between her bulging thighs, he buried his face in her shaved armpit and took a deep breath.

"Aaaaaaaaaaah!"

The body-heat steamed out of her until she smoked. He ran a hand over the immense globes of her buttocks and slid it up her crotch, fingering the two openings to her body. Moving his face down her throat he knelt beside her and kissed her huge pointed breasts, taking the nipples between his teeth and biting them. She moaned. He moved further down and rubbed his cheeks on her belly, kissing the soft black maiden-hair faintly scented with soap and urine. Then he tickled her mound of Venus with his lips and blew into her. She tossed her head from side to side on the pillow and groaned loudly. He kissed the softness of her inner thighs and moved down her legs, kissing the flat, whitish soles of her feet and sucking her toes, one by one. Then rolling her over, he went back up her legs and kissed the heavy black melons of her ass.

"I—want—you," she groaned.

She felt his penis as he came into her and moved back and forth with savage piston and cylinder regularity. He screwed like a Playboy rabbit. The bed knocked against the wall in short steady skidding jerks. She was Bess—he was a three-legged Porgy. The act without a hymen. "Ooh!" she screamed. "You gotta bone in that cock!" The world spun around—love made it—around and around. "I've got yuh by the short hairs now, baby!" He pulled them hard. She tightened her bottom and shoved his foreskin down.

Later, after he had wiped himself off on the bed sheets, she kissed the tip of his penis.

"I thought it'd go right up through my throat!" she said.

He chuckled and brushed a drop of moisture from her lips.

"*Sweet* Georgia Brown . . ."

"Well; it's brown all right," she said. "I used to keep a picture of a naked white boy in my dresser under the bras and panties. Some nights I'd take it out and look at it and goose myself with a brush handle . . ."

"Brown is down. And cunt is up. But hindsight is better'n foresight. That's what the queen says."

"What queen?"

"Of England."

"I had a lesbian roommate in college," she said. "A blonde chick. Just *crazy* about black meat. Sometimes I let her suck me in bed. Christ. She brought herself off against my thighs six or seven times a night."

A picture of Earla and the blonde girl, naked and together in bed, unreeled across his mind. He groaned softly and his penis stirred, without rising.

"She sure had small tits," she said. "I've seen *men* hung heavier'n her. Good-lookin' legs, though."

"Um."

"Did you ever fuck a man?"

"Shit, no," he said.

"*Never?*"

"Never."

"My brother did. He was in the Air Force and he hadn't seen a woman in six months. Then one night this guy cruised him on the base. He said he was out to get some fish, so my brother took him to a hot-bed-barracks and did it off on him behind. Felt just like a woman he said. Then, later on, he let the fag take it in his mouth . . ."

"Yeah?"

"Sure. The fag was gone on the stuff. My brother told me he said it tasted like salmon."

"Does it?"

"Shoot . . . it don't taste like *nothin'*, man!"

A spurt of white semen hit a beer glass and ran down its side. On the night club's dance floor Earla took her bow and walked out backwards with the microphone in her hand. If she had been sitting down the men at the tables would have fought each other for a chance to sniff and wallow their faces along the spot where her buttocks had been. Odin watched a man run after her with his fly open, only to be held back at the exit by four husky bouncers. The man struggled furiously in their grip, screaming—"Lemme fuck her! Lemme fuck her! I got money, I tell ya! Lemme fuck her!"—but the bouncers locked the door and dragged him back to his table.

It was a hot night. Odin spread his legs. Sweat stuck to his balls and ran down between the cheeks of his buttocks. He cursed and raised himself from the bar stool, shoving the cotton of his boxers into the wet crevice. Then he sat down. Does he or doesn't he? Only his right hand knows for sure. A fag in Capri pants swung a cocked hindleg over a stool next to the wall and seated himself, smiling. If there ever was a fag who looked like a man, this was it. Six-foot four, black hair, two-hundred and ten pounds, and *handsome.* His eyes moved over Odin light and quick as finger tips. He licked his pinkie and smoothed his left eyebrow with a little spittle.

"Mighty hot," he said.

It certainly was. Odin felt the sweat sticking under his hair. He watched the fag quietly. Their eyes locked and held.

"Your fly is open . . ."

The man looked down quickly. He blushed. He had left it open on purpose. How *very* Gay!

"Oh dear!" he said. "How careless of me!" He zippered up his pants to half mast.

"Why don't you wear 'em ass-forwards?" said Odin.

"*What?*"

"With the zipper in back—"

The fag raised his eyebrows, the left one higher than the other.

"Is that a new style?"

"For you it should be."

They regarded one another soberly.

"Get your tongue outta my hole," said Odin.

The fag opened his mouth in a perfect O, like a fish. He started to say something, but Odin cut him short.

"Blow, Josephine . . ."

"*Well!*" The fag stood up and walked majestically towards the men's room, his nose in the air and his ass wobbling heavily in his tight pants.

"Hincty sonofabitch . . ."

Odin swung around in surprise. Earla was standing behind him, leaning an elbow against the bar. "Hello, man," she said.

"Hello, woman." He looked her over slowly. She had on a tight knit wool dress that showed off all of her curves.

"All right?" she said. Her white teeth flashed in a smile.

"Copasetic." He put an arm around her waist and explored the shape of her buttocks.

"I like your dress," he said. "It must be wool."

She grinned. "What're you? The American Sheep Council?"

"Yes," he said. "I wanna *ram* you."

The night was dark. On the outskirts of town an old barn rose gaunt and stark above a grove of moss-hung oaks and rusted bathtubs. In the knee-high weeds that surrounded the trees, crickets cheeped and gnats spun and whirled madly among myriad drifting fireflies. A colored albino with kinky white hair as tightly knotted as a sheep's coat held a lantern over his head and grinned at them.

"Show's jest about to begin, folks," he said.

Earla strained on Odin's arm like a leashed panther. Inside the blacked-out barn a circle of bug-swirled gas lanterns hung from nails in the ceiling. As they walked into the light half a hundred male eyes followed them.

"Over here, daddy!" whispered Earla.

"Um."

They moved through a cluster of men with yellow halfmoons of sweat under their armpits and large straw hats on the backs of their heads. Earla leaned her hip on a fowlcrate and Odin placed a foot on the crate's rungs and leaned on his knee.

"Bill yo' birds!"

The referee was a big fat Negro man in a collarless shirt complete with collar-button and gold-plated diamond studs. He waved a hand ringed with sapphires towards the darkness beyond the circle of light. Two handlers came forward and met in the center of the floor, each holding a rooster in front of him at arms length.

"*Pit* yo' birds!"

The cocks slashed out viciously at each other's eyes, but the handlers pulled them back and placed them on the floor behind two chalk lines—facing one another.

"*Pit!*"

The handlers let go and backed away, to stand outside the glare of light, watching. The two birds approached each other slowly. Their small heads strained forward with neck feathers ruffled and tails held stiffly erect. One of them was a young black rooster—the other was an older white bird, a "blinker": with one eye and an empty socket full of gray, scarred tissue. Both birds had sharp, inch-long steel gaffs tied to their legs with leather straps.

Earla looked up at Odin excitedly. Her enormous pointed breasts rose and fell within her dress like Brunhilde's bubs—the soft mammalian udders.

"Let's pick the white one, daddy!" she said.

"Why?"

"He looks like he's had plenty of experience. That dark one's just a punk."

"Um," he said. "That old cock is full of shit."

A slender mulatto with gold teeth came over and leered at Earla. He wore a white linen suit, a black tie, but no shirt.

"You layin' down some bread, baby?" he asked.

Earla looked at Odin. "Are we?"

"The black one," he said.

The mulatto sucked his teeth and printed laboriously in a child's blue-ruled school book. Then he pulled his tongue out from between his teeth and licked the end of the pencil.

"How much?"

"Fifty bucks."

He wrote that down and closed the book on his forefinger. Bugs spun about them. Suddenly there was an explosion of dust and feathers as the two birds came together on the floor. The blinker flailed and slashed at the black bird's chest with its metal spurs. The black bird squawked and jumped back—just as one of the gaffs shaved its breast. A fine line of blood bubbled out through its feathers. The blinker came down hard and its spurs hacked splinters from the floor. Without waiting it lunged forward again and pecked at the other bird's eyes. The black bird kicked out with its feet and crushed down on top of the blinker's wing. There was a sharp *crunch*—the wing broke. The black bird stabbed furiously at the empty eye socket. The blinker thrashed on the floor, blood spurting thickly from its hole. Then suddenly it was up again, its broken wing flapping at an angle from its side as it slashed at the black rooster's throat with its steel gaffs.

"C'mon cock!" Odin jerked his head forth in his collar.

The black rooster bit into the blinker's face and dug out its single eye with the point of its beak. The white bird was blind. It slashed out again and again. Blood gushed from the socket and washed down its front. The crowd roared. Suddenly, the black bird was on the floor with its legs in the air. The blind rooster jumped two feet off the ground and landed on the younger bird's chest, sinking its gaffs deep into the heart.

"Cock—!"

Odin bit into his tongue and tasted the salty blood. The mulatto was doing the Italian *mano morta* bit. Having placed a dead hand on Earla's hip halfway through the fight, he was now moving it slowly and appreciatively over the rounded curves of her butt.

"Take your hand off my ass!" she said. *"Odin!"* He looked over at her in surprise. "This man has been bothering me ever since the cockfight started. I don't think you should pay him that fifty!"

Odin took his foot down from the chicken coop. He curled his toes and stamped his shoe in the bird droppings. His foot was sleeping. Stinging needles.

"What you doin', man?" he said.

The mulatto backed off and made small, placating gestures with his hands.

"Take it easy, mister. I didn't mean nothin'!"

Odin followed him through a mass of black and white faces that gleamed with sweat. In a corner of the barn a toilet was improvised by a bucket and a plastic shower curtain. Over the curtain a pair of pliers hung from a nail in the wall and Odin took them down and opened them with a squeaking, rusty sound. Then he picked the mulatto up by his black tie and pinched him hard in the ass.

"Pizzicotti!" he said. "How you like *that*, buddy?"

He opened the pliers and pinched him again. The mulatto screamed in pain like a woman.

"Pizzicotti!" said Odin. *"Pizzicotti!"*

He pinched the man again and again. First the right buttock, then the left. Then right, then left. Then left, then right. Then right again.

"Aw Aw Aw Aw Aw Aw Aw Aw Aw Aw Aw Aw Aw!"

The man screamed like Joe E. Brown. Then the blind cock

started to crow. Crow on crow, its head stretched toward the roof as it stood on top of the dead bird's breast and flapped its wings. After a time, the referee walked over and casually twisted its neck.

Odin gave the mulatto a final pinch and tossed the pliers into the john. Then he walked back to Earla where the referee stood holding the dead white bird in his black hand.

"We got a nice Cheshire Pile comin' up," the referee told them, "and one Irish Gilder that just—"

"No." Odin shook his head. "It's too hot. I'm going to take a drive."

"Battle Royal tonight," the referee said. "Twenty birds!"

"Some other time."

The referee shrugged and threw the dead bird into the garbage pail.

"Come on, baby." Odin took Earla's arm and led her out of the barn.

"Where we goin', daddy?"

"For a swim."

"I don't have no bathin' suit!"

"That's why."

She laughed as he slapped her bottom and shoved her into the Ferrari. Up ahead a black cat miaowed and ran across the road with its tail erect.

Their world was deserted.

On the beach a rowboat lay on its side, half buried in the sand. Over the water the moon stood full and pale, casting the boat's shadow a tremendous distance along the shore. The ocean was dark and flat like a mirror—its mooned path narrowed to a point on the horizon. In the sky a sea gull drifted motionless beneath the stars.

"Sure is quiet out here," Earla whispered.

She held on to Odin's shoulder and stood on alternate legs, removing her high-heeled slippers. Then she dipped a foot into the greenish-black water that surged among the rocks and lapped at the shore.

"Uuuuuuuuh!" She shivered.

He put a hand over her left buttock, squeezing it.

"C'mon. Take off your dress."

"I will not!" she retorted.

He massaged and patted her gently.

"Come on."

"What if somebody sees us?" she whispered.

"Nobody'll see us."

She picked up a shell and examined it.

"Do you like oysters?"

"No."

"Why-y?"

"Slimy.   Like something an old man coughed up."

"Oh."

He bent forward and kissed her on the shoulder.

"Take off your dress."

"N-No—"

"Come on."

He buried his face in the base of her throat, his hand up her back, searching for the zipper.

"No," she said. "No—"

He jerked her dress down and unhooked her brassiere. Her huge, pointed breasts burst free and knocked against his chin.

"Yes!" he murmured. He moved down quickly and kissed the hard brown nipples, wallowing his face against them, embracing the hot black breasts and sucking them off until she moaned.

Suddenly he leaped up on her like a gorilla, wrapping his legs around her waist—climbing her.

"Oooooooooh!"

She staggered and fell backwards in the sand, with him on top.

"Wait!" she cried. "Wait!" She mounted an elbow.

He worked furiously, tearing her nylon step-ins down her thighs—pulling off his own pants—goosing her.

"Wait!" she cried. "I got my *Kotex* on!"

"Christ!"

He ripped the napkin from between her legs and shoved her back on the sand, holding her pinned beneath his body with her arms stretched above her head, his hands on her wrists.

"C'mon," he panted. "C'mon."

She spread her thighs and raised her hips toward the root of his belly. Then, digging her heels into the sand, she held her cunt open with two fingers and felt his erect penis as he came into her.

He straddled her, on hands and knees, shoving his phallus into her black hole with a sudden stallion-like surge.

She moaned and her knees began to quiver. His penis went further and further up her hole. *God* how he shoved it in her! It was as though he could not get it far enough up in her womb—her uterus, the place where men grew and came *out* of!

He started to withdraw—then suddenly he shoved it forward. Then back again, then forward. Back-and-forth. Back-and-forth. She moaned at each thrust and withdrawal. The sand ground into her buttocks. The ocean surged. Waves rose and fell. She saw stars. Palm fronds clashed. The moon! She felt his deep-sunk manhood—the springing seed. Black water slapped and whispered at her feet.

"That's what I like about you," he said to her afterwards. "You always act like a virgin getting her cherry copped."

She moved her fingers down his belly and grasped his penis in her black hand, jerking it upwards.

"What've you got in that cock?" she said. "Arch-supports?"

Later, after he had chased her down along the beach, nude and with his balls swinging like a cock's wattles, he flung an arm around her waist and threw her into the sand, mounting her from behind like a stud, while she, wild as a black mare, drew up her legs and kicked at him, her rump letting out a terrific fart against his stomach.

"You remind me of Mr. Clean," she told him, later. "With the other studs I always feel so *dirty* . . ."

"GREEN GIANT," he said, *"Hump! Hump!"*

"Green Pecker!" she laughed.

"I wonder what happens to all those little *green* peas?"

"Up the Giant's," she said, shoving her forefingers into the air.

He glanced down at himself.

"Christ. It's smeared all over!"

She wiped her hand on the blond hairs of his crotch.

"Better go wash it off," she said.

He took a handful of sand and trickled it into her hole.

"Within this limit is relief enough. Sweet bottom-grass and high delightful plain. Round rising hillocks, brakes obscure and rough . . ."

She shoved his hand away.

"What the hell you doing?" she said. She brushed the sand off the soft maiden-hair that hung to a point between her legs.

He leaned over and tickled her nipples with his tongue.

"Her breasts, like ebony globes circled with blue. A pair of maiden worlds unconquered . . . ."

"She-it!" she said. "You trying to suck me off with Shakespeare now?"

She held her breasts with her two hands and shoved the big brown nipples into his mouth, one after the other.

"U-m-m-m," he said, "U-m-m-m-m!"

He worked his finger up her rear.

"Cornhole me!" she said.

"Wait."

He stood her up, flat against the rowboat, like a swimmer getting her stomach pumped over a barrel.

"Giddy up!" she cried.

She whinnied like a horse.

He jumped in the saddle.

"Ride me down, cowboy!"

She bucked like a bronco. He grabbed her around the middle and pulled her heavy posteriors against his chest. *Whoaa!* She laughed and kicked back at him. He stood her on her head. She doubled up. He inserted his .45 into her rectum and *Bang!* cocked the hammer between the cheeks of her butt.

"That ain't no .22, daddy-o!"

He ejaculated. She farted. His penis came out limp and brown and rested on the boat. She tried to do a handstand as he held her ankles. He leaned forward and kissed her between her legs. She laughed and collapsed in the sand. He dragged her up again by her ankles and made her walk toward the water on her hands—pushing her along like a wheelbarrow.

"Let's do it like the goldfish," she said. *"Underwater."*

He turned her over and lay in the surf with his head between her legs, burying his teeth in the soft black cunt. She moved down and kissed his feet and thighs, running her tongue up his legs and under his balls and around his penis. Then she pushed her tongue up into his anus and he climbed halfway out of the water. "Christ!" he said. She took his penis in her mouth and moved her head back and forth, sucking it, caressing the eye with the tip of her tongue. Then suddenly she rolled on top of him, her feet twined around his neck, her wet crotch pressed against his face. She moved her head up and down on the end of his erect organ. He shoved his tongue in and out of her hot pussy.

Her voice was penis-smothered.

"You got *sand* on your dick—"

"U-m-m-m."

"It's *gritty!*"

"U-m-m-m-m-m-m-m."

"It's a *gritty* dicky!"

"U-m-m-m-m-m-m-m-m-m-m-m."

He came off in her mouth. She coughed and swallowed the semen. He pushed his penis against her ear. She gave him a tongue bath around the testicles. He rubbed his penis in the cleavage between her breasts. She sucked his thighs. He licked her vulva. She turned him over on his belly and gave him soft intra-buttock kisses. He groaned. She got on her knees and spread his legs apart. He looked back over his shoulder. She stuck her tongue deep into his rump. He ejaculated. She tickled his scrotum. He shot off like a string of firecrackers. She moved her tongue around in his anus. He crawled forward like a turtle. She followed him. He panted. She fastened her lips to his hole. He let his tongue hang out. She shoved it in *"AAAAAIIIII"* up to her teeth.

*   *   *

The loose folds of skin became engorged with blood and his penis slowly rose under the water and snapped to attention as a sudden constriction of the veins cut off the circulation. She stood upright, treading water, holding his long erect organ in her hand.

"Oooooooooooh!" she said.

She pulled the foreskin back and a little drop of lubricating fluid came out of the uretha and slipped between her fingers.

"Your *eye*," she said, "it's underneath your dick! I can *feel* it!"

"Ummm." She fingered the little hole in his glans.

"Shouldn't it be at the tip?" she said.

A spurt of sticky white fluid shot into her hand. She closed her fist and brought it over the surface of the water. She opened her hand and sniffed it.

"M-m-m-m-m-m," she said. *"Fish!"*

She let the little drop of semen float on the water.

"Just think!" she said. "There are MILLIONS of cute little sperms swimming around in there!"

"All lookin' for your little pussy," he said.

She picked up a piece of seaweed and hung it on his pecker.

"A hatrack!" she cried.

"You got a dirty little ass I'm just crazy about," he whispered.

Their shadows were monsters in the water. They kissed.

"I think you're the nicest white liar I know," she said.

She spat a stream of water into his ear. He cursed and leaned his head over to the side, tapping it with the heel of his hand. A pelican came out from the shore, floating through the sky with no motion of its wings. Suddenly it stopped in mid-air and plunged downward, hitting the water with a tremendous splash. A moment later it climbed into the sky again, the tail of a fish hanging from its enormous beak.

Earla grasped his arm and her fingers dug into his flesh.

"There's a shark right under us!" she said.

He looked down at a long dark shadow that drifted motionless in a stream of phosphorescent fire bubbles six feet below their legs. The great pectoral fins moved lazily in the queer blue light that loomed up from the bottom.

"Start swimming towards the beach," he said calmly.

He watched the shark move under his legs, its jaws slowly opening and closing—its small catlike eyes white and gleaming with phosphorus. It was so close that he thought he could see the lice and sucker fish that clung to its sides like leeches.

"It's your white skin," she whispered. "The moon is shining right on it!"

"Shhh!" he said. "Get away from here!"

"I'm not going to leave you," she said. "We'll swim back together . . ."

"You crazy cunt!" he hissed. "Get away from meeee!"

The shark moved up and nudged his legs. Earla screamed and slapped her cupped hands on the water. He kicked the fish in the snout and shoved Earla towards the beach as she flailed her feet up and down on the surface.

"Shout under the water!" she screamed.

"Get up on that fuckin' beach!" He shoved her ahead of him and turned as the shark came head-on, protruding its upper jaw so that its entire head rose up into an ugly Reaper's hood above an open grave bristling with row after row of flashing white teeth.

"*ODIN!*"

He drew back his knees and kicked at the shark. His toes caught the hard ridge above its nostrils and he gave himself a powerful push with his legs, leaping two feet into the air and landing with a terrific *smack* on its back, as the jaws snapped shut. Earla was in the shallows now, crawling and clawing her way across the slimy rocks and deep patches of sand, her large buttocks shining in the moonlight. The shark tried to wriggle after her on its belly until it was almost out of the water—but Odin grabbed its fins and pressed his heels into the sand, holding it back. The shark lashed out with its tail and shook its head furiously, as though tearing fifteen or twenty pounds of meat from her ass. His fingers bit into the tough skin and the cords of his neck stook out like steel wires. Earla was on the beach now. His eyes bulged and his breath whistled through his throat. He pulled his fingers out of the shark's snout and slipped and plunged across the shallows to where she was standing.

"God!" she said. She pulled his arm around her neck and caught his waist, helping him across the last few steps to the beach.

His blond hair was glued to his skull. Hers hung limply around her face in black waterlogged tendrils. They collapsed in the sand and lay side by side, gasping for breath.

"That motherfucker came after your ass like a buzzsaw," he said.

"Daddy!"

She rolled over on top of him and put her arms around his shoulders. Her mouth enveloped both his lips and her tongue pushed between his teeth and went halfway down his throat. She forced his mouth open and sucked him off with the soft insides of her lips. "*M-m-m-m!*" He ran his forefinger over the tip of her erect, nipple-like clitoris until a slippery secretion seeped from between her thighs. The fluid was thick, viscous, and he tested it with his fingers. Then he spread the lips of her vulva and inserted his penis in her vagina. She moved to the left on top of him and the walls of her canal adjusted his organ to a better position. He tickled her in the crotch and suddenly thrust his manhood deep into her vagina and held it there, revolving it slowly inside her canal with a circular motion. She dug her nails into his shoulders and fastened her teeth in the side of his neck, straining her hips against his to draw him even deeper into her body.

"Now," she said. "Now!"

The deep thrust of his penis had shoved his foreskin back so that it bunched at the base of his glans like a Goodyear tire around a Python. But now, as he started the in-and-out rhythm, his foreskin pulled back and forth across his glans, covering and exposing it as the skin bunched in folds and stretched out flat, rippling the walls of her pussy, exquisitely, like a tickler.

"Oh daddy! Oh daddy!"

She was an ocean of dark waves rising and falling, her womb throbbed, her sea-grass trembled, foam rose about her outer lips. Then without warning her sphincter muscle gripped and milked his penis, clenching it hard, expanding and contracting. She pulled her legs back and suddenly flung them forward—as if trying to draw his whole body into hers.

"Fuck me, daddy! Fuck me!"

He rolled her over on her right side with her right leg between his thighs and her left leg lying knee bent across his hip. For a moment they lay motionless, panting, his penis deep in her body. Then he rolled her over on top of him, his legs clasped around her thigh. "No-ooo!" She groaned. He shoved it in, *hard!* up to the hilt. A tickling sensation started in the head of his penis and ran up towards his scrotum. Suddenly it burst in a series of convulsive jerks and spurts as his seed sprang deep into the mouth of her uterus.

"*Eeeeeeeeeeeeeeeeh!*"

She screamed and bit his neck, raking his back with her fingers. Her eyes rolled upward and closed. A hot little brush of fire started in her clitoris and continued to burn, the flames running up higher and higher into her vagina, skyrocketing until suddenly it burst in her womb—explosion following explosion, a fiery pain of pleasure lifting her—up, up—out of her body, and then dropping her down as the shower of sparks fell on the sand, spluttering—cooling—leaving her spent.

"Daddy!"

They lay panting, a striking contrast in black and white—both lost, thinking of nothing, not even each other. Her vagina was around and surrounding his ivory, holding him tight as blood drained from the erectile tissue and left his penis shrunken and soft—inside her body.

"Earla . . ."

He withdrew his penis slowly. There was a little smack of her lips as he left her. *The lollipop that made the world go around: red at the tip.* He panted softly against her breast and rolled off and lay beside her, placing his hands behind the back of his neck.

"Now, who says a nigger can do that better'n a white man?" he said.

"Whoo-eee!" she said. "Ah sho don't!"

They both laughed.

She looked at him. "How much you got there, sweet man?"

"Sixteen inches."

"Sure doesn't look like it now," she said. She stroked his groin firm and close. The soft penis stirred in her hand like a live eel, but did not rise.

"I guess it's above twelve feet now," he said, looking down at his blond body in the moonlight. She laughed.

He grabbed her ankle and tried to bite her big toe but she broke away and kicked sand in his face. He cursed and got up as she ran down the beach, laughing and calling him names. He went after her—running hard—galloping, as madly as a wild stallion, his eyes fixed on her twinkling black buttocks—his testicles swinging from side to side between his legs, like dinner bells.

"*Yaaaaaaaj!*" she taunted. "You can't catch me!"

She bounded along like a gazelle, leaping into the air. He panted and leaned forward, running hard with his phallus lifted. Suddenly she turned and plunged into the water, her heavy female thighs working furiously, a streak of scum breaking on each side of her body. There was a steamer—far out at sea—moving across the mooned path, its screw kicking up a ball of glittering white foam. He plunged face-down into the ocean and grabbed her legs, pulling her down. She laughed and kicked loose of him, swimming away. He paddled after her like a dog. Suddenly she disappeared. He treaded water and looked around, confused. A little fish darted between his legs and nibbled at his penis with soft teeth. "*Aiiiih!*" Below the surface her head was grotesquely distorted. He grabbed her by the ears and pulled her up. She spat a stream of salt water straight into his face. Then she laughed. "*Whee!*" He drew her towards him and she clasped her legs about his waist. "*On the road to Mandalay-ay . . . Where the flyin'-fishes plaay!*" Bubbles slid from between her legs and floated up their chins. "*Mothah!*" he yelled. "*It's a long, long way to Tipperary!*" Yet—water did not enter her body where his member sealed it like a 4-centimeter cork in a champagne bottle.

* * *

They stood side by side in the shallows, water running down their naked bodies—a study in ebony and white.

He touched the dying shark with his foot.

"Ugly bastard, isn't he?"

She put her arm around his waist and leaned her head on his shoulder.

"Now we know what it feels like," she said. "Under water."

He picked up a piece of driftwood and shoved the pointed end into the shark's mouth. *CRUNCH!* The branch splintered to matchsticks between six rows of ivory teeth that lay in a bed of soft, pink tissue.

"Granny," he said, "WHAT BIG TEETH YOU GOT!"

He picked up another piece of driftwood and struck the shark across the nose hard, with his closed fist. There was a click of teeth as it slashed at him but he reached his hand into its mouth and wedged the plank lengthwise between its upper and lower jaws: holding them open. Then, taking his penis between forefinger and thumb, he urinated into the huge yawning orifice.

"Christ!" she said. "It could have bit your hands off at the wrists!"

He laughed and shook the last drop of urine into the gaping hole.

"There's a Porki in a pool back there," he said, jerking his head toward the beach. "Let's get 'im."

"Porki?" she said.

"Here. I'll show you."

They walked back to a pool of moonlit water that lay between slimy rocks in the shallows. He squatted on his heels and picked up a small porcupine fish with two pieces of wood. Then, holding the little fish in front of him, he carried it back and thrust it into the shark's mouth forcing it past the six rows of teeth and then shoving it down its throat with the sticks.

"What you do that for?" she asked.

He knocked the plank from the shark's mouth and the enormous jaws snapped shut—like a steel trap.

"That Porki'll make his insides so full of holes he'll think he's a cancelled check," he told her.

She embraced him from behind and rubbed her clitoris against his left buttock. "It's going to die anyway," she said, flicking his ear with her tongue.

"You can't tell with this spring tide," he said equably. "It might wriggle out to deep water again.

"So what?"

He smiled. "I once caught a hammerhead shark in the Gulf of Mexico. It had a big bulge on its side, and when I cut its belly open, a man's head fell out."

She laughed. "I don't believe you."

"You don't believe *nothin'!*" he bellowed. "I might've had to slit this motherfucker open and pull you and your black ass *both* out!"

She bit his shoulder and he turned around, facing her.

"Did you ever get laid on a shark?" he asked.

She stared at him, her eyes wide.

"Well," he said. "You're going to now."

He picked her up in his arms and carried her—struggling, around the shark, dropping her onto its blue back. She mounted an elbow and tried to rise, but he swung her legs over his shoulders and sank down on one knee before her.

"I—I'll stink like a fish!" she stammered.

"You already do."

He pressed his face into her dripping black crotch and moved his lips over and around her knob-like clitoris: tracing the letter O in the soft, buried parts below with the tip of his tongue.

"ODIN!" she screamed.

His tongue entered her vagina, withdrew, re-entered quickly, moved around in a circle, ran over her inner lips and tickled the tip of her clit.

"AaaaaaaaaaaaaaaaaH!"

Her flesh trembled in the perineal area between the anus and the vaginal entrance. He moved up on her—still on his knees and still holding her legs raised over his shoulders—the back of her buttocks juxtaposed to his belly.

"Odin!" she groaned. "Oooooh-din!"

The shark thrashed beneath her as it got its first taste of death.

She stared up at him from between the reddish-brown nipples of her breasts, her eyes half-closed and floating in sperm. Then her mouth curled—showing the underside of her lips, like a monkey.

"You white motherfucker!" she gasped.

He thrust himself against her, using the weight of his body to drive his penis into the glossy black crack between her legs. She groaned and raised his hips and suddenly he went all the way into the crimson center of her vagina. They ground together and burned their flesh into each other, furiously, soldering hilt to sheath until her sphincter muscle cut off the circulation at the base of his penis—like a rubber band—preventing the blood from leaving his flooded organ. He tried to pull out again and start the to-and fro-going, but she held him locked painfully between her thighs, like a dog with a knot in its engorged phallus.

"Let go!" he panted.

She laughed and squeezed his manhood hard with a milkmaid's cruel grasp, choking him at the root of his belly. He shoved at her hips and humped his buttocks, but she held him tight between her legs. There was a furious tug of war. *"Lemme outta here!"* He rolled his eyeballs like the colored chauffeur in the Charlie Chan movies. "Whoooooooooooeeeeeeeeeee!" She laughed so hard that she almost let him go.

"C'mon, baby," he said.

"No!"

Her legs and arms tightened around him. Suddenly the shark tossed onto its back throwing them both ass over appetite along the rocks.

"Christ," he moaned. "You broke my pecker!"

He pulled out of her gingerly and examined himself with the tips of his fingers.

"Aha ha ha ha!" She lay back on the rocks and rolled from side to side, laughing. "Let's put a splint on it, baby . . . A mothah-flippin' tourniquet!"

He sat up and gave her a reproachful look.

"It's nothing to laugh about," he said, rubbing his crotch. "I might be crippled for life!"

"Oh, you poor baby!" She got up and crawled toward him on her knees. "Let mama kiss it. Mama knows just how . . ."

"Keep your goddamn liver lips off'n me!" he shouted.

She took his phallus in her hand and brushed the underside of the glans with her tongue. Beneath the skin blue veins rose and bulged as blood poured into the erectile tissues—like meat shooting from a machine into a factory-made sausage. His penis filled and surged in her hand, rising up, stretching toward her lips like a live fish. She kissed and bit the pink head, pulling the foreskin back completely and scrubbing her teeth up and down its surface. Then, pressing her lips together, she slowly withdrew his organ. There was a little *smack* when he left her.

"She eats and wipes her mouth and says '*I ain't done nothin' wrong!*' " he said.

She kissed him on the tip of his penis. "Every Black will have its White, motherfucker." She grinned.

Suddenly she thrust half the organ into her mouth and took his balls in her hand. She pressed the flat of her tongue hard against his urethra, touching him everywhere with hot hot lips. Then slowly, she shoved him all the way in, sucking the shaft. His breath came out in a long, low whistle. Sperm shot halfway down her throat, she swallowed hard. Suddenly he changed position, still in her mouth but turning slowly like a wheel on its axle until they lay in a French 69—performing lip service on one another. After a while she pulled away from him and raised her head, her lips dripping. "See . . ." she laughed. "It wasn't broken at all."

"Um. After what it's been through tonight, it *should* be."

"Sugar," she said. "When it went down my throat like that—I thought it was going to come out of my asshole!"

"Well, it ain't *that* long."

"Felt like it, though."

She moved around until they lay cradled, spoon-fashion, he with his legs drawn up and she behind him, fitting herself into the contour of his body. Her chicken-tongue clitoris protruded downward between her thighs and she rubbed it moist against the cheeks of his ass. Then her arms went around his waist and her long dark fingers stroked his phallus.

"That fish sure is wild," she said.

"Yeh. The Porki's stickin' him fulla holes all right."

She slipped the foreskin back and forth across the head of his penis.

"Your cute uncircumcised cock."

She grasped his entire organ in her two hands and started the rhythmic motion of intercourse.

"You can't squeeze another drop outta that thing," he warned her.

"What thing?"

"This thing!" He grabbed hold of her black hands and shook his shaft like a joy stick. "Odin!" She tickled the velvet tip of his glans and he ejaculated but weakly, a drop of clear spermless fluid oozing out between her fingers.

"You can do better than that, honey." She rolled his erect penis furiously between the palms of her hands, like a girl scout trying to start a fire with a stick of wood.

"Christ!" he said. "What're you tryin' to do? Reshape it?" He looked down at his milk-white shaft in her black hands. The head was dry and shining. Flaming red. Less than a quarter of an inch from the tip his eye stood wide open—gaping, like the mouth of a fish. Dying.

"Your hole is further down than other men's," she said and touched his eye lightly with the tip of her forefinger.

"You complainin'?" he asked.

"No." She ran her fingernail into his urethra. "The head is split," she said. "I like it that way. It's like a built-in feather at the tip. A *tickler!* Real crazy, man."

"It's a groovy dick . . ."

She looked at him. "You better take me home now, you dumb shit."

"What for?"

"So I can get a nigger to pump some sperm into me!"

"I pumped enough sperm into you for a *hundred* white babies."

"That's what I mean," she said. "A Negro's sperm and a white man's sperm will fight each other inside a woman's pussy like crazy. They kill each other off."

"What?"

"Sure," she said. "Didn't you know that? I *always* take on a black stud after I've had a white man . . ."

"And vice versa."

"Exactly."

He shaped his mouth to say liberal black asshole, then got up and looked at the ocean. "What the fuck is *that?*" he said.

"What?" She turned around and followed his gaze. The water was boiling furiously in the shallows behind the shark. Suddenly a long black whip slashed across the surface and a pair of enormous black wings glinted in the moonlight.

"A devilfish!" he breathed. "Look at those *fins!*"

"That thing must be *twenty feet* across!" she gasped.

"Maa-n!" He walked along the shore and rubbed his hands on his thighs. "That sonofabitch will come down on top of a diver and hold on to him with its fins. *Eating him!* It won't let him go. It'll drop down to the bottom—enveloping him—still eating him. Kee-rist! I can still see that boy bubbling and screaming behind his face mask!"

He picked up a piece of driftwood and tested its point with his thumb. Then he ran towards the water.

"I can still see that sonofabitch lying on top of the boy—watching me—and eating him. *Eating* him!"

The manta ray moved out of the moonlit shallows, its wings flapping and the snake-like tail striking and slashing in every direction. He ran after it and dived into the water—fantastic shades of deep brown, greenish-black and purple surrounding him as he blew two air bubbles from his nostrils and gently pressed them into his eye-sockets, for use as goggles. All around him between the strands of staghorn coral, red squirrel fish darted in and out among the reefs and spoon-shaped parrot fish grazed on the ledges. The enormous manta ray swam steadily ahead, its huge, shadow-like wings moving up and down with slow regularity above a forest of swaying yellow and purple sea fans.

On the beach Earla staggered to her feet and ran after him.

"ODIN!" she screamed. "YOU CRAZY WHITE MOTHER-FUCKER! COME BACK HERE!"

JETT SAGE

Jett Sage is a mysterious figure whose only known work is a huge, vivid, wildly original manuscript which was delivered to

Maurice Girodias one night by a Hell's Angels motorcycle messenger, and out of which came the two books Crazy Wild *and* Crazy Wild Breaks Loose. *His present whereabouts are unknown.*

William Burroughs III

SPEED

*T*he next image I can remember was the two of us, there we were in Greenwich Village, part of the great phenomenon, just arrived and celebrating on a couple of hot dogs. Things started rolling right away. We hadn't been there six minutes before a familiar face floated free of the crowd and told me that an old friend of mine was living with her just around the corner.

Gary was one of the people I used to fool around with in Palm Beach before he became unsavory and had to leave. As we hove into view, he was sitting on the steps of his hotel chewing the fat with a little psychologist who was running a survey. There was a girl there who was saying why no, she wasn't ashamed of being a lesbian, no, of course not, why should she be? "Well, how about you?" said the good doctor, turning to me. I like to answer questions about myself, so I went along with his quiz until all of a sudden he started pestering me to come to Bellevue so he could show me to a doctor. He said I wouldn't have to stay if I didn't want to and that I wouldn't be committing myself in any way. Well, I damn near laughed my ass off. He got kind of upset at that and walked off down the street looking over his shoulder.

All this time, I was saying hello to Gary and introducing him to Chad and both of us to the girl. After the nut left, I told Gary we were dead on our feet and asked him if he knew where we could get some methedrine. As a rule, it never occurred to us to sleep while we were in New York; we just figured that when we needed it, it would come get us and isn't nature wonderful? Chad stood in awe of the human body. Anyway, Gary said with a manly flourish that we'd come to the right place and sold us a dime's worth for a nickel. We did it up and suddenly he started looking very strange and I sat still, breathing carefully. When I stopped sweating, I said wow and how much did he want for a gram? Fifteen dollars, and off we went to find it.

On the street I remembered a girl named Vicki that I'd grown up with was supposed to be attending N.Y.U. We walked into the first building we came to, and there she was, so help me God, and taking a twenty-dollar bill out of her purse. I promised her that I'd come to her hotel for a visit soon, and we went back and copped from Gary. And it didn't even seem strangely simple at the time.

Half an hour later and thoroughly stoned, we stood laughing our heads off on the street trying to think about where we were going to spend the night. I spat once, with an effort, and bubbles flew away on the wind. I watched them go, moving fast, and the street was blurred behind them. The Washington Square Arch shot by. So we went and blew most of the money we had left on beer, twenty-five cents the glass at some famous old pub with sawdust on the floor.

A little later, Chad called those two girls uptown and found out that they wouldn't be back until midnight. We decided that it wouldn't be manners to arrive then—without notice anyway—so we started down to the East Side in hopes of ferreting out a poet friend that I thought might render temporary aid. But we got hung up. Down around Avenue C I spotted a colored guy sucking an orange and swishing in a crouch from side to side. Crazy as hell, and I said to myself, "I gotta ask this guy." So I did and he pointed to a window above us and said, "Ask him, WooEEE!" I turned and looked at an empty window and he told me to wait a minute. Then a pale wild-eyed guy came and leaned out like he was looking for something. I asked him if he knew where this friend of mine lived, and he said, "Yeah, vaguely, wait a minute, I'll be right down, you can help me move!" So a minute later, he staggered down onto the street with an enormous pile of trash and gave some to each of us. That's me, Chad and the laughing man with the orange, and we started walking back to the West Side. By the time we got to his place, we were on pretty friendly terms and he invited us up to try some wonderful speed he'd been saving for a special occasion.

We fell into his ten-dollar-a-week, bloodstained closet all out of breath from seven flights of stairs and stepped around the plastic syringes that littered the floor. He got them legally because he was diabetic, but you could say that he misused a few of them. He had all kinds of odd drugs lying around and he couldn't have been more generous or desperate for company.

So we sat around shooting the shit and talking, dissolving this in that, and all of a sudden it came out that he'd been going with a fashion model named Victoria, that I'd loved in Florida. Out of all the people in New York, the chances were pretty big against my running into him, but the way things were going, the coincidence didn't rate much more than a smile. His name was Fred and I told him I wanted to see her right then that minute, and I jumped on him to tell me where I could find her. But he got all wall-eyed at that point and said, "Uh, well, we're not exactly in touch right now, but I'll try to find out for you." It was a long time after that when I finally got ahold of her by calling her at her hotel and catching her when she happened to be in. But I'll get to that, anyway, we kept getting higher and higher, and Flip, the orange-eater, was getting laughing hysterical and going, "Wow! WowEEE! Wow! WowEEHEEHEE!" So we decided that it was time to get on the street and walk some of it off. Flip played the bass and was crazy to get to the Village and find one. We did, and we listened to him play for about an hour, then he hollered like he was drowning for us to go on because he was hung up and we could find him there later, no doubt about it.

We were walking down the street and I was saying that I wished we had a joint to take the edge off it, when I looked down on the ground and found one, so help me. I said, "Saints Preserve!" and we cut down an alley to smoke it.

It was excellent grass and all three of us got high but it really fetched Chad. We turned a corner and he kept on going straight and didn't answer when I called to him. I told Fred to hang on a minute and caught up to Chad to ask him where he was going. He looked at me through terrified eyes and said he didn't understand why I was doing this to him. I thought, "Oh Jesus!" and what I should have done was let him go find those two girls uptown. Then he wouldn't have known he was crazy and could have gotten some sleep. But I thought about the subway, which scares me to death anyway, and how he might fall on them electric tracks or something. So I tried to get him to come with us but he said he couldn't face Fred and Flip. I thought he was just embarrassed and told him that they'd seen crazy people before, or something just as tactful. I was in no great reasoning condition myself and all I knew was I couldn't let him out of my sight until he started to come down, and that he'd disintegrate completely if I acted like a caretaker. Well, he wouldn't come back, and he wouldn't come back, so I hollered to Fred that we'd meet him back at his place later, and started walking around trying to talk it out of him. He kept saying he knew what was happening all right, oh yes, but he didn't understand *why*, which seemed like a pretty common affliction to me.

Bushwhacked by a sidewalk joint, for the next four hours we followed a zigzag course from the East Side to the West and back maybe fifteen times. Every direction I'd start to go, he'd say, "Oh no! You're not getting me to go *that* way!" The fourth time we passed through the Bowery, I found three dollars neatly folded on the sidewalk and considered myself apologized to.

Chad was afraid to go back to Fred's apartment because he thought we were going to kill him there. We went back and forth, both of us getting more and more tense with him leading the field until finally, he got to where he wouldn't go up or down the street, and he wouldn't talk at all coherently, and he wouldn't shut up. At that point, I screamed at him for being an idiot who couldn't even go crazy without being rude and accusing about it. Part of that got through, and he agreed to go back to the apartment house if I'd walk in front of him, but then he balked at the door for another hour. I am no rock of sanity myself, and will react heavily off of nuts when I'm not completely together, and he kept giving out with this frightened snarl that scared the daylights out of me. His face rippled like a stream with torrents of emotions and reversals and ideas and in the middle of all this I saw the moon floating through a fire escape above the tenements and I had to grab a lamppost to keep from giving up and wailing. I thought about the people all around us who were eating, sleeping, fucking or slashing their wrists, and right then, a cop drove by looking at us real business-like. Quick then, I begged to Chad that we were a couple of lunatics and if that cop came back and asked either one of us the simplest question, we'd try to cover it up and wind up in Bellevue. That, thank God, sank in and we went inside, me getting a better grip on myself, and Chad staring around at things I couldn't see. We made slow time up the stairs for fear of ambushes at every landing, and the seventh flight was more hollow than the rest, giving out with a booming noise that was good for another ten minutes of panic and confusion.

At right angles to the hall at the top of the stairs and one step down was another, only three feet wide and very short with a floor of corrugated aluminum. I didn't like the looks of this spot myself, and Chad made an unprecedented noise that was very expressive. But Fred's room was there, so we went and banged on the door. They had been lying down, resting if not sleeping, and it took them a lifetime to open the door while Chad wondered what they were preparing.

The room was about six feet wide and twelve long with a bed along one side and a table by the window at the end. Immediately we got in, Chad whipped over and sat on the table and I expected him to flip out the window like Lloyd Bridges any minute. Flip sat on the floor, and Fred and I on the bed, all of us moving slowly and talking cheerful. I was all fagged out from walking so much and fixed up a big one, but I was so nervous I jerked the vein around and raised a lump half the size of a golf ball. I yanked the needle out and it was followed by black blood and a loud, victorious, "AHA!" from Chad. Fred and Flip were being as sympathetic as possible, not to be patronizing but it didn't seem to be doing any good. One minute he'd stare, then stretch and grin, then shiver, then sweat. Over his shoulder and through the window I could see a taxicab parking lot and a occasional pedestrian. It was very late. Fred took off, and in a rare spasm of cleanliness, shot the leftover blood into a piece of cotton instead of on the floor. This brought Chad bolt upright saying we couldn't fool him, goddamn it, he saw that trick with the cotton and what's in it? I told him if he'd pay attention to what was happening instead of acting so crazy, he'd know what was in it. I wasn't about to say blood. I was getting a little sick of all his accusing me of plots and felt like knocking him over the head so he'd sleep a while. Then he said, "I'm not as crazy as you think. I know you're going to get me drugged and try to kill me, but why? I don't understand *why!*" All the while he eyed the piece of cotton that Fed had then thrown cleanly into the corner. About this time, Fred got to thinking just what the situation could come to, and he announced that it was time to move the show out of his room. As we got up to leave, Chad said, "Oh, no! You're not leaving me here!" and made for the door after us. But he was too frightened to go out in the hall. After a minute, he followed us down the stairs, peering around the banisters like a lunatic caricature. We walked self-consciously around the street for a while, with him faltering around behind us, and finally he said in a somewhat steady voice that he wanted to go uptown. I went to give him subway fare but he wouldn't let me get near him, so I set it on the curb and backed off. He snatched it up and ran around the corner.

WILLIAM BURROUGHS III

William Burroughs III, son of the famous writer whose first book Naked Lunch *was originally published by Olympia, and grandson of the Burroughs of calculating machine fame, was born in Conroe, Texas, raised by his grandparents in St. Louis, and attended high school in Palm Beach. He spent four months in the Federal Narcotics Hospital at Lexington, Kentucky, followed by six months catching salmon in Alaska. He is now twenty-two, attends Armstrong State College and was recently married.*

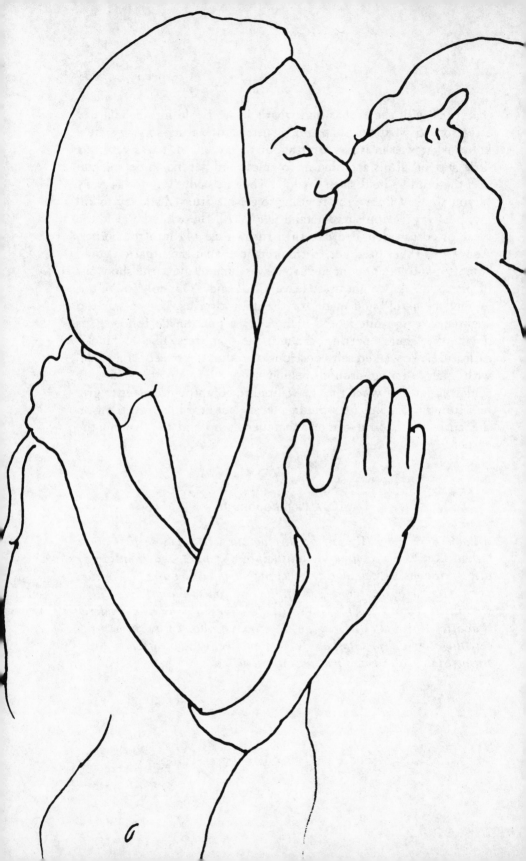

Norman Singer

Curtain of Flesh

One afternoon about a week later Paula Fabian left her office a little after five, and upon reaching the street grew annoyed to see that a swirling snowstorm was about to grip the city. She pulled up the collar of her sparse cloth coat which, she reflected grimly, was already two seasons old and wearing thinner by the day, and dug inside her pockets for her gloves. It was then that she saw a strange man approach her and strike up a conversation; which, in itself, wouldn't have been so objectionable to her. However, not at an hour when she was otherwise scheduled, nor so close to the building which housed her professional identity.

And then she saw that it wasn't a stranger after all, but a relative of one of her clients. Relieved at not having to circumvent a transient encounter which might have proved rewarding elsewhere, Paula affixed to her eyes the filtered neutrality which she reserved for all attractive men with whom she must deal platonically.

Max looked immense and overpowering standing before her in his camel's hair greatcoat, clutching one of his long ornate pipes and puffing on it for dear life. "Hi, Miss Fabian, remember me? Maxwell Sinclair!"

"Yes, of course I remember you . . ." smile waxen. From a distance she let herself hear the rough whiskered husk in the voice, the knell of virile timbre, and knew that soon she must look at him, must look at the man. And knew it was out of the question here and now, for there had been no masks assigned, no categories rehearsed. And to continue filtering such swarthy vitality would become a limited process. She must hurry away.

"You're Anna's big brother. And also a TV personality. An acrobat, or a dancer. Am I right, sir?" clipped, polite.

"Hell no!" Max frowned. "I'm a writer. Don't you watch TV on Friday nights?"

Trying subtly to edge around the hurdle and the swamp of him, she said, "Sorry, I have class on Fridays."

"Aw, from where I stand you got class every day!" Max waited hopefully for a laugh, wincing when he got none. "Look, I do most of the writing for 'My Three Muggers.' Number four on the Trendex just last week."

"Perhaps my mother watches it . . ." her eyes, starting out perfunctorily apologetic, were suddenly not. She saw. Saw the succulence of square jutting man's jaw under the wide generous smile of him, the flashing white teeth of him . . . saw the devil's stud of a phallic widow's peak . . . and thick rippled masses of unruly black hair . . . brows slashing shaggy jet . . . cheeks ruddy and lean . . . and felt the looming breadth, the contoured heat . . . Male in the night. Male on the street. Sorry, sir, I do not sup without place-cards. And wondering how long since the last time. Weeks? No. It must be days or I wouldn't still be here. I'd be in a 42nd Street movie-house finding a safe one.

"Well hey, now that we're old friends, let me give you a lift home." Max pointed to his low, long Cadillac convertible parked half-way up the block. "I mean, in this weather a gal might turn into the abominable snowman before she made it to the subway."

Again the sensual dizzying smile and Paula not turning away from it. "But Mr. Sinclair, I live a good distance uptown. Yorkville," still the therapy-tones.

"So, I'll send you a bill for the gas. Come on, let's get in that car before I freeze my options off!" then wincing, "Oops, slipped in a little blue stuff there . . . ."

Bumptious, she thought. Crude and plundering and undoubtedly oversexed to a point of cultism. Probably hangs around girls' playgrounds waiting for skirts to fly. Unleashed tiger species, needing to be taught and harnessed and removed. A pity that he knows me, knows my work and my name. This one's for using . . .

Max took her arm, but she pulled away and hurried on ahead through the crowd, waiting for him at the car.

They drove in silence for a moment. Intermittently, Paula felt his eyes on her, darting and curious as he angled for a line.

"This'll give me a chance to thank you for what you've done for our Anna-banana. I mean, six months ago that girl was ready to foam over."

Paula stole a quick glance at the profile, ripe waiting silhouette . . . stevedore's rumble of a voice . . . and slid her body away, pressed and hovered against the door. Trembling. Her throat constricted and crowded with fear. No . . . not to be cornered by something wild that had words and recognition . . . Jump from the car at the next light. Jump and escape.

"Yep, without you it would have been the rubber room and the whole *schmear* for Anna . . ." Max was determined to tell her his whole life-story, even though it looked like he was giving her some kind of an allergy. But he might never get another chance, so this had to be an all-out effort. "She's the only girl in the family, and not being exactly a Miss Rheingold type, my Ma was never too patient with her. She let us boys grow up like crabgrass, but wanted to make a regular nun out of Anna, with the convent and the baldness and the whole *schtick*. Real character, my Ma. She said: 'Any daughter of mine who looks like that's gonna marry Jesus Christ!' " Max glanced quickly at Paula. "Not religious, are you?"

"Hardly."

"Well, we're a bunch of roarin' Catholics, but I never do much about it. Too many production numbers, and I get enough of that at the studio.''

Silence again as they waited for a light to change. Max gave her a sidelong glance, saw that her face was turned away, almost shoved against the window. His eyes travelled down her throat as he tried to make out the breast-mounds under her coat. And succeeding, saw that they were more than ample, but decided he'd have to blast to get to them. Then he looked at her lustrous hair so severe and pulled back, and wondered what she'd do if he reached over and took the pins out.

She turned and caught his stare. "Why are we waiting . . . the light has changed."

Max couldn't take his eyes off her mouth as she spoke, and suddenly blurted it out like some kind of subnormal spastic case . . . "Miss Fabian, you have got the most beautiful mouth I have ever seen on a woman!" And then saw her cringe and go pale and turn her face away again.

"That's in bad taste, Mr. Sinclair, and I'm in a hurry." Why must he speak, she thought . . . why must any of them speak?

Although the midtown traffic was still heavy, Max decided to oblige the lady and maybe get arrested for speeding, as relentlessly he plowed on. "Did I ever tell you what a big family we've got?"

No answer.

"Five boys and a girl, although me, Anna and my brother Joe're all that's left in New York. The others shoved off to California a few years ago. Poor Ma, she sure misses 'em. How many kids in your family?"

Resigned sigh, still looking away . . . "Only child."

"Aw, that must have been lonely."

"It was perfect." Oh God, hurry and get me home behind a lock, behind my books. And then later when Mom's asleep I'll find someone who won't wage a campaign. This one is too close and greedy with what he knows. Expects a role fulfilled, idolatrous and handed to him. Oh, the big gross audacious bastard, how many defenseless young girls has he ripped bloody with that ego-thrust between his legs? Cocky muscle-bound clod all bravado and girth, so positive that everything he is is prime and top priority. Should be chained when they're like that . . . segregated, encamped . . . Oh hurry, hurry . . .

"I'm the only one in the family who never got married," Max went on, "and I'm the eldest. Five years ago I moved the folks uptown to Riverside Drive. Real elegant, wall-to-wall everything. My Ma's old-country Dublin, and Papa's old-country Milano, and down our way it wasn't too easy to mix wops and micks. You oughta get them to tell you the story sometime, how their families fought like blue murder to keep them apart. Like Romeo and Juliet . . . or maybe we should call it The Lower East Side Story . . ." Oh man, he thought, with her every word's a bomb; why doesn't someone just shovel the dirt over me? . . . "And you know, when my folks get a few beers in them and feisty enough, they still roll around the kitchen floor like they were back on Second Avenue . . ." The storm grew into a full blizzard now and Max prayed for a big traffic tie-up, because maybe with more time he might find the right combination. He just couldn't be this sunk on some plugged-up little man-hater; nor could he let it end like this . . . "Miss Fabian, I'm going to level with you. For what it's worth, I like you. I mean . . . I like you very much . . ." he cleared his throat . . . "that's right, very much. First time I saw you, nearly five months ago . . . well, whew man, you really shook me up . . ." Oh you meathead, ya fuckin' slob, why can't you talk all beautiful and romantic like you do with those Eighth Avenue chippies! . . . "And, like I was saying . . . or as I was saying, ever since that . . . uh . . . ever since then, I mean . . . well, I have been thinking about you a heap of a lot . . ." Heap-of-a-lot, Max died inside, where the hell'd I learn that, Zamboango?

Then he asked her for a date, dinner that evening.

"My mother's expecting me."

"Oh? Bet you've got a real nice mother too . . ." Shut up Max, shut the hell up your big mouth, Max! "Well then, hey, how about tomorrow night?"

"I'm busy."

"Then the next night?"

"Class."

Waiting for another light now, Max made a desperate lifeline of a maneuver and groped for her hand. Paula clenched her fist and pulled it away, wondering why they must all be such atavistic frauds, surrounding and impaling with their lordly bombasts, cupidinous wars . . . .

"I guess now I've really offended you," he said miserably.

Paula saw that they were at last nearing her block, although the snow whirling against the window nearly blinded her vision. "It's not important," she told him.

"Okay, prove it and let's have a lunch date . . . a luncheon date; tomorrow, huh?"

"I don't date, Mr. Sinclair."

Oh now man, this was too much . . . this was where he was gonna get the needles out and go jabbing for blood . . . "What're you, puttin' me on or something, Miss Paula Fabian . . . Miss Brainhead? I mean, what is that. 'I don't date' . . . what kinda bit is that? Either you're frigid or a les, right?"

"Mr. Sinclair, do you think your underprivileged mentality excuses you for being insulting?"

"Oh swell! Fine! You get an A-plus for that one. I'll even skip'ya a whole semester . . ." Damn her, what's so repulsive about me . . . and why does she make me come on like King Kong when I'm smooth, Goddammit, smooth! Think I'll kick her out before I start bawlin' . . . but first maybe I'll grab myself a big fat kiss. Oh hell no, I don't beg no broad . . . any broad . . . never . . . ever : . .

They pulled up to her apartment house, Max clutching the steering wheel in a bullish mass of brooding. "Could I at least have your phone number?"

Not answering, Paula found herself staring at his hands on the wheel, the black curling hairs on his wrist, her eyes dropping for a fast fever-glimpse of the long preposterous straddling legs under the dashboard . . . odors of tobacco and gasoline tunnelling so much back to her. Childhood goodies . . . treats for little Paulie Fabian 'cause she's the smartest . . . And then fleeting pain of the present as her eyes went to his face and she flung open the door and ran out into the snow.

Jolted by her sudden flight, Max roared out: "Holy shit!" and gaped after her. Then yelled, "How'd you find out I'm really Jack-The-Ripper, huh? Ya crud, go home, you mudder wants ya!" Then he saw her slip and fall in the snow. "Oh hell, wait honey . . ."

Max clambered out of the car and hurried to help her up, bending down to take her by the arms, their faces so close that his wisp of beard brushed against her cheek.

Paula struck out a hand against his shoulder with such force he nearly lost his balance. "Move back," she ordered him. And when he saw those flints of steel in her eyes it scared the hell out of him, almost scared him enough to pee right there in the snow.

Paula rose to her full five feet seven inches and he watched her shoulders go back, watched the gym-teacher's posture of her as she grandly brushed the snow from her coat.

Max ambled back towards the car, kicking furiously at the snow-drifts as he walked, turning and looking back several times with a couple of really rapier parting shots . . . "All right, Queenie, that's it then. *Fini* and you've had it, sweet stuff . . . and you can save it for the worms . . . you eggheads all got halitosis anyway . . ."

She'll remember that one, he thought, getting into the car. Before closing the door he grabbed for his pipe and went into a tense and nervous lighting process.

Paula hadn't moved. Stood there in the snow gusts watching as Max sat behind the wheel, legs big and spread, trousers tightly cloaking new mysteries . . . as old schoolgirl jingle sang in her ears . . . "wonder what that one's like . . . and that one . . . and the one next to him . . ." The flare of the match illuminated Max's face for her and her eyes narrowed and explored. Cameo raw and exposed. Beacon of need's light . . . as removed and untenable as a star.

No. Eyes lowering. Why the face of *this* one, when all the others had been hooded?

Max reached to shut the door and saw her standing there. In that moment the blustery winds tore at her hair and loosened it. Flowing dark cascades swept and hurled and tousled as she stood there, the transfixed voyeur.

Aw . . . look at her like that, he thought. Christ, I can't stand it. What's she gonna do now? Maybe she fell on her head.

He said nothing. Turned and stared straight ahead. Left the door open. He didn't know what was bugging her, but he still wanted her to feel welcome. After a minute, still gazing ahead and puffing on his pipe, Max visualized utter defeat . . . She's inside her house now . . . going up in the elevator . . . fallin' in her Mommie's arms and telling her how she got away from the big bad man . . .

Then turned and saw her seated next to him. Saw the firm graceful lady's hand reach out and slam the car door. Max watched the supple, resolute face, his eyes fierce with questing, his mouth dry, licking his lips, saying something . . . "Whaaa?"

Paula looked down the street. Dinner hour. Quiet. Deserted. "Drive around the corner," she said.

Throat dry and parched, his words scratched for logic . . . "We . . . had the wrong address?"

"Don't talk. Do as I say."

Watching the lips move in soft command, Max started the car. Slowly drove around the corner.

"Here," she said.

An empty lot.

Max went a little sweaty . . . Jesus, what is this . . . she gonna pull a knife or something? All I did was hold her hand.

They parked under a huge snow-laden tree.

He waited. His hand on the door-handle, ready for attack.

Then felt her fingers gliding at his knee and gave a sharp intake of breath. And looking down, saw her hand trailing upwards . . . slowly, the length of his leg, nestling into thigh and biceps.

"Ohmygod!" he groaned, and swirling about he plunged in on her, taking her in his arms, his hands grabbing at bouquets of her hair . . . "Aw honey, you are the biggest surprise package of my career!" Unbelieving, but so soaring and ready as his mouth rushed down and covered hers . . . thinking, umm . . . hell, it's happening. Soft, baby . . . soft.

And wrong again as she shoved him away from her. "Oh for God's sake, stop that!"

"Jesus Christ, what did I do? I want to kiss you, Miss Fabian . . . such a sweet beautiful mouth . . ."

"I don't kiss," her eyes on the parted full moistness of his lips as she spoke. "It's decadent."

He glared down at her, clenching a fist. "What're you, on the needle or something? Oh man, you gotta be the end. You don't date, you don't kiss. Well let me tell you something, I kicked playing Doctor and Patty-cake when I was ten; I mean, I don't need anybody to play with me, honey, 'cause I can play with myself . . . and . . . and what I need is you, dammit!"

"Not so loud," she said, and moved forward to switch on the car-heater. "Does this seat move back?"

"Sure."

"Move it."

He did.

"Get out of that heavy coat," she said.

He eyed her face for a second, nodding, "Yes," and kept his eyes peeled on her as he took the coat off, watching her remove hers, then tossing both garments in the back seat.

Paula looked at him, eyes nurturing the gangling lounging darkness of him. "Now everything."

Max swallowed. "Pardon?"

"Strip to your shoes, please, and don't speak."

"Okay," he started undressing, hungrily watching her watching him. "But this means you like me a little bit, doesn't it?"

She held a finger to her lips . . . "Shhh . . ."

And seeing her purse her mouth like that Max grew too shaky to undo his tie and simply tore it from his neck, his eyes planted on her as she removed the jacket of her suit and slowly undid her blouse, and he perspired there in the dead of winter as button after button revealed what he'd been trying to X-ray for months, those damned packed and hidden bursts half-spilling out of her bra as he got out of his shirt and saw her eyes on his hands fumbling at his belt-buckle as he followed her squirming movements to get out of her skirt, and with a gasp he saw the reason for her heavy woollen suits, because as far as he could see there were no panties . . . there was only . . . "Unnn!" Max said, and following his eyes Paula slumped down and winged her legs apart for him and his throat went so dry he hacked out a little cough as he quickly scooted up in the seat to slip out of the trousers which she seized and threw in the back. Max wore no undershirt and seeing the bearish naked chest Paula reached up and fiercely pulled out several hairs . . . "Ouch!" Max said, and trembled and muttered, "Oh Christ . . ." and tugged at his swelling briefs, but she said, "Wait," and he felt her warm light tapered hand flat against his abdomen, slipping so goddam slowly down inside his briefs that he was afraid he might stop breathing . . . until the hand touched and gripped and prodded his big hurting tong of an erection that had been straining against the fabric and could pop ten times over every time he looked at her mouth and those twin volcanoes still strapped and hiding in the bra which he wanted to rip off and save and keep under his pillow . . . and now feeling her hand caressing and pulling off the briefs . . . he watched her head lower and softly press his anxious acting prick against her cheek like it was a giant rosebud . . . "I'll be darned," he commented . . . and she held it and wielded it and murmured, "This is you, stranger; not up there, down here . . ." Then raised up and let her bra drop to the floor, and Max's eyes went so sincere they burned and teared, as he swallowed and then coughed again and stared at what was waiting . . . what was so alive and free and lush it had to be forbidden, but with a small whine Max reached for them . . . "Oh sweetheart, that's perfect like that . . . aw God, look at that . . . just perfect . . ." In his hands and palmed and rolling firm full high breasts and rising nipples of a big beautiful scholar all for him, in his hands, pressed against his mouth . . . and she said, "Move back, I want to see again . . ." and he slid off and away and felt the heat-rays of her aristocrat's eyes between his legs and the longer she looked there the more it ached, but she said, "Stay waiting and holding like that . . . the best moment to watch, most personal profile of all . . ." Then she reached up and pulled him swiftly down and inside as he gasped and yelled . . . "Ohmygod, Miss Fabian!" her legs flung high and pleading and ensnared him like a vise, grindings humid, teasing . . . "Farther," she ordered, "deeper . . ." and he said, "I don't want to hurt you," and she said, "Don't lie," and her heels pounded and pummelled at his haunches as he lunged more fully, circular thrusting strokes now, her legs wrapped and sucked and drawing him in tighter . . . wrenching her face away from the searching persistence of his mouth, insidious crippling softness of kisses so eager to capture and seal the brand . . . but locking him to her, clamping and absorbing the prescription and the remedy of him, using what she knew to be the best of him, the role of him . . . guiding and riding and directing the instrument for her own personal joy, the phenomena which she found nearly as beautiful as being alone in her fancies . . . not hearing Max's whimpered sobs of groans as he felt himself sinking and lost in the giddy wonder of newness and first experience . . . half-fainting from the tumbling fire and force of what writhed beneath him . . . and despite all the tearing passion of the woman, what Max found was cleansing, was right, as he swept full and deeply in and up and sliding fast and back and in and now their moist explosive sharings streamed and joined as they rolled and pressed and coveted the interlocking . . . denying an end to it . . . still caught by lingering waves of the attack as their bodies remained sealed and committed, and Max had to say it, "I love you, Miss Fabian . . . aw, I'm in love with you," and she tore her face away from his dreaming mouth, saying, "Be quiet, you fool, don't you know what you're ruining?" But kept him on her because within minutes she was near again, her hands beating, tugging at his back, as she felt him slung and raiding up inside where the contentment lay, and the ease. Then, a moment later, accompanied by Max's own fresh and heaving sighs, it was over and done with and she pushed him away.

Paula reached behind for her clothes and began to dress. Stunned by this speeding shift of mood, Max thought maybe it had been a dream after all, his honey of a storybook-lady so naked and grappling. But no . . . his body still echoed her clinging and her wanting. Let her deny what they'd given each other, let her try.

Her voice was suddenly full of caution. "It's dangerous here. It's stopped snowing and there may be squad cars," her eyes on the sustaining boldness between his legs.

"It didn't have to be here at all, you know," he said. "I do have a home."

She said nothing. Looked away from him and continued dressing.

God, he felt like such a big stupid ass sitting there not being able to move or make a decision, so immobilized by the quick coldness and change of her . . . There's something so great here for us, why does she want me to feel like garbage, like manure . . . when it's a lie, damn her, a lie!

"I'm finished business now, is that it?" he asked.

Paula let herself look at him again, saw the same brawny pugnacity, his body still owning and exuding everything they'd done together, his flesh still alive and reeking with what she'd discovered and made hers. But offerings not yet dead. Tremulous brute-feasts still waiting and there. And although she'd instructed herself to end it and blot out, the taunting of it still grew and pulled at her. Chemistry, Paula pounded at herself . . . accident of genes and glands, for desire is a decision that is always mine.

Watching her eyes roaming and bitter, Max heard a small cry escape her lips of which Paula was unaware. And then she shrieked at him, "Why don't you get dressed, you look so disgusting!"

He reached for his clothes and quickly started dressing, knowing she watched his every move . . . the briefs, the pants, the zipper, the belt; and he loved the excitement of her eyes on him, but wasn't too sure now that she did, though she did not turn away.

"I suppose you'll be telling everyone about this," she snapped, "telling 'the boys' about how I put out . . . about the new notch in your belt, this hot piece of ass you dug up who has the whole world believing she's a germ-free scholar-lady . . . but man, who's really the cheapest horniest little pushover . . ."

She hurts, Max thought . . . oh Christ, how she hurts . . .

"I don't discuss my private life with anybody," he muttered. "Your secrets are safe with me, if that's all you're thinking about . . ." Abruptly he faced her and met her eyes and she looked away at once. And Max knew . . . She's so unhappy, he thought, and I can make her happy. How can I tell her if she hates the words?

In control again, Paula decided to face what had really happened. The man was unusually equipped to satisfy. Really the most successful and therapeutic session she'd had in months. She'd been working exceptionally hard lately, so perhaps more of such tension's ease was indicated. More than the usual quick hour this time. A purging talent like his might be worth it. A prowess so native. Latin and Irish, that might be it. Astounding dimensions; that, too, might be it. Whatever it was, Paula wanted more.

Her choice.

"Do I drive you home?" he said.

For an answer Paula's hand went between his legs, unzipped and came quietly to rest on the warm bulge of his briefs. Gasping, Max thought he would never get used to a woman doing something like that so casually. Before it had always been his hands making the move, jamming courteously up their skirts and turning on the heat and being the aggressor like men are supposed to.

"I know a hotel that's quite safe," she said.

"Oh wow, honey . . . Oh Jesus, you had me scared!" for now Max didn't care how she wanted to play, and he lovingly pressed the sweet reconciled hand at his crotch, pressed and held it and was quite ready to hold it wherever she wanted to put it, even though she tried to pull it away now with the feel of his hands on hers. "But look, we don't need a hotel. We'll go to my place. I live alone. No danger there."

Good God, what is he raving about, Paula wondered . . . is it a foreign tongue? She never went to their apartments. Never gave them the role of scavenger, the advantage of recruiting her so that she'd have to pay court and perform and do a slum-service, at *their* leisure, for *their* amusement, in the conquering midst of *their* security-trappings. "Mr. Sinclair, I am not a whore. I go only to hotels when I meet someone at night. And *I* pay for the room. Have I made myself clear?"

Holy Christ, he thought . . . she wants to make a fuckin' pimp out of me. Oh God, this is never gonna work . . . oh no man, not for Maxie-boy . . . not that slimy route for ol' Max . . . not even if she stays stuck in my craw the rest of my life, I don't play ass-licker for nobody! And damn her, if what she wants is a man, she's gonna know right now that she's got one.

He reached across her lap and opened the car-door. "Out," he said, "right now. It's stopped snowing, so take a hike."

Tensely, Paula thrust out her chin and threw back her shoulders and arched a superior brow, and although Max saw her mouth tremble, he wasn't going to give a bitchin' inch.

"Idiot," she said crisply, "you'll be playing with that thing the rest of your life thinking of all you missed tonight."

She flung the door wide and stepped out onto the snowy pavement. And stood there a moment on the pretext of adjusting her coat, knowing that he couldn't close the door with her in the way. Stood there and glowered in at him, her face straining for great poise and victory. But as she watched the hulking fury of the man behind the wheel, her words refuted all attempts at composure . . . "I wouldn't be able to stay very long, Mr. Sinclair."

The voice sounded so small and young to him Max could barely hear her, but he turned and smiled, his face full and beaming at her, as she looked down at her feet. Primly. "My dear Miss Fabian, sweetheart, you can stay as long as you like."

As he drove, Paula sat beside him, regal and controlled. Remained silent, neither looking his way nor touching.

Max sneaked furtive glances at her quiet profile, her princess face . . . so distant and away; and with each look he knew and realized the finality of what was in him . . .

I love her. It'll never be anyone else for me now. Maybe if I hadn't met her, if there hadn't been this past hour; but not now. She's the one.

Max's apartment was in the East Sixties near Lexington, and after a cold sweeping glance at the decor Paula neatly hid her surprise at not finding it the gaudy tinselled bachelor pad she had expected. It was an enormous and impressive three room arrangement, done in tones of subdued and contemporary walnut. One vast wall of the studio livingroom was panelled and lined with books, while the other offered a stunning array of original paintings. Renoir, Modigliani, Picasso. Overhead hung a crystal chandelier of such delicate artistry, Paula decided then that the place wasn't his at all but that he'd sub-leased it. At the center of the room was a magnificently built fireplace, which Max immediately proceeded to light.

Paula went directly to the telephone to call her mother; grateful, as always, that Marta Fabian never checked on her daughter's stories, due either to faith or fear, Paula had never been sure which. Tonight the piquant little woman sounded increasingly distressed over the Hungarian uprising which had begun only a few weeks before. Marta had heard nothing from her sister, who still lived in Budapest with her husband and three boys. After calming her mother's fears as only she could, Paula went on to explain that she would be spending the night with Gretchen, her co-worker at the clinic, who, she said, had been taken suddenly ill. Marta praised her for her charitable heart and said not to worry, she would have dinner with her neighbor, Hilda.

Max poked at the fire, cherishing that fleeting glimpse of appraisal he'd seen Paula give the room, for he was proud of his apartment. Some people said he wore his home like a badge, but Max had known from the start how he'd wanted the place. No scrapbooks or autographed pictures of stars he'd never met or weird Martian mobiles hanging from the ceiling or a bunch of low-slung slats for chairs. Something solid and comfortable. That was the pitch. Something his.

Later, he'd mix Paula a drink and they'd sit and talk, and she'd see they had so much more in common than she'd ever expect. Not many people knew that he collected rare books, for instance; especially books on humour dating all the way back to old Rabelais himself, as well as all of Shakespeare's comedies and Moliere. Then he'd show her his record collection, which admittedly contained a lot of jazz albums, but quite a lot of long hair stuff too. Mostly operas. Max went absolutely ape over Puccini. And as for Verdi, he got a lump in his throat just reading the programs.

Seeing Paula put down the phone, Max went over to her and asked what she'd like to drink.

"Nothing," she replied. "Where's the bedroom?"

And her hand reached out and grabbed him there again like an involuntary reflex, and hell, she wasn't even smiling.

"Yeah . . . I know," he said, bumping politely backwards and clutching her hand away as subtly as he knew how, "but first I thought we'd have a drink and chat awhile . . . and . . . and I've got quite a collection of books, Miss Fabian, would you like me to play a few . . . uh . . . records, I mean, not books. But I have books too, see up there on those shelves?" Aw Christ, he thought, I still sound like the prizewinning clownhead of all time!

"Bedroom," Paula said again, and as she moved away from him he saw that she was, actually, headed in the right direction.

Max gave a forlorn backward look at his library and his Hi-Fi and his record racks. "Puccini!" he called after her. Then pointed across the room. "And Pablo Picasso in his mauve period! Oh hey,

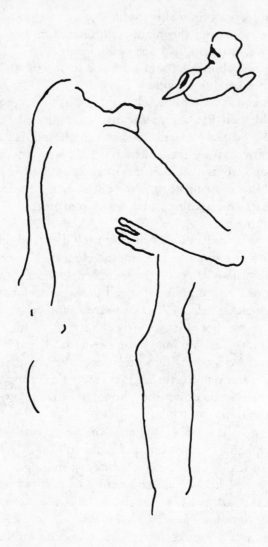

wait honey, I want to show you around the place first; we don't have to rush."

As Paula walked into the big sumptuous bedroom, her heels sank into the thick carpet. Luxury, she thought as she stripped. He writes TV nursery-drama for mass idiocy and gets paid like this. Then thought of all her years of study and scrimping to remain in school, and thought of the cramped cubicle of an apartment she and her mother shared. And, nude now, rubbed her thighs together and waited for him.

Max stood in the middle of his beautiful living room, feeling like he was about seven and a half years old and all the kids in his neighborhood had suddenly moved . . .

Oh nuts . . . she didn't look at a single book. Not even *The Would-Be Gentleman;* that would have gotten a rise out of her. Pretty sick psychologist to be making a house-call. Never saw such a one-track mind. Anything above the belly-button's off-limits for her. Well shit, that does it for her; I don't need a freak like that to get my jollies—I can get all the lovin' I want. I'm going in there and give her such a screwin' blast, her little vibrator's gonna twitch all the way home. Then I'll toss a couple of bucks in her face and dump her in a cab . . .

When he reached the bedroom he saw her lying naked on the white chenille of his king-size bed, as if she had been mounted on a great big plaque. Max stood in the doorway and swallowed and stared for a second, and Paula squirmed and rolled full-circle as he caught rippling flashes of pliant buttocks and pubis, her body lithe and long and full, nipples rigid and aimed . . . topping the loveliest creamiest peaks Max had ever seen from such an angel. Like soup's on and the table's set and pull up a chair and a spoon. Like . . . "unnn!" . . . how could he ever throw anything like that away when she was so pretty everywhere?

Shuffling towards her like a sleepwalker, Max started undressing. But she rose swiftly and met him en route. Told him to stand perfectly still. And, her fingers full of nubbing grace, undressed him, deftly fitting him with the condom she'd found in her purse. And Max was helpless and no longer tried for conversation, with her hands ladling all those places on him like everything of his that she unveiled was some kind of jewel and should be insured.

And then . . . the newer expanse and freedom of their bodies heaped together in his bed, the stream and stretch and crawl of limb's embraces which was once again a communication more eloquent and articulate than anything either of them could have said to deny the special power. And as Paula saw the stricken ardour on his face and watched the body as it hovered over her and descended, she saw the length of all of him, really, the total man—but opened up and received what her body insisted was his sublimest value. Attachments applied. Cause and effect. Sensory friction.

But soon her catchwords blurred and dissolved as time left the room. It was a world of feeling, a tender plateau . . . more mutual than either of them suspected.

There were no beginnings or boundaries or endings. Climaxes interwove and relayed, each becoming the fresh starting flux of another. The thought of not touching was absurd and unbearable, was pain. Daylight beamed through the blinds and the warm addictions still clung to them, as they lay drunk and senseless with what they held, with the awe and novelty of simply staying near.

Max knew that he would never have the words to tell her what an assault these hours had been. The heady scope and variety of her body-needs, and the exquisite teasing torments she added to his, always the surprise attack or turn or movement, the perversions which she handed out like royal edicts . . . sinuously cruel one moment, breathlessly soft and waiting the next.

And for Max it wasn't enough. It was only the surface of what he wanted from this woman. And before she left his bed he swore to himself that he would show her what he meant. And convince her that without it they were like children playing in a sandpile. He meant kisses for his love. Kisses for the dear child-woman mouth that twisted away from his even when she was at her highest reaches of the wistful lunacy.

He chose a moment when she was near again and ready, when her eyes looked somehow innocent and humbled by the gift she found within her. And he asked, "Again, baby? Now?"

Paula nodded, her face raised and rapt and unseeing.

Pinning her arms behind her, Max quickly seized that face in his two hands, cupped and firm, and kissed her, his mouth partly open and crushing to still her cries, his mouth staying and becoming law; and he knew at once the perfection he'd been waiting for. Felt her thrashing twisting legs beneath him, but he was still inside of her and plowing . . . and now it was too late for either of them to dwarf the heights they were about to achieve, for he knew there was nothing she could do to stop the flow of this moment despite the forbidden mouth on hers, as Max held her flat and powerless and made her mouth a part of him, a part of all that had passed between them . . . breathing words against her lips, the savage mumbles . . . "kisses and orgasm, baby . . . kisses and orgasm . . . one and the same . . . no segregation . . ."

Max felt her tortured moans against his mouth as they came, and in the next instant Paula freed her left arm and made a fist of the hand on which she wore a large signet ring—a class ring. And with all her strength socked a gashing blow at Max's cheek that hurled him off her body and sent him stumbling half-way across the room.

Jesusgod, the bitch, he thought, she probably knows Karate too, and with an infuriated howl he stood there and glared at her, blood slowly streaming down his cheek. As if afraid to approach her in his fury, Max didn't move, but flung out an arm and pointed at her . . . "Get up and get out," he roared. "Get out of my house if you don't want to be loved." He stood there and waited, fists clenched, his face full of shock and rage.

Rising, Paula moved across the room and stood before him, the slim trace of a smile on her lips. "You have no further use of me?" she inquired.

"You heard me!" his voice clung desperately to the hostility.

Her eyes lingered down towards familiar terrain, viewing it only a second before she saw the rising. "You're contradicting yourself," and with a long manicured nail she jabbed at the tip of the evidence, and Max swore and hit her in the face with the back of his hand, and to keep from falling Paula had to reach up and grab on to his shoulder, slumping towards him and striking out another blow on the same spot where her ring had cut him.

Then, clumsily, they touched and mauled in the contempt, bodies tossed together in a recklessness of nubile intimacy neither of them had intended. Awkward sliding flesh-raids as his penis prodded crazily against her stomach and the hair of his chest became a curling jungle growth against her throat. And words were somehow gone again and anger became a fatuous irrelevance, as once more the entrapment cloaked, and Max gently lifted her in his arms and carried her back to the bed. A few drops of blood dripped heedlessly on his shoulder as Paula ripped at the hairs on his chest and madly kicked her legs in the air to make herself heavier to carry. Placing her softly on the bed, her victory smile meant nothing to Max, and his arms held all the flesh of her she was willing to relinquish, his arms taking possession in embrace. Max hugged and prized the body of her and his lips went to her breasts and made love there, as he remembered the truth of what she had become for him . . . I love her, love whatever she is . . . and I'll kiss my love wherever she'll let me. As long as it is her and we are close. And maybe someday she'll find out who I am and won't be so afraid to look . . .

Paula did look in that moment, looked down at his face, the mouth so abject and nuzzling; told herself the only reason for watching his lips' moist sensuous caressing was to scoff at his indignity and defeat and lowering. Yet, though unaware of it, as her eyes remained on the boyish searching lips that lay against her breasts and beseeched there, telling herself it was a servile process, a bowing and a nursing, the result of the conquering use she'd made of him . . . Paula's hand went to the back of his head and with a detached and lingering softness, lightly held and cherished there as he kissed, her fingers playing and sifting through the thick black hair that felt warm and tumbled to the touch . . .

And, abstractedly, drowsily, Paula watched everything the mouth did. The mouth that was such a danger for her own. Watched the face. Watched Max.

Max knew that with Paula he'd have to find all his hidden persuaders in bed, because if he wanted any sort of an audience with that queen he'd have to go through her body to get it. It seemed strange to him, using orgasms to brainwash his own wife, but then, not strange at all when you thought of Paula. So, on the pretext of wanting to spend some time writing new material, Max told his agents not to book him anywhere for the next few weeks. It was true that this was how he occupied himself during the day, but late every night he left himself free to perform at home.

Knowing that sex still remained Paula's first overture for reaching, he glutted her with it nightly. A plowing, unrelenting chain of attacks, more frenzied than ever because now he was the one dishing out the big surprises, engineering all the raging oral assaults which she had initiated; but without the hostility now. With tenderness. Every lunatic squirm and twist of flesh she wanted Max gave her, leaving her gasping and tremulous with the new satieties he'd brought to her. After the first week of such massive doses he felt the stunned and clinging joy of her as she pressed and held him to her, speechless except for the small whimpers of incredulity, as if she were being presented with something too fulfilling to be trusted. And her hands did more than prod or grip or claw—they caressed the gift of him, made love to his bestowals. Anchor-man, lover man . . . and soon-to-be father-man, all wrapped up in the same lovely nonsectarian package. And that's what he had to see, that it was all part of the same action. No specialized compartments for love, but one big sweeping urge . . .

Their nights went on like that. Soon Paula skipped a few classes to begin earlier. Missed several nights at the Center. Wanted to take advantage of the cycle. Not questioning it, or discussing it. He half-expected her to gloat over what she might term his new debasement. But neither of them found words for it. Except that body of hers, he thought . . . oh Jesus, that sweet-tasting body never shut its mouth! Told him everything. Made love to him in languages that couldn't be written or thought or even stammered.

After a few weeks she told him she would have to pass up a night or two for the usual reasons, but said she would come to his bed anyway. Wanted her hands on his body. Wanted to do things to him as a spectator, with him lying perfectly still and letting her. And wanted a dim lamp turned on so she could see the prize that she fondled. Max decided the time to strike must be drawing near if even her period didn't scare her away from him.

Another week passed before he felt primed, felt the courage stemming from his body to hers and back to his again. An April night. The rain beating against the windows made everything seem right to him somehow; cozy and sheltered, wonderful time for nesting. Max lay flat on his back as her fingers trailed and encircled, eyes seeking the thrust of what the soft light reflected. Then her hand fiercely gripped his warm and jutting fullness and with swift up and down strokes she began an undulance and an urging.

"Hey, watch it!" he tried to stop her.

"No Max, let me please . . ." hand faster, insistent . . . "want to see the fountains at Versailles . . . want to see the ripples and the geysers . . ."

"No . . . oh honey . . . oh hell, wait!"

And Jesus, it was such a helpless naughty *spritzing* feeling to let it happen like that, but who the hell cared as long as it excited her to watch? Then, not giving him an instant's respite, she slid her body under his and moistly rammed up deep inside of her what was still firm and staying, and while plunging above her Max told himself that after this one he would finally tell her what they both wanted, what their flesh could do for them besides . . . Oh but now he drew back, jabbed forward, hoisted her higher, held her sweet pearly-white ass in his hands and slammed crazily up and swirling, their tangling becoming as urgent as if it were their first time . . . but going somewhere now, a real adult destination in all that ruthless surging . . . scouring for new villages to plunder and populate, fresh juices to flow into man's image . . . until, at last, the brief locked madness . . . then sighs explosive . . .

They lay still, her fingers toyfully dabbing at his tentative softness. "Amazing," she said, cradling the length of it, watching its ascent once more, "how this triples its size with just a touch. Phenomena of the ages . . ."

He reached over and brushed his beard against her breasts, then pressed his mouth between them and blew hot breath there. "You look at it as if it had a life of its own," his lips raising and brushing the rigid nipples, as he hoped that line hadn't been too subtle a beginning, because tonight she had to get the message.

"I look at it and think where it's been, what it's done," she said lazily, "that's where the wonder is. It looks so inanimate now, but think how its mood can rear up and change . . ."

Max lay back down on the bed. Took a deep breath. He was ready now, and dammit, it wasn't going to be like changing the subject. No, it had to sound like the same subject. "Honey?"

"Hmm?"

Oh Christ, suddenly he was so tense with it he almost felt like bawling, and what the hell would he want to go and do a thing like that for . . . because why couldn't he let it out easy and natural, even though there was so damn much at stake and he knew it could never be the matter-of-fact conversation piece it might be with other couples, he still didn't want it turning into a fight, didn't want a bunch of screaming insults growing out of all that wonder she was talking about without realizing what she meant . . . "Honey . . . you're right," he began again, "it does have a life of its own."

"I didn't say that, Max, you did. I just meant it was a huge lovely appendage, and possibly the only status symbol I've ever hunted."

"No, I know . . ." he muttered. "I'm the one who said it had life," his words rushing, tumbling . . . not cool, dammit, but all sludging and emotional . . . "Power of life. I mean, it can give life, Paula. It can . . . triple its size by producing a lot more just like it . . . I don't mean more pricks, for God's sake, I mean . . . well, you know what I mean?" Aw hell, he sounded so clumsy and backward he wanted to die . . . because it meant so much and he knew he was starting to shake with how much it meant. But goddammit, it *had* to be done with words, didn't it . . . and right here and now . . . not drawing up diagrams or writing it in a poem . . . had to be said. But gently, you sonofabitch Max, gently!

He felt the slight change in her, a shifting. Felt her switch roles. Could almost hear that brain of hers clickin' and fartin' away. Her hands left his body and her eyes went to his face. "What's wrong with you, Max? You look like you're about to . . . to cry or something . . ."

Oh Jesus, and all he'd felt was a goddamned lump in his throat. But it was true! He felt his eyes and they were wet. Snotnose little kid wants to be a father, does he?

"Honey, you said two years . . . and it's more than two years now dammit, and I want kids!" Listen to him, shouting at her . . . listen to the gentle growling bull playing it sweet and easy . . . and he couldn't stop the sound, the slob and whining sound . . . all wrong and getting worse . . . "I'm not gonna wait . . . 'cause you're the only woman I'll ever love, so damn you, Paula, you're my only chance. So I want us to start a family and the quicker the better!"

Paula lunged up and away from the spectacle of foolish tears streaming down his cheeks. It was a startling, uneasy sight for her, this instrument of desire so quickly transformed into an object of erosive pity, and she felt disgust and embarrassment for him that he would let himself be seen like that. But more than anything, she felt she'd been used. "A family! So that's why you've been courting me all these weeks with that throbbing brute of a body of yours . . . trying to melt me down, get me ripe for the kill."

"No, don't you use words like that for it . . ." He grabbed the sheets and mopped at his face. "I know I'm saying everything wrong, but maybe I want this so much I just can't talk about it . . . 'cause it chokes me when I try to get it out in words, but . . . but dammit I'm thirty-three years old and I'm Irish and dago and I gotta have kids!" Max was suddenly standing up in bed, his body naked and writhing with what he wanted from her . . . "Babies are the only answer for both of us, Paula . . . babies will set things right, and you'll know what I mean as soon as you hold the first one in your arms, 'cause you'll love it on sight . . . and it'll make things right . . . make this right . . ." pointing down at the bed.

"I don't require little child-crutches to justify my pleasure, Max. At the moment I'm not ready for children. I want to think about it. Want to plan for myself. At least another year."

"All right, you take time and you think about it, Paula, and then if the answer is no as well, I'm not going to let it stay no, 'cause I'm not letting us go on like this forever . . . screwing and grinding my nuts off . . . banging our lives away till there's nothing left but slime, because I want you to see me like I am, instead of some heavy-hung moron you turn on and off like a fire-hose 'cause goddammit, look at me, Paula, I'm not a thing, I'm a man . . . not just a piece of meat, but a man . . . so you look at me for once and see something else besides this . . ." he clutched between his legs and waggled it at her.

"Oh for God's sake, Max, have a little pride! If you want to go to pieces, do it alone like a dignified human being. This is all so pointless of you, and so . . . so unattractive . . ."

But as she went into the bathroom for a robe which hung on the door and draped it around her, Paula knew that she wanted him in this moment, standing there like that, all loose and damp and lumbering, wanted him, the damned brawling howling ape! Then, before she could retreat into her own bedroom, Max raced ahead of her, blocking her path and yanking her back into his bedroom. "I'm not finished with you yet!" he yelled at her, slamming the door behind her. He saw the tight battle readiness in her face, and knew that he'd lost the ball, at least for this one night that was going to be so crucial for them, so full of promise . . . thinking maybe the only way to get her pregnant was to catch her with a gadget-free cunt some night and fuck the livin' hell out of her, and keep fucking her until she was gorgeously knocked up . . . and maybe she'd leave him, but he'd keep the kid . . . Aw no, Christ . . . what was he thinking of? They both had to want it, wasn't that the deal? Wasn't that everything?

"Max, I'm really ashamed for you. You look such a mess. So . . ." she swallowed. ". . . undesirable . . ."

"Tough shit in spades, baby, but I happen to be a human being and I am not ashamed who the hell sees me cry. Tears are not a crime, Paula. Animals wish they could cry like we do, but they can't. But sure, honey, I cry . . . and it's about time you knew exactly what you married . . . I cry and I bleed and I sweat. And what's more, sweetheart, I shit and I fart and I fuck and I suck, as you well know, Princess Bangtail, as you well taught me!"

He saw the trace of a smile on her face, as her voice went gentler . . . "Max, we'll both give it some thought . . ." one hand going involuntarily between his legs to hold the loose heaviness there, while the other dabbed at his eyes with the sleeve of her robe.

She wants me to think about sex again, he thought, because she's physically afraid of the rest of me, the way I grabbed her, the way I'm yelling my filthy-mouthed head off. Thinks I'm going to beat her up. Oh hell, what happened, he wondered, moving out of her reach; how did I let it come to this when it was going to be such a simple homey little fireside chat . . . and why the hell do we start screaming at each other as soon as we're out of bed . . . as if we blame each other for how much we like it . . .

"Of course, you do see that shouting won't solve anything," she went on smoothly.

"Okay, okay, humor me, I got it coming." He went to the closet and put on his pajama-trousers, thus hiding those distractions she always relied on whenever things threatened to get too personal between them. "But listen, Paula, you know my family, so just think how I feel. My brother's two years younger than me and already he and Elsie got six kids . . ."

"That sow of a wife of Joe's?" she shrieked; and with a start, Max turned around, unable to believe the roaring, trembling sound of her. "Is that what you want for me, Max? You want me to look like that . . . that walking dung-heap?"

"Oh now wait a minute, don't you start diggin' at my family again . . ."

"That blob of a female," she began pacing hectically about the room. "Oh that . . . glandular dumpling, that eruption, that vegetable!"

"Shut your goddamn mouth, they love each other . . . they're happy!"

"They are obscene."

Seeing her detachment dissolve into such a flaring rage, Max found himself caught up in this rarity, the phenomena of disturbed emotional fury. Not disturbed between her legs, emotionally . . . and showing it! Where's her brilliant control, he wondered . . . and what finally got to her, mentioning other people's kids? Christ, look at her, slashing around the room like she's ready to set fire to the place. "Paula, they're a good example of what we could be if we gave ourselves the chance," he said. "Joe says a man with lots of kids has the whole world in his lap. He's got respect and prestige that nothing can take away from him."

"Sweet Mother of Christ! He should be the gagwriter, not you!"

"He says a man with six kids can walk like a king, no matter what happens to him."

"Oh God, I don't believe it," she glared at him. "Where could that mountain of bad manners and bad breath walk like a king? My God, to throw in my face the nauseating couplings of those two dinosaurs as an example of communal superiority! It's obvious how they hate each other's bodies or they wouldn't keep having children . . ."

"Don't insult them, they've got more love in their . . ."

"A toad of a spineless jellyfish like your brother Joe has six or seven household orgasms and this unique feat, which is copied in barnyards the world over, this alone is his sublime contribution to society, after which he does nothing but sit on his . . . fat testes and point to these babbling discharges as his sole claim to fame."

"Holy Christ, where did all that shit come from?" Max was jolted by her cynicism, yet still full of wonder at the soaring vehemence of her. "There's nothing babbling about his kids. They're great kids, every one of them. And having a big family means a helluva lot more than just fathering these babies; a man raises his kids, and supports them and . . . watches them grow. That's the big job, just being there when they grow up."

"Disabled veterans, that's what they're like," she went on, "Demanding preference wherever they go, practically stopping strangers on the street to brag about their fatherhood status . . . 'Please be nice to me, Sir, I'm maimed—got a wife and six kids at home.' And what happens to the little woman after eight or nine pregnancies?"

"She's fulfilled."

"Gutted, you mean. I see them by the dozens at the Guidance Center . . . not even thirty, some of them, but dazed and wallowing blimps in a state of arrested shock. Well thanks a lot, King, but not for me. Sex isn't going to make a victim out of me . . . turn me into some sort of brood mare dropping mutations all up and down the countryside . . . draining my individuality . . . dissipating my progress . . ."

Max sank down on the bed, hearing the echo of those edicts, the finality . . . Sounds like the end of the argument, he thought. Meeting adjourned. Lecture-group go home and sack out. No more to be said about babies. Ever. And I can't leave her because she's with me every minute and I love her. What does that mean, that I'm stuck with only a body because she wants the rest of her to rot? Desperately, he groped for some logic behind all those violent fatherhood aversions. And then Max remembered something personal and tried it aloud. "Look Paula, I know how hurt you must have been by your own father, the way he failed you, ran out on you . . ."

Her face went livid. "Oh you liar, this had absolutely nothing to do with my father!" her voice rising again as she stared hatefully at him. "I was being completely impersonal tonight."

He met her stare. "Impersonal," he nodded. "Oh brother, that's the word all right. Shooting your head off about everything but us, about trends and . . . and social conditions, when all the time it happens to be very personal with you, Paula, because you are blaming me and practically every other guy for what your father did to you."

"No . . . oh you don't know, you don't know!" She rushed over to the bed where he sat and struck him in the face with the back of her hand. Catching both of her wrists and holding them, Max rose. "Jesus, it sure looks like I've been hitting you where you live tonight, Paula, and I don't know what the hell any of it means, except that you don't want my babies."

"You're goddamned right," she said, tearing free of him. "Babies from you, Max . . . little tadpoles of lust and greed! Men like you and Joe shouldn't be allowed to have children . . . defective, Mongoloids . . . brawling jungle-types, beating your chests

. . . creating nothing but your own sperm . . .!"

"What's left for us, then, huh, Paula? You think we oughta be gassed maybe, or castrated . . . or put on the rack, or burned?"

"But it's quite true, you know," she said, backing away from him towards the door, "Any offspring of yours would be reciting Joe Miller at three, table-hopping in Lindy's at six, and after that, Max, he'd dress like you and . . . talk like you and clown like you . . . another boor, another buffoon!"

In a fast leap Max seized her by the wrists again, pressing his face close to hers. "Or it could be a little girl, Paula, and take after you. Fuckin' everything in pants by the time she was twelve!"

At once Max saw the transformation in her face, slight, only the barest essence, but a falling, a bailing out. He let go of her.

"Oh . . ." she murmured, and absently brushed a strand of hair from her forehead. Then a brief tremor about the eyes, lips parted, stricken, and she turned to leave the room.

Frightened by the look of her, by the shattered haunted thing that had entered the room and settled on them like a mist, Max was caught up in a sick and mournful remorse. Everything strong about her had gone weak and lost in that moment, he thought, hurrying after. "Oh Paula, listen . . . I didn't mean to dig into you like that. It's just . . . well, you say something bitchy to me, so I gotta say something bitchy to you, but please don't look like that . . . because anyway, it's not such a great big worry. I mean . . . it's not hereditary or anything . . ." Oh God no, he thought; why were they hanging themselves with words tonight?

Paula gazed up at him, eyes bemused, uncomprehending. And Max saw that she was, somehow, away. Removed. Taken from him. As in a small voice she inquired, *"What isn't hereditary?"*

She's not accepting the word, he thought, cancelling out the whole subject. "Oh honey . . . God, I . . ." He put his arms about her and it scared him even more because she didn't push him away. No resistance. He held her softly and she leaned there, reclined there in his arms, expressionless . . . What *are* the words for loving, he wondered, if we found all the words to kill tonight? "Paula, please forget everything we said . . . tomorrow we'll start fresh."

"I'm . . . tired, so tired all at once," voice not agitated, not tense, not hers. Her body seemed to go limp in his arms as he lifted her up, carried her into her bedroom, wishing to God that she'd kick and fight to get free. But Christ, she let him carry her to bed like a baby . . .

"Sit there a minute, honey, and I'll get your nightgown."

She was obedient. Waited. "Don't know when I've been so tired," she murmured, "So silly, isn't it?" He took off her robe and she stood up, nude and still, letting him slip the nightgown over her head. The he lifted her again and slipped her under the blankets, tucked her in, fluffed up the pillows for her. She let him do this . . . And oh damn, it wasn't fair, he thought, the way he had to hurt her and tear at her to make her sweet and pliable, make her a girl to protect. How could he be happy about it when he thought of what he'd had to do to get her like this? Jesus, I'm so hooked on this baby. Kids or not, I have to stay, have to hang around . . .

But tonight was too rare, and he'd already been such a bastard, so maybe he'd press his luck and take advantage. He crept in beside her under the covers, taking her hand in his, breathless with new hoping. "I . . . better stay with you tonight," he said softly; and then in a whisper . . . "darling."

Paula said nothing, lay still. And he was afraid to believe it, in her bed like this, so calm and right. But a moment later the fancy crumbled. "You've helped me enough for one night, Max, go get your rest." Not mean or sarcastic, not with any feeling at all. But definitely said.

"Okay," he said, crawling out on the other side of the bed. "I am tired, honey. You sleep well." He headed for the door.

"Max?" she called faintly.

"Yes?" he turned, and she said no more for so long that he started getting scared all over again. "Yes, honey?" he spoke again.

"Breakfast," she said. "See you at breakfast."

"Sure!" he grinned across the room at her, but she switched her nightlight off and left his smile in the dark.

Max went back to his room, not bothering to stop the new stream of tears, letting them roll and trickle but wishing he were built more like a rock inside than he was out so maybe he could take the kind of torture his love was turning into, take it like a man. But no, he couldn't take it, not without letting go . . . because oh, how she looked . . . oh God, how she sounded like a stranger, like a foundling . . .

He sat on his rumpled bed and thought about the night.

Mission demolished. I can't change her, and can't replace her. But wait a minute, dammit, let's look on the bright side. Love is bigger than fertility, isn't it? What're we, a couple of breeding factories? Hell no, we've got more . . . Jesus, there's so much more we have to live for. Got our jobs, haven't we? Careers? Goals? Meaningful roads ahead to pave and trod and pile up the old bankroll, and build together and grow rich and old together . . . Hell, it's such a stimulating future! Space Age coming and us climbing every mountain . . . He shoved a fist in his mouth to hold back the rocking grief, clog up the sobs . . . buried his face in the blankets to stop the spineless slob sounds of him . . . kids do this when their toys are stolen, not men . . . so hold them back, you clod! . . . Plug up the crawling chicken-shit noises because they're not gonna help her . . . Your tears can't do a thing for her, so shut up . . . so . . . Oh you Goddamned crapper, stop crying . . . now, save it, dry it, stow it, shove it . . .

But the sobs stayed. His body shook with them.

UP TIGHT

Carl Ross

Dear Walt:

*A*ctually, what this is, it's a wedding invitation. Now I know right away that blows your mind a little, right? I mean, me of all people. You think it's a joke. Old Kenny, he's putting you on again, but you're not going to fall for it. Well sit down and get ready for a shock, buddy; it's real.

Now I know I said I'd never take the step, unless maybe I was like eighty years old and senile, needed somebody to push me around in my wheelchair or something. Marriage is for squares and all that. With all the sweet young things running around loose out there, a guy has to have a loose bolt someplace to tie himself down to one chick. Etc, etc.

Okay, I'm a fink. But I haven't really gone square. (Can you picture me in the gray flannel suit bit? Not yet, friend.) It just happened that, like they say in the movies, the right girl came along. Don't vomit all over this letter, please. Not yet. Because I want to tell you just how it happened. It was all pretty wild, and you might get a bash out of it.

It started while I was still out in San Francisco. You remember I was living in that crazy pad on Haight Street. That was while the scene was still pretty groovy out there. I'm told it's kind of draggy now, all tourists and kids from Podunk who think they're where it's at because they see a beard once in a while. But at that time it was the real thing.

Well I was sharing this place with Frank the Fish. I don't recall if you ever met this guy, but he was one of the old characters from the North Beach scene, back when Ginsberg and Kerouac and those guys were around. I don't know why they called him Frank the Fish, maybe because his name was Frank. Anyway, he was an interesting type to talk to once in a while, but if you spent too much time with him it got to be Boresville pretty quick. Luckily, the way the place was set up, we each had our own private part of the pad and didn't have to see each other too often.

So one day I'm up there painting away like mad, like I usually did early in the afternoon, trying to get this picture I was working on to come out something like what I had in mind—which is always a hopeless cause anyway—when Frank comes to my door.

"Hey, Kensington," he says. Frank always has to do his own thing with people's names, he can never call then Joe or Jack or whatever, he has to fancy them up. I'm Kensington, don't ask me why.

"Frank," I say, still daubing away with the old brush.

"You busy?"

"Yes." I didn't really expect that to make any difference to him, and I was right. He comes in and plunks himself down on my bed, because he knows from experience that the one chair in that room, which I picked up off the street when somebody was throwing it out, was likely to come apart when you sat in it.

Frank is this very tall, skinny type, with stringy blond hair always falling in his eyes. "Listen, kiddo," he says. "I got this chick over in my room."

"Congratulations," I say.

"No, listen, the thing is she wants to meet you," he says.

"What for?"

"I told her you're an artist, see? She's a model. At least, she's not really a model, but she wants to be one. She got real excited when I told her my roommate was a painter. She wants to know if she can model for you."

"You gotta be kidding," I tell him. "You know the kind of stuff I do, Frank." I wave my hand around the room to show him all the paintings hanging around the place, all abstractions. "I'm strictly non-representational. None of that figure crap, man; that stuff's been dead for centuries."

Frank makes a face. "You know, Kensington, you're a drag when you start with this serious artist jazz," he says. "I mean here's this broad, she is no dog by any means, she's ready to come in here and pose for you. Now I didn't go so far as to ask her if she wants to pose in the nude, I'm a little more subtle than that, but hell, that's what models do, right? You're gonna throw this opportunity away because of your goddam aesthetic principles?"

I was starting to get interested, I have to admit. "She willing to pose for nothing?"

"Hell, she's eager. She says she wants the experience. If you ask me, she just wants an excuse to take her clothes off. Who are we to interfere with the girl's career?"

I look over at him. "You, I suppose, are planning to stick around and watch while she poses."

"You know it. Sort of like a commission for bringing her, you dig?"

"I dig, I dig." I look kind of wistfully at my uncompleted picture, then shrug. "Okay, what the hell. What's this chick's name?"

"Emily, she says. I call her Emilina."

"Naturally. You wouldn't call her Emily just because her name is Emily, right? That would be silly."

"I'll bring her in," he says, and goes out.

After a minute he is back with this chick, and I can see right away he is right about her not being a dog. She is maybe eighteen or so, with this very long brown hair and big brown eyes and cute little dimples in her cheeks. Medium size, and a very curvy figure. She's wearing one of these simple dresses that just kind of hang down and stop short in the middle of the thigh. They look great on shapely-type girls with good legs, and this kid qualified, no doubt about it.

"Emilina," Frank says with a grand flourish, "this is Kensington."

"Call me Ken," I tell her, "like the rest of the peasants."

She grins at me. "And I'm Emily."

"What's in a name?" Frank says. Which coming from him is very funny. "I've told this young lady that you are without a doubt the foremost undiscovered artist of our time. And other lies. Even so, she expressed a desire to meet you." He talks like that when he's trying to impress a chick. Sometimes it works, too, which I've never understood.

"Frank tells me you're a model," I say to her.

"Well, not really," she says. "But I'd like to try it out. It would be so interesting, I mean . . . to be the inspiration for a real artist. But—" She's looking around the room. "You don't seem to paint people much," she says in a disappointed voice. "I guess you don't use models, do you?"

Well this gal doesn't strike me as being particularly bright. "Oh, yes indeed," I say, very sincerely. "But you see, I try to paint the inside of what I see, rather than the outside. That's why my pictures may not look like people at first glance. I paint their souls instead of their bodies, but the body is always the starting point."

"Oh," she says, very impressed.

"This one, for instance," I say, pointing to a picture composed of bright orange and purple lines, which I call *Opus 397,* "this is called *Nude in the Afternoon.* And this—" I move to a canvas filled with red and black squares. "This is *Nude on a Bicycle.* And this one over here is called *Nude Lying Down.* And so on."

"I see," the chick says. She moves over to stand in front of one of the paintings and looks at it closely for a minute. "Yes," she says, "I can see what you mean."

She's better than I am if she can, but I don't tell her that. Frank winks at me approvingly behind her back, and I press on. "As you can see, the nude figure provides the catalyst through which the artist gains access to the nude psyche." I'm even starting to impress myself now, and I figure she's got the idea. "So I'd be happy to have you pose for me, Emily."

She smiles happily. "That's wonderful!" she says. "Can we start right now?"

"Why not?" I say casually. I take the picture I've been working on off the easel and set up a clean canvas. I do a few artistic-looking preparations with paints and brushes, then I look at her expectantly and say, "Anytime you're ready, Emily."

Well this girl is cooperative as all hell. With another big smile she reaches back and unzips the dress, then pulls it up over her head. She's wearing this white bra and little black panties, and she is the curviest thing I have seen in a long time.

"Can I hang my dress up in your closet?" she asks me.

"Oh, sure," I say. "Go ahead."

She walks over to the closet, setting all those curves in motion. I watch the breasts jiggling under the tight brassiere, and the rippling of those sexy leg muscles as she walks. She hangs up the dress and turns back toward me, reaching around to open the bra.

I am trying to act casual about the whole thing, but Frank is staring at her like he can't get his eyes open wide enough. But she doesn't seem to mind at all, she is still smiling when she pulls off the bra and tosses it over the back of the chair. I am beginning to think that Frank was right about her wanting an excuse to take her clothes off. Maybe she is some kind of an exhibitionist or something. But who's complaining?

She doesn't really need the brassiere, because her breasts are nice and firm and stand out invitingly from her body without support. They sway gently as she bends over to slide her panties down. She steps out of them and puts them with the bra, then stands up straight and watches us as we look at her. She is still smiling, but there is something else in her eyes now, a kind of excitement.

"Will I do for a model?" she asks anxiously.

I clear my throat. "Yes, I think so," I say, looking her up and down with what I hope looks like professional detachment. I walk around her slowly, studying her body from all angles, and buddy, that is the kind of studying I go for. "You'll do fine," I tell her. "In fact, you're just perfect for a new picture I have in mind. I've been waiting for the right model to—ah—embody this idea for a long time."

"Really?" Emily says. "How wonderful!"

I'm beginning to wonder now just how far we can get this gal to go in the name of art. Her body was inspiring me all right, but not with thoughts of painting her picture. A scheme begins to form in my mind.

"This painting is to be called *Nude Waiting For Her Lover*," I say. "It will be a portrait of the excitement and anticipation in the soul of a beautiful young girl anxiously awaiting the caresses of the man she loves. I want to capture the conjunction of the spiritual and physical longing as they fuse into desire."

She is watching me, so she does not see Frank as he shakes his hand back and forth like Art Carney on TV. I have trouble keeping a straight face, but I manage. "Do you understand, Emily?"

"Oh yes," she says. "It sounds beautiful!"

"Good," I say. "Then we can get started."

"Where do you want me to pose?" she asks.

"On the bed," I tell her. "Just like you were actually waiting for your lover. You understand, the reality of the setting must be as strong as possible in order for me to pierce to the heart of the abstract." Whatever that meant.

"Of course," she says.

I turn to Frank, who has not taken his eyes off Emily since she finished undressing. "If you don't mind, Frank . . ."

He reluctantly gets off the bed and goes to the chair, where he sits down very slowly and carefully, still not looking away from the girl.

Emily walks over to the bed and lays herself down on it, and what a sight that is! Her breasts stick straight up in the air even when she's flat on her back, and her round little stomach moves up and down sexily with every breath she takes.

"Like this?" she asks.

"That's fine," I say. "Now pretend you're waiting to be made love to. You're all worked up and ready. Your lover is coming to you. You're abandoning yourself to his caresses. Can you do that?"

"I'll try," she says. And she does, and I want to tell you she puts her heart into it. First she kind of wiggles her body a little, to get in the mood I guess. Then she throws her arms up over her head. This pulls those breasts taut, and I'm starting to get a little taut myself.

Then she moves those fine legs apart—wide apart—and she lies there all spread out like . . . well, like I don't know what. I mean there is nothing you can compare a sight like that to. Nothing in the world. It's all by itself. I can feel my heart start to beat faster, and at the same time I hear a funny little noise from Frank. I figure his eyes must be just about popping out of his head by now, but I am not about to waste time looking at him.

Emily doesn't seem to notice. She's just lying there concentrating on doing her best in her new career. It might have made a great picture if somebody really had wanted to paint it; but like I say, my thoughts were on a different level.

I decide it's now time for Phase Two. I walk over to the bed, still trying to look objective. I sit down on the side of the bed, partly to get closer to her and partly because I'm afraid it's becoming obvious that my interest is more than artistic.

"That's excellent, Emily," I tell her. "Really excellent. Now just a few details and we'll be all set."

"Details?" she says.

"To make it more real," I explain. "So I can really get the feeling of excitement that I'm after. Your nipples, for instance. You're supposed to be really aroused. All worked up, like I say. Your nipples should be hard. They should stand out."

"Oh," she says, and she looks down at her nipples like they had betrayed her or something.

I take a deep breath. This is the crucial point. "Let me help you," I say, and put my hands on her breasts.

I more than half expect her to object, but she doesn't, she just lies there watching me. Her breasts feel wonderful under my hands, soft and firm at the same time. I move my fingers over the nipples, and sure enough, they start to get stiff. And you know what else is getting stiff.

I keep this up until I've got her nipples standing up on the tips of her breasts like little red sentinels, and still she hasn't said a word. Also her breathing is beginning to get a little faster, which is a good sign.

"That's better," I say. My voice sounds a little shaky to me. "You see, the more you can get into the mood, Emily, the deeper the reality that will come across."

With this I slide one hand off her breast and start moving it down slowly over her stomach. Man, that smooth warm skin under my hands is making my head swim. But I figure I better keep making with the artistic talk before she gets mad and stops the whole thing. So I keep jabbering away about reality and aesthetic perception and stuff like that, and all the time my one hand keeps playing with those crazy nipples and the other one is sliding around on her stomach, working its way down.

Soon I can hear her breath going in and out and her eyes are getting a little glazed-looking. I don't really know what I'm saying by this time, but then maybe she doesn't either.

Now my hand has reached her leg, and I'm caressing the

beautiful softness of her upper thigh. Her eyes go halfway closed and at the same time her cute little mouth opens slightly. Her lips are soft and inviting. I croak something about how her lips should be moist, and with that I bend my face down to hers and run my tongue slowly over her lips, tracing the circle of her mouth. She gives a soft little moan, and so I do it again, and at the same time I slide the hand that's on her leg very slowly to the inside of her thigh and then up to the soft moistness of her crotch.

She gives a tiny little gasp and another moan. I move my face away from hers and let my fingers explore just a little bit, experimentally. Her eyes close the rest of the way and her breathing gets louder.

Now I'm starting to tingle all over, because it looks like I've got it made. But just at this point Frank decides to join in the fun. He gets up — carefully — off the chair and starts coming over to the bed. I give him a fierce look, trying to warn him off, but he doesn't pay any attention, the bastard. He goes around and sits down on the other side of the bed.

"I want to help out," he says, winking at me. "Anything for the sake of art." And he puts his hands on Emily's legs and begins to stroke them.

Well, I am sure the stupid fart is going to blow the whole scene and I am ready to knock his teeth out. But Emily does not make any objections. In fact, she reacts beautifully. Her body starts to twist a little, and I feel her hips raise up a bit under my fingers.

So it looks like four hands are better than two after all, and I let Frank play around with the lower part of her and I concentrate on the top part. Between us we cover every inch of that juicy body about a hundred times over, and we are having a fine time for ourselves, but that chick is really flying. In a few minutes she's squirming around on the bed like crazy and making little whimpering noises in her throat.

I didn't think those nipples could get any harder, but now I can practically see them throbbing. I bend down and take the nearest one into my mouth, running my tongue around it. She makes a funny gurgling sound.

Then one of her hands moves down, kind of like it's got a life of its own, and starts groping at me. She touches my chest, then goes lower. And lower. Finally she finds what I guess she's been looking for—she could hardly miss it by this time—and I guess she likes it, because the gurgle turns into a low moan.

She clutches at me through my trousers, then starts kind of squeezing and pulling at me, while I continue to feed on her breast. Out of the corner of my eye I see that Frank is keeping himself busy. His mouth is moving over one of Emily's legs, his left hand over the other one, while his right hand is buried high up between her thighs. Her hips are churning. Her breath sounds like a bellows.

I feel her busy little hand unwind itself from me, and then it heads straight for the waistband of my trousers and plunges down inside. Her fingers find me and curl around me again, this time with nothing between us. I straighten up with a gasp.

Emily moans again, tugging at me. "Please," she breathes hoarsely. "Please."

Well, as you know, pal, I am not one to turn down a lady, being the chivalrous type, so I skin the hell out of my pants and shorts, and while I'm at it I throw my shirt off too. Then, naked, I lie down on my side next to her and pull her over to me. Frank makes some kind of protesting noise, but he could be in Bermuda for all I care at that moment.

The chick brings that whole body up against me, and whammo! I mean it is like being hit over the head with a very soft sledgehammer. Those wonderful breasts are mashed against my chest, the nipples practically boring holes through my skin. I feel the soft stomach, the strong hips, the legs against mine; and it is all one squirming, twisting, moaning mass of girl-flesh — ready, able, and willing as hell.

Now don't you wish you were a painter?

Well, our mouths come together and her lips are sweet and pliable and sexy and the inside of her mouth is like a blast furnace. Our tongues clash and wind around each other, and in the middle of this I feel her leg sliding over the outside of mine. Our loins meet, and we wriggle around a little bit until we find each other and make the connection. Our mouths pop apart as we give a simultaneous gasp.

And then the chick really starts to blast off. Usually I like to kind of take it easy at first, but this kid doesn't know the meaning of the word. She wraps herself around me like an octopus, and she is writhing and moaning and pumping away nineteen to the dozen.

I'm not exactly complaining, you dig, it's terrific; but like I want it to last a while, so I have to hold on and grit my teeth to stay with it.

Well, at one point while this is going on my eyes come into focus and I see that Frank has taken his clothes off too, and he is lying down on the other side of Emily, obviously intending to join the festivities. I yell something at him about keeping the hell out of it. But Emily has different ideas.

"Oh, yes," she gasps. "Him too. Please. Him too."

Frank smirks at me and cuddles up behind her. Emily's hips stop moving for a minute as Frank puts his hands on her buttocks and spreads them apart. She buries her face in my neck with a little whine as he positions himself carefully. Then he pushes at her, and I feel her teeth bite into my skin and she gives a cry of pain. But the next instant she is groaning with pleasure, and then she starts to move again, harder than ever.

Her teeth are still in my neck, but I don't even feel it now. All I am aware of is the fantastic sensation as her body jerks back and forth between the two of us like a puppet whose strings have all gone haywire. But no puppet ever felt like that, or made the noises she is making.

It goes on and on. The room starts to whirl around and I know I can't hold out much longer. I can hear Frank grunting like a pig in rhythm with his movements. Emily's cries start to get higher and higher, shriller and shriller, until she doesn't sound human any more. Then suddenly she goes all stiff and jams herself into me, shuddering all over, again and again. Her scream is muffled in my neck. At about the same time I feel the top of my head come off, and my brain explodes out of it and starts flying around the room.

In another minute we all fall away from each other and lie, gasping and panting, side by side on the bed.

The room gradually stops spinning around, and as it does I become aware that Emily is asking me something.

"What?"

"I said are you going to paint the picture now?"

e find Harry at his pad with his chick, Louise. He is surprised as hell to see me, and nearly knocks me over with his enthusiasm as he pulls me inside and starts firing questions at me exuberantly. He is a medium-size, dark-haired guy, and he never seems to be able to stand still for more than three seconds. Louise is one of these very quiet, ethereal types, with long brown hair and delicate features, but a hell of a good figure. I tell Harry I need a place to put up for a while.

"Christ, man, we got nothing but room," he says. "There's nobody staying here now but us and Big Marvin."

"Is Big Marvin around?" Big Marvin is this spade cat who's been on the scene in one place or another for about as long as I can remember. He's a poet. He doesn't get published much, but I really dig his stuff.

"Sure," Harry says. "He ought to be back any minute."

I introduce Joanne to them. "She needs a place to stay, too."

"She's got it," Harry says. "Welcome aboard, honey."

We sit around rapping about this and that for a little while, and then there is a knock on the door. Louise opens it, and this very square-looking, middleaged type is standing there. He's got kind of distinguished grey hair, a business suit, tie, the whole bit.

"Hello, Mr. Nelson," Louise says to him.

"Hello, Louise."

"Is it the first of the month already?" Harry asks.

"Yes, it is," the guy says.

"All right," Louise says. "Come on."

He comes in, and she takes him into another room and closes the door.

"Who's that?" I ask Harry.

"That's the landlord. He comes around every month to collect the rent. Only we practically never have the bread, you dig? So Louise lets him make it with her instead." He grins. "I bet that cat collects half the rents in this building that way. He probably loses money on the place, but he has a crazy sex life."

"Don't you mind?" Joanne asks. Then she looks like she wishes she hadn't, because he will think she's square.

Harry shrugs. "Hell, I believe in spreading the good things around." He turns to me. "The cat has this crazy game he likes to play to get his kicks. It's wild. You want to watch?"

"What? How?"

"C'mere." He takes me over to the door of the room the two have gone into. It is kind of battered up, and I see a narrow crack running halfway down the middle of it. "I broke this thing up while I was on a bad trip one time," he says. "Go ahead, take a look. Louise don't mind."

I put my eye to the crack and I can see into the room. The middle-aged guy is undressing. He takes off all his clothes and hangs them neatly over the back of a chair, while Louise stands watching him. When he is naked he goes over to the bed which stands against the wall opposite the door—it's just a box spring and a mattress— and lies down on it on his back, his head propped up on a pillow.

Louise walks around the bed and stands facing him, just far enough back from the foot of the bed so he can see all of her.

"How much is your rent, Louise?" he asks her. His voice comes faintly through the crack, but I can hear the words clearly.

"Eighty-five dollars," she says. Their voices have a kind of ritual quality, as though they have been through this many times before.

"You are a very pretty girl," the landlord says. "I will deduct five dollars if you will take off your blouse."

Louise's hand moves slowly to the top button of her blouse, and lingers there. "I will for ten dollars," she says.

"No," the guy says. "Ten dollars is too much."

Louise's fingers leave the button. She rubs both hands over the hills of her breasts, massaging them in little circles, her eyes on his.

"Seven dollars," the landlord says.

Louise opens the buttons of her blouse, one by one. She pulls it slightly apart, enough to reveal a narrow strip of white skin, broken by a patch of bra. "Nine dollars," she says.

"Eight."

"All right." She pulls the blouse off.

He gazes at her. I can see his chest going up and down with his breathing. "Your skin is so light," he says fervently. "It's like cream."

"Do you want to see more of it?" Louise says.

"Yes. I will deduct another eight dollars if you take off your slacks."

Louise unbuttons her slacks at the side, and pulls down the

zipper. But she holds them up. "I can't," she says.

"Why not?"

"They won't come off over my shoes."

"Take the shoes off."

"That's extra."

"No."

Louise lowers the slacks about an inch, just enough to show the rounded beginnings of her hips. "Yes."

He swallows. "All right. "One dollar."

"Three."

"Two."

She kicks her shoes off, then lets the slacks drop and kicks them off too.

The landlord's dick begins to rise as he looks her over. "Sexy," he says. "God, you're sexy."

"Thank you," she says.

"What's under the brassiere, Louise?"

"You know what's under it."

"Tell me."

"I'll tell you for a dollar."

"All right."

"My breasts," she says. "My naked breasts."

The guys prick rises further. "Take it off." His voice is hoarser.

"For how much?"

"Ten dollars."

"That's not enough." She pulls one of the bra straps off her shoulder.

"Twelve."

"Twenty." She pulls the other strap down.

"That's too much. Thirteen."

"To see my tits?" she says. "You know how much you like them. I'll make the nipples hard for nothing."

"Fifteen," he says.

She shakes her head.

"Sixteen."

"Well . . . " her hands go behind her. "Say please," she says.

"Please, Louise. Please."

She opens the brassiere and drops it. The breasts are surprisingly full for her slim frame. She brings her hands to them and brushes her fingers over the brown nipples until they stand out.

"Oh, you sweet thing," he says. "I want you."

"I know."

"Take off the panties."

"But I'll be all naked."

He moistens his lips. "Yes. I want you naked."

Louise doesn't move.

"Fifteen dollars," he says.

"Fifteen! You gave me sixteen for my bra."

"Sixteen, then."

"Don't be cheap," Louise says. "Twenty-five."

"Eighteen."

"Twenty-three."

"Nineteen."

"Twenty-one."

"Twenty."

"Twenty dollars and fifty cents," Louise says.

"All right. All right."

Louise slides her panties down.

A small noise comes from him. "You're lovely," he says. "Lovely. And so young. God, those tits. Those legs. That fuzzy little crotch. But do you know what I like best about you, Louise?"

"Yes," she says. "My hair."

His eyes close. "Say it again," he breathes.

"You like my hair best," Louise says. "You want me to let it hang loose for you. You want to touch it. You want me to touch you with it."

"Yes. Oh, yes." His eyes open. "Go ahead. Do it. Please."

Louise's long, straight brown hair is pulled back and gathered at her neck with a little ribbon. She reaches back and pulls the ribbon out. Her hair comes loose, flowing around her shoulders. She takes her hair in both hands and pulls it over her shoulders so that it falls down in front of her, hanging below her breasts.

"Aahh," the landlord says softly.

Louise now walks around to stand by the side of the bed. The landlord's prick is fully erect now, and throbbing. He looks up at her hungrily.

"Please," he says.

"Twenty dollars."

He frowns. "How much have we deducted so far?" he asks her.

"Fifty-five dollars and fifty cents," she says immediately.

"There won't be enough left for . . ."

"All right," she says. "Fifteen. Just this once."

"Yes."

She bends her head forward, leaning over him, so that her hair falls down in a brown waterfall over his face. He gives a little cry and buries his hands in it, clutching it to him, rubbing his face in it, drawing long shuddering breaths as he inhales the odor of it.

Then, after a minute, his hands drop. Louise moves her head from side to side, brushing the hair across his face a couple of times. Then she moves downward, stroking it over his chest. He begins to moan as she sweeps the soft strand back and forth on him.

Slowly, he moves downward again, the hair dragging across his stomach. His moans grow louder. His hands are clenched into fists. She continues her journey down, but deliberately bypasses his crotch. The hair glides over one of his hips, then slowly down the length of his leg. She drags it back up over his other leg. She pauses teasingly for a minute as he holds his breath, and then lets the silky hair flow over his straining prick.

With a groan he arches his hips from the bed. He continues to writhe, moaning loudly, as the girl's bowed head goes into a pendulum motion above him, stroking the brown tresses rhythmically back and forth over his genitals.

His excitement seems to build more and more as she goes on, and I am wondering if he is going to come that way, when suddenly he pulls himself away.

"The chair," he pants. "The chair, Louise."

She straightens up, tossing the hair back. The guy gets up and walks over to a straight, hard-backed chair near the wall. He sits down on it. "Come on," he says. "Hurry."

She walks toward him slowly, swaying. "You sure you want me this way?"

"You know I do."

She reaches the chair and turns around. He grabs for her hair again, stroking it. She sits down on his lap, her back to him, he reaches around her body to cover her breasts with his hands. He buries his face in the hair of her head and rubs himself against her with a side-to-side movement, obviously glorying in the feel of her long mane, caught between her back and his chest.

She hitches herself up a little and reaches beneath her, finding his cock. He moans as she guides it to her. She inserts it and settles down on it slowly, until she is sitting tightly against him, all of it inside her. He squirms, but her weight on him prevents him from moving very much.

"Now!" he groans. "Now!"

"Will this take care of the rest of the rent?" Louise says.

"Yes. All of it," he gasps.

"And will you pay the gas and electricity bill this month?"

"Yes."

"And the telephone?"

"Yes. Yes!"

"Okay," she says. She spreads her legs, sliding them around to the sides of the chair, and hooks her feet over the rungs. Using them for leverage, she begins working herself up and down steadily.

The landlord's groans and cries fill the room as she jounces on his lap like she is riding a galloping horse. He pulls her back against him tightly by her breasts, rubbing her hair into his chest. I can see the swollen underside of his prick as it moves in and out of her. Louise reaches down again and puts her hand there, giving it a quick stroke with every upward movement of her body. Very soon the landlord makes a loud rattling noise in his throat and throws his head back as his climax rips through him.

I pull my eyes away from the crack in the door. Watching this, I have damn near forgotten where I am. Harry is grinning at me, Joanne staring curiously.

"Did I tell you it was wild?" Harry says. "You'd never think it to look at him, would you?"

"I'd never think it to look at her, either," I tell him, and he laughs.

A few minutes later the landlord comes out, fully dressed, and heads for the outer door.

"See you next month, Mr. Nelson," Harry calls.

He mumbles something and goes out.

"What went on in there?" Joanne wants to know.

Before I can answer, Louise's voice calls from the room the landlord had just left. "Harry!"

Harry gets up, grinning apologetically. " 'Scuse me," he says.

"He always leaves her kind of worked up. I better go take care of it. Make yourselves at home." He goes into the room.

I find myself wishing Pat was there.

After a minute Joanne gets up, tiptoes over to the door of that room, and puts her eye to the crack. I start to say something to her, but then stop myself. What the hell am I going to say? Tell her not to do what I was just doing? Anyway, they probably wouldn't mind. So let the chick get her kicks. After all, I tell myself, that's what it's all about, right? Right?

I get no answer. The hell with it. I decide I'm hungry, and start looking around to see if there's any food in the place.

CARL ROSS

Carl Ross is the pseudonym of a poet and writer who was born in Brooklyn, educated in New York and Pittsburgh, and says he spends most of his time trying to figure out ways to avoid writing. He likes to watch old W. C. Fields movies, and afterwards, practices in front of the mirror; however, he can't get the nose quite right, preferring, like so many of his peers, amphetemine to alcohol. When pressed for further revelations, Ross reluctantly admitted that he liked girls. He lives in New York.

Only Skin Deep

George Kimball

*L*ater that spring of my Junior year I first met Larry. Of course, I'd known who he was and all—after all, every girl in school did. Tall, handsome Larry was the star of the football team and the heart-throb of every teeny-bopper at LHS, from the cheerleaders right down to the scabbiest little pimpleface in the Junior class. Which happened to be me.

It was a well-established fact that Larry had a steady girl. That was Stephanie, the Homecoming Queen. She wore gobs of makeup, had rather massive boobs, and a round little butt which she continually wiggled—particularly when Larry was around. She was kind of catty, if you know what I mean, and none of us girls really liked her very much for that reason. Well, they (the other girls, I mean) didn't exactly like me that well either, but I guess they sure liked me a lot better than that creep Stephanie.

To digress for a moment, before telling you about Larry, and only, really, to illustrate a point about Stephanie before I just leave her behind altogether, there was one time when we girls all had a slumber party at Judy's house: me and Judy, Margie, Debbie, Lynda, and of course, that horrible old Stephanie. We were all sleeping on the floor that night, since Judy only had one bed in her room and she didn't want to look like a pig by sleeping on it if she was the only one . . .

Well, you can guess what happened. That Stephanie was in the damn bed before you could say Larry Sheridan, which happens to be Larry's full name, and before it was even ten o'clock she was telling us stories about things she and Larry did together sometimes in the back seat of his Ford Galaxie.

That Stephanie certainly has a dirty mind! I wouldn't even repeat some of the things she said, but let me tell you that she went so far as to act out some of the scenes for what I guess was supposed to be our benefit. Anyway, while she was writhing on the bed in the midst of her vile narratives, she subtly enticed Margie and Lynda over into the bed with her and when she described how Larry stuck his "bad thing" into that cute little butt of hers (that's exactly what she said, although her rear end is actually somewhat flabby; Judy would have been Homecoming Queen but for her braces), and made her squirm, Margie even shrieked a little bit.

Then she started talking about some other really dirty things, like Larry sticking his face and nose right up her smelly old snatch, and even lapping up the goo with his tongue and running it all around her little love button, right up by her old pee hole. (Stephanie is so crude! She knows *nothing* about the finer points of love—just what filthy practices she conjures up by pure animal instinct!)

Well, I don't even have to tell you what happened next. Before she even got around to the part about how Larry made her come in rippling torrents down her fat round little legs, that dirty-minded Stephanie had Margie doing all these same things to Lynda. Like, Stephanie would talk about the sensation of Larry's slimy tongue between her legs and sure enough, there'd be Margie, kneeling on the floor before the bed with her face buried in Lynda's lap, licking her little point of sensitivity while Lynda, legs tucked beneath her, shuddered in tremors as she simultaneously listened to Stephanie, copped a head from Margie, and performed digital clitoral manipulations on that creepy Stephanie. Debbie sat across the room in the rocking chair, performing autoeroticisms on her own little fur-pie.

I can't begin to describe how disgusted Judy and I were by all this. Clutching one another tenaciously, we rolled under the bed and proceeded to ignore—as much as we could—the entire proceedings.

After we came together, Judy and I agreed that we'd never have anything to do with that gutterminded Queen ever again. She was hopelessly degenerate!

After Judy fell asleep, I slipped back into my silk panties with the pink flowers embroidered on the crotch and thought. Obviously, just *ignoring* her was too good for Stephanie. She was a horrid bitch, and she *certainly* didn't deserve Larry's love. But what could I do? I walked silently to the bathroom without awakening the other girls—Judy, Margie, Debbie, Lynda, and that awful Stephanie—to plan my course of action.

I pondered the consequences likely to result in each of several alternative approaches as I stood before the mirror, squeezing blackheads and otherwise manicuring my face. Then, suddenly, it came to me like a vision from out of nowhere! I would induce Larry to fall in love with *me!* I licked off my fingers and tiptoed silently back to the bedroom, hoping I wouldn't choke to death from the perfume emanating from that smelly vain Homecoming Queen.

Now, I don't mean to convey the impression—or even *begin* to imply—that I was naive. As a matter of fact, I was quite well-read for my age. I had never *been* in love before, but for the most part, I knew how it was done.

Judy and I had conducted considerable research into several Classical and Oriental studies of the art; we'd read THE LOVE BOOK, and we'd practiced lots of the things we'd learned on each other. Still, it wasn't the same as being in love with a *boy*, especially Larry.

It was common knowledge that Larry was one of the most well-endowed specimens of masculinity ever to strut the Dairy Queen parking lot. When he wore a basketball uniform, even those silly athletic supporters couldn't hide that big bulging thing between his legs. Sometimes when the games got real tense, Larry would also, and believe me, *that* was something to see. His dong would swell up like a telephone pole, and there sure were plenty of girls at LHS who'd have traded their left titties to be in love with

Larry just once.

Naturally I didn't sleep too well that night. I was far too excited over the prospect of being in love with Larry. I knew a thing or two about being in love that that slut Stephanie didn't know! As I said before, I'd read lots of things, and I knew all about the magical acts of Fellatio and Cunnilingus and the seventy-nine positions of the mystical Oriental instructional manuals of love, and plenty of other things that Stephanie probably couldn't even spell, much less perform. Although she claimed to have been in love several times before (all with Larry, if you believe *her* which usually isn't a wise thing to do), she—by her own implicit admission—only knew a couple of ways to do it. *I'd* show her . . .

I thought so much about being in love with Larry that night that I soaked my silk panties (the ones with the pink flowers) right through! I dreamed about that big throbbing column of sensitivity. I could almost feel his hot, demanding love-pump magnificiently gushing up and down within the protective folds of my educated little slit. It was almost real, and I even came there as I writhed on the floor in sweet agony. The first time I'd actually achieved orgasm without Judy, there was a wonderfully authentic feeling about it, which extended to a mental simulation of a monstrous spurt emanating from my vision of Larry Sheridan's rocket-pole.

I could hardly wait to be in love! I finally drifted off into a confident slumber, almost oblivious to Stephanie's existence.

Well, the next day was Sunday, and of course I couldn't get Larry to fall in love with me then, since I had to go to Sunday School in the morning and help Mother with sewing my prom dress in the afternoon. (Although I still didn't exactly have a date, Mother could always get me one with Alvin, next door, who was even uglier than I was.) Frankly, I'd even then (somewhat presumptuously) allowed my thoughts to stray occasionally to what still seemed only a wild glimpse of fantasy and hope—that after falling in love with me, Larry might even break his prom date with Stephanie and take *me*.

Stephanie, too, was in attendance at Sunday School, and that sanctimonious bitch actually sang a solo in church at the 11 o'clock service. She can't sing anyway, in the first place, and she shouldn't even be allowed in church at all, since she's such an immoral piece of crap. She sang, though, and then, the worst part of all, Reverend Atkins shook her hand after the service. I can't begin to see how he could even stand to touch her!

Anyway, Monday was the slowest day I've ever experienced. Algebra seemed to take hours, and History was even worse. English wasn't quite so bad, for as I've already mentioned, I'm very widely read and I guess it's my favorite subject.

At lunch I noticed a horrid new pimple on my forehead, and my heart sank a bit. I managed to cover it up pretty well, though, and it's a good thing I could because the next class wasn't really a class at all but *Study Hall*. There were some Seniors in my Study Hall, and I don't even have to tell you who had the desk just three seats from me, one aisle over.

Running his huge, manly hands through the shiny gleam of the Wildroot in his long, curly black hair, a surpentine bulge running the length of his jeans nearly to his knee, picking at the one cute, festering little pimple on the tip of his nose, sat none other than my own true love.

I couldn't decide whether to make a move then, or to wait until after basketball practice. Since, I reasoned, Larry might not recognize my name if I passed him notes, I might as well wait.

I just couldn't take my eyes off him that whole hour. I'd make a half-hearted attempt to do my homework, but my eyes kept drifting over to the man of my destiny, and, as in synchronized movement, my hands crept up my legs. By the time the bell rang, I was in a veritable trance, drooling down the front of my dress and wetting my thighs as a river of anticipation sprang from my moist little bush. I wondered if Larry noticed. I didn't really care.

The hours dragged on and on. The last class over, Stephanie left for a meeting of the Prom Committee at her house and I lingered behind, alone. How Stephanie ever got on the Prom Committee I'll never know!

As dusk began to settle about the LHS campus, the gym doors at last opened and the first members of the team started filing out. I stationed myself by Larry's car and waited for his appearance. Though it was getting dark, I could identify Larry the moment he walked out. He was so clearly distinguishable from all the others!

After what seemed to me like an eternity, Larry freed himself of the hangers-on and walked briskly to the car. I held my breath, smiling demurely as I fixed him with an intent and loving stare.

"What the fuck do *you* want?" asked the love of my life.

"Precisely!" was my well-intentioned reply. "Oh Great Larry with member so worthy of Ganesha, god of the elephant-penis!"

But my darling misunderstood. "Look, bitch, I don't know what the hell you're talkin' about, but quit leanin' on my car. If you put so much as one scratch in my candy-apple-red finish, I'll split your underaged cunt from top to bottom!"

"Would that thou wouldst perform that very act with your massive and competent cannon of iron, O my Lord and Master . . . as only thou art capable of doing, sweet Larry of my dreams," was my ingenious rejoinder.

Larry still hadn't gotten the point. "You," he said, "are crazier than hell, and ugly to boot." Between my trembling thighs, my teenage clit quivered perceptibly.

I was becoming exasperated. Love was at stake. I called upon memory for some more colloquial phraseology.

"You want a blow job?" I blurted out.

In less than ten minutes we were parked on a dark, romantic, and secluded road. I was gorging myself with as much of Larry's gigantic, overstuffed phallus as I could fit into my fifteen-year-old mouth. Flame-orange lipstick lent color to that delectable object, and as I raised and lowered my head in seemingly perpetual motion, it was almost as if I were adding a new coat of cadmium hue to Larry's lovely lizard with each new thrust. My tongue frantically groped for whatever it could find there as thought and deed became one, and an unstoppable flow of saliva leapt forth from my inspired glands, bathing us in a literal bath of passion.

There was no distinguishing between the quickness of my own head-and-tongue movements and Larry's writhing and stabbing deeply into my throat. Ah, the sweet taste of first love!

The precision with which I performed the fifty-third precept of the Litany of Tung Goo, ancient and venerable instruction in the art of love dating from a 4th Century B.C. Southeast Asian Fuckee-Suckee cult, belied my tender innocence, even to my love. After far too short a time for me, my giant-lover rallied to the occasion, spewing and gushing forth a veritable river of his existence, that creamy fluid of life itself, onward into my desire-prodded oral suction-cup. I drained my man! He burst, he moaned, he groaned.

He clearly showed, had anyone been watching, that our experience had been profound indeed, and it was apparent to me that he could never again entertain serious ideas about Stephanie; certainly, at any rate, he could never again reconcile thoughts of her with thoughts of real love. Never ever again. I'd make certain of that; after all, all's fair in love and war.

GEORGE KIMBALL

George Kimball was born in Grass Valley, California and educated in Europe, Texas, Kansas and Massachusetts. Following literary tradition, he has been a dock worker, cab driver, ski-lift operator, bartender, ride operator in an amusement park, dope peddler and rock-n-roll singer. His poetry and fiction have been published in the Paris Review, Manhattan Review, Gust, The World *and elsewhere. He is the author of a book of poetry,* The Origin of Feces, *published in 1965. At the present time he lives on Wolverton Mountain near Lone Star, Kansas, with poet Jim McCrary, his dog Wayne and "several-mistresses." Kimball and McCrary built the house themselves and live more or less off the land.*

My Sister My Sin

Terence FitzBancroft

My blood was so hot and throbbing, my body still so sweetly aroused, that when I hit the water it felt as though I was diving into the contents of an ice pack. Sandy squealed as she came up, and began swimming like Tarzan. She had opened up a tenlength lead on me by the time we reached the shallower part of the stream, and when she lifted her naked body out of the water and began to run upstream I gave up all hope of catching her and just trotted along, content to watch the resilient twitching of her pink buttocks.

Then, with a squeal, she fell. I raced up beside her and helped her to her feet.

"You all right?" I asked.

"I don't know," she said a little breathlessly, "I guess so." I looked over her perfect body. Her knee was chafed and there was a cut near the nipple of her quivering left breast. Cupping it with one hand I put my mouth to the wound and licked it free of blood; then sucked some more of the hot, salty red juice from her body.

"I want to drink some of your blood too, Terry," she said.

"I want that too." I picked up a sharp-edged rock and handed it to her. She cut a shallow wound in my chest, beside the nipple, over the heart, and then began to lick the blood and suck it from my body.

She lifted her head, her eyes sparkling in the sunlight. "That tastes good," she said.

"It ought to. It's the same as yours."

She brushed her nipples across mine—both pairs were red, erect and prickly—until both wounds were touching and our blood-streams mingled.

"Just like the Indians," I said.

"Now we really are brother and sister," she said.

"And married, and friends, and everything!"

So she wouldn't see me starting to cry like a kid again I pulled her mouth to mine and kissed her fiercely.

Then, holding hands tightly, every sensitive center of our two bodies throbbing with excitement again, we waded splashing up the chill stream in mottled sunlight to the weeping willow where our clothes were piled.

"Let's not put them on yet," she said. "I want to stay naked with you."

"Me too," I picked up the heap of clothes. Hanging on to each other as if our bodies had grown like vines from one root, which they had, we headed back toward Grandma's house.

Everything around us now seemed so much friendlier than ever before, as if we really were creatures of the forest, as if we finally understood—with out bodies and our hearts—the deep mysteries we had so feared as children. The birds—wrens, white-throated sparrows, goldfinches, red-faced warblers. Bohemian waxwings, blue-gray gnatcatchers, red-eyed virios, black-eared bushtits, bluebirds, tufted titmice, little chickadees, larks, yellow-bellied flycatchers, yellow-bellied sapsuckers, hairy woodpeckers, red-shafted flickers and ruby-throated hummingbirds all seemed to forget their predatory preoccupation with worms and bugs in order to sing for us. Squirrels, chipmunks, a rabbit—rodents all—twitched their upper lips and greeted us with big, vegetarian front teeth. The wildflowers—white pussytoes, yellow tickseeds, pansies, sneezeweeks, goldenrods dripping with pollen, blue monkeyflowers, cowslips, forget-me-nots, nightshades, milkweeds, white rose-pink gentians, bearberries, one-flowered wintergreens, hemlock, marsh-mallows, wild-lettuce, orange touch-me-nots which didn't scream when Sandy picked a handful, flax like her hair, the white bloodroot poppy, and in the sun as we neared the clearing wild strawberries with ripe, red fruit—all offered up their succulence and carpeted the forest floor for our naked feet.

"Look at all the strawberries," Sandy said.

"Let's eat some. They want us to."

We knelt down and picked handfuls of the plump, luscious berries, stuffing them into our mouths. Like my sister, they had just reached their first full ripeness.

"I can think of a better way of eating these things," I said.

"What's that?" she asked, and a bright look of curiosity infused her sly smile.

"Lie down on your belly," I said. She complied, giggling, and I joined her. "Now squirm around and roll over a few times. Get them all over you."

She giggled more, and squealed as we writhed and rolled in the soft fruit. When her body was bloodied with red pulp and seeds Sandy lay panting on her back. I crawled over toward her and straddled her thighs, my knees pressing into her buttocks.

"You look delicious," I said, "Some dish."

"You can eat all you want."

I grabbed a handful of berries and put them between her lips, then leaned into her mouth. Our tongues and lips thrashing together crushed them, and together we drank of their juicy sweetness, licking each other's lips and tongues and gums clean.

I moved my mouth down along her white throat and began to lick up every drop of syrup and suck up every morsel of crimson pulp on her round shoulders, licking downward to the sweet hollow between her breasts and sliding upward over each mound, doing my best at each point to suck up the hard strawberries of her nipples.

Slowly I moved downward across her flat belly, where the juicy pulp was rich and thick. Some of it had impacted into her navel, and I lingered there lovingly, emptying that sweet hollow of every last seed.

I lapped all across her abdomen and down across her hip bones to the soft resiliency of her upper thighs. Licking slowly inward across the smoother and smoother skin of her inner thighs, which now began to spread invitingly, I reached home.

Sliding my arm out sideways, I picked a handful of strawberries with one hand while spreading her red erected lips with the other. I crushed the fruit with my hand and gently pushed it up into her hot vagina.

I kept both lips spread with my hands and lowered my mouth to them while Sandy moaned and clasped my head with her thighs. I sucked, and slid my tongue inside her, lapping up the juice of the strawberries and her own intoxicating succulence.

The more of the fruit I retrieved from her cunt, the more juicy she seemed to become, until I could feel her start to quiver and buck under me. She cried out and stiffened up into my mouth and I could feel all her new juices come carrying her ecstasy into me.

I started to pull away, but she said, "Wait, Terry, stay just like that."

I stopped.

"Now just spin around. I'm hungry too."

Pivoting my tongue, I moved my body around so that my stiffened cock was brushing her mouth.

"Roll over," she said, and we did. She picked more berries and smeared them on the insides of my thighs, over my balls and up and down my prick, up and down and up and down and up.

Cupping my balls lightly, she lapped around underneath them, then took them into her mouth and sucked them clean. She slid her tongue to the base of my cock, then licked all the way up its throbbing underside. When she reached the tip she said, "Look at this big strawberry," and took the head into her mouth, sucking fiercely. She slid her mouth down to the base and back up and down and up and then, holding the head with her hand, licked the rest of the strawberry pulp and seed from every pore with her furiously active tongue.

I had become so excited licking and lapping her that I was near the point of climax when she stuffed me back into her mouth and I could feel her beginning to come again too. As I felt her force her pelvis down juicily into my face, pinpricks of pleasure started to stab me all over the loins and I thrust up toward her throat only to feel her withdraw her mouth and use her pistonlike hand to pull me up to a blazing climax.

She had pulled her thighs away from me and was milking the last droplets onto my strawberry-smeared belly and abdomen.

"Now for dessert," she said.

"What do you mean?"

"A strawberry sundae with whipped cream."

She bent over me and, starting at the base of my abdomen, licked upward, not missing a morsel of the strawberries nor a drop-let of the cream.

When she reached my mouth we kissed long, fluidly and peace-fully, as if our bodies were one, which they were.

"We better get back," she said.

"What for?"

"Grandma must have lunch by now."

"I don't want any more lunch."

"She'll be hurt."

"It'd be like—I don't know—I just wouldn't want to spoil the feast I've just had."

"What would it be like?" she asked tauntingly.

"I don't know—it'd be like going to some old second-hand stale bread store to eat after you've just had a huge wedding banquet."

She laughed, got to her feet and dragged me up with her.

"You've still got mush on your ass and your back," I said.

"Do I?"

"Yeah. I better lick it off."

She turned around and I started at her ankles, working all the way up around her ass and through its furrow up to the back of her neck. Then I turned around and she did the same for me. Only she lingered a little too long at my backside and when she inserted her tongue into my anus I shot up with excitement all over again. When she finished at my shoulders she put on her panties and shorts. I just stood there.

"Come on, Terry, get dressed."

"I don't feel like it."

"I can see what you feel like. Save some of it for later. We've got all afternoon, all night and all summer."

"I want you now. Besides, there's plenty more where that came from."

She pulled on her jersey and slipped on her sneakers.

"Well, if you're so excited you can stay here in the strawberry fields and play with yourself forever. I'm going back." With this she took off running.

"Hey, wait," I yelled, pulling on my shorts, grabbing my tee shirt and sneakers without putting them on and dashing after her. "Wait for me!"

TERENCE FITZBANCROFT

Terence FitzBancroft, like the hero of My Sister, My Sin, *is and has been inveterately hooked on incest since his first pubic hairs began to blossom. However, his mother is now too old and his sister (the heroine of his memoir) is married with two daughters and no longer of interest to him. Mr. FitzBancroft, therefore, will have to wait until one of his little nieces is available or, better yet, until he spawns and raises a daughter. In the meantime, he writes books, sleeps all day, goes to the movies and has a fondness for street waifs.*

Never Piss-Fight With A Skunk

Peter Rabbit

*I*saw water & birds / wind & waves / cloud formations that I've never forgotten / waterspouts &
sails / fish & dragons / suns & moons

There is a big moon / pretty / she is / rising / it was a cold
night / it would have been sharp if it was not for the stars / they
sit / dull frogeyes / looking out to each side & blinking / as a frog
folding & unfolding his eyelids / stars in the mountains are
snaketongues of light

The man sat there / he didn't know I was watching / & then
the tattoo on his arm came alive / she separated herself from his
arm & stood there shimmying

Eating crabs / oysters / shrimp / crayfish / we had just left the
theater / we came to a bar / there was a fat ugly woman in the bar
suckin on a crab claw / How much are your crabs / we sd / Crawbs
/ crawbs / we aint got any goddam crawbs here / she sd

There was a poster in the bar advertising BLOOD
WEDDING / we walked around the block between acts / a small
dog leaped out at us / then slouched back whimpering after I'd
kicked his head / the humidity has broken with a cooling late night
shower / the day after the rain it turned cold / the Lady left for her
studio early

There were a pair of oars standing in the corner / I was going
to steal a rowboat & drift down to the mouth of the Mississippi to
an abandoned lighthouse below Pilot Town / delta of fish fur &
waterfowl / I never made it / got hung up with a steel hulled ketch
named LADYBIRD / fixed her up & sailed her to Florida

Children in the sunny schoolyard & their games / & outside /
& inside only spots of sun / the crone schoolteacher with her heavy
bell / I was taking the census / red haired girl hung up her blue
apron & ran joyous to play in the sun / little girl fell in a dive down
a flight of stairs / she was good & scared but not hurt / then a little
boy stooped with his ear to a door / What are you doing there little
boy / I sd / listening at that door / Listening / he sd / listening / &
when he turned his head it had no eyes in it / only empty
sockets / then he stumbled off / perhaps crippled too / or maybe
just wary of bashing himself against walls

And other nights / warm / with no rain / Tonight / I sd / I'm
going to write no matter what / but she took off her wet clothes &

dried & rubbed till her skin was pink & her hair smelled of the rain or the flowers in the air / & while we crossed the streets the streetlights picked up our shadows & with them broadcast our coming / there were trees & shrubs shadowing this walk & we disappeared into the shadows / an old woman gesturing & muttering to herself clomped by without seeing us / & I running from blossom to blossom / hibiscus / or splashing from puddle to puddle / I demand that the dogs announce our coming / fear sanctifies my excitement / & sometimes I sneak / the great red Indian of the night / always night / & the cat screams in recognition of my power / a squirrel fell still galloping from the very top of a palm tree & the cat killed him with two neat throat punctures for being a squirrel & living in & falling out of a palm tree

Streetmarkers / milestones / etc. / so many gone by without notice.

Night again & there is music & a broken curved postured spade kissing a fat greasy old Italian shopkeeper / rubbing her BELLY against his paunch / telling him to put his olive oil fingers in her red HAIR / you can do it with me / she sd / you can do it with me / but his dick was as floppy as the pants around his ankles / she shook it desperately / SAFE

The night before I pressed my hardick against her asshole redhaired asshole / WAIT / she sd / I didnt / & the next night / & the next night / this night I was GLAD

*   *   *

The sky is clear / there is a lizard in the house / I go to the creepy titty movie in the Quarter when I'm supposed to be working & jack off into my handkerchief / the Lady is pregnant / the water in the canal is clean at night & there are two chugholes along the path / I'm always afraid a snake will jump out of one of them at me / two days ago Pete saw a cottonmouth by the faucet & speared him with a blue pole just as the tide was going out / he was pinned to the mud / Are we gonna have trouble with you / Sonny sd jabbing & twisting the snake on the pole / the snake writhed & snapped his body into the air with his fluffy white mouth wide open & fanging / I'm cruel / he sd

Little girls who kiss with their eyes open / hardbrown summer legs / nights rocking gently on the berth with her thighs clapping out all sound / my lips full of clit / she stood with her absurd sunglasses on & stared at me scraping tar for a full five minutes / her blouse was tailored to her young body like wet / without smiling or even showing interest / just staring / then she got on her bicycle & rode away

She wore black & a green sweater / her belly butt thighs tossed to the music & her hair kept coming down out of the bun at the back of her neck falling over her shoulders & one eye / she'd repin it never missing a beat / once while the hair was down I leaned out far enough to kiss & smell it / sweet / as she passed by / sweat made huge dark blotches under her arms / poured off her forehead streaking her mascara into black tears on her cheeks / they stopped / she looked around / dazed / her partner went back to his youngman friend who was dressed as Jane Avril who was giggling & waving limpwrist / I grabbed her & out we went into the panic carnival streets / as often as I could I pushed her into doorways to kiss & kiss / grope & grope / I turned to catch her a trinket / THROW ME SOMETHIN MISTER / I turned with a junkglass necklace / turned back to put it around her neck & touch her hair again & pull out the pins the better to smell & kiss & kiss / she was gone / I saw her dancing off toward the band with another faggot / heavily made up / loosehipped

*   *   *

The sun dissolved into the lake behind the causeway casting the water blue / purple / then green / long after the sun had become part of the water coral cloudroses lit the horizon / a mosquitospray-truck fogged by / off we went sailing a little white sloop / whitesailed whitesloop / whisper of a breeze / whispered hard alee changing tacks & the squeak of the sheets in their blocks / off the amusement park lights from the ferris wheel rollercoaster loop the loop lit the water with kaliedoscope snakes / other boats sail ghosted by / I tumbled overboard from the windward rail / the warmth of the water held me between its breasts / a line from the boat / I let them drag me / stretched on my back / long & skinny as the line / with water over my ears so I could only hear the gentle cracked bell tinkle of water / see only the stars / two searchlights & the peak of the sail

Didnt it rain / every coonass in Louisiana was prayin for it / the ground & lake had a fresh smell / I stood on the deck leaning on the mizzenmast while it came down watching the radiating circles begin / overlap / again / the whole world a confusion of concentric circles / water circles / Old Gar liked it too / coming to the surface to feel it splat on him / he came up even before he'd finished his lunch / he had a perch held lightly between his jaws stuck on forty needle teeth / the ducks in the back pen banged their approval & grouped together going round & round banging at the tops of their voices / then after the rain / the stillness / it might have been death except I heard the earth sucking life / never a breath / the heat hung over everything / shimmery steamy mist to quiet the ducks & insects / not a cloud moved except now & again a ragged black fringe descended in the distance & the cooling sprinkle resumed / I walked home with the sweeps across my shoulders / wet & humming

The locust calls / slow to crescendo / it seems to die away quickly / silence / silence / there aint no mocking birds / five delicate shapes / each living / absence of real light / rocks or clam shells / glowing green-blue / purple / It's the best thing youve ever done / he sd to her / want it

Eyes in the black face that night / refusing to focus / FOCUS / riding / riding from face to face light to light bottle to bottle / carried on by the song on her lips

* * *

I saw water & birds / wind & waves / cloud formations that I've never forgotten / waterspouts & sails / fish & dragons / suns & moons

Mississippi Sound about six miles offshore on a clear day / the seas were moving in long easy swells & we were steaming toward Ship Island / then there was an apparition in a pirogue / six miles at sea / a beard & hair with toothpick arms & legs paddling as casually as if he was in the Bayou St. John / I took the GHOST off auto-pilot & eased alongside of him / Stand off ya coonassed mothahfuckah / he yelled / yull swamp me / Are you OK / I sd a little embarrassed / You blind as well as bein stupid & a menace tuh peaceful seagoin folk / he sd / Beer / I sd / Beer / he shouted / & a tongue appeared out of the lower half of the growth on his face / he came aboard & gobbled two cans without breathing / Here here / I sd / where / he sd / More More / I asked questions / his answers were rapid movements from where an adams apple might be & slurps & grunts

In the middle of his sixth beer a heron became a distinguish-able shape in the southeast coming from the island / he stopped gulping & stared / his eyes following the bird from horizon to horizon / all was dead to him except the heron / he jumped into the pirogue & paddled off without so much as a faretheewell or a kissmyass following the flight path of the bird / I swear he made a bow wave / all in the direction of the Louisiana Marsh

We steamed on to the island / Who was he / we asked the spade caretaker on the island / O hem / heyuh heyuh / dat Deoj / be a troppah / he a feddah troppah / he trop dem beeg buuds / he fugg dem beeg buuds too / heyuh heyuh / he cotch um ina trop / he tah a streeng roun dair weeng ina beeg bow / he grob um roun dair feets / he stick he pekkah in dair asshoe / he pool dat streeng / bub-ubububububububububub / go dem weengs / ain dat too much / heyuh heyuh / main dat are too much / he sd / & his eyes rolled laughing toward the Louisiana Marsh.

* * *

The children were asleep / their mouths opened into a yawn / a small sound fell out of each mouth / the hand of one twitched / the leg of the other twitched / their bodies are now all breathing curves & masses / they are together in that

I see / I see / I move in & out of houses & rooms / I have friends / we are of the tribe of Ishmael / we are mild men / we have been circumcised in the flesh of our foreskins

"And the Lord smelled a sweet savour . . . for the imagin-ation of man's heart is evil from his youth . . ."

I saw a woman all in white driving a big Dodge car with her midriff showing / O for a woman all in white / then the sun set in the Gulf & the moon lay upside down at noon

Cancer has black hair / Cancer has white skin / Cancer has

bluegray eyes / let me touch your skin your hair / let me kiss your eyes / Cancer sits behind a steel desk / sometimes she is a he / either way they wear sterile clothing & they wait for the world to be a better place to live in

I keep seeing this girl in a sexmovie / she has such big tits / ordinarily I like asses but this chick has monster tits / she takes off her clothes & stands there idly fondling herself waiting for me to get out of mine / she is very blonde & I walk to her slowly / slowly / she opens her arms / my body just fits in between her tits / my arms squeeze them together against my sides / they flare out with the nipples getting red & extending / then I disappear

I want another mad odyssey with white & yellow roadslashes flipping away / telephone poles / on my back in the back seat watching the wires rollercoaster / the insulators wink / trees blur distinct / blur distinct blur distinct HHHUUuummmmHHUUmmm HHUUmmmmHHUUummm / just like that.

PETER RABBIT

Peter Rabbit, poet, mystic and well-known underground figure, was one of the earliest inhabitants and a leading spokesman for Drop City. The years spent in this commune of writers and artists in South Central Colorado provided the background for a current book-in-progress, and taught the author enough about the advantages and problems of this kind of life to help him found his own commune — that of Libre, in Gardner, Colorado, where he now lives with his wife and child.

SCREEN

Barry Malzberg

What I did was to go out to the track. The track is not the movies, has nothing whatsoever to do with the movies, has no relation to the movies at all but at a moment of stress, some time ago, I went out and lost $45.00 on three races and the feeling of perfect disaster and foolishness that swept over me was sufficient to obliterate the more complex histrionics that had sent me there. Perhaps it is all the same: the track, the movies, I have not thought about this deeply or often and, certainly, if they were exactly the same, the movies would not outweigh the track; I could go to them equally, parcelling out favors, and might be tenanted equally by jockeys. But that moment the track seemed the solution; I had a long, long weekend yet to come—while the usual course of the weekends was to be far too short for everything that I had to put in them—and I had no idea of getting through it; no idea of how to get through it, in any event, in the same condition in which I had entered it; this was not a usual problem. It would have been easy enough to have called Barbara, of course: a bang was there any time I wanted it and there were other things as well, other intimations which might have been touched in the process to make it a truly interesting weekend, but I didn't want it, no part of it at all. In the first place she wasn't that good-looking, and in the second place she could not possibly have any idea of what was really going on; to have told her would have been to have taken us to a very difficult and dangerous kind of alteration of circumstances in which anything, literally anything at all, might have happened; I couldn't afford it. I couldn't risk it. The basic point, I suppose, is that for one of the few times since it had started, the inside things were not all in their place but were all bucking and clamoring to become part of the outside and I couldn't bear that. I couldn't put up with that at all. In order to put up with it I would have had to admit that I was insane and I didn't want to be insane: not quite, not yet. There were better alternatives than insanity to living somewhere in the middle of the twentieth century in America; I wanted to find them. Insanity could be a safer bet, a kind of protection possibility lurking somewhere in the background, but it was nothing to try until you had tried the other alternatives first; I hadn't exhausted them. On the asphalt of the road, battling with cars side by side to find the exit road to the track I found myself surrounded by the floating, suspended faces of movie stars; stars I had known and not known, looking at me impenetrably, opening and closing their eyes in a wink which came close to collective obscenity. I fought my way through to the access road to the track, hearing the knocking and hammering of overheating in the car engine, wondering if the proper way to spend the weekend, ultimately, might not simply be to roll to a dead halt and spend the hours camped under the open hood, the smell of burning and futility wafting back over me with a stench so complete that it would make other thoughts impossible. But the car was in good condition; the car wouldn't overheat on me, the car was a 1956 Cadillac, exactly the same car that Paul Muni had driven himself to the lot every day that year, the dealer had guaranteed me a good deal on it and for the first time in history, a dealer had come through because even though I was not Paul Muni, the car ran. I parked it in a private lot, a little nearer to the track than the big public lot so that I would have a fast exit if I needed it and I gave the old woman who, along with a dangerous juvenescent who had the broad, flat eyes of a maniac was watching the cars as if they might explode, two dollars, and I walked all the way into the track itself, a gigantic, off-shaped candy box thrown up on the flats of a suburb; the sounds of slaughterhouse already vaguely in the air. I bought a tipsheet and a newspaper and had a beer when I got inside, which left me with something like thirty-five dollars to bet. The place was littered with filth of all kinds; it was fifteen minutes until the first race and already the air was heavy, heavy; heavy with some foreshadowing, perhaps, of everything which was to come, heavy with the smell of the 17% track cut-in which sooner or later would demolish everybody inside there if they only came and came again. Most of them looked as if they would. Most of them looked as if they had no other place to go.

I posted myself between two middle-aged men on one of the benches and looked through the tipsheet and paper without real interest; what I wanted was not a horse which would only win but a horse which, in beating the field by dozens and dozens of lengths would somehow, in the process of carrying my money home, bring home also a solution; a solution so vast, so enormous in all of its implications as to free me from whatever had brought me to this track in the first place; whatever muddling of doubts and gloom and flight and loss which had perpetrated themselves upon the paper I was holding in my hands, the muttering of the men to my right and left. The age of this crowd was old; old, they were not the people you saw in the movie houses or driving on the highways or working in most places, but rather the kind of people with whom you could find yourself riding back in the subways at some damned hour of the morning, people hunched over paper bags and newspapers with a quiet apprehension; people who had gone through all the events of the day and knew truly, then, that nothing that had happened to them was better than what had happened before or, for that matter, any worse; there was only a trundling in tubes from one kind of gloom to another with the occasional shriek of whining of brakes functioning as a reminder of mortality. The people in the subways when they ran out of reading matter would look idly out of the windows, staring at the grey walls as if, in full speed, they might clap over the train and squeeze it and finally bring a disaster so total, so totally immersible that it would negate whatever else they were struggling with: would make the giving-up and the joining a pleasure rather than the worse. The people on the subways had huge flat eyes and would look at you now and then as if they thought you might have the answer and if they were sure you did they might come over to you, all seriousness, all deference, and tear your body open to find it. But these people at the track never looked up, when they stopped reading—which was often, because there was a fine, high, nice calculation of choices to everything— they would cup their hands over their eyes and put their elbows on the knees, tracing back to some kind of equivocation which might have its own answer; if they weren't doing that, they were looking up at the tote board overhanging the benches where all the possibilities, if not the answers, were given. There was a magic in the tote board and I could understand its purpose at last; when you looked at it, you knew where you stood if not where you were going; you knew exactly where you existed in relation to everything else that was going on within the contained sphere of the one race. The man whose horse was 10-1 was either better or worse than the plunger who was putting $100.00 on the 3-2 shot to finish third, but his relation to that other man—if he could meet him, if they were together, if they were being friendly in the crowd—was precise and it was defined; there was a basis upon which to be because the man with the 10-1 shot had the ability to thrust himself further outside the shell of immediate possibilities; could grasp visions that the other man could not and was therefore subtly expanded over him, at least for the terms of that one race. It was possible—it was more than possible—that when the 10-1 shot ran sixth while the 3-2 shot came in a galloping winner that the adventurer would have different thoughts for the next engagement and would join his more limited opponent; in this case there had been a metaphysical alteration. It was possible too that both horses would finish nowhere and both men would then have to make an intricate speculation upon personality, speed and its role in the universe; it was even possible that both might win or the adventurer alone might win which would mean that for the time contained in that one sphere, a kind of reality had been conquered and another one put in its place. But the fact was that, no matter who you were, you knew where you stood in relation to all of the others and in only a little while you would know where you stood in relation to the universe itself and that was good; that was definitely a reality. It was better than the other way because the other way you could contain nothing, you were split off and gone somewhere; gone, gone into miserable calculations, miserable obsessions. Yes, the races would have been much better than the movies if I had been constructed that way but the fact was that I was not; I was turned in another direction. It was my loss because I was not involved in simplicities and I never knew where I stood, not in relation to any of it. The easier way would have been the way I had been trying to take this afternoon but I was not geared for it; I had to launch myself inside rather than outside and in that tomb there was nothing but doubt; doubt forever.

I was not constructed for the enlargement and projection of possibilities; no, not at all. Everything had to come down to a hard center with me, one last spot where I could identify and touch the enemy-lover groping for me, but the terrain was difficult and the drive itself was limited by fear; so all that it came down to was old scatology, old myths, old jokes behind the curtains; I could see now that there was probably no solution in anything that I was doing because all that it would come down to, sooner or later, was a dirty joke. The further you voyaged inside the nearer you got to the central dirt, the more central facts, whereas if you went outside you came against other problems but they were the stones and mire of existence, a far easier manifestation than what was going on in the self. But there was no way to make sense of this; no way to equate the insight with need and I could sense, dimly, that I was probably in real trouble; that I was in the worst trouble of all because now I knew it: I knew beyond questioning exactly what was going on and maybe even what was gone wrong and yet I was going to do absolutely nothing about it except try to balance off the inside with the outside so that I could get back easier. It was frightening to the degree that I was able to be frightened; I had other things on my mind. More than that, it was simple: it edged in to a final explanation of everything that was going on; there must be some way—if I had been able to talk to anyone—that I could make it clear that the tote board and the movie star were the same thing and that I was the only difference; that the one or the other co-existed with the spirit forever, and that in the last analysis, after the gravestone had been hurled up and sanded down and engraved, it probably made no difference at all; voyagers and conservatives, seekers and followers, 10-1 and 3-2 shots alike huddled one by one under the sod, facing in the direction of the sky, everything else that had happened to them in abstraction. I folded up the tipsheet and newspaper and bought a program so that I would know who the tote board was saying was what and went to the windows to make a bet.

It was crowded in there; crowded already with a kind of apprehensive gloom, people piled back from the windows in lines that could not have been more dismal if they were on the way to a private and final solution and I looked up at the inner tote, suspended on high wires near the ceiling, to see that there were only two minutes until post time; it was getting close, one could see the despair on these faces accelerate to necessity as they moved slowly forward, patient because impatience meant possibly losing a bet but the knife-face of violence protruding through the flesh of all those faces because if they had a winner and got shut out they would most likely kill themselves; nothing breeds violence like internal violence. I was going to bet on the three horse, something called Carte Blanche, but as I watched the tote on line the odds went up, taking in one flash from 12-1 to 20-1 and this meant that very few people in the crowd had any faith in Carte Blanche; very few people believed that he was a good horse who was going to win today. I did not want that; I desperately wanted, for that moment, to be on the side of justice, truth and honor, huddled with my fellows on the back of a horse who we all agreed deserved to be the best and so I went instead to Cake Maker, the 7 horse, a horse listed as 7-5 which meant that Cake Maker was definitely the favorite in this twelve-horse field. I bought two two-dollar win tickets on Cake Maker and then found that I had just enough time to get to the $10.00 windows and take two tickets on him to show, which meant that $24.00 of faith and community were on the side of the legions of truth in the person of the favorite. Then it was time to go out to watch the race but the hall was crowded, still jammed with people, all of them moving slowly like stunned, scattered fish, in no particular direction, a few trying aimlessly for the exit doors to the infield, but being blocked by the drift of bodies at the door; a few, trapped in small pockets of space in the center of the crowd still looking aimlessly up at the tote board as if, behind its hard assertion, rested some larger mystery which might, in the blast of the public address system calling the race, explode to unleash from a height upon the crowd a nest of dwarves or elves or gremlins who would carry the good news all the way to the salt flats beyond the track and further than that. It was impossible to see the race or even to hear the call so I allowed the crowd to move me, by presses and surges, near a closed-circuit television set where, from a great distance, I was able to see the race as if spotlighted at the end of the tube; there appeared to be several horses running in a group and then one horse alone and then another, larger pack; I hoped that Cake Maker was in one of those groups although I didn't particularly care which one. Around me people were shouting and jostling; their faces had broken open and coming out from all corners of those faces was an emotion which might have been like grief if there had not been so much liability in it; it alternated between that and a child's anticipation. The set showed the horses getting near the wire and then the race was over and it blanked out. It was impossible to gather who might have won it; the numbers were not visible from this distance. I supposed that it was very important for me to care; there was no reason, after all, to be out at the track in the first place if I didn't care who won a race I was betting on. Not to care hinted of psychosis, of a whole fine network of breakdown which I might crash to and bounce upon if I didn't care. So I said to the short woman standing next to me—she was creasing her newspaper and alternately slapping it in her hand and placing it between her teeth—"Who won the race?"

"You didn't see? You didn't see?"

"I couldn't."

"I thought *you* could tell *me* who won the race. You can't see a damned thing in here."

"It's the angle," somebody else said. "They give you the wrong angle so that you can't see a thing, the crooked, cheating, lousy sons of bitches. I tell you—"

"The three," a tiny man said. He might have come up to my chest with difficulty, his small head bobbing wisely, viscously on the slump of his shoulders. "The three had it all the way at the wire."

"The three?" I said. "You mean Carte Blanche."

"I told you. You get away from me, sonny; you hear that? I don't want to talk to you any more, you got something to tout you take it somewhere else. Just stay out of the old man's way, Johnny. The three, didn't I tell you the three, there it goes right up there, it's official."

The set had gone on again and now, since there was a close-up of the tote board I could see the figures. The three had won it. The PA system said that the race was official. More figures went up. The three paid $45.10, $12.80 and $7.80 to show. The seven was fourth.

"Didn't I tell you?" the little man said. "Didn't I tell you the three was an easy winner? Why don't they listen to me? Nobody listens to me; nothing I say gets paid any attention; what the hell is the point of any of it if nobody listens to you anyway? What's the point?"

"Oh, shut up, Harry," the woman said. "Shut up and leave the kid alone, will you? Can't you look at him? I bet he went off the three himself."

I got away from them moving through the increasing, ever-darkening density of the crowds and got to a bench outside, found a small space and got in. The benches had space because everybody was either cashing their tickets or tearing them up or still hanging around at the base of the infield or the grandstand hoping impossibly for a disqualification or an alteration of the results, hoping that a voice, perhaps, would come out of the PA system and say: LADIES AND GENTLEMEN, HOLD YOUR TICKETS PLEASE, THE RACE WHICH YOU HAVE JUST SEEN IS NOT A REPRESENTATION OF A PARTICULAR KIND OF REALITY WHICH YOU FELT YOU HAD TO HAVE: IT WAS A MYSTERY, A PRIVATE PROJECTION OF YOUR INMOST DESIRES IN WHICH THOSE WHO WANTED TO WIN AT HEART DID WIN WHILE THE LOSERS—THOSE BELOVED OF YOU WHO KEEP US GOING BECAUSE YOU NEED AND NEED TO LOSE—WERE ALSO GRANTED THEIR WISH BUT NOW WE SHALL MOVE AWAY FROM DREAMS, DEPTHS AND POSSIBILITIES AND INTO THE CLEAR, FINAL MOMENT OF RECKONING ITSELF; A MOMENT OF RECKONING IN WHICH THE TRUE, THE REAL, THE MEANINGFUL RACE SHALL BE RUN AND THE FAVORITE SHALL WIN BECAUSE FAVORITES ALWAYS DO WHEREAS THE LONGSHOTS, YEA EVEN UNTO THE LEAST OF THEM, SHALL TRAIL THE FIELD BECAUSE WE KNOW IN THIS LIFE—OR DON'T WE KNOW, LADIES AND GENTLEMEN, DON'T WE KNOW ALL OF THIS REALLY AND TRULY—THAT LONGSHOTS NEVER WIN. HOLD YOUR TICKETS; HOLD YOUR TICKETS PLEASE BECAUSE THE JOCKEYS ARE GOING UP AND THE RACE SHALL BE RUN TRUE AND FINAL OVER ITS DISTANCE AND HERE AT LAST FAIRNESS AND

EQUALITY SHALL TRIUMPH; THIS RACE WILL NOT BE A PROJECTION OF YOUR NEEDS BUT A STATEMENT, ONLY, OF THE WAY IT IS IN THE WORLD AND ALL THINGS WILL COME OUT EVEN IN THE END. HOLD YOUR TICKETS LADY WRAITHS AND GENTLEMEN ALL HOLD YOUR TICKETS, OH HOLD YOUR TICKETS BECAUSE BEFORE YOU NOW IN THE STILL GREEN OF THE PADDOCK WHERE EVEN THE BIRDS PAUSE IN THEIR FLIGHT TO GIVE HOMAGE AND LOOK WITH PRIDE; HERE IN THE STILL GREEN OF THE PADDOCK ONE BY ONE, LIGHT AND PRANCING, WASHED WITH ALL THE COLORS OF THE DAY, THE HORSES ARE COMING OUT.

But there was no such announcement: nothing like that had ever happened—although there was no saying that it never would—and I looked at the tickets in my hand; pretty tickets of many colors and then cast them in twinkling flight against the stones where they landed with the patter of many birds. I went back to the program and the tipsheet and the newspaper, balancing out the one thing against the other; the two things against the third. I was twenty-four dollars behind; a day's wages, that was, or the price of twelve pornographic books. I needed a winner. I needed to get ahead.

It went the same way before the second race as it had gone for the first except that it was darker and things seemed to be shut into a complex, somehow more enclosed space; so much energy having already been burned up, taken from its possessors and strewn to the infield gulls, who seemed to be so well fed on it that they flew easily to the benches in the back, the small contrived park, strewing themselves on all of us. We could hardly have noticed. I could feel within me now pulsing the second and more important emotion of the racetrack; the sensation that was always the successor whether it came early or late and was, perhaps, the more satisfying of the two because it had roots and connections with reality that the feeling of mystery did not have and this was the sensation of rage, of loss, of entrapment; a feeling of irretrievable scattering. Not only energy had been burned up and forever lost in that first race but all kinds of possibilities as well; even if you got even—which, of course, you never, never did—you could never recapture the money you had lost and the hopes you had had but would only find a more equivocal kind of recovery; a recovery of a different sort, the darker recovery because it came out of the waste of age. One aged many years at a racetrack in the course of the afternoon because everyone was an adolescent when he came in and an old, old man when he came out; along the way were littered the catastrophes and removed successes of distant contemporaries because someone, after all, was collecting that $45.10, someone by the law of statistics had to; you didn't know what he looked like but he was there right at the payoff windows, dining on the ashes of your own futility, ashes phoenixed into reward by numerous unspoken disasters, a number of tickets in his hand, his large face beaming. One could see This Stranger, one could see and hate him the more because he had accomplished what he had only at your expense, but the hatred, like everything else at the racetrack, hit a bottom level of exhausted futility and then rebounded; you might be able to do to him the very next race what he was doing with you on this one. The Stranger was not the Enemy. The Enemy—if, at this stage of life, you were able to think of anything or anyone as The Enemy; perhaps the horror was that there was none and one would have to go looking in some other place entirely for the explanation of why everything had wound up this way—lurked within the tote board, dwelt at the heart of the giant machines figuring out the odds; the Enemy chuckled and nestled at the base root of the machinery himself and had no eyes and no ears and no sensations whatsoever; he was only dealing in percentages. So one could hate the enemy as well or more; hate him with twenty-four dollars worth of intensity. I felt severed, elated, launched to some final plane of insight which would mark recovery. The second race was almost upon us; it was a second race feeling, no thinking of the senility and disuse of the fifth or sixth or seventh. No, before the second race you were 24 years old or so, a little battered, a little broken inside because now, having passed through juvenescence and its dreams you realized that you would probably never, after all, be able to fuck Sophia Loren; that if you got into the same bed with Sophia Loren even after fucking her you wouldn't know what to say to her, and you may not even have been able to come; the second was knowing that you were 24 and what was within reach was infinitely more desirable than what was not because at least you had access; the second was the superseding of the rage and pain of adolescence when if you drove yourself hard and harder against the wall of self, hard enough to break through the flesh and pour the waters into the density of an imagined receptacle, you could come to terms with the movement of the suns themselves against the canvas of space; it was the superseding of all that because by the second race you knew that the wall of self was impenetrable but, perhaps, you would be able to do things inside it; it was all a matter of testing, of resting, of coming to terms. I decided to go with the four horse, the second favorite, 3-1 on the board, a horse which had used to run in better races before something happened to it—senility? disuse? a seventh race of the spirit?—and it began to drift down to a lower and lower kind of horse; a kind of horse which, had it been a person, it would have felt itself demeaned: the second favorite, the four horse, was the horse for me because he had been in better places and had acquitted himself with dignity and honor but now he knew the truth and the truth was that it was better to come to terms with yourself as you were than to batter and batter and break. I bet six dollars on the four horse to win, finding the lines as congested as before but more knowledgeable somehow; there had been a subtle raising of the level of general consciousness between the first and second races and now people did not seem to be in such a hurry to bet; rather, they stood diffidently, almost queasily on the lines, holding their money in cupped hands as if it were a hat; their eyes saying, for the most part, that if the windows closed before they could get there it was perfectly all right with them because they knew the truth anyway; the truth was fine and clear and perfect regardless of their participation in it and they could come to accords with their world as long as it seemed capable of acknowledging the presence, if not the dire necessity, of that truth. I took the tickets away from the window cupping them to look at their colors against the changing flashes of the tote and then I went out to the infield—I had more time this time; time enough to get another beer and push myself through the rising urgency moving the other way—and found a spot on the rail near the stretch turn, feeling myself wrapped by the heat and the fluttering of the gulls, into another private space, and while there I watched the post parade and the call to the colors and the workouts of the horses themselves as, straining against the jockeys, they permitted themselves to be turned at the head of the stretch and to move slowly by, their frames flattened out against the sky and the black of the infield pool; their eyes sad, serious, intent with knowledge. It was possible to sentimentalize the horses and to feel that they at the root knew more about everything than the rest of us; it was possible to do this if one were not very bright. One had to see the horses as objects, virtually nonexistent; all that mattered was the tote. I felt myself growing into maturity as I watched the odds on the four horse drop to 2-1 and then even money as he was installed as the favorite. I had placed myself far out beyond the rest, testing myself against the ultimate possibilities and I had won. I was correct. Most of the people believed as I did that the four horse was a good horse; that what he had seen and known could be applied to the present situation. I had the whole thing beaten. There was no need whatsoever to run the race.

But the race was run, of course; all races must be run—the final completion of the metaphor—and I watched the four horse take a long lead on the backstretch; as they came past me in the stretch turn I could see his fine, wide nostrils spread out against the air, sucking valorously as he tried to hold his lead and instead lost his action, his joints and limbs seeming to tumble in upon one another like a clown's collapse, a diminution as violent as the shrinking of the prick after completion and a damned bit quicker and the horse fell, fell gracelessly to the ground, the jockey bouncing harmlessly off him and landing easily on the turf, rising from his knees, a hand extended as if he had not just disgracefully lost the race but had, instead won it right there and was now about to accept the victory token as well as some of his own winning bets. But after a while the triumph faded from the jockey's face and a kind of exhaustion seeped into the high, dark bones as the horse—the four horse—thrashed around the ground in an intricate kind of agony and a truck came out with two men riding it sidecar, one of them holding a shotgun, the other wearing dark glasses. Far, far down the track, a thin roar went up; probably the results had been posted on the tote and even those people around me in the stretch turn area turned their heads to see what was going on and then walked away mumbling, but I was still fixated, fascinated, upon the horse; he was rolling from side to side on the ground, his mouth open, something dark running out. It was hard to tell that a few moments ago he had been an even-money favorite against the field; a horse who had known better trails in his other times, and even perhaps, had touched a kind of greatness; the qualified greatness of allowance races in any case; where the horses that weren't quite good enough to be the best but could beat almost anyone else played with themselves, before the big races themselves were run. Now, it was as if I had a kind of tunnel vision; everything to the left and right of me was blotted out and I was peering down a long, dark pipe at the horse; the horse and I staring at each other against some wide space and I saw the pain come into his eyes; it was as if the pain was something special, very unique that he needed to communicate to me and in the intensity of that moment, I felt that the horse and I were alone, quite clearly alone and apart from everything else; communing with one another over the rail and through the sun, but then the two men walked over and the one with dark glasses lifted the horse's head the way a baby's chin might be chucked and stared at it and then began to pat his hands absently, alternately, down the horse's flank. A high, shrill scream cut into the air; a scream which could have been human except that nothing human screamed at the racetrack, and the horse struggled against the ground and tried to get up, its legs scrabbling, the head flailing like a misshapen hand and then, somehow, it did achieve its feet with a whine of agony and, yes, it was quite clear, the left rear leg was broken, dangling at a precarious angle against the ground, the haunches seeming to shrivel around it. The man with dark glasses shook his head and made a pointing gesture at the man with the shotgun who had stood respectfully by the inner rail all through this, smoking a cigar and looking down the line at the tote.

"They're going to shoot that horse now," somebody next to me said. It was a plump woman with large, discolored patches of flesh running on her upper arms and palms and her eyes, turned toward me against the sun, showed a kind of utter apprehension of everything that was going on and would go on at this racetrack throughout the day; a sodden, ninth-race kind of post-senescence had settled upon her face; it was a face that looked as if it expected no surprises, none whatever, for quite a long time.

"I lost the double on that horse," she said. "You see?" She took a large wad of tickets out of her handbag and pushed them at me. "I had everything in the first race wheeled to that bastard; he was the day's best bet. If he runs even a little bit I'm hooked into a two hundred dollar double but no, that can't be, he's got to break himself around a turn. The son of a bitch can lie there and die as far as I'm concerned. But they're not going to do that; they'll shoot him."

"Well," I said, "they have to. He's in pain and he isn't much use anymore."

She shook her head. "They could save him," she said. "Pain is nothing and if you can keep them off their feet with drugs for the first couple of days in the cast, you can save them. But they don't want to save him. They want to shoot him. I'm glad. I'd shoot the bastard myself if I knew how to handle a gun."

The man with the gun walked over slowly, lightly, moving somewhere near the balls of his feet and crouched beside the horse, looking at him, then reached out a hand to touch the mane. The horse whined again and fell slowly back to one side, his flanks heaving. The man with the gun shook his head and backed off.

"He deserves that and more," the woman said. She seemed to have nothing more to say after that but handed me the tickets and walked away, swinging her bag, the uneven texture of her skin making her look like a cartoon character as she diminished in the distance. At the fact of the shooting, a small crowd seemed to have gathered around the area; it was a crowd just like the ones lining up at the last moment to bet except that they seemed a bit younger and their faces blunt rather than shabby. Some of them took tickets out of their pockets and scattered them on the ground, others slapped pencils against their cheeks and seemed to be abstractedly figuring out the next race while they waited for this one to end. The gunman moved back against the rail and centered his rifle while a larger truck came past the grandstand and parked behind the horse in the line of fire, half-blocking the view. Some in the crowd got down on their knees to see under the truck but I settled for putting a foot up on the rail and then half-vaulting myself; from that perspective, I was able to see everything. The horse was demolished with two bullets which seemed to hit its chest and neck and its body seemed to turn to water, flowing out on the hard, bright dirt of the track although there was no blood anywhere at all. The crowd seemed to sigh and the man with the gun put it down to foot-level and, dragging it away on the ground, went back into the smaller car. Meanwhile, someone in the larger truck threw a canvas over the animal's body so that it was now completely covered.

"Fixes the son of a bitch," someone said. "He'll never do that to me again. Did it to me two races running but now he's finished."

"Caught him clean," someone else said. "Usually these things can get messy. But he levelled him real nice."

"Level him nice, level him messy; the point is that this is one bastard who's never going to put it to me again."

"You think so? They'll take him back to the barns and put a machine into him and fix him up nice and he'll be right out to race in the third tomorrow. And he'll be odds-on under his new name and you, you bastard, you'll bet on him and he'll go down the pipe and you'll say 'hey, I think they oughta shoot that horse.' That's how it's going to work out."

"Doesn't it always?"

"Isn't that the way?"

"They're going to tow the son of a bitch away, now."

"Why couldn't he have broken it a furlong later; I would've sent roses to his funeral."

"He breaks it further than a furlong you wouldn't have enough money to send roses to his funeral. That horse wasn't going to win. He didn't have a chance. Not a chance."

"You say that?"

"Sure I say it. Didn't you see him stopping in the stretch turn anyway? He was beat."

"He was laying close in the backstretch. He hadn't even made his move yet. He was starting to make his move on the outside when he went down."

"Doesn't make no difference. That horse was finished."

"Maybe he broke it on the backstretch. Maybe he was running that way all the way through."

"Maybe you broke it on the backstretch too. Maybe you'll have a quarter left to go home. What do you like in the next race?"

"What's the difference? I liked this one in the second."

"So give me your choice. Maybe we can lay odds on he drops dead of heat stroke or something."

"They don't open the windows on bets like that."

"With you around they'd make an exception."

"It was really something when they shot that horse. Wasn't it something when they shot that horse? I never seen anything like that in my whole life. I was never out on one of those days before."

"All part of the game, baby. Just be happy they didn't shoot you. They got a special policy; they do all that with the big winners."

"Well, I don't have to worry about that."

"Yeah. Anyway, what you like in the third?"

I had about five dollars left. It would have been enough because I had gas in the car and a fair expectation of reaching home without disaster—and there was always plenty of money at home; I saw to that—but I was sick of it, then, sick of it with a ninth-race sickness; dwindled and shrunken and already far removed from all of it; I wanted to go home. Whatever I had had to solve out here was either solved or would never be—I couldn't tell the difference; there was no way at all of telling the difference; this was one of the main troubles with the track—and I wanted to go home, wanted to put myself in a small, enclosed space because I felt myself dimly, then, to be on the verge of other projects, other intuitions which, however related to whatever had happened to me this afternoon would end up so remote as to seem to have no connection whatsoever. There was no such thing as an uneventful day at the track; what happened was always meaningful and compartmented and the right metaphor for whatever had driven you there in the first place but the best part of the knowledge you tried to gain was to know when you had had it; when you had to go home and apply it in other areas. I needed to go home, but the crowd was thick and angry at the edges; a furious crowd, a raging crowd, a third race crowd standing out there in the infield: losers all of them because if they were winners they would either be inside cashing their tickets or at the bars having a drink, but losers not without a fairly good idea of precisely what had done it to them and what they could do about it. I felt hands slapping at me aimlessly, reaching out as if I was not only an obstruction but, perhaps, a vessel of some information which, if only given to them, would negate everything which had happened to them already and restore them, clean and juvenescent, to the moments before the first race themselves when, all equivocation and despair cast aside, they could make their bets encased in a kind of quiet nobility because they had been given a Second Chance. But I had nothing to say to any of them; I barely had anything to say to myself. The PA system went on again and said that the winner of the third race was Number 7, Beau Champion, a three-year-old bay gelding by Swaps-Nashua's girl, the second horse was number nine, March Militaire and the third horse was number one, Table D'Hote and announced that the time of the next race would be 2:31 and in the next race there would be no changes and then clicked off. In the brief hush that followed, I could tell that they were waiting around me for another kind of announcement from the system, this one would say: ALSO, LADIES AND GENTLEMEN, THE EVEN MONEY FAVORITE IN THIS RACE WAS DESTROYED AT THE STRETCH TURN DUE TO A BROKEN LEFT LEG BUT THIS IS NOTHING FOR YOU FINE PEOPLE TO WORRY ABOUT: HE WASN'T GOING TO WIN THE RACE ANYWAY AND EVEN IF HE HAD IT WOULD HAVE MADE NO DIFFERENCE AT ALL TO THOSE OF YOU WHO BET HIM BECAUSE THERE ARE SEVEN RACES LEFT THIS AFTERNOON AND ALL OF THEM ARE BOUND TO BE VERY DIFFICULT. SO DON'T TAKE ANY OF THIS PERSON-ALLY, LADIES AND GENTLEMEN, PARTICULARLY DO NOT TAKE THE FACT THAT THE ANIMAL WAS DESTROYED PERSONALLY BECAUSE HE WAS AN ANIMAL IN THE FIRST PLACE NOT ANY OF YOU AND IN THE SECOND PLACE THE RACING ASSOCIATION DOES EVERYTHING WITHIN ITS POWER TO MAKE YOUR DAYS PLEASANT AND COM-FORTABLE AND REWARDING AND UNTROUBLESOME BY DESTROYING ANY HORSES WHICH DAMAGE THEMSELVES DURING THE RUNNING OF THE RACES. CRIPPLING, DIS-ASTER, MISINFORMATION, THE BLASTING OF HOPES: THESE HAVE NOTHING TO DO WITH YOUR BENIGN RACING ASSOCIATION WHICH HAS RESOLVED TO BLAST THEM FROM THE FACE OF THE EARTH WITH RIFLE OR WITH EXACTAS: WE REALIZE THAT THERE IS ENOUGH TRAGEDY IN THE WORLD AS IS WITHOUT MORE FAILURE AND LOSS BEING HEAPED UPON YOU. THE WINDOWS ARE NOW OPEN FOR THE THIRD RACE AND REST ASSURED THAT IF YOUR HORSE DOES NOT PERFORM TO EXPECTATION BY REASON OF SHATTERING INJURY OR BROKEN BONE WE WILL SERVE TO MAKE AMENDS TO YOU PERSONALLY AND BEFORE YOUR VERY EYES WHEREAS IF HE PERFORMS POORLY BY REASON OF MYSTERY AND NOT FACT WE

WILL RETURN HIM TO THE BARN TO RUN ANOTHER DAY, MORE SUCCESSFULLY. MYSTERIES ARE FRUITFUL, FACTS ARE NOT: WE OF YOUR RACING ASSOCIATION ARE GEARED TOWARD THE ACCULTURATION AND PROPITIATION OF MYSTERIES. ONTO THE SHROUDED GREEN, UNDER THE SUN ITSELF, SEE NOW, WATCH, FOR THE HORSES ARE COMING OUT.

But I was not listening to it; not even in the channels of the mind was I listening to it, I was trying to get out. I got through the undergrandstand once again, small pockets and tumors of people billowing around me and into one of the alleys which lead downstairs and outside of the track. The coolness came up over me then as I trotted down the stairs; a total and almost final coolness; all of the heat and energy being alternately drawn and dispersed within the acres of the track itself while the surrounding areas, having no kinesis, lacked heat as well. I got downstairs and outside the grandstand and handed my program, tipsheet and newspaper to a small man who thanked me and offered me a quarter and asked who had won the second. I told him I didn't know but the four horse had been destroyed.

"Really? What happened?"

"Broke his leg on the stretch turn."

"Be damned. Finished out of the money then, right?"

"Right."

"I'm a lucky son of a bitch, I swear. I was pushing myself like mad out of the office to get here in time to bet that race. I wanted to bet that horse. I thought he was a sure thing. I would have lost a hundred dollars on that horse."

"You are lucky."

"Just proves that you can never figure horse-racing, don't it?"

"That's what it proves."

And walked then past the umbrella of the ticket-takers window, past the stands where tipsheets were still being sold, where people were still coming in from the subway, a first-race look upon them seeming shockingly irrelevant against even the faces of the tipsheet sellers who now, in the afternoon's first gloom, seemed to have already learned something. I got to my car, feeling the dreadful humidity of the flats pouring in through me, soaking all my garments together in a consistency which felt like glue, trying to keep my mind perfectly blank because again perhaps I had learned something and I wanted to keep that knowledge intact to me. I got to my car and the wild-eyed juvenescent asked how I had done and I told him I had lost, had lost everything, had broken myself utterly, which was probably the right angle to take in any event because he was a man whose tote board was all internal, and if calculations seemed to drop to the proper odds for a course of action he was considering he could have done it; he could have done anything at all. The car started easily and I got out onto the roads, deciding to take the back alleys and service accesses all the way home; no turnpikes or highways for me. I tried not to think.

F riday, it was YESTERDAY, TODAY AND TOMOR-
ROW. It was playing at the Jewel, a battered, faintly odorous theatre somewhere near the slaughterhouses in the business district of the borough, but the business of slaughterhouses
didn't bother me at all. I was not, after all, purely on a pleasure
trip.
YESTERDAY, TODAY AND TOMORROW, all things taken
into account, isn't too bad. It's the least titillating of all the truly
hot movies of the 60's but then again it's in fast company. There's
the Sophia Loren breast feeding business in the first part and all
those fine necrophile overtones in the second and the theological
overtones of the third are really dirty. Putting an ecclesiaste of any
gender in proximity to the likes of Sophia Loren is in itself promising. All in all, it isn't a bad deal for the kind of film it is. Of
course, there was nothing much else playing the city that night; I
had checked it out. There was the underground stuff, of course, but
I'm no pervert. My purposes are not frivolous.
So I went out to the field, then, at about two in the afternoon,
visited two dreadful old men living together on Old Age Assistance
for fifteen minutes—getting credit, then, for two visits that way
instead of one which would almost get me through the afternoon
anyway, even if I was playing it straight—and got back to my apart-

ment at about a quarter after three. I opened a can of beer and watched a panel show while I checked the movie clock to see that the most convenient showing would be the one at 4:30 because then I could see it through three times and still have the evening ahead—and then, at about four, just when I was getting ready to go, the phone rang. I knew right away that it was Poirier, the supervisor, calling to check on me, waiting for me to pick up the phone so that he could ask me why the hell I wasn't in the field; what I was doing at home over an hour before clock-out time. That was all right with me. I didn't mind hearing from him in the least at that point. I picked up the phone and making no attempt to disguise my voice—an old, usually successful trick but too damned childish —said hello.

"That you, Miller?" Poirier said.

"That's me. I'm right here."

"You're supposed to be in the field."

"I finished up early."

"You checked out at 2:00 and you're home already? That's pretty serious, you know."

"I got sick in the field," I said. "I'll take sick leave from three on, which is when I finished my visits. So I'm not trying to steal any time from you."

"You declare sick leave before you leave the office, not after; you know that. You know all the ropes. You've been with the department for three and a half years so how do you expect me to believe that?"

"It was my gut," I said. "I got sick to my gut. After I saw those two old bastards sitting together in that room—"

"A lot of people here are gunning for you, Miller. There's a lot of heat on you now. Why are you making more trouble for yourself?"

"Why did you call me? There'd be no trouble if you hadn't called, isn't that right?"

"You know better than that. I've got to protect my unit, the clients it services. You're in trouble, Miller. You're in bad trouble. They had a conference here this morning upstairs about a lot of people and they want to let you go. They want to bring charges."

His voice had that flat, hard, anxious edge which always came into it when he was either trying to give one of his investigators a hard time or trying to close a client's case. I could imagine his hand, moistening slowly to the excitement of it all, grasping the receiver even more closely to his ears. I had dealt with Poirier for a long time, with middling success. Now we were approaching the last act.

"Well," I said, "let them bring charges. It takes a long, long time to make a dismissal stick in this department, Poirier. Besides, I don't even know if I care to have the job anymore. I might just save all of you a lot of problems and quit. Become a free-lance researcher."

"You're a fool," he said, his voice moistening along with the hand, as he thought of the Department. "You're a fool to throw over a good, secure job like this. If you get fired you'll never get another position in civil service. Besides, you know how the department is coming along; how improvements are being made in services, how salary increases are in the works. I can't see a man like you—who has nowhere else to go anyway—doing something like this to himself."

"How do you know I have nowhere to go?" I said, taking up a new can of beer and opening it one-handed, not a very difficult thing to do if you have any practice and any serious interest in getting at the beer. "For all you know, I might have something in industry all set up for myself. It so happens that one of the largest movie producers in the country and I are talking right now about a position in the east coast casting department. It could come through for me any day. How much difference can it make to me what you people do?"

"Well, listen, Miller," Poirier said, stopping to think that one over only slightly; there is not, among supervisors in the Department of Welfare, a great interest in the arts or crafts, "if you want to go, you go. But you go clean now: just put in your resignation form and quit. Don't play around, have them making me call you Friday afternoons to check you out. Stop complicating my life and everyone's, okay?"

"Well," I said, "well, we'll see. I'll be by on Monday morning and I might just have a surprise for you; I might even have a little two weeks notice. We'll see. We'll see."

His voice went to a new level. "You quit, you have your caseload absolutely cleaned up, you understand me? No loose ends, no evictions, no new pregnancies or anything like that."

"No problem," I said. "I've got the neatest caseload in the

whole east side. I'm on top of it like a big, throbbing drum. Be talking to you on Monday, then, Poirier; have a good weekend."

I hung up on him.

It put the tag end on the week.

After that, and because I already had the can opened, I figured I might just as well sit and finish off the beer; I could still make it to the Jewel on time or only a little bit late and since I was going to see it through three times anyway it wasn't as if I would miss much. Of course, it would leave a few loose ends in the plotting, but nothing I couldn't work up fast. All that I wanted to do was to sit and think quietly for a short while, try to purge Poirier, his conversation, the people upstairs, and the whole Department of Welfare out of my system for the weekend. Never a man for fast transitions, I needed a few more minutes to catch up on it.

About five minutes after that, some publicity stills came special delivery from Warner Brothers anyway and it was fortunate that I was there to sign for them; I had obtained them by advising the studio that I was publicity director of a large freelance critical bureau and it would have been the end of me at Warner Brothers if the envelope had been returned UNKNOWN or NOT AT HOME. So I thanked the mailman very much and gave him the thirty cents postage due and put the stills in the bottom of my dresser drawer with everything else to be sorted out sometime later and then I went downstairs to my car and went over to the theatre.

I was practically the first person into the place. The old woman in the window gave me that peculiar intense look mixing stupefaction and contempt which only ticket takers in neighborhood movie houses truly know and went past an even older man guarding the inner doors who was so numbed that his hand was barely able to reach out and make connection with the stub I handed him. Then, at last, I was inside the cool spaces of the theatre itself; irrelevant preparatory music bleating out from the lighted space under the closed curtain—they were holding back the start after all—and with a feeling of gratitude I found a seat in the middle of a middle row and camped into it. There were only two other people in the house; a teenage couple sitting down in the first row, already necking. The girl had long, thin arms which, coming bare out of the sleeveless sweater to encircle the boy assumed, in the muddled light, the aspect of chains; I wondered how he could stand being in there. But before I had too much time to think about it the music cut off with the kind of high whine which meant that the needle was being drawn over the record and the lights went down and the different kind of music began.

So I leaned back, taking my shoes off, and propped them on the back of the seat in front of me looking at the screen, at a higher, more intense angle now, suspended above the people in the front row so that, for all intents and purposes, they no longer existed; suspended above even my own memory and the dismal events of the afternoon. Now, in the blackness, all things were truly possible: it was possible that I would go in to face Poirier on Monday morning and hand him my identification card and say, *listen, kid, I've had it; after three and a half years of escape and loss I've found my own private way out and I won't be taking this on any more;* it was possible that in the mail on Saturday or at the very latest on Monday, before I went to work, there would be a letter telling me that my application for a position in the promotion department had been carefully considered and found to be acceptable and that I could report for work one week from the date of the letter; it was even possible that not once this weekend would the phone ring and the girl named Barbara, the one in my case-unit, would be on to ask me if I had any particular plans for that afternoon and whether or not I didn't want to try to straighten out and make a go of the job. Everything was possible in that first darkness of the theatre; that was the lesson I had learned a long time ago and held closely to me ever since; the permanence of dreams in the first fastening. Now the curtains were parting and past the title I could hear the voices of people, could see the people themselves, could see the girl, the first intimations of her breasts coming through the angle of the dress she was wearing; could hear the music, the sounds, could hear the bands playing and the familiar sweeping passed through me then, all the way through and out to the other side, and I was suspended somewhere in the overwhelming continuity of history moving forward, moving forward, always moving forward. I must have cried again with the shock of it, and then I had passed through.

In the mirror of the bedroom I could catch the reflection of what I had become and it was fine; it was completely in order and I had to think of it no more. Sophia turned to me, the harsh blackness of her dress striking against the whiteness of her arms and legs and the bedsheets and said to me, "What are you doing with yourself now? Can't you ever pay any attention to me? You look perfectly all right, now stop it!" Her voice speaks English with only the slightest laboring on the vowels whereas my own English is marred by harshness on the consonants; this strangeness somehow improving the way that we go together.

"I merely want to look well," I said to her, clucking slightly. "This is not an unimportant party you know. Possibly, my entire future in the organization hinges upon the impression which you and I give before these people tonight: so pardon a fastidiousness which is only a question, this one time, of being sensible."

"But Marcello, you are always this way. A big, big peacock." Over her face comes the familiar pout, half-leer, half promise. It is really too bad that I have long ago lost most of my passion for her, because she is a splendid looking woman. Time was when I could induce an orgasm—a very strong orgasm—simply by thinking about her for a long time and then touching her, very lightly, on the flesh of the shoulder; the stored release would come with a mingled sigh of pain and necessity. But for the last few months there has been a distinct falling off; a clear feeling that whole areas of thought and connection to her have been blocked off as if by slamming doors. It is a thorough pity, of course, but there is really nothing that I can do about it; I have other things on my mind.

"I am not a peacock," I say. "I am an executive ascendant which is something entirely different. The one makes an end out of appearances. The other makes an appearance out of his destination. I guess that that didn't come off very well, did it?"

"No," she says, "it didn't," and tumbles back on the bed, now all hair and flesh, a whiteness on whiteness, her breasts, undisturbed by the fall, peaking tightly from her dress. "Why don't you come here and make love to me now?" she says with a smile. "We will have plenty of time."

"Because we would have to take our clothes off completely and it would ruin everything. You know how long it took me to dress."

She draws a finger over her lips. "No we don't," she says. "We can make love with our clothes on. All we have to do is to make certain adjustments." She hitches the skirt delicately above her legs, places a finger inside her exposed panties. A splendid woman, she has no need whatsoever of other undergarments.

"I wouldn't even have to take them down," she says. "I could just turn them to the side." She does so, showing me a slight patch of her pubic hair, the dark circle concealing the darker circle within. She raises her other hand, squeezes and envelops her breast, motions to me. "All you would have to do," she whispers, "is to let down your fly and support yourself on your hands with your feet hanging over the bed. We wouldn't disturb a crease in your jacket then; you exercise more drinking a cocktail. See, I'll even do all the moving." And her thighs began to gesticulate subtly, their curved inner surfaces coming together and parting, a suggestion of moisture trapped between them, then spiralling out onto the bed. Yes, I cannot deny it: despite myself, despite my cold, focussed perception of what she is trying to do to us, I am excited by her. And yet with the idiot temptation to move upon her whatever the consequence to the evening's appearances, is the realization that if I do I have truly conceded some point to her; a point which is such a mystery that I will not be able to understand her victory for a long time but which, nevertheless, has sent her in this way on the evening. "Sit up," I say, trying to be reasonable. "We have other things to do this evening. Later tonight, who knows?" It is true; later tonight, now, I would go to bed with her with joy and completion as if for the first time but now, despite the rising throb of my genitals there is a darker undercurrent, need, persuasion, the events to come. But it goes beyond her.

She drops the hand covering her breast onto an inner thigh; begins to curve and stroke it alternately, moaning slightly. "Marcello," she mutters to me, "are you such an entire fool that you cannot see my need?" And elevating her hips slightly she draws the panties down below her knees.

And now I see the whole of her; I see the whole of Sophia Loren exposed before me, her rounded ass, the soft curvature of the thighs, the secret of the mons veneris pulsing out its slow confession on the bedsheets and even though I am a movie star it proves to be too much; entirely too much for the likes of me . . . even though the party tonight will be splendid and magnificent and crucial to any definition of my outcome, it is still too much for me. I remove the cigarette from where it has been dangling all this time between my pursed, quizzical lips, and putting an indolent but quivering hand on my fly, I move toward her. Now, in that intensity of anticipation I can feel the room itself contract, literally contract around me and there is that feeling of slow contraction in space which I have felt so often in screwing Sophia, and maybe this is one of the primary reasons why I originally lost interest in her; she is too intense. But those are all post-coital thoughts; what has seized me now is the outspokenness and idiot need of lust itself and, kicking my shoes off tentatively, one by one, I vault myself onto the bed and hang carefully above her, my body suspended on my clattering knees, reaching for my fly. She moves a hand upwards and helps me with it, there is an almost fatal snag halfway down and I think for an instant that I will have to wrench off the pants themselves, commit all of the evening to a kind of penance, but then the fly comes down easily with a slow wheeze, much as if it had made a difficult but determined choice and resolved to cooperate.

Hovering above her now, swimming in want and retrospection, I see her face. The eyes are closed and she once again has entered that slow passage where only the connection matters; I wonder, absurdly, as I poke and pry below, how many men have seen Sophia like this. Certainly, both in and out of the worlds she portrays in the cinema, both as creation and reality, she has never been seen like this; the eyes shuttered, the cheeks faintly puffed, the mouth itself curled in that slow, blinking sexsmile which both denies and implements what is going on below. For a moment, I would reach my hand out to seize her breasts, hold and remove them slowly from the low bodice but I must be firm, firm, so I think of her nipples one by one instead and remembering that we must be leaving for the party in no more than ten minutes, now, I hasten myself into need.

"Oh, don't you like this?" she murmurs, my actress, my nemesis, my wife, my tool, as I hover over her, "isn't this nice? Don't you wish, Marcello, we could just screw all the time and not get involved in those silly, contrived plots, this childish nonsense?" and her arms come around slowly in procession to enfold me as I plunge deeper and deeper into her network, finding an obstacle, withdrawing from the unseen, push, getting it past another way and now at last I have moved inside her all the way and delicately, tentatively, have begun my dance upon her, still wondering absurdly about creases in my clothes, loss, need, urgency, as I feel the convulsions from below. "I just wish we could get out of this movie and live our lives without things always getting in the middle," Sophia murmurs to me and I open my mouth to tell her, then, that she is wrong, wrong: that only the interception and contrivance matter, that only the interruptions are meaningful, lending taste and balance to this other, darker side, but I am unable to speak. Her breasts rise against me, her dress glides against my pants with a tearing, zooming sound and I feel myself spend to the last inch and then begin to drive clear in the high, white, detailed sensations of orgasm. I poise out over her, extended now in the need to plant, to generate and she spreads even further before me and then begins to reciprocate with a slow unfolding of her juices. I hear her moan and grunt and ease out below me. I feel the shudders of her hands passing slowly over my shoulders and the exhaustion comes on top of the coming but I cannot collapse over her; I cannot ruin my suit and thus my reputation and so I manage to part from her quickly, already overcome by the old revulsion, the old boredom, and pass off her side to the floor itself where I stand already instinctively rearranging my clothing. Her body curls out on the bed and then unwinds slowly. I can see between her thighs the first trickling indications of what we have done together.

"Oh, my," she says, "oh, my, my, wasn't that good?"

"Get dressed," I say, "we have to go to the party."

"But wasn't it? Wasn't it? Didn't you like it?"

"Yes," I say, "yes, yes," feeling that I must comfort her or the evening itself will be lost in the aftersulk. "It was all right, Sophia But now I insist that we leave; we have things to do."

Drums clatter behind us and I sense we are ready for a transition. We hang in an undefined space for a time while I feel her assemble beside me, something that seems to be a thick, continental fog embraces us and takes us to its center. When it releases us from that grip, we are standing in a ballroom with several hundred people around us, being introduced. Sophia's garments cling to her now, it is apparent that she has done one of the most effective of all her reconstructions. In the crowd there seem to be some people I know: Fellini, Magnani, a couple of minor British directors and perhaps—although I cannot be sure—Elizabeth Taylor and Richard Burton themselves are there, entrapped somewhere between the hors d'oeuvres and a group of large, red-faced men who seem to be alternately shouting at or clawing them. It is that kind of a party.

It is precisely that kind of party; now, as I assemble myself toward its unfolding I can feel the decay slip through me, the corruption, the loss, the waste; the feeling of a Europe gone far and irretrievably past its best possibilities, now useless and irrelevant in the heart of its industrial wastes, sinking deeper and deeper into crime, pollution and elegant parties which can barely shield the rich, indolent and beautiful from the pain of knowing they are themselves. I inhale this feeling with a stricken and rising feeling of familiarity; this is what I know best, that is what I do best. Next to my increasingly provocative stream-of-consciousness, and my superb if rather mechanical performances with Sophia, the thing that I do best of all is to center myself at such parties, accepting with my swollen, descending eyes both the best and worst parts of myself; moving through them like the idealized gnome of conscience itself as I drift into the rising inebriation, the rising despair, the settling remorse that these parties become. Casual, inflating slowly to the cloak of my attitude, I turn to Sophia who has stood loyally beside me, lifting my elbow slightly and say, "This is one of the worst parties I have ever seen in my life. The bankruptcy, the depression; the waste of all of this. Where have all the real people gone?"

"You insisted that we go. You said it was vital to your professional career. Now that we are here, stupid, it should be quite clear to you that no one takes any interest in us at all; they are all playing their own pursuits." She is holding a very large martini in a glass the shape of a barrel and she takes a slow, dramatic sip, looking at me. "I could have told you all of this but you never listen, Marcello."

"Listen, listen, nobody listens!" I say, rather loudly, and feel the old rage move in somewhere under my mood, vitiating the situation, at a stroke, of the best of its possibilities. "Nobody listens to anything anymore at any time whatsoever; we drift ever further into obscurity, into masks, wine and chatter; the reality only a sceptre to guide us, staggering, through the last door of night. No, I cannot say that I like this. Why did the partners insist we come? Why did the partners say my appearance at this party was so vital to them? Surely, we would be better off in a small room, holding one another, moving past one another, looking slowly into one another, looking slowly through one another, blending and joining in the silence of postwar Europe, moving forward to creating itself; the candles wickering past the bedside, the moaning of doves—"

"Marcello," she says, giving my elbow a jog, "you are sometimes full of the most paralyzing kind of misconceptions. Really, you often make an impossible thing of yourself."

I am hurt. What Sophia does not understand, what she has never understood, is that this particular kind of plot imposes certain exigencies which, while they make the actors unhappy, cannot be helped. It is a postwar sequence with which we have very little to do; we are, after all, only there to commit a certain portion of imagination to reality. But this would be too deep for her. Everything is too deep for Sophia; all the publicity to the contrary, she is a simple, religious creature, numbed to the first level of response, more comfortable with ritual than with manner and thus obsessed with the need to define everything with which she comes into contact in terms only of a kind of ceremony. As this intricate thought hits me—and with it a kind of depression that I will, in no way, be able to make Sophia see this; were I to seize her breasts from behind, cup them urgently and do a tattoo on her buttocks she would still think that the world was a kind and simplistic place—I feel a severe depression and with it a necessity for flight. The fact of the matter is that I am sick of Sophia. I have been married to her for several years, I have done my duty; past routine fornication I have no more interest in her and I have already taken care of that for the evening. What I want to do now is to dismiss her.

This is less easily accomplished than thought; we are at a party populated by most of the reigning personalities and libertines of the continent but she is, nevertheless, my wife, and I am condemned by the contrivances of the plot to work out the evening with her at some basic level of contact. But there is a way around this, of course, which has to do with the accessory of plot. This is something which ordinarily I dislike trying because it breaks a certain consistency; causes even my handsome, knowledgeable features to grey with a kind of insecurity, but on the other hand, there are alternatives here which I feel it is vital for me to pursue. Besides, I need make no apologies; I have already gone to bed with her. I have performed sublimely, that is to say successfully. Past obligation, I assure myself, I have no further commitment.

So I walk away from her rather quickly, balancing a cocktail glass which someone has placed in my hand unevenly in the curve of my fingertips, heading for the cluster of people in the area of the Richard Burtons which, as I approach, dwindles; red-faced men with dim expressions of woe scurrying for the sides as they witness my coming. It is usually that way; it is not so much that I consciously want to be mean to potential rivals as it is a profound kind of inequity which embarrasses other men into retreat at my faintest gesture. It is not something which I would have willed that way; it simply happened. Behind me, through the haze and gloom and the thump of two prematurely copulating bodies already settling to the floor in a huddle of coats, I imagine that I can hear Sophia crying to me: *Marcello, Marcello, why must you wander? Cannot I alone satisfy you; there are so many people who think I am an entirety of woman,* but I pay it no heed. Sophia is like that. One must be very determined to escape her, as my superfluity of appearances with her in the public domain should long since have proven.

I am standing by Elizabeth Taylor herself now; her husband, shrunken by this engagement to realistic proportions stands grinning rather vacuously at the two of us and, attempting to show that he is not discomfited, awkwardly gobbles an hors d'oeuvre, most of which glances off his cheeks and onto his clothing. Demolished by this—the more so because he has been betrayed by manners rather than choice—he shrugs vapidly and says, "This is just one of those terrible, terrible parties. It would drive you to drink, that is what it would do. Drive a man to drink, that is if he had a drink fit for the drinking which is precisely what the scum here will never offer you. I recognize you; you come from this country, don't you?"

I shrug, not committing myself and reach out a finger to caress Elizabeth's shoulder lightly; coming out of the blue, strapless gown she is wearing it is enormous, an explosion of near-white rippling skin against the tighter sheen of her throat, the pearls casting their mysteries in reflection off the chandelier. "I come from all countries," I say to her. "Decay, waste, loss are universals rather than particulars, at least in the society which we have come to inherit. Wouldn't you think so?"

"Oh yes," she says, looking at me quickly, then back to her drink which is a muddy orange in color; it sets her dress off nicely, to say nothing of those large, bursting, Madonna's breasts fighting unsuccessfully through layers of bone to reach an accommodation with the good free air. "I couldn't agree more with that. Richard and I were saying to each other just before you came over that we hadn't the faintest idea why we were at this party at all; someone sent us this silly invitation by mail and because we had absolutely nothing better to do this evening we came. But it's so American, the whole scene here, that you could just throw up, that is if you were the kind of person to get easily nauseous. There is something about what Americans do to every place they tenant that can kill a good party."

"Nothing else to do?" I say, stroking the softness of her arm again and letting my eyes glance off her breasts, sensing dimly in the background her husband's recession. It is almost as if, in the extremity of this contact, he has ceased to exist: despite all his contracts, all his notoriety, all his literacy and fame, some complex apprehension has stripped him to the soul and left him vacuous. "Do you mean to say that you had nothing else to do this evening?"

"Well," my madonna says, "we could have done all kinds of things. But we didn't. Richard likes to go to parties and drink. That's his worst fault."

I look upon her fully now, let her see the knowledge growing in my eyes, the sensitivity of my face, that strange, piercing, glowing quality which reduces contacts with others to the level of a uniform and depressing pretension. "It all depends on the marriages, yes?" I say, "and the persons who are married to one another. Sometimes there can be too much to do, am I right?"

"And sometimes not enough."

I finish my drink in a remorseless gulp, my eyes like glass now, inspecting her, looking through the sheen and fullness of the dress to the skin underneath; the tired, workmanlike honesty of her body which I know, now, waits to receive me. I crumble the glass to ash between my fingers, cupping it beneath my hands, feeling the fragments sift like ash and silt over the corruption below. "Let's get out of here," I say.

"And go where?"

"Does it matter? To some clear quiet place by the sea, perhaps, where we can look upon the purer spaces of the moon and grasp ourselves. Anything away from this sadness."

Her eyes twinkle and I remember, gazing at their lost translucence, how beautiful she was in NATIONAL VELVET; how far she has voyaged from there and yet how inextricably, how peculiarly, she is bound to her past; like all of us doomed to act out small parodies of her history in lighted corridors. "My husband," she says. "You must understand how Richard feels about this kind of thing."

I shrug, another inexpressible, consuming Italianate shrug. "Where is he?" I ask. "I haven't seen him around for a long time, now. He seems to have disappeared."

"He drinks. He drinks all the time, Marcello. May I call you Marcello?"

"Yes. And I will call you Elizabeth Taylor."

"You can call me Liz."

"No," I say, liking the fullness, the rightness of it; the enormity of that devouring. "You are Elizabeth Taylor."

"He drinks more and more. I don't really know how to control him. It's like he goes out into a world of his own and I can't even touch him. Sometimes," she says, running her palms over the surfaces of the dress, the flesh of her upper arms trembling slightly at the effort, "well, sometimes I don't even know if he thinks of me as a woman."

"That is terrible," I say. I take her hand. It is time. "We cannot have you go on feeling like that, it does not befit you. We must show you that you remain a woman."

Her palm glides into mine, rapid, discrete, somehow self-enclosed, but she comes with me quickly. "Oh, I wouldn't say that I don't think I'm a woman," she says. "You've got to understand that a woman of my background doesn't have too many worries that way. No, it's just that sometimes, I think, the whole American corruption has gotten to poor Richard and it beats him down."

"Disastrous," I nod, with a journalist's briskness. "Absolutely disastrous."

We pass from the party that way, the two of us joined by our hands, her gown trailing over the floor; the rapid patter patter of my expensive shoes setting the basic rhythm of retreat. The crowd, which has been assembling in an ever-increasing horde around the now invisible copulating couple on the floor, moves aside slightly for us to pass through, purring in acknowledgment. Sophia herself is huddled somewhere near the hors d'oeuvre table, two pieces of toast clasped to her breast, her glass somewhere in the invisibility of the spaces between her breasts, tentatively balanced there. Once again I think I hear her reproach, sense her dimly saying something to me above the sounds of pain and mingling on the floor, the faint crows of delight that echo through the room, but I am secure now, centered to my purpose, far beyond her capacity to reach me. Besides, I wish to do nothing to embarrass Elizabeth Taylor; we are, after all, on a first date. So I leave a smile and a wink in my wake for Sophia to pick up and interpret as she will and we pass through the clattering, shuddering doors of the ballroom, into something that looks very much like the corridor of an apartment building and out into the cool, desiccate air of a muddled landscape.

"Take my car," she says urgently, producing some keys from the space between her breasts. "I want you to drive my possessions; it will excite me far more than anything else you could do."

"Where shall we go?" I ask, taking the keys, feeling their weight in my hand, reaching up a palm to graze her shoulder.

"Away from here. I know an old couple in the next town who rent out this room. We can go there and be alone."

"Well," I say, "that's perfectly all right with me." Old couples, young couples, middle-aged couples, I think . . . when will this corruption cease? We get into her car, a large Cadillac, from opposite ends and she slides close to me on the plastic of the seat; I insert the keys and start the motor.

There is no transition. We are on a long, flat grey road moving past the parking lot, moving past refreshment stands, past used car auctions, past drive-in eateries where adolescents turn numbed faces in the twilight to watch us glide past, food poised at their mouths. If it were not that I knew so much better, I would take the scene for an American rather than Continental embroidery and this fills me for an instant with distress—is the reel breaking up, are they about to jolt me from the camera's flash?—but it occurs to me that in the broken loss of the postwar, all landscapes have become America, a generalized country of the heart, and this idles my anxiety, fills me with a questing peace. I have a fine, analytic journalist's brain even though, from my performances, one would never think so: I perform vaguely "creative" duties I know and have even written some essays upon the metaphysics of decay. Some day, far away from all these useless women, I will have to think more on this.

We pass through forests ringing us on either side, the lights of cars halving our bodies with their beams and Elizabeth drifts over to me, takes my hand again, leans her shoulders heavily on my chest. I can feel the throbbing of her heart through the even rising of her breasts and on an impulse I free my right hand from her embrace and slip it into the cold crack between her breasts. The smoothness and fullness of the skin assaults me, a faint crack and smell of gunpowder drifts through the car. It is not every day, after all, that one touches the breasts of an Elizabeth Taylor; even though she is 38 years old she was very beautiful as a young girl in NATIONAL VELVET and won an Academy Award for having such large breasts and almost dying with them in the bargain. I feel my lean, perceptive loins quiver and she drifts a hand over them, pauses at the outer ring of my genitals and then works a tender thumb into a crevice she has created. I begin to bounce upon the seat in childish glee, pumping the brake pedal furiously, my despair and disillusion for the moment—for all moments, perhaps, while feeling and being felt by Elizabeth Taylor—forgotten.

After a long time, a long slow passage through this connection, the car seems to slow of its own volition; I see that we are approaching a large, twinkling farmhouse on the near side of the road from whose windows two absent, unrecognizable faces peer like doughnuts, looking down upon us. Elizabeth takes her hand away from me and stretches on the seat, moves up to a more proper position against me. "That's it," she says. "That's the place. They're always waiting for visitors here."

Superbly, careless of my accomplishment, I bring the car imperceptibly into the curve of the access highway, move it slowly through rubble toward an enormous gate which swings open before us, move through the plowed, brown spaces of the field into a small parking cubicle which sits before the house. I cut the motor and the two of us get out slowly; an old woman confronts us from the porch.

"Good evening," she says, before I have had a chance to properly introduce myself, to say nothing of Elizabeth Taylor. "Have you come to pay us a visit?"

The crone's features shift in the twilight and she assumes for me, then, an aspect of familiarity; if I were not absolutely convinced otherwise I would be sure that I had met her before; perhaps in one of my earliest comedies playing the role of a vaguely religious character. It is evident too from the way in which she looks at me that she feels this connection. But she passes through the moment with a gesture of dismissal which implies in its totality almost everything which I have been thinking this evening and says, simply, "How long do you want to stay?"

Elizabeth huddles more closely to me, her face against my shoulder. "As long as I need," I say, and then, as I feel her tremble, I say, "I mean, as long as the lady wants to."

"Is this lady your wife?"

"Of course. Do you wish me to produce evidence?"

The woman shrugs and turns away. "It is not necessary. The two of you will want the master bedroom, of course. That means that I will have to displace my husband for the moment."

"Oh, listen," Elizabeth says, "we wouldn't think—"

"Nonsense. You people come; you take the master bedroom. It is only fitting. Pepe is quite used to it by now; besides, he needs the air." She calls his name twice and a large man wearing loose-fitting garments, peers from an upper window, motions to her.

"Come down," she says. "The people are here again."

"I was just doing the crossword—"

"You do it in the kitchen. Hurry, Pepe, we do not wish to offend these young visitors."

The man withdraws, moves away and Elizabeth, still against my shoulder, gives a small cry which might be pain or pleasure mingled; might be simple embarrassment. I fold an arm more tightly around her, watching the woman inspect us, possibly for signs of infestation. As she recognizes us—and I can see the knowledge sifting into her honest face with the interminable slowness and inevitability with which the sun must huddle, every evening, behind her house—a twitch of an eyebrow affects a shrewdness and she says, "Of course, it will be very expensive."

"What will be expensive?"

"The use of the room. Pepe is a sick man; he is under doctor's orders not to come out of doors except during the evenings and then escorted, always escorted. Really, the quarters are quite pleasant, even luxurious. We will need at least several billion lire for its occupancy."

"How much would that be?"

"Twenty dollars."

I take out my wallet, give her two tens clutched against one another with tender familiarity, brush my hand over Elizabeth's shoulder. "We must not be disturbed."

"Of course not. We are very discreet people."

"Nothing must disturb us," Elizabeth says.

Pepe emerges from the house now, a small, spry man whose spirits and demeanor seem to render questionable his wife's gloomy medical report. He smiles at us, waving the newspaper. "Visitors?" he says in a shrill voice. "I love visitors. They are so profitable."

"Quiet, Pepe," the woman says.

"Perhaps you would know a four-letter word synonymous with *egress?* The puzzle is very challenging today."

"Later, Pepe," the woman says, showing him the tens and taking him by the elbow in a gesture similar to the clutch of my hand on Elizabeth but lacking the urgency of lust. "These nice people must not be disturbed. We can wait by the trees."

"I am merely trying to be friendly. The word is not *door*; I tried that already. I think it begins with —"

"Now, Pepe," the woman says determinedly and leads him away. His little legs scuttle over cobblestones, alternately losing and reasserting their balance; he weaves unsteadily in their wake. "I'll talk to you later," he says.

"Have a pleasant time, children," the woman says, leading him somewhere behind our parked car and from then on, as far as we are concerned, out of our lives forever. I increase my pressure on Elizabeth, lead her slowly toward the house. We move into its cool, small interior, feeling surrounded by wool and old odors, up a thin dangerous stairway and get eventually to the room itself, a neat room with a bed, a nightstand, two ashtrays, a washbasin and a strange contraption which might be a toilet or some kind of purging mechanism. I close the door and turn to Elizabeth. She is shaking slightly.

"Oh, no," I say, feeling the old, creeping, Sophia-dismay rising within me. "You're not going to get nervous or depressed now and spoil everything, are you?"

"No," she says, sitting on the bed. "You know me. Of course not. I love good times. The only thing is that it makes me feel kind of cheap and spoiled."

"There's no reason for you to feel that way. We must find our love where we can and this is a lovely room."

I am distressed that Elizabeth Taylor, of all people, is behaving in this manner. It makes me suspect her publicity, not that I would be so unkind as to say anything of this sort to her. Instead, I lean forward and kiss her gently on the forehead, at the same time working with my hands to free my belt, feeling it part with a crunch and underneath it, somewhere in obscurity, my pants. "Of course, she knows," I say. "That woman knows more about the human soul than Stendahl or the very famous Alberto Moravia. That woman has entertained, in this very room, the cream of Continental and American society."

"That crone? That hag!"

But this does not disturb me because I know that Elizabeth is known for her sharp tongue and cutting judgements of people; it is a blunt honesty which I expect to see complemented by frank and open passion in the bed. "She is a very wise, understanding woman," I say, "and she has done more for the betterment of society than even Freud himself.".

"Well, it makes me feel very cheap."

I kick myself considerately out of my pants, working now on my shirt. "Come, come, Elizabeth," I say. "Free yourself of your clothing, as I am, and it will be beautiful. In the early gathering of sunset this room takes on the rich and dark hues of an immortal Autumn."

She sighs at this—I know her taste for poetry—and stands limply from the bed, begins then to work on her garments. The dress, which I had envisioned to be astonishingly complex, turns out to be a very simple, almost childish kind of thing similar to those bathing suits which small boys and girls will wear to the paddling pools on Sundays, for there is a zipper concealed in the folds of a side panel, and with one truly majestic sweep, she has taken it all the way down, the dress parting itself completely to reveal her standing before me only in her brassiere. She has worn no pants or other undergarments whatsoever. The rich, light scent of her—what I had taken to be in the car the smell of sweet auto grease between the axles—comes out frankly to fill all the spaces of the room and I look upon her with wonder, struck, even in the center of my own reputation and accomplishment, by the beauty of this international movie star. She bends a hand back awkwardly behind her brassiere, shaking her head slowly.

"Sometimes I wonder why you men are so insistent upon

having all the clothes off," she says. "Richard is the same way. He won't do a thing unless we're both naked with the door locked somewhere. Just because animals make love without any clothes, must humans as well? Clothes, after all, are what bring us closer to the Divine; why can we not accommodate ourselves to them?"

I let this speculation pass. My shirt off, stripped to my multicolored garters and socks, I have found myself seized by excitement at the sight of her breasts tumbling before me; the nipples bursting to flower, the strange, hardened surfaces of the aureolae a mystery themselves; the thick whiteness of the under-breast trembling slightly in the heat of the room. Now, as she raises her arms over her head, I find that I can literally no longer control myself; as debonair, assured and despairing as I must surely be, my cock sings a different tune at the sight of my lovely Elizabeth, kept for joining in this room, and I whisk toward her, both calves flying and grip her in a hard embrace, feeling her body slide up and against me. I hear her mumble something about the shade, about the need to get the shade down, about the light that is coming into the room but I cannot permit myself to release her—it is like a dream; were I to release her I might awaken and all of it would be gone—and so, instead, I sidle over to the shade still maintaining that grip, our surfaces bumping and jogging against one another, the touch of our toes and calves adding a not unwelcome and highly relaxing air of *commedia* to the proceedings. With my left hand I manage somehow to undo the string from its place on a post and get the shade down; I manage to do all of this while, belowships, my cock is making urgent, tentative contact with the hard, moist surfaces of her sex. She gives a squeal, somewhere between dismay and need, and still locked in that joining we prowl to the bed and fall upon it like a pair of assassins, her hands groping to raise her breasts to my lips. I stretch my palms into the small of her back to raise her into me and then, for a very long time, I feed upon her, feast upon her juices, swaddle my contemporary despair in the darker fluids that are rising all within and without us.

I am doing it to her, then, and with the keener, finer, more histrionic and detached part of my mind I am able to depart from the linkage to the degree that I can look upon it almost as a voyeur—I have always had this streak of perversity; it shows even in the mildest of my films—and this thought, this realization, rather, that I am doing it to a very big star, to a very important actress: that I am doing it to Elizabeth Taylor herself, enters me much as my cock must be beginning to prowl her and I swim with excitement and lust. There are not many people, after all, who have been fortunate enough to have been in this position with Elizabeth Taylor; this is something that has been restricted to relatively few men and it increases my excitement to no small degree. Thinking of this, lapping on her huge breasts, making myself believe that there is milk in them that will emerge in a matter of seconds and fill my mouth to bursting, I speculate what most men would think of me now; men, that is, who possess dull wives and no outlet—as could have happened to me if I had not known better than Sophia—men who had no wives and less outlet, men who came alone in the darkness to movie theatres and watched this woman on the screen, trying somehow, in an extension of their muddled hopes, to place themselves against the celluloid and so find the softness. As I bite her nipple, hearing her small wickering cries I think now of men who sit in movie theatres all over the world, men with grey coats covering their laps to conceal the frantic busyness of their hands from view; men who, immersed in the terrible economy and brutality of image, try to flog themselves through and into another level of feeling while I, Marcello, have the reality itself poised against me, sobbing something about the dense air in the room as I move further and further on top of her, deeper and deeper into her spaces. I think about these men and as I do so it is not with arrogance nor even with pity but only with the kind of massive resignation and sadness with which one thinks of a brother fallen upon an evil, disastrous end, an old friend fallen into an unsuccessful speculation. It is, after all, partly luck that I myself am in this hole; I came from a very mediocre background.

Elizabeth shifts against me, her breasts still seized in her hands but pulled out of my mouth and as she begins to work on my ear with insistence she is whispering about her thighs, the necessity to go to her thighs, to enjoin them for cooperation, and so I move below, blindly now, shutting my eyes against this good fortune and bury myself, all the way to the tongue in the fur and odor of her necessity. Her hips thrash wildly, her thighs straining to engulf me and for a tense moment I think that I might actually be immersed; that I might swim and die in those foreign spaces but then another rocket of energy tears me loose, my tongue clinging to bits of hair and I return to her breasts, feeling like a voyeur's dummy—because all those departed brothers and friends indeed might be looking at me—but no less excited for all this explosion of good luck. Her breasts are before me again, this time without the benefit of support from her hands and in their massivity they roll off her chest, diving into sheets and pillows as I seek to recover them, all willing and neat, with my agonized mouth. She begins to murmur to me again: this time she is murmuring gracious obscenities with a hint of Brooklyn practicality behind them and so, then, I rise a little; I rise upon my knees; I swim in the channel of darkness I have created, I rise up all the way and then I plunge into her, the first strokes vapid and languid, then, as I accommodate myself to her contours, picking up in rhythm; moving faster and faster in that invisibility, the visitation coming to a clamorous end and I feel myself moving up all the way in her. Her face is turned to one side, her eyes closed against the load of Italianate ardor which I am about to place in her furthest spaces and then as she sighs and stretches back, her stomach and genitals pulsing in a lostness of their own I squeal—I can distinctly hear myself squeal but it is a delicate European shout; there is nothing animaline about it—and throw my load all the way into her, gasping.

And yet it does not stop there; this is Elizabeth Taylor and for her I carry on the longest sustained orgasm I have ever had in my life; far, far longer than the ten or twenty-second specials which I have managed for Sophia; it is as if the mysterious hidden triggers are blocked inside me on OPEN and I hang at the very crest of it for an incredible, for an almost frightening extension of time, feeling that because this is Elizabeth Taylor herself this time, I may literally never stop coming and my hands reach again for the remote hugeness of her breasts and I subside finally, breaking upon her, all sobs and shouts, mingled in the warm and sheltering spaces of the room.

After a long time, we disentangle. There is really nothing to say. We have solved our anomie in difficult and separate ways, blended together for an instant's shout. I light cigarettes and hand her one, slightly chilled by our excesses and trying to show her, now, by the poise and control of movements that I could not possibly have been the one who squealed like a goat; no Mastroianni would be capable of something like that. No, it must have been an illusion, must have been her own shout hurled back at her; it is known that I come silently and with great force and control, my face twitched at the crest in a quizzical, correct, interrogatory sneer. She begins to fumble for her brassiere, her face open now with the renewed knowledge of love. There is a knocking on the door. We are both beautiful people; there is nothing to fear from our discovery. I get up from the bed, go to the door and open it. Pepe is standing there, a newspaper flapping. His face apprehends slowly the state of our clothing and condition but it does so without lust; rather the multifarious creases and curves seem to settle even more deeply upon his skull. He shows me the newspaper.

"I found the word," he says, showing it to me neatly written in in a painful, senile hand and I agree; he has certainly found the word. "Can I come back in now? I'd like to rest on the bed."

"Well, we could use a few moments—"

"Doctor's orders," he says and puts a wiry elbow into my ribs, brushing me to the side and proceeds toward the bed.

I look back of me to tell Elizabeth that it is perfectly all right; to comfort her but—not surprisingly—she has already gone, disassembled completely and vanished. This is not the least of her witchery. I would think upon it further but I feel a wrench at my own vitals.

Creased into the seat, so deeply riven into the folds of it that it took me a long, wrenching effort to get free, I slowly reoriented myself, hearing the thud of music behind the screen, the sound of iron curtains closing. Before me, the teenage couple seemed to have disappeared below seat level, only an occasional flying ankle or arm indicating that, like me, they were still with the picture and themselves, but my view was cut off by the heads of two old ladies who had, apparently, come in sometime during the movie and it was difficult to see. It was even more difficult to move but self-discipline was vital—it is only by a deliberate excess of movement after a movie that I find myself able to be restored and I have no desire, even at this point, *not* to be restored—and I managed to get a wrist up, check my watch, which said in sly luminescence that it was 7:00 and that, apparently, I had already sat through two showings of YESTERDAY, TODAY AND TOMORROW. Between my stomach and head there was a vague feeling of disconnection, probably caused by the beer I had had with nothing following—it is a very bad idea for me to go to a movie having had nothing to eat—but I was able to fight my way through that and forced myself into a standing posture, and then into a vague, shambling, somewhat terrified walk which took me out into the empty aisle and through into the lobby. It was an unusual day, there was no question about it for I had rarely felt so drained. Usually a double feature or a consecutive showing of one film will leave me vaguely chilled and in severance from any real sense of past for a few moments, but the weakness, the sense of drainage this time were something entirely new. It had been one of the most powerful exercises yet; a sheer vault past the extraneous into the center of need itself and abetted no little by the women themselves; it was very rarely that I possessed more than one woman during the span of a movie, let alone two beauties such as these. It was too much for me. It was, all things considered, simply too much for me. It was, all things considered, simply too much for me. I had the feeling that one of my clients might have had if his welfare check went scuttling from him on payment day, lost purposes dwindling down the street, his feet in hopeless comic flight; in just such a fashion did I feel myself trailing, unsuccessfully, after my consciousness. I paused before the candy counter and looked at the glow of winkage of the popcorn machine for a few minutes, then decided that it was probably not popcorn which I was after at all. There seemed to be a wind in the lobby; a feeling of being a gnome trapped in a small, bat-strewn cave. I turned and saying *the hell with it, the hell with this; I'm tired, I don't really know what I want to do so I better get out*, left the lobby and came into the warm, dim spaces of the street and finding my car in the parking lot, starting the motor and moving out slowly, I decided that all the experiences of the evening having been equal—as they usually, usually were—I might as well get the hell home.

Commentary

Maurice Girodias

The Olympia Press should have emigrated from Paris to America much sooner than 1967, ten years before, in the late fifties I would say. Immediately after the publication of *Lolita* in 1959, it was proven that the old puritanical order in the United States was fast disintegrating. By publishing *Lolita, The Ginger Man,* Henry Miller's books, the works of Samuel Beckett, Jean Genet and William Burroughs, plus the de Sade translations in English and piles of modern fancy pornography (including masterpieces such as *Candy* and *The Story of O*) we had contributed powerfully to this cataclysmic change.

But we had also built up a backlist so impressive in the process that I could have turned it into a vast publishing empire if I had been wise enough to leave Paris for New York ten years or even five years before I did. But wisdom is one quality I may never find the time to learn and so I stayed in Paris to see my backlist being stolen from my hands by legions of scavengers and my authors turning away from and then against me because I had ceased to be of any use to them.

As, when I signed a contract for an original work, I usually acquired world rights (all the more easily as no one thought in the early 'fifties that "such books" could ever be reprinted in other countries) it became a sort of routine for my authors to sue me in order to regain their freedom when offers from American publishers came in. Or sometimes they would simply sell the American rights to their books (as was done in the case of *Candy* for $1,000!) and *then* sue me, as a kind of afterthought. One thing was sure to happen: I would lose my case automatically in the Paris courts.

I was anathema to French judges. I had only to *appear* in court and the magistrates would turn green, would pointedly fall asleep every time my lawyer opened his mouth, then wake up just before the end with that familiarly insane grin on their faces . . . and clamp down on me a monstrous sentence. Since all of my books were published in English and since my judges did not have knowledge of that alien tongue the whole process was made even more bizarre: One day, after having been given three months for a book I hadn't even published, I could not resist muttering, "This is like something out of Kafka." "Kafka!" the judge snapped. "Nine months! Next..."

All of these legal vaudevilles cost me an incredible amount of money and energy since the persecution had started with the bans of *Lolita* and *The Ginger Man* at the end of 1956. I had sued the Minister of Interior to have those bans reversed, won my case in February 1958, saw my victory reversed shortly after de Gaulle's *coup d'Etat* in May 1958 and became the pet victim ever after of every judge and gendarme in the country. A parking ticket would cost me ten times more than it would an ordinary, non-pornographic citizen . . . and I was even summoned in 1962 to serve two years in the army! I was forty-three and grey-haired but in spite of the obvious mistake I had a hell of a time getting out of that one.

You don't believe me? Ask my lawyer; he doesn't lie.

My lawyer, Leo Matarasso, dear and faithful friend, was my constant savior during those years of trial and misery. Managing by hook and by crook, *and* a fabulous imagination, to dazzle the courts, Leo would rescue me at the last minute, not unaided by an almost encyclopedic knowledge of the law. He would invent unprecedented delaying tactics, negotiate, compromise and so insure, literally from day to day, my right to freedom. Many times when he would appear in court at my side with a modest smile on his face the judge would roar, "But didn't I send your client to jail for one year . . . three months ago? Is he still free?" And Leo would lower his lashes in sweet confusion, with an expression conveying shy embarrassment and the simple desire to please. I would shake in my shoes with delight.

The fact that most of my authors were published pseudonymously did not help either. It was my basic professional commitment to them that I would never reveal their identity since most of them were young expatriates, living strange lives in an alien land. But I had, each time I was prosecuted for another book, to answer the routine question of identity. Of course I had no choice but to

say that I had written the book myself. Thus I became the
pseudonymous familiar of Carmencita de Las Lunas, Akbar del
Piombo, Pauline Réage, Marcus Van Heller, Miles Underwood,
Pierre Angélique and a legion of others equally genteel. My claims
were received with constabulary sniggers ("That's twenty-five books
you say you wrote in 1956, eh?") and were considered to be
further insolent defiance of the court.

Well, perhaps there *was* a bit of that.

When I began publishing *Olympia* magazine in 1961 it was my
idea to create a house organ and its function was mainly to attract
new talent and aid in its discovery. But I was working against
insuperable odds and each issue of *Olympia* marked another date
in my struggle against fate. In fact, only four issues of that alleged
monthly were printed between 1961 and 1963 and each at the cost
of Herculean efforts.

A literary magazine is, in itself, one of the most doubtful
ventures imaginable. How many have been conceived in a burst of
enthusiasm which never took them through their third issue?
Co-editorship turns the best of friends into mortal enemies. What
appears, in manuscript, to be a treasure of originality suddenly
reveals itself as entirely hackneyed when displayed on the printed
page. Then, of course, there are all the material details, no less
complex then if one were running (and losing) a hundred-million-
dollar business: the undelivered paper, the unpaid printer whose ink
somehow never dries, the binder who goes bankrupt or closes for
the summer holidays on the eve of delivery, the elusive subscribers,
the world-weary bookseller who compliments one's faith and
courage with pointed irony; and the forever unsatisfied contributors,
one's former friends and supporters, who now rave, urge, protest,
criticize, deride, denounce and generally do all they can to hurt one in
every possible way with an unlimited volume of spite and
malevolence.

But those are only the classic problems.

Olympia had many other and more original odds against it.
When I decided to publish the magazine I had already been the pet
victim of the French censors for five or six years. Still, I did
not anticipate that strange wave of Gallic puritanism striking an
enterprise as dedicated as *Olympia*. How wrong I was! Three days
after the first issue had been released the magazine was banned

forever, by which I mean that the ban did not apply only to *that* issue — but to any subsequent ones I might have hoped to publish!

Naturally I wrote to the Minister of the Interior, Monsieur Frey, to protest against what seemed to be an error. No answer. No comment. Then I went to see an official of that ministry who acts as advisor to matters involving the press and publishers. He listened to me with an expression of complacent boredom. When I asked him whether he thought *le Ministre* would perchance suppress the ban, he simply answered that he did not think he would. I was beginning to lose patience and I asked if he personally thought that such a ban was fair and whether it was not a rather unseemly restriction against the freedom of the press. He merely smiled absently as if he was thinking of more important matters and shrugged. I became quite angry and asked with a shaking voice if the magazine had not been banned simply because *I* was the publisher. At last I got his attention. *"But of course, cher Monsieur,"* he exclaimed with unfeigned joviality. *"C'est évident!* You know very well that you are not well-noted by this administration, so you should not be surprised if your magazine has been suppressed as a matter of routine. And now if you will allow me," he concluded, half standing and showing me the door with a perfunctory flourish.

I was floored. Was this France? Franco's officials were more scrupulous, less presumptuous. But perhaps I had been a fool not to understand from the beginning what was happening to my country. It was so obvious! I could not have missed it!

I was still mulling over these dark thoughts when I entered my office to find a summons from a magistrate on my desk. I was being indicted for having published, in the first issue of Olympia, excerpts from two books previously banned by the French administration: *Candy* and *The Woman Thing.* Simply to kill my magazine was not enough for the French administration, they had to crush me, to stamp me out of existence.

On top of the ban, then, I was sentenced by the lower courts to a stiff sentence which was later confirmed by the Court of Appeals. As was my right, I further appealed, to the *Cour de Cassation* and forgot about the case until my lawyer informed me that I had won a half-victory: the *Cour de Cassation* had cancelled the previous judgement and in keeping with the rule set up by

Napoleon I was to be tried again by a provincial Court of Appeals a few months later.

On the eve of the appointed day, for some obscure reason, I had had too much to drink and when I met Leo at the station on the day of the trial I had a splitting headache. I could hardly see, my speech was blurred and incoherent, and none of the medication he forced on me during the two-hour train ride had any effect on my hangover.

We looked for the courthouse, Leo half supporting me with one arm while carrying his robes under the other, and we finally stumbled to the front of a great romantic building of 18th-century style which was graced by a monumental stone staircase covered with moss and weeds. This image of abandon brought to mind poems of Novalis or *Le Grande Meaulnes,* with visions of dead loves and hopeless pursuits. I was beginning to cry silently when Leo tugged me by the sleeve saying that it seemed a tragedy indeed but that we were going to see if we could find some trace of humanity inside, and ask where the real courthouse was. A door was opened in the east wing. Inside, crepuscular light half revealed walls covered with century-old legal posters, the floor strewn with masses of ancient files lying under a thick blanket of dust. From far away we heard the creaking and uneven noise of a man coming toward us, pushing a wheelbarrow loaded with refuse. Leo asked for the courthouse; the man silently pointed to a staircase.

Two floors up, three doors to open, and we found ourselves in a gigantic hall, apparently taking up the entire width of the central part of the building; freshly painted walls, outsized statues shining white, immensely tall windows and doors; and no one in sight. But obviously the old courthouse was being redecorated, and all we had to do now was to find the right courtroom. We opened a door at random, and gasped. It looked like a courtroom, but a courtroom for Zeus himself, certainly not for mortal justice. Everything was outsized, empty, silent and new. At the far end an immense and majestic podium covered with a dark green carpet held a long table of unusual height, hidden under heavy drapes of the same hue. Three gigantic thrones, the middle one higher than the others, increased the impression of awesome majesty; their design was curvaceous, but any frivolous implications such shapes might have carried were smothered under the thick protection of bottle-green plush. To the right and to the left, armchairs of more reasonable proportions flanked the central edifice, and placed at a lower level on each side of the tribunal were the green-draped pulpits of the public prosecutor and the court clerk. Facing the podium, at a respectful distance, were lawyers' benches, of an unusually handsome design. Far away, at the back and on the sides, were the benches reserved for the public. The walls and the large square pillars were painted white, but their bases, up to eye level, were decorated in dark green imitation marble.

We tiptoed inside, not daring to speak. Suddenly Leo pressed my arm; I looked in the direction of his stare and stifled an exclamation of surprise. A ray of sunlight was falling from one of the tall windows and revealed a strange figure: a man dressed in long, black robes was standing there, totally immobile, his colorless, emaciated face and skull completely shaven, with the unblinking stare of a hermit painted by El Greco.

This was a little too eerie for me and I vaguely sensed that Leo himself, a staunch champion of logic and the Cartesian approach, felt his reason sway. He whispered something, made me sit on a bench, and walked hurriedly to the door half-hidden behind the tribunal. I was beginning to doze off when he came back with a large grin on his face. I woke up completely: the man in black had disappeared. Leo explained that he was nothing more than a minor court official, whose function was to carry papers around, and that he was quite old and slightly out of his mind, so he had been permitted as a special favor to wear that strange medieval costume which he had copied from an illustration in a history book . . . *"No harm in that!"* Leo chuckled; then looked worried again. He said: "Listen, I have just seen the judge and his two assessors. He does not look like a bad judge as judges go, but . . . *Enfin*, I must ask you to be very quiet and very polite when you see him. You are in no condition to make speeches anyway. All you have to do when they come in and call for you is walk to the bar over there, on the floor. Answer *yes* or *no*, look contrite and that's all. Leave the rest to me. *You understand?"*

I shook my head. I understood — obscurely. But why was Leo so worried? What was the matter with my judge? I was still hazily puzzling over those questions when the El Greco character in black robes re-entered the room, walked to the middle of the floor and, facing an imaginary public, intoned the usual inaugural phrase in a creaky voice: *"Messieurs, la Cour."*

Two or three lawyers in funny, outmoded provincial robes and bonnets, and an awe-struck peasant family then revealed their presence by getting to their feet. I stood up with difficulty — but nearly fell to the floor in hysterics when the door opened for the hierarchic procession of court officials: the head judge was a dwarf — or so small that the dimensions of the decor made him appear like one. All the others behind him looked approximately normal, but I thought that I detected ill-concealed grins on their faces; a sick fantasy, no doubt, and I caught Leo's look of concern, pleading with me silently to keep cool, quiet, and in control of myself.

The judge sat down, the other members of the court sat down, the three members of the public and the four lawyers shuffled to their seats. All there was left to see of the judge was the top half of his forehead. His assessors now looked slightly embarrassed and peevish. Then the judge cleared his throat; he spoke! And his voice was a tiny squeak — like a little girl's voice would sound if she had a sore throat. I collapsed with repressed giggles. But Leo was looking at me again with desolate intensity, and that sobered me: All right, I would do my best. And I knew it would be tough! There was a long silence and the little voice spoke up again, calling my name.

I stood up and staggered forward on the highly polished parquet floor in the direction of the bar, my right hand extended to grasp the thin rail which would safeguard my uncertain balance. The attorney-general was looking at me strangely. When I reached the bar, after what seemed an endless ordeal in slow motion, it lurched forward under my weight, to the left, then slowly back to the right, and I realized that the bar was held up by two thin sticks that had been only loosely fixed to the floor; someone had not had time to finish his job! And I was to inaugurate that bar! I felt great tears rolling down my face, whether of mirth or horror I did not know. I told myself: "I am certainly acting quite emotional today," and I sensed the attorney-general's gaze on me, and Leo's anguished stare on the back of my head.

I had just enough in me to answer a strangled *yes* or *no* between sobs, and I was told to return to my seat in a tone of voice in which I fancied I could detect a trace of pity.

Then the attorney-general stood up and spoke. I could not

understand what he was saying, but I was able to study him; he was a youngish man, he would be zealous in his job — as his ambition was obviously to be promoted to a Paris court. He was making gestures in my direction with his hands and chin, and I did not have to hear his words to know that he was fulminating against me in the name of Society, of Tradition, of Family, Religion, Fatherland and so on. Legal arguments would have no place in his diatribe. And it did not matter a bit, what he said, not even to himself: he knew that perfectly well, and the others knew it, and they knew that *I* knew, or if I was too drunk or stupid to know, at least my *avocat* was supposed to know: It's all a game.

Then it was Leo's turn. Leo has a sense of humor. He proved it in his choice of literary references; he spoke well, slowly, stopping every time he saw one of the magistrates closing his eyes or looking out of the window. He spoke firmly, but respectfully, with humor, but also with simplicity. I found myself listening to him, and understanding everything he was saying. Wonderful! A real master!

And so also thought the attorney-general! He was bristling with impatience, turning in his armchair, fingering papers nervously. Leo, his gaze shifting slowly from one opponent to the other, spoke of the old tradition of the courts, of culture, of the debt of society to its artists, of *La France, patrie des arts,* of the extraordinary occasion for such an enlightened court to show its moral courage and independence, when such a regrettable mistake had been made by a Paris Court of Appeal.

The attorney-general was now shaking with uncontrollable emotion and he was trying to interrupt Leo with his gestures, brandishing an open copy of *Olympia* magazine in his direction. Leo rounded up his speech and then sat down. I was mentally applauding; the magistrates seemed subdued. I had lost sight entirely of the judge's upper skull.

Then the attorney-general stood up again and begged permission to make one final remark. This was granted. He then asked the magistrates, now alert and watchful behind the high green wall of the tribunal, if any one of them could read the English language. The answer was no. The attorney-general seemed to have expected as much. *"Eh bien,"* he exclaimed, "with the Court's permission, I can read that language. Oh, certainly, I am no expert, but I know enough to judge the quality of this infamous publication. Literature! Pah!" he spat. "This is simply disgusting, no poetic inspiration, no redeeming qualities. Beatnik stories. Your Honor, look at this story, for instance, *The Woman Thing*. You have these two young people, an American girl and a Scottish sculptor, who never works. They have been spending weeks on end in a bed, practically without going out. The sheets are complacently described as being in a revolting state. Then they talk, those two young foreigners, they exchange remarks, most of which do not seem to make any sense at all. And all of a sudden, do you know what the man tells the girl? I am sorry, Your Honor, I am most sorry if I have to wound your sensibilities, but you must know what is written ... Naturally it will not be recorded ... Well, the man," the attorney-general roared, "the man turns to the girl and says: *'Look at all that shit on the floor.'*"

The dramatic gesture of the right hand indicated the floor of the entire courtroom. Treated thus, the metaphor became much too scatologically vivid. The magistrates winced, their nostrils twitching in open disgust. Leo closed his eyes. We had lost our case. Yeah.

In 1957, I moved the offices of the Olympia Press from the small, murky, historical rue de Nesle — west of Place Saint-Michel — to the slightly larger, but even more ancient, murky and historical rue Saint-Séverin — east of Place Saint Michel. I took possession of that 17th-century building which was hardly more than a ruin, and assessed with a great movement of the heart its ancient, melancholy charm, its long-deserted horse stables, the dark labyrinth of its corridors, stairwells and cellars, and the many vintages of secular dust and grime shrouding every object in sight.

Since I had now too much space for my publishing operation, I decided to use at least half of it to create a nightclub such as one finds only in dreams. It took two years to put the place in shape, and much money, and at times the whole venture became more of a nightmare than anything else.

It opened in 1959, which was the year of *Lolita's* triumph, and I naïvely decided to call the place *Chez Lolita*, a silly homage: Nabokov cabled his agent, threatening to sue if I did any such thing. Perhaps he was right .... I finally settled for *La Grande Séverine,* and inaugurated one of the most harrowing, insane, drunken, funny and soul-shattering periods of my life.

Five years later, and after many trials and tribulations —
including a fire, several floods and other sub-divine interventions —
the resulting enterprise consisted of several exotic units: a Russian
nightclub, *Chez Vodka* — a Brazilian one, *Batucada* — a jazz club,
Mae Mercer's *Blues Bar* — and the last born, the eighty-seat *Café
Théâtre,* which had been installed in a sumptuous 13th-century
vaulted cellar, its rough stones brought back to life by the crystals
and the velvets.

During all that period, from 1959 to 1965, *La Grande Séverine*
absorbed all my energies, my time, my imagination. She was the
fatal mistress who kept me away from my duties and, true enough,
it is during that period that, instead of becoming a grandiloquent
and catastrophic nightclub owner, I should have fled the ugly
police-infested Paris scene, and followed my authors and my books
to America. It was so clear, so evident. What awful blindness...

And there I sat, night after night, year after year, doing a job
for which I did not have the least disposition, drinking myself to
death, designing new rooms, opening new nightclubs within the
main nightclub, adding entire floors, changing them, talking to
other drunken people, being robbed, plundered and ridiculed — and
nevertheless caught into my own creation, dazzled by it like a
hydrocephalic child by a Christmas tree, unable to wrench myself
away from the silly fascination.

The more it went, the more I was losing money, and the more
stubborn I became. What started as an innocent fantasy turned into
a hard and dreadful reality. Every night I would convince myself
that I was close to breaking even, that things would soon go better,
that I had been right to be persistent for those two years, three
years, four years, five years... And then, at dawn, I would finally
stagger to bed, my brain drowned in liquor and sick optimism, and I
would catch two hours of sleep before resuming my daylight
activities: my publishing career. Hurrah, the brave young man!
Consider the inhuman plight of the born optimist.

And my publishing career, at that point, had nothing much to
do any longer with publishing books. Nothing at all. It had to do
with desperately trying to hold together the last shreds of the
business, to fight tedious lawsuits, to literally invent money where
none could be found, to supplement reality with alibis, syllogistic
exercises, absurd dreams and bad checks.

The Algerian war was extending an atmosphere of thick desolation and confusion over France. A knock-kneed police state was coming to life, a senile dictatorship was suddenly revealing all the latent pestilence of the French bourgeoisie. Smiles were gone from the faces of the street people, the wonderful grace of Paris springs was lost in the fetid air of politics. Cops were everywhere, armies of them, dour, stolid, expressing the new reality with all the bland hate written down on their square pasty faces . . .

Lolita's triumph in America, in 1959, had brought to Paris its publisher, Walter Minton, who had only recently become president of G.P. Putnam's Sons after his father's death. For that steady and not too progressive publishing firm, to publish *Lolita* appeared as an act of unprecedented and slightly cockeyed courage. Whatever the reasons for that act, *Lolita* brought a much-needed influx of hard cash to Putnam's and consolidated Walter Minton in his new function at the head of the board. *Time* had told the story of *Lolita,* explaining that it had been discovered by a Latin Quarter chorus girl acting as literary scout for Mr. Minton, and they printed the little lady's picture — which was a nice way to dismiss the book. (Ten years later it is equally nice to see *Time* devote one of their meticulous, painstaking cover pictures to Vladimir Nabokov, now being promoted as the darling of the Establishment press.)

In any case I was glad to see Minton, and he arrived flanked by the girl in the picture, a rather sweet girl, I decided, never having had any previous contacts with Latin Quarter book-reading choreographers. I took them to lunch; Rosemary opted for *La Tour d'Argent* and acted like a true little lady. An interesting little lady, it soon appeared: she brought Walter into the open during the meal and maneuvered him into admitting that he had not yet had time to read *Lolita.* I took a good look at him, trying to figure out the person. But there was nothing much to read there apart from the repressed anger. Are American publishers like that, I wondered naïvely.

I took them to dinner also, then to a picturesque sleazy transvestite place, *La Montagne.* Rosemary was rather impressive in evening garb, but the tension between her and Walter had perceptibly risen since lunch time. It's not always easy to be a literary scout, I'll say . . . . The evening ended with a sudden, brief scene: she insulted him, he slapped her, she wrenched his glasses from his face and sent them flying to the dance floor. I took the hissing and screeching pair speedily back to their hotel, not wanting any part in other people's drunken scenes, since I felt I was doing those things in much better style myself.

However, the next day, I called the hotel at a decent hour. Rosemary answered, said that Walter had decided to fly off to London, and from there back to America and his suburban family; and also that she expected me to take her to dinner.

That meal was different from the previous ones. Rosemary stayed a few days in Paris, and when I took her to the airport, her parting words were: "In three months I will be back." Which I did not believe of course, until, three months later, the Maitre d' at *La Grande Séverine* told me that a lady was asking for me — and sure enough, there she was, true to life, svelte and tremulous . . . .

Barney Rosset I met in Paris also, a little later, through my friend John Calder. He was definitely an intriguing person, impressively nervous, self-centered, alternating between moments of catatonic near-slumber and bouts of frantic speech and activity. Bizarre. The convulsive, grating laughter, coming as it did at unexpected moments, broke any possible continuity in the conversation. This man was as ambiguous as they come; there was a ferocious insanely possessive and ruthless child hidden somewhere inside; and on the outside a reasonably friendly person, well-meaning, clever, daring, sometimes witty, and apparently devoted to all the liberal causes of the time.

Barney was the son of two seemingly powerful persons, a dead millionaire father, and a very much alive mother with a few ideas of her own.

The first phase of Grove Press, 1953-1959, dedicated to arduous, useful, ill-conceived projects in which much money was sunk and lost, would no doubt be seen by any psychologist as inspired by Barney's will to defy and surpass his progenitors on their own level; but it didn't work since he was not at all interested in ideas or in creation, but only in the exciting side of business — gambling, maneuvering, conquering . . . The second phase started shortly after we met. Barney discovered a whole new area in which to redirect his publishing activities: to fight for freedom of expression was as good a cause as any. And it might make money as well. He was further stimulated in that endeavor by Minton's publication of *Lolita* in 1959: in 1960, Barney published *Lady Chatterley's Lover*. My two American associates had become rivals, and I was not going to end up being the winner.

Before the transition, Barney had offered to publish the American version of a book to which I had devoted many months of arduous work, *The Black Diaries*, a biography of Roger Casement. I was grateful for that offer, since I knew that the book could hardly be expected to make money, and that disinterested gesture sealed our friendship.

After Barney published *Lady Chatterley*, I wrote to suggest that he should try to publish Henry Miller's *Tropic of Cancer* — a pretty obvious next step. He replied that he would like to, but how to get the rights?

The rights were controlled partly by Miller himself — who always rejected with great finality any suggestion that he should ever allow his books to be published in America, — and Hachette, the French publishers, who had tricked me out of the control of my former publishing firm, *Les Editions du Chêne*, which had been and still was the co-owner with Miller of those rights.

I took immense pains to gradually convince Miller to adjust to the idea of having his books published in America — and to accept as his American publisher an unknown firm, Grove Press. I managed to get Hachette's approval to the plan. I went as far as preparing the contracts between the three parties, Miller, Grove and Hachette, and even typing them myself. As Miller was still undecided, I went to visit him in Frankfurt where he was staying, taking my prettiest girl friend with me. And there we met, in the cold German winter, in a comfortable inn, with Heinrich Ledig-Rowohlt, Henry's German host and publisher, doing double somersaults over the bottle-laden table.

At the end of the friendly and slightly erratic meal, Henry told me: "About Rosset, you can send him a telegram and say that, yes, I'll sign the contract."

One year later, Henry Miller was suing me in Paris to have my contract with him cancelled. I controlled the rights of several of his books, *Sexus* and *Plexus* in particular, which I had published in the early 'fifties. I had had to fight many costly battles to protect Miller's books against French censorship, ever since 1946 . . . Miller was suing me when I was at the peak of my difficulties in Paris, on the verge of total collapse, because I was unable to pay him a few thousand dollars that I owed him in royalties. When he really needed that money, he had never had any idea of suing me. He knew in what sort of a mess I was, even if he disapproved of my reasons for being in it. I just could not believe it! . . . Henry, a tramp one year before, a rich man today thanks to my absurd devotion, and protecting himself behind his agents, his lawyers and his butlers! Mr. Miller sitting by the side of his newly-acquired heart-shaped California swimming pool, like any other local tycoon, and refusing to even speak to me on the telephone? That was too much!

I could not believe at the time that Henry Miller was truly and personally responsible for that ugly business. Even when I read (in *Time*, where else!) that *"No less an authority than Henry Miller recently denounced pornography as 'a leering and lecherous disguise that has helped make sexuality joyless,' "* I cannot believe that old age has turned Henry into a cynical businessman as well as an Establishment clown. But Henry is helpless in the hands of whoever counsels him: and that will do as an explanation of his attitude in that miserable circumstance. In any event, my friend Barney has now become the owner of the publishing rights of *Sexus* and *Plexus*, which were forcibly taken away from me as I have just described. Someone at least, at the end of those obscure transactions, is showing a clear profit!

The publication of *Tropic of Cancer* by Grove Press in 1961 was to precipitate a major battle between the friends and the foes of freedom. Very few men would have taken up the challenge and assumed it with as much clairvoyant courage as Barney Rosset did. The fight was gruelling and dangerous. The fact that Grove was in a precarious financial position at the time made it a nearly desperate risk, a rare gamble. The issue was money. The pro-censorship groups, being in a position to start a nationwide offensive, forced Grove to invest large sums of money for the defense of the book in several dozen local litigations. At the same time, those litigations created all the publicity needed to increase the sales. Finally, however, that vicious circle was broken by Grove's final victory at the Supreme Court. Grove had become one of the potential new powers in American publishing, and the sexual revolution was well on its way. Three writers: Nabokov, D. H. Lawrence and Henry Miller, had become the first symbols of the new era.

Barney Rosset's victory had made Minton jealous and hungry. It was *his* turn. But this time, he would not be silly enough to *buy* something from me, he would simply take what he could. The easiest choice was *Fanny Hill*, of which I had been selling my own edition for years in Paris, compiled from the two known first editions. But whatever the similarities between Putnam's edition and mine, it would be difficult for me to establish a valid claim since *Fanny Hill* was so completely in the public domain.

Putnam's edition was intensely successful, but was also subjected to harassment. This gave to the Supreme Court a chance to enlarge the definition of the new freedom: although it was admitted that the book was not a literary monument, and had clearly been written as a work of pornography, it was judged to have enough "redeeming social value" to receive constitutional protection. I never understood what was meant here by redeeming social value, but never mind. *Fanny Hill* is a nice little book as well as a model of its kind.

Barney then had another good look at my catalogue, and decided that it was time to give a chance to the Marquis de Sade in America. But it is an extremely arduous and expensive collection of works to translate. It had taken me ten years to have the various novels translated — nearly entirely by one man, Austryn Wainhouse, who appears on the title page of my editions as Pieralessandro Casavini. Austryn was therefore approached by Grove, and sold a second time to Grove (of course without my knowledge) the translations which he had done for me on a salary basis, and which were the exclusive property of my company.

Later Grove applied the same technique to acquire the American rights of *The Story Of O* from the publisher of the French version, my erstwhile friend, Jean-Jacques Pauvert. I was resigned to accept that last fatality, as I had accepted all the previous ones; but Pauvert thought fit to sue me before the Paris courts. That case is still pending. Pauvert affirms that he was forced to take that action by Grove Press.

Then Walter Minton felt that he was losing too much ground, and he decided to try for something big. One of his editors, Peter Israel, told him about *Candy*. He met the two boys, Terry Southern and Mason Hoffenberg, and bought the U.S. rights of the book from them against a $1000 advance. In the contract he added a clause stating that if ever any edition besides his own were to be sold in the United States, he would be free to stop paying any royalties to the authors. Of course, I was the original owner of the rights, having commissioned the book from Terry and Mason in 1956. But, being practically out of business, how could I start suing Putnam in New York?

Meanwhile Vladimir Nabokov was beginning to sue me to have our contract concerning *Lolita* abrogated, and the various litigations concerning *The Ginger Man* were following their course in London as well as in Paris. When Terry and Mason found out that they could not sell the film rights of *Candy* as long as they were still bound to me by contract, they started suing me in the Paris courts also for breach of contract, on the grounds that I had been late in paying them $200 in royalties. They won; but at the same time I had just obtained a copyright certificate from the U.S. Copyright Office in Washington for my edition of *Candy* which would have enabled me to prevent the sale of the film rights, and so we made a settlement. And now we are good friends again, eh, chums?

It became more and more obvious that I would perish as a publisher if I did not manage to re-establish myself professionally outside of France.

America was my dream, of course, but I could not conceive how I could leave Paris, leave my nightclub, my friends, my girl friends, my life, my city, my youth, my illusions. How could I start in America on my own, without money, with no knowledge of the country? The only way to do that was to find a good American partner. Perhaps I would share my time between New York and Paris. I had to find myself a partner.

Who? I had forgiven each of Barney's bad actions and, whatever he did to me, I still had a recurring weakness for him. He really was a master of duplicity, but that was the way he was: he was an artist, I was a fool, so what?

On every possible occasion I indicated my hope that one day we would be partners. He never said no, looked thoughtful, and never said yes. And no doubt, inwardly, he was gloating over my imbecile masochistic mania.

One day I received a visit from one William Becker, a smartly-dressed New York businessman who had been sent by friends, and who, after introducing himself, asked me point-blank, firstly, if I could introduce him to a girl because he hadn't shot his load in three days (and, *man,* he couldn't wait one minute more); and, secondly, if I would be interested in going into business with himself and his partner, a Mr. Sol Stein, who was in the process of establishing a new publishing firm in New York with his wife, Mrs. Pat Day, under the logical imprint of Stein and Day.

To make an unnecessarily long story short, I signed a contract with Sol Stein. It was not what I wanted, but it was better than nothing, since Barney was still hemming and hawing between yes, no and maybe. Those of my books that Sol would consider both "safe enough" and "good enough" for America in 1962, would be selected and would come out under S & D's well-meaning imprint, with Olympia being mentioned somewhere in small type. Sol was a heavy, a pretentious and an obstinate man, wily but not too bright. Not an ideal partner, for sure, but I had no choice.

Since the major books had already disappeared from my list to enrich others, our selection was pretty limited, all the more as Sol was mortally afraid of litigation. We started with a pleasant enough book, *Bottoms Up*, re-named by Sol *The Shy Photographer*. Nothing to write home about, but not bad. The second book was to be a rather funny black sex novel by Chester Himes, *Pinktoes*.

Chester, a black writer living in Paris, was a sweet fellow and a good friend, although his drinking habits made him often difficult and always unpredictable. It was nice to be able to announce to that struggling minority of one that I would be able to ensure the publication of his book in America. He liked the idea. And when I told him that we would pay him an advance of $7,500 he looked at me with real big eyes. Then Sol sent me a cable to Paris to say that something awful had happened. Letter follows. Regards.

Thus I learned that, although Chester had signed an option agreement with us, which was perfectly valid and binding, he had since received an offer from another publisher with a $10,000 advance, accepted it and signed a contract! Who was the publisher? Who else: Walter Minton.

But, proclaimed Sol when I next saw him, that Mr. Minton is not going to do something like that to *me*! No sir! It's time that someone cooked his goose for him! The disgrace of the book trade! My lawyers tell me, etc.

Three months later the book was out, under Putnam's imprint. I went to see Sol one last time in his office.

"Well, you must understand, Maurice, after all Minton has lots of money now — thanks to you, by the way! — and I am only starting. A litigation like that would have been awfully expensive, and even though we were entirely in our right, well you never know, you know. So I decided to settle with Minton, you know. You know what . . . "

That was the end of my association with the house of Stein & Day. The outlook appeared bleak indeed in Paris. Bankruptcy was just around the corner, creditors were closing in, no escape route left. But the nights were more than ever rich with friends, balalaikas, drinking, and dreaming, talking, hoping, until the break of dawn, until the banks opened, until the hell of daylight and reality took over again.

To print anything in France was out of the question anymore. So I decided to print some more books, some hard-hitting shockers that would be sure to sell fast outside the country. I chose Denmark, the most liberal country in the world. I had friends there who found a printer for me; but I would have to pay in advance for the six books I wanted to do. To find the money was a clear impossibility; however, I did, paid the printer, sent the manuscripts, corrected the proofs, and waited for the books.

Denmark has been the first country in the world to take an intelligent and modern stand on the issue of censorship by abrogating its censorship laws — in 1967. In 1963, when those books were printed, there still were censorship laws in existence, but the authorities in Copenhagen were very lax and reluctant in their use of them. Besides, my books were in English, not in Danish.

However, the reader of these lines will not be surprised to hear the conclusion of the story. The French police heard about my new stratagem, and prevailed on their Danish counterparts, through the channel of Interpol, to do something about it — as a friendly gesture. A good cop never forgets! And the Danish police obliged, raided the printers, and confiscated all the books, in finished or half-finished state. A first in Danish legal history!

But, somehow, we never quite give up, do we? John Calder had suggested that one good way for me to make a pile of money and reverse the situation, both financially and professionally, would be to sell the rights to an anthology of Olympia Press writers. It could form a pretty impressive compendium of erotico-literary masterpieces, and might become a best-seller in America, and even in England.

He introduced me in London to Ian Ballantine, who offered me a $30,000 advance on the paperback rights for the United States alone. A miracle! At last, a genuine break!

Before getting a formal contract, though, I had to put the book together, of course. That in itself was an enormous job. My brother Eric made a first selection of texts within a few weeks while I was writing notes on the authors, and while our friend Norman Rubington worked on the illustrations. All that was done at top speed, so great was the hunger and the despair. However, there was another hurdle: the book, Ian had clearly specified, had to be published first in hard covers by a legitimate and qualified American publisher, and Grove Press was his choice.

I had to approach Barney then, and I found myself in the extreme predicament of having to beg him to publish *The Olympia Reader.*

Of course he loved that situation. He was looking at me with a little light of merriment shining on his glasses. Ah rascal, he was thinking, you thought you could escape! . . . And he was saying at the same time:

"Sure, Maurice, I'd like to help you. You know how I feel about you. But frankly, that's a terribly expensive book to print. There are all those copyrights to clear. And, whatever you may think, it might not sell that well."

"But Barney, it's a *sure* thing, you know that! Listen, you know the terms of my contract with Ballantine. Well, I will give you one third of the $30,000, and one third of everything we make on Ballantine's edition on top of that. OK?"

"OK," said Barney. "Let's sign a contract."

Every year in the early 'sixties, I would receive the visit, in my Paris office, of a middle-aged New York publisher, Walter Zacharius, who had been introduced to me by some obscure friends. He had a salesman's way of ingratiating himself to me in order to justify those visits, varying from rather dull forms of flattery to offers of small services. But obviously he was after something more concrete than just proving his uninvited friendship. He was co-owner of a struggling paperback publishing firm, Lancer Books, and he was always questioning me about possible projects on which we might cooperate. But our normal production was much too rough, in those days, for his paperback line, and it certainly did not qualify as a vehicle for the books by our better authors. So, after each visit, Zacharius would leave me with the same saturnine, disappointed look on his face.

His last appearance took place in the spring of 1964, a few weeks after Putnam had released their edition of *Candy*. I was smarting under the blow, and beside myself with disgust and indignation. Zacharius became automatically alert to the potential benefit he could draw from that interesting situation. He offered to sign a contract with me immediately, and Lancer would release, on our license, a paperback edition of *Candy* at seventy-five cents, which would steal the show (and the profit) from Putnam's six-dollar best-seller. I did not even stop to consider his offer, as I was still convinced that Terry and Mason could be persuaded to settle with me: I thought that they had acted like misguided, spoiled children, but that they would realize they could not really *do* that to their old friend and supporter, and would agree to an over-all settlement with all concerned – including Putnam and my own firm. Even Minton could not be such a leech as to oppose a friendly solution, since it would be a wise one as well.

However, I thought that I could use Zacharius' offer in such a manner as to improve at least my bargaining position. I took another look at him. He was handing me a contract form with one hand, and a check for one thousand dollars with the other, a hungry calculating look in his eyes. It was tempting. But I did not like the myriads of money-grubbing second thoughts I could see in those eyes; the man was not to be trusted. Definitely not a gentleman.

"Really, Walter, I can't do it just like that, on an impulse. It is true that I have financed those two idiots for two years to write the book I told them to write, and the book belongs to me, no question about that. But I just can't sign a contract with you today, it wouldn't be ethical, and it might not be legal. So I'll give you a one-month option on the American paperback rights, with no money attached, no terms specified. You go back to New York, you discuss it with your lawyers, and you send me an offer on the basis of what they recommend. If it looks fair to me, *then* I will sign the contract."

I typed up the option myself, signed it, and gave it to Walter who pocketed it with his usual chagrined, preoccupied look. He got up without another word, leaving the blank contract form on my desk, but of course not the check. I accompanied him to the door. I had a last look at the man, going down the medieval staircase. Seen from the back, that chamberpot skull was even less appealing. There was something both sour and twisted about the fellow that made me feel really uncomfortable. I began to suspect that I should not have trusted him even with that meaningless piece of paper.

Two weeks after his visit, I wrote to enquire about his legal consultations. His answer was evasive. The option expired, and I considered the matter closed.

Soon after that, I arrived in New York for one of my periodic campaigns of negotiations to find myself a new American partner to replace Stein & Day. I had hardly settled down when a friend called me and asked me if I knew that Lancer was going to publish *Candy* before the end of that week.

I was dizzy with outrage. I took a cab to Lancer's office on Madison Avenue, and asked to see Walter. The receptionist looked at me nervously. A French accent, an angry-looking man — who else? She didn't even ask for my name; she had been warned: Girodias.

So of course I was informed that Mr. Zacharius, unfortunately, was out of town.

"What about his partner?" I shouted. "What's his name, Irwin Stein?"

"Mr. Stein will not be in the office today," she answered uncertainly.

"I don't care about what you've been told to tell me, I'll wait for them," I said, opening the door to the main office somewhat forcefully.

After a long moment, Walter's secretary came in, expressed some routine sympathy, and told me that truly she was sorry that, since

I was not expected, nothing could be arranged for me to meet her principals; but I could speak to Mr. Stein on the phone. She handed me the receiver, and I heard Stein's voice, presumably speaking from the next room, behind lock and bolt.

He confirmed that, yes, they were preparing to release *Candy* the next day. No, he did not think it was an unethical thing to do. It was a business decision, he added, as if that was the answer to my question. And no, a meeting was unnecessary, it was a matter for our respective lawyers to discuss at this stage, if I thought fit. "And, what? Oh, *of course,*" he exclaimed. "We are acting on our lawyers' advice on this! *You bet!* Our lawyers say that the book is in the public domain, so we publish it.

"And let me add this," he added to consolidate his victory, "Who are you to insult me and question my honesty? You gave an option to my partner on a book that's in the *public domain*, you've been trying to get *money* from us on false pretenses! Goodbye."

The next day Lancer's edition was out, and I learned that, simultaneously, a West Coast firm called alternatively Greenleaf or Reed Enterprises, had put out its own million of seventy-five-cent pirated copies on its side of the U.S. market, by arrangement with Lancer. It was hardly a consolation for me to imagine Walter Minton's rage, to see his own best-selling six-dollar edition blown up in thin air like a kid's balloon. He was reported to have sold close to 150,000 copies in three months, and could still have sold twice as many, and after that negotiated the paperback rights for a sale of many millions of copies.

I was the inventor-promoter of *Candy*, and here I was, looking like a real fool. The authors, for the price of deserting me, had received one thousand dollars from my friend Minton to share between them; sure enough he would use the escape clause in his contract with them, and never pay them another cent in royalties. Minton himself had made a huge amount of money already on the book, but he could have expected to make three or four times as much, had the book not been pirated.

It would have been easy to avoid piracy. I had a legitimate copyright on my edition of the book, enforceable in the U.S. courts. However, since it was a foreign copyright, I had to obtain a copyright certificate from the Copyright Office in Washington before I could initiate any litigation in this country. I obtained that certificate, in fact, but more than one year after the book was pirated: the Copyright Office, because of the unprecedented situation created by Putnam's edition (for which Minton was also trying to get a copyright certificate) needed time to examine the problem from all angles, and I must admit that the problem was indeed complex.

Thus greed and stupidity, plus the advice given to Terry and Mason by their lawyers, agents, girl friends, wives and buddies, created a situation whereby we jointly lost a few million dollars. Amen.

But the worst aspect of that sleazy micro-tragedy is that it had turned the notion of literary piracy into a big thing. The story of *Candy* was bound to give ideas to all the denizens of the American underworld, the perennial sharks, the two-bit gangsters. They had always thrived by adapting their natural gifts and appetites, from season to season, to the peddling of moonshine booze, the pushing of dope, together with pimping and usury; and now they would call themselves publishers, and spread a little bit of profitable culture around them! The fact that they could hardly read did not disturb them at all.

Barney Rosset's and Walter Minton's example had made others sick with envy: Zacharius, Irwin Stein and Hamlyng, the owner of Greenleaf, had decided that, why not, after all, why shouldn't they get their slice of the Olympia pie? Their lawyers, Stanley Fleishman in Los Angeles and Greer Marechal in New York, had explained to them that, thanks to the incredible intricacies of the American copyright system, they could just go ahead and copy all the books published in Paris in the 'fifties, and no one would stop them. The copyright statute contained a special disposition, the *manufacturing clause,* which had been meant by some lobbyists of genius to protect American printers against foreign competition, and the clause was *it.*

That clause did very effectively deprive American authors from practically all copyright protection in their own country, for books first published (and therefore printed) outside the United States. Under a number of very restrictive and formalistic conditions, an author placed in that situation could obtain a five year "ad interim" copyright, which *could* eventually be extended to the statutory period of twenty-eight years, but only if the book was reprinted in the United States within that five-year time limit. Failing that, the book fell into the public domain and the author lost all his legal rights of ownership on it. *Candy* was not in fact in that situation, since it had been copyrighted in the name of my firm and not in Terry and Mason's names: but as I have just explained, I was unable to take advantage of the fact without a regular U.S. copyright certificate. From the pirates' viewpoint, *Candy* was not the ideal situation. It would be easier to steal my other books.

It's not clear if that American copyright system has ever proved of help to American printers, but it has certainly had the most damaging effect on American writers living and writing abroad. The works of Henry Miller, for instance, were technically in the public domain, and they were indeed saved from total appropriation by the pirates only because they were released by Grove at a time when the significance of the manufacturing clause had not been fully understood by most. And yet Greenleaf had already tested its virtues, in the early 'sixties, by pirating their own unauthorized edition of *Tropic of Cancer*. No one had tried to prevent them, since litigation would be pointless in any event. And they had been steadily building up a complete library of Olympia Press books. A day would come when all that wonderful material would become permissible in America, and they wanted to be *ready!* Oh boy.

Every year the Congress is requested to reform the law, and put an end to a situation which puts the United States on a par with Formosa, fatherland of literary piracy. Every year Abraham Kaminstein, head of the U.S. Copyright Office, denounces the shameless system under which he is forced to operate. And every year Senator John McClellan manages to postpone all reform bills, under the pretext that they are not yet complete and trustworthy enough.

Meanwhile, I was still fumbling through the last phase of my Parisian adventures, which meant more to me than all the fortunes made by those American entrepreneurs.

And it came to pass that my posthumous alliance with the Marquis de Sade, to conspire against General de Gaulle's austere régime, was concluded by a memorable and resounding defeat at the hands of the General's Vice Squad. Here is the rambling story of the creation in Paris, in October, 1964, of a play drawn from de Sade's famous work, *La Philosophie dans le Boudoir*.

Being in the tightest spot in which I had ever found myself, I was moved by some mysterious astrological spring to respond with an additional provocation. I had already produced a few mildly unconventional plays on the little stage of *La Grande Séverine*, including one by Boris Vian, but I was tormented by the growing need to spit squarely into the flabby face of the Gaullist bourgeoisie. De Sade, de Sade only had the virulence I needed to express my revulsion for that race of pudgy slaves. De Sade was the only antidote; only he was possessed of the mad, fiery iconoclastic rage which is the mark of the truest French genius; only he could address the degenerate grandsons of the French Revolution in a suitable manner.

And thus I asked my brother, Eric, to turn his talents to that meaningful enterprise. His dramatization of de Sade's *Philosophie* is no doubt a rare achievement. To make a light, vivacious entertainment out of that heavy treatise, to express the long slabs of rhetoric with the roundest ease and concision, to turn the apocalyptical fulminations into a graceful ballet — and without losing the meaning — well, who will ever dare try to do the same with Plato's *Banquet?*

Nicolas Bataille, who had been the director of most of Ionesco's plays, gladly agreed to participate in our venture, and we were lucky enough to recruit a perfect cast of actors to play the band of extravagant libertines who undertake Eugenie's education. Elisabeth Wiener, who created the part of the diabolical ingénue, was catapulted to instant stardom as a result.

De Sade wrote *La Philosophie* in prison, in 1795, six years after the beginning of the revolution in which he had played a real, although somewhat erratic part — before being locked away by the Republic, as he had been by the monarchy up to the liberation of the Bastille prison, and as he would still be under Napoleon till his death. *La Philosophie* was conceived as an attempt to influence the leaders of the revolution, and to impregnate their effervescent ideology with his own ideas. The intellectual ferments were such at the time that de Sade's ideas do appear nearly reasonable by comparison with some of the many philosophies and political utopias then in fashion. But de Sade was not really imprisoned as a conspirator, or a madman, or a criminal, but more simply as "a dangerous person". Even the revolution was not ready for a dialogue with him — and thus did him the great service of jailing him, which forced de Sade to put down on paper the words which would have been otherwise lost in the wind of fruitless discussions.

A decadent nobleman, a cosmic anarchist, the dedicated crusader against human society, what better home could he hope for than the many prisons and asylums where he lived, worked and died?

As we went along with the rehearsals of *La Philosophie,* I became more and more enamoured of our creation, and more and more oblivious to the scandal it was bound to set off. Journalists called me, and asked their questions with the precautions they would take when dealing with a criminal lunatic. I could not understand why. The play was lovely, wonderfully witty, clever and elegant: who on God's earth could possibly object to it?

The first public performance was given for a select number of guests, who were asked to come in full dress, and masked. It was a beautiful, exhilarating triumph, and I did not perceive the least reservation in the applause. The cast was literally transported, transfigured, all the fumbling and errors of the last rehearsals had been ironed out as by magic.

In the papers, the critics were unanimously praising the quality of the show; but their voice was soon drowned by the mounting and persistent rumble set off in the gossip columns. A man called Philippe Bouvard wrote in the very influential super-bourgeois daily, *Le Figaro*; he had not seen the play but would print, every morning, snippets of misinformation with huge provocative titles such as *SADE BRAVE LE PREFET!* in a manner well calculated to set in motion the heavy arm of the law. And true enough, on the second night, in came two policemen, one of them the second-in-command of the Paris Vice Squad, a man with whom I had had some unpleasant previous encounters occasioned by my satanical publishing activities. They wanted to see the show, and I had no choice but to let them in with as sweet a smile as I could manage.

I caught up with them on their way out, and suggested that we have a drink in the Russian nightclub. They hemmed and hawed, and finally agreed to "sit down for a minute". It took quite a bit of effort to make them accept a drink as well; but they sat on stonily, their eyes well away from the lovely-looking orchestra, as if stealing a glance at the luscious Potemkin sisters would instantly corrupt them away from their duties. Two brave cops on a dangerous beat!

In came Marpessa Dawn, who had just finished her *Black Orpheus* song and dance routine in the Brazilian room, and I had her join us in the hope she would be more successful in unfreezing them. The official jowls trembled slightly, but I could still get no word out of them. After a while Marpessa herself became somewhat nervous over the lack of human response, and eventually the two gothic zombies got up stiffly, prompted by the same internal trigger, and marched out of the room, leaving me with an ominous feeling of brewing horror.

The next night the tension had grown near to breaking point. Just before curtain time, the actors sent for me, and declared flatly that they would refuse to play if I did not have the two nuns who were sitting in the front row immediately removed. I looked through the curtain, and sure enough, two nuns in full costume were sitting there, very neat and demure. The excellent actor who was playing Dolmancé (and who I had been surprised to learn was a devout Catholic — what actors won't do!), appeared to be close to hysteria. I entered the room, went to the two nuns, and tried several approaches before I could get one word out of them, and that word came on a whisky breath, immediately followed by an explosion of giggles. In the shadow of their immense white wimples, I then identified the cheerful countenances of two familiar drinking companions, to whom the absence of make-up gave an unusual saintly appearance. I was only beginning to weakly respond to the joke when someone called me from upstairs, where two policemen were asking for me. After politely flashing their badges, they explained that they were sent by the Vice Squad to see the play. The feeling of horror was steadily mounting.

It did not diminish the next day. Two more cops were already waiting to be admitted long before the show was due to start — again the Vice Squad. They were given their seats, and immediately after that, I was again called to the door: this time it was a police commissioner sent by *la Présidence de la République* who was asking for me, with a whole retinue of policemen. I felt that sinking feeling coming back to me again; I was beginning obscurely to realize my immense, my desperate and inexcusable folly; but it was too late to abandon myself to such maudlin weaknesses, and I went to meet my tormentors.

There was a big fat one with a handle-bar moustache, and a hat down to his eyebrows, a thinner one next to him with a trenchcoat and shades, plus two cops in uniform. I started to expostulate that I had already two of their colleagues downstairs, waiting to see the show; meanwhile the fat one was sniggering at me and, his elbow on the bar, he was downing large glasses of whisky which he was ordering in quick succession from the terrorized bartender.

When all that liquid finally happened to unglue his false moustache, I found myself ridiculed once more: laughing at me like two idiots were Jean Castel, and his companion in debauchery, Jean-Marie Riviére, perennial lords of the Paris nights. As to the two cops in uniform, I did not know them. I was later to learn that they were genuine cops, who had been recently seduced away from their beat by Castel, and were on the third day of a memorable drinking bout, with obviously no hope of retaining their jobs once they eventually zigzagged back to their precinct. I tried once more to decide that my friends all had a terrific sense of humor. I tried and tried.

As the signs of the impending disaster were growing so fast, I had decided on a desperate move. I had invited, for the next day, a roomful of famous people, from both the political and the literary worlds, for a private gala show, hoping that they would give me their support to fight an eventual ban. But during the afternoon, I was summoned for an interview with one Commissaire Simbille, the reigning chief of the Vice Squad. He told me with a pinched face of the official displeasure my play had provoked, and that he advised me to discontinue my shows until some decision would have been made in the high places.

We nevertheless showed the play, that same night, the fifth night, after many nerve-racking hesitations. It went like this: First I decided to ignore Simbille's crude pressure. Then some friends argued with me that it was utter madness to do so, and I decided to listen to their advice. Since all our guests were already seated, eager and waiting, I had to come on stage and apologize for the last-minute cancellation. I was interrupted in the middle of my speech by the news that a policeman had dropped in to say that I had finally been allowed to give the play this one last time. The news was received with explosions of joy by the actors, and with a polite murmur of satisfaction by the public . . . The show went like magic: never before had it been so good. And when we were nearly finished, I was again summoned upstairs to meet another cop.

That one was an elderly man. He was alone, he had arrived in a minuscule car, he was panting and apoplectic. He literally shouted at me: Showing the play had been an insane provocation, he was going to arrest instantly the actors and whomever he found in the theater. I looked at him. The man was even more insane than myself, I reflected. I tried to calm him down, to explain that he could not take one hundred people in his little car to police headquarters, or wherever, let alone arrest them all by himself. I managed to hold him up for five minutes of surrealistic dialogue during which the play reached its happy and immoral conclusion.

A thunder of applause suddenly rose up from the cellar. The policeman looked stunned. Then the first spectators emerged, still laughing and exclaiming. In the first group were a well-known journalist, and a bevy of politicians. Next came Edgar Faure, one of the top personalities of the Gaullist establishment, who complimented me with great warmth. The policeman was still standing next to me, identifying one by one all those famous people, his natural superiors, his bosses, his bread and butter. His brow was marked with a painful line. And when the last of the guests had finally gone, he left in turn, without a word, and climbed back into his little car, a beaten man, a crushed man.

But the next day of course, I was summoned once again to Mr. Simbille's office. He had a truly terrifying smirk on his face this time, and he seemed to relish every word he said to me. *La Grande Séverine* was closed down, he pronounced, as of this very minute. It would be the decision of "le Ministre" himself to let us reopen the rest of the establishment one of these days — perhaps — but the theater, hah, never. All those decisions were of course documented with pages and pages of official papers, stamped and sealed in every conceivable manner.

The rest of the story is simple enough. Several weeks later I was allowed to reopen part of the club.

After *La Grande Séverine* was allowed to reopen, theaterless, all the creditors moved in, clamped down, and made our life a little more intolerable. Some of them would obtain warrants and send court marshals at three in the morning to seize the contents of the cash register, right in front of the last flirting and drunken customers. I had to borrow money from my own cooks and waiters, in the vain hope of being able to carry on. Carry on I did not.

In December, 1964, both *La Grande Séverine* and Olympia Press were declared bankrupt, although the nightclub was allowed to continue operations under the control of a court-appointed receiver. I managed to find a buyer for the club, a lady who paid about $40,000 to acquire that delirious establishment, which had cost me well over $600,000.

The price she paid allowed me to buy Olympia Press out of bankruptcy, by making arrangements with the company's creditors. And once Olympia Press was nominally on its own again, on May 30, 1965, I asked myself for the thousandth time: and now, old boy, what next?

I had been flying from Paris to New York many times to try to find a partner a little more substantial than Sol Stein, a backer, a distributor, anything that would get me started one way or the other in that country. Every time a new possibility would present itself, life would resume its rosy course; six weeks or six days later, or sometimes only six minutes, the hopeful edifice would be dashed to the ground. What could be so wrong? People seemed to find an association with me a wonderful idea at first; then they would change their minds for no understandable reason at all. Perhaps I was too exotic for American businessmen? A bit freakish maybe? The truth of the matter is that during those years I started not less than forty-three unsuccessful negotiations. I never had that much trouble with girls.

The longest and most suspenseful attempt was, once more, with Grove Press.

Their edition of *The Olympia Reader* had been published quite successfully. This had caused Ballantine to pay the $30,000 advance — just in time for our part of it to be swallowed up and lost in *La Grande Séverine* bankruptcy. But that was the past, everything was in the past, and Barney was assuring me now that it had always been his heart's desire to work with me, his dearest and only friend, his only true friend in the whole wide world. His dear, dear friend . . . Those excessive, disturbing declarations, usually made at the end of a night of drinking, sounded awfully strange of course. But I knew that Barney was not *all* bad, and that one half of his split personality did like me, and that the elusive "good Barney" was being lamentably truthful when he was mouthing those maudlin words. But since the good Barney looked exactly the same as the bad Barney, I was always letting myself be caught in the game.

The would-be arrangement with Grove consumed a whole year of negotiation, starting in 1964, and five trips on my part from Paris to New York in order to finally sign a contract, which was never signed. Each time, at the last minute, more changes would be demanded, more concessions on my part, until there was absolutely nothing left for me in that contract but the certainty of a final disaster if I signed it. Those final requests and demands would rarely be made by Barney himself, but mostly by his entourage. And the entourage I really did not care for: people whose only true function was to satisfy Barney's sadistic tendencies, to let themselves be tortured and brutalized by him with beatific smiles, and then to sing his praise, humiliate themselves even further, and sing his praise again.

The procedure was therefore simple. Barney's minions were given a victim, the best available, a real old-time stag-at-bay, Girodias himself. And we would play the Game of Contract — we negotiate, we sign, we don't sign, let's start again . . . Barney would sit back contentedly, shaking with hacking laughter, and enjoy the sight of his victims victimizing his dear, dear old friend.

At the Frankfurt Book Fair of 1965, I met, through John Calder again, the two picturesque young men who were running the New English Library in London, property of the powerful *Times-Mirror* group and, indirectly but very effectively, of the Chandler dynasty.

Gareth Powell was the top man, not a bad boy for sure, but so loud, so ill-mannered and so shaking with speed and self-adulation that it took me a little while to adjust. He was as objectionable as the worst American publishers I had ever seen; but of course his reason for being like that was, precisely, that being nothing but an uneducated lad from the Welsh lowlands, he was desperately trying to *look* like an American publisher — in order to hide his natural shyness, his youth, and his general lack of social graces. After I had made those adjustments, I managed to overcome my initial reluctance, and I finally discovered a certain naive charm in that fractured personality.

Christopher Shaw, his second-in-command, was a very rotund, rosy gentleman whose girth and prematurely bald pate made him look older, much older than his age: he was in his mid-twenties.

After only ten minutes of negotiation we had an agreement: NEL would publish the Traveller's Companion series in England, under its original plain green cover and under my editorship. One week later, we had signed a contract. I had wanted America and I was getting England; well, that was better than Bosnia and Herzegovin.

But there was a hitch. The two boys had failed to let the whole truth about our contract transpire up to the highest reaches of the *Times-Mirror* empire before they signed it. The original idea was to make a lot of money very fast by publishing d.b's in England, where a liberal trend was asserting itself. But the name of Chandler could not possibly be connected, however remotely, with the unabashed commerce of pornography, since that Chandler family happens to be, so to speak, the conservative backbone of California, and has more natural sympathies for such symbols of Hollywoodian law-and-order as Governor Reagan, than for perverted agitators such as myself.

So our venture was dead before it started, and I spent two years, two more vital years, trying to shake that ugly still-born thing into some sort of life. There was nothing I could do really. I was presented in NEL's publicity (textually) as *"The Genius of the Publishing World,"* but I was not given the slightest say in the editorial decisions. The selection of books was indifferent, trite, silly, and reflected the stupidity of that impossible compromise: to sell books as alleged erotica, and at the same time carefully suppress any trace of lasciviousness in them. Even after NEL's editors had taken away the poor books' vitals, NEL's printers were allowed to go through them in turn with a fine comb, plus scalpels, pincers and tweezers, and delete anything that might have offended a hymn-singing spinster of Claxton-on-the-Brine. The British censorship system, it is worth noting here, is indeed so extremely elaborately Machiavellian that the printer, being held theoretically responsible for what he prints (and although no printer was ever sentenced in England, to the best of my knowledge, just for printing obscene writings) — is thereby given a clear mandate to blackmail, terrorize and generally abuse and torture his natural enemy, the publisher. Printers have thus become the unofficial censors in England, and many printers' estimates stipulate the printer's right to remove anything from a book that he might deem objectionable as per his own personal standards. The courts hardly have to lift a finger: their job is done by those vigilantes, the printers.

Two horribly vivid memories emerge from that era. A speech I was forced to make at a Foyle's Literary Luncheon, as part of our promotion campaign, and at which in spite of Angus Wilson's help (bless him), I made a fool of myself (and where most of the four hundred little old ladies in the audience remained convinced to the end that the whole thing had to do with the Olympic games, since they had of course never heard of the Olympia Press). And a debate at the Students' Union in Oxford, where I was to be the main speaker in favor of the "freedom of expression", my opponent being John Trevelyan, the British film censor-in-chief, and as delightful a censor as I have ever met (bless him also). I survived thanks to the gracious help of my adversary, since John Trevelyan is (hardly secretly) even more fanatically opposed to any form of censorship than I am myself. An elegantly paradoxical gentleman.

After we had published a dozen books with NEL, Gareth was fired, and sold his Rolls Royce and disappeared in Australia; he was replaced by his second-in-command, Christopher Shaw. Shaw, who had an even larger responsibility for my association with NEL than Gareth, gave a rather absurd interview to *The Financial Times,* in which he declared that one of his first reforms would consist in putting an end to NEL's contract with me, and thus dispose of *"the image of a publisher of dirty books."*

And so my contract with NEL came to its natural end. But at the same time I was being disposed of, I was told by NEL's lawyer that Shaw wanted to buy the British rights to *Candy*. NEL offered $20,000. I closed my eyes, agreed and signed, and received only $14,000. Better, again, than nothing at all.

Of course, NEL could not take a risk and publish *Candy* as it stood. Not only did they have to cut it practically to death, but they had to find someone else to publish it first in hard covers. Since no responsible publisher in England would lend himself to such a ludicrous operation, they decided to make an offer to Mr. Bernard Geis, the famous Gotham-based publisher of *Valley of the*

Dolls. Mr. Geis smilingly bowed his silver pompadour, and was in his turn promoted by NEL as *"The Genius of the Publishing World."*

The rest of *Candy's* regrettable career in England can be read in the papers. Clearly NEL needs a lot of outside geniuses to supplement lack of same. And my congratulations to Christopher Shaw in whose hands everything turns to gold: to thank him for his loyal services, the *Times-Mirror* hierarchy have now elevated him to the post of ruler of World Publishing Company.

I was feverishly covering the body of Manhattan, up and down, still hoping for miracles. To be a Jew is wonderful, not to be a Jew is marvellous, but to be half-and-half, I don't know, it seems to me that it makes for strange destinies. A self-generating superstition perhaps?

Stalking up and down Manhattan with a parched mouth and dusty shoes. Thirty years of inventive publishing behind me, and destitute of the twenty cents for the subway token. Ahem. Miles and miles of more and more aimless walking. A distinct touch of alienation attacking my purpose, my identity, my rhythm of life. This pure, sordid city, floating like a piece of greasy paper in a frozen December. Whirlwind, angel and beast, that you could see either as a solar ship made of a thousand cathedrals, or as the world's sewer disgorging infamy, depending on your mood and your angle of vision. The silent winter mornings spent in the contemplation of the perfect geometry lesson, the window framing the methodical deployment of rectangles of snow reposing against the intergalactic blue of the sky. The little vivid people in the streets, the makeshift chromosome compounds, the gaiety and the frank insanity, and on every face the obvious knowledge that the word normal means just nothing at all. The tenderness, the pretensions, the self-derision, the self-delusions, the beautiful openness and the clear simplicity of manner of the damned.

New York has always appeared to me as another image of Paris — an extravagant, barbaric image of Paris projected, at the same time, in the pre-formative past and in the nebulous future — but a strong and vivid image, which helped me live and adapt myself gradually to my new surroundings. As if, suddenly, I had been sent back to live in the Paris of a thousand years ago, when the first city was emerging from the marshes, the fields and the muddy banks of the river, when a freshly-welded race of men was inventing a new language, a new society, a new definition of mankind.

In New York I was learning to test and taste America, whose gods were not Venus and Apollo but rather Walt Disney and the Stock Exchange, whose breasts were feeding not Romulus and Remus, but rather George Wallace and Norman Mailer. Here the world was being entirely reinvented, with fragments of the old world mixed with good Indian earth, pickled in the white man's firewater and smoked in the smoke stack of the red man's hallucinogenic peace pipe. I was coming from a country which had attained absolute self-definition, and had been able to freeze itself into total classical immobility, France; and I was arriving in a land where everything was movement, chaos, and everyone was obscurely struggling to achieve the first version of the archetypal dream, America. The contrast shook me alive, shook me out of my past. I was shedding a half century of dead years behind me, I was coming to life again.

One morning just before eight o'clock, the telephone rang in my room at the Chelsea, and a voice said, "McShane here. Are we coming to your room or do you prefer downstairs?"

"I'll be with you in a minute," I answered, dropping my laundry bag, and simultaneously realizing that this unknown voice was the police, and it was the police to the point that it did not even have to say so, and that I, the fugitive, was expected to automatically understand, tremble, feel guilty, and invent my own crimes so as to give them the satisfaction of catching me, and start the old game going again. But, as I have just proudly said, my past was behind me. I ordered my stomach to stop squirming, and in the thirty-second elevator ride I had prepared myself for my first encounter with the American police.

We shook hands in the lobby, sat down. There were three of them, representing the Post Office, the D.A.'s office and the F.B.I.; one looking like a healthy Irish farm boy, another one bland to the point of invisibility, and the last one an emaciated version of William Burroughs. They started by reminding me that I had started litigation against one of the American pirates of my books, and that was the reason why they were checking me. I did not remark how unusual it seemed to me, that they should be investigating *me* rather than the pirate, but why waste time on platitudes since, beyond their official excuse for seeing me, what they wanted to find out really was what I was doing in this country.

Since I was the new Girodias, no longer the victim, I told them a valid version of the truth, in a perfectly detached, friendly and businesslike manner. Never, never before had I been able to achieve this style of delivery! It worked wonders, and in less than one hour we were trading jokes like any other group of straight citizens; and then they bade me a warm goodbye, and disappeared from my life forever.

My stars were shining in harmony at last. In the summer of 1967 a Long Island distributor, one of the forty-three with whom I had unsuccessfully negotiated before, said suddenly, yes, why not, let's have a try at it, I will distribute the books and I know a man who can print them.

It looked good. Just when I was going to throw the sponge in, just in the nick of time! However it did not work out quite as easily as all that. At the moment when I started printing my first books in America (all of them being reprints of books from my Paris backlist), the Supreme Court had just come out with a decision that was taking the last teeth out of the censor's jaws. That decision said in effect that practically any book could be printed, however salacious, obscene, perverse, crazy. Censorship was dead and gone — at least on the Supreme Court level, since local authorities could be expected to continue their harassment of retailers and little people.

And as a consequence, all of a sudden, all hell broke loose, and for once that's not a figure of speech. Lancer did not go any further into the piracy business, but Greenleaf did: all the old Paris Olympia Press books that they had been collecting over the years now represented an incredible pirate's treasure. Smaller people in turn joined the rat race, one Milton Luros, founder of an establishment named Brandon House, and one Marvin Miller, founder of the Collectors' Publications (and who was not content to just copy the books themselves, he went as far as duplicating our trademarked cover); and then even smaller people started to imitate Luros and Miller.

The taste for piracy is really deeply ingrained in the American business mind! Each time I was bringing out a new edition of one of my old books, I was sure to find three or four pirated ones on the market the same day. The situation was further complicated by the fact that my distributor also distributed the pirates' productions. And finally, when my printer sent me his first bill, the rate he charged per book was double what had been verbally agreed on at first. Since he had been careful never to send me any written estimate or contract, and since I was dependent on the distributor to pay the bills the printer was sending me, it did somewhat look like the old days again.

But my faith in the new Girodias was so great that nothing at all could stop me. I found a larger distributor, an honest printer, and then found myself a partner — for the first time in my life. A real businessman! And one who was not only able to understand and condone my ways, but with whom I was able to work in perfect dynamic harmony. Had I met David Young thirty years before, I would have gone by now through a lifetime of professional success. Well, I didn't.

Two years after its American rebirth, the Olympia Press will have given a new proof of its vitality with the publication of this second *Olympia Reader*, which lists a large number of new writers of unquestionable talent — writers who we are convinced will be as important in the seventies as those launched by Olympia in Paris in the fifties.

But this new selection is both more dense and more systematic than the one we had in the first *Olympia Reader*. More dense because it represents the new authors and books discovered over a period of *two years only*, 1967-1969. And also more systematic because it is totally and willfully erotic in intent. Even in the case of books in which the erotic element is secondary (with only two or three exceptions), we chose passages in which it is represented in the strongest manner.

We took that option for two reasons: first of all to offer to the public a selection of totally enjoyable reading material. And also to prove our point, and demonstrate what good erotic writing can represent, as opposed to the distressing kind of pornographic fiction that has been flourishing as an aftermath to the "sexual revolution" in the United States.

All the debates that have taken place in recent years, in and out of court, on the issue of obscenity vs. freedom of expression, have illustrated time and again that the definition of such notions rests exclusively on individual taste, intelligence and culture — and that no two individuals can share exactly identical views and feelings on that issue. In a totally confused attempt at simplification, the notion of "community standards" has been introduced, which means in effect that the provincial spirit pervading the hinterlands is given precedence over national culture, and that any local chief of police or religious leader has enough power to condemn and destroy a work of art on the grounds of pornography.

In America the "fight against smut" has become one of the greatest and phoniest political issues ever invented, flaring up again regularly with each election, and forgotten again as soon as it is over—except of course by the salaried vigilantes of the League of Citizens for Decent Literature and other such Comstockian associations. The political exploitation of "smut" has become in fact much more scandalous than its commercial exploitation; when elsewhere, in Denmark, one of the wisest and most constructive governments the West ever had decided that the whole issue was obsolete, childish, and in consequence abrogated all its censorhip laws for good and ever. It does not seem that the courageous decision has caused the least harm to the Danish people; and it has at least gained its government the incomparable merit of stating for the first time that the freedom to write and to read is one of the most practical, elementary liberties in a modern democracy, and must suffer no limitations — community standards or no community standards. After all in a free society anyone who hates obscenity remains free not to read obscene books.

What the Danes achieved with intelligence, humor and dignity was imposed on the American public after years of pompous judicial disputes, grotesque scandals and degrading injustices. All this unhealthy attention given to what was so long forbidden created an enormous tension, a totally disproportionate curiosity for the objects of those endless trials and prosecutions. The fortune of such books as *Lady Chatterley's Lover* or *Tropic of Cancer*, or such films as *I Am Curious*, is due exclusively to the good work of the harebrained censor. And since this is America, where the taste for plagiarism, piracy and imitation is so deeply ingrained, the commercial fortune of those few noble books rescued from the clutches of the censors opened the appetite of dozens of improvised publishers, and the country was invaded overnight by a formidable wave of the most repulsive kind of sex fiction.

Ex-convicts became novelists, ex-bootleggers became publishers, and a billion-dollar industry was artifically created in lightning time: non-books by non-writers, produced by non-publishers for non-readers. All this being based simply on the fascination of the forbidden, bolstered equally by the gutter press and the decency leagues, the courts and the churches. In a book entitled *The Seven Minutes* Irving Wallace devoted 600 pages of his richest prose to that laboratory drama: the trial by a Los Angeles court of a famous dirty book — whose pseudonymous author is finally revealed to be a member of the U.S. senate, an ex-judge and candidate for the Supreme Court . . . That Mr. Wallace could have crashed his way to the top of the best-seller list with this extravagant saga of pornography (in which even the Pope and the President of the United States are made to play a part) is indicative enough, it seems to me, of the totally psychotic nature of that collective American delusion: the lure of obscenity. Obscenity is truly an invention of American provincial puritanism, and the traumatic myth of pornography reigns supreme in the American libido; it exercises on the masses a fascination even greater than such masochistic symbols as Joe McCarthy or Jackie Kennedy ever did.

And that is the reason which makes us persist in the program we inaugurated in Paris fifteen years ago. Our primary object then was to dismantle censorship; today, with the sexual revolution well on its way, our aim is to normalize the situation, and help integrate the erotic side of life in creative writing, as being one of its most natural and essential components. The idea of "pornography-for-profit" is only kept alive today in and through the imagination of the censors. What matters now is to move ahead, to take the next step, and let writers write *normally* about sex, about desire, about the erotic dream which permeates and molds our lives — no longer as if it were a shameful and secret aspect of our psyches, but on the contrary, as the richest, warmest and happiest realm of the human reality.

Erotic writing, as represented in this anthology, may give the reader an idea of what it may become in the future, when more creative effort will have been devoted to its development. The search for erotic accomplishment starts here and now; and it will open new worlds to us, and serve as the foundation for a new culture closer to man, closer to life.

Having been reborn in America, the Olympia Press is now in the process of giving birth to affiliated enterprises in many other countries. The phenomenon of mental and moral liberation which started in 1958 with the publication of *Lolita* in New York, and which so radically overturned the thinking habits of the American society in less than ten years, is suddenly extending to Europe and other parts of the world; which shows that it has a universal definition, related not to the evolution of the American society *per se*, but more generally to the transformation of the world we have known. It seems, today, that most Western countries have traversed successfully the initial phase of their liberation (usually in the form of the trial and acquittal of *Fanny Hill*!) and that they are ready now to embark into the inevitable process which leads to total freedom — whether by following the neater Danish example, or the chaotic American method. As a result Olympia is fast becoming an international, multi-lingual publishing firm, which will reflect in the years to come not American trends only, but an infinitely more varied picture of the movement towards the crowning utopia of a universal culture. From Japan to Brazil, from Finland to Italy, we hope to be able to express both the diversity and the unity of purpose of the movements which will come to life.

And this, we hope, will produce the program for our next *Olympia Reader* . . . a few years hence!

Maurice Girodias
July-November 1969